Praise for *Kabul*

"An expeditiously compressed and simplified—and quite splendidly mounted—action and angst version of the tragic and tumultuous recent history of Afghanistan (1973–1979), as lived through, and influenced by, the members of a Western educated, highly placed family, who through their various political stances and painful family relationships wound and betray one another. Meaty, invigorating, politically speculative . . . with a clutch of giant family members—intelligent, aching and doomed." —*Kirkus Reviews* (starred)

"An exciting and absorbing novel set against the background of the intrigue in government circles just before the Soviet invasion of Afghanistan." —Doris Lessing

"*Kabul* is the compelling story of one family caught in the tragedy that is Afghanistan. With great sensitivity it explores the conflicts of a traditional society in the modern world and that country's subjugation by a ruthless superpower. Hirsh has done a first-rate job."
—Theodore Eliot, Jr., United States Ambassador to Afghanistan, 1973–1978.

"Interestingly flawed Afghans . . . present many points of view, from Islamic fundamentalism to the tilt toward socialism of many educated women fighting for rights. *Kabul*'s plot is tightly woven. An accurate reflection of today's Afghanistan, torn by dissension, confusion, and misplaced good intentions." —*Los Angeles Times*

"Riveting. Whether one reads *Kabul* as romantic saga or searing docu-drama, this contemporary novel will not disappoint its readers." —*Atlanta Sunday Journal and Constitution*

"Gripping . . . gives a human face to events of which most Americans are only dimly aware." —*Booklist*

"A gratifying and vibrant description of a family and country torn apart by political strife." —*Publishers Weekly*

Also by M. E. Hirsh

Dreaming Back

A NOVEL

M. E. HIRSH

Thomas Dunne Books / St. Martin's Griffin 🟦 New York

THOMAS DUNNE BOOKS.
An imprint of St. Martin's Press.

KABUL. Copyright © 1986 by M. E. Hirsh. All rights reserved. Printed in the United States of America. No part of this book may be used or reproduced in any manner whatsoever without written permission except in the case of brief quotations embodied in critical articles or reviews. For information, address St. Martin's Press, 175 Fifth Avenue, New York, N.Y. 10010.

www.stmartins.com

ISBN 0-312-30173-1
First published in the United States by Atheneum
First St. Martin's Griffin Edition: June 2002

10 9 8 7 6 5 4 3 2

To my family
and one Afghan family,
with gratitude and love.

Note:

This novel opens at the end of what *The New York Times* has called the Golden Age of Afghanistan, when Kabul was a sophisticated international capital with a coed university drawing faculty from around the world.

Subsequent events described herein set the stage for the Soviet invasion and the years of devastating war and international abandonment which ultimately led to the rise of the Taliban. This portrait of Afghanistan's not too distant past explores the tensions that came to polarize the country.

On July 17, 1973, Afghanistan's last king, Mohammad Zahir Shah was deposed by his cousin and brother-in-law, General Mohammad Daoud Khan, who announced the first Republic of Afghanistan.

Five years later, Daoud and his family were killed, with approximately two hundred other people, in a Leftist coup led by Nur Mohammad Taraki, Babrak Karmal, and Hafizullah Amin following the assassination of their associate, Mir Akbar Khyber.

Taraki and Amin were executed in subsequent coups mentioned in the Afterword of this book, and the Soviet "Christmas Invasion" of 1979 installed Babrak Karmal as president of the country.

The Kerala massacre, the Herat uprising and the women's demonstration actually occurred.

The final image is of the king's former minister, Omar Anwari, flying back to Pakistan to try to mediate among warring factions and families embroiled in power struggles in Peshawar, which are again in play as this 2002 edition of Kabul goes to print.

The family Anwari, however, and their friends and servants are fictional characters. Any resemblance they may have to actual persons is coincidental.

KABUL

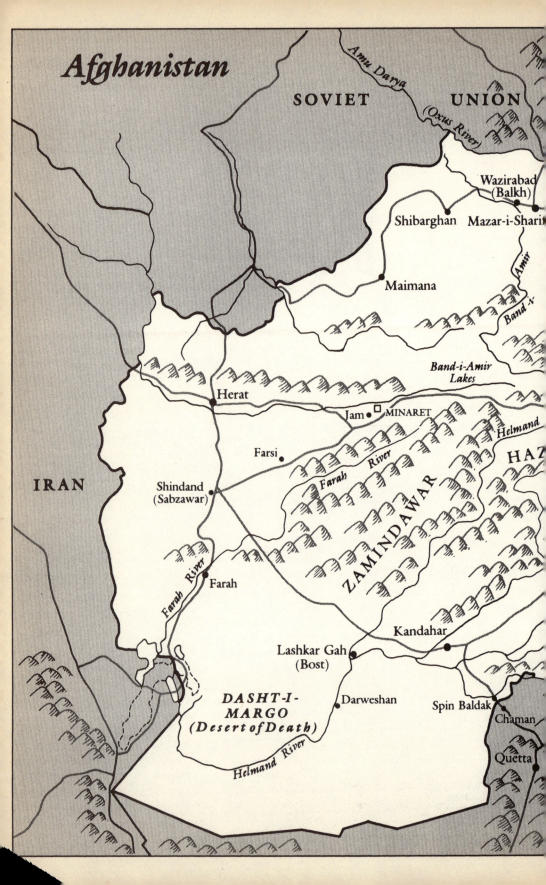

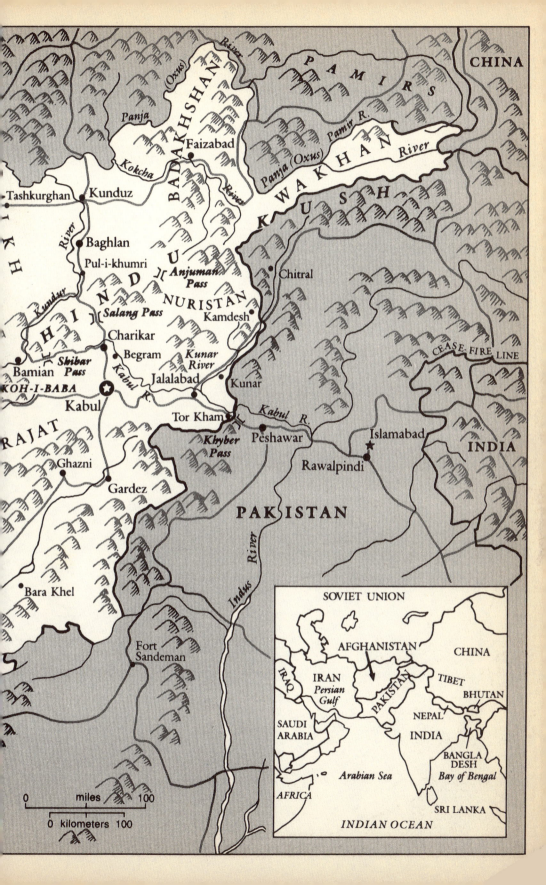

Part One

*Your face is a rose and your eyes are candles;
Faith! I am lost. Should I become a butterfly, or a moth?*
—*Landay, Benawa, 1958*

JULY 1973
Kabul, Afghanistan

One

WHEN TOR Anwari came into the stable his horse pawed the floor, then stood with forelegs splayed, ears quivering in anticipation. He was a silver Waziri, with the grace and speed of an Arabian, and he had no name. Grand-uncle Yusef claimed Tor's first word had been a pet name for horse, Aspi, and Tor called him only that, like a whistle of wind.

Aspi kicked the stall gate, nodding his head in wide impatient arcs, and Tor threw his arms around the stallion's broad neck. "We're going out, alright." But closing his eyes, he let his weight relax against that solid warmth, breathing in the mix of straw, manure and leather oil with Aspi's own smell, acid and familiar. This was their place, no one else ever came here. No one but Karima. Who, according to Mummy-jan, was just the servants' daughter and not fit for him to love.

He pressed a hand hard along the gleaming coat. It was impossible to hurt Aspi, he was so strong, and he never got upset. "I wish I were a horse," Tor said. "You never feel like this."

Mummy screaming at him... "In this case, it's you who's not good enough, Tor!" But if she'd caught him with a rich girl, he'd be the one getting married tomorrow instead of perfect big brother Mangal.

Besides, Mummy was American. They were supposed to believe in freedom. Hadn't she bragged a hundred times that she'd married Daddy-jan even though his Uncle Yusef and her parents didn't like the idea? What a hypocrite!

Tor's fingers touched something sticky on one wither. "Aspi, where did that come from?" He opened the gate. "We're always getting in messes. You're as bad as they say I am."

Choosing a metal curry brush, he began to work on the mat, carding it out in stiff clumps. Before Mummy-jan burst in last night, he'd brushed Karima's hair, curling it around his hands and covering his face with it, so soft and sweet.

Karima liked it too, he knew that much. Mummy made it sound as if he'd forced her into bed, but she liked it even if he had tricked her that first time, saying he'd brought her a secret present from Pakistan. It was only a necklace—and there was only one reason why he wanted to give it to her in his room. That soft hair of hers, and those smooth round arms reaching up to comb Aspi's mane.... Karima had groomed Aspi all year while he was in Pakistan, and her letters were like pictures he could think about in bed at school—how she bandaged Aspi's cut leg and picked sweet grass to mix with his hay. Karima was the only one who cared. Mangal had wanted to send Aspi away to the Paghman house until she offered to look after him. Brave Mangal was afraid of horses, no matter how much he tried to hide it.

Tor put down the brush. "Let's get out of here."

Something was growing inside him, black and angry. When they were out riding in the hills he would feel better, but... still, it was so unfair. No one ever told Mangal what to do. Oh no, he was "the eldest." Mangal with his three-piece suits and little colored notebooks, acting so important about his newspaper job. It was always, "Mangal-jan, will you be home for dinner?" And, "Mangal-jan, is there anything you need?" His only sister was flying in from the States tonight after years at Radcliffe, but Mangal had "too much work" to meet Saira at the airport. Some excuse, when Daddy was cutting short his secret mission for the king in order to greet her.

And because of the wedding, of course.

Mangal's wedding tomorrow. That's what all the fuss was for. "Such a brilliant boy!" His fiancée, Roshana, was a big brain too, a college teacher, yakking about politics all the time. How could they stand it? And everyone said, "Oh, Tor, why can't you be more like Mangal!"

Because I'm not dead yet, that's why, he thought, leading Aspi into sunlight. Why can't I be happy my own way?

Reaching over his cavalry saddle he took down the high-horned BuzKashi saddle hanging on the dark wall by the door. Today they would really fly! Then he smiled. In the old days, men stole brides on horseback, in the middle of the night, just rode off with them. If Mangal ever tried that with Roshana, he'd fall right on his fat nose.

But I could do it, Tor thought.

He fit the silver-studded bridle over Aspi's head. And what if I did, he thought, what could they do about it? Karima would be "ruined."

So what? She already was. And he was eighteen now. A man.

He felt his stomach turn. Why not? They could sneak out tonight, disappear for a few days, and then everyone would just have to accept it. Things like that used to happen all the time. Mummy would be watching him, but he could slip Karima a note and she could answer....

He knew what she'd say. Exactly what Mummy said: Never. After last night she wouldn't dare make them madder, even though Mummy had promised not to tell anyone so long as it never happened again. "Never! You aren't to go anywhere near her! Do you hear me, Tor?"

Now that Karima knew she'd got into Kabul University she wouldn't come to his room so often anyway. She wanted to be "honorable." But they wouldn't let him marry her, or even stay in Kabul. That awful school at Lawrence College in Pakistan...that was so he could go to Harvard next fall, or Columbia, or Moscow, or the Sorbonne like Mangal. "And if you don't behave, it will be Moscow, Tor!"

Everything he loved was here: Karima's glowing eyes, the strength and beauty of Aspi, and Saira—she was coming home. It could be so much fun. But never mind, Tor, go away and just be miserable.

They wouldn't even miss him.

Grabbing the horn, he swung up into the saddle. They were such a bunch of liars. Mummy said: If you love her, Tor, you must never, never, never. Mangal was supposed to love Roshana, but when did he ever touch her? And Karima...at night she claimed to love him, but sometimes the next day she'd hardly look at him, always claiming she had to study. As if he'd never read a book and that was so much more important. None of them knew what feelings were, they just used his to stuff him into a box of "You can't, no, never, I have to *study*, Tor!"

If that's their love I might as well hate them, he thought, kicking Aspi's flank.

As the horse leapt forward someone called out—Mummy-jan, on the terrace, "No, Tor, no!" A dark red Mercedes was coming at him, Miss Roshana driving, making such a face, and that was *Karima* beside her. Aspi reared back and Tor was looking straight down at them, two scared little faces behind the windshield under Aspi's plunging hooves. But Aspi was bucking hard—he was frightened too, and turning him, Tor dug in his heels, feeling nothing but a rush of air as he galloped down the drive and out of the compound.

Damn them. They could all go to hell! Even Karima, if she was going to side with Mummy. He wouldn't even think about them now, but only ride with his legs free in these long stirrups, not bent and cramped like in those stupid English saddles they used at Lawrence College. He could post, but why would anyone want to? Bounce, bounce, bounce like a goose in those silly breeches—that wasn't riding. No wonder the British had never conquered Afghanistan.

Dar-al-Aman Avenue stretched out flat in the hot sun, edged by high compound walls. He trotted Aspi quickly through its border of trees, out of their district, Carte Seh, toward the old palace and the brown hills beyond.

Mummy was right about one thing. He felt too much. Sometimes he even wanted to cry to stop the pressure in his chest. But men never cried. He'd be alright if he let the feelings out, as he had in Pakistan when he rode ahead of the class, dropping his feet from the stirrups and spurring his horse until it knew it could run free with Tor light on his back. That always made him feel better when he was mad or scared about something, but it didn't seem to help too much with love.

The whole thing was unfair, confusing, maddening. There were only three people who mattered, and now Mummy-jan, whom he could always count on, was pushing him away. He'd been miserable in Pakistan, and instead of comfort her letters were full of: You must, you must, you must. Then there was Karima. Till two years ago it was fine that they were friends, but suddenly everyone started saying it was wrong. "You're both getting older, Tor, you can't play like children anymore. You must have more respect for Karima now." Instead he felt angry, betrayed by the curving hips that took her away from him.

At the same time it was exciting—his own body answered the new gentle sway in her walk with so much desire it almost made him sick. For a while that made him frightened, and disgusted with himself—for spying on her like a sneak, peering down from the roof while she dried her long hair in the sun or cut herbs with a little silver scissors, each one very carefully, as though they might have feelings too.

Everything Karima did was sweet and graceful now—things they used to do together—and he missed her smiles and teasing, wanted so much just to trace the side of her throat with the tip of one finger, and maybe for a second let his hand fall down to touch the soft breasts pressing against her blouse. Watching from the roof was bad, but it was better than nothing. It made him happy to whisper things and pretend she could hear. "Karima-jan, you're the prettiest girl in Kabul and I'll love you till the day I die"... though whenever he met her by accident in the garden or the hall, he jabbered like a fool, trying desperately not to look at her body and not in her eyes either, because she would see what he was trying to hide.

But finally in Pakistan, he just stopped feeling guilty. He did respect Karima, that was why he loved her—it was as if she'd grown beautiful just for him. That seemed so true he couldn't believe it was wrong. Why should they want him to love a stranger instead? At Lawrence College he'd spent many nights imagining she was beside him whispering in the dark, and this summer, touching her, loving her, had been the strongest thing in his whole life. He'd had sex once in Pakistan on an adventure with his friend Satpal and it was fun, but not so exciting as riding Aspi through the mountains and nothing compared to how he felt with Karima. That was like being lost, unbalanced, even scared, but knowing what to do in that instant, not thinking or looking past it, but being alive. He could be good if he also had that clash like a fall knocking the air from his lungs, leaving him quiet and empty for a while. With Karima and Aspi he knew what to do, Mummy had got that backward too. It was spying, sneaking around that was bad—that was why Karima wouldn't talk to him. If they got married everything would be alright again. Why couldn't they understand? He loved her and wanted to marry her. What was wrong with that?

Maybe Saira could help, he thought. At least he still had his sister left. Saira, little nightingale, her voice was just that sweet. She never shouted, "Oh, Tor," and always took his side against Mangal—though of course they could never contradict Mangal to his face. Why should being born first give him the right to be such a bully? Mangal talked about respect as if it were something only he deserved, and Tor was there just to be stepped on. But Saira would come to comfort him, resting his head on her shoulder and smoothing his hair, singing little songs she made up to make him laugh, about how Mangal's nose was so big because he even made the bees mad and they stung it. Then Mangal, who hadn't heard the words, would tell her how nice her singing sounded!

The day Saira left for Radcliffe, Mangal said, "Well, Tor, you won't have her to run to anymore." And that morning at the airport was the first time he'd felt like crying. Instead he hugged her close, copying Daddy-jan's deep voice. "You're the flower and the honor of our family, don't forget that!" But he'd meant it, and he still did. Now she was all he had left.

He clapped his knees hard against Aspi. "Come on, I'll find some grass for you later. Let's go now—Saira's coming home tonight, and I might even let her ride you!"

At the turning of the Chilsitoon road his good mood shattered and he reined Aspi in tightly. Two old friends from Habibiya High School were standing at a tiny fruit stall buying melons. The tall boy, Farouk, had been his best friend before he went away to Pakistan, but now Farouk spent all his time with this idiot, Abdullah. Even now Abdullah was laughing... and then Tor saw why.

By the side of the road an old Hazara was trying to move a donkey loaded with fruit baskets, but its knees were locked, its eyes rolling wildly, it was starting to lie down. Sweat spilled from creases around the old man's slanting eyes to stain the edge of his turban, and every time he scrambled back jerking on the lead, Abdullah and Farouk laughed even harder.

The Hazara tribe was treated as the lowliest of the low—people said their Mongolian features were inherited from Genghis Khan, and a year ago, Tor thought, he might have laughed at this too. But today he felt as distant from his friends as he guessed that old man must. Abdullah and Farouk didn't have their own horses, but in every other way they were lucky. Their fathers weren't important, so nobody watched them and they didn't have to be home for afternoon tea. Abdullah and Farouk could go to Kabul University. They might never leave Afghanistan at all.

He remembered running to see Farouk the day he got home from Pakistan, when instead of a bear hug Farouk embraced him stiffly as if he were Mangal. Tor teased him about it, and gradually Farouk relaxed enough to ask about the rifles used for target practice at Lawrence, and what the universities in America might be like. But each time Tor tried to steer their talk back to old companions, Farouk just smiled and shrugged. "Ah, you know, it's the same. It will always be the same with us. But you, Tor, why, you've already traveled to the States! Tell me about that again." In despair, Tor had recited descriptions of the New York he had seen years ago, exaggerating to amuse his friend.

"And the buildings are really a kilometer high?"

"Oh, several. You can't see the tops! They disappear into the sky. And the women wear no clothes."

Farouk's grave eyes widened. "None at all?"

"Well—" Tor marked his thigh. "Only a little skirt that comes to here. And people drink wine on the street corners and the restaurants never close. You can dance till two in the morning! Or see five cowboy movies in a row on TV."

He had said all this before. It was a story Farouk loved to hear. But that time the telling had a ghostly sound, as if he were already gone. Even Farouk seemed to be pushing him toward some grim hopeless future, and though he spoke of it with awe and called Tor "fortunate" there was a wariness in his voice that said Tor could no longer be trusted. Stung, he had not visited Farouk again, and watching him now, he was glad. If Farouk preferred this Abdullah's company to his own, well, they could just have each other. He would never beg for anything again.

The Hazara's donkey skidded forward, and Farouk and Abdullah turned back to their fruit. Swerving to avoid them, Tor loosened Aspi's reins and started toward the Dar-al-Aman palace.

This palace, with its domes and arched windows, was ten times as beautiful as the one in Pashtunistan Square, even though poor King Amanullah never got to finish it. That was what happened when you did things from your heart, when you tried to give your best to other people. Amanullah had been pushed out of the country too, and Daddy-jan's parents, who worked for him, were murdered for their wonderful ideals. Daddy-jan was only twelve years old then.

Now Daddy-jan worked at King Zahir's palace in Pashtunistan Square, but it was like a fortress, ugly and forbidding—and if that's what people needed, Tor thought, then they deserved it, but he would never be part of it no matter what anyone expected.

He imagined walking solemnly across Pashtunistan Square with a briefcase and laughed out loud. No, that would never work. They could send him away now, but by the time he finished college he'd be too old to push. Maybe he wouldn't come back at all. Why should he? To find Karima married to someone else? To be saddled and driven like that donkey? Maybe he'd stay in the United States and dance till two in the morning. Grandmother and Grandfather Lowe should like that—hadn't Mummy promised to send him there for a while, as she had Mangal and Saira? That must be why she wouldn't let him stay in Kabul. She was just as scared of making them mad as Karima was of her.

Well, I'm not afraid of any of them, he thought, they can all shout all they want.

Bending low, Tor whispered, "Aspi! Aspi! Aspi!" to urge him up the steep brown rocky slope. Then they were in an open space and he gave the horse its head, scattering birds and butterflies into the air. This land was a military target zone, forbidden, but it was good for riding and the danger added spice. He could pretend to be a cowboy, or one of his Pashtun great-uncles at the Khyber Pass swooping down on English soldiers with his rifle blazing, or that he was playing BuzKashi... one of maybe four hundred men lined around a field, their horses the best and fastest in the country—a calf's headless body heavy with water lying in a shallow ditch waiting for the signal when they would all race furiously toward it... one man, faster than the rest, bends to snatch up the corpse, and pulling it across his saddle, gallops for the goal, but the others are on him, dragging it away, a stormcloud of riders and horses sweeping the plain. Spurring Aspi, he made for a low shrub, leaned to grab it without slowing down, but another rider came at him too quickly, reaching for the prize, he had Tor's bridle....

The man was in uniform and angry, holding Tor's reins. "You aren't allowed up here! What's your name?"

He was angry, but he could see that Tor was someone of importance.

Tor drew himself up in the saddle and glared back just as hard. "Let go."

Uncertainty flickered in the guard's eyes as they moved from Tor's shiny leather boots to the gold rings on his right hand, the silver-studded bridle. Beside Aspi, the guard's horse was nothing. Tor watched envy pinch the young face as he coolly returned its study—because in spite of all the fake brass on that shabby uniform, Tor guessed now, this soldier was no older than himself. And he was sweating, Tor could smell it, see it on his forehead, even his limp mustache looked discouraged. He was just a boy with rough peasant hands who would never have a good horse in his life.

Tor stared pointedly at his frayed cuffs. "No, you tell me your name! My father's a minister in the king's cabinet and he'll want to know who you are when I tell him how his soldiers act. But maybe you don't have a name, just a uniform, is that it? Now let go of my reins."

"Pah!" The guard spat. "You people think you can do anything! Laws are the same for everyone, didn't your father teach you that? If not, I'll teach you right now."

"If you try, you'll have a very short career."

They were head to head; the guard's breath reeked of mutton and there was a streak of grease on his collar. "But then," Tor said, "you're going to have a bad career anyway. Just look, your uniform is a disgrace!" There was a mole on his cheek too, as big as a coin. Ugly.

The dark eyes narrowed. "Because I work! I'm not a parasite like you, all perfume and rosewater. Go ahead, tell your rich father how 'his' soldiers act. You'll both find out soon enough anyway. We're not all so stupid as you think."

"Oh, so I'm a *parasite*!" Tor smiled. "That makes you a Communist. You'd better tell me your name so I can report you." Maybe they would fight, he thought. This boy looked stronger than he was, but he felt mad enough to beat anyone today. Clenching his fists, he met the guard's gaze hotly, but just as that tense body strained toward his own, Tor saw something change, some fear come into his eyes—not of fighting, his muscles were hardened for that—but of Tor himself or something he had said.

Quickly, Tor moved a foot from one stirrup to kick the guard's hand away. "Good-bye, little soldier, I'm going to finish my ride now, and if you bother me again I *will* report you!" Still smiling, he turned Aspi back in the direction they had come.

"I'll remember you!" the guard shouted. "You and I will meet again one day!" The hatred in his voice was like a cool breeze at Tor's neck, but he kept on smiling, riding straight ahead. There was nothing that boy could do to him. Nothing.

Tor felt sweat trickle down his chest. That was alright though, it had been fun. Maybe he'd come back every day to make the guard's life miserable. Why shouldn't he remember Tor?

After all, he was an Anwari. He had certain privileges. If only he were sure what they were. No one in his family would condone what he had just done, but the people expected it. They seemed to respect him only when he was arrogant. Why did it work? he wondered. How could he be so brave with strangers when Daddy and Mangal made him feel so small and worthless? Only because he cared what they thought. And the women, Mummy, Saira and especially Karima... was their love so important just because they knew him well? He'd rather fight a hundred guards than one cold look from Karima. Any risk was better than that.

Well, hadn't Mummy-jan deserted him, sending him off to Pakistan, and hadn't that taught him something? The Lawrence College motto was "Never Give In," so 'he'd taken it seriously—after all, he had the blood of generations of Pashtun mountain tribesmen. With his Sikh friend Satpal he cut classes and gym, sneaking out to prowl the nearby village or lie telling stories on the pine forest's soft floor. When they were caught, they were given fatigues to perform—hours of crawling, somersaults, hopping around like chickens—until his body grew hard as Aspi's. The more they punished him, the tougher he got, so by the end of that year it was almost impossible for them to hurt him at all.

Kabul, Afghanistan

Tor smiled, running a hand through his long, tangled hair. Mangal would love Lawrence College with its bells between gym and breakfast, between military drills each morning, between classes, bells and more bells that made him want to scream. Mangal was like that donkey, but jerking himself around by his own lead, so serious, no one ever said, "Oh Mangal, why can't you be like Tor!"

But Mangal was a liar. He was more like Tor than they thought, because even Holy Mangal had secrets... those little colored notebooks he never put down, then growing a beard like Grand-uncle Yusef's, now even wearing different clothes. He had seen Mangal in the bazaar yesterday. It was Mangal alright. But he was trying hard to look like someone else.

Two

Mangal tied the dark blue turban low on his forehead, cursing. His hands had forgotten the rhythm learned in childhood, and the thick material slid between his fingers, still slick from the brown tanning oil he had rubbed into his face and neck. But when he finished, Ahmed's cracked mirror told him the effect was not too bad. In this loose white tribal costume, the itchy beard he'd grown made him indistinguishable from thousands of Pashtuns crowding the streets of Kabul, so if anyone had seen Mangal Anwari enter the shop, they wouldn't recognize him when he left.

He frowned at his reflection. It was nerves, not oil, that made his fingers clumsy. Mangal Anwari, the great nationalist who couldn't tie his own turban. I've had four months of practice now, he thought, and it still either falls apart or I get it so tight I look like a Sikh. And what have I done with my cigarettes?

The rear of the bazaar shop was storage for hides, and he'd hung his Western suit behind a rack of half-sewn saddlebags. Now, fumbling through the redolent leather to his jacket pocket, he cursed again. The box of Marlboros was gone, left somewhere... on the table at home at lunchtime, that must be it. Mummy-jan's questions about his evening "meetings" had cut a bit too close for comfort—or was he so rattled he'd just imagined she was looking at him strangely?

Never mind, he told the bronzed face in the mirror, this is your last performance. After tonight it's finished, and with any luck we'll get away with it and Roshana's little extracurricular civics class will graduate with honors—one illegal, quite articulate dissident newspaper on the streets tomorrow morning.

But there was still tonight to get through.

If anything went wrong, his own paper ought to welcome his father home with the headline MINISTER'S SON ARRESTED FOR SUBVERSION. Then, perhaps in smaller print, "*Times* Editor Fired for Inciting Students." Wouldn't Daddy-jan love reading that story! Not to mention Roshana's father and the few hundred other people who held invitations to the wedding tomorrow night.

But the *Kabul Times* isn't my paper, he thought. It's in English, which I write perfectly, thanks to my Western mother, and being an editor gives me lots of prestige, thanks to King Zahir who loves the West so much. At bottom though, the *Times* is a government whitewash like every other "legitimate" publication. And as long as that's true, the only platform the students have will be the streets—more strikes and riots, eighteen-year-old bodies lying in the sun.

He glanced at his watch, then took it off and put it in his pocket. In ten minutes he would leave. Drawing back the edge of the curtain, he saw Ahmed showing purses to a pale woman in a huge sun hat, and changing his voice he called, "Forgive me, sir, but have you any tobacco? I've lost my pouch."

Without looking up, Ahmed said, "On the table, donkey. And hurry up, I can't spend all night bargaining with you."

Mangal stepped out to grab the pouch, then retreated behind the curtain. Better smoke than this stink of leather. Rolling cigarettes was another skill he was learning from necessity, though he couldn't manage it with one hand as Ahmed did, flicking his tongue along the flimsy paper and twisting it up in one motion. Trying again, he spilled tobacco on the floor. His hands were bad today. By this time tomorrow he would be either in jail or safe again and wearing Grandfather Anwari's wedding shirt.

Safe again, he thought bitterly. No, it's my father who will be that, since I've lost my taste for safety after a lifetime of it, after six years of sitting in Paris lecture halls while students here were getting shot in demonstrations. I was sitting in cafés on the Seine, drinking just a little of only the very best wine, passing judgment on the Paris workers' barricades, the movements at Columbia and Berkeley—anything but what was going on at home and especially with other Afghan students at the Sorbonne, who I'm sure quite accurately called me a coward. If it weren't for Suzanne and then Roshana I might be happy even now writing for the *Times*.

Suzanne... he could still vividly recall his first reaction when she came to lecture on the role of the press to his political science seminar. She was thirty-five then, a journalist for *Le Monde* who had spent several years in Asia, and he hadn't been able to use his father's job as an excuse for not answering her pointed questions. Later, with some other students, he had visited her apartment on Rue Mouffetard, where she disturbed him even more profoundly. She was outspoken, laughed too loud, the blue jeans on her long legs were too tight, she had no hips at all. In fact, she seemed hardly a woman. Worst of all, when he wouldn't join in their arguments she took to calling him Mangal-jan, but as if he were a baby, or else Your Highness, which was even more infuriating, reminding him of Tor. But because she was so intelligent, he told himself, he went back again to watch the twining of her long hands, the almost masculine stride—poised to attack flaws in her reasoning and then shocked by the petulance in his voice. She recognized the source of his hostility before he did, and teased him, *"Tu es trop sérieux, mon petit.* Come another time, when you're more relaxed."

It had taken weeks and many walks along the Seine to find his way back to Rue Mouffetard. After all, he told himself, he'd come to Paris to study, not to act. He had planned this for years, choosing Kabul's Istiqlal High School, where French was taught as a second language, just so the Sorbonne couldn't segregate him with other foreign students on their separate campus. He was conscious of representing his country, that Paris was hardly the place to air Afghanistan's laundry, and more, that the time was simply wrong. It might be tempting to move with the gusts of revolution sweeping the cafés and dormitories—talk that came to nothing—but if he were politically active the news would precede him back to Kabul, embarrassing the family and bringing suspicion on himself. Suzanne knew enough about Afghanistan to call him Mangal-jan, but couldn't possibly understand his position in relation to his father, or how seriously even talk could affect his future. How dared she presume... and then he started wondering why she bothered him so much. It was more than her talk, it was her physical presence that contradicted every notion he held of femininity. Slowly, he admitted his attraction to both the woman and her words, and on the night he went back to Rue Mouffetard he didn't sleep in his rooms. Not that night, or many others.

Mangal rolled another of Ahmed's cigarettes. He should be grateful for his years in France, he thought. Now there was very little time or choice. Suzanne had predicted that, in her fatalistic way, when she drove him to Orly airport for his final journey home. "I'll write to you," he said, and she shrugged. "It's finished for you here, Mangal. But you've been well prepared, *mon frère*. For your work, and"—she whispered in his ear—"for your marriage too?"

She had also predicted his engagement to Roshana Haidiri, urged him to it since the day in 1970 when he'd translated bits of a letter from his "old friend" about a demonstration she was organizing to protest the violence that Islamic fundamentalists were still visiting on unveiled working women. Suzanne had listened, nodding, then pushed him playfully. "Hey, Mangal, you should marry this one! How many of her kind are there in Kabul?"

He shook his head, embarrassed, unwilling to define his feeling for Roshana. "After you? How could I marry anyone else."

Kabul, Afghanistan

She smiled archly, "It will be difficult, yes. But I'm serious, Mangal. This woman is your peer. Perhaps more than that?"

Because of Suzanne's interest, he noticed earlier than he might have that Roshana's letters had stopped. Then Mummy-jan wrote that during the demonstration, Roshana and several other women were badly burned with acid thrown by men screaming quotes from the Koran. That night he walked for hours, his chest exploding with frustration. Her courage made his reasoning seem more than ever the tool of cowardice. At midnight, he found himself on Rue Mouffetard; and after she had listened, Suzanne said flatly, "It's as I thought, this woman's more than your equal. You'll have some catching up to do, my friend." She turned from him, rigid with anger. And he had stood still, ashamed of his own failure to feel rage before self-pity.

Roshana, my "old friend," he thought, crushing out the cigarette on Ahmed's tin tray. All through high school we were special to each other in the same way Saira and Ashraf and how many other couples were—not engaged, not quite "intended," just encouraged in our interest by both families—but if I loved you I didn't want to hear what you were telling me even then. Your politics made me nervous you might not be the "right sort of wife" for an aspiring bureaucrat like myself. Well, look at me now.

When he first returned to Kabul, Roshana had refused to see him. By then he thought she must despise him, but that was just more self-absorption. "Her face is scarred," Mummy-jan reminded him. "And for a girl of twenty-three...if her mother were alive it might have been easier, but...I know she cares for you, dear."

The next morning he had parked across the street from the Haidiri family compound and waited for an hour until she came out through the gate. She was walking away from him so he couldn't see her face, but it was Roshana in that red dress, the only daughter of a Mercedes-Benz dealer, who traveled on foot wherever possible. She moved with a new forcefulness that made him hesitate. Then he climbed out of his car and started after her.

At the second corner she glanced over her shoulder, stopped short and then turned slowly, tossing back her hair to face him, proud Roshana—they had always been just the same height. Roshana wasn't thin like Suzanne. Her beauty was strength of feature, the sculpted planes of her face and deep expressive eyes that, like Suzanne's, could be intimidating. He stopped at arm's length, looking straight into her eyes and not at the band of rough white shiny flesh that ran from cheekbone to jaw. It didn't seem to matter until she smiled at him with the left side of her mouth only. "Well, Mangal-jan, I was wondering when I'd see you. Did you get that fancy suit in Paris?"

When she spoke, the outer corner of her right eye was pulled down as if with sadness, so that smiling, her face showed two moods and he wasn't sure which to trust.

"Roshana." He swallowed hard. "Why...wouldn't you talk to me?" That was an idiotic question. She was talking to him. But he felt farther from her than he ever had in Paris. There were new lines on her forehead the years could not account for—she had been barely seventeen when he left home, an earnest girl, and looking at her now he could only guess how much solitary pain had gone into the making of this splendid woman. If anything, she was more handsome and her eyes asked no reassurance. He hadn't been here when he was needed, so she had no need of him.

"You see, Mangal? I'm like a politician now. I can talk out of either side of my mouth." Her smile faded. "I didn't answer your calls because I wanted to make it easy for you not to feel obligated to me."

"But if you wouldn't—" he stammered, "I didn't want to—"

"What? Embarrass the victim? Listen to me, Mangal." She pointed at the scar. "I'm over this. I'm still myself. I don't feel bad anymore and I never want to again. Only you could make me feel that way, do you see? I might want to be beautiful for you. And I never can be."

"No." He shook his head. "Now you can only be magnificent." Gently, he touched the scar. "This... this is nothing but a tiny defect to keep you from competing with Allah."

She laughed. "As I recall, you always had a gift for words. I may have a good use for that talent. Would you like to come in for tea?"

They walked back to her house.

Roshana said her injury held one advantage: her father had despaired of her marrying anyone in their circle, so instead he gave her freedom. Arguments about her political involvement had ended.

"Of course"—she smiled when the servant left them—"he'd rather not know what I'm really doing. Since the university's been on strike all year, I'm obviously not teaching now. I am doing some work for the new women's cancer clinic, which is something he can tell his friends at least. He thinks my life is ruined and he loves me, so he wants me to be happy however I can. And I suppose he doesn't think I'm capable of much."

"With all respect, he must be blind."

"Not really." She frowned at the tea she was pouring. "My sex is still an obstacle. For instance, I'm the only woman in our group."

He took the cup. "What group?"

"Wait."

Standing up, she went to the door and closed it, then came back to the couch. "Do you know what's been happening here, Mangal? Eighty thousand people died in the last drought, and more than half the livestock in the country. But what are a few peasants as long as the king's strawberry beds didn't suffer! Nothing was done for the villagers, naturally. They can be counted on to starve in silence. But in Kabul—there have been dozens of strikes since you left, by workers and students both, and the government managed to spring to life long enough to kill a few of them on purpose. Six months the university's been closed now, with no end in sight."

"And you don't like being out of a job."

"That's right." Her mouth tightened. "I kid myself that learning's as important here as it is at the Sorbonne. And I don't enjoy watching my most idealistic students being manipulated by people like Babrak Karmal, who doesn't care what happens to them afterward."

"Roshana, I was joking!"

"You can afford to. It hasn't touched you."

"Alright. That's fair enough. So you're having classes on your own?"

"In a manner of speaking." Impatiently, she brushed a wisp of hair off her forehead in a gesture he remembered. "The problem is, the students' demands are as absurd as they were in '65 when Babrak used them to cause trouble in Parliament. Shut down the university, fine. Break up the legislature, even better. Never mind that all they're asking for is total control of the curriculum, no such thing as a failing grade, and that every official who studied in the States be considered a CIA spy. If the demands were reasonable, they might be met, which is the last thing the radical Left wants. Babrak's Parcham crowd looks more to Brezhnev every day. And Taraki's Khalqis too, though at least he seems a decent man."

"But since political parties are illegal, they're automatically romantic, right? I don't know why the king doesn't see that."

"His Majesty never looks out the window. He lets other people tell him what the weather is." She folded her arms tight against her red dress. "So how do Babrak and Taraki work? By making martyrs of themselves, starting papers that are very quickly banned...." She smiled. "Well, I shouldn't argue with that. It's what I'm planning to do with my group. Ours will be banned too, of course, but first they'll have to find out where we are. Who we are. And we need a good editor. Like you."

"Ah." He'd been watching with pleasure while she spoke. The scar made her speech seem wry. Now her eyes were challenging and he shifted in his chair. "Roshana, as long as my father's in the cabinet I can't say a word against the government. Don't you understand? It's just..."

"Impossible. I know, Mangal. I respect your father very much. He's too honorable, if there is such a thing. And I'm not asking you to do anything but tell us where we're wrong. Really, we haven't got to the newspaper stage yet. It's just a study group now, and we won't be ready to publish for months. But it's past the point where my brains are enough. I'm all used up, and I can't stand to think this could fall apart." She touched the scar. "It's my only revenge."

He nodded. "But didn't that come from the other side? The Islamic Brotherhood?"

"Well yes, but..." She bent closer. "I'd hate to have to choose between them, wouldn't you? And that's what's going to happen if we can't make a middle ground." Her eyes seemed more compelling, given that immobile cheek.

"Who's 'we,' exactly? Tell me all of it."

"Have your tea first. And try one of these pastries, or the cook will be insulted."

While she filled their cups again, he thought: she knows I feel guilty enough right now to go against my better judgment. That's why she looks so cheerful.

As if reading his mind, Roshana looked up. "I wanted to write to you about it, but I didn't dare. Not that it's so much. When the university closed down this time, I couldn't stand just to do nothing. Again. So I collected everyone I could trust who I knew felt the same—mostly students, a few teachers, some provincial officials who were at the university during the other strikes. The class of '65 and '66 and '68." She grinned. "Sixty-seven was a fairly quiet year. But they're brave, committed people, Mangal, and we could really use your help. I didn't grow up in your house. I don't have your information or your access. And when we do get around to publishing, I want it to be very good, that's the point."

"So you have meetings, and you want me to...what?"

"Right now, just come and listen. Later, if we get that far, go through what we put together and criticize it. Is that so much to ask? You wouldn't have to do the printing, and there won't be much risk till then. Now we're only meeting once a month, and people read papers they've written in the meantime that will be articles later on, I hope. Won't you come at least once?"

And if I don't, he thought, how will you look at me then? You'll have no need of me. Again.

Roshana was smiling crookedly. "Since this scar makes me...memorable, I wear a chadri to these meetings. That's right, a full veil, and I have to try very hard not to trip on it. Wouldn't you come, only to see that?"

After a moment he nodded. "I just might."

So he had gone, and been pleasantly surprised. For the first six monthly meetings he'd done nothing but listen and discovered he liked every member of the group. He couldn't think of another time that had been true. Roshana he came to love again with an intensity that tore his soul: by honor, once her people moved from talk to action he would have to withdraw, and if they married, she would also owe that loyalty to his father. In March, when he proposed to her on New Year's Day, they had struck a bargain: he'd help through the first issue of the paper. After that, they would both be model subjects for a while.

Since March he'd worn this disguise to their meetings, now held after dark in the back room of a teahouse a short walk from Ahmed's stall, and in four months they'd drafted enough material to fill a dozen broadsides, so that after tonight putting out the paper would involve only two or three people. But there was still tonight to get through and the danger would not end here—a fact that had spurred his painful decision to move from the family compound to a new house after the wedding. He and Roshana might be accused at any time. Demazang prison was designed for suffering, not rehabilitation, and if any member of the group was caught, a confession would be extracted. By appearing to split with the family he could at least reduce the potential threat to them.

For himself and Roshana, exposure would mean the end of all their plans. Sympathy for their families might get them out of jail even if they were found guilty of incitement, but then there would be no jobs open to them, no direction to move in—Kabul's small circle would have closed against them. During his single year of high school in the States he had been amazed by the sprawling cities where anyone could disappear to live in anonymity. Here, all prospects were tied to what work your father did, the lands your father owned, and if with great effort people from the countryside might climb up the ladder, there was no real way for either him or Roshana to move down it. They could only choose to retreat to the family's winter house at Jalalabad or the summer house at Paghman—where we'd do what, he wondered, raise chickens?

He checked his watch again. It was time to go.

Slinging the saddlebag of notebooks over his shoulder, he opened the curtain and stepped into the front of Ahmed's shop.

Two customers glanced up and went back to their shopping. Going over to Ahmed, he said, "I've looked at your skins, but they're too small for what you're asking. We wouldn't pay that price."

"You'd steal from me then! Rob me!" Ahmed snarled. "Tell your dealer to send you back when he's ready to be honest."

"Why? We can do better anywhere else. If that's your final offer."

"Yes, it is. So be it, then. Be gone, you donkey."

Mangal backed out of the stall.

It was dusk and all around him men were closing down their shops, moving into the teahouses. A tang of roast lamb floated on the smoky purple air, and here and there small rugs were being quickly unrolled by people late for sunset prayers. The afternoon crowds had drifted home, even the flies had abandoned the sides of meat hanging in the butcher's stall. It was so quiet he could hear sheep bleating along the riverbank.

The bazaar was its own universe, he thought. In these stalls of carpets, leather, brass and pyramided fruit you could find anything from Roman coins to canned sardines and pay almost any price for either. Tonight would be the last time he could wander here unnoticed, and he knew now he would miss that very much. It was good to be invisible, sandals caked with dung, knocked around by wagons in the street, watching people and talking to them without being marked by his gray suit and laced shoes. Yesterday, smuggling in paper, he'd passed within a meter of Tor and not been recognized in this costume, which increasingly made Western dress feel confining as a harness. For years now, Daddy-jan had put on tribal clothes to read in the evening or work in the garden, silently, as if his deepest nature grew from the rugged landscape, and seeing him then Mangal always felt their differences less sharply.

At the Sorbonne, he had been afraid Paris would spoil him, but Gothic cathedrals might have taken their inspiration from the vaulting Hindu Kush, and the Seine was no more precious than the Kabul River, bringing life to desert. In France, he'd read a long article by an Englishman asking why anyone would *want* Afghanistan except for strategic reasons, since it was so hot, dry and flat, or else so mountainous and cold, but in any event too filthy, poor and difficult to interest civilized countries. Now, trying to picture Suzanne here, he knew she would have to feel its beauty, the grace of that small boy leading his donkey, a red sun setting behind the Paghman mountains, the haunting cry of a blind singer calling the end of day.

How would Kabul have looked to Mummy when she came from Boston in 1946? Or to Daddy-jan, for that matter, after sixteen years of schooling in England and the States? He'd said that when his parents were shot, Granduncle Yusef sent him "into exile in the name of Western education" so he could take up their fight—and then been shocked when he chose a blond Radcliffe student to fall in love with. Catherine Lowe and Omar Anwari: there were photographs of that grim little wedding party. Grand-uncle Yusef tried to stop their courtship by bringing Daddy-jan home "on the king's orders" to work on the Pashtun border dispute at India's partition. And in duty, in honor, Daddy-jan had come back—but with twenty-one-year-old Catherine, who hadn't yet learned a word of Pashto, or the Dari that Uncle Yusef called "the purest form of Persian." Even now, Daddy-jan insisted they speak English at home, to preserve the family's privacy against his public life, so it had become their language for fighting, telling secrets, and finally, writing in newspapers.

But not this paper, Mangal thought, smiling. Not tonight.

The bazaar edged the old quarter—a labyrinth of mud-brick houses climbing the rock face in ragged tiers. Stooping as if to adjust a sandal, he glanced behind him, then slipped down the alley in back of Khalid's tea shop.

Six tense faces looked up from the table as he came into the room. Tonight only a fraction of the group would participate, to minimize the risk, and except for Ahmed they had all arrived before him. Since tea shops were still a male preserve, Roshana always carried in a basket, like a delivery, and it stood filled with peaches in the center of the table. A pleated gray silk chadri was folded over the back of her chair.

Only Khalid stood to greet him, smiling through his heavy white mustache, then moving to the door to wait for Ahmed, who followed seconds later. Khalid and Ahmed were old friends, and though neither could read or write well, their contribution was the most crucial: like most people, they relied on gossip for uncensored news, on the drifting rumors of the bazaar, and after tonight they would spread the stories in "the paper my cousin read to me" as well as judge the response to it.

Khalid and Ahmed were also least likely to suffer consequences, Mangal told himself, unpacking his spiral notebooks. Their illiteracy and long years in the bazaar should protect them. But the others... his glance moved along the table. There was Professor Durrani, perhaps the country's greatest expert on Pashto language and literature, reaming out his pipe again, too thoroughly for that to be the casual habit he tried to make it seem. Durrani was fifty-nine, a hard brown nut of a man who wore woolen vests even in summer and could speak eloquently on a hundred subjects. Mangal thought: he'll be lucky to teach reading in a village school after tonight if we're caught.

Roshana's hands were folded. Her skin glowed against her white cotton blouse and her eyes held no anxiety. This was the moment she had waited and worked for now for over a year, and he wondered if any threat could touch her deeply again.

She pushed the basket to Durrani. "Professor? Have a peach. Everybody eat one. I picked them myself this morning. We have to relax."

Mangal sat down opposite her. There was hardly room to move around the table. The walls were filled with shelves of pots, plates, cups, enormous dented samovars, sacks of tea and rice—the only open space now taken up by the typewriter and outsized mimeo machine a provincial official, Abdul Rahman, had brought down from Begram.

All their attention seemed captured in the circle of yellow light thrown by the overhead lamp. The close air was already thick with smoke. As the basket was passed from hand to hand, Mangal found himself studying Nur-Ali, the farm boy from Herat province whose older brother had been killed in the strike of '69. It was Nur-Ali and his fellow students from the countryside who had most to lose. Expulsion would bring dishonor on the families who had worked so hard to send them to Kabul, on fathers who cherished the hope that one son might rise through the great gift of a university education—though the jobs they envisioned were really so few as to be nonexistent. So much learning would be a precious resource to their village even if that son did finally follow his father on the farm, in the cement or cotton works, but to be sent home in disgrace, to have abused that privilege... Mangal felt sure there was little sympathy in the countryside for student disruptions, and Nur-Ali's father had already lost one son.

Nur-Ali was grinding a peach pit between his teeth, looking as always as if he were about to jump up and murder someone. He was as wiry as Tor and as impetuous, Mangal thought, but Nur-Ali's anger sprang from an almost fanatical need to avenge his brother. Roshana called his inclusion in the group protective custody: If they didn't make him do this, he would find something far worse.

She tapped a pencil on the table. "Are we ready to begin? It's so noisy in your shop tonight, Khalid!"

"Yes," the old man said. "I invited half of Kabul in, to cover the sound of that machine. And there will be music later too, Bibi Roshana."

"Good work. Now, Khalid and Ahmed will be putting our case to people who move around the country—bus drivers, traders and so forth—as well as through the bazaars and tea shops, so please everyone, go slowly tonight and if there are questions let's settle them here. Nur-Ali, you can spend some of that energy on the typewriter, cutting stencils. As soon as a piece is finished it goes to you, so read first and then get started. Zalmai, if you keep smoking so much we'll all be dead before morning."

Zalmai ground out his cigarette, laughing nervously. "But what's the name to be? We left that honor up to you last time. What name has Mother chosen for this infant?"

Zalmai was the son of a wealthy merchant and so notorious a playboy it had taken Mangal time to see his self-indulgence was a pose. He'd claim to have wrecked his car in the forest—until it turned up driven by an old servant of his family. And his graduate thesis was a model of deception: on the surface, a rather boring study of the uses of foreign aid—but closer reading suggested large sums of that money had been diverted to private projects of the Royal House. Still, watching his grin now, Mangal felt uneasy. Zalmai's motives and loyalties were more obscure than the others'. He was generous, yes, but he could afford to be. Why should he work against a system whose rewards he so obviously relished? And he looked jumpy tonight, which was unlike him, unless this hadn't seemed real enough to frighten him before, or unless he knew something...Mangal felt a stab of anxiety. This was Roshana's hand-picked group. He'd never questioned whether one of them might be an informer.

"There was a paper in 1951," she said, "the first to call for the removal of the Royal Family from government. It was named *Homeland*. I thought we'd title ours *New Homeland*. Are there any objections?" She looked around the table. "No? Then I'll consider that passed, thank you all very much. Abdul Rahman, you may as well set up that machine. Let's use both the Islamic and Western dates to make it clear we aren't godless Communists. Nur-Ali, will you read, please?"

He spat out the peach pit and stood up with his wrinkled notes. Mangal turned to face him fully. Through several meetings, Nur-Ali had protested that he couldn't write or study, had never wanted to come to Kabul and saw no value in words, but only in guns, since his brother had gone unarmed and been shot. Then grudgingly, at Roshana's prodding, he began to draft a paper opposing his own wish for bloody rebellion, and at its last reading only the beginning needed further work. Nur-Ali was more surprised than anyone else by its quality, though he still looked angry to have contradicted himself so well.

"I'll just read the first part, the rest is the same." He pulled at his shirt and raked a hand through his thick hair. "I'm calling it, 'Balancing on a Sword.'"

His delivery was like machine-gun fire—a list of reasons why outright revolution would profit Moscow more than anyone else. But ending with the question: Has our Royal House become just a symbol that no longer serves?

Nur-Ali's face was dark. "The rest goes on about the reforms that never happened."

"That's good!" Roshana said. "It's clear and effective. You can put that on page one."

"And you?" He turned to Mangal. "Do you like it? You should. It's everything you said." His hands clenched, crumpling the paper. "I just wrote it down! I don't believe it."

Deliberately, Mangal reached for Zalmai's pack of Lucky Strikes, offered one to Nur-Ali and lit another for himself. "Don't try to blame that all on me. You don't believe any of it? Not even about the Royal House?"

"Well..." His thin mouth twisted in a half smile. "Yes, that part I do."

"But?"

"Not... this!" Nur-Ali swept his hand over the table. "It won't work! It's just a lot of nice-sounding words we tell each other hiding in stupid little rooms."

Trembling, he swiveled toward Khalid. "Forgive me, Khalid, with all respect, this is a fine room, but we shouldn't be hiding. We should stand up as men. The king won't listen anyway, he'll just throw us in prison. I'd rather be shot in the open like my brother than go to jail like a dog for writing words."

"Ah!" Khalid patted his mustache. "How sweet to talk of death when one is young. And to think words are nothing when one can write them. I do this so my grandchildren in Badakshan may learn to read and worship Allah both, not one or the other. Tell me, what did your brother gain by dying?"

A muscle was working in Nur-Ali's jaw. He spat, "Nothing! Just dirt on his face."

Khalid smiled gently. "As we would, in an open fight. There are too few of us now. Words are better than guns. They'll win us friends."

And words are what Roshana and I are good at, Mangal thought. But if they fail your time of guns will come.

"I don't believe the rest of it, either." Nur-Ali fanned his papers on the table. "These reforms! Why should the king want people to learn to read? They might cause trouble when they find out how they've been taken advantage of. And land reform..." He shoved one page under Mangal's nose. "This is the only reason I'm with you instead of the Parchamis—it's the only thing I know enough about to see the lies. They say: cut up the land and give it away in little pieces! When many families share a horse or plow or donkey? That won't work! So maybe the rest of what they say is just as wrong. I don't know."

"Nur-Ali—" Roshana touched his arm. "I know you're frustrated. So are we all. This is a very indirect way to work, but right now I don't see another. What we're doing is putting on pressure in the hope that things will change, but if they don't, we're also putting ourselves in the game, so anyone who wants power will have to reckon with us. I think that takes more nerve than being a target on the street, but what you do is up to you. Do you want to withdraw your paper?"

"Well..." His jaw relaxed. "I guess *you* have the right to say that. You're not afraid. That's why I trusted you. If you really want it, Roshana, I'll put it in for you."

Hmmm, Mangal thought, and maybe a little out of pride? I'll bet that's the best work you've ever done.

Nur-Ali moved to the typewriter, and Roshana said, "Zalmai? Would you just summarize your piece, unless that's impossible?"

"Of course! Whatever Mother says." Grinning, Zalmai ran a finger under the tight collar of his pearl gray Western shirt. He had made no effort to disguise himself, and Mangal thought he would look quite at home on the Champs Elysées in those clothes—therefore highly conspicuous in Kabul. Again he felt a twinge of apprehension.

"Now listen carefully, class, this is about the Royal House and the executive branch. Roughly as follows." He spoke without consulting his paper. "For decades, our government has been run by a clique, all intimates of the Royal Family—the same people just reshuffled through the cabinet. This has led to corruption on every level... bribery, personal investments, misuse of public funds, a feudal land system that benefits the few at the expense of many. The executive seems to exist only to serve the Royal House. We're just coming out of the worst drought in our history, and no help was given to people in the countryside. The bureaucrats were all too busy doing favors for Prince so-and-so. Then there's the fact that over ninety percent of our people still can't read. As Nur-Ali said, literacy is the enemy of weak government. Right now there's hardly a factory in the country working at even half capacity. Minus the detail, that's basically my line. It's called, The New Democracy: Ten Years of Stagnation."

"I hope your details are pretty specific," Mangal said uncomfortably. "That's hardly true of everyone in the cabinet."

"Such as your honored father?" Zalmai bowed. "Don't worry, Mangal. Everyone knows Omar Anwari's reputation. I've named the right names and traced their sins carefully. Here, see how you like it."

Mangal took the paper. "Roshana? I'm beginning to think Nur-Ali may be right about this land reform question. We ought to have an editorial giving both sides of the picture. Could you collaborate with him on that, Abdul Rahman? Zalmai can type his own."

As Nur-Ali squeezed past them smiling triumphantly, Mangal skimmed through Zalmai's paper. It was like his thesis. Excellent. Even Daddy-jan would agree with this, in private at least. Then why was Zalmai still looking so nervous?

"Saleem," Roshana said, "the last piece is yours. Go ahead, and take your time."

Mangal tried not to smile. Zalmai could hurry, but Saleem should take his time, otherwise he might faint from embarrassment. Professor Durrani had practically dictated his paper after several failed attempts by the second-year history student. Saleem was plump, in every way the opposite of Nur-Ali, but Roshana thought Saleem also had a personal ax to grind here. She had a folder of completed articles from more able students who preferred to avoid tonight's risk and manual labor, but she said Saleem needed to do something courageous.

"The name of my article is, 'The 1964 Constitution: Beautiful Lies.'" Saleem nodded with each word for emphasis. "There are three bills the king refuses to sign. I say that until those promises are kept, his 'new democracy' is only words on paper."

"What?" Nur-Ali hooted. "You mean he's as pitiful as we are?"

Just then the thrum of a tambour filtered through from the tea shop, joined by a man's voice rising in mournful song. Khalid sighed with relief.

"As I was saying"—Saleem scowled at Nur-Ali—"first, political parties are still illegal, so there are no power bases in the legislature. They haven't had a quorum now for eighty-two sessions! Each man acts only for himself, or at most, his tribe. It's a madhouse!"

"And Senate." Roshana chuckled. "I'm sorry. Go on, Saleem."

"Second, city elections haven't been held. Mayors are still appointed by central government, and their loyalty is to Kabul, not their own people. It's disgusting."

Professor Durrani said quietly, "I believe you should delete that last remark."

"What?" Saleem looked stricken. "Oh, the disgusting? That's not written down, Professor, I just said it."

"Good." Durrani was lighting his pipe for the tenth time. "Though I agree with you, Saleem, it is disgusting. Please continue."

"Finally"—Saleem swallowed—"one-third of the Senate is missing. How stupid do they think we are?" He looked at Durrani. "That's not written down either, Professor."

"I know. You just said it?"

Saleem's head bobbed. "Every province is supposed to send a senator from councils that still don't exist, so half the Senate is appointed by the king now. Maybe that's his idea of balance of powers."

"I hope you did put that in," Durrani smiled. "Perhaps you'd better read us the whole thing, Saleem."

Fine, Mangal thought, you listen, Professor. I'm going to have another Lucky Strike. Don't tell me about the constitution, Saleem, I was there when they wrote it. And that was the last time I felt Nur-Ali's passionate certainty about anything.

In fact, he thought now, it had been the signal event of his own adolescence—sitting, thin and serious, day after day on a low wall outside the hall of Salaamkhaneh, watching delegates come and go from their deliberations and wondering at the babel of tongues and varieties of complexion... bearded mullahs in flowing robes with younger men in Western clothing, sturdy Tajiks and Uzbeks in tightly rolled turbans walking beside tribal Durrani, Ghilzai and even Mangal Pashtuns from the east whose turban tails fell over their shoulders; Oriental-featured Kirghiz from the mountains bordering China and Mongolian Hazaras in carved wooden clogs, the assortment of long shirts and colored turban caps marking men from the western plains to the deserts of Baluchistan, bare felt contrasting with the gold embroidered caps worn by mirror-shirted Kandaharis, the high sheepskin hats of sunburnt Turkomen, and most striking, the Nuristanis with bright daggers in their belts, rolled chitrali caps and knee breeches worn over their long gathered leggings, some with the light hair and blue eyes—thought to be a legacy of Alexander's soldiers—he had heard rumors of but never seen before... watching in that cool October air until finally, after hours of waiting, Daddy-jan or Grand-uncle Yusef came to tell about the day's events.

And of all that, he still most remembered the day Prince Daoud had stopped to talk, questioning his knowledge of this great assembly, the Loya Jirga, when in answer he had babbled, "My father says, and my grand-uncle tells me..." The prince brought his heavy, hawklike face close. "Think of me as your uncle too, Mangal. I call you Bechaim as if you were my son. And it's a fine thing to honor your father and uncles, but you must also learn to form your own opinions." Mohammad Daoud had just resigned as prime minister over the issue of Pashtunistan—the same border dispute that had only grown worse since Pakistan was created. Twelve million Pashtuns, divided by a line that was never meant as a permanent boundary. After years of struggle, Daddy-jan had given up that fight, saying trouble with Pakistan caused too much dependence on the Soviet Union. But Daoud called the border a bleeding wound that could never heal as long as families were cut off from their lands and relatives, and at fifteen Mangal had chosen him as a hero. Finding his courage, he'd said, "Uncle, my opinion is, you are right! The British drew the Durand Line, and it must be erased. The Pashtun tribes should be united so we can be one people in one country." Nodding, Daoud had cupped his face in one huge hand. "Then see to it, Bechaim."

Daoud was also an army general, and Daddy-jan grumbled that his brains were all in his uniform. But he'd been a brilliant prime minister, Mangal thought, playing the West off against the Russians with a sure touch that seemed lost to the present administration. Maybe that was why Daddy resented him so much. Asking Daoud-jan to stand as a witness at the wedding had caused some black looks at home, but it would have been cowardly not to, and if the prince had taught any lesson it was to act on belief and take the consequences.

Mangal looked down the table to where Professor Durrani sat smoking quietly over the corrections he was adding to Saleem's paper. Durrani's own contribution would be a stirring defense of Pashtunistan and tomorrow Prince

Daoud would read it, though not in Durrani's fiery Pashto.

"Professor? I apologize again that our typewriter speaks only Dari, but have you translated your piece yet? We have to start printing."

"Yes, with one addition, unless you're afraid of leaning too far north. I've mentioned that both Khrushchev and Bulganin supported a plebiscite on the subject."

"Can't we afford to bend toward Russia again after kneeling to the West for ten years?" Mangal smiled. "Abdul Rahman, show me how your machine works. We can start to lay this out."

For the next few hours, while the mimeograph ran its slow rotation, the singer's voice poured through from the tea shop in songs of endless longing. All our songs are sad, Mangal thought, always about an unreachable place or person, just as we're wailing back here and probably to no more effect.

Then, suddenly, he froze. Some vehicle was coming down the alley behind the shop, getting closer, stopping just outside the door. He glanced at his watch, it was two o'clock, too late for any business. Surveying the littered room, he saw Khalid's face draw tight with fear, the others standing like statues, hands in midair, listening to the creak of a hinge, quick footsteps, then a sharp knock on the door.

Zalmai got halfway across the room before Mangal grabbed him, hooking one arm around his chest and covering his mouth with the other. Nodding toward Khalid, he jerked his head at the overhead lamp. The old man tapped his chest, then pointed to the door, and in the instant before the room went black Mangal had a final glimpse of his face, grim but no longer afraid.

Zalmai was struggling and Mangal tightened his grasp. Three rapid knocks came again.

"My kitchen's closed," Khalid called irritably. "Go away, whoever you are."

There was a fresh tattoo, this time louder, and Mangal heard Khalid moving toward the door. "Come back tomorrow. I'm sleeping now. Go away!"

But from somewhere near the door there was a faint rasp of metal against metal, the sound of a dagger being drawn, and Zalmai was bucking under his arms, almost breaking free.

A bolt rattled and as the door opened, a sliver of moonlight fell across the room, holding Khalid in profile. "What do you want..."—then his right arm shot out and a tall male figure hurtled into the room, with Khalid on top of him. They were on the floor....

Mangal said, "Close that door and get the light!" But Nur-Ali was already at the door. Someone else stumbled into the table, and then Mangal found himself looking down at the gaping face of Tor's friend Farouk Zadran, and Khalid's dagger glinting by his neck.

"What?" The old man threw down his knife in disgust. "It's another baby! Am I running a school?"

Releasing Zalmai, Mangal cursed silently. Farouk's father was also in the government, a civil servant with the Ministry of the Interior.

"It's all right!" Zalmai said. "He had to come now. Please don't be angry."

Farouk stood up slowly, rubbing a sleeve across his face. "No, Zalmai, it's my fault, they're right to be careful. But you are very strong, old man!"

He extended a hand to Mangal. "I'm sorry. Zalmai warned me tonight wasn't a good time to join you. I'll go quickly, but we have to bring something in first. It's on a cart and I'm afraid to leave it."

"Does Tor know about this meeting too?" Mangal was struggling to control his voice.

"Oh, no!" Farouk shook his head. "Respectfully, your brother's a good friend, but not a... serious person, I think. I've been careful not to talk to him since he came back from Pakistan. No one knows but me."

"Then what is it that couldn't wait? This is very bad, Farouk."

"Help me...." Farouk turned to Khalid. "You help me, it's very heavy. Just pretend it's a box of teapots. Come, we have to hurry, before someone sees."

They went out, returning with a large wooden crate.

"Zalmai told me what you're doing," Farouk said. "A newspaper's a good thing, only most people can't read. But many people have transistor radios now." He was prying at the top of the crate. "I've wanted to join you for a long time, but I was afraid. For my family, as you must be. Then I found this thing. My father took me on a tour of a factory in Kandahar, and I saw it lying in the basement. I don't think they knew what it was. Now I'm pretty sure it's left from World War II. Anyway, I like to play with machinery so I went back and they sold it to me for three hundred afghanis. I've been working on it secretly in the back of my father's garage, but this morning I found out they're buying another car tomorrow, a surprise for my brother, so I had to get it out."

Farouk set aside the lid and removed a packing of paper, exposing a slightly rusted panel studded with knobs and meters. "It's a radio transmitter. An old German make. And"—he beamed—"in very good condition, now. If you set it up high outside the city, it should have a range of thirty kilometers."

Durrani caressed the metal box. "This is wonderful, Mangal! We can broadcast every day if we like, in Pashto and Dari both."

Roshana said, "Mangal's in shock."

"You're right." He managed a smile. "And so are you, Professor. Congratulations, Farouk, it is wonderful. Zalmai, I owe you an apology. But you should have warned us."

"I wanted to." Zalmai's taut face opened in a grin. "But I was afraid it would make everyone too nervous."

"But when you were so nervous, I thought..." Mangal shook his head. "Never mind. I'll tell you this, though, what you say with it had better be well chosen. Get a sense of reaction to the paper first, because once you start broadcasting they'll blow up the mountains trying to find you. Can we store this here, Khalid, or would that make *you* too nervous?"

The old man scowled. "I must be stupid, but alright, you may." He pointed to a shadowed archway. "Put it under that canvas."

"After this, we'd better go with the copies we've printed." Mangal turned to Abdul Rahman. "Pack those machines now and leave. You too, Farouk, when you've covered that up. Ahmed"—he smiled—"be gone, you donkey. I've been waiting all night to say that. Saleem and Professor Durrani, good evening. The rest of us will finish here. Zalmai, you're very brightly dressed for a night of crime."

"But they're used to seeing me like this, driving around late. And Nur-Ali will do the jumping out and running with the bundles . . . but he should have a turban for that."

"I forgot," said Nur-Ali. "I can't remember everything!"

"Here." Mangal lifted off his blue turban as a piece. "Take mine. I won't need this again and it won't show as much as a white one."

"Then you have this." Ahmed pulled off his own. "Yes, Mangal, I insist, or you really are a donkey. You still have to get home."

Tying it on, Mangal smelled leather and tobacco as he watched the others leaving one by one.

When Zalmai and Nur-Ali were ready with their bundled newspapers, Roshana said, "Be careful, now. It's all for nothing if you're caught."

"The king's in Italy, remember?" Zalmai smiled. "So the police are all asleep. But don't worry, Mother, we'll go like mice. And tomorrow will be a new day!"

The moon had almost set when Mangal walked out with Roshana. The air was chilly for July, the sun a clear wash of scarlet in the east. Roshana wore her veil and carried the basket again. There was no reason why one of her family's servants might not be up early, shopping for eggs.

He looked around for Zalmai's car. "I hope they don't expect too much from this."

"If it's so little . . . why were we afraid? And if reason can't change anything, that's a lesson worth learning. I feel satisfied. But you? What happened to the piece you were writing all month?"

"I couldn't finish it. Anyway, it's too soon for my wishful thinking."

At the door to her compound, she said, "So now we go back to our velvet cushions. No more dusty back rooms." He couldn't see her eyes through the narrow grillework of silk.

"Roshana"—the question was nagging him again—"are you sure it's not too much to give up?"

Her hand moved under the veil as if to touch him. "Not if I think in terms of the next fifty years. I love you. But tonight was good. Everyone did well. And it won't be the last time, Mangal, I'm sure of that. We'll just be on sabbatical for a while." She opened the gate. "Good night and good morning. The next time you see my face I'll be your wife."

It seemed she had taken his last energy with her. He walked home in a daze. These clothes, he would have to get rid of them, Daddy-jan would be there. And hide the notebooks, especially the yellow one filled with drafts of the piece he had finally rejected. "The Coming Republic"—but Nur-Ali's title was better. It would be like "balancing on a sword" to find a safe way between the factions jockeying for position now, and in the end there was only one man he could follow. A brilliant progressive, and a devout Muslim who still owned the loyalty of the officers corps, who understood the uses of force and tact... and who in roughly fifteen hours would be a witness at the wedding. He smiled. Roshana, haven't we earned it.

She was right, their strengths were complementary. Roshana had an organizer's sense of what would work, but no patience for detail, teasing him, after one of his lectures, "You're supposed to be a journalist, Mangal. Will you please give us the lead to this story?"

Still, there was an odd restraint between them. They'd kissed for the first time the night he asked her to marry him, and he wondered if they would ever share the passion he'd known with Suzanne when there was no specter of future or children, risk or family to consider. It was as though he and Roshana had already given birth to a difficult child who needed all their attention, and the implications subdued them both. They'd been walking a knife edge of tension for months now. Would that end tonight?

It has to, he thought. We'll get free of this in Europe, and after the wedding trip we'll have the new house, our isolation ward, the illusion of a new beginning, and if not safety, at least time to laugh and make love and plant a garden. I almost wish we *were* being banished to Paghman, so we could lie in bed with the windows open watching the sun come up. Well, starting tomorrow we'll have time together at least, and the rest should come. Didn't we both want a traditional wedding?

In Kabul now, it was fashionable to be married in white lace and tuxedos. Instead, he'd be wearing clothes much like these—Grandfather Anwari's wedding costume. Grand-uncle Yusef hadn't offered it until after Daddy-jan left on this mission. Would it be an unwelcome surprise?

Daddy-jan had been married in a Western suit, gray Oxford flannels, and even at twenty-eight some gray hair showed at his temples. All those years of carrying his dead parents' weight and Uncle Yusef's obsession from one continent to another... no wonder he'd wanted to bring that other self, whom Catherine Lowe knew, home with him. As a kind of protection, like speaking English in front of the servants? But she'd wanted to come. And she was beautiful, from a prominent Boston family. She was the only one smiling in their wedding pictures, and they still looked at each other that way. Before he'd been made a minister without portfolio, she even wrote his cabinet speeches.

For them, the differences worked well right from the beginning. On their first anniversary, Grand-uncle Yusef had given Mummy-jan his most prized possession—a crystal globe the size of a grapefruit, inlaid with colored shards almost two thousand years old from an excavation on the Silk Route. She said that was to remind her Afghanistan had been a crossroad of cultures while Boston was still swampland.

Bringing home a Western wife in 1946 might have been easier than now in some ways, though. More shocking, maybe, but less politically charged. He hadn't considered marrying Suzanne. She'd never have said yes anyway.

Would Mummy-jan, if she knew how much she'd be left alone in Kabul? First it was Daddy-jan's failed referendum on Pashtunistan, then his trade and cultural tours, United Nations missions to Cairo, Athens and Kuwait. ...He's been away for half my life, Mangal thought. We were almost as fatherless as he was.

It seemed now that waiting for Daddy had been their chief excitement as children. So much anticipation. Ten minutes' ecstatic reunion. And then the arguments would start—weeks of criticism doled out in a day. Tor caught the worst of it, had even been beaten for kicking his tutor or stealing the car at night. One way or another, Tor got the attention he needed. But Saira ...Saira was too good, and so was overlooked.

Little Saira, twittering around in one of her hundred pretty dresses, trying to keep everyone happy and being trampled in the process. Would Radcliffe have changed that? She had only come home one summer, while he was still in France, and her letters were always charming and apologetic.

Mangal thought, if I'd seen how uncertain she was...but I was just a child then myself, with my own need for approval, which I got by burning my brains out studying to have good marks to show Daddy-jan. Only now we don't agree on anything. He thinks patience will win what he wants, but if the king doesn't move soon, he'll be moved against and my father will go down with him. I guess that would be one way of ending our competition for his time.

Maybe it was too late already. This latest mission...even Mummy-jan didn't know what it was—for the first time in their marriage, she said. In May, without warning, he'd canceled their trip to Saira's graduation and he hadn't been home since. Two cables came from Zurich last week, but now he was back in the country, traveling in the northern mountains. What could it be about?

Nothing the *Kabul Times* would report, that was certain.

Mangal let himself in through the garden gate. Poor Mummy. She'd been stuck with most of the wedding arrangements, and for the last month, with Tor, who caused twice as much trouble when Daddy-jan was gone. Saira would be home too now, feeling neglected...but Mummy never got caught up in family eruptions. They joked that she was more Eastern than any of them. After a day of calmly sorting through everyone else's crises, she'd sit up while the house was quiet, reading till four in the morning.

Let's hope she didn't have insomnia last night, he thought, glancing down at his clothes.

His hands were black with ink. Turning the kitchen doorknob carefully, he found himself looking into the astonished eyes of his father's driver, Ghulam-Nabi.

Three

"Toryalai, you can't wear those today!"

Saira stood in her bedroom doorway, watching him, wrapped in a pink robe still damp from her shower. Tor strutted in front of her, modeling the tight, faded jeans. "But they fit so well, Saira-gak! How did you know?"

"I didn't," she smiled. "I just got them to fit me and washed them every time I did my laundry. They shouldn't shrink any more now."

"But *you've* shrunk, Saira! You're as skinny as I am. Didn't they feed you in Boston?" He took her right hand and examined it, nodding. "I can count all your bones!"

It was sheer luck the jeans fit, she thought. Tor had grown. But what she remembered most about him hadn't changed: the extravagance in his voice and what she called his dangerous smile—meaning he was in trouble again with Mummy-jan or Mangal. Well, he'd tell her soon enough. No one else ever listened to Tor.

"Yes, they fed me, Tor, but the food there is boring. They don't use any spice. And then on Christian holidays the staff went home and I had to live on boiled eggs." That was true, anyway.

"But didn't your roommate's family give you dinners? You were with them a whole month. If they're so rich, they must have a good cook like Raima. Is California as wild as people say, Saira? Did you meet a lot of movie stars?"

He was looking at her almost adoringly, and bending her head she unwrapped the thick red towel, letting the coil of wet hair fall over her shoulder. Tor was such a good liar himself that he was quick to sense evasiveness, and her nonexistent trip to California was the least of what she had to falsify. She shook out her hair. "No, Toryalai, no movie stars. I'm sorry. But I did bring you two other pairs of jeans. Do you think you can manage not to wear them out till you get to the U.S. to buy some yourself?"

"I'll try." He hugged her. "Thank you very much. Did you bring some for Prince Mangal too?"

He winked at her and they both laughed. The idea of Mangal in jeans was ridiculous.

"Oh, look!" Tor pointed down through the hall window. "Raima's putting up lights!"

Closing her robe tight, Saira went over to the window. In the flagstone courtyard below a new fountain shot water from Daddy-jan's circle of white rose trees, and beyond the orchard and vegetable gardens, Raima was moving slowly along the mud-brick compound wall, fixing an electric cord to pegs. Her daughter Karima must be in school today. Would she look as grown-up as Tor now?

He swung open the window. "And after the Nikka ceremony the guests will start arriving, to stuff their honored faces full of Raima's food. The king's uncle, Prince Wali Khan..." Tor curled over, twitching, and gazed around vaguely. "He must be at least a hundred! They say he runs on batteries now. But still, he never misses a wedding. I guess they don't feed him too well either. Then of course, His Excellency, Mangal's great idol, Prince Daoud..." Hunching his shoulders, Tor swaggered down the hall grunting monosyllables. "He's the real robot, if you ask me. But guess who I am now!"

He bent to shake her hand, looking just past her and tugging at an imaginary tie. "So nice to see you again, my dear"—he scratched his head—"whoever you are!"

"The American ambassador!" She chuckled. "But that's mean, Tor. I like him. He reminds me of my old history professor."

"And why not? Our Doctor of American Intelligence! But he's not the real CIA, they have a new 'political attaché' for that. The guy only has one leg, though, which shows you how much they prize Afghanistan."

"One leg?" Saira laughed. "I don't believe you!"

"As God is my judge! Well, maybe two legs, but one of them's in a brace or something. He does a Nazi goose step, like this. And you should see his glasses, he must be half blind too. But wait till you hear the funny part. His name is Jonathan Straight. Honestly, Saira. Jonathan Straight, our very own CIA cripple. But wait...." He was looking through the window again. "Isn't that Ashraf's car coming in now? The boy who used to make you blush? The one who wears a different suit every day," Tor pirouetted haughtily. "So elegant! And look at you, little nightingale..." He weighed her long hair in his hands. "Your feathers are wet!"

Her stomach clenched in a knot. "But he's so early! Why?"

"For the Nikka, silly. Signing the contract! This is a business deal, remember? Mangal invited him for you, jan. If Ashraf's going to be part of the family, Mangal wants to show him how to do things right. Meaning his way, of course." Tor shook his head. "So the guests are coming and Daddy isn't here yet. This morning he told me he'd be home in an hour, but he's been saying that every day all week."

"Yes," she said, "I know." She'd taken his call that afternoon and his voice had held nothing, as if her coming home were an inconvenience.

Down in the driveway, Ashraf got out of his red Fiat and stood for a moment adjusting his suit. Stepping back from the window, Saira recorded every detail of his clothing, the tall slender frame and thick mass of curling hair. It was two years since she had seen him, could they possibly still feel the same? After all that had happened, after Jeffrey... but Ashraf will never know about Jeffrey, she thought, because I'll never tell him, and soon I will forget him too. Charming, blond, empty Jeffrey, who made me feel shamed, whom I could kill right now if he were standing here. Ashraf, forgive me.

But just before she left Boston, her Indian friend Devika had said: Do you think this Ashraf of yours has been so pure while he was at Cambridge University? Don't tell him, Saira, but remember, if sex is a sin he must be guilty of it too. Why should you suffer, when he won't?

Tor was gazing at her queerly. "Will he be, Saira? Part of the family, I mean?"

She forced a smile. "Not if he sees me like this. Come on, we have to get dressed, Tor. Go take those off and I'll give you the other pairs. Hurry now, we don't have much time."

"Alright. I have a present for you too!"

He spun off down the hall and she watched him go. Tor had grown alright, he was positively sexy, and she found that somehow upsetting. Had Jeffrey spoiled her trust in all men now, even her own little brother?

She took a last look out the window. Ashraf was lifting a brightly wrapped package from the trunk of his car. Then again he smoothed his cream-colored suit, glanced up at the house, straightened his tie and finally started toward the door. So he was nervous too, maybe bracing himself in case she was downstairs to greet him. But she knew when they met later they would both pretend an ease that neither felt, exchange polite regards, respectful compliments. It might be days till they could really talk. And then, she thought, I'll have to lie and lie and lie, be the Saira he remembers, who doesn't exist anymore.

Shutting the bedroom door behind her, she found a comb and began to tug it through her damp hair. The room seemed sad and empty without her wall of birds—finches and canaries mostly—in their pretty cages. More than twenty of them, rescued one by one from the dark cavernous songbird market in the bazaar. Now her room looked as bare as the stripped studio where she had spent this last month, wanting only to come home, going wild until she sought out Devika Ray, who'd been almost a stranger before that night.

Ashraf, she thought, how I wish we could be friends in the way that woman was to me. Not judging or expecting, just listening to one another, holding up a mirror.

Two years since she had seen him. And even that last time, that summer when she knew she loved him, they had not been very honest. She hadn't asked: Did you make the same mistakes I did when you first went to Cambridge? If they could have laughed about it then... but they were both too proud, and at any rate Cambridge sounded more elegant than Harvard, much more formal. They probably had sherry parties there instead of mixers, and if Ashraf's clothes were wrong he could have worn his academic gown while new suits were being sewn. He made a point of being correct, to cover his shyness.

She had expected sherry parties at Harvard, so wore her best silk dress to the first mixer—and found everyone else in jeans. It seemed now she should have known better. Harvard Square looked like a war zone that first year, with all the bank windows boarded up and buildings sprayed with red painted slogans: "Strike!" or "ROTC Off Campus" or "No Dow Chemical Recruiters." That frightened her. In Kabul, students had been shot for doing less.

The sudden freedom of the U.S. was just as disconcerting. She'd had some hope that going to Radcliffe would make her more like Mummy-jan, more decisive, sure of her self. But the girls in her dorm were so independent she could never catch up, and in spite of their kindness it was humiliating to have to ask help with the smallest things: registering, cooking meals on holidays, running the washing machine in the basement. There was no need to lie when she came in late, but no protection either. Boys she had never met called her up for dates on the strength of her picture in the Freshman Register, and even after her roommate, Nora, told her that was customary, she had to struggle to keep horror from her voice when she said no. The subway made her nauseated and meals were a worse problem. It was unbearable to sit alone in the cafeteria, so when there was no one to go down to dinner with she lived on oranges. And though the Harvard strike had ended just before she came to Radcliffe, the antiwar demonstrations grew more frequent and violent, till near the end of that first year four students were shot at a college in the midwest.

She remembered wanting desperately to come home then too and talk it over with Mummy, but she had promised Grandmother Lowe to spend that summer on Cape Cod.

Saira put the comb down, smiling. If she'd known then she would have to wear a bathing suit... but that hadn't really occurred to her until Grandmother Lowe took her shopping. They settled on a white one with a small flounced skirt, yet in spite of its comparative modesty it took all her pride and will to drop the terry cloth robe and follow Grandmother toward the waves that surged up suddenly, unbalancing her and sucking her into the murky surf where slimy plants reached to coil around her legs. She'd smothered a cry, then felt hot with embarrassment walking back to the blanket, expecting to find Grandfather laughing, half expecting even the rage and disgust her costume would have caused in Kabul. Instead, when she reached him, he shook his head. "Aphrodite from the sea!"—smiling with approval. "Now, my girl, you just have to learn to swim!"

It's funny, she thought, it's the ocean I'll miss most here, floating on my back and looking out across that glitter, with sea gulls circling overhead.

She had learned to swim and loved it, and hunting along the beach for shells. Grandfather Lowe apologized for not having a sailboat, "but I sold our last when your mother left, she was my best crew." It was more, Saira thought, that he was ill, he seemed always to be cold. At night he taught her to play chess—while also trying to convince her to study international law—and by August she knew the Cape was just what she had needed, that ocean and a total lack of conflict. When she went back to school the Lowes presented her with a down parka and a dark green bicycle, and through sophomore year she felt more relaxed. Her brown eyes and long waving hair were commonplace in Cambridge, if her olive skin was not, and finally she had the right clothes. But though she sympathized, she still refused to join the antiwar demonstrations, refused dates with all but a few Iranian or Indian students, who mostly wanted to talk politics. Even with them she was guarded, but it was something of a relief. Only the Jewish girls in her dorm seemed to have any real idea of what was going on in the Middle East.

And then, she thought, there was you, Ashraf, when I came home that next summer, you with your fresh engineering degree and new car and new job, and a thousand plans that made me feel guilty for studying languages instead of something more useful to the country. But you said I should be the first woman prime minister, meaning you wouldn't try to make a housewife of me, and you gave me a sweetness and respect that I hadn't realized I needed, and you talked about the house you wanted to build, with an aviary for a hundred birds. I began to think one day we'd do something wonderful together, some project of our own that would leave everyone impressed. And if I couldn't say that to you, I bored poor Royila silly about it.

Saira saw her face contort in the mirror, a hand move to her throat. My best friend, Royila, she thought, it was you, not Ashraf, who packed me off to Jeffrey. He had everything to do with you. I just didn't see that then.

Royila had been two years behind her at school, so was just about to graduate the summer Saira came home, and when Saira finished listing her complaints, Royila quietly announced that her parents refused to send her on to Kabul University. Which was a shame, Saira thought. Royila had more spirit, was a better athlete than any other girl she knew, and if that frightened her parents, it was what Saira liked and envied in spite of her family's relative poverty. Royila with her reddish-brown curls, huge eyes and small pointed chin... like many of her cousins she'd worn the veil briefly to show she was no longer a child, and claimed to like it, said it made her feel invisible. So one day Saira put it on to walk secretly through the bazaar, and felt a rare exciting sense of privacy. Royila joked that they could use it later for romantic assignations, but they agreed they enjoyed it only because they were free not to wear it. "Do you know how lucky you are?" Royila asked. "You can be anything, Saira, a doctor, a lawyer, a journalist.... What can I be now? A first-grade teacher? Until I start having children myself?"

It was Royila, she thought, who should be the lawyer. She herself was not forceful enough. But Royila's thwarted aspirations and Ashraf's ambitions weighed on her in junior year while she struggled through Chekhov, Tolstoy and Lenin in her Russian classes, so when Grandfather Lowe offered her a summer job in his law firm's library she eagerly accepted. That June she also accepted her first dates with Western men, young lawyers from the firm. Spending long days at the beach, she was fearless in her white swimsuit, but showed with every gesture that she was not to be touched, feeling, perhaps, that this freedom was what Royila wanted to taste.

But what Royila had done... Twisting her hands in the pink robe, Saira turned away from the mirror. Royila hadn't written, so there was no chance to help. That August she had received a letter from Mummy-jan saying Royila had killed herself rather than face the marriage her parents had arranged with a first cousin. Saira knew that boy and he was dull and stupid, impossible for Royila.... Why had no one done anything?

She was crying again as painfully as she had all last month in Cambridge, and there was no time for it today, she had to stop. In Boston she hadn't been able to grieve properly. The Lowes and her roommate Nora were very kind but had never known Royila, so couldn't really mourn her. Was she crying for Royila now, or for herself, for Jeffrey, for all the misery of this past year? It seemed impossible to separate Royila from Jeffrey, or Jeffrey from Ashraf, who was waiting downstairs, who had also known Royila. What could she tell him—yes, I consoled myself by letting a man I barely knew make love to me?

She'd been coming from a mid-term that late fall afternoon when she first saw Jeffrey speaking in Harvard Yard, and had stopped at the edge of the crowd listening to his pronouncements on the "oppression of third-world peoples." His blue eyes found and held hers, and for a minute he seemed to be speaking just to her. Royila had surely been oppressed. But when he began an attack on the Shah of Iran she had to turn away. She knew all about the SAVAK—among other things that they photographed foreign students at demonstrations like this, and since those pictures sometimes found their way into print at home it could embarrass the family if she appeared to be participating, in old jeans with her long hair free.

On Mass. Avenue he had come up behind her, touching her sleeve. "Did I say something wrong?"

He was so tall she had to step back to look at him. "Wrong? I'm sorry, I don't know what you mean."

He smiled. "You're Iranian, aren't you?"

His eyes were clear blue in a tanned angular face, his hair the color of wheat, his corduroy pants and tweed jacket worn but of obvious quality, and he radiated the energy she had come to think of as wholly American.

"No," she said, "I'm Afghan." But her tone was wrong, as if the question were offensive. "And half Bostonian too. My mother grew up here."

Half American. Wasn't that the point of coming to Radcliffe, to find that other side of herself? And what had she done for three years but hide behind aristocratic distance, in fear of being touched, confused, of becoming too much like the women in her dorm, whom she admired but who'd never have to be judged by Afghan standards, as she would again very soon.

He shook his head. "You look like a Persian miniature. I'm afraid all I know about Afghanistan comes from *King of the Khyber Rifles*." He stuck out a well-manicured hand. "I'm Jeffrey Carleton. Listen, could I buy you a cup of coffee? There are a few things I'm puzzled about that you might be able to clear up."

She smiled but didn't shake the hand. "I doubt I could be much help." Then, suddenly not wanting him to leave, "My name's Saira Anwari. Actually, I was just going to have tea somewhere. If you'd like to join me, that would be alright."

See how clever I was, she thought. I turned his invitation around. I allowed him to come with me. I made every step of it seem my choice, the queen of self-delusion.

At the Blue Parrot, he'd rolled crisp denim shirt sleeves to his elbows, and while he talked, endlessly it seemed, about the Shah, SAVAK, the Kurdish question, she found herself trying not to stare at the golden hair on his sinewy arms. He didn't need her to answer him, she understood finally, but just wanted her to appreciate the effort that he, an American, had made to inform himself of such things. That was alright, it helped rationalize her quickly growing attraction, gave a reason to say yes when he asked her to come and read a news article he was writing on the upheaval in Iran.

But at what point, she wondered now, had he consciously started telling her what she wanted to hear? He was the first student she'd met in the States who knew as much about world politics as she did.

In contrast to his careful grooming, the apartment was strewn with books and folders that he had to move so they could sit on the couch. She read three pages of his writing, then put it down. "Yes, it's true, things have changed much too quickly in Tehran and not enough in the countryside. But it hasn't been all bad, you know. Particularly for women." And she told him about Royila, the story pouring out—was that so he would touch her? She didn't want to talk but just to be insensible, curled in the dark against some stronger warmth.

When she finished, he gave her hand a squeeze, saying, "What a waste. It's tragic. You poor kid!" with such vehemence it seemed to justify her need—for what? To be a child again? Then he added, brilliantly, "No, I'm sorry, that sounds as if I don't respect your customs." And seeing her startled gratitude at that recognition, he went on for hours and days about cultural evolution, class struggle, the emancipation of women, freedom as a thing that must be seized ... a world of ideals in which it would have been immoral of her not to return his love completely. And when, after weeks of turmoil, she had gone to bed with him, "Saira, why didn't you tell me you'd never done this before?"

Why did I go with you at all, she thought. Because I wanted to be bruised, I'd been numb for so long, but I couldn't admit what I was doing. I needed to feel alive again, to climb out of Royila's grave. And I was afraid of coming home, even to you, Ashraf, I was afraid of being buried too.

Through that winter and spring, life had consisted of books and making love. It seemed an imposition even to go across the river for Sunday lunch at the Lowes' house on Beacon Street. Jeffrey said that because he was her first lover she would never forget him, and he wanted to be worth remembering. He was flattered, as if she'd chosen him above all others; her virginity seemed to drive his passion. He wanted to teach her everything, be first in everything, so that any future man would compare unfavorably, she thought now. And she had cooperated, given herself in ways it was her curse she never would forget, though not once had she overcome her sense of shame or felt more than a frightened kind of pleasure.

And then of course, Jeffrey's phone would ring, or he'd jump up to make a call. He never went anywhere without a sheet of phone numbers folded in the pocket of his shirt—deans, politicians, heads of national organizations— he seemed to know everyone from the Kennedy family to the Weather Underground, and if he went to the moon she had no doubt he'd be followed by a string of messages. His concerns ran from apartheid to the Church in Latin America, and it was exciting to work on articles he wrote for the *Old Mole* and the *New Republic*—her thoughts, discreetly rendered under a by-line he never offered to share. But when he tried to add Afghanistan to his list of causes, reading field reports on the country and cross-examining her, she only smiled and said nothing. Jeffrey prided himself on his analytic abilities and she had no wish to be a specimen informant.

Would he have been interested in her at all, Saira wondered, if she hadn't been a minister's daughter? Because in spite of so much talk about "the people" she never met any of them through him. He teased her about her servants, but sent his own clothes out to be cleaned—separate clothes for different roles, like an actor's wardrobe. Jeffrey's messy apartment was a smoke screen for conceits she now saw as more personal than political. Yes, all the signs were there, she thought, I just wouldn't read them.

She had never mentioned the possibility of staying in the States, but turned the idea over like a coin in her pocket. Why not marry Jeffrey and live Mummy's life in reverse? At home there was Ashraf, but there was also Royila, and Ashraf's terms might change once she was really his wife—that happened fairly often. She'd given herself to Jeffrey and he loved her. Every night he made up stories about adventures they could have if she weren't going back. He was getting a master's degree, and to give the decision time she agreed to go camping with him after commencement. So she wrote home that she'd be visiting Nora's family in California for the month of June.

And then, a week before graduation, she came back from a party to find his apartment strangely neat, her belongings piled on a chair, Jeffrey blushing, twitching, holding out his hands. "I really didn't anticipate this, Saira. I'm sorry, but there's nothing I can do."

He'd neglected to tell her that he already had a girl friend, a woman he had been with for years. "My regular woman," that's what he called her—as if she herself were abnormal. This "regular" woman was studying at the London School of Economics, but had decided unexpectedly to come back for commencement. Surprise. She was flying in that night.

Saira remembered picking up her things and walking straight out of the room, down the hall, the stairs, in spite of her shaking knees and dizziness, down Green Street to the corner of Putnam Avenue, where she blacked out, clinging to a fence. She still couldn't recall getting back to the dorm. The next thing she remembered was Nora pacing in front of her, cursing, "That bastard! And he's the one who's always preaching about truth and justice! Oh, God, Saira, don't cry, he isn't worth it!" Nora crouched in front of her hugging her knees. "Listen, maybe this is for the best. You would have split up anyway, so now you'll have a month to get over that creep. Some time to decompress. I *would* take you home if I didn't have to be in Paris, but I'll find you somewhere to stay, don't worry. Saira, it would have ended anyway. Maybe it's better if you hate him."

But it was hatred of herself that consumed her all that month spent in the studio apartment of one of Nora's vacationing friends, alone with a growing knowledge of her self-deception and the ghost of Jeffrey's "regular woman" whom she'd seen at graduation—a girl with a braid of blond hair and cool blue eyes like his own. The Lowes often came to Harvard Square and she was afraid to go out and risk meeting them, until Jeffrey's letter drove her in near hysteria to find Devika, a graduate student from Calcutta whom she barely knew, but who was the only one around who might possibly understand.

Nora had seen him, Jeffrey's letter said, and "read him the riot act," but he was only sorry about how things ended. Not telling her wasn't the same as lying, it was "elitist" of her to be so possessive. He had liberated her—

didn't she really enjoy sleeping with him too? "Saira, admit it," and "be grateful" and "remember all the good things."

She remembered very well but found nothing good in either of their behavior, or in his "ideals." She'd crumpled up the letter, then smoothed it out to show Devika, and now had decided to keep and read it every day of her life so she would never make that same mistake again.

"Never," she told the streaked face in the mirror. "But you'll never have the chance, you're such a mess."

There were airline towels in her knapsack, she remembered, along with the brandy she'd bought in Paris for her nerves. Lifting the pack onto her bed, she found and opened one foil envelope, pressing the wet lemon-scented paper over her forehead. She was home now, it was over, it must be over and forgotten.

But she hardly looked like someone who had just spent a lazy month on the beach at Santa Barbara.

The rust-colored silk and a little makeup should help. Her dress was hanging on the door and Raima had ironed it beautifully, its handkerchief points seemed to flutter in spite of the heat. But this was dry heat. In Boston the fog was so dense at times that she could put up her hands and touch it like a wall.

"Saira?" It was Tor knocking. "Are you dressed? I want to give you my present."

"Alright. Come in!" She let him see her mopping her face with the towel, but he wasn't fooled.

"Jan, have you been *crying*? Your eyes are all red." He was holding his hands behind his back. "Is something wrong, Saira?"

"No, it's just the heat, silly. But don't you look handsome!" His high cheekbones were sunburned and his hair was much too long, but at least he'd brushed it. He was wearing an oyster-colored suit, a white shirt and red silk tie. He was beautiful. Little Tor?

He grimaced. "Don't say that! I hate these clothes. Now, shut your eyes and put out your hands."

She did and felt something like a prickly box touch her palms.

"Alright. You can look now!"

It was a bamboo cage, a very small one, and from inside it a red-factor canary glanced up at her cheerfully, first with one bright black eye, then the other. She laughed. "Oh, Tor, he's just adorable!"

She carried the cage to the window and Tor followed. "He's a genius! Wait till you hear him sing! This is a bird of great understanding, Saira, he deserves a much better cage. I didn't have enough money for that but we can buy one together this week." He bowed his head. "I felt so bad about your other birds dying."

Inexplicably, she had thought that he had killed them. But Tor would never do that. He loved the birds as much as she did.

"I gave them lots of greens," he said, still looking down at his shoes, "and fish bone, and put them outside in the sun, but I guess they just missed you too much. So did I, jan, I should have died too."

He was always saying things like that: I wish I were dead, meaning, love me, love me, love me. She wondered if he even knew what he meant.

"Come on, Tor, it wasn't your fault. Besides, now we can start again. I could almost wear him on my dress tonight." She held up the cage and the bird's fluffy salmon breast and darker bronze head and wings contrasted beautifully with the rust silk. Tor giggled.

There it was again, that odd high note in his voice. He sounded almost as crazy as she felt.

She hugged him. "Thank you, Toryalai, you couldn't have given me anything nicer. But I have to get dressed now. Your jeans are in my pack."

Setting the cage on her dresser, Saira remembered the brandy, but turning quickly saw it was too late. Tor was spilling out her pack and the newspaper-wrapped bottle slid out on the coverlet. He picked it up, curling back the paper. "What's this? Rémy Martin Fine Champagne Cognac? Ooh, Saira, you've drunk some! What would Daddy say? And look what you've wrapped it in...." He pretended to squint, "God save us, the Progressive Labor Party! Saira-gak, are you a Communist now? Or did you bring this for Prince Mangal to read? Does it say the masses should unite?"

As he peeled off the paper, a white envelope fell to the floor and she felt her throat close with panic. Jeffrey's letter, she must have stuck it in there on the plane.

Tor looked from her face to the envelope, but just as she moved for it, he dove, snatched it up, was waving it over his head. "So!" He squinted elaborately. "Why, this looks like a *man's* handwriting! Could it be a love letter?" He danced away, keeping it out of reach. "Hmmm. The return address says J. Carleton. Who's J. Carleton, Saira-gak? Should I ask Ashraf? Maybe he knows!"

"Tor! Give that to me! It's private!" But showing fear would only make him more curious. "Come on," she said evenly. "Do you want those jeans or not?"

"A bribe?" He was grinning. "This must be quite a secret! Alright, I'll trade. For a sip of that whiskey." But he handed her the letter as if he'd measured her anger. "Honestly, Saira, I've never tasted alcohol." He twisted up the cork. "Just one sip? I was only playing. You know I wouldn't read it."

"And you won't tell anyone I've got this.... It's cognac, Tor, not whiskey. I only bought it so I could sleep on the plane. I had a four-hour layover in Paris, and six hours in Tehran...."

His eyes were shining with excitement. "Of course I won't tell! French Champagne Cognac! And a Communist newspaper—is that how they teach Russian at Radcliffe? But wait, I'll get a glass."

He was gone before she could stop him, returning in an instant. "And you'll need the rest to help you sleep in Kabul, right? No, don't get mad again, I mean it, Saira. I'm going out of my mind too." Tor put the bottle to his nose, inhaling. "God save us again! It's turpentine!"

She smiled. "But Tor, you can't have that now. It's very strong. They'll smell it."

"There's mouthwash in the bathroom. Besides, this is supposed to be relaxing. Isn't it?"

As he poured it out, she reached to grab his wrist. "For heaven's sake! That's ten times too much!"

"Okay. Watch this—I'm a cowboy!" Tipping up the glass, he emptied it in one gulp.

She shook her head. "You're supposed to sip it!" But her voice broke with laughter because Tor's eyes were already pink and startled and he was holding his chest in an effort not to choke.

Collapsing back on the quilt, he blew out air as if he'd been running. "Oooh, Saira, I think I'm on fire! I can feel it all the way down to my toes." He glanced up. "Aren't you going to have some? I'm on fire, but it's nice! I don't think I can get up, though. But I don't want to anyway, let's just stay in here. They can have the stupid wedding without us." He craned his neck to look at her. "It's been so lonely here without you, jan, you're the only one who makes me feel good. Oh, but I feel good now."

His eyes were very red, she saw. It had been stupid to let him do it, especially on an empty stomach. He'd been out riding all through lunch. "You're probably drunk," she said acidly. "You just had about five shots. Tor, you're going to ruin your clothes. You have to get up now."

"Drunk? Am I drunk? No, I'm not." He rolled over to face her. "Tell me about J. Carleton, Saira. I want to know about J. Carleton."

He was frowning with an exaggerated concern that frightened her. If he was drunk, it was her fault. She'd sensed the fragility of his control the first minute she saw him last night. There was some new anger in him that she didn't understand yet, no doubt another battle with Tor against the world, and this morning she had consciously kept him at a distance so he wouldn't try to open his heart and be comforted, make her choose again between him and the rest of the family. But Tor was like some volatile gas, always on the verge of exploding, and that was the last thing she needed now. Why did he force all these conflicts? In an instinctive, shrewd sort of way, he saw her more clearly than anyone else, but now she didn't want to be known, or engulfed by his emotion. And there really was no time....

"No, Tor, I have to get dressed now. Come on, get up."

The impatience in her voice seemed to wound him, and she ruffled his hair. "We can talk later."

"No!" His face was stubborn. "Don't treat me like a baby. Tell me about J. Carleton. I won't leave till you do. Really, Saira, I want to know."

Sighing audibly, she said, "What?"

"He was your boyfriend?"

"For a while."

"And did you love him?" He was watching her eagerly now.

She shrugged. "I don't know, Tor. I thought I did. Look, I'll just tell you, alright? His name is Jeffrey. We met almost a year ago. And we broke up"—she smiled bitterly—"a week before graduation. When I was half dead from writing my honors thesis. It was sudden and I really don't want to talk about it. Understand?"

Tor caressed her cheek unsteadily. "Yes, oh yes, I understand. All the pain inside! Tell me, did you make love with him too?"

He asked it gently, but his voice had that edge again and it made her nervous. Tor loved tripping other people up, to justify his own sins.

"How could I?" She teased, "Don't you remember? You practically hung a sign around my neck when I left. Saira Anwari, Keep Off the Grass." But she could see her lie reflected in his eyes.

He took her hand. "You can tell me, Saira-jan. You see, I've also known a great love."

Leaning back on her elbows, she studied him and his expression was almost comic. Of course this was the point: to pry at her so he could confess some trifle of his own, blown out of all proportion by his eternal feeling of martyrdom and heroism. With Tor, everything came back to himself. But that was alright this time, since it let her off the hook.

She said dryly, "A great love, Tor?"

"As God is my judge." He nodded solemnly. "The greatest love a human heart can feel. It's a good thing you didn't make love with this Jeffrey"—he glanced at her sideways—"because then you'd never get over it. Like I never will." He pointed to the floor. "Do you know who's getting married down there? The wrong person, people . . . I should be the one. Mangal could never feel a love like mine. I wanted to marry her too, but Mummy-jan won't let me. She doesn't want me to be happy. No one here does but you. Why do we suffer, when we're the most sensitive, while they get everything they want?"

This is ridiculous, Saira thought. She felt like screaming, It's not sensitivity, just stupidity, Tor. Don't include me in your conspiracy. Instead she asked, "So, who was the object of this great love?"

Her irony seemed to escape him. Closing his eyes, he shook his head. "Who could it be, Saira? Who's the only girl I've ever loved as much as you? It's Karima, my beautiful Karima-jan. And they want to send me away from her and ruin both our lives." He buried his face theatrically in his hands.

"Karima downstairs?" Saira realized she'd whispered the words. So that was it. No wonder Mummy-jan looked so pale and tired. Raima and Ghulam-Nabi had lived in\the compound for twenty-five years. If Tor had dishonored their daughter, both families would be shamed. And she was so sweet, Karima, so sincere... and no doubt vulnerable to a "man" of the house, charming Tor, with his big brown eyes and lies and promises. But wait, she thought, I may be wrong.

"Do you mean to tell me," she said, "that you slept with her? With Karima? Oh, Tor, how could you do that?"

He was staring. "What? I didn't 'sleep' with her, I made love with her. I love her."

"Love?" Saira felt her cheeks burn. "What does love mean to you, sex? Karima's still a child, Tor, you both are. You can't marry her! If you thought about it ten minutes you'd know that. And if you didn't think, it's worse because you're lying to yourself as well. Is that how you got her into bed with you, by promising to marry her? When you knew very well Daddy-jan would never allow it?"

"I didn't know! We could run away!" Tor punched the mattress. "Even Mummy-jan said if Karima lived in their old village she'd probably have kids by now. I wasn't lying. I do want to marry her!"

"Yes, but since you know you can't, that's a nice safe thing to say, isn't it. If Raima and Ghulam-Nabi were our in-laws, they couldn't work for us anymore. Then what would they do? So Mummy-jan knows about this?"

"Yes." He glared. "She caught us. Now she won't even let me talk to Karima."

"Well, someone has to protect her! You obviously don't care what happens. When she meets someone she *can* marry, how do you think she'll feel? Does she tell him and risk a public disgrace? Or not, and live with a lie all her life? You pick, which is better? Of course you'll never have to worry about that, will you? You're a sacred, holy male who can do exactly what you please!"

"Except marry Karima!" He jumped up. "You're disgusting! You're even worse than Mummy! You should understand! My heart's broken and instead of trying to help..."

He was shaking, his mouth hanging open, she could see the red underside of his lip.... Tor in one of his rages, snorting and shivering, looked just like Grand-uncle Yusef's black horse, she thought, and suddenly it was funny. They were both funny, both ridiculous. She for imbuing Jeffrey with every virtue on earth when everyone else knew he was a fake, a fraud, about as reliable as a lizard, and Tor with his prince-and-beggarmaid romance, a "great love" just as absurd as all the rest of his emotions. She started laughing helplessly, in spite of Tor's scowl, his darkening face, the anger growing and flashing in his eyes. She reached for him, "Tor, it's funny, don't you see..."

But he stepped back. "You! Alright, go on and laugh! So you're so brilliant and I'm still a baby, is that it? I'm so funny? Good, I'm glad you're laughing! I thought I loved you! I thought you were one person I could always trust. And instead, when I tell you... Oh, never mind. I hate you now. Good! I want to hate you. I hate everybody and you all deserve it. I hope you go to hell, Miss Grown-up Two-faced Idiot. You're just a big liar like everyone else." Wheeling into the hall, he slammed her door, then opened it and slammed it again.

Saira sat up straight, wiping her eyes. It *was* funny. At least she still remembered how to laugh. And Tor was right, she was a liar, though not in the way he and Jeffrey were. "I only fib in self-defense," she said, and started giggling again. Stop it, Saira, calm down.

Reaching for the cognac, she rolled it up in the now-smeared copy of P.L. She had bought that paper because of something Devika said, but found she couldn't concentrate on it on the plane. It sounded too much like Jeffrey. Tor and Jeffrey had quite a lot in common really. So warm, both of them, as long as you agreed. As long as you smiled and nodded you were allowed to be part of a magic circle. But suggest either of them might be wrong and you were hateful, elitist, a two-faced idiot. Devika called that emotional blackmail, sheer manipulation, and now it was transparent to her too. No, Tor, she thought, if you're looking for sympathy, you've come to the wrong place. After last month I don't have any left.

Standing up, she found the letter and put it in her pack with the cognac, then carried that to the back of her closet. Jeffrey and his so-called ideals... But no, the ideals were right. He just perverted them, used them as a license. Inside his scaffolding of "politics" there was no Jeffrey at all.

Her hair was almost dry now, and sitting at the dresser she began to brush it hard. Devika had also said: Let's face it, Saira, you were his third-world experience. I've heard this story before. In three years' time he'll be working in a bank. Now find your pride again and put it on like a suit of armor. You can still go home and be happy.

Devika, it seemed, could not go home, because of a similar problem, which she never fully explained, except to say that her affair caused a public scandal and she'd chosen to leave rather than be stigmatized forever as a woman of no virtue. "Perhaps that's why I'm a Communist," she had said, smiling faintly. "Oh, I'm sorry, does that shock you?" Leaning forward suddenly, she grasped Saira's wrist. "Let me tell you something. Between two forms of oppression, if one has a marginal benefit, it's that one you will choose." Then she smiled again, wryly. "But you don't have to choose. I can tell you how to counterfeit virginity. Women have been doing it for thousands of years. Tricks and games, Saira, that's what we teach each other, but maybe it's worth it if you love this Ashraf so much. And if he loves you. Go home and take the chance while you still have it."

Well, I'm home now, she thought, not even Tor can spoil that. And Ashraf ... he may not be as passionate as Jeffrey, but he does truly love me, Devika. He wants to give me a home, work, children, for always, not just six months of lies.

Maybe Jeffrey had been partly her rebellion against Ashraf and the kind of "arrangements" Royila had suffered. Both sets of parents had pushed them together since childhood—all those joint family picnics. And if she wanted to see a movie with Ashraf that was alright, but if it were someone else, well, they thought she had too much homework. Yet now it seemed they were right in doing that. They'd never have forced her to marry him, and in the meantime it gave her life grace and order. The very worst of Jeffrey was losing dignity.

She peered at her reflection—would Ashraf think she was too thin? And later, might he guess she wasn't a virgin? Even Daddy-jan had harangued her about sex, to their mutual embarrassment, saying that as a woman she would be judged differently even now. So she'd have to lie and that was undignified too, but thanks to Devika no one need be the wiser. Poor Daddy, she thought, and Ashraf and Tor, poor me, poor everybody.

Carefully, she brushed on a little rouge, a touch of eyeshadow. Her eyes looked as big as Royila's these days. Daddy-jan. She could count the pieces of advice he'd ever given her on the fingers of one hand. In the single conversation when she'd tried to probe his experience abroad, that sophomore year she came home so upset, he'd praised her grades and Ashraf's work and warned her to keep her virginity. If she had changed, he didn't want to know it. Her confusion was temporary, like a head cold, it would disappear, and coming back for good would be the fruition of her life, as it had been for him.

Untying the pink robe, Saira found the lace bra she'd also bought at Orly airport. And a bronze slip, to go under the silk. It was possible to have a conscience and not wear hiking boots and denim—the one favor Jeffrey did her was to make Ashraf look wonderful by comparison. She and Ashraf would be quite a handsome couple tonight. Mangal would be proud.

Slipping on the silk dress, she fixed its wrapped waist and felt the handkerchief skirt move lightly around her legs. Yes, Mangal should definitely approve. All the way home, she had looked forward to seeing him... or rather, to having him see her as more than a baby sister. He'd made fun of her shyness and lack of purpose, but now four years had passed. This morning there had been no chance to visit. He'd slept late and then been sort of jumpy when he got up. Wedding nerves, probably, and rather sweet. Mangal was the least sentimental man on earth.

Dark stockings. And Grandmother Lowe's pearl necklace—that had been Mummy's graduation gift to her. She smiled at her reflection. The dress was just right and her hair looked fine too, swept up by twin gold combs. At the party she would talk to Mangal, make him see how much she'd grown. It was funny, before she left home she had felt much closer to Tor, but now it was Mangal's company she wanted.

She jumped as a car door slammed shut in the driveway, then heard Ghulam-Nabi's voice. Could this be Daddy-jan finally?

Walking out to the hall, she bent through the open window—and for the second time that day stepped back numbly. It was her father. But he looked horrible, sick and exhausted, older than Grand-uncle Yusef. And Ghulam-Nabi was half carrying him toward the house.

Four

"Mummy-jan?" Catherine looked up. "Careful, or you'll break a leg in those shoes."

Saira ran downstairs holding the bannister. "But I saw Daddy!"

"Shhh. Yes, he's here now."

"But he looks..."

"Your father's fine, Saira. He just had a dizzy spell on the road. Knowing him, he probably hasn't eaten all day."

Ghulam-Nabi was coming toward them carrying towels and a steaming water basin, and as he slipped into the study Saira leaned to look over his shoulder, but the old man closed the door quickly.

"Saira, dear..." Catherine took her arm, steering her away. "Everything's alright, he only needs a minute to unwind. You look lovely. Those pearls were made for you! Now, would you do something for me?"

"What?" Saira was frowning, hurt at being shut out, but Omar was in no state yet for a reunion.

"Everyone's waiting in the living room and I want you to go and be hostess. Just apologize, say your father was delayed and we'll be in right away. Roshana's uncle's name is Aziz Haidiri, the same as her little brother. Her father will introduce you to their witnesses. Now, scoot."

"All right, Mummy-jan. I'll do my best." Shaking her head, Saira crossed the foyer and started down the hall, straightening her posture and smoothing her dress.

Good girl, Catherine thought. My beautiful daughter. You should have a better homecoming than this.

Grasping the study doorknob, Catherine took a slow breath. Whatever had happened, they would find a way around or through it. But Omar's face had frightened her, too.

What time was it this morning when he woke her up? Stretched out beside her, propped on an elbow. "No, I'm not a dream, my love. More like a nightmare. I'm going straight to the palace, but I had to warn you first."

"Of what, Omar? Where have you been?"

"It doesn't matter. I'm just hoping you still love me, since I may be home a good deal after today. Could you stand it if I retired a little earlier than we'd planned? No, don't turn on the light." He leaned over her, kissing her. "Anyway, try to get used to the idea. Now go back to sleep. I'll tell you the rest of it later."

In their twenty-seven years together he'd never kept secrets before, and that had been a constant ache through all the wedding preparations.... Finding Tor in bed with Karima didn't help either. But there were guests here who would have to be greeted soon, with at least a semblance of harmony, no matter what was said in the next few minutes.

Tucking a loose strand of hair back up into her chignon, she opened the study door.

Omar stood by the fireplace in his shirt sleeves with his back to her, and the instant before he turned she had a glimpse of his reflection in the gun cabinet's glass—thick gray hair falling over his forehead, the face below it slack, eyes closed. He looked asleep on his feet, supported by the hands clenched at his hips. Then with a jolt he opened his eyes and she saw him construct a smile for her as he pivoted on one heel. "Well, I suppose there's an uproar out there. I'm sorry to be so late. I've asked Ghulam-Nabi to bring my clothes down here so our guests won't see a ghost."

"I'll do that now," Ghulam-Nabi said. "Excuse me, Mrs. Anwari."

But even after the servant left, neither of them moved. Omar's smile was so strained she knew it would be better not to touch him, however much she wanted to hug him and hear the same reassurance she had just given Saira.

Things were not alright though, she knew that from the tired flesh under his eyes, the lines carving his forehead even more deeply than this morning. At fifty-five, Omar was leaner and more muscular than at thirty, brown from his hours of working in the garden. But his hair had been gray for a decade, and now there was white growing in at the temples, making his eyes seem sharper and less kind. For the first time she saw how he would look as an old man, gaunt, with a wreath of silver hair like Uncle Yusef's, unsubstantial but for those eyes.

She stepped closer. "Omar, did you do it?"

His hands were in his pockets and he thrust his elbows out, smiling, in the same too bright way Tor did when something was irretrievably lost. "What a funny world we live in, Catherine. As fast as one hand builds things up, the other tears them down. You know, I'm almost glad about all this. I want to laugh instead of worry for a while." But his voice was brittle and he turned away. "There was a new manifesto out in the bazaar today, have you seen it? Here, I brought you a copy."

Watching him sift through his briefcase, she remembered the time when Tor had climbed a poplar tree and she couldn't tell him where to put his feet and had to wait for him to find his own way down to her again. Omar had kept his secret too long to tell it easily.

"This one's called *New Homeland*." He held up some folded pages. "Tell me, how does one have a 'new homeland'? By becoming God, to make it rain and put oil in the ground? And land reform—they admit they have no answer, but why not toss another coal on the fire and with any luck we'll have a conflagration."

Crumpling the paper, he threw it across the room. "Till I was twelve, the mosque was my only school. Now we educate our children and they're idiots. I don't know which team put out this particular tract, but it's asinine—they complain about Pashtunistan on the one hand, and a slow legislature on the other, somehow failing to see that our troubles with democracy come from the very tribalism they're so sentimental about. And literacy! The Germans were all literate under Hitler. We've got too many graduates and too few jobs as it is. That's what makes revolutions. It's elementary de Tocqueville. Is that what they want?"

He was close to raving and she reached for his hands. "But couldn't you almost have written that yourself? You've made all those complaints at some point. Omar, for God's sake, did you see Moosa Shafiq?"

The name stopped him. Nodding, he smiled thinly. "Yes, my love. You're married to a man of leisure. I gave my resignation to the prime minister at noon, and we've been arguing ever since. Poor Moosa Shafiq—he didn't want to accept it with the king out of the country, but of course that's why I insisted. To spare His Majesty asking me why, since he'll know the answer as soon as he hears I've stepped down. He knew what I was looking for in Zurich."

"Did you tell the prime minister? Will you tell me now?"

He pulled her close. "Only you. Poor Catherine. I wake you up and mumble and then run off.... But I wasn't absolutely sure this morning. I had to sit at my desk and go through it all over again. After that, it wasn't hard to decide. How could I stay in the cabinet and turn a blind eye to this, when today's *Times* has a page-one article by my son about pay-offs in government. I don't want to give Mangal any more ammunition." His arms were tight around her and she felt their tension.

"I told Mangal they wouldn't print that." She hid her face in his shoulder. "What you said this morning was that you never thought you'd be buried by a pile of lapis lazuli."

"And emeralds. And rubies. A good share of the profits from the mines in Badakshan. Going straight into Swiss bank accounts connected to the Royal House."

"Oh, no, Omar. Good lord. No wonder you've been so frantic." The king's strong-featured face rose in her mind. Was Zahir Shah capable of such a betrayal? He'd always seemed an honest man, as did his cousins, Mohammad Daoud and Naim. But "connected to the Royal House" could mean anyone from His Majesty to some nephew or business associate—even another minister, though Omar would hardly resign to save a colleague's skin. She said, "You must be feeling pretty badly used. Who was it? Tell me, so I can strangle them."

"You might just do that." He shook his head. "No, Catherine, don't ask. It would make you an accomplice too. This has been the hardest choice I've ever had to make. Let's leave it at that for now."

"Alright. Maybe it's better if I don't know. But how on earth did you trace it? Especially the bank accounts. I thought that was impossible."

He laughed. "It is, theoretically. I did a spy routine with an old Oxford tie who's there now. You know, 'Let's have lunch again tomorrow, and if my guess is right just don't show up'? Since neither of us was specific, I don't think he felt too compromised, but I'm in the same position. If I stayed in the cabinet, I'd be obliged to act on this information."

"And why not?" She stepped back, looking into his face. "Why should you be the scapegoat? Let whoever did it be tried like any other criminal. That's simple justice. It would do the king honor."

"Yes, except the government would fall." Opening the alabaster box on his desk, he lit one cigarette from the other in their old way. "I didn't tell Moosa Shafiq because he's too damn good at his job. He might be tempted to take over himself, before this gets out and someone else beats him to it."

"Really?" She took the cigarette. "The scandal would be that bad?"

"I think so." Pushing aside a green onyx lamp, he sat on the edge of his desk. "If this could happen, why should we be trusted with all that foreign aid? But it's more the climate than the crime, Catherine. There are too damn many groups just waiting for a wedge to use against the king—the Khalqis, the Parchamis, even some members of the Royal House. Well, I won't give it to them. We've built too much, but more than that...you know how I feel. If the monarchy falls, that's the end. All we've got is a little bit of hard-won stability, and if we lose that we'll be just another banana-less republic. Just a dog's bone. King Zahir's the only glue holding the country together now, and he's respected internationally as well. So, no, I'm not about to force a trial over this, but neither can I stay in the cabinet. That would mean complicity. And if it came out later, they could hang it all on me, like...

who's Nixon's fool? John Dean? We couldn't survive a Watergate here now. The irony is, my resignation equals silence. I can trust that the king will put a stop to it, but I may never know that for sure."

"And in either case he'll accept you as a sacrificial lamb."

"With deep regret." Omar smiled bitterly. "What a wedding present for Mangal! He'll think I've come to agree with him. And he'll be free of my long black shadow. Unless he's fired, of course. Since ministers resign so rarely, there may be an assumption of malfeasance in some quarters, especially when I won't talk about it. Will you mind that very much?"

"Only why you had to do it. I won't miss writing your reports. Frankly, infrastructure doesn't exactly fascinate me. So, what will we do now? Keep bees? You always said you wanted to try that." Resting her forearms on his shoulders, she looked down into his face. He was very tired, and angry, understandably enough, but he didn't seem wholly unhappy. We'll be alright, she thought, we can start something new, and at least Omar will be here for a change. Haven't I been wishing we could all be together again?

Someone knocked twice on the door and Omar called, "Come in, Ghulam-Nabi." He kissed her quickly. "Yes, I'll keep bees, and get to know my wife again, and my rather unpleasant sons. No, I don't mean that, Catherine, don't scowl. Has Saira grown up behind my back? Not too much, I hope."

But she was looking at Ghulam-Nabi, who had put on his most elegant tribal costume and combed his beard in two long careful points. Almost surely, there were tears in his eyes.

Omar stood up to take the suit his driver was holding. "I've warned Ghulam-Nabi he may be bored from now on. He claims he can live with that."

"Because I don't believe it," Ghulam-Nabi said with disgust. "You'll probably start a factory by next week. You can't sit still."

"Hah!" Omar laughed. "I've been out of office four hours and already my servants are rude to me. But speaking of manners, Catherine, you'd better go pacify our guests. I still have to shave."

It hasn't really hit him yet, she thought, and when it does... at least we'll have got through the wedding.

"Alright," she smiled. "Don't hurry so fast you cut yourself."

But she felt dizzy, and as she moved across the room its dimensions seemed distorted. Yes, she thought, closing the door behind her, and it's only starting to hit me.

Just outside the living room, Saira had stepped behind the Indonesian statue to look in without being seen. Be hostess, Mummy said, which sounded easy enough until she caught sight of the mullah standing apart from the others, raking a bony hand through the white beard that fell to the waist of his gray robe. Suddenly her dress and jewelry seemed too bright and noisy, and again she felt the panic that had gripped her on the plane when, circling over Kabul, the city had appeared dwarfed and trapped by its girdle of mountains. Concentric circles growing smaller, from the sky to the bowl of the valley, to the ordered family compound, and now to this circle of men.

Tor's mimicry had made them seem harmless, almost funny, and walking down the hall she'd pictured herself coming into the room gracefully, like Mummy, smiling apologies and receiving warm appreciative glances, even admiration. In Boston, it was possible to wear one's pride like armor, as Devika said. But this gathering in the living room belonged entirely to Kabul, and for an instant she thought her sins would be as obvious as a can of red paint spilled on the carpet, so shocking the guests would fly out of their chairs and crash against the ceiling.

They were all men except for Roshana, who must be sitting in the armchair Mangal was touching. Next to him, Prince Daoud stood in full-dress uniform, with fringe and medals and ribbons that seemed flimsy under his huge, bullet-shaped head. He was practically bald now, with heavy black eyebrows that shadowed his expression.

To his left, examining one of the Buddhist hide paintings was a strange man, the tallest in the room—and the only one besides the mullah wearing a turban. That must be Roshana's Uncle Aziz, the famous tribal khan from Paktia province. And there, by the glass door to the garden, sat Grand-uncle Yusef, so frail and gentle in his old age that she felt her nervousness replaced by love. He'd never judge her. He would, she felt sure, forgive her anything, if only because she was his dead brother's grandchild. Then as she watched, Ashraf came up behind him from the garden and looked straight to where she was standing, with a smile that began as surprise, changed to a question, then seemed to know the answer. She saw his lips form her name.

How could I have forgotten that face, she thought. How could I ever have wanted anyone else.

What was Ashraf seeing now? Even he must be wondering how she had changed in the States, how different they both were after five separate years broken only by that one summer. It might have been easier to meet again at a sherry party. Instead he'd flatter her, and it would be for her to reverse the compliment, honoring him in terms that sounded extravagant in English.

All the others, too... they would welcome a sister and daughter, not a "defiled," opinionated woman. To enter this final circle she'd have to contain her voice and gestures and there was the risk of diminishing with them, becoming inconsequential again. By making her hostess, Mummy-jan had asked her to play a part, but Mummy was American. They would be thinking: Is Saira too, now?

Ashraf had caught her hiding, so she pretended to be tightening the sash of her dress, then stepped out, across the threshold. "Good evening, everyone! My parents will be here in just a minute. My father was delayed at work...." But the men were standing, Mangal moving to offer her a chair; then, as she passed, he whispered urgently, "Where's Tor?" Shaking her head, she suppressed a smile as she remembered Tor's wisecrack about the Nikka being a business deal. Mangal did look like a flustered executive in that three-piece suit. Maybe when he put on the loose wedding shirt he would relax.

She wanted to go to Grand-uncle Yusef, but that would mean greeting Ashraf as well, and there were too many eyes watching her now. So she followed Mangal's introductions, welcoming the mullah, who was less forbidding at close range, then Roshana's father, brother, and muscular uncle, all obviously pleased with the marriage, and the two familiar Kabul merchants who were the Haidiris' witnesses. Prince Daoud bowed slightly. "You had a safe journey, I trust?" She felt his acute glance appraising her, then he nodded once and his eyes were hooded again.

Roshana kissed both her cheeks, grinning. "I'm so glad you're home. I've always wanted a sister!" The scar on her face, which had been livid two years ago, was white now, like a long irregular vaccination mark. Yes, Saira thought, and scars are honorable, I almost envy her that. She's even respected by people who hate her—vaccinated against criticism. Maybe she can teach me not to mind it.

Returning the kisses, she smiled. "Me too. Especially an older sister, most especially one like you. My brother's a very lucky man."

Roshana's father laughed. "Well spoken, Saira! But both our houses are blessed."

As the guests went back to their talk she made her way to Grand-uncle Yusef's chair, touching his shoulder. "No, Grand-uncle, don't get up."

His eyesight was bad now and he cupped her face. "Saira-gak? You've grown so much I hardly know you! They must be blinder than I am in the U.S. to let so pretty a girl as you leave, but we all thank Allah they did."

Finally she stood to greet Ashraf, fixing her gaze on the center of his blue silk tie. "Ashraf-jan, it's been much too long since I've last seen you."

"Kabul's a poor place when you're not here, Saira." He added quietly, "You're radiant enough to be a bride yourself."

"No," she said. "It's your eyes that are beautiful." Then looking up, she saw delight and amusement in them, as if from a shared private joke. Their exchange had been Afghan, in spite of their Western clothes and colleges, and Grand-uncle Yusef nodded with approval.

Ashraf's features were stronger, less boyish than before. But his skin was still like honey, and the intelligence in his dark eyes seemed to count her own changes without question. Smiling at him, she knew he wouldn't quiz her, maybe because he had sins too, as Devika had said, but more, she thought, because he loved her and could tell she had come back to him. He touched her hand, squeezing it quickly, out of anyone's sight, and she turned back to the room so he wouldn't see her blush.

Raima carried in a tray of sugared almonds, and behind her Mummy-jan was walking down the hall looking pale and distracted. Again, the men rose and there were introductions and a long embrace for Roshana, but then she came to give Saira a hard hug, and kissed Grand-uncle Yusef, stroking his back as if she were comforting him. He must have felt something odd too, because he said, "My dear, we're gaining a daughter!" And her face brightened. "Yes, I couldn't be more proud!" But she glanced around, puzzled, and Saira guessed she was looking for Tor.

She was about to ask if she should go find him when she heard her father's voice. "Bechaim, you're growing so fast we'll have to get you new clothes again." He strode into the room with a hand on Tor's shoulder, and she thought: Mummy-jan was right, he's only tired. He always looks sad when he's tired.

Tor seemed dreadful though, with his face red and sullen and his hair plastered down from a wet combing. When she smiled at him he turned his head away.

After greeting the others, Daddy-jan held her at arm's length, "Can this be my daughter? No, she's only this tall." Measuring the height of his hip, he hugged her, lifting her off the floor. "My Saira, welcome home! The house has been very gray without you." Releasing her, he nodded to the mullah. "I'm sorry I've kept you waiting. I apologize to you all." He clasped her arm. "Go sit down now. We can begin."

He'd looked in her eyes and smiled and touched her. Then why, Saira wondered, moving toward the couch, did she still have the feeling he hadn't seen her?

The mullah studied the contract, his beard twitching as his lips suggested its words. Then he gave copies to Prince Daoud and Ashraf, and the Haidiris' witnesses, and while they read it she saw Grand-uncle Yusef and Roshana's uncle exchanging glances, thinking perhaps of the Pashtun code of honor and the price for breaching a marriage contract. It was funny to imagine them battling it out over some slight to Roshana, yet she had no doubt if it came to that, they would. Not inside the compound, of course. That would break the law of hospitality. But later, if Grand-uncle Yusef were twice as old, he'd still fight for his family's honor and die happy.

Mummy had said Roshana's dowry and her bride price were equal, since Mangal and Roshana were almost socialists, and they were having the Nikka mostly for Roshana's father's sake. And for Daddy-jan. It was expected. The document the mullah unrolled was beautiful, though, decorated with birds and flowers.

He was saying, "... and what is listed under these provisions will become the sole property of Roshana Anwari in the event of her husband's death or desertion. Do her witnesses approve the terms as written?"

They answered, "We do."

He turned to Prince Daoud and Ashraf. "And with regard to the bride's dowry, do you approve?"

"Yes," said the prince. "We bear witness to what is written."

"Roshana Haidiri, so you agree to these terms of your marriage?"

She was looking down at her folded hands. "I do."
"And Mangal Anwari, do you agree?"
Smiling, he glanced at Roshana. "Yes."
"Then the contract can be signed."

Mangal offered Prince Daoud a pen, looking happier than he had all day. He must still be religious to want such a traditional wedding, in spite of what Mummy said. Would his children also hear the Christian beliefs that had been added to their own Islamic instruction? Probably not. But then, what did she really know about Mangal after seven years on separate continents? Only that he'd chosen Roshana to marry.

The mullah's dark eyes followed the witnesses' signatures. Then he unwrapped the cloth covering his Koran and began to read, "...Your wives are as a tilth unto you; So approach your tilth when and how ye will; But do some good act for your souls beforehand...."

A tilth, a plowed field, passive, broken open—Roshana was more than that. And she looked tense now, as if she were only waiting for this to be over, as if she might have reservations about the prayers too. Those doubts seemed to go with being half American, Saira thought, and Roshana had never been out of the country. But hadn't the men who burned her shouted quotes from the Koran?

"...And fear God, and know that ye are to meet him, and give good tidings to those who believe..."

Her parents were standing so close together she could feel the energy flowing between them. How much did they believe in anything else? Once Daddy-jan said that when he tried to pray in England it only made him feel lonelier, but occasionally she had found his small rug unrolled on the study carpet. Mummy said: There aren't two Gods in this house. If we don't practice publicly, it's so you'll understand that.

"...And make not God's name an excuse in your oaths against doing good, or acting rightly, or making peace between persons; For God is one who hearest and knoweth all things. God will not call you to account for thoughtlessness, but for the intention in your hearts; And he is oft-forgiving, most forbearing..."

And there was Tor, with his head down but his hands still clenched at his sides, Tor who always said, "As God is my judge." Peace between persons, Saira thought, forgive me, little brother. I punished you for my sin. We may have been stupid about Jeffrey and Karima, but our intentions were alright. Maybe even Jeffrey's were good to start with, but he hurt me so I hurt you.

Then she wondered why, since the prayers disturbed her, they could also bring her peace. This was their first real family ceremony, and looking around she felt glad Mangal was following these old customs, restoring her to this place, these people whose warmth and love filled the room. The wedding party would be like a welcoming celebration too, for herself, Daddy, even Tor....

Kabul, Afghanistan

Closing his Koran, the mullah smiled and said something to Mangal and Roshana, and suddenly everyone was shaking hands or hugging, laughing and grabbing handfuls of sugared almonds from Raima's tray to shower on the bride and groom. Ashraf and Roshana's brother Aziz scrambled to pluck the nuts from Mangal's pockets, the way bridesmaids in the States tried to catch the bouquet, and Ashraf shot an almond at her, grinning as if he meant: next time it will be us.

She was about to throw it back when she saw Tor behind him, motionless and glaring at the floor. Of course, he wanted to marry Karima, this must have been hard on him. *And I laughed in his face,* she thought, *just to make things worse. Poor Tor, I'd better try to cheer him up.*

When she went to hug him though, he pushed her away muttering, "Leave me alone, you traitor!" and darted through the garden door.

Saira followed a few steps down the path to the stable, then stopped short. Consoling him there would mean ruining her dress and probably manure on her shoes. *No,* she decided, *not tonight, let Aspi comfort him now. Oh, Tor, just let me be happy for a while!*

In the living room, the guests were leaving to change their clothes and Ashraf came to say good-bye, "but only for an hour." Raima brought a broom and started sweeping up nuts.

Saira felt someone pull her hair and twisted around to find Mangal smiling, elated. "My little sister, you aren't so little anymore."

"I was hoping you'd notice that." She laughed. "I really want to talk to you, Mangal."

"Later, I have to get dressed now. And I could use another shower." Kissing her cheek, he started across the room, just as Daddy-jan moved to block the doorway.

"Wait, Mangal," he held up a hand, "I have something to say that concerns you. Everyone, sit down. Prince Daoud, please stay for another minute. This is probably common gossip at the palace by now, so you may as well hear it too."

Reaching back, he closed the door.

Five

Mangal took a step backward, turned uneasily and walked over to the couch. He had seen that chilly wounded smile on his father's face just once before; he couldn't recall the occasion, but it had not been pleasant.

Mummy-jan folded her arms and was staring down at the rug. Whatever this news was, she must be aware of it. Only Grand-uncle Yusef seemed not to have felt the urgency of the words. He had lifted the crystal globe on the coffee table off its lapis lazuli base and was turning it slowly in his hands, gazing down at the shifting pattern of colored shards for what must have been the millionth time. Saira stared, bewildered, and Tor...Tor was nowhere in sight, as usual when things mattered.

"First, Mangal, I apologize if it's selfish of me to be making this announcement on the day of your wedding. I could have postponed my decision, I suppose, but I thought both of us should start with a clean slate tonight. I want you to know how things stand."

With his hands in his pockets, he started pacing the carpet. "I have to ask you all one favor, which is not to question me. I can't answer, so you'll simply have to trust my judgment." He stopped by the garden door. "Right. Here it is then. I've resigned from His Majesty's cabinet as of today. I did it of my own free will, over an issue involving my honor, and it's no disgrace—rather the opposite, I think. King Zahir isn't aware of this yet, unless the prime minister's called him in Rome, but I'm sure he'll be the first to say my name hasn't been compromised in any way. Again, I hope rather the opposite, and that's really all I can tell you." Smiling, he walked stiffly to the couch and held out a hand. "Come, Uncle Yusef, come up with me and have a rest now. It's going to be a long evening and our guests will be here soon."

Mangal saw that Grand-uncle Yusef looked as stunned as he felt himself. He was gripping the crystal globe. "But, Bechaim... this must have been a very sudden decision! You haven't spoken to me of any trouble."

"Yes, it was sudden." Taking the globe, he set it back on its base. "Which means there's a lot of planning to do, and I'll need your advice. Which is why I think you should rest now." He helped the old man to his feet. "Catherine, you might ask Raima to bring in tea for His Excellency. Please excuse us, I'll see you all later."

Watching them leave the room, Mangal thought: he'll tell Grand-uncle what his reason was, he tells him everything. Mummy knows, and the prince will hear it from the king, so it's a secret only from me.

Glancing up, he met Daoud's frowning quizzical eyes and felt a bubble of crazed laughter start in his chest. Yes, that was the other time Daddy-jan had smiled so bitterly. Ten years ago, when Prince Daoud resigned as prime minister and Daddy-jan said, "Forgive me, Mangal, I'd forgotten how much you admire him. Would it comfort you to know that Nikita Khrushchev also is sorry to see that impressive uniform leave office?"

"Please, Mrs. Anwari, don't bother with tea." The prince went to where she was standing with her arms around Saira, who looked shaken. "I'm sure you'd all like some privacy for a little while at least. But I'd like to say"—he seemed to be weighing his words—"this is a great loss to the government, to all Afghanistan. Your husband is one of the most able men who's ever served our country. We need more of his kind in the cabinet, not fewer." Turning, he fixed Mangal with another long, questioning gaze, then walked out to the hall. Mummy-jan followed, and Saira, holding her hand.

Mangal escaped to the garden.

Darkness was gathering in shadows cut by squares of light from the house, and the small electric bulbs strung along the wall shone emerald under the foliage. Tables had been arranged around the circle of white rose trees, centered now by a fountain throwing jets of clear spray, and moving past them he let himself out through the gate and stood looking at the sunset.

Behind him it was dusk, but all across the plain the sky was hot and glowing with color. At the horizon the Paghman mountains were an inferno of scarlet, peach and golden light. The earth was pale, dry as dust outside the compound, and the sunflowers drooped with their own weight. A slight breeze carried the scent of roasting lamb and spices from the kitchen.

"An issue involving my honor," Daddy-jan had said—but one that apparently hadn't damaged his friendship with the king. He must have found something very wrong on this mission though, perhaps connected with some project he had overseen in the past. What in heaven's name could it be?

So Daddy-jan should get the headlines, not himself, at least in tomorrow's paper. CABINET MINISTER ANWARI RESIGNS AFTER TWENTY-FIVE YEARS OF SERVICE. Except that if that news embarrassed the Royal House, it wouldn't be reported. Later of course there might be more, even, FORMER MINISTER'S SON ARRESTED FOR SUBVERSION. At least now Daddy-jan wouldn't suffer for that scandal.

Unless they became linked in people's minds. There could seem to be a relation. If Daddy-jan knew about *New Homeland*, that his son and daughter-in-law were guilty of a criminal attack on the monarchy... he wouldn't shield us, Mangal thought, but however much he disapproved he would never betray us either, and given that conflict of loyalties he might resign than choose between them. And he might announce it just that way—coolly, publicly, "I want you to know how things stand." Then nothing more, above all not the satisfaction of an argument. His favorite weapon was always silence.

Would Ghulam-Nabi have mentioned he'd seen Mangal at dawn wearing stained tribal clothing? The old servant had said nothing then, but all day he'd been watching as if he were trying to decide. There was Tor's friend Farouk, too, whose father worked for the government, and Zalmai and Nur-Ali—any one of them could have been caught. How would I know, he thought, I slept half the day.

He jumped as the kitchen's screen door banged. Was that Ghulam-Nabi now? Maybe he'd only been waiting for a quiet confrontation. Well, I'll give it to him, Mangal decided, because whatever Daddy-jan's reason was, I'm on my own from here on out. For the moment, at least, Roshana and I are free—to stand, fall, go to jail or burn down the palace, so I may as well find out which wind is blowing.

Slipping back through the gate, he surveyed the garden and saw no one. It must really have been the wind, and just as well, given the hour.

He was almost at the door when he heard a sound like someone moving outside the kitchen, and called, "Who is there?" But got no answer.

Again, "Ghulam-Nabi, Raima? Toryalai, is that you?"

The sounds had stopped, and impatiently he walked down the gravel path, squinting from the brilliance of the sunset. At the junction of the house and compound wall there was a white streak, and coming closer he saw it was a woman's skirt reflecting light from the kitchen window—Ghulam-Nabi's daughter Karima, crouching with her face concealed by her long dark hair.

"Karima? Why didn't you answer me?"

She curled away from him, and touching her shoulder, he felt it shake under his hand. "Karima? Why are you crying?"

"I'm sorry!" She hiccuped. "I couldn't help it, I felt so bad, but I didn't mean to bother anyone. It's just so awful, and your mother..."

"Come on, it's not the end of the world." Taking her elbow, he raised the girl to her feet. "My mother's very strong, and they've been through hard scrapes before. It was his decision and he's very resourceful, so you mustn't cry about it. I know it's a shock, but things will look better in a few days, I promise."

"But will he be punished? He won't be, will he? It wasn't all his fault."

"No, of course he won't be punished." Mangal could hardly see her face in the dark. Does she know more than I do? he wondered. Karima might have overheard Daddy-jan and Ghulam-Nabi talking.

Smiling, he turned her toward the light. "Why should he be? What would ever make you think that?"

"I know it was very bad, Mangal." She was wiping her cheeks with a crumpled handkerchief. "But he does things without thinking sometimes. I do too. And I don't mind being sent away, I'm even glad about it, but I don't want your mother to hate me."

I must be going crazy, he thought, this can't be what it sounds. "Why would you be sent away, Karima? I don't understand you. Why on earth would my mother hate you? Stop sniffling and talk to me."

"You mean you don't know?" She stepped away from him, looking nervously toward the house. "No, Mangal, I shouldn't burden you with my problems. Not on your wedding night."

"Not even if I can help?" He clasped her shoulders. "Just because it's my wedding night, whatever your trouble is, I vow to try to set it right. You believe me, don't you, Karima?"

She nodded but would not look at him. "Yes. I'm just so ashamed. Your mother found us...together...and now she's sending me to Herat to stay with my grandfather. He's very sick. My parents think it's kind of her to be so concerned. They don't know the real reason. But I'm afraid she'll never forgive me and I'll never come back here, and she'll punish Tor and he'll hate me too."

"Tor? You mean she found...you and Tor." Of course it was Tor, naturally it was Tor, he'd been slinking around like a whipped dog all day...as if there wasn't enough to cope with.

Karima was still glancing over at the figures moving in the kitchen window. Even blurred with tears, her eyes were lovely. Damn Tor, Mangal thought, can't he leave anything alone? And she's supposed to be so bright.

"Let's take a walk through the orchard," he said, steering her down the path. "Now tell me what happened. My mother found you in Tor's room?"

"Yes," she swallowed the word. "In the dark. It was very late. And then yesterday she told me I'd have to leave and she'd find a tutor to keep me up with my studies."

Fine, he thought, but that doesn't quite answer the question and I'm not sure how else to ask it.

"Karima..." He stopped and waited for her to turn. "You realize what my mother must think. Is she right about that?"

She was twisting the handkerchief. "Oh, Mangal, now you won't respect me either! I'm so frightened. What if my father finds out? I know it was wrong, but I missed Tor so much, I was so glad when he came home...it just happened, and now everything's ruined. And what if...if I'm..."

"You mean...not already?" But he heard the shock in his voice and, regretting it, said more gently, "You're afraid you might be pregnant. Have you been...involved with Tor ever since he came back from Pakistan?" I'll kill him, Mangal thought, he'd better stay very far away from me or I will murder him.

Karima was trembling, crying silently again, but he thought she had nodded yes. So it was over a month now—he wanted to curse. Why couldn't Roshana have found her?

"Listen to me," he said. "Stop that. Someone will come looking for one of us in another minute and we haven't finished yet. Karima, I'm sorry this happened. It's not good, and trouble may come of it, but my mother certainly doesn't hate you. We all respect you very much. I'm sure she's only sending you away because she trusts you to keep up with your work, and she can't trust Tor at all now. You still want to go on to study...at the university, don't you?" He realized he had no idea what her interests were, but only that she was an honors student at Rabia Balkhi High School, as Saira had been.

"Yes, if I can. I know I like school more than Tor does." She held out her hands. "Believe me, Mangal, I wasn't trying to trap him. I know your parents would never let him marry a servant."

No, he thought, you're right, they wouldn't, and why you should want him is beyond me.

"But you won't be a servant, not if you finish school." He took her hands. "If you married Tor you would be, and his second mother, and I'd bet you'd get tired of that in a week. I promised to help you and I meant it, but you have to do what my mother says now. Don't go anywhere near Tor. And if there's a problem later, come straight to me. Will you do that, Karima?"

"If you say so, Mangal." She was staring at him, he could see her round eyes gleaming in the dark. "I don't know why you should bother about me. Especially now."

Why, he thought? Because I'm the great liberal who always said you were lucky to live here. Too bad if you can't have any part of our world, or your own either after this.

"Don't be silly," he smiled. "I'm Tor's older brother, naturally I'm concerned. So, you're going to stay with your grandfather? Think how happy he'll be to see you. It's not going to be much fun around here this summer anyway."

The living room door creaked and she tried to pull away, but he held her wrist to keep her still.

"Mangal?" It was his mother's voice, "Are you out there? We have guests!"

"Yes, coming!" He turned to Karima. "When I get back from my wedding trip I'll write to you in Herat. We have a cousin there who can look out for you, so try not to worry too much."

"Alright, I will. Thank you, Mangal. And if I may say this, all blessings on your marriage."

"Thank you too, Karima. Go back in now, and remember, we have an understanding."

There are an awful lot of promises being passed around tonight, he thought, watching her walk up the path. When she reached the kitchen he started back toward the living room door.

"Mangal?" Mummy-jan was peering at him. "The guests are coming. And you still haven't changed?"

Over her shoulder he saw Raima at the other end of the hall, taking wraps from two women in evening dress.

"No, sorry, I'll just be a minute. But this has been quite a day for bombshells! First Daddy-jan, now Karima—have you got any other surprises?"

"She told you. Oh, I wish she hadn't."

"For heaven's sake, she didn't 'tell' me, I found her crying into the spearmint. She's scared to death and I don't blame her."

"I'll take care of her, Mangal. The main thing's to get her away from Tor."

"And from the house? So if she's pregnant it won't be too embarrassing? But she'll have a tutor, how fortunate. She'll be the only unwed mother in Herat who can do advanced trigonometry." He had kept his voice low, a smile on his face, and one of the women down the hall waved gaily.

"You can be very cruel, do you know that? I'll be responsible for Karima. But Mangal"—she shook her head—"you mustn't say a word of this to your father. He's completely exhausted, I think he'd snap."

"At Tor? Why shouldn't he? Why do you always protect him?"

"It's your father I'm protecting right now. And Karima. I mean that, Mangal! And don't talk to Tor about it either, he's upset enough as it is." She sagged against the doorframe and he thought: poor Mummy, she's always having to clean up one of our messes.

"I swear it," he bowed. "But tell me this. How long have you known about Daddy-jan? Did he tell you why he resigned?"

"Not the specifics. And only since this morning. You know I can't break his confidence, please don't ask me to, dear." Her eyes were very dark gray tonight, and angry... at him?

"Can I ask what we should say to the guests then?" He reached to smooth back a wisp of blond hair escaping from her chignon. "This could be awkward."

"I doubt it. The only people who know will be from the palace, and they won't have the bad taste to bring it up at your wedding. Are you planning to be at your wedding? If so, you'd better hurry."

"I will." He held her at arm's length, studying her simple blue silk dress. "You're the one who's exhausted, but you've disguised it very well. You look beautiful. Very elegant. I'll see you in five minutes."

The hall was empty now, and crossing the room, he turned quickly up the stairs.

There was no time for a shower. Sponging off in the bath, he went through the opposite door to his bedroom. And there it was: Grandfather Anwari's wedding costume—so full and light it seemed to be the only thing in the room. White silk embroidered over fine white cotton that had been worn just once in the last century. Raima had hung it high on the Indian screen as if this unknown grandfather were gigantic, and touching the soft long shirt Mangal realized he no longer had the heart to wear it.

Even yesterday, choosing this costume seemed a safe statement to make ...safe, because only half true? But tonight what he'd meant as a symbolic claim to that grandfather's nationalism felt more like a violation. These were Daddy-jan's clothes by right, his inheritance, and he hadn't been home to give his permission when Grand-uncle Yusef offered them.

Dammit, Mangal cursed, he'll think I'm mocking him with my freedom. Why can't he understand that I love him? He made me in his image, and now he can't bear to see how much we're alike.

Well, it was too late to do anything else. Roshana would be wearing her late mother's velvet wedding dress—an antique passed through several generations.

He stepped into the loose pantaloons, tied the waist and was reaching for the shirt when someone knocked twice on the door and Ghulam-Nabi called, "Mangal? I've brought you the turban cloth."

The servant came in smiling dryly. "Raima thought you should have the original. It's fragile though, and she's been bleaching it for days, so you'd better tie it carefully. But I don't need to show you how to do that."

"I don't think so." He took the folded cloth. "Please thank Raima for me."

"I will." Ghulam-Nabi cleared his throat. "I believe you also have some rags to be burned. I heard your mother say she wants to help pack for your wedding trip. You surely wouldn't want her to soil her hands on those foul things you were wearing this morning." His dark eyes were inscrutable.

"No." Mangal returned a blank gaze. "They're in the bag on the floor of my closet." Pulling on the shirt, he asked softly, "Did you tell anyone about that?"

"Such as your father? Would I bother him with such nonsense today? If I told him everything I knew about his sons he'd be even more unhappy." Ghulam-Nabi retrieved the bag and stood watching Mangal tie the turban. "Your grandfather was a man of great wisdom, as is your father. For your wedding, I wish that blessing for you too." He touched Mangal's shoulder, adjusting a button, then went out closing the door.

Mangal studied himself in the mirror. This might be the first time in ten years that a member of the so-called upper class had been married in tribal clothing, and some would call it affectation. But the fit was good, the richly embroidered shirt fell exactly to his knees—Grand-uncle Yusef at least would be proud. And it had been his decision too, so how could Daddy-jan object?

He left the room and started down the stairs.

In the hall below, the family stood to receive the stream of guests—his mother's blond head beside Saira's dark one, with their blue and russet silks fluttering like plumage, Daddy-jan's hair the exact shade of his pearl gray vested suit.... But where was Tor? He should be there. As Mangal walked down to them, he heard his mother say, "Omar, look at your son."

"Bechaim!" His father's smile froze. "What is this?"

"Grand-uncle Yusef thought wearing these clothes would honor your father," Mangal said quickly. "They used to be his. I was wondering if you would have worn them if you'd had them with you in Boston."

"They were... my father's?" His gaze was fixed on the shirt. "My father's. So." He nodded shortly. "Well, that's reassuring. I didn't know whether you were supposed to be a peasant or a khan."

Ashraf and his parents came up the path, and while Mangal welcomed them he felt his father's eyes studying him, skeptical of his motives. But a string of dignitaries followed Ashraf's family—the French and Italian ambassadors with their wives; the limping American official, Jonathan Straight, whom Tor called Mr. CIA—and now it was his turn to watch Daddy-jan greeting guests, speaking their own language to each, showing no emotion when they called him "Minister," perhaps for the last time.

Tomorrow they'll be gossiping about him, Mangal thought. He knows that, and then he'll have to sit around while they ruin his life's work.... How can he stand this?

As if Daddy-jan had heard his thoughts, he turned after greeting Jonathan Straight and said, "To answer your question, Mangal, no, I wouldn't have worn them in Boston. If we'd been married here I might have, but not half so... convincingly as you? Uncle Yusef did well to give them to you, and I'm sure Roshana's uncle will also be pleased." The words were clipped, decisive, his expression nearly proud, but there was new pain in his eyes. He'd have to let go of everything now, accept anything, he had no choice, Mangal realized, and it would be an agonizing struggle.

Around them, the house seemed alive with motion, long bright dresses and glittering jewels. The procession through the front door had stopped at last and Mummy-jan said, "I think we can go in now."

The large reception hall was rarely used, but tonight it was warm with flowers and the glow of candles. At one end of the crowded room, Raima was fussing over a long buffet. At the other, a dais had been raised with a couch and table at its center, and beside that four musicians began to play as the family came in, the stringed sarod and duruba joined by a harmonium and a tight-skinned tabla. The band members were also wearing tribal clothes, and Mangal thought: I'll be taken for their singer.

But as he mingled with the guests, his spirits began to climb. There was no murmur of criticism, and moving from table to table he collected kisses and compliments with growing pleasure. When the American ambassador and Jonathan Straight admired his costume, he joked that they should have come dressed as mullahs—after all, wasn't that the CIA masquerade in eastern Afghanistan now?—and led them laughing to the buffet, where an elaborate dinner was being served.

"I'm afraid I don't know what most of this is." Jonathan Straight smiled apprehensively. "You'll have to tell me, Mangal. That's a whole roast lamb in the middle?"

"In a pilau of raisins and nuts, yes. The platters beside it are emerald pilau—rice cooked with spinach—and orange pilau, with pistachios and orange rind. Don't worry, there's nothing very hot here." He felt a sudden sympathy for this pale young American with thick glasses and wispy red hair. If Straight did work for the CIA, he must have been chosen for his visibility, for that disarming limp. He seemed accessible, even harmless, but his green eyes were quick and shrewd. Had he wanted to come to these mountains, Mangal wondered, or was he hoping for a European capital where he could go to concerts in the evening?

"Here, may I serve you?" He picked up a plate. "There are ten kinds of kebab down there if you want something simple. My favorite's kebab-i-seekhi, little bits of broiled lamb marinated in garlic yogurt. But first, try this ashak, it's traditionally served to honored guests."

"Well, thank you." Straight glanced at him uncertainly. "I'm honored to be here, Mangal. That looks like ravioli—come from China along the Silk Route?"

"Hmmm, but ours are stuffed with leeks or lentils and dressed with gravy and yogurt and mint." Feeling mischievous he added, "It's true of course, we owe a lot to each of the superpowers. Unfortunately, only the Chinese know how to cook. Here, have some of this too, it's called do-piaza, two onions, but as you see the name's deceiving, like so much else in Afghanistan. The pancake's chapati, like pita bread, with meat, salted peas and thin onion rings marinated in vinegar. And if you can tell me the origins of that, you deserve a promotion."

Moving along the table, even he was amazed at the number of dishes Raima had set out. There were stuffed chickens, platters of lamb and ground beef kebabs with chilis, a dozen different vegetables and half as many salads, all beautifully arranged. Hired servants offered pitchers of juice and bowls of puddings and other sweets sprinkled with chopped nuts and syrup. But the rows of mounded fresh fruit were most striking—dark red pomegranates, sweet and sour cherries, apricots, blue plums, strawberries, apples, yellow pears and every kind of melon gleamed in the candlelight, as though Raima meant to represent every variety in the country. This was her wedding gift, he realized. She had taken pains with the smallest details, and catching her eye, he smiled appreciation and had the pleasure of seeing her shy grin. When he finished serving Jonathan Straight he went back for a plate of his own.

Just then Prince Daoud stepped out from behind a marble pillar and also picked up a dish. "I've been looking at the tapestries when I might more profitably have been admiring the dinner. I don't know when I've seen such food."

"Not since last night at the palace?" Mangal chuckled. "But thank you, Your Excellency. Here, aren't you especially fond of the khattah pilau?"

"If you remember that, you must also know I haven't lived at the palace for years. And I dine there very seldom—less and less as time goes on, which may be why this uniform still fits. But don't you call me 'Uncle' anymore, Mangal? You used to, before you went to France. Have you forgotten that too?"

The prince's tone was teasing, but his keen eyes could say more than a speech by anyone else, and Mangal saw impatience in them, a wish to brush aside formalities and talk more openly than the situation allowed. Was he distancing himself from the palace in the hope of learning why his cousin's favored minister had resigned? Or did he know why? He could easily have called the king in Rome. Mangal thought: one of us is about to be disappointed.

He said, "With your permission, Uncle, I'll never forget the respect and affection I've held for you since—"

"I know." Daoud's full lips suggested a smile. "Since that day ten years ago when you spoke to me so passionately of Pashtunistan!"

"You must have thought me ridiculous, Uncle. Would you like some of this chicken?"

"On the contrary, I was very moved that day, Mangal. And impressed with your understanding—which is why I encouraged you to form your own opinions. Thank you, no, I have quite enough to eat. There's a free table in the corner. Shall we sit down?"

Mangal followed him to a small table that was not only empty but in shadow and set apart from the others, behind the pillar where the prince had first been standing.

Daoud unfolded his linen napkin. "Reading between the lines of your articles in the *Times*, I'd say you've learned to trust your judgment very well. Which makes me even more honored that you asked me to be your witness— particularly given what you're wearing. I was sad to hear your father's news, tonight of all nights. But things happen in their own time. He felt he had no choice."

"That's alright." Mangal focused his attention on the chicken he was carving. "I wouldn't have wanted him to wait. Not for my sake."

"Perhaps"—the prince shook his head—"one might call it symptomatic.

Unfortunately, it's only the last of many recent symptoms—as in the final stages of an illness. I'm sure my cousin will be most unhappy."

So he hadn't spoken to the king yet. Mangal nodded. "We were all hoping His Majesty might celebrate with us. It's too bad he couldn't be here."

"Yes, I think so too. But then, he and I often disagree about what's important. About Pashtunistan, for one thing." Daoud smiled faintly. "And press censorship for another. But I haven't congratulated you on your bride yet, Mangal. Roshana's a remarkable woman. I've been watching her with interest for some years. I should honor you too—there aren't many men who'd choose a wife with her strength of will."

"Or with her scars? Thank you, Uncle. I'm lucky she accepted me. As you probably know, she gets along very well on her own."

"I wasn't thinking of her scars, Mangal. She wears them well. In my eyes they don't disfigure her at all." He was cutting lamb methodically. "Isn't it odd, though, how in one moment someone's life can be changed forever? But of course that's an illusion, since each moment grows out of all that came before. In Roshana's case, her tragedy was preceded by a Parliament made up overwhelmingly of mullahs. That created an atmosphere... well, I don't have to tell you. Since they own so much land, my cousin thought they could be managed, but the mullahs have to be handled very carefully. I wonder if you have any idea how difficult it was when I acted to remove the veil?"

"My father explained it to me, Uncle. He admired your strategy. I was only eleven then, but I was there." Daoud had still been prime minister in that scorching August of 1959 when President Nasser of Egypt came to celebrate National Independence Day. The prince had issued no edict, so there could be no advance opposition. But that day on the fairground, when women of the Royal House and wives of ministers filed into the reviewing stand, they were unveiled—in public for the first time since King Amanullah's abortive effort in the twenties—and a collective gasp had gone up from the crowd. Mangal remembered women around him weeping, calling it shameful—confusing for a boy whose mother had always gone unveiled. And then, of course, the mullahs did protest, but Daoud had done his homework, presenting Islamic scholars who justified his action. A few of the most vitriolic mullahs had been arrested, but apart from that the official unveiling passed into history as a fait accompli. Now the chadri was chiefly worn by upward-striving families who mistook it for a symbol of idle affluence.

"You see, Mangal"—the prince was watching him over his glass of cherry juice—"it's possible to interpret the Koran liberally, if great care is used. Here change can occur only within the principles of Islam. Since everything creates its opposite, of course, there's a far worse threat from the Left now. My cousin doesn't take that seriously enough either. He thinks by pacifying the mullahs and muzzling the socialists he can keep them both at arm's length. But communications being what they are today, controlling the press doesn't work. We're past the time when truth can be manipulated. As a journalist, wouldn't you agree?"

Mangal picked up a ground beef kebab uneasily. The pressure in Daoud's voice was leading somewhere. He seemed to be inviting criticism of the king, calling him "my cousin." Why?

"Frankly, Uncle"—he made his voice light—"I'd hate to lose my job for saying this, but yes, I do agree."

"I thought you might," Daoud smiled. "Particularly when it forces our brightest children to commit crimes simply in order to be heard. For instance, I came across an illegal paper in the bazaar today—called *New Homeland*. Have you seen it, by any chance?"

The kebab had not quite touched his lips. Mangal bit into it, shrugging. "There are so many papers..."

"Mostly of no importance, yes. But this was different. Quite distinctive. Obviously the product of highly educated minds. And when people of that caliber are ready to take large risks... well, that's a serious matter. As is your father's resignation. And the fact that our long-awaited elections may never take place. I don't think my cousin has any intention of signing the required legislation. Yes, I have great sympathy for the author of *New Homeland*."

Mangal noticed the prince had taken very little food. "Surely there must have been many writers. Could I get you some kebab-i-seekhi, Uncle?"

Daoud waved away the offer. "Even so, Mangal, a unified work must be the product of one intelligence. Speaking, in this case, with the strength of many voices. And their arguments were so persuasive I'm sure thousands more will be convinced. The juxtaposition of elements, the writing alone... a rare talent. Invaluable." Resting folded arms on the table, he hunched over them smiling. "I picture a trained journalist with strong nationalist sentiment. A young man who would look well in tribal clothing."

So he knows, Mangal thought, but he won't do anything about it. He just wants me to know he's found me out.

He met the prince's gaze. "You have a great imagination, Uncle."

"Hah!" Daoud laughed. "May I take that to mean you see me as a man of vision?"

"Please do. It's why I asked you to be my witness tonight."

"Good. Very good. I'm honored to officiate. Tonight begins a new generation of Anwaris, and your family record is the history of Afghanistan."

Now the prince had changed his tone, deliberately, Mangal felt sure. His eyes were still watchful in spite of his laughter.

"Tell me, Nephew, where are you going on your wedding trip?"

"To Europe. France, Italy and England."

"And when are you leaving? Not tomorrow, I hope."

"Yes, in the evening. We're flying into Paris. Roshana's never been abroad."

"So." Daoud shook his large head sadly. "I was hoping you'd stay for a few days to visit with her relatives from Paktia. I can understand, of course, after all this, why you'd want to get away, but you put me in an awkward position. It's your wedding night. I don't want to upset you."

"But?" Mangal pushed his plate away. "You're the third person who's said that today. If there's something wrong, please tell me, Uncle. Are you worried about my father?"

"In part. And about you, and me and the rest of the country. We're in a state of crisis, Mangal. It's not a good time to travel. If something were to happen... if the borders were to be closed, well, you might not be able to come back for several months. And you're needed here."

The words had been almost inaudible. Mangal pulled his chair closer. "If what were to happen? I don't know what you mean."

"Can I speak to you in absolute confidence?"

"Of course."

The prince glanced over his shoulder. "I wish I could wait to say these things, but like your father, I have no choice. Because of your father I have no choice. And because of *New Homeland*. We're at the point of revolution now, Mangal. And when a king leaves his country at such a time, power can be seized. The question is, who will win it? A Marxist rhetorician spouting clichés? That would mean disaster. The Left here is too young, with no experience of leadership and no understanding of the importance of religion to our people. But the alternatives are worse. The mullahs would drag us back to the fifteenth century. The new prime minister, who has ambitions, would only continue the same facade of democracy we've had for ten years now. You and I have something in common. Do you know what that is?"

Daoud's voice was low and urgent and Mangal felt sweat trickling down his sides. He shook his head. No, Uncle.

"Because of your father, you've had to mask your talents with an illegal newspaper. I'm in a similar quandary with my cousin. One of the things *New Homeland* complained of was the '64 constitution. When I resigned as prime minister in '63, I fully intended to go on working in some other capacity. Then Article 24 of that constitution was passed."

"Which... prohibits members of the Royal House from holding government posts?"

"Exactly. A ridiculous sop—intended to mislead people into believing that power was being decentralized. For these ten years I've been able only to watch, and every nerve in my body has screamed in frustration. There's so much that could be done—oil exploration, land reform—instead of which the country's almost bankrupt and swords are drawn on every side. Power will be seized, and if a man has any stake in the outcome, he must act. Even if it's repugnant to him. It does no good to weep after the fact, don't you agree?"

As Mangal watched, the room beyond them seemed to fall away. Only yesterday he'd said Daoud was the one man he could follow, but this was incredible—did he really mean to overthrow his own cousin? Why would he advertise that? Unless he was really working for the king, asking for trust to win an admission of complicity in some rebellion they thought was brewing.

"Uncle," he said tightly, "I agree, position brings responsibility. Most people can stand by and weep after the fact, but not men of influence."

"Or men of talent! This threatens us all. You realize, some fanatics would gladly execute the whole cabinet along with the Royal House."

"My father..." Mangal spread his fingers on the table. "My father's out of it. He didn't resign on a whim. Whatever his reason, I'm sure he won't change his mind about it. He won't go back into government again."

"Yes." Daoud's eyes were piercing. "Which leaves his son free to do so. Didn't I just say that in an instant one's life could change forever? That happened for you tonight. In these ten years my contacts with the Left have only grown deeper, Mangal. I've been aware of what you and Roshana were up to for some time, and believe me, if that Pashtunistan article had been written in Greek I would have known it was my old friend Professor Durrani's work. The point is, power can be taken by force, but to be held, maintained ...the cause must be righteous. And that must be communicated—those reasons and motives—to the people, well and simply, as in the *New Homeland*. Because in the end, success depends more on words than guns, wouldn't you agree?"

"Success depends on the loyalty of the people, yes."

"Your father owns that trust—to an unusual extent. Many would consider him a serious threat. I don't, and I think I also have their loyalty. The Left is with me, the army's with me, and I believe the people also will be. But I want you with me too, Mangal. I'm a man of action, not words. I need your youth and talent, and your friendship. Our views are the same. Why shouldn't we work together to solve the problems described in *New Homeland*? If we don't, I promise you someone else will try. The threat of revolt's always greatest when reforms start to take root, and since I initiated most of them myself I feel obliged to step in now. As your father's son and the author of *New Homeland*, you're also accountable. Our families laid this groundwork and it's up to us to make the next leap, to true democracy. Tomorrow night you can either get on that plane, or write a speech announcing the new Republic of Afghanistan. Which one will it be?"

"So soon? You mean, really tomorrow? Forgive me, Uncle, yesterday I dreamt of this and now I can't believe it." He was studying Daoud's face, his worried eyes under the slash of dark brows, the heavy folds of skin and thinning hair...well, why shouldn't it be now? The prince was aging, how much longer would this be possible for him? And there was no one else.

"Dreams are dangerous if you aren't prepared for their consequence, Mangal. What do you think Roshana will say?"

"On her wedding night? That your timing couldn't be worse." Yes, he thought, and then she'll say: If he's going to move, do we have a choice? If we aren't with him, he'll think we're against him. Your father won't like this any better a year from now than he will tomorrow. You'll wait forever if you want his blessing."

"And after that?" Daoud bent closer. "I hate to push you, but I must know your answer now. If I can't have you, I'll need to make other plans quickly."

"Roshana gave up her work to marry me, Uncle. I think she'd sacrifice a trip to get it back."

"You're saying yes, then?"

"I suppose I am, if you're sure I won't disappoint you. I've never written speeches."

"No, but you've studied your father's, haven't you? I've already outlined a draft, but it's clumsy. It needs your trenchant phrasing—and in Pashto, Mangal, not Dari. After tomorrow we'll have no more court language, no titles and no crown. But there's one other thing you must do. I want this to be a peaceful transition, and it can be, if the police aren't nervous. You'll have to tell your associates in *New Homeland* not to put out any more papers. Today's caused quite enough disturbance."

"Professor Durrani wanted to do one after we left, so it would seem we couldn't be involved." He smiled. "That was going to be their wedding gift to us."

"Then for their own safety, you'll have to stop them. I'll have troops in the streets after dark." Suddenly, his lips stretched in a peculiar grin. He was pushing back his chair and standing. "Well, it's Miss Anwari! You do look lovely tonight. I hope I wasn't too short with you before, Saira."

Mangal felt a light hand on his shoulder and saw another clasp Daoud's—how could they not have seen her coming? But looking up, he guessed she hadn't heard their conversation. She was beaming at the prince. "Thank you, Your Excellency, and don't worry. I knew this would happen when I came home. Oh, Mangal, what a wonderful party!" Daoud drew up a chair and she perched on the edge of it, smoothing the pointed sleeves of her dark orange dress.

"Mmmm. Raima's really outdone herself. What did you know would happen?" Retrieving his half-eaten kebab, he took an unenthusiastic bite. Not small talk with Saira now, for heaven's sake.

"That I'd say the wrong thing to everyone for a week or two. The trouble is, I don't know when I'm doing it or why what I've said is wrong. I asked His Excellency what he thought the state of women would be today if King Amanullah hadn't been deposed. It was a great accomplishment, taking off the veils, but if it had happened forty years ago, Roshana wouldn't have suffered. Or my friend Royila." She gave Daoud a wry glance. "His Excellency told me Amanullah was a fool for not strengthening the army. And then he said he didn't really mean that."

Looking from her bright face to the prince's grave one, Mangal saw Daoud's lips tighten with annoyance. He must be very edgy if Saira could provoke him, and she didn't seem about to leave.

Kabul, Afghanistan

"As Mummy-jan pointed out yesterday"—he smiled—"if Amanullah had lasted, Daddy wouldn't have left Kabul and you and I wouldn't be here. Just count yourself lucky. There were no veils worn in this house."

"Lucky? Do you think that was so easy for me? I'm neither fish nor fowl, as Grandmother Lowe says. It was like that in the States, too—there was so much going on there, and I couldn't really get involved in any of it. Not directly, at least. I did do some writing, but I couldn't put my name on it. Didn't you feel that way in Paris, Mangal?"

Her eager chatter was grating. He said irritably, "I didn't do any writing. What are you talking about?"

"Well." Daoud folded his arms. "Another journalist."

"Oh no, Your Excellency," she flushed. "I don't think so. My articles weren't about Afghanistan. I never even discussed affairs here, except with my grandparents. That's partly why it's so good to be home again—I can stop watching every word I say. Mangal, thank you for giving me such a brave older sister to learn from. Roshana's wonderful. I want to work for the country too now. Of course with Daddy..." She lowered her voice. "Well, it's time I did something on my own for a change. But forgive me, Your Excellency, I'm being rude again. Is your wife with you tonight?"

"Yes," Daoud nodded, "she's over there. I know she'll be glad to see you. But please call me Uncle, Saira. Titles are so formal."

Mangal took the cue. "Would you like to come and see her now? I was just going to get us some tea."

"In a minute. I came over to see you, big brother. Otherwise we might not have a chance to talk before you leave, and there's so much I want to ask you. I'm not sure whether to look for a job or do volunteer work, like Roshana."

"Why don't you wait and discuss that with her when we get back then? There's no hurry. I'm sure you could use a little time off too."

"But I feel like I need to make up my mind. If I found a job I'd be at least partly independent, but I'd still have to live at home, so maybe I should just face up to that and do volunteer work somewhere." Saira shook her head. "I wish I were a man, so I could go off and work in the countryside. That's where the worst need is, and whatever I do, I know Daddy won't approve of my ideas. I liked the States, but Afghanistan's not America. We aren't industrial. Russia's faced the same problems we have, though—trying to modernize an essentially feudal society. I believe, Uncle, you favor their models? In agriculture, for example?"

Textbook jargon, Mangal thought. Who's she trying to impress?

"Don't misunderstand me," said Daoud sharply. "What I value most is our independence. It would be very unwise, especially now, to favor any power disproportionately. But what's all this talk about politics? You should be thinking of marriage! I have a feeling your friend Ashraf is doing just that."

Mangal saw a nervous tic pulse at the corner of the prince's eye, and realized with a start why Daoud was so jumpy. Anything he said now would surely be remembered, and repeated, after tomorrow.

"Saira's been reading Russian literature at Radcliffe," he teased. "Too much Tolstoy—which is probably as close as she's ever come to a feudal peasant. But maybe they discussed collectivism in the snack bar."

Her smile quivered and the color in her cheeks deepened. "That's not fair, Mangal. I studied Marx as well. We read Trotsky and Lenin, and all last year I went to meetings. You aren't the only one who can think."

"Then think, for heaven's sake! But don't go on about Marx. Talk about the Politburo. Forget Trotsky. Look at what Stalin did in the name of ideology. Those students in the States are just dilettantes, Saira, playing at being socialists. What Roshana did here was real!"

"Don't you think I know that? I was Miss Third World for four years! I know the real work is here, and I also know I'll do it better because of some of the things I learned there. One of which is not to be patronized by men who think they know everything." A gold comb was slipping out of her hair and she pushed it back with anger, then as if to prove her words, took it out again and pinned it carefully.

"So," Daoud said, "it seems you've decided on a career in government, Saira?"

"No!" She glanced up, startled. "I didn't mean that, Uncle. One thing I learned in the States is that it can be faster to move a government from the outside. And I don't just mean the antiwar movement, Mangal. There were groups who did organizing in Cambridge, for poor people, and a sit-in for a women's center—I didn't work with them, I only watched, but I think some of their tactics could do well in Kabul. If you can get people together around a common problem and they make enough noise, it may be in the government's interest to make concessions to them. I'll bet Roshana would agree with that, if you don't. And as far as what you said about Trotsky—if he'd lived, and Stalin had been murdered instead, there might not be that kind of Politburo now."

"Yes, the state would have withered away," said Daoud dryly. "Isn't that the idea? Well, Mangal, what do you think we have here? A Bolshevik, or a Gandhi?"

He smiled. "Let's hope a Gandhi."

"I'm flattered by the comparison," Saira said, but her face was stony and Mangal realized he'd never seen her so angry before, hadn't looked at her today apart from the pretty dress and jewelry that made her seem so young. She wasn't, though. Her eyes had a hard determination, an insistence he found unsettling. He hadn't considered that she might be a problem.

Folding her hands tight in her lap, she looked down at them. "Laugh, it's alright, I'd rather be Gandhi than anyone else. Maybe good leaders don't make the best generals, but does that mean whoever's most ruthless is right? I don't know if you read about the Weather Underground in the States, but they were mostly rich kids planting bombs and killing people—that didn't help the poor. But groups who took time to organize at the grassroots made a difference."

Daoud coughed, and Mangal read the clear message in his eyes: Stop this, for God's sake.

"Uncle"—Saira smiled tentatively—"don't you agree, in spite of what you said before? Maybe Amanullah should have strengthened the army, but he wasn't a fool in any other way. He was a great innovator... like yourself. You built up the army, and even my father admits you could have led a coup instead of resigning in '63 if you'd wanted to. He says it's to your great credit that you didn't."

As Daoud's hand closed in a fist, Mangal laughed. "Didn't they teach you anything at Radcliffe? Sure, ideals are wonderful, just don't confuse them with politics—not in this world, anyway. You asked how I felt in Paris? I'll tell you about coming home. I didn't understand anything about the realities here, and you know even less."

"Mangal," Daoud interrupted, "your mother's waving at you. Perhaps Roshana has arrived?"

Glancing at his watch, Mangal stood up with relief. "That's right, it's almost midnight. Oh, come on, Saira, don't sulk, it'll give you wrinkles. How old are you, twenty? Don't you think you still might have a little more to learn? Now cheer up, it's my wedding—no more arguments allowed." Patting her shoulder, he turned to the man who would be called president after tomorrow. "Would you please join me, Uncle, I'm sure to forget some of the details."

Together, they started across the room.

Catherine watched Mangal come toward her smiling tensely. Prince Daoud, walking beside him, also looked agitated. Had they been discussing Omar's resignation? Beyond them, Saira was sitting slumped at the table they had left, arms clenched at her waist and her face, taut with emotion, focused on her brother's back. So they'd fought about something, and that would be Mangal's doing. This wedding had turned him into a bear.

She held out a hand to the prince, "Your Excellency, we have one more thing for you to do, if you don't mind. Would you hold the Koran with my husband, please? I don't think Uncle Yusef could manage it tonight." And Tor has disappeared, she thought. I wouldn't want to be in his shoes when he decides to turn up again.

"I'd be honored to, Mrs. Anwari. I take it the bride is here?"

"Yes, she's in the study."

"I'll speak to Omar now, then. Excuse me, please." He gave them each a nod and strode away.

Mangal's smile softened. "How does she look?"

"Very lovely, dear. I wish her mother could see her. I'm sure she'd be as proud as I am. But Mangal, what on earth did you say to Saira? Even from here I can tell she's upset."

"Oh, she's alright. She was trying to impress Daoud-jan with her incisive grasp of world history, and I just suggested she might not know exactly everything yet. Have you seen Tor? He's supposed to escort me."

"No. I've been telling everyone he isn't feeling well, but I'm pretty sure he's out riding. Frankly, if this weren't your wedding party, I'd be just as glad he's not home. He looked frantic at the Nikka. I thought he was going to have a fit and I'm still afraid that could happen. Of course, your father says if Tor's not back for the ceremony he'll wish he were dead by tomorrow. And he hasn't said another word about it since. You know what that means."

"Yes, that he'll smile cheerfully while he breaks every one of Tor's bones. And since it *is* my wedding he's spoiling, I'll applaud."

"Please don't make this any worse, Mangal. They're like a pair of bombs already. I'm going to ask Saira to see if Tor's snuck back up to his room, but I've also asked Uncle Yusef to escort you in any case. I'm just worried about how he'll manage those steps. Keep a good hold on his arm."

"I will. I'll keep him on my right. Then I'd better go find him now. And Mother..." He bent to kiss her cheek. "Thank you. Everything's beautiful."

His beard had a faint oily smell. Had he started using pomade? She smiled, "I'm happy you approve. Go on, now, and I'll just see Saira."

"Alright." He turned toward the dais, and quickly she threaded her way across the floor.

Saira was pulling apart a matchbook, and when she looked up, Catherine saw she was on the verge of tears.

"Oh, sweetheart, you mustn't mind him!" She cupped Saira's trembling chin. "He bit my head off too, and Tor's. It's wedding jitters. He'll get over it."

"No." Saira shook her head angrily. "He had no right to do that! Why did he? I asked perfectly good questions and he humiliated me right in front of His Excellency. Daoud-jan *did* favor collective farms, I know that, I thought he'd be pleased I remembered. And Mangal treated me like an idiot! What I said was true, and he insulted me! I'm not stupid. I didn't say stupid things."

It was probably Mangal she had been "trying to impress," Catherine thought stroking Saira's tight shoulders. "I'm sure you didn't, dear, any more than I did. We'll just have to declare him temporarily insane."

Gazing down at Saira's face, she was struck by the beauty that had flowered in this daughter in two years. Only Saira had inherited any resemblance to her American relatives, and that just in the lighter cast of her skin, the straight nose and arched lips that might have been copied from the portrait of Greataunt Jane Lowe. What would Omar's mother have seen of herself, looking at this girl? Delicate Asian bones and almond eyes under winglike brows, dark glossy hair that sprang out from her temples and fell almost to her waist. But in the day Saira had been home it was already clear she was more Western now in other respects. Her voice and gestures, the way she walked—she had lost her timidity and gained an assertiveness Catherine realized she herself no longer had.

I was afraid of having a wholly Afghan daughter, she thought, I was afraid we wouldn't understand each other. And I'm glad she's stronger, but it's not going to be easy for her to live here after Cambridge. Maybe it was selfish of me to send her to Radcliffe.

"I knew someone at Harvard like Mangal," said Saira bitterly. "I just wish I'd figured that out sooner. It would have saved me a lot of trouble."

"Someone arrogant, you mean?" Catherine smiled. "I suspect that's epidemic among ambitious young men. But Saira, dear, will you please run upstairs right now and see if Tor's in his room? The ceremony's starting any minute, and if he isn't here there's going to be trouble."

"Okay." She stood up abruptly. "I'll do anything you want. You're the only one who seems to care a damn that I've come home."

"That's not true, and you know it." Hugging her, Catherine chuckled. "And I wouldn't swear in front of your father, if I were you. Not tonight, anyway."

She kept an arm around Saira's waist as they made their way through the guests who were moving up toward the dais now, and felt her relax as people called out and touched her, welcoming her back. But when Mr. Nawabi hurried over, she turned Saira away. It still seemed impossible to be civil to this man whose wife had been kindness itself for so many years. His first wife, that is, since he'd taken another last September, a girl from Kandahar whom he decorated with expensive jewelry.

"Mummy-jan?" Saira glanced up, surprised. "Mr. Nawabi wanted to speak to you. Didn't you see him? He's certainly gotten fat! Which daughter is that with him? I thought they were all younger than me."

Stopping short, Catherine fought the anger rising in her throat. This had happened before, though never to anyone so close, and it would have to be accepted. But looking down at Saira, she thought, no, my girl, I'm glad I didn't protect you. Be uneasy. Be suspicious. You may not be so lucky as I was.

"That's not his daughter, Saira, it's his second wife. I hear she's pregnant now."

"His second...? But what about Bibi Nawabi?"

"She's still alive. They didn't divorce. Physically, she's fine."

"Oh, no, how could he!" Twisting, Saira glared over her shoulder. "How could he bring her to this house in place of Bibi-jan?"

"I only see her if I go to visit her now. Or she comes here. I'm sorry if I've startled you, dear, maybe I should have written, but as you see, I can hardly talk about it."

"I'd never stand for that!" Saira was crimson. "And who'd want to be a second wife these days?"

"It may not have been her choice, Saira. I don't suppose she's very comfortable here, either."

Her jaw tightened. "No. She looks nervous. She can't be much older than I am. That ought to be illegal. It makes me sick."

"I know. And I agree. But Saira, I don't think you have to worry about that where Ashraf's concerned. I trust him." She smiled. "And if he had two wives he wouldn't be able to keep himself in such nice silk shirts."

"Oh, he doesn't care about those!" The tension in her face broke. "I know he'd never do it. That's why I like him."

"I do too. Now hurry up and see if you can find Tor."

Saira climbed the stairs carefully. The heels on her black sandals were really too high, Catherine thought, turning back to the crowded hall.

By the door she felt a sudden wave of dizziness again. Everyone needed so much, took so much ... how could she be expected to supply it all? Mangal and Roshana were right for each other, wonderfully so, and for the next few hours she must think only of them, but still, even in Kabul these weddings had an undertone that brought out her Yankee squeamishness. The double-meaning jokes the men shared, laughing, the henna, signifying defloration—Roshana's bed would not be checked for proof of virginity, but at many weddings the bride did seem like a lamb prepared for slaughter. Tonight's wedding was simple compared to those classic three-day-long affairs with ritual meals and visits, games, wrestling, the singing of suggestive songs and endless symbols of fertility. It was only in the last few years that men and women celebrated together instead of sitting separately—and visiting, being entertained always separately had been her hardest, angriest adjustment, though in fact she had preferred the company of women after so much talk of government at home.

Crossing the hall, she took her place in front of the carpeted dais. The silk cushions on the velvet couch were antique brocade, the lacquerware table four centuries old and the blue and yellow flowers she had arranged around them scented the close air. They'd struck a tasteful compromise, she thought. Some modern weddings were incongruously Western, with flashing electric lights on the henna tray and photographers everywhere.

Now Omar and Uncle Yusef would lead Mangal to the dais—and from the flurry behind her it seemed they must be coming. Yes, the crowd was parting and there was Uncle Yusef, walking straighter than he had in years. Mangal moved easily in those loose clothes, looking calmer than before, and even Omar's face was less drawn. At their own wedding he had worn a gray suit very much like this one, though there had been no smiling throng. Was he remembering that, the old minister, the narrow aisle in King's Chapel, and later the champagne toasts he'd felt uncomfortable drinking in front of his solemn uncle, whose presence in Boston had sparked their hasty marriage?

I could use a glass of sherry right now, she thought, and if my side of the family were here they'd want a good deal more than that. The time they did come, Dad unpacked his bottle of Scotch before anything else—then wandered around shaking his head and asking me if I knew we had some valuable art in this house. What was he expecting, a mud hut strung with chilis? It's too bad he can't see this.

Mangal had reached the dais and deftly supported Uncle Yusef up the steps, then let himself be settled on the couch where he sat facing the guests, smiling openly, the silk threads in his shirt reflecting light. Some poor woman must have spent a year on that embroidery.

Now again the crowd was turning as a little girl cousin of Roshana's came out bearing the candlelit henna tray, and then behind her Roshana appeared walking between two aunts, looking fragile in her transparent veil and heavy red velvet dress. The band began the wedding song, Ahesta-buro, the singer throwing back his head, "... Go slowly, you go slowly..." When Roshana had joined Mangal, Omar and Prince Daoud moved to hold the silk-wrapped Koran above their heads.

As one of Roshana's aunts lifted back her veil, the other presented a round mirror so the couple could glimpse each other for the "first time," indirectly in its glass, and Catherine shivered remembering how often that had really been true. At some weddings, the bride and groom would never have met before this moment, and in spite of warnings to accept their parents' greater wisdom in such matters, she had seen more apprehension than delight in those young eyes.

Mangal and Roshana were grinning at each other in the mirror, then composed themselves to read a passage from the Koran aloud together, and the mullah began his questioning. As Catherine listened to them promise, yes, they would take, provide for and make one another happy, the verses from her own service echoed in the minister's thin voice: "My beloved spake, and said unto me, Rise up, my love, my fair one, and come away. For lo, the winter is past, the rain is over and gone; The flowers appear on the earth, and the time of singing of birds is come, and the voice of the turtle is heard in our land." The Song of Songs was filled with images that might have come from this country—flocks and vineyards, black goatskin tents, pomegranates. Maybe it hadn't seemed so foreign to Omar after all. Besides, he'd been to other Protestant services in England.

Roshana had chosen to stay in Kabul rather than go abroad to college. Would her wedding trip to Europe make as great a contrast as coming here from Boston had? Not possibly. She knew English, and some French and Italian, and she wasn't twenty-one and frightened.

Marrying Omar on three weeks' notice, when he was ordered home, had been a lucky gamble. He'd managed to convince her that anything else would be boring in comparison. Then he'd left her with her language books in an empty house and bare garden for six months while he fought with Mountbatten over Pashtunistan.

Since her parents hated the marriage, she wouldn't admit her loneliness or that descriptions in her early letters home were taken from books: "Afghanistan's shaped like an oak leaf, about the size of Texas. Mountain spurs run through the center, the Himalayas and the Hindu Kush turning west into the Koh-i-Baba range. The north is a wide plateau, with occasional oases. The south is mostly desert land."

She hadn't written, "This country terrifies me. It's too barren, wrenching, demanding. Even where it's green, even here in the Kabul valley, all life seems unbearably tenuous." But when Omar came back from Delhi she'd shouted for joy in spite of his failure. "Good," he laughed. "I was hoping you'd feel that way. Let's go, I want to show you the biggest statue you've ever seen." For the next month, words on paper came to life in a landscape so extreme it silenced her completely.

They'd driven up from the wheat fields of Kabul past the site of ancient Kapisa and the Begram excavation that had yielded the relics in Uncle Yusef's crystal globe—Indian ivory, Han dynasty red lacquerware, green Phoenician glass, a piece of Roman stonework and Greco-Egyptian bronze—all from one first-century point on the Silk Route.

Further on, at Charikar, three rivers ran together, and unveiled nomad women in black billowing dresses were setting up tents for summer, tethering their camels nose-to-tail by crumbling caravanserais now overgrown with yellow fennel and early roses that mingled with the scent of mint and rhubarb blowing down from the mountains.

Then green fields gave way to the climbing red rock Shibar Gorge and the spectacular pink sandstone cliffs at Bamian—honeycombed with monastic chambers and flanked by two statues of the Buddha that stood over a hundred and fifty feet tall—towering, massive figures with mutilated faces guarding the place where twelve hundred monks had settled by the fourth century, only to be slaughtered later by white Huns riding down from the north.

She had climbed to the top of one statue to look for the faint paintings her books had described as the first expression of Buddhist art, owing a Greek influence to Alexander the Great. But standing by that scarred, gigantic head in a shadowed grotto where the only sound was of the wind buffeting the empty cells, she'd felt cold, as if surrounded by ghosts in a huge mausoleum. The magnitude of what had been, and of its destruction, made the irrigated valley below seem like a window box on one of the pyramids.

To the north, the land grew wilder—pure strong streams rushing down granite hillsides bright with juniper and roses, the broad stretch of the Oxus plain where remnant arches rose like spectral doorways to the endless brown horizon, so when they reached the Blue Mosque at Mazar-i-Sharif, its obsessive detail made sense. The intricacy of its innumerable tiles and concentration of design seemed a human attempt to hold the desert in balance, to answer the greater, incomprehensible order of Allah. Each pattern contained a tiny defect in deference to his perfection.

They drove west to Balkh, Alexander's ancient Bactria, where again new life had grown up from the ruins left by Genghis Khan's hundred thousand horsemen. Marco Polo passed through here on his way to China, then Tamerlane, who rebuilt the city—which fell, finally, to an invasion of cholera. King Amanullah, the great reformer for whom Omar's parents worked and died, had laid out modern Balkh's wide avenues and evergreen groves close to the Oxus River, now called the Amu Darya, marking the border with the Soviet Union. But though, as with the Durand Line, the tribes there had been cut in two, the Uzbeks and Turkomans had no hope of mending that scar, hoped only, after so much warfare, to be left in peace.

King Amanullah also commissioned part of new Herat on the western border with Iran, where the British had deliberately demolished a renowned Islamic college to create a "field of fire" against a Russian incursion that never materialized. In the sixteenth century, nine hundred poets and artists had gathered at Herat to work, producing, among other things, the exquisite Persian miniatures that now lined Omar's study and their entry hall. She had bought them in Herat, spent days selecting them. By then she felt a need for small, ordered landscapes, to sit in the Persian garden of the Park Hotel drinking tea and writing letters while butterflies and bees fed in the red and yellow flower beds around her.

On the way there, they were caught in a dust storm—a dense, gritty cloud that swirled up lashing into the car and filling her mouth and nose before she could raise the window. Choking, she panicked, and then what looked like a crumpled newspaper hurtled straight down toward the windshield, but it was a buzzard coming for shelter and she screamed at its hideous talons, at the dust, the disintegrating earth that seemed about to split open, spewing out the rag-and-bone victims of Russian, British, Mongol and Timurid armies. Afghanistan was simply in the way and it would always be. The pretty shards in Uncle Yusef's crystal globe came from a graveyard, and if Omar disappeared in this dust, she'd be left with her few words of Dari to try to find her way back to Boston. But the people here would probably speak some other language and never have heard of America.

Then had come the last long push across the vast dead Helmand valley to the old walled city of Kandahar, named for Alexander, from the Arabic Iskandar; then east and north again to the mountains of Paktia and the infamous Khyber Pass, whose tribes, Omar said, sold protection and the force of their arms to the highest bidder.

They hadn't crossed the Durand Line into what was then still India, but by that time she could see why these artificial borders were causing so much strife. It was absurd to think of anyone saying Boston or New England with the fervor that these tribesmen spoke the word Pashtunistan, or Nuristan, or Baluchistan. The tribes belonged to their lands and vice versa, Omar said, as they had for thousands of years—which was why his family was so passionate about this idea of sovereignty. Without a monarchy, there was too much danger of these tribal areas' being drawn and quartered by the Russians, Chinese or anyone else who could benefit from their instability.

Omar's family fort was in Paktia, inhabited now by some second cousins who showed them the overwhelming hospitality central to the Pashtun code of honor, killing lambs she was sure they could ill afford to spare and serving endless pilaus with minted yogurt and heavily sweetened tea and the flat crusty bread called nan, which they baked in domed clay ovens. For the first time she was taken into a compound's inner courtyard, and sat surrounded by women who laughed and pointed at her pale skin and simple clothing, so different from their long embroidered dresses and tinkling jewelry, and after consulting her Pashto dictionary she guessed one old woman was telling her with pride that this was not the first yellow hair she'd ever seen. They embraced her as a sister and showed her their daughters, looking for her approval, and it was only later that she realized three of these women shared one husband, and two more another, and they expected she would have a similar fate. But they were happy for each other's company and she found it hard to leave them, resolving that when she returned she'd speak Pashto well enough to contribute jokes and stories of her own. The turbaned men in baggy pants and loose shirts never addressed or looked at her directly, but Omar assured her they thought her a great prize.

The only part of the country remotely like New England was their final stop in Nuristan, Rudyard Kipling's Kafiristan, where evergreen forests blanketed the mountains and the houses were made of carved timber instead of mud brick. As they sat by a stream glittering with mica, an old woman in black with a silver hair band and bangles climbed down a steep slope balancing a load of wood on her back to offer them a handful of wild strawberries like a reward for having survived the trip.

In opening her hands to the fruit and that smiling rugged woman, she felt, idiotically, as if she were accepting everything she'd seen, and on her tongue the hard berries burst with a sharp tang and sweetness. Poverty and illiteracy were taken for granted here, and disease sprang from open sewers and the animal dung used for fuel and plaster. Progress had no value in a place where any change was seen as a threat, and Islam, the only law in much of the country, left thieves with stumps for hands, sentenced adulterers to be stoned and women to lives of shadow behind the heavy medieval doors of Kabul's old quarter. But Omar said the law of the desert, however in need of mending, prevented the law of the jungle. The counsel of women was more respected than in Boston. And after centuries of devastation, the people had a toughness and humor she could only hold in awe.

There was no waste, nothing was taken for granted, least of all the Afghans' fierce pride in their faith, strong families and the eerie beauty of the mountains and bright sky. That day in Nuristan she began to see the country through Omar's eyes—not as some cultural game preserve, but as a fascinating, unique society trying to survive intact in the twentieth century. He had studied the landscape as if it were full of messages she couldn't read, but now she also saw a camel caravan as in hopeless competition with paved roads, another problem whose solution would demand subtlety and great care.

Without medicine, children would continue to die unnecessarily; without better fertilizer and breeding, the crops and livestock could never supply the country's needs; without more education and industry, Afghanistan would lose any chance for self-sufficiency. But advances had to be made in terms acceptable to people whose traditions had gone unbroken for hundreds of years, who were mistrustful of any interference in tribal rights and loyalties.

If only Mangal could understand that. Kabul was farther in time than distance from the countryside.

It was useless to lecture Mangal about patience, though. His father didn't show him any. Visions of the future had driven Omar's life, and he couldn't think the children anything but lucky for having a real home, herself, and each other. Too much, he reserved his intimacy for her, and Mangal in particular resented that, responding with a coolness of his own.

Roshana was helping ease their tension. She made them laugh in spite of themselves. Why did Mangal have to be so pig-headed about moving out of the compound? He said that some traditions were only for close families. At his age, Omar had no family.

Omar's resignation might turn out to be a blessing, Catherine thought. It will give them time to get to know each other.

Omar was watching Mangal with a mixture of pride and amusement now. Roshana's face was serious as the mullah closed his Koran. Beside the dais, Saira stood holding Uncle Yusef's hand. When Catherine caught her eye she frowned, shaking her head to say that she hadn't found Tor, but her cheeks were warm with excitement again—perhaps because Ashraf hovered close by. At least Omar approved of his children's romantic choices. He said Ashraf's father was already making inquiries and that neither of them would mind writing another marriage contract soon.

On the dais, Prince Daoud was bending to paint henna on Mangal's little finger, tying it with a satin ribbon, and then Mangal repeated the ritual with Roshana, rather daintily for him. Traditionally, the proceedings would stop here with the eating of breadcrumb pudding, but since Roshana was staying in this house tonight they had decided to include the leavetaking rite as part of the ceremony, and her aunts and girl cousins came to cover her with veils.

The final seventh veil, of fine silk, was carried by her male relatives and had something tied in each corner—sugar for prosperity, saffron for happiness, cloves for purity and a coin for security—and after holding it up, the men undid those knots and lowered it, weightless, over her head. Roshana's Uncle Aziz took the coin and spices while her father with mock severity tied the seventh veil to a green turban cloth, then passed that around her waist, symbolically releasing her in chastity and reminding her to shine with honor always.

He turned her to face her husband, so Mangal could lift back the veils, his face soft with emotion. Roshana blinked, and to Catherine's joy he gave his bride a very Western kiss, as her aunts hurried out with bowls of sherbet and malida pudding to sweeten and make their union fertile.

Mangal fed some to Roshana, and when she returned the favor, blushing with the first embarrassment Catherine could remember seeing in her, the room erupted with laughter and applause and the band began to play again, wildly, in celebration.

"Mummy-jan?" Saira had come up behind her. "We have to serve the malida now. And that's my only part in this. Oh, Mummy, wasn't it wonderful? I'll remember tonight as long as I live!"

Catherine hugged her, but she was watching Mangal and Roshana walk down from the dais smiling with all the happiness she wished for them, and the strain she'd felt in managing so much tradition vanished in the face of its meaning. Never had two people seemed more truly married, and as Mangal crushed them in a bear hug she murmured, "So will I, Saira, every minute of it."

It was perfect, it was over, it was just beginning, and against her chest Saira giggled, "Mangal, you're wrecking my hair! And I've got work to do!"

Saira handed her empty malida tray to one of the hired servants and collapsed at a littered table. Her ankles ached. It was months since she had worn such flimsy shoes.

On the other side of the room Mr. Nawabi was waving his fat hands under Roshana's nose. Mr. Nawabi with his big belly—how could that girl stand him? Maybe Bibi Nawabi was relieved.

Roshana looked beautiful though, in that dress. She looked ancient. There should have been coins sewn into it to jingle when she moved. But Mangal, next to her, talking to Prince Daoud's wife, seemed to be in a daze. Twice now he had lifted a spoonful of malida halfway to his mouth, then looked at it and put it down again. Mangal...had he meant to be so nasty before? Maybe she had interrupted his conversation with Daoud-jan, but was that such a sin when she hadn't seen her brother in so long?

Maybe he was angry about something else. About Daddy? That still didn't seem real—it was like a joke. What if the king wouldn't accept his resignation?

Farther down the hall, Ashraf was sitting, drinking tea with his father. The cup in his hand almost touched his father's. That was like him, instinctively warm, not surrounded by some electromagnetic field no one could get through. How did Mangal act with Roshana when they were alone, she wondered. Would he go on about politics the way Jeffrey had, or did she bring out some secret playful side of him?

Now Daddy-jan came up to Roshana carrying two bowls and said something that made her laugh sharply, as if he'd caught her off guard. Saira saw Roshana shrug, and then nodding, he turned still smiling to walk in her own direction, holding out one dish.

"Some malida for my little girl!" He sat down beside her. "You were so busy serving the guests, I thought you might like some yourself now."

His face was closer than it had been in two years, but he had aged more than that. His eyelids were wrinkled now and there was white hair mixed with the gray around his ears. Behind that smile he was upset too; it looked plastered on, artificial. He probably just wanted to go to bed.

"Thank you." She took the bowl. "Maybe I could eat a little. But it's so rich, and I had such a lot of dinner!"

"It's supposed to be rich. I was just telling Roshana I hope she has a child for every grain of wheat in it, and the sooner the better. You too, Saira, before long. I'd love a houseful of grandchildren now. I expect after being in government, they'll all seem like geniuses to me."

"Not when they've messed up your study for the hundredth time." She tasted the thick pudding. It was too sweet, cloying, but she tried to look pleased. "Anyway, what if Roshana doesn't want to have a baby yet? She may want to teach a while longer."

"Oh..." He pursed his lips. "You think I'm rushing her. But they're going to have children, you know, so why shouldn't they start now? They'll have all the help they need."

He was annoyed and she said quickly, "I didn't mean they shouldn't. Only that it's up to her, isn't it?" This felt like talking to Tor, she thought. When either of them was overtired they snapped at anything. She took another swallow of malida.

"You've been away a long time." He frowned. "I hope not so long that you've forgotten what's important. There are only two things that matter, Saira—work and family, nothing else. And the honor that you bring to both. Besides, it's a very good thing to have children while you're young enough to give them time and energy."

Did he think that had been true of him? she wondered.

"Yes," he nodded. "You've been gone four years. I expect many things here are strange to you now. I certainly felt that way when I came home, and I know Mangal did too. You have to give yourself time to readjust. It can be frustrating at first, but I'll offer you the advice Uncle Yusef gave to me: the best thing you can do is watch and show respect while you get used to being home again. I had to prove myself doubly because I'd married an American, and some people will be suspicious of you too. So you have to be cautious. For instance, I was watching you with Ashraf earlier. If you flirt with him like that, you'd better mean it."

He said it lightly but his eyes were stern. What had she done that was so shameful? "We were just teasing each other," she said. "We always do that. Can't I have fun anymore?"

"Of course you can. Just be aware of how Ashraf may interpret your behavior. You're twenty now, not sixteen, and I think he's serious about you."

"And I'm serious about him! Don't you know that? I thought you liked Ashraf."

He was looking at her intently. "Do you really mean that, Saira? In every sense of the word?"

"Of course I do. For heaven's sake!"

"Good." He grinned. "No, don't look at me that way, I had to find out for sure. Ashraf's father isn't well, Saira, he's had trouble with his heart all year, and he's been very anxious for me to speak to you about this. I suppose it's natural enough to want to see one's children settled, and he's very fond of you. But I had to know how you felt first."

"Daddy, I've only been home one day! Do you mean he asked you to propose to me? It's 1973, can't Ashraf do that for himself? I love you, but I'd rather hear it from him."

They both were laughing, and she was glad to see him looking happy again.

"No, no," he wiped his eyes. "I'm sure you'll get a highly romantic offer from the gentleman in question. His father just wanted to know if you'd be open to it. And...well, you know how traditional his people are. I expect they have all sorts of wild notions about what goes on in the States. He wants my assurance that there would be no bar to such a marriage. You know what I mean. It's an embarrassing question to ask one's daughter, but customs are what they are. Can I tell him you're amenable and the same honest girl you've always been, Saira?"

She felt her stomach twist in a knot. The same honest girl, meaning: virgin. No bar, meaning: virgin. Well, if he used euphemisms, she could too, but it was disgusting to think of Ashraf's father asking whether she was "alright" or "intact" or "preserved," as if otherwise she would be worthless, as if all her value and honor depended on that one condition of flesh—which she would have lost in any case after marriage, but then it would be "alright." Where was honor, what was honest in this? It made her furious.

She smiled coolly, "I can't say I'm exactly the same. For one thing, I'm not a girl anymore. But you can tell him there's no bar where Ashraf and I are concerned, and that I'm interested, yes. I love Ashraf. Why don't you tell him that too." Or isn't it important, she thought.

"I must say I'm delighted, Saira! You know, I've had nothing but work all my life, and it's really a comfort now to look forward to spending some time with the family, including Ashraf and Roshana, whom I think so much of. That's a blessing for which I'm grateful. Perhaps it's true that when you lose one thing you always gain another."

She wanted to say: but we were always here, you were just too busy for us. Or: yes, I lost my virginity, but I learned a lot in the process. It was hopeless though; to him she would always be a "girl" who had to be "cautious." He wanted only respect and comfort, so why not let him have it. After all, he had suffered too.

"Come on, let's find your mother," he said. "I've hardly seen her all evening. Or do you want to finish your malida?"

"No." She smiled again. "I'm afraid I'll have a baby for every grain I eat. Did you really say that to Roshana?"

"I'm afraid I did. Should I apologize?"

"No. We'll just wait and see what happens."

He laughed and she stood up to go with him. He was happy now, and if it was because of a lie, did that really matter? If she'd told the truth, would he have answered, fine, I just don't want to mislead them? No, it would have hurt him, humiliated him... and anyway, she thought, I do want Ashraf, I love him more now than I could have before Jeffrey. I've known him all my life and he's just what I need, a friend to play with and to work with. But I'm not a girl anymore, Daddy-jan, and you're going to have to accept that. You have to understand me too.

"There's Catherine, with Ashraf and Mangal," he said, quickening his step. "Now what are they all giggling about?"

Mangal was laughing so hard that a few drops of cherry juice flew out of his glass to stain the edge of his sleeve.

"But you *have* to, Aunty," Ashraf was saying. "For the mother of the groom not to dance the Atan... it would seem you have no happiness in your new daughter. Of course"—his eyes twinkled—"the bride's family is supposed to be very sad. But I don't think they're too miserable, do you?" He nodded toward Roshana's father and her uncle Aziz, who were beaming at each other as if they had solved a major problem.

"Please dance, Aunty," he prodded. "It's very simple, really, you've seen it done. And Saira will be dancing with you."

"The answer is *no*." She smiled. "I'm Afghan only by marriage. Omar, rescue me please. I couldn't dance now if my life depended on it."

"Alright." Ashraf surrendered. "Saira, you'll have to begin it alone then. You don't want to insult Roshana." He clasped her shoulder, and the warmth of his hand through her thin silk dress was vibrant and distinct from the heat of the night. She had never felt his touch so acutely, and soon it would be hers forever. Why had talking to Daddy made that seem so real?

"Saira can't do the Atan," Mangal grinned. "She's hardly Afghan herself anymore. Maybe she could do that new American dance I've read about— the Bump? But I suppose you'd need a bumpee for that."

Saira was looking at Ashraf and saw his eyes react as angrily as her own must have done. What was wrong with Mangal tonight?

"That's silly," said Ashraf firmly. "She can dance it as well as anyone in this room. Don't you think so, Aunty?"

"Yes, if she wants to. But that's up to her. Would you care to uphold our honor, dear?"

Ashraf gave her a squeeze for encouragement. "Don't worry, once you start the others will join in. Please, Saira, for me? No"—he shook his head—"I mean, for Roshana, of course."

Nodding, she turned to face Mangal. "Yes, I'll do it, Ashraf."

"Then I'll signal the band. Good for you!"

Passing Mangal, she walked a few steps away from them and stood still to ready herself. It was stupid to fight Mangal with words, he could always get the better of her that way. He seemed to take pleasure in ridiculing her as if she were still a child, as if it were her fault she had ever been a child, her sin to go to school in Boston instead of Kabul like Roshana, whose father wanted nothing more for her than a society wedding. Roshana was blamed for being too forceful, she for her weakness.... Daddy with his lectures, Daoud-jan telling her she ought to be thinking of marriage, as if her brain could hold only one idea at a time or she wasn't fit for anything but domesticity. Royila, Devika and Roshana, all were punished for wanting more than that—and Mr. Nawabi's new wife too? But Roshana was still working to free women from the bonds Mangal seemed willing to inflict on his own sister. Why? So he could feel sure of his superiority?

Not Afghan anymore, he said. Well, this would show them. The important thing was not to be afraid, not to let them intimidate her. Roshana and Devika set their own terms and commanded respect.

But her legs felt like wood and her hands were sweating.

"The Atan!" Ashraf called. "Led by the groom's sister, Saira!"

As the people around her drew back to form a circle, she stepped out in her high-heeled sandals trying to remember.... Usually it was done by many people moving in a ring and clapping, first slowly, then bending deeper, spinning faster and faster. She felt herself blush, but the point was just to dance not caring what anyone thought, to find energy and freedom in the music as she had once or twice at Radcliffe, and forget everything else.

Glancing at the band, she saw the tabla player smiling and drumming with emphasis to give her the beat. She thought, I can begin however I like, just moving to the rhythm. Then she walked out into the circle of expectant faces with her hands down and elbows bent, feeling strength in her arms, the floor hard under her feet, and suddenly she knew it was going to be alright, she wouldn't look at anyone, just let the music enter her body and sway with it till her spine moved freely like a length of rope. As other instruments joined the tabla she flexed her knees and started swinging her hips and shoulders in counterpoint, but still her arms were down, head bent forward as she listened, absorbing sound and letting it radiate through her limbs. Slowly, the tension was melting, her legs felt warm and alive and it was no longer the simple drumbeat she followed, but the more complicated notes of the harmonium. She was spinning in a circle, dipping almost to the floor, then gradually her arms came up making widening arcs and now others were joining in, clapping in unison, surrounding her with a wall of noise and a kaleidoscope of color. The men stamped so hard the floor was like part of the dance, knocking her feet higher and shaking her whole frame until her head snapped back and forth with the wild rhythm. She felt each instrument playing through her, vibrating as if in one more instant her fingers, hands and arms would fly away, running after the chords into space. And as the music reached a crescendo her hair fell loose from its combs, billowing around her shoulders like a veil to cover her finally with softness and silence.

She stood still with her eyes closed, but inside the darkness, nerves and muscles trembled in a frenzy. Then someone was touching her, hugging her, and people were shouting approval.

When she opened her eyes, there was Mangal, surprised, and Roshana and her uncle smiling... but where had Ashraf gone?

Scanning the room, she couldn't find him—until she glanced over toward the hall, and with a sinking feeling saw him hurrying out the front door. And Tor stepping out of shadow to close it behind him. Next to her, Mangal cursed softly. He must have seen that too.

Bowing at them with a hateful grin, Tor spun away to run up the broad staircase.

Six

AT THE TOP of the stairs, Tor leaned against the wall to catch his breath. So Saira and Mangal had seen him. So what? They wouldn't send a search party now. He was too much in disgrace. "Oh, Tor, how could you? Oh, Tor!" Well, let her say it. He had seen her too down there, whirling around like a dervish with her skirt flying up so anyone could have a look at her skinny legs. What a hypocrite!

He'd been creeping down the hall, about to slip upstairs, when Ashraf caught his arm. "Tor, my father's not feeling well and I'm going to take him home now." So worried he looked, the little gentleman. "I don't want to bother your parents. Would you make my apologies? And Tor, please tell Saira she danced the Atan better than Mangal ever could. Will you do that for me?"

Tor made his face a mask of concern. "But of course, Ashraf-jan! I hope your dear father feels better very soon. Here, let me get the door."

He could play that game too. That's what none of them understood. It was easy. It meant nothing—to him or them either, it was just a nice way of telling lies. The funny thing was, when he pretended the way he just had with Ashraf, no one ever saw that he was faking. He could copy their expressions and tone of voice—even use the same words—and they always thought he was serious. Well, everyone but Mummy-jan. But she was a big fake too. Half the time when people thought she was listening, he could tell her mind was really somewhere else. Except when he talked. Then she listened like an owl—criticizing everything he said.

What a good boy Ashraf was, taking his father home. Really, a fine fellow. Ashraf was probably never "in disgrace."

Missing the wedding was bad though, everyone would be mad. So what could they do, beat him to death? Good, let them try. He felt like beating up someone himself—had even ridden back to the target zone looking for that guard with the big mole on his cheek, but there were half a dozen soldiers there, all officers, and watching from hiding he had decided they were up to something and he'd better get out of there fast. Riding Aspi hadn't helped much tonight anyway. He was even madder now than before. ...Prince Mangal acting so virtuous, he and Roshana, so holy, then Daddy-jan coming up and jerking that stupid necktie. "I want you to behave!"—as if he were some kind of wild animal, lucky to be let out of his cage. And Saira was the worst. She was supposed to be his friend, and he'd been waiting for her to come home...the one person he could always trust! But all she could do was scream at him about Karima, and then run down to make cow eyes at Ashraf and dance with her skirt up around her ears. She and Ashraf hardly knew each other, but so what? They were "intended."

It was going to be bad alright, he could see that now. While he was riding, nothing mattered but the wind against his face, but even then something seemed to be chasing him. Yes, it would be very bad. "Oh, Toryalai, how could you!"

So, what should he do about it? Run away? Hide? No, he wasn't a coward. He'd left because he couldn't stand being there, and if they didn't like it they could drown themselves. But he hadn't fought with Daddy in a year. He was out of practice. He'd have to calm down and set his nerves the way he had at Lawrence College, so nothing they did could hurt him.

Yes, he needed to relax. Then when they came for him, he'd just smile. Too bad, all of you, screech all you want, I don't care.

Maybe some more of Saira's cognac would help...Fine Champagne Cognac. French always sounded so nice.

Turning down the hall, he opened the door to her room. It was dark. Good, he'd leave it dark. There was a little lamp in the closet. If he shut himself up there, even if someone came looking they wouldn't see him.

The closet smelled good, like that French perfume she wore. And all her pretty silk dresses felt so soft. Karima never had anything made of silk.

It was hard to open the knapsack on top of Saira's shoes, there were too many strings and buckles. Maybe if he just stuck his hand in through the side....yes, that was the bottle, the glass felt like velvet.

He pulled it out. There was hardly any gone. The black label said Rémy Martin. This didn't look like the bottles cowboys drank from in the movies, but cognac must be as strong as whiskey, and at least it had a cork like cowboy bottles.

Pulling the cork, he smiled at the sound it made—like when you puffed your cheeks up with air and then smashed them down hard with your fingers. He tried that, then the cork again. Just the same.

Alright, here goes, and this time right from the bottle. Oh, he liked the way it burned! How many cowboy movies had he seen in the States, maybe ten altogether? When they drank in saloons they used little glasses and threw the whiskey down their throats in one gulp. But sometimes they drank out of the bottle too, sitting around the campfire. Then they wiped their mouths on their sleeves, like this.

In Kabul there were hardly ever cowboy movies, which was too bad. And of course whiskey was "forbidden." That was too bad too, because it made you feel so nice, so...comfortable. Pashtun tribesmen were a lot like cowboys, sitting around their fires, or riding through the hills and shooting, wild and free. That's what it meant to be a man! Not this phony "Oh, so-and-so, dear, would you mind if I...and forgive me, but...and let's all sit down and have tea." Nobody ever said what they meant, and they didn't like it when he did. They could drown themselves.

Fine Champagne Cognac. He tipped up the bottle. It hardly burned at all anymore, and his whole body felt tingly. It still hurt his stomach a little, but the next swallow should stop that too. Glug. Another nice sound. Wipe your mouth on your sleeve...and why not get more cozy?

Pulling down Saira's thick pink robe, he crushed it into a pillow. Yes, from now on he'd just be a cowboy. "Oh, Toryalai, dear!" The liars! Except Karima, who had nothing made of silk. And look at all Saira's dresses! Blue, green, yellow, red...this one felt the softest. It slipped off the hanger right into his hands, and he rubbed the silk against his cheek...mmmm. They should all belong to Karima, and that French perfume too. Maybe he'd just give them to her. Saira didn't deserve them, she was the worst liar of all. Did she think he was blind?

One more drink. That letter of hers...did she think he was stupid? The letter, that's right, she had put it back in the knapsack too. J. Carleton, her great love—whom she forgot as soon as she saw Ashraf, like a toaster changing its plug. Let's see about J. Carleton...quite a long letter! Jeffrey, that's what the J. stood for—Jeffrey wanted to know why she was making such a fuss.

What? Tor squinted. Of course! He'd been sure of it. That liar! There it was in black and white: "You enjoyed sleeping with me too, Saira, admit it. But having sex with someone doesn't mean you own them forever. It was your choice. I never forced you, and I think you're so angry because you feel guilty, because you liked it too. But you're supposed to like it, Saira, even though they don't tell you that at home. So be grateful you can, and just remember all the good things—until you forget me completely, which I'm sure you will before long."

So this was Saira's idea of love! Sleeping together, having sex—and it had been *her* choice. Ugly, ugly. Nothing about love at all. She was disgusting, making fun of him and Karima! The way she was dancing when he came in—that was for her next victim, of course. This Jeffrey was smart. She'd forgotten him alright, the minute she got off the plane.

The cognac was half gone and it was making him feel sick, but he could see things much better now. Yes, that dance of hers, with her skirt flying up and all the men watching and clapping...she must have loved it! And Ashraf even smiled at that, poor fellow. He didn't know anything.

It was getting dizzy in here...not enough air. Open the door a crack. She'd been sitting right there on the bed, laughing at him and hugging herself ...laughing at Karima! He could kill her. And Karima was so beautiful, she loved Aspi too, and now he couldn't even talk to her anymore. Sleeping together! Karima never stayed all night to sleep with her long hair across his chest—no, she had to run back to her room. They'd always been friends, and then her body, this summer...that was love, and now he couldn't even look at her.

His head felt ready to crack, he was so mad. And Saira laughed! Yesterday all he'd wanted was for her to come home—as if she'd ever help him! Good, hate all of them, especially her. They could all go to hell.

Usually when he got upset, he'd just ride away. Not this time. The whiskey made him feel strong enough to beat them all up now. Mummy and Daddy-jan...they didn't matter so much. They would hate him no matter what he did. But Saira...she was disgusting, a liar and a traitor—and so happy about it, laughing and joking with Ashraf. What if someone told Ashraf the truth? Would he still be smiling at her?

Ashraf, the little gentleman, taking his father home: "Tor, please tell Saira..." The sneak! And Prince Mangal was a big liar too, sneaking through the bazaar in those old clothes...probably going to see some other woman. They both thought they could get away with anything.

Not this time.

There was only a little whiskey left. Toss it back, like a cowboy. If only he'd read this before Ashraf left...She'd been upset to see him leave too... she and Mangal making such faces. They didn't know why Ashraf left. Only he knew why. "Tor, please tell Saira..." He was the only one who knew, and he'd never tell her now, let her think whatever she wanted. But he should have told Ashraf....She wouldn't get away with this. Not after laughing that way. He'd fix her. He'd fix all of them. Yes, why not? Give the liars their lies. That letter...

He grabbed her dresses to pull himself up, but they came falling all around him. There was something in his hand. It was silk...a sleeve. Throwing it down, he reached for the doorknob and finally got up on his feet. Oh, he was dizzy. It was hard to walk, after the closet. But that was alright, because now he knew exactly what to do.

Omar shut the front door behind the last few guests and glanced at his watch. It was three o'clock, but the hall was still hot and hazy with tobacco smoke. Tomorrow they'd have to give the house a good airing. Tomorrow ... there would be time for everything.

Catherine touched his arm, "I've asked Raima to serve us mint tea in the living room. Everyone's overtired and I think it will help us get to sleep. But if you're too exhausted, go on up now and I'll say good night to the children for you."

"No, this is Roshana's first night in this house. I'd at least like to welcome her." His lips felt thick as rubber. Had he ever been so tired? I'm getting old, he thought, I'm used up, spent, and what has it been for? After all these years...

He smiled. Ah, so I'm bitter now. Add that to the list.

At some point during the evening he had begun to watch his symptoms, guarding them so no cracks would show in his wall of pleasantries. An initial euphoria after resigning had taken him through the Nikka. But the strain of the wedding, the endless smiles, sheer fatigue had worn him down until he started to resent the need for artifice, the enforced, oblivious merriment and even Mangal himself. Light-headedness, petulance, anger, and now a swimming exhaustion that made his feet clumsy, crossing the hall.

Soon I'll be a catalog of symptoms, he thought, if I don't find something to do. Maybe I should start an export company for lapis lazuli.

Raima passed him, carrying a tray that she set on the coffee table, pushing aside Uncle Yusef's crystal globe. Uncle Yusef had already gone up to bed, but the rest of the family was there, draped across the furniture while Catherine poured tea. All except Tor... But tomorrow there would be time to deal with Tor. How had he forgotten it was Tor who had made him so angry?

Stretching out in an armchair, he took the cup Roshana offered. She and Catherine both were smiling, pleased with the quality of the evening. They'd done very well without him, in spite of Catherine's protestations—which came as no surprise. She had arranged the wedding as competently as she ran the house, raised the children and taught at the university. He would probably just be in her way, underfoot at home now, but at least the children were more or less settled, and they could be alone without speeches to write or receptions to manage. Poor Catherine, how many pots of tea had she served in the last twenty-seven years?

Saira was lying back in the other armchair, yawning with her eyes closed. Well, she had good reason to be tired. Not five minutes after he'd warned her to watch her behavior, she had danced the Atan like some kind of gypsy in that pointed skirt... not three minutes after he told Ashraf's father that marriage proposals could be made. Everyone praised her dancing, but he'd found it disturbing—provocative and defiant. She hadn't listened to anything he'd said. And Ashraf's father had turned and walked away.

Glancing at Mangal, he felt another stab of annoyance. Mangal in that costume, whispering with Prince Daoud all evening, following him around like a puppy.... Who did the children think they were in these clothes? No doubt Mangal pictured himself a champion of the masses—though he rarely drove outside of Kabul. And after four years at Radcliffe, Saira had come back looking like a kuchi dressed in Paris. That must be fashionable then, in the States now.

I merely brought home a Western wife, he thought, but at least I was conscious of what I was doing. And right now I want to be alone with her so we can make it all seem absurd.

"Saira"—Catherine passed her a cup—"you saw Tor come in? What time was that?"

"About an hour ago." She sat up straighter. "And he looked like he'd been through a war."

Roshana laughed. "I don't think Tor likes ceremonies very much. Or neckties, for that matter. I don't blame him."

"Well, I do," Mangal growled. "Half the guests must have seen him too, and after I'd been telling them how sick he was all evening!"

"Never mind that now. Was he all right? I don't like Tor riding after dark, it isn't safe." There was real anxiety in her face, and Omar said silently: Don't worry, Tor won't have that horse to ride after tomorrow.

"He's fine, Mummy-jan." Mangal shook his head. "Don't tell me you're going to let him get away with this."

As if in answer, Tor's voice chirped, "We'll see who gets away with what, Prince Mangal-jan!" He was peering in at an odd angle from the hall and his eyes were very bloodshot.

Omar gripped the arms of his chair. "So, Tor, you've decided to honor us?" His anger returned in a rush. Tor's shirt was hanging open, and there was something spilled down the front of it. "Come in here where I can see you, Tor. Right now."

"Yes, of course, Daddy-jan!" But he spoke too loudly, and his steps were an exaggerated tiptoe. Why were his eyes so red? Then came the sharp smell of alcohol.

"What? Is that you? Get over here..."

But Tor had already fallen down on his knees, and throwing back his head, blew fumes toward the ceiling. "It's Saira's new French perfume, Daddy-jan. Don't you think it's nice?"

"Saira's...?" He turned to look at her, and found her gaping too.

"Saira's French perfume..." Tor smiled crazily, swaying as he tried to stand up.

"It's just—" Saira stammered, "I just bought a little cognac in Paris, because I just couldn't—sleep on the plane."

"Oh, a *little*! You liar," said Tor venomously. "A whole bottle, this big, and she gave it to me for a bribe. But I'm not a liar like her. I'm going to tell!"

"What's going on here!" Omar heard himself shout, and from the corner of his eye saw Roshana staring. "Tell what? And what possible excuse could there be..." The room was spinning around him. "You're drunk! And you..." He glared at Saira. "You gave it... you brought alcohol into this house and gave it to him?"

"No, I didn't! I only..."

"Yes you did, you liar!" Wrenching himself free, Tor swiveled toward her. "And that's not all, either! Sweet little Saira. Saira-gak! You want to know what she's really like? I mean, what she really likes?" He was fumbling in his pocket and Saira's mouth fell open as he held up a crumpled sheet of paper. "Listen... this is from her boyfriend... her lover! Know what he says? That she *loved* going to bed with him! He says having sex was all *her* idea," Tor was shrieking, "and he didn't even like her! He wants to know why she's making a fuss, when it was all just for fun!"

"Stop it, Tor! Shut up!" Saira had been watching as if paralyzed, but now she jumped up grabbing for the letter, striking at him blindly and screaming. "Give that to me! It's mine!"

"Both of you, stop!" Catherine started up and Omar moved, but Mangal was already out of his chair, darting between them. He had Tor's arm... "And Prince Mangal here, too, you think he's so holy, but I saw him in the bazaar yesterday..." Cursing, Mangal pulled back, slapping Tor's face so hard that he careened into the coffee table, tipping it over with a crash that brought silence to the room. On the hearth in front of the fireplace, Uncle Yusef's crystal globe lay shattered in bright pieces.

Tor lay smiling where he'd fallen, blood trickling down one cheek from a scrape at his hairline. His head must have hit the corner of the table. Mangal turned to Saira, but she had picked up the letter and slid to the carpet, weeping.

"My God!" Omar felt numb with shock. "I don't believe this!"

He stood up, pulled Saira to her feet and sat her in a chair. "You stay there! Roshana, what must you think of us, and on your wedding night. Please forgive this. Why don't you and Mangal go on upstairs now."

"Yes, we will." She stood up quickly and put out a hand to Mangal. "The wedding was lovely. Thank you so much. Good night."

When they had left the room, Omar walked over to the hearth and picked up the shards of glass, slowly, deliberately, not trusting himself to speak. Catherine had got Tor to the couch and was pressing a napkin against his cut. It was important not to look at Tor now. This globe had been Catherine's, and she had meant to pass it on to Roshana.... But if Mangal hadn't stopped Tor, Omar thought, I would have in another second, and then he'd be lying here in pieces.

They'd had everything, these children, a home, stability, family... everything he'd had to live without from the age of twelve, and he had even spared them Uncle Yusef's suffocating lectures on duty and honor. Too much of everything. He'd pointed to the young princes as an example of privilege abused, but were his own children any better?

"Alright," Catherine said. "Let's get to the bottom of this. Saira, you gave Tor that cognac?"

"I bought it..." She squirmed in her chair. "But I didn't give it—"

"Liar!" Tor grinned. "Yes you did too, so I wouldn't tell about that letter!"

"But only a sip, not the rest! He must have taken it when he came back."

"Oh, well, that's very commendable." Omar turned to face her. "You planned to finish it yourself, then?"

"Daddy-jan, it's legal in the States, and almost everywhere else! I'm not a baby anymore."

"Clearly. Is what Tor said about that letter also true?"

The color left her face, and closing her eyes, she shook her head. "Oh, God."

"Does that mean yes or no, Saira?"

"Yes! It means yes! Yes, yes, yes!"

"Omar..." Catherine said in her warning tone, but he stopped her with a glance. She would plead for the children as she always did, and he'd listened too often for too long.

"As you say," he turned back to Saira, "that's perfectly 'legal' too. You're half American, and you have every right to live like an American woman. But then why come home? And even if you've chosen different standards, you're still well aware of my definition of honor. You did *not* have the right to lie to me, and worse yet, cause me to lie to Ashraf's father. You used me and manipulated me, and that's something I can't accept. Not from you, or His Majesty, or anyone else. If those are your values, as far as I'm concerned you can take the next plane back to the States."

"Saira, dear," said Tor sweetly, "I told Ashraf, too. Yes, I did. I showed him that letter, and he knows all about your carryings-on with Jeffrey. Why do you think he left so early? He'll never marry you now." Tor's head drooped forward and he closed his eyes. "Never, never, never!"

"No, Tor!" Catherine shook his shoulder. "Tell the truth, wake up now! You didn't do that."

Moaning, Saira spun away. "Yes, yes, he did! I saw them talking in the hall together, and then Ashraf just walked out! And Tor made this horrible face at me.... Oh, God, what am I going to do?" She ran sobbing out of the room and up the stairs.

Omar sat down, feeling suddenly lost. The world had jumped off its axis and he was too tired now to sort out the reasons why. Apparently he had failed in everything, and he could not, did not want to try to understand any of it. Not tonight. Not even tomorrow.

Slowly, he turned his gaze to the boy who was, unbelievably, his son. Tor was worse than the young princes—not only spoiled, but calculating and destructive. And he was almost grown, there was no longer time to punish, and humor, and hope.

"Tor," he said, "you've had everything, every chance in the world. And in spite of that, or perhaps because of it, you've turned into someone I don't even like. If it's my fault, I'll have to live with that. The point is, I don't care anymore. You've tyrannized this family with your moods and tantrums, and we've actually rewarded that behavior. You've had horses, money, special tutors—all the freedom and attention in the world, while a stone's throw away from here, people starve and struggle. But you wouldn't know about that, would you, Tor. You haven't learned to appreciate anything. So now we'll have to balance one extreme with another. It's very tempting to send you off to New York and get you out of our hair, but I'm not going to do that. Next month, you'll start the six-year program at Moscow University, and you'll stay there until you finish if it takes you ten years. You won't like it there, Tor. It's very cold, and very strict, and when you scream and cry, no one will listen. Including me, Tor. Do you understand that? Now get out of my sight."

"But Daddy-jan..." The effects of the liquor seemed to have worn off. He looked sick and shaken, holding out his hands. "You haven't heard my side yet! It's Saira's fault! She gave it to me...."

"It's always someone else's fault, isn't it, Tor? I told you to go now, this minute!" He thought in one more instant he would slap Tor himself, but the boy jumped up and bolted like a rabbit.

Catherine's eyes followed him. "This doesn't make any sense, Omar. We'll have to talk to them both again tomorrow. I know you're exhausted, and it's certainly a mess..."

"Don't try to humor me, Catherine. Tor's going to Moscow, and that's final. He obviously needs more supervision than we've been able to give him, and in the States he'd have none." Omar rested his head against the back of his chair. He was beginning to feel ill himself.

"But I can't believe he showed that letter to Ashraf. Even Tor wouldn't do such a thing."

"After this performance, how can you say that! He's half crazy, Catherine, can't you see it? I'd just like to know what set him off. He and Saira must have argued about something."

She was sitting hunched over on the couch, looking desolate. "All I wanted was for us to be together, and happy. Then there was your resignation and now this."

"Darling," he said, "come here, please, I can't move."

He shifted in the chair to give her room, and put his arms around her. "Tor would be gone by next fall anyway. We agreed he shouldn't stay in Kabul. There's too much trouble at the university, and if he gets caught up in it, he could ruin all his chances."

"Yes, alright, but Omar, you didn't mean what you said about sending Saira back? She's just come home. She needs to be here, and I need her to be here."

But he did. However tired he was. If she'd been drinking and having affairs, she would be better off in the States. Why had she even bothered coming home? He said, "I can't stand any more deception, Catherine. She lied to me, so I lied to Ashraf's father. I'm not about to call him up and tell him so, and given the state of his health, I doubt Ashraf will either. But I can't keep any more secrets or make any more excuses. Besides, if Saira's been living that way..."

"What way?" She stood up abruptly. "We don't know anything about that yet. Alright, so she isn't a virgin. Neither was I, when you married me."

"That was different. We were in love and thinking of marriage."

"So? Maybe she was too! She probably trusted the wrong man. Is that such a crime?"

He wanted to soothe her anger, to touch her and speak gently, but even that seemed impossible. Getting up, he walked over to the open garden door.

"Omar?" There was pain in her voice, and accusation. "Don't you remember how it was with us?"

"No!"

The word exploded from his chest, and he knew, yet couldn't tell her, that it was no answer, but rather denial and rage at the shambles their lives had so quickly become.

The sky was lightening, in another hour the sun would be up. He stood gazing out at the garden, breathing its clean air, until finally he remembered very well.

"Alright," he said, "Saira can stay. Everyone's entitled to one disaster. From Uncle Yusef's point of view, you were mine, and we didn't turn out so badly. Tor goes, but we'll see if we can't stick Saira back together again. Agreed?"

He held out his arms and she came to him, nodding.

But who, he wondered kissing her soft hair, who is going to do that for me?

Tor clamped the pillow tight around his head, shutting out the first rays of sun. He felt ready to suffocate, but even dying would be better than this. The pain was like an ax in his head, with voices screeching all around it. What were they saying? He couldn't tell.

He remembered crouching in the bathroom, trying to throw up, hanging over the toilet retching nothing for what seemed like hours. Now he was shivering in a cold sweat. Something terrible had happened. A big fight... and he'd hit his head. The goose-egg still throbbed by his right ear. Why?

"Toryalai?"

He was biting his lip to keep from choking again. Go away, whoever you are.

"Tor?" The door opened, and lifting a corner of the pillow he saw Ghulam-Nabi come in.

"Drink this, Tor, it will help you." He was holding a cup. "I heard you being sick. This will make you feel better." Handing him the mug, the old man reached to prop a pillow behind his head, then sat at the foot of the bed watching him mildly. Tor sipped the hot liquid. It was some kind of herb tea, and it made his mouth feel cleaner. Well, at least he had one friend left.

"Toryalai, do you know what happened here last night while you were out?"

"Mangal's wedding. And a fight. I can't remember why, though."

"That is not my concern. No, I meant earlier, right after the Nikka."

His stomach turned again, and he took another sip of tea. Had Karima told on him after all? He stole a glance at Ghulam-Nabi, who was frowning now. "I don't know what you're talking about."

"Your father resigned from the cabinet yesterday, Tor. He gave up a lifetime of work for the sake of your family's honor. For your sake as much as his own."

Tea was spilling over his hand and he watched a red patch come up on his skin. Resigned? Why would Daddy-jan resign?

Something terrible had happened. What? Aspi... he remembered being in the stables, saddling Aspi... but after that nothing but some screaming.

"Why didn't you know that, Tor?"

He looked up. "You just said..."

"Yes, that you weren't here, when it was important. So out of ignorance you hurt your father, and your sister, but most of all you hurt yourself. Because you were asleep."

"No, I was out riding! But why did he resign?"

Ghulam-Nabi shook his head. "That's your father's business. But I want to tell you this: you can't go on sleeping while trees fall around you. Tor, I owe your father very much. I'm a Tajik, not a Pashtun. My people are a minority, but your father cares nothing for that. He helps all people equally. He's a great man, and you bring him nothing but pain. To your mother too, and now your sister."

"You forgot Mangal," Tor joked, but tears burned his eyes. What had happened? And why was Ghulam-Nabi looking at him as if... as if it was all his fault? He couldn't help crying, with the cup pressed against his mouth, and the old man just watched his shame.

Then he felt Ghulam-Nabi take the mug from his hand. "Toryalai, let me tell you a story. Lie down, now. That's better. I want you to listen to me. This is a very old story, from the days before the Prophet Mohammad came, peace and blessings be upon him! Some young men were seeking the truth in those days, looking very hard, but since the True Message had not yet come, of course they could not find it.

"Allah, the all-merciful, knew that they were good men, and he wanted them to witness his message. So one night while they were dreaming in a dark cave, he put them in a magic sleep."

His voice was low and gentle now, not mad anymore. "Six hundred years passed, and still the men slept! Then finally, Mohammad, blessings be upon his name, came with the True Message, and when he heard about these sleepers, he sent four of his Companions to instruct the young men in the truth."

Shadows were growing in the loose white folds of Ghulam-Nabi's shirt. Tor closed his eyes. "Go ahead."

"After this instruction, the Companions offered to return the young men to Arabia. But the sleepers looked at each other and said, 'Allah has preserved us to learn the True Message, so now all that remains is Paradise!'

"So the sleepers returned to their cave, and Allah in his wisdom put their bodies back to sleep, and took their spirits up to Paradise."

Yes, Tor thought, that was a very nice story—like the ones Ghulam-Nabi used to tell him. Paradise! But the old man went on.

"The Companions flew back to the Prophet, peace be upon him, to tell him of this miracle. And he asked, 'How many sleepers were there?' To their amazement, one Companion said three, another said five—they each gave a different number!

"The Prophet, praise be to him, said, 'The ways of Allah are wondrous, and only he knows how many sleepers there are. Only he knows when one will awaken. The world is full of seekers and only Allah knows their number and when they will awaken.'"

Tor couldn't talk or open his eyes or let go of the old man's coarse shirt. He wanted to say he didn't understand; he wasn't looking for anything. Besides, the "Message" was already here. What did that story have to do with him?"

But it was too dark now to say anything at all.

Seven

"SEE, MANGAL? It's dawn." Roshana turned from the window. "We've been up all night. That's traditional, at least." She had changed from the velvet dress to a raw silk robe, a pale shadow he saw more clearly than her face in the wavering light of their single candle.

Walking to the bedside table, she lit a cigarette. "I should be happy about this, shouldn't I. After all that work, the best hope we've had is suddenly coming true. It's like a gift. I ought to be ecstatic."

"We don't have to do this, Roshana. I mean it. I'll tell Daoud I've changed my mind, and we can fly to Paris tonight." At first he had been surprised by her reaction, but as they talked the room had filled with unpleasant questions and now he was frightened too.

She shook her head. "No, we've been all through it. At this point it would be more dangerous not to go with him. Oh, but I was looking forward to Europe so much, not to mention a few years of peace. When you said if I married you I'd have to behave myself for a while, I think I was secretly relieved. I've been living on politics and not much else ever since my mother died. Is it terribly bourgeois to want a family of my own again? You, and a house and a garden, and then maybe a child or two?"

"But we can still have that." He went to her, gently lifting back her long black hair. "You're the most important thing in the world to me. We're married now, the house is almost finished, and I'll say it again: we don't owe Daoud anything."

"Or Nur-Ali? Or the professor? Don't we have any responsibility for what we've written and all our fine speeches? I believe those words, Mangal. Right now I almost wish I didn't, but we can't just disappear when it's time to stand behind them. We wanted a republic and it seems we're going to have one, so it's more crucial than ever to stay in the game. Only I'm mad because I had this golden vision of what our life could be like, and now we've lost that chance"—her voice hardened—"Oh, God, listen to this silly woman feeling sorry for herself, when she ought to be dancing for joy."

"I know, Roshana, I know." He put his arms around her and found that under the loose robe she was shaking. How many nights, he wondered, must she have spent like this after the demonstration, when he was in France and she'd been alone and hurt, with no one to honor her sacrifice. Even he had made an icon of her courage, as if it meant she were superhuman and so not in need of comforting.

"I'm sorry," she said. "It's just that I thought I'd have something of my own for once. I'm a freak, Mangal, a female anomaly, and I've lived in that house with my father's disapproval for eight years, being hated and pitied and gossiped about. And now we have to start fighting all over again with both our families against us." She was wiping her eyes. "See what a hero I am?"

"No, you're right! Oh, Roshana, I love you. Let's forget Daoud and go on our wedding trip." He held her tight, for the first time feeling all her warmth against him, and then he was kissing her cheek, ear, eyes, tasting salt and smelling sandalwood. Roshana, she was his now, his first responsibility, and he'd seen and understood nothing of her pain.

"How can I be so lucky?" he said.

"No, my love, it's I who am that. Let's hope it lasts for one more day, at least. And one more night."

She turned her face up to his mouth and all the desire trembling under his tension sang along nerves raw with denial. If only for this moment, they were beyond the reach of others, and the scent of her swept through him, spreading like fire.

"Roshana, shall I put out the candle?"

"No, Mangal," she whispered, looking into his eyes. "Let's have now. Whatever happens, let's have this."

He touched her scar. "I don't want to hurt you."

She smiled, "Do you think after that, I'm afraid of *this*?"

Her body was lean and ripe and in an instant he would have been lost if he hadn't remembered the times with Suzanne when they had gone slowly, not afraid to look or touch.

He had tried not to think what this would be like, and it was beyond imagining, and he forgot Suzanne and everything but Roshana.

She moved sinuously with him, and he wondered how he had been able to keep from it before, the silk of her skin feeling suddenly more familiar to him than the sound of his own breathing.

Roshana gave a frightened, surprised laugh. Her hands were tight on his back, "My love . . ." And when the moment came, he pushed beyond it, pushed her beyond it, and she arched her back to meet him. There was nothing but Roshana, rocking him, letting him go, until the yellow tip of the candle flame swayed in his eyes again.

Tilting her face toward the light, he brushed back a damp strand of hair, smiling. "Do you know how beautiful you are? And I was afraid we'd be polite and shy and hide under the covers."

"Maybe we should have. Under your mother's nice blanket." Her eyes were bright and she was smiling too.

"I'll hang it on the compound wall to prove your honor. Roshana, I'm sorry I hurt you. I won't always. I promise."

"Hah, you should have heard what my aunts predicted!" She laughed huskily again. "They spent all yesterday telling me how awful this would be, and how I should bite the pillow so your parents wouldn't hear me scream. But it was pleasure too, Mangal, so much! I don't know what happened, but the minute you touched me it was like nothing could stop it. Oh, I love you."

"You just wait." He kissed her softly. "One day we will spend the whole day here. Just the two of us, and there won't be anyone to hear. I didn't think it was possible that I could love you more than yesterday." Reaching down, he covered them both with the blanket. "I don't even want to go to Paris. Let's stay right here for a week."

Snuggling against him, she rested her head on his shoulder. "I wish we could, Mangal. Maybe soon we can, after things calm down a bit? But I'm worried about tonight. I couldn't live if I lost you now."

"Daoud swears it will be the least violent coup in history." He was tracing the curve of her ear. "I don't want to think about that now. I've never been as happy as this."

"But we have to think about it. What time does he want you there tonight?"

"At six. That gives us nine hours to decide."

"Not if you have to see the professor." Roshana frowned. "I must say the timing of this is very convenient. For everyone but us. A nice, neat coup while the king just happens to be in Italy. If he weren't, that would put Daoud in an awkward position, wouldn't it. What could he do, throw His Majesty in prison?"

"That's why you don't need to worry about me. There won't be much resistance." But something in her tone made him sit up to look at her. "Are you thinking they planned this together?"

She shrugged. "Well, they're cousins. They've run the government for forty years. And it would certainly be one way of keeping power in the family, since Daoud as much as admitted that if he didn't move, someone else would. Ironic, isn't it. We've been telling Nur-Ali that one voice is better than none. Why shouldn't the Royal House feel the same way? Or this house."

"Oh, no." He was lighting a cigarette. "If it were any one but Daoud, I wouldn't want to be on the inside. He's still the only man I'd trust. But Roshana, if you want, we can fly to Paris anyway. I was an afterthought. He doesn't need me."

"Maybe. But we aren't the only ones involved, Mangal. There's the group, our families... If we don't go with him now, I think we'll all have to wait at the end of a very long line outside his office. He's just as proud as your father. I think he'd pretend we didn't exist—no work, no permits, no visas, period. Oh!" She propped herself on an elbow, pulling the blanket around her. "Mangal, we have to get Saira out of this!"

"Saira? What's she got to do with it?" His hand moved down Roshana's arm and he felt a new stirring of desire. "Let's lie down. You'll catch cold."

"No, I'm serious!" Her eyes were haunted. "I don't want Saira to suffer the way I did. You said you heard your father shouting that he wants her to leave, and if that's what he thinks, she should. You don't know what it's like to feel trapped and at the mercy of men who treat you like a pariah. The borders will be closed, she won't be able to find work.... You won't be in any position to pass out jobs for a long time, least of all to your own family. If Saira has to spend six months shut up here with your father and Tor, waiting for Ashraf to call, it could destroy all the confidence she's gained."

"And you don't think Ashraf will call." An engine started somewhere outside, and he wanted to get up and close the shutter, to preserve an illusion of night.

Roshana shook her head. "Not soon enough, anyway. Not before Saira knows she's a prisoner. Everyone will be nervous of your family after today, and it would be nice if some of that distance were real. Why don't you tell her I'm sick and we're going to postpone our trip, and give her our money and tickets? Get her right out of it. Knowing your father doesn't want her here must hurt pretty badly, and this may be her only chance to leave."

"Oh, for heaven's sake!" He blew smoke toward the window. "Why do you always have to think of everything? Isn't there enough to cope with? Besides, I doubt she'd listen. She's angry at me too."

"Then you'll have to be cruel and just make her go, since you can't tell her the truth."

Crushing out the cigarette, he tried to picture that conversation. "Not even part of it? I'd need some kind of argument. Maybe I could say there's a rumor the borders will be closed, and let her make up her own mind."

"But she's almost hysterical! She's been up all night too. Haven't you heard her in there?" Roshana shook her head. "No, Mangal, we have to be responsible for Saira—for all of it, if we decide to do this thing. She may hate you until she knows your reason, but then at least she'll have the choice to come back or stay away. It's Ashraf who needs to make up his mind."

Sliding an arm around Roshana's waist, he drew her down on top of him. "Have you decided? Are you sure?"

"Yes." She smiled wryly, "I don't like the alternatives. Your father won't speak to us for a year, but after that I'm sure he'll have quite a lot to say. I do want to see Europe someday, though, my husband of ten hours."

"We will. You can be an ambassador, while I lie around on cushions drinking tea." He kissed her, and her hair covered his face and it was night again, a yellow darkness that seemed to hold them closer than ever. A child could come of this night, he thought, born, with the republic, and both would have to learn to walk on very unsteady legs.

Roshana drew her hair back and she was grinning, trying not to laugh out loud. So many times he had seen that, and how radiant she was then, and now he knew why. Everything she had been kept from saying, from being, shone in her eyes. "You're like that Landay you said to me the other day. Do you know which one I mean?" She was collecting these Pashtun couplets for a book, and filling his head with them.

"I think so. But I meant it for you. 'Your face is a rose and your eyes are candles. Faith! I am lost. Should I become a butterfly, or . . . ?'"

"A moth!" he laughed. "You *do* look like a moth right now, with your soft wings of hair."

"Then yours is the wool I will feast on! And I'm very hungry, Mangal. I couldn't eat a thing at the wedding. Especially once I saw you cheek to cheek with Daoud Khan."

"If it's food you want, maybe we *should* go to Paris. Where snails are a delicacy." He hugged her. "Do you know how amazing you are? I thought it might take months for us to be together like this."

"It must be the coup, then. Being afraid. And if that's true, let's stay in Kabul." She was smiling, pleased with herself. "I can feel things again! When I got burned I think I locked myself up inside so I couldn't be hurt anymore. It's wonderful to let go of that. It's like being let out of prison. Thank you, Mangal."

"No, you did it, not me." Kissing her, he pulled away gently. "How am I going to keep my mind on Daoud's speech tonight, knowing you're in my bed?"

"But I won't be in bed. I'll be right over there on my knees by that window, listening and praying." Her face opened in a grin. "I'll pray we have fifty years to practice."

"I'm going to close that window. There won't be anything to listen to till after midnight, and we ought to try to get some rest."

He got up to close the shutter and there was only the candlelight.

As she moved to straighten the blanket, he was struck by how defenseless her bare body seemed. He was leading them both into danger, and if Daoud made one wrong move, there were men in the king's service who would welcome the chance to torture defiant, proud Roshana. He slid in beside her. "If I were a woman, I'd be a coward."

"Then I'm even more glad you're not." Her head was heavy on his shoulder and he pinched out the candle flame. I'll wait till she's asleep, he thought. Just for a few minutes, then I'll get up.

But it was long after noon the next time he looked at his watch. As he moved, Roshana opened her eyes with a start, and he tucked the sheet around her. "You stay right there. Don't wake up. I have to take a shower and call Professor Durrani."

"And talk to Saira? Please, Mangal." Yawning, she stretched like a cat. "I really am tired, which may be just as well if I have to pretend I'm sick. But I feel guilty. You must be exhausted too."

"I'll have plenty to keep me awake. Just rest, and after I've seen Durrani I'll come back to say good-bye. I only hope I can reach him. It's almost one o'clock." He bent to kiss her. "Close your eyes and don't open them till I say so."

"Alright. Give him my love." She curled up in a ball, and walking to the closet he put on his robe and chose a pair of khaki trousers and a white shirt. Slipping out to the bathroom, he discovered in the shower how painful losing her virginity must have been. And then he found himself praying this would be the only blood shed today.

Downstairs, the house was quiet. Even the servants were asleep, and no wonder—the party debris had already been cleaned up. He used the desk phone in the study and Durrani answered at the second ring.

"Professor? It's Mangal. I need to see you today. Can we have tea?"

There was silence. Then, "Are you mad, Mangal? Weren't you married last night?"

"Yes, thank you. But that's not all that happened. Can we meet at Khalid's shop? It's important, and I can't talk from here."

Durrani grunted. "You want to share your bridegroom's blush with me, is that it? Alright, let's say in one hour. Will Roshana be with you?"

"No, I'll come alone."

"I'm glad to hear that she at least is still sane. I'll see you later then, Mangal." He hung up, and replacing the receiver, Mangal walked out to the hall. Who would be harder to lie to, he wondered, Saira or Durrani?

Daoud had said repeatedly that no one but Roshana could know, and she was right about Saira, it would be unbearable for her here and she was too upset to be trusted with this secret. Durrani was a different story, though. He was the sage and soul of *New Homeland*, and it was the paper that had drawn Daoud's attention—the paper that now had to be suppressed.

But tomorrow he'll understand why I lied, Mangal thought, climbing the stairs. And Saira will know why I've seemed so heartless. I only hope I don't have to wake her up first.

The shrill song of a young canary came through her door. How had she found new birds so quickly? With relief, he heard her walking across the room, and knocked twice, "Saira? It's Mangal."

She stopped but didn't answer him.

"Saira?" He knocked again. "Can I come in, jan? I have to talk to you."

She said something unintelligible, and turning the handle he opened the door a crack. "What was that? I couldn't hear you."

"I said *yes*. Sure, sure. Come in."

She was wearing a thick pink robe and her dark hair streamed out in long waves from her head, making her face and body look fragile. But her eyes were smudged and frantic, all her energy was there. She stood woodenly. "What do you want?"

"Just to talk." He felt awkward, unprepared. "I heard you banging around in here. We were up all night too." The lie came easily. "Roshana isn't feeling well."

"Oh. That's a shame. Please give her my sympathy. I don't feel so great myself."

"I know. We've been talking about you." He closed the door. "That's why I'm here."

There was a strange, nearly amber light in the room. Only one shutter was open, by the table where a bird jumped in its cage. The bare walls dimly reflected sun from the orange garden shed.

"Tor went in my closet," she said. "Want to see what he did?"

Pivoting, she wrenched the door open and he pursed his lips with anger. Lamplight spilled over the rifled knapsack and tangled heap of shoes and dresses on the floor. An empty cognac bottle lay on its side by the threshold, next to a scrap of torn blue silk.

"Tor should be locked up," he said. "I swear it. He's a menace. But I feel responsible too. You came all the way from California for this."

She shook her head. "I wanted to come home. That's the joke. I couldn't wait to get back, and now in just one day..." She gave the empty bottle a little kick and it rolled down to the pile of clothes.

Don't cry, he thought, please, Saira, there isn't time.

"I know, jan. That's what I'd like to talk to you about. You can't want to stay here after this."

Her gaze turned toward him slowly, "I can't? What do you mean?"

"Well..." He looked away, back to the wreckage of the closet. "Wouldn't you like to get away from Tor and Daddy-jan for a while? And Ashraf, for that matter?"

Smiling grimly, she pulled the sash of her robe tighter. "Is that a hypothetical question, or just a rhetorical one?"

"It's a real question, jan." Her eyes were brilliant, glassy with tears or fatigue. "Don't you think it might be a good idea to go away for a month or two, and give things here a chance to calm down? Tour around for the rest of the summer—I did, when I finished college. Or you could stay on Cape Cod with the Lowes. Then by the time you come back, Ashraf will be dying to see you again. Of course he will. I'm sure of it."

"You are?" She stepped closer to him. "Why?"

"Well"—he swallowed—"because you won't have argued and made things worse in the meanwhile. You both need to sort it out rationally, and you can't do that now. It's been a shock, and you're both upset. But I know Ashraf will come around if you give him time. He loves you and he's a sophisticated man." What a string of clichés, he thought, why couldn't Roshana have done this?

"My, you really have been thinking about me!" She pushed her hands deep in the pockets of the robe. "So you think we'd communicate better if we were thousands of miles apart."

He nodded. "It would be easier by mail. You don't say the kinds of things in a letter that you might face to face. That goes for Daddy-jan too, Saira. The minute you leave he'll want you back again."

"Oh?" She cocked her head to one side. "How did you know he told me to go? You must have been eavesdropping, Mangal. You couldn't have heard that from your room."

The hostility in her voice made him defensive. All this was Tor's fault, and her own, for giving him the cognac. "Of course I listened. I was concerned. I am concerned. I'm your brother."

"I see." Saira paced around him in a circle. "Then tell me this, my brother. Why are you being so thoughtful now, when last night you treated me like a public embarrassment?" Walking to the canary's cage, she stood with her back to him, pouring seed from a packet into its dish.

"I'm sorry," he said. "Maybe I'd like to make up for that. I'm offering you our trip money and our tickets, and they're a gift, not a loan."

"You mean I should leave today? On your plane?" She spun around. "Is that what you're saying?"

"Well, why not?" He managed a smile. "Roshana won't be able to travel. She thought we could tell people you had to make up an exam or something. No one else needs to know what happened."

"But I just got home, Mangal!" She put the packet down. "So Roshana agrees with you about this?"

Saira admired her, he remembered, and it was Roshana who had sent him on this mission in the first place. "Yes," he said. "In fact it was her idea."

"And Daddy's idea, and your idea," Saira singsonged. "Everybody seems to have the same idea—that I should get out of their way." She came toward him slowly. "You know what I think, Mangal? I think last night you were being honest, and this is just a different tactic. I've disgraced you, haven't I, and you can't afford that as an up-and-coming editor of the *Kabul Times*. It's better to get rid of me. I suppose if we were poor I'd just have to kill myself, like Royila. No one offered her a plane ticket."

Dammit, he thought, I have to be harsh now. But in a week she'll know why I've done this and she'll thank me.

"Don't be so melodramatic," he said. "For heaven's sake, I'm trying to help you. Daddy-jan told you to go. Do you want to stay after that? Do you want to live in the same house with Tor all summer, waiting for Ashraf to call, when you could be in Paris or the States? I can't wave a magic wand and make this disappear, and it's going to be like an armed camp around here with all of you furious at each other. You haven't even unpacked yet, and isn't your visa good till September? Why don't you use it while you can."

Saira sat down on the bed. "Yes, and this fall I'll be twenty-one. I could choose American citizenship and you'd never have to see me again at all."

"Oh, come on, Saira. I'm not suggesting anything like that. I'm offering you our vacation, and I think you'd be stupid not to take it. I can promise you this: If you don't, you'll wish you had."

"Because everyone will make life so miserable for me, right?" She peered over her shoulder. "Do I have to decide right now, Mangal?"

"Well"—he clenched his fists with frustration—"if I turn back the trip money and our tickets it would be harder to arrange. Besides, the next few weeks will be the worst. I'm surprised you're not happy for the chance."

"Happy!" She laughed bitterly. "Maybe even grateful? For a graceful exit, so no blot will spread over the family name? I had a friend in Cambridge, an Indian woman. Do you know what she said? That she refused to live under any terms that defined her as a woman of no virtue. Maybe I should refuse to leave under those terms."

Mangal glanced at his watch. It was 1:30, he would be very late, and his head already ached with tension. "Alright," he said. "Be a martyr if you want to, but I think that pose will wear thin pretty quickly. Your Indian friend had a point, Saira. Maybe you'd better consider it."

"That's all I've been doing for the past five hours." She ran her hands through her snarled hair. "Asking myself, can I live here now without being crushed again? Asking myself, can I love Ashraf if I feel he doesn't respect me? Wondering how I can ask him to forgive me, when he's probably done the same thing himself. But the best part is, Mangal, I've been sitting here wishing I could just escape somehow, just get away long enough to answer all these questions. Doesn't that make you happy?"

"Then for God's sake, why were you fighting about it? Now you're admitting I'm right!"

"No!" She jumped up violently. "Those are my reasons, not yours. Don't you think I know you're turning them around on me for reasons of your own? You've been picking at me ever since I got home. Alright, you and Roshana want me to leave, Daddy-jan wants me to leave, and I'm sure Tor would agree. Even I want to leave, so hooray, I'll go! But I understand what you're doing, my dear brother who is so concerned. I know who you're really worried about. What time does the plane leave, tell me that?"

"At six." He felt lacerated. "Saira, I'm very sorry about this. I don't blame you for being upset. But you're wrong about me, and I hope you'll realize that soon. I'm not trying to get rid of you. I really think this is the right thing to do."

"Sure. I suppose you'll also be happy to drive me to the airport?"

He looked down at his watch again. Daoud wanted him at six. "Can you be ready by four? We ought to go early, in case there's trouble with the tickets."

"I guess so. As you pointed out, I haven't even unpacked." Glancing around the room, she shook her head. "So I'm going to spend another two days sitting in airports. I've been home less time than that. What a joke."

"You'll be back soon. And things will look better then, I promise." But the words seemed an echo, and he remembered he had spoken them before—last night, to Karima.

Standing up, she moved to open the door. "Good-bye, Mangal. Don't worry, I won't keep you waiting. Come up here and get me, though. I don't want to see Daddy or Tor."

"Alright. But take it easy, jan. Everything's going to be fine."

He went out and she closed the door behind him.

Twenty minutes later he turned off the Jada-i-Maiwand and parked across from the Ministry of Health. Tonight there would be soldiers here and at all the ministries, and it was odd to see the secretaries passing, unaware that this might be their last day of work. In all his talk of a republic, he realized he had never considered the specifics of transferring power.

The bazaar was lazy in the sun. No merchants beckoned him over, and he made no attempt to avoid their gaze. Two men were arguing in the narrow alley behind Khalid's shop, and brushing past them, he let himself in through the back door. Then he stopped short. Durrani was not alone. Beside him at the long table Nur-Ali sat, smiling unpleasantly. "I knew it! When he tried to get rid of me, I knew I shouldn't go."

"I ran into our young friend outside." Durrani waved his hand. "He's like a fly, buzzing around. I've been trying to explain the difference between a secret meeting and an unexpected one, but that subtlety seems quite beyond him."

"Nevertheless, he'll have to leave." Mangal sat down across from the boy. "I want to talk to the professor in private. That's my right, and also your right. But you'll have to make your own appointment."

Khalid stuck his head in from the kitchen, stroking his white mustache. "Can I bring you some tea or food?"

"No, thank you," Durrani said. "Take this child and put him in one of your pots instead."

"I want to know what this is about!" Nur-Ali pushed his thin face close to Mangal's. "Do you tell us one thing and him another? You say, 'Trust me' and I have, even though I know I shouldn't trust anyone. If you're here because of the paper, I do have a right to stay. I'm involved too!" His face was flushed. "Is it about the paper?"

After a moment, Mangal nodded and fished in his pocket for a cigarette. Nur-Ali had a point, and maybe this would make things easier. He had considered telling Durrani the truth but now he'd have to lie, and so his promise to Daoud would not be broken.

Nur-Ali grinned triumphantly. "Then what!"

"The professor wanted to put out another edition tonight, after Roshana and I were gone. As it happens, we aren't leaving. Roshana's ill and I'd rather he waited a few days, till we get some reaction to the first one."

"But there's been plenty of reaction! All day, people were talking about it." Snatching up the cigarettes, Nur-Ali lit one with shaking fingers, "I was proud, but I was worried too, that someone would find out."

"All the more reason to wait, then." He looked at Durrani, who was frowning slightly. "Don't you think so, Professor?"

Durrani's sharp brown eyes met his and Mangal saw questions in them. "Well, it would seem you've negated any reason for putting out another one so quickly. Are you satisfied now, Nur-Ali?" The professor was not, that was clear, and Mangal felt his belly tighten.

Nur-Ali puffed on the cigarette as if debating his answer. Then he squinted. "But how can Roshana be so ill? She was very well yesterday."

"You're being impolite," Durrani said acidly. "They were married last night, and she hasn't had any sleep for days."

"Then if she's sick, you shouldn't have left her." Jumping up, Nur-Ali walked around the table. "Why would you do that, unless you were afraid of another paper coming out while you were still here! Maybe you're afraid of getting caught with us?" He turned toward the professor. "I'll bet he knows something we don't know! His father's a minister. He must hear everything."

"That's why he *had* to leave Roshana," Durrani scowled. "He can't talk on his house phone." But suspicion deepened the lines in his face, and Mangal remembered that he too had been skeptical of the urgency for this meeting. "If I gave you my solemn word of honor, would you trust it?" the professor asked Nur-Ali. "Because if not, I want nothing more to do with you."

The boy studied Durrani and then nodded slowly, "I'd believe you. Mangal is too rich for me to trust."

"Fine." He called, "Khalid?"

When the old man came to the door, Durrani smiled, "Would you show this child out now? I need to talk to Mangal alone. Nur-Ali, I'll speak with you later, and I give you my solemn word of honor that if there's anything to fear, you'll know it."

"Come," said Khalid. "You can help me move the samovar, which is falling over as I stand here."

"Alright." Nur-Ali crossed the room reluctantly, "I'll wait for you, Professor."

As soon as they were out of earshot, Durrani folded his hands on the table. "What is this, Mangal? I've seen Roshana sick before, and unless she were dead nothing could keep her from going on her wedding trip."

Mangal got up and went to the kitchen door, looking out at the front of the shop. It was full and noisy, and he pushed the door shut. "You're right. She's fine, but I couldn't talk with Nur-Ali here." And I'd forgotten how shrewd you are, he thought.

Sitting across from Durrani, he lit another cigarette. "I've been sworn to secrecy about this, though. You'll have to give me your oath not to repeat it."

Durrani took out his pipe. "Could I make such a vow in good conscience without compromising the others?"

"Yes." Mangal watched him ream out the bowl. "There's no danger to them, and they'll know about it tomorrow anyway."

"Alright. Go on, Mangal."

"Prince Daoud is taking power tonight. He says it will be peaceful, but he'll have troops in the streets so he asked me to stop the paper." Leaning forward, he grasped Durrani's wrist, "Professor, it's true, it's finally come! Tomorrow we'll be a republic, with a president who's given this country the best leadership it's ever had." He felt his enthusiasm returning, "It's what we'd stopped hoping for, and now it's here!"

The pipe dropped with a clatter and Durrani sat back in his chair. "So, he's finally making his move. I can't say I'm surprised. But how do you know this, Mangal? From your father?"

He shook his head. "My father resigned last night. I don't know why yet, but Daoud felt that left him free to talk to me. He told me at the wedding."

"I see." Durrani gave a small smile. "Did he also ask you to join him, by any chance?"

Mangal colored under his gaze. But why should I feel guilty, he thought, and why isn't the professor more pleased?

"Only to help write his speech. Aren't you glad? I know it's sudden, but I thought you'd be delighted. Do you know, he recognized that Pashtunistan article as yours? He called you his 'old friend.'"

"Yes, very old." Durrani picked up his pipe again. "I lost the unceasing optimism of youth a long time ago, Mangal. But if you'll give me a moment to take all this in, I probably will be glad. I don't completely share your high opinion of Prince Daoud, because like your father, I'm suspicious of the military. But he may well be the best man to forge a republic, and that's a wonderful prospect indeed."

Just then the kitchen door flew open, and Nur-Ali bounded into the room. "I heard that! I heard all of it! So you're going off—"

Khalid came up behind him and gave him a hard push, then pulled the door shut, cursing. "Do you want to put us all in prison, boy? Remember where you are." He nodded toward Durrani, "I'll keep watch, but you'd better go quickly, someone may be curious about all the shouting."

When he'd left, the professor glared at Nur-Ali. "So you ask for my honor, but have none yourself! Eavesdropping like a spy!"

"But he's a traitor!" Nur-Ali hissed. "He's going without us, to help a prince take over! I was right not to trust him!"

"And what would *you* have to offer such an effort? You're nothing but a bad-tempered boy." Turning, Durrani waved at Mangal. "Why don't you go along now. And I'll spend the rest of the day trying to explain to this ill-mannered child that the reason he's so angry is because he has no power. That under a republic, he and his father will have as much say as anyone else about how the government's run, even though they're farmers and not princes or mullahs. That under a republic they might not have suffered so much during the drought, and now they can work to make sure that never happens again. Do you think he'll understand any of it? Perhaps even that Prince Daoud is a better choice than anyone else to bring such a momentous change to pass? Never mind. I'll try. I will stay with him and try. I wish you luck, Mangal. And be careful. I don't believe in bloodless coups. Go now, and may Allah be with you."

Mangal felt rooted to the floor, but looking from one taut face to the other he knew it would be best to leave that lecture to Durrani.

"Alright," he said. "And Nur-Ali, tomorrow you'll be a citizen, not a subject. Your brother died fighting for freedom. Don't forget it."

Crossing the room, he walked out into sunshine.

Damn Nur-Ali! Now his own nerves were raw, and it was too early in the day to succumb to that contagion. But Durrani understood. He had even made a point of saying he'd stay with the boy—which was generous, given his temperament—so there should be no more trouble from that quarter.

Summer dust had settled on the dark red Mercedes, and taking a brush from the backseat, he wiped a film off the windshield, then drove home hoping no one else would be up yet. Daddy-jan usually slept around the clock after one of his trips, and Tor had been drunk and Mummy-jan exhausted. No, Saira, he thought, I don't want to see them any more than you do.

Parking in the drive, he entered through the kitchen. There was no sound in the house, and opening the refrigerator he poured a glass of sour cherry juice. But he'd eaten so little the night before that his stomach turned in protest. Putting down the glass, he walked out to the hall and up the stairs.

Saira's door stood open. She was sitting on her suitcase with the knapsack resting against her knees, looking down into the garden. As he came in she turned to give him a cool appraising glance. "You're late, Mangal. I just went down to try to find you. I didn't know you were going out." Her white slacks and yellow silk tunic seemed incongruous with the battered pack, and her hair was pinned with combs to fall over one shoulder. She looked like a stranger and he realized that if he hadn't known her, he would be curious to meet this sullen, beautiful woman who wore bright red bracelets and an air of disdain.

"I had to pick up something for Roshana. Are you all ready, jan?"

Standing up, she slung a white leather bag over her shoulder and took out a pair of black sunglasses. "Let's go."

"I have to see her for a minute first. Why don't you take your pack and I'll bring down the suitcase. I left the trunk unlocked."

She put on the square dark glasses. "All right, Mangal. But you'd better hurry up."

Nodding, he turned back to the hall and went into his own room.

Roshana was lying curled away from the door, sound asleep. He crouched beside her, tickling her cheek until she opened her eyes. "Hello, I was just having a dream about you! We were in Paktia...." Her smile faded. "Oh, Mangal, you've had a bad time."

"I feel like a monster," he said. "And this is just the beginning."

"If Saira stayed here, she'd feel like a monster by next week. How did it go with the professor?"

"Alright. Nur-Ali was there and he had a fit, which reminds me, what about Tor? He saw me yesterday. He could still cause trouble."

"I think he'll be too sick." She took his hand. "But if not, I'll say those clothes were practice for your wedding costume. I'll manage things here, Mangal. You just worry about yourself. Will you be at the Bagh-i-Bala all night?"

"Through the worst of it, at least. Once they've taken the radio station, Daoud and I will go over to tape his speech."

"But that means driving through Pashtunistan Square!" She sat up. "You didn't tell me that before."

"You didn't ask." Smiling, he sat down next to her. "I'll be safe with Daoud. Now give me a kiss. I have to go."

Her arms were tight around him and he caught the scent of sandalwood and lovemaking. "Oh, Mangal, that frightens me! Why do you have to go with him?"

"I must be in the wrong house. This can't be the same woman who led a demonstration through the Square." The touch of her bare breast aroused him and he was glad of the darkness. "Roshana, my love, I'm late already. And in one more minute I'll be back in bed with you."

Drawing his head down, she kissed him and he remembered everything from before, her hair and the way she had moved with him. "Don't be brave, Mangal. Be careful. I don't want to be a widow."

He pushed her back gently, pulling the sheet around her. "I'll be fine, Roshana. I'll call you as soon as it's over. In the meantime, send me strength, and give some to my parents too. They'll need it, if they wake up."

"I know. I will. Go ahead, Mangal, I'm alright now."

Kissing her forehead, he whispered good-bye and went quietly down the stairs.

At the kitchen door he was startled to see Mummy-jan standing in the drive, wrapped in a blue robe and gesturing at Saira, who was sitting in the passenger seat. She heard him and looked up, "What's the meaning of this, Mangal?" Her face was anguished, haggard in the hot white sun. "Saira, get out of that car!"

"I've explained it all to her," Saira said. "She doesn't agree with you, Mangal. I'm sorry, Mummy-jan, but I don't care anymore. I want to go, I really do."

"You can't! I won't let you! Mangal, you have to talk to her. I don't know what you told her, but it's wrong of her to go. And you weren't even going to say good-bye to me?" Her voice rose, "I'll get your father. He didn't mean it, Saira. After you went upstairs, he promised me you could stay!"

Mangal threw the suitcase in the trunk and walked around to the driver's side. If Daddy-jan came down, they'd never get away.

Saira laughed bitterly. "Oh, he said that, did he? That he'd *allow* me to live in his house? That's very kind, but I'd rather go where I'm wanted. Will you call Grandmother Lowe and tell her I'm coming?"

He opened the door. "We have to go now, Mummy-jan, or we'll miss the plane. Talk to Roshana about it, and you'll see why this is right." Climbing in, he started the ignition, "I'm sorry, we don't have time to go all through it."

He backed down the driveway and left her standing there, watching after them with a look of incredulity.

Saira sat half-turned away from him, staring out the window, answering his questions with monosyllables. Glancing down at the pack, he said, "Do you want me to stop so we can put that in the trunk? I told you it was open."

She shrugged and he turned onto Sher Shah Mina road. "Do you know it's all ripped at the bottom? Something might fall out." He reached down to point out the tear, but she knocked his hand away.

"I know it's torn. I cut it myself. I took the bird, Mangal, all right? If I'd left him there, Tor would kill him."

"You mean it's in your pack? Oh, for God's sake!" Was she trying to seem pathetic? "You can't take a bird through customs, Saira. That's ridiculous. I'll be glad to keep him for you."

"Thanks, but I'd rather take my chances. If it doesn't work, that's my hard luck. What do you care, anyway?" Her tone refused conversation and they rode in silence until they reached the airport.

"You'll have to change that money in Paris, if you're going on to Boston."

She showed him a profile, "I realize that. Just drop me at the door, please. I don't want you to come in." Bending down, she pinned the torn flap shut. "I can carry my bags alone. A little humor goes a long way here. I'll do better on my own." She climbed out and struggled into the pack while he got the suitcase. "Thank you, Mangal. You've been so considerate. I'll never forget you for this."

"Saira..." He touched her arm, tempted to tell her everything now that she was safely on her way. But a guard was watching them, and she stepped back coldly. "Good-bye, Mangal. Have a nice life."

Turning, she walked away from him, erect in spite of her burdens, and the guard stepped out to open the glass door.

Lighting another cigarette he didn't want, Mangal watched until her yellow tunic disappeared from sight. There was nothing more he could do here, though, and once again he was late.

I'll write to her tomorrow, he thought. It will be the first thing I do.

Getting into the car, he drove back down the Bibi Mahro road, past the radio station, which looked deserted at this hour, and further on, the Habibya sports ground, where in spite of the heat boys were playing soccer, finally coming into Pashtunistan Square. The traffic was heavy and there was a bright summer crowd outside the Khyber Restaurant. Stopping at a light, he glanced over at the palace, wondering how many members of the Royal House would be there tonight and what Daoud had planned for them. It seemed impregnable, its tan rock face reflecting sun, and throwing the shift he turned right onto the Sharara road leading toward the Bagh-i-Bala, the Moon Palace, the old summer palace of Abdur Rahman.

It sat on a hillside surrounded by vineyards and was visible from the highway—a two-storied white building with gleaming blue domes and carefully restored nineteenth-century trim. Now it was a restaurant with small function rooms upstairs, and Mangal remembered laughing when Daoud had named this as his headquarters. For a while he and Roshana had considered having their wedding here, as many of their friends had done, to spare the family that headache.

Parking the car, he climbed the long flight of stairs and stood on the veranda looking back at the city. From here it was hazy with dust. A mountain ridge hid his own district, but he could see the Bala Hissar, the old citadel, and a glitter from the few high office buildings. Tonight there would be tanks in the streets, mass arrests, and shelling at the Bala Hissar if the Kabul garrison remained loyal to the king. And tomorrow? he wondered. Few people would understand the implications of this change, though many should welcome Daoud's return to power. Popularity from his decade as prime minister ought to carry him for a time, until he could start the reforms that would make the advantages of democracy clear. But they'd have to come quickly to justify this night, Mangal thought, even to me. Tomorrow will truly have to be a new day.

Turning, he went inside, and when the host approached him, said he was with the private party on the second floor.

"Ah yes, His Excellency's dinner meeting! Forgive me, I assumed all his guests would be in uniform. Please go right up."

Mangal smiled. Daoud's logic was simple: an apparently secret gathering of the officer corps might draw attention, but a noisy buffet in a public place would go unremarked. The Bagh-i-Bala was well away from any military target, and the downstairs restaurant would have closed hours before the coup began.

A man whom he recognized as one of Daoud's hand-picked protégés, Lieutenant Qadir, was standing at the head of the stairs reading a newspaper. He nodded and said, "Come with me, please," and Mangal followed him through the door on the right.

Half a dozen young officers were clustered at the end of a conference table strewn with cups and papers, listening closely to Daoud, who raised his hand toward Mangal, but didn't gesture for him to join them.

"There really is food across the hall, if you're hungry," Qadir said. "It's going to be a long night." But Daoud had started over holding out a hand. "Mangal, I'm glad to see you. What do you think of our window dressing?" There was a film of sweat on his high forehead. "Now I'll show you what's behind it." He walked to open a side door leading to a smaller room that seemed to have no other access, and as soon as they crossed the threshold Qadir closed it behind them.

"This is where you'll be tonight. I hope activity doesn't distract you. Isn't that supposed to be the test of a professional writer?" Daoud swept away some clutter. "When this is cleared up you'll have more space."

The walls were covered with maps—detailed drawings of the center of Kabul, Pashtunistan Square and the ministries, a blueprint of the airport and a floor plan of the radio station, even street maps of Jalalabad and Kandahar. A soldier in rolled shirt sleeves was bending over a canvas bin meant for restaurant linen, extracting pieces of what seemed to be a communications system. At the other end of the table stood a typewriter and a brown leather briefcase.

"Please sit down." Daoud reached for the briefcase and took out a thick file folder. "My notes are handwritten, I'm afraid, but I think you'll be able to read them." He held out the folder, then changed his mind and put it down on the table. "I take it Roshana had no objection to postponing your wedding trip?"

"To that, yes, but not to this. She sends you congratulations, Uncle."

"I hope they aren't premature." He was unbuttoning the jacket of his uniform, and also, Mangal sensed, turning the focus of his attention fully on the matter at hand. His eyes moved from the folder to Mangal's face. "Yes, I'm very glad to see you. Qadir thought you might not come. But I felt sure you'd find the challenge irresistible. I'm sorry, though, that you couldn't tell your colleagues at *New Homeland* about this, since we seem to agree on every point. Well, tomorrow we'll all be able to stand in the open, with no more need for secrecy."

"That will be a relief, Uncle. Even in terms of my father."

"And my cousin? No, Mangal, it won't endear us to our families. But to your young friends, yes, and Durrani. I'm curious, were there others of his caliber on your editorial board?"

He chuckled. "No, Uncle. The rest were students, except for a few provincial officials. And our membership was getting younger by the day. The night we put out the paper a friend of my brother Tor's showed up—Farouk Zadran, you know him. His father's in the Ministry of the Interior. He even brought an old German radio transmitter he'd fixed up, as a sort of initiation fee."

"Really? A radio transmitter?" Daoud ran a hand along his jaw. "It seems I didn't underestimate your appeal then. You were meeting in the bazaar, of course, but where could you find to print anything there?"

"In the back of Khalid's tea shop, by the silversmith's. It's very noisy. We share the same reasoning, Uncle."

"On many levels, I hope. Well, it's quite a tribute to your authority, if no one questioned your decision about tonight's edition."

Remembering Nur-Ali's thin angry face, Mangal laughed involuntarily. He and Daoud couldn't be more different. "I can't take all the credit. If Durrani hadn't been there... do you know Roshana's great admirer, Nur-Ali? The one whose brother was killed in the strike of '69?"

"The boy from Herat? Yes, that was tragic." Daoud was playing with the knot of his tie. "If Nur-Ali's like his brother, I'm sure he did have objections, and no doubt my friend the professor had to mediate. Well, he's very good at that. I'm sure he defended what I'm doing."

"He practically gave a speech about it."

As soon as he had said the words, Mangal realized his mistake, and looking into Daoud's keen eyes he knew the admission had been deliberately drawn out.

"I thought so." Daoud set his lips grimly. "No, Mangal, don't get upset, I expected as much. After I left you last night it occurred to me you'd have trouble deceiving Durrani. Was anyone else with you today?"

His mouth was dry. "No, Uncle. And Nur-Ali wouldn't have been either, if I could have helped it. But they won't do anything, I swear it. Durrani said he'd stay with the boy."

"Mmmm," Daoud nodded. "Did you hear that, Qadir?"

"Yes, General." He'd been standing so quietly by the door that Mangal had forgotten his presence. Now he stepped forward. "Shall I pick them up?"

"Yes, all of them. And be sure you get that radio transmitter too. Where is it, Mangal, still at the shop?"

He pushed his chair back, "Uncle, don't do this! They'll support you! They're not a threat."

"Nur-Ali," said Daoud, "and old Khalid, and Farouk Zadran and his father. I'm afraid you'll have to bring in the professor too. He may misunderstand what I'm doing in arresting the others. Go now, Qadir. Time is short."

"No, wait, listen to me!" Mangal jumped up, but Qadir had already slipped through the door.

"You listen, Mangal. Sit down. Do you think I'm playing a game? I said tomorrow there would be no need for secrecy. Tonight that need is absolute. I won't jeopardize this to save anyone's face. If you hadn't come tonight, I'd have you picked up too. If your father hadn't resigned, he'd be arrested soon along with the other ministers, much as that would pain me. I can't risk any surprises. Do you understand that?"

"But they're harmless! Really, Uncle..."

"What you mean is, they'll feel you betrayed them. An angry boy with a radio transmitter is not harmless. I could also say that you betrayed me, and we could sit all night arguing about it, but the simple fact is that you chose a certain course, which has this as its consequence. For the sake of our success, your friends will spend one or two nights in discomfort. I don't think that's a great sacrifice, given what hangs in the balance, but if you'd prefer to be with them, you could choose that too. And Mangal, if you think I'm being hard, consider this: I'll have to put my whole family under house arrest tonight, and they won't thank me, either."

His shoulders sagged, and Mangal relaxed a little. That was true enough.

"Do you know what many people will say about me?" Daoud shook his large head. "That I took power from a woman. If only dear Queen Homaira had gone abroad with my cousin! But I'd rather hear the insults than be responsible for the violence that would be inevitable if Zahir were here. Well, what's your decision, Mangal? Will you stay with me or join your friends?"

"I guess I'd better stay here, Uncle." He tried to smile. "At this point, it's safer."

"Good. And don't berate yourself. I was still a bit naive too at twenty-five. Have a look at my draft now. I need to speak to the others before they leave." Pushing the folder across the table, he stood up and buttoned his jacket. "We'll start just after midnight with an armored division from the Pul-i-Charki cantonment. The radio station will be their second target. That gives you roughly three hours to work on this, and it will be busy in here soon, so you'd better get started." Walking around the table, he bent to examine the console the young soldier was assembling, then nodded once and went out. The other room was crowded now and Mangal saw all eyes turn toward Daoud in the instant before the door closed behind him.

He lit a cigarette. Naive? No, he had trusted the man.

Then he did smile. It was too much like this afternoon's exchange, and in fact, Nur-Ali had been shrewder. I may have patronized him, Mangal thought, but Daoud played me like a chess piece.

A wave of self-disgust rose in his throat and he swallowed hard. He had let his guard down completely, with very little coaxing—so Daoud would admire how well he'd done with limited resources? And this was a lesson the others would have to pay for. All he could do now was work to make their "discomfort" worthwhile. It would take confidence to write the speech.

Opening the folder, he pushed away the image of Durrani answering his doorbell, taking Qadir's measure and saying, "Bring a book, Nur-Ali. We're going to be guests of the new government, it seems." He would guess what had happened though, and wouldn't be afraid. Nur-Ali would have the pleasure of having his worst suspicions confirmed, and Khalid... he would not understand, and might be very frightened. But if they were held together, Durrani's dry wit should make the time bearable, and admittedly, Daoud was right to leave no margin for error.

He turned toward the overhead light. Across the top of the first sheet was written: Proclamation of the First Republic of Afghanistan. Skimming through several pages he found no mention of the king, but a criticism of the stagnation of the past decade, with references to the constitution Daoud had proposed as his last act in office and his growing determination to establish a "real and reasonable" democracy, granting complete rights to the people while maintaining national sovereignty. The language was clotted and whole paragraphs had been crossed out and rewritten in tiny script.

Mangal moved to the typewriter. It would take three hours just to make all this coherent.

As he played with the material, his concentration focused and he was only dimly aware of other movement in the room, the crackle of the radio and glasses of tea the young soldier set by his hand. Daoud had written strongly, calling the system corrupt, vile and rotten, and describing the despair and poverty of the people, the "bitter facts" of society and economic bankruptcy. In places it was tempting to soften his words. How would Daddy-jan feel to hear his beloved constitutional monarchy condemned as a "despotic regime" based on hypocrisy and class interests? But this was Daoud's speech and it was exhilarating finally to set tact aside.

When Daoud reappeared at the door, Mangal smiled. It was midnight and he had just typed, "Dear Countrymen, let me inform you that this system has been overthrown and a new order, a republic, has been established which conforms to the true spirit of Islam."

Sifting through the pages, Daoud nodded. "This is excellent, Mangal. And the rest should be easy enough—it speaks to nonalignment and our wish to live in peace, even with the Pakistanis once we can solve Pashtunistan. But let's push this table against the wall. We'll need the space here now."

Qadir came in behind him. "The ministers have been arrested, General. And Mangal's associates too. I told them we were keeping them in protective custody. They'd moved the transmitter, though—the tea shop owner was nervous about it, and they won't tell me where it is. Shall I convince them to answer?"

Glancing at Mangal, Daoud shook his head. "Never mind. I had my car radio on, and no one's used it yet. I'm more concerned about our own transmitter right now." He turned to the soldier. "How's it working?"

"Perfectly, sir. There should be no trouble."

"There had better not be. Alright, Qadir, take your receiver and get up to Pul-i-Charki. And let me know when you've finished at the airport."

Saluting, Qadir picked up part of the apparatus and left.

"You see, Mangal"—Daoud bent to help him move the table—"I'm not so cruel after all. Do you know where we're holding the ministers? At the zoo. Won't that amuse your father!"

The door flew open and a stocky air force lieutenant came in. "Your Excellency! I have news from Babrak!"

"Just a moment," Daoud cut him off coolly, "I won't have anarchy in here, and my title is General tonight. Alright." He folded his arms. "What's the problem?"

"One of the jet pilots is having second thoughts. There has to be a substitution."

"Babrak Karmal?" Mangal stepped forward. "Is he part of this too?"

Daoud cursed. "Then tell him to use his discretion, but he'd better be very sure this time."

When the lieutenant left the room, Daoud nodded. "Yes, Mangal, Babrak and his young Parcham friends have been very good at convincing some of their peers in the army. I've been out of office for ten years now."

"But he's..."

"What? A Communist? Don't you think I can handle that?" His mouth tightened. "You and I may have been educated in France, but almost every officer involved tonight was trained in the Soviet Union. If I didn't lead them, someone else would. No, Babrak is exactly where I want him—working under me, and out where I can see him. He's respected, but the Soviets could use him very easily. Would you say the same is true of me?"

Mangal wondered if that reasoning also explained his own presence. Slowly, he shook his head.

"Then stop worrying about Babrak and finish the speech. I'm going to secure the palace now. That won't be pleasant. In an hour or so I'll come back and we'll go in to the radio station."

Opening the door, he called in two captains who, it seemed from Daoud's orders, had been assigned to coordinate operations. One would stay in constant contact with the armored division, while the other recorded progress on the maps and kept track of the national situation.

Mangal moved back to the typewriter and started working, but as the radio came alive it was harder to concentrate. The young soldier, leaning over his console, relayed items tersely: the armored division had split to take the airport and radio station, both of which had fallen without bloodshed. The Bala Hissar had been surrounded to prevent the Special Forces Regiment from joining the Palace Guard, and they were being "contained." One tank had gone into the river. A taxi driver had been killed accidentally, and the men in the tank were presumed dead also. The ministries had been taken and all major routes blocked, but two tanks and an armored car were overturned on the Jalalabad road. It wasn't clear how that had happened.

At one o'clock came the deafening roar of MIG fighters swooping over the city, and moments later, three muffled explosions.

"What do you think that was?" Mangal had started toward the door, but just then Daoud opened it, his face flushed with anger.

"The imbeciles! They've shelled Shah Wali's house and my grandniece has been injured. I told them no unnecessary force!" He strode over to the maps and drew a series of lines and circles, then seemed to relax and shook his head. "Oh well, for our purposes it's been successful. There's some trouble with the police but we'll have to hope it's settled, because I want to get word on the radio now. Are you set, Mangal? Then come."

He followed Daoud down the stairs to an armored car, feeling shaken but not daring to speak yet. Daoud was chewing on his lower lip, oblivious of anyone else, making short impatient gestures with his hand. As they came down from the hillside the staccato of small arms fire grew louder. Suddenly, Daoud laughed. "Do you know what my cousin's last official act was? He dined with the Queen Mother of England. Imagine how..."

The jets screamed overhead, drowning him out, and Mangal peered through the small window. The military hospital was brightly lit, and there were two tanks outside the British embassy. Windows had been blown out of the Inter-Continental Hotel, live power lines crackled in the gutter, and every bank and ministry they passed was under heavy guard. Troops were running through the streets shouting, and he could make no sense of that, since there appeared to be no opposition. On the corner of the Sharara road an overturned jeep was burning, orange flames devouring a black skeleton. The square stone palace compound was circled by tanks.

As they turned onto the Bibi Mahro road, a new eruption of gunfire came from the southeast and he said nervously, "That sounds like it's in my district."

"No, that's at Demazang Circle, police headquarters." They had reached the radio station and a phalanx of armored vehicles parted to let them through. "I've put a patrol at your house, Mangal. Don't worry about your family."

A lieutenant stepped forward, saluting. "It's quiet here, sir. There's only one technician and he's praying on his face."

"We'll get him up. Come with me."

"Sir!" He saluted again. "On behalf of these men and the nation I congratulate you, President Mohammad Daoud. May you never be tired!"

Daoud lifted his head in acknowledgment and there was pleasure in his eyes. "And may you live long, my friend. Now let's share this news with our fellow citizens."

He made his way to the control room as though he had been there before. The technician was sitting in a chair now and jumped to his feet when they came in. He was, Mangal guessed, about his own age and wearing very similar clothes.

"Do you recognize me?" Daoud waved the guard away.

"Sardar!" The man held up his shaking hands. "Of course, Your Excellency! They didn't tell me!"

"I want to tape a speech, and when that's done I want you to read a bulletin to the people."

The man's Adam's apple bobbed. "But I'm not a broadcaster, Excellency. We're off the air now. I'm just here to fix equipment."

"I see." Daoud smiled. "But you also know how to use it?"

"Yes, Excellency. Most assuredly."

"Good. Then get us back on the air." He swiveled toward Mangal. "I don't want to broadcast the speech yet. It's too long. People won't know what they're hearing with those planes going back and forth. But I've written a short message, which should clarify matters at least. You can deliver it while I tape the other."

"With all respect, Uncle"—he stepped backward—"I've never spoken on the radio in my life."

"Yes, but you were planning to, were you not? So you'll learn now. I need a strong voice, Mangal, a sure voice, not a mouse squeak, do you understand that?" He jabbed a finger at the engineer. "Get me some martial music, and show this man how to interrupt it with live broadcasts."

Reluctantly, Mangal sat down in front of the microphone. It couldn't be very complicated. But he cleared his throat, nervous of how he'd sound. Daddy-jan might be listening. Even if he had slept through the whine of the jets, the gunfire at Demazang Circle would certainly have jolted him awake. What would he think was happening when he saw flames on the horizon, and heard shooting and shelling coming from so many different points in the city? He'd be frightened and probably run downstairs to unlock the gun cabinet, calling to Mummy-jan, who would come down in her blue bathrobe, and then Roshana might offer them the unwelcome reassurance that they'd be safe because their son was involved in the coup. Would Daddy-jan say: In that case, he is no longer my son?

The engineer came back with a reel of tape, seeming eager now to help. "Excellency, we've used this for many state occasions. It should be suitable." Threading it onto the spindle, he pulled the power switch and pointed out two knobs on the deck. "This will start and stop the tape, and this the microphone."

Daoud was sorting through his folder. "Here's my message. You should enjoy reading this, Mangal. Run through it once or twice and then begin." He clasped Mangal's shoulder. "And congratulations to you too, Nephew. As of today, you're my Special Aide for Public Communications. So think of this as baptism by fire." Nodding toward the engineer, he started across the room. "Now we'll make the tape recording, and after that you'll call me President, not Sardar. Doesn't that sound agreeable?"

They left the studio and the spring door snapped shut.

Mangal studied the scribbled lines. They were barely legible, and he turned to call Daoud back. But no, he thought, as of now this is my job, so I'd better do it.

Switching on the music tape, he took out his pen and wrote a clearer version. It was Roshana who would turn on the radio at home—first the transistor set in the bedroom, then the receiver in the study, while the others stared at her in disbelief. Tor would be excited, cradling a rifle and hoping for a chance to use it on the guard Daoud had put at the house. They'd all be in the study now and Roshana would have to face their anger, without excuses or apologies or any hope of being understood, much less consoled. Daddy-jan might accuse her of lying, say we'd been with Daoud from the start, since he'd never believe this alliance could have come about so quickly. What would Roshana answer? Probably, "In a sense you may be right, but we didn't want it now any more than you do."

Then perhaps she and all of them would recognize his voice, and he must think only of her to do this well. She would need to believe in these few words tonight.

He cleared his throat again and said, "Roshana, this is for you. Instead of Paris. May *you* never be tired, either." His voice was steady, and fading the music down he opened the microphone channel. There was no going back. They had worked for this and it must be worth the price.

"My countrymen." He felt an unexpected surge of pride. "It is my privilege to announce the formation of the first Republic of Afghanistan! Stay off the streets and don't interfere with the soldiers. There is nothing to fear. This day brings new hope for all our people, in accordance with the highest principles of Islam. Join with us in welcoming it. Long live the republic and long live Afghanistan!"

Part Two

If leadership rests inside the lion's jaw,
So be it. Go, snatch it from his jaws.
Your lot shall be greatness, prestige, honor and glory.
If all fails, face death like a man.
                              —Hanzala of Badghis, 9th C.

FEBRUARY 1978
Moscow

Eight

Pushing open the window, Tor inventoried his supplies. Two half-liter bottles of vodka stuck up out of snow banked along the ledge. Yesterday there had been four. Most of a jar of herring and another of pickled cucumber, both frozen where they faced the wind. But the noon sun was bright now, illuminating a sky too blue to be made of air, brilliant and stunning like the Blue Mosque at Mazar-i-Sharif. It made the sea of matchbox dorms pathetic. Closing his eyes, he turned his face in offering to his ally against everything Soviet. No wonder people had worshiped the sun. And Moscow might as well be a desert.

Vodka at noon? Comrade, you should be in class! You'll get another warning, be expelled from another department. How often can you change careers? Animal Husbandry, to Psychology, to History, to Journalism—soon there won't be any choices left. But never mind, they'd find something. As long as there was any political value to having him in Moscow, concessions would be made. Not for his sake. He was just a handle. An Anwari. An Afghan pawn.

But not a little lamb, he smiled.

Shaking snow off the vodka, he made a face at the jar of herring. It was too sour, but he needed something for a chaser. There was no more salami and only a small chunk of black bread gone stale in his desk drawer, so herring would have to do. He'd been sick once too often, and in five minutes this new customer Ivan would come. He wasn't sure Ivan could be trusted.

Tor arranged implements on his nightstand in precise order. The shot glass, his army knife, herring, bread—but no, it was hard as a rock. Peeling the foil top off the vodka, he filled the small glass carefully, then skewered a slab of fish with his knife. Ready: exhale, one fast gulp, herring. He had to be quick. Even now, roommate Petrov might be sneaking down the hall to catch him drinking, the Komsomol snoop! Komsomol, the youth party, and With Lenin All Things Are Possible! Every room in this dorm had a Petrov: four foreigners and one spy. Just to keep an eye on things. Repeat: breathe, swallow, fish.

He could feel veins pulsing in his neck and temples, and in his eyes, which were always sore. The pink never left them these days. Now even his ears were starting to tighten, all his senses turning inside out until his brain throbbed against his skull. Why did vodka hit him this way, when everyone else got so jolly? It was as if the tension in his nerves and muscles was rushing up to explode out of his head. But after that stopped, the quiet would come and only then would he feel calm and relaxed, able to concentrate.

Without vodka, he worried too much. Doubts came like little gray Soviet soldiers, row after endless row. And when you had to deal with the Ivans of the world, who might be setting traps of their own...Tor's hand reached automatically for the bottle, tossed a shot straight down. If he had a horse he might not need vodka. But his room was a box in a larger box, and outside that an ocean of robots. You couldn't get away on foot. Vodka made a wall of privacy, even when his room was full of people drinking and laughing, counting up the day's profits and looking to him for their next scheme. He'd smile back while his brain arranged their talents in new equations, like a spider spinning webs out into space.

But lately he was making small mistakes, because it had all grown so boring. Only private jobs were interesting now—the odd piece of antique jewelry some professor wanted to trade for Mozart records or a book by Solzhenitsyn. You could even barter for grades in Moscow, which was a good thing since the program ran so long—one year of intensive Russian and five more of study. There were still eighteen months to go, and he'd been starting to wish vodka did make him drunk when this deal with Ivan came up. It could be beautiful. It would make him the envy of all his competition. But if Ivan was a plant...Tor realized he was holding the bottle and raised it to his lips. Yes, he would have to be very careful, very cool. Because this just might be a setup.

The police hadn't bothered him so far, he guessed, because things were shaky at home. The Soviets wanted every possible control over Daoud's government, and at some point Tor might be useful. No, better to let him get in plenty of trouble until his file grew thick as a book. Then when some delicate issue came up, they could trap him and negotiate his freedom with Mangal. Did they think he was too blind to see that? Roommate Petrov overlooked too much in return for time with one of the girls.

The crime they finally caught him at would have to be serious, though, warranting several years in jail. Hah! As if Mangal would care. In a way Tor almost wished it would happen. It was fun to picture Mangal squirming and sweating under his three-piece suit. Family honor would require him to rescue his younger brother, but how he'd hate it. He might have to make a compromise! Mangal, the voice of virtue. His letters... that letter...

Suddenly Tor's stomach convulsed so violently he bent double, almost falling off the bed. Grabbing the nightstand, he pulled himself up and ran down the hall to the bathroom. The pain was searing this time, as if he'd been stabbed, and he hung between the partitions weak and shuddering. Mangal's first letter, arriving just a month after he had come to Moscow... and only in the last paragraph, so casually... "While Karima was visiting her grandparents in Herat, she met our second cousin Nadir, and they've since decided to marry. They have all our blessings, and I'm sure you will also wish them happiness."

Now Karima had three children. Well, what a nice surprise! He used to think she liked making love because it was with him, but instead she turned out to be just like Saira—changing plugs as soon as he was out of sight. Of course, Karima had also almost finished college. Nadir had magically found a job in Kabul, and Mummy-jan wrote that Karima was "fitting classes into every spare minute. What determination!" No doubt Prince Mangal had arranged all that—family honor, again. It was alright for a poor-relation Anwari to marry a servant if her social status wasn't *too* embarrassing. Tor laughed harshly. Well, to hell with the bunch of them! He'd "changed plugs" himself a hundred times since then.

Ripping a page from the math book on the floor, he wiped herring juice off his hands. There was never any toilet paper in the Soviet Socialist Republics. He hadn't been really sick because his stomach was so empty, but the vodka must have started burning holes down there. He had to remember to buy bread.

Outside the open door to his room he stopped. An unfamiliar jacket was draped across the foot of Petrov's bed. So Ivan had already come. Tor felt shaky, out of focus, and that was bad for business—he'd have to get some more vodka into them both, and quickly. With Ivan he'd need to seem cool and awake, but also charming. Disarming. Ivan had to be relaxed so he could be watched for that indefinable something... the slip that would betray him if he was lying.

Tor took a deep breath, stretching his arms toward the ceiling, then twisted his face into a conspiratorial grin as he crossed the threshold. "Comrade Ivan?"

The big blond man had taken possession of the bed where Tor obviously had been sitting. A good ploy, but a revealing one. He couldn't be as stupid as he looked.

"Tovarich Tor!" Standing up, he offered a broad palm that made Tor's seem feminine by contrast. Ivan was very tall and plump, though his handshake showed there were hard muscles under that layer of fat.

Tor thought, a peasant. And he bites his nails. It would take a lot of vodka to fill him, and Ivan might not want to drink. But there were some toasts a Russian couldn't refuse.

Ivan's light blue eyes flickered toward the half-liter on the table, and Tor smiled. "Forgive me, Comrade. That's left over from last night." Opening the window, he emptied out the clear liquid casually. "But I have a fresh bottle, to celebrate the friendship of our countries."

The Russian watched stone-faced as Tor poured two drinks. They both chose pickled cucumber over the herring. Lifting his glass, Tor said solemnly, "To peace and brotherhood between the Soviet Union and the Islamic Republic of Afghanistan!"

Nodding, Ivan tossed back his shot. Before his glass hit the table, Tor filled it again.

"And to prosperity, for both our peoples!"

"Oh, yes. To prosperity!"

Again.

"And to the great October Revolution, which points the way to the world!"

Ivan smiled. "Certainly, Comrade. To the Revolution, which makes capitalists like yourself such a necessity in Moscow."

"Comrade Ivan!" Tor gulped his drink. "I've learned everything at the knee of my Soviet mother!" He poured again, returning Ivan's smile. "As a visitor in your country, I would like to toast your hero, Vladimir Ilyich Lenin!"

Pain, like a hot needle, was starting in his stomach again. Maybe they'd drunk enough?

"Of course. To Lenin!" Ivan was studying him, and the empty glass he held out looked like a thimble between his fingers. "Now it's my turn, Comrade. To the success of our endeavors!"

Gritting his teeth, Tor nodded enthusiastically. The liquor stung like pure acid now.

"And to hard currency, Comrade!" Ivan banged his glass on the table. "To dollars, pounds, marks and yen! Which can be used in the beryozka shops to get wonderful things rubles can't buy. To French underwear, Comrade! To Italian boots and Japanese cameras! Drink, Comrade Tor, drink!"

"But Comrade Ivan!" Tor put down his glass, pretending shock. "The beryozka shops are merely an expression of Soviet hospitality to foreign visitors! Special shops, with only the best goods."

"Yes, which good Soviet citizens can't get their hands on. At least, not people like me." Ivan's thick blond eyebrows met in a line. "Let's speak frankly, Tor. You drink well for a small man, and I always see you with girls. Well, I have a girl of my own, Comrade, and she's much too pretty for an ordinary Soviet citizen like myself. So I'd like to buy her beautiful presents, but I have no foreign money or the certificate rubles that also can be used in the beryozkas. Because I'm of no importance. I have only this."

He stood up to get his jacket and took some folded papers from its inside pocket. As Tor reached for them, he noticed a beading of sweat along Ivan's pale forehead.

"You see..." The Russian hesitated, his eyes fixed on the page Tor was reading, "You can see, they're Intourist memos. My sister works for Intourist, planning itineraries for foreign groups. I've heard your people like to meet foreigners, to exchange their money for rubles at black-market rates?"

Tor returned his gaze steadily. He'd say nothing himself until he put some loud music on the stereo.

"Well..." Ivan was smiling. "That's a good thing! A good bargain all around. Our visitors get more rubles than the government would give them, and you get hard currency, yes? But there are problems too. Most foreigners don't speak Russian, and even though many of your...friends speak other languages, you can never be sure when Aeroflot will deliver Americans, or Japanese, or Germans, am I right? But with these memos, Comrade Tor, you *would* know which planes were bringing whom. And when they'd be at Lenin's Tomb, and when at the Pushkin monument! You see? Those papers schedule every minute."

"Yes, Comrade Ivan, I see that." Tor flipped through the printed sheets casually, but his mind was racing. It was true. You could always find groups of tourists lining up at Lenin's Tomb, but it was impossible to predict which currency they'd have. Frequently, it had already been exchanged. With Ivan's lists, they could be met somewhere on the street or outside their hotels— much less conspicuous than bargaining in Red Square. And figuring the exchange rate would be no trouble either, if he knew which nationality to expect.

Ivan's blue eyes were straying toward the bottle of vodka. Tossing aside the papers, Tor said, "Forgive me, Comrade," and poured them both drinks. No toast this time. Tor appraised the big man coolly. He was in shirt sleeves and the trousers on his thick legs fit like skin, so he carried no hidden tape recorder. But why, Tor wondered, had Ivan been so insistent on meeting here, when it was much safer to talk business outdoors in the Quad or one of the parks? Was he more afraid of being seen? Tor lit a cigarette. This morning after everyone else went to class he'd gone over the room from top to bottom looking for bugs and found none, but that hadn't made him less suspicious. It might only mean they were very well concealed. So far Ivan had done all the advancing, and so openly that he must be either a spy or stupid after all. It was time to find out which.

Opening his notebook, Tor scribbled, "Pay no attention to what I say."

Ivan read the words and looked up quizzically.

"Comrade!" Tor sounded indignant. "What can you be proposing? I'm sure it's against the law!" He wrote quickly, "We may be overheard."

Horror widened Ivan's eyes and one hand fluttered to his cheek. Jumping up, he opened the hall door as if he expected to find someone crouched there, then seemed to realize Tor was referring to mechanical ears. His glance moved wildly around the room and Tor saw he was trembling. Yes, his fear looked genuine enough.

Bending to put a record on the turntable, Tor said, "Have you ever heard Van Morrison, Comrade? A very decadent Irish singer." He turned up the volume and set the needle on the first track, "Come Running to Me."

"I never talk business without music. It is more peaceful, don't you think? I'm sorry if I scared you."

Ivan took a step forward and Tor's hand closed around the sheaf of papers. "Don't worry, I never betray a trust. You know that, or you wouldn't have come to me. Here, I'll incriminate myself too. In exchange for these schedules, you want hard currency. Say, twenty percent of our profits?"

Gaping, Ivan grabbed the pencil and wrote, "Fifty!"

Tor shook his head. "Comrade! We take all the risks!"

"But my sister!" Ivan threw down the pencil. "I have to split with her. We need at least forty between us."

"I'll give you thirty," Tor said, "and I bet she'll only see ten. Do we have a deal?"

After a moment, the man nodded once and Tor smiled inwardly. If Ivan were less nervous he could have struck a better bargain, but now he wanted only to leave.

"And you'll bring me her lists each week? What day?"

"Monday," he said resentfully. "At lunchtime."

"Good." Tor clasped his arm. "But not here, Comrade, outside is better. At the Exposition of Economic Achievements? Let's meet at the Fountain of Friendship of Peoples. That seems appropriate."

Leaning toward him, Ivan muttered, "Tor, if I'm caught..."

"Oh, are you still frightened? I'm glad. It's good to be worried and on guard. That way neither of us will be careless. Here..." He offered the papers. "Take these back, if it will make you feel safer. Since we can't start till Monday anyway, you could always change your mind. But think of your girl friend, think of all the pretty things in the beryozkas. And I'll see you four days from now at noon. Shake on it, Comrade?"

Ivan took the memo eagerly but his handshake was limp and moist. Tor watched, amused, as he scooped up his jacket and hurried out down the hall.

Another glass of vodka, to celebrate. Closing the door, Tor sat back on the bed and kicked off his shoes. Unless Ivan was really an actor... but no, he didn't seem bright enough even for the KGB. No one that big could be too smart. Anyway, these Russians were all the same, bluffing and bragging until there was a chance of getting caught, and then they cried like babies scared of their own little games. This Ivan was no different. He'd be simple to manage now.

And that, Tor thought uncomfortably, was the problem.

How long would it take to get the system working on its own? A month at most, and after that he'd be right back where he started—richer, of course, but bored again. What was the point of making money, when everything except vodka came in trade? He'd turned Moscow upside down and shaken it out. There was nothing here to want.

Maybe this was the right time to expand his private practice. There were a few jobs he'd refused before as too dangerous, but...why not? He had more experience now. That Egyptian student Magdi's gold—that was the big one. Selling gold was the riskiest business in Moscow. Only real devils like Gregori Kirov bought gold, and they rarely let anyone walk away with much of their hard cash.

Smiling, Tor stretched lazily in the sun. Right now he wanted a girl. His skin was warm, and after the strain of a deal he always needed sharp feelings. But not in the sun, never in the light, close the curtains and pull down the shades. He didn't want to see their smiles, their eyes asking him questions, and he didn't want them to see him. Not once, in all his time in Moscow...

But even sex was getting too easy. Girls slept with him from curiosity—the Black Wasp, who always turned out the lights. Well, they were never disappointed. A few had fallen in love with him—girls who reminded him of Karima so much that he let himself whisper things in the dark. But that had ended finally two years ago. Now his policy was not to sleep with the same woman more than once. That way, everyone was happy. No jealousy, and no confusion.

Reserves were getting thin, though. In fact, there was only one he really wanted now, the girl he called Queen Victoria, and he wasn't even sure why he found her attractive. She despised him, Miss English Elizabeth Sutcliffe—he knew her name. He'd found out all about her after the first day he saw her in the cafeteria, when she brushed past him as if he were a piece of garbage in her way. Maybe that was why he wanted her...just for the challenge. She wasn't beautiful and couldn't be worth the trouble it would take to talk her into bed. Because talking would be what she liked—he'd decided that months ago. She was a big brain, just like Mangal, and probably didn't know she had a body.

But those high breasts under her cashmere sweaters were what had caught his eye to begin with last fall...yes, they looked very nice. It had been tempting to use his Lawrence College manners then, to show her what a proper little gentleman he could be, only it turned out she roomed with Nadia Lermontova, so he had changed his mind. He'd broken his "once only" rule for Nadia last year—until he found out her father worked on the staff of the Politburo. That was the end, and she didn't take it well, the spoiled Komsomol brat.

Now he and Nadia were friends again though, and last week she had told him Elizabeth wanted to sell some things. Then yesterday in the library, sure enough, Queen Victoria gave him a tight little English smile. Wasn't it funny how people changed when they needed this or that. She must think he was stupid.

Well, he'd play any game she wanted. Whatever happened, it wouldn't be predictable at least and it might be fun to sleep with an intelligent girl for a change, even if that went against his policy too. It could take some doing, but he had the element of surprise in his favor: knowing his reputation, she'd expect him to be crude, and instead he would be sweet and charming and very helpful, and then maybe she'd want to save him from the terrible life he led, so he could become another English colony.

Alright, now to plan it out. What else did Nadia say about her? That she studied all the time, which meant she ought to be in her room tonight. And that her father was some famous Russian history professor who'd been invited to the Kremlin twice, only now he was very sick. Maybe that was why she wanted to sell things. Maybe she needed comforting. He'd bring a bottle of good Spanish sherry and be very sympathetic.

After all, he didn't dislike Elizabeth—it was the other way around. She could be very pretty if she ever decided to use some makeup and took that cold expression off her face. Her hair was silvery and fine but her body looked strong, not soft like most Russian women's. Mmm, wouldn't it be nice to have Queen Victoria here right now, his hands tangled in her hair, and those gray eyes... no, he remembered, it was her eyes that disturbed him. But at night he wouldn't have to see them, and in another hour it would be dark.

Nine

THE DORM WAS oddly silent tonight. No footsteps in the hall. Elizabeth gave up trying to study and lit a cigarette. Pretending not to be worried was only making her more jumpy.

Lubyanka prison would be a quiet place too, and that might be her next address, as her father had warned her. He'd forbidden her to smuggle anything more than Yelena's poetry through customs. Perhaps he'd been squirreling out the dissidents' work for years, but since he was a guest of the government, his luggage was treated gently. Why should anyone interfere with Professor Asher Sutcliffe, who had an admiring letter from Brezhnev in his passport case?

Unfortunately, his daughter had no such protection.

Even without it though, and in spite of his cancer, he'd find some way to bring this new manuscript out if he still had the stamina to do it. Now it seemed unlikely he'd leave London Clinic again. What better gift to give him than a public vindication of the war he'd fought in private for so long. He could write the Introduction. It would be the crown of his career. And there was no one but herself to act as courier.

It had taken Yelena's network seven years of theft and bribery to assemble what they hoped would be a breakthrough book in the West: the first fully documented record of the psychiatric abuse of political dissidents in the Soviet Union... Kopolev's three hundred shock treatments, the brain-destroying drugs administered to Rostov and Lubya—whose work had become internationally respected thanks in part to Dr. Sutcliffe's cleverly made briefcase.

Now that could be said. His days in Moscow were over, as with luck her own would be soon. But the manuscript was five hundred pages long, and so far she hadn't found any good camouflage.

She and Yelena had argued over how much to tell him about it. If they weren't desperate, Yelena said, she'd never think of putting her friend's daughter in such danger, since being caught might well mean a convenient, fatal accident to prevent even the fact of the manuscript's existence from reaching the West. But with the coming Olympics, KGB crackdowns were growing more frequent and vicious. All Yelena's people were under threat of arrest now. So if Elizabeth was willing, they would have to use her, but her father must at least be told this was a longer, riskier work. Otherwise, he might die without knowing what had happened to her, or why.

At Christmas, the first hints she gave had made him smile. "A novel, you mean? Showing up that nonsense about the equality of Soviet women? Yelena always said she wanted to try one." Was he a little in love with her? Elizabeth wondered. Then quickly, his interest turned to distress and more agitation than she thought his health could stand. She had promised: I won't do it if there's any risk. If I can't find a safe way. Not a word code. Not a false-bottom case. Almost as a joke, she had mentioned Tor Anwari, prince of the black market at the university. Tor was supposed to be able to get anything in or out of the country—even crates of shoes and stereo sets—so a manuscript should be child's play for him.

Tor Anwari, the so-called Black Wasp, who traded in everything from blue jeans to Picasso prints in staggering quantities, who strutted around the Moscow University campus in a long black cape, with six girls hanging on him. Half the time he was drunk too, like his gang of junior crooks... embassy brats, most of them.

Her father had grinned. "You're not suggesting you'd compromise your virtue?" Because Tor was only a joke then. She crossed her arms on her chest. "Never!" But next day she'd gone out to buy a miniature tape recorder, a Nikon camera and the George Harrison *Bangladesh* album that sold for a hundred pounds in Moscow. Tor ought to find them irresistible. And the truth was, for some mysterious reason, the authorities left him alone. He'd probably bribed them all. If she could get him drunk and flatter him into giving away his secrets, they might be well worth learning. Besides, it would be a pleasure to outmaneuver the little twit.

Elizabeth pushed her chair back from the narrow dormitory desk. Last month, in England, that hadn't seemed a bad idea. It might even have worked. Yelena wouldn't have liked it if they'd had the chance to talk, but as a last resort she might have agreed. Except that Yelena had vanished. Was she in Lubyanka prison now? And the manuscript still under the floorboards in her kitchen? Her apartment had been searched twice in December.

Moscow

They were supposed to have met two weeks ago, in line outside the state department store, and if that meeting failed, to try again at the same time the next Saturday. Waiting for hours in the cold, she had seen hallucinations of Yelena go by—clipped chestnut hair, her flat cheekbones and wide green eyes, a mouth always trembling with hurt or anger, the passion of their cause ... or perhaps now with the dread Elizabeth felt in her own body. Today at lunch in the cafeteria, Yelena's young friend Kostia Ivanov had come up behind her whispering, "Stay in your room tonight, please."

His voice was hard and urgent and she felt it then, this chilly prickling of fear. Something must have gone wrong, perhaps with Kostia too by now. It was eight o'clock already. Well, it was snowing, she told herself, that could have held him up. And it might not be Kostia who would come anyway, since it was almost as dangerous for him to be seen with foreigners as it was for Yelena.

Opening her roommate's refrigerator, Elizabeth took out an apple and some yellow cheese. Maybe some food would take the edge off her nerves, though she didn't feel hungry in spite of missing dinner. Anyway, rooming with Nadia had spoiled her for the leaden cafeteria meals. In the classless Soviet Union, Nadia was kept supplied with whole roast chickens, smoked salmon and fresh fruit that she begged Elizabeth to help her eat so her Politburo father might not guess that dear Nadia spent every weekend at her latest boyfriend's apartment.

But it was Nadia's other privilege that had come as a real stroke of luck. She was the only girl in the dorm with just one roommate and Nadia seemed far less concerned about supervising her English "guest" than with concealing her own transgressions. If only it were Friday instead of Thursday, Elizabeth thought. Then Nadia wouldn't be in all night. Please, God, let her stay out late—at least long enough for Kostia to get away safely.

Because if Nadia even suspected what was going on, she'd call in the KGB. There was no doubt of that. She might be generous, but she wouldn't take risks with her family's political standing, however much she criticized the government herself. The knife slipped through Elizabeth's fingers and she swore out loud. How could she hope to smuggle Yelena's manuscript through customs, when just thinking about Nadia made her drop things?

As she bent to pick it up, a soft knock came on the door. Moving too quickly, she hit her head on the edge of the table and swore again. The thing to remember was not to speak or react in any way, to take her cue from Kostia or whoever it was and not get rattled.

Crossing the room she turned the lock and then stepped back, startled. Tor Anwari was standing in the hall, smiling. "Hello, I was hoping you'd be here." He moved his arm under the black cape and she realized he was holding something. "Can I come in, Comrade? It's cold."

She kept her hand on the doorknob. "Well, actually, Tor, I'm busy tonight. I'm expecting someone...."

"That's right. You're expecting me. I won't take up much of your time." His face was serious now. "I snuck up without leaving my card at the desk, to save your reputation. Please let me come in."

Was it possible, she wondered, that Tor could be involved somehow with the dissidents too? He looked different tonight, composed and determined, his finely drawn features not fuzzy with drink.... Reluctantly, she let the door swing open. "Alright, just for a minute, then."

He shut the door behind him. "My, this is quite a palace you have here! Compared to my room, that is." His eyes settled on the stereo. "Wouldn't you like to put on some music? Just for a minute, of course. Something noisy, if you know what I mean, Comrade."

Bending to the stack of records, she had a sense of dislocation. The timing of this visit must be sheer coincidence. Tor couldn't be a courier. But he acted with such assurance that she didn't dare risk being wrong, and in any case could not afford to be very rude, she remembered. It seemed years now since she had spoken to Nadia about Tor, since she'd even thought of him. After Saturday's broken appointment only Yelena had been on her mind, but Tor might still be important to them later.

When she turned back, he had taken off his cape and was holding out a brown bottle. "For you, to remind you of England. Nadia said she thought you were homesick. I don't blame you, Comrade, I've felt that way for the past five years."

Elizabeth smiled at the label. "Nadia can't have told you Domecq's is my favorite sherry."

No, she thought, of course he wasn't a courier, he had just caught her off guard. And now it would be the devil's business to get rid of him without being offensive.

"Good, now we can really talk. I've wanted to for a long time." He sat down in one of the armchairs. "That's perfect music for bugs. What is it?"

"Vivaldi. It's sort of a Moscow family heirloom. Do you like it?"

"I don't know yet. Want a cigarette?"

She shook her head. "Thanks for the sherry, Tor. I'd offer you a drink, but I simply can't tonight. Could we get together on the weekend instead?"

"Let's have one drink. Then I'll go if you want. I'd like to see the little tape recorder Nadia mentioned, but if your date shows up I'll leave right away. I'm very stubborn, Comrade, so you may as well give in."

It would probably be quicker to agree, she decided, and went to get some glasses. "Alright, just a taste, then I have to get back to my books."

He filled the glasses almost to the brim, smiling guiltily. "Don't be mad, I'll drink it fast and you can sip yours while you're reading."

She sat down opposite him. "I thought that under Islam it was a sin to drink alcohol."

"Ah, but in my case, I drink to keep from sinning! If I drink, I sleep, and if I sleep I can't sin." He pushed a mass of glossy hair back from his forehead.

"But here's to our exile in Moscow! May we both be free some day."

Lifting her glass, she said, "Cheers! Do you hate it here so much? You seem to have more fun than most people do."

"With all respect, you must be going blind. I'd rather be anywhere else." Reaching for his cape, he took a red enameled lighter and a pack of cigarettes from its pocket. "Are you sure you wouldn't like one of these? They came from Istanbul yesterday."

"So Turkey's part of your empire too? Alright, yes, I would." The sherry was delicious and she felt her tension ease a bit. Tor seemed manageable enough, he would leave if Kostia came, and he was hardly an informant after all.

"At least my 'empire,' as you call it, is only commercial, Comrade. I just try to make everyone happy however they like. But I guess you don't approve of that."

"Since I want to use your services too, I could hardly disapprove." She took the cigarette he offered. "Is that a Dunhill lighter?"

"Why not the best? As Jimmy Carter would say." Settling back in the chair, he stretched out his legs and blew a plume of smoke toward the ceiling. His gray flannel slacks and pale blue sweater were as impeccable as his grooming tonight, and with his olive skin and almond eyes he looked, she thought, rather like King Tut dressed by Savile Row.

"Are you keen on Carter, then?"

"Not exactly." Tor had almost finished his drink. "I think he's a mullah in disguise. Do you know what a mullah is?"

She nodded. "A Muslim priest."

"Right. This Carter's a very good priest. He prays five times a day."

"I suppose you got that from reading *Pravda*."

"No, from the *Guardian Weekly*. That's an evil English newspaper full of capitalist propaganda, right?"

"Blimey." She laughed. "Do you actually smuggle the *Weekly* into Moscow? How could you do that?" After a moment's hesitation, she poured him a little more sherry. If he had some way to get papers through, why shouldn't it work in reverse?

"Ah, that's a professional secret!" He was beaming as though the fresh drink represented a victory, and she could have kicked herself for being so direct.

"Here's to you, Comrade," he toasted her with a flourish. "I'll tell you one of my secrets. I think you're the only interesting person in this city."

"Really? Well, you have good taste." But she was so distracted the words sounded pompous instead of wry and she took a sip of sherry, watching him over the rim of her glass.

The low table seemed to hold them in delicate balance. Tor tapped his foot impatiently. "Elizabeth, it's quarter of nine. Maybe your friend isn't coming. If he's not here in fifteen minutes, I humbly invite you to have dinner with me. There's a restaurant near Red Square that serves good Uzbek food, and I'm feeling awfully homesick tonight."

He looked it too, she thought, and perhaps that was how he had charmed Nadia and the rest—with this sudden show of vulnerability. His brown eyes were warm now, appealing. "No, Tor," she said. "I've just told you, I have to study."

"But you've got all weekend for that!" Pushing up the sleeves of his sweater, he rested his elbows on his knees. "I'll tell you what. If you come with me, I'll let you see all my *Guardian* weeklies. Before I give them to my history professor in return for a passing grade. Oh no, I forgot, your father's a historian, so you won't approve of that either."

She couldn't help smiling back at him. "That depends on which professor you have. But I can't, Tor, honestly."

"Because you hate me very much." He was gazing straight into her eyes and the intimacy unnerved her.

Standing up, she pushed the cork back in the bottle and set it on the desk. "That's a rather large conclusion to jump to. I've just said we could go out some other night."

He was right though, it was almost nine o'clock. Where in God's name had Kostia got to? The later he came, the more conspicuous he'd be and he must certainly know that. Pulling back the curtain, she peered down through the frosted window at the path leading up to the front of the dorm.

"I wonder why I think you're beautiful," Tor said. "I never did before."

She turned, surprised. "Well, that's honest! You go for the skinny model type, I've noticed. Which probably means you're stringing me a line."

He was leaning forward with his hands clasped, "I mean, I wonder how I could find you attractive at all, when I know you have no respect for me." He pressed his lips together, and watching him, she felt sure he hadn't planned to ask that particular question, or at least not so seriously. He covered his embarrassment with a grin. "Never mind, Comrade, I just admire your muscles."

"It's the novelty, I expect. You probably thought all those other women were beautiful, until you got sick of them." But her own voice sounded strange too and she felt exposed by his steady stare. The whole situation was a bit eerie, really... waiting for Godot with this Tor, who seemed so much more subdued than usual and unsettled by that himself, as though in taking off his cape he had unwittingly shed his gaudy Black Wasp bravado. If they'd met for the first time tonight she might not have guessed it was a studied technique.

"Oh, I respect some of your talents," she teased, trying to break the spell. "In fact, let me show you that tape recorder. It's the smallest one I've ever seen."

"I'd rather just talk for a while if you don't mind. I haven't had a chance to use my English since last summer. Maybe you don't like me much, but we have some things in common and there can't be many interesting people in Moscow for you, either."

Was he claiming to be lonely? Tor Anwari? "You have more friends here than anyone else I know," she smiled. "Except Nadia, that is."

"Yes, and they all bore me to death."

She felt more confused now. Was he asking for sympathy as a prelude to seduction? But if he could even affect being this straightforward it must exist somewhere in his character, and she found that an unwelcome revelation. It would be easier to play games with Tor than to confront him as a person—one whom she could never trust in any case. She had pictured getting him drunk one night and coaxing information out of him, while he now seemed bent on showing her how civilized he could be.

Then as she opened her mouth to speak, someone knocked twice on the door.

"Dammit." Tor smiled, but he didn't move to put on his cape.

She went to answer it, scolding herself for having let him in at all.

This time it really was Kostia outside, his thin face twisted with anxiety. When she glanced over her shoulder to say she wasn't alone he made no effort to come in, just looked down the hall and then held up a note for her to read without letting her take it from him.

It said: "Last Friday Yelena was admitted to the Serbsky Institute of Forensic Psychiatry. Since they have no crime to try her for, it's easier to declare her insane. Now, we can only pray. The manuscript is still in her apartment but I haven't found a way to get it out. Come to the GUM store on Saturday and stand in line for the sale on nylon shopping bags. I may have more news by then."

Giving her a short, agonized smile, he crumpled the note into a ball and turned quickly toward the stairs.

Stunned, Elizabeth stood watching him go. The Serbsky Institute! It should have been called the Serbsky Chamber of Horrors, since that was where half the records in Yelena's manuscript had come from. What would they have done to her by now? She'd been there a whole week, and prison or exile would seem pleasant compared to the "drug therapy" and shock treatments that might not leave her with enough brains to write her own name.

Behind her, Tor said, "Don't tell me you play my games! Notes, in case of bugs? Have you been stood up after all, Comrade?"

He was smiling with satisfaction, thinking he'd won again, no doubt, and her fright gave way to mounting anger. Showing that would be foolish, improvident, but neither could she carry on chatting as if nothing had happened, and it would be harder than ever to make him leave now.

I have to get out of here, she thought, I can't say another word until I've pulled myself together or God knows what will come out of my mouth. If we walk, though, I won't have to talk, even to make excuses, and some cold air is just what I need.

She nodded. "That's right. No date after all. We could go to dinner if you like."

There was something wrong with her, Tor knew, he'd seen it from the first minute, and whoever this mysterious visitor was he hadn't made things any better.

But what difference did that make, she was coming with him and he felt almost stupidly grateful. An hour ago, when she had opened the door, she looked as if he were the last person in the world she wanted to see. She couldn't have been expecting a boyfriend, though. Her eyes were scared and since then she'd been so tense he thought she was going to jump out of her skin. Somehow that made him feel protective of her and more curious than ever, and he wanted to get her out of Nadia's bugged room and have her all to himself. Now she was putting on her parka and he didn't care that she still looked shaky.

Because in spite of that, he could sense no weakness in her. Comrade Liz exuded power like a faint electrical charge, and that, he guessed, was what had raised his hackles every time he'd seen her—his own strength, in opposition. He could almost laugh now, remembering his fantasy of conquest. If he and Queen Victoria ever made love, they would be like lions.

He held the door and she went out ahead of him. The lobby of the dorm was so crowded it was easy to slip by the desk attendant.

They walked along Vernadski Avenue to the Lenin Hills metro station and stood looking down through thick glass at the frozen river. Elizabeth had hardly spoken since they left her room. Who was it who had made her so upset? Well, that would be simple to find out—when he took her back he'd have a look at the desk register.

Her lips were moving faintly, as if she were very far away, and he studied her profile in the beam of light—straight blond hair cut to the curve of her cheek, a short nose and gray eyes almost too serious to be pretty. There was something in her face that made him want to hold her, comfort her, and then he was surprised to discover that feeling didn't scare him. Tentatively, he touched her hand and she twitched, then glanced up with an odd little smile as if he were a stranger she had bumped into by mistake. He kept his fingers just touching hers, turning his attention to the black ice below until a hiss of steel announced the train.

"Quite a tribute to the Revolution, Comrade, wouldn't you agree?" Tor took her arm as they stepped onto the Marx Prospect platform. "The Moscow metro is the finest *in the world*!"

She smiled. "Yes, they've rather an obsession with that. Everything's got to be the biggest or the best. I have to go along with some of it, though. Saint Basil's, for instance. It's magnificent."

"Tell me about Saint Basil's!" She was more relaxed now, and he felt wildly happy. "Open these peasant eyes!"

Outside, the red star above the Kremlin quivered in the freezing air. It's crenellated walls marked the expanse of Red Square with towers and cupolas rearing into darkness. Saint Basil's stood at the opposite end, looking, Tor thought, like an assortment of spires robbed from several churches and bound together. Its swirling onion and pineapple domes seemed huddled against the blast of white artificial light.

"Well, it's mid-sixteenth century," she said, "commissioned by Ivan the Terrible. What else would you like to know?"

"One man built this?" But he was looking at her.

"They think so. One Posnik Yakovlev. Amazing, isn't it?"

"So this Yakovlev predicted the embrace of the Soviet state. He must have been a true genius!" Afraid his sarcasm would silence her, Tor said quickly, "Please go on. Did you learn all this from your father? Nadia told me he's very famous." No, dammit, he remembered, her father's sick. Why did I have to bring that up?

"Yes, from him and from a course I took here." Her voice was wooden. "What does your father do?"

I set myself up for this, he thought, fishing in his pocket for a cigarette. But he could feel Elizabeth's eyes on his face. "My father's an apiarist." The red lighter flared. "He keeps bees. Come on, let's go now. The Uzbekistan's over on Neglinnaya."

They went back along the endless facade of the GUM department store. Across from the red granite slab of Lenin's Tomb a man was pouring vodka into the engine of his car. Trying to recapture their gaiety, Tor called, "How many degrees, Comrade?" But when the man saw they were students he waved them away.

As they joined the line outside the restaurant, Tor smiled genuinely. At any other time he would have passed a bribe of twenty rubles to get in. Through steaming windows they could see a crush of people sitting at tables littered with bowls and bottles of vodka, and he caught Elizabeth's arm again. "See those three? At the corner table on the right?"

"In the dark shirts and white ties? Yes, they look a bit like Bedouins dressed up as American gangsters."

"Those are probably the first ties they've owned," Tor grinned. "They're Afghans, from the provinces. I call them Abdullah One, Two and Three. The first time they saw a hot shower here, they thought their Russian roommate was trying to gas them and I had to go running over to calm them down." He choked back laughter. "The one in the middle—see the white thing on his glasses? That's the maker's label. In the countryside, it's a sign of prestige to leave the tags on things, to show that it's new, your best. Oh damn, they've seen us now."

Skinny Abdullah One was already getting up and moving toward the door. Which meant, Tor knew, they were in for it. Well, this would have happened in a few minutes anyhow, since he could hardly have dragged her away at this point.

"Toryalai Anwari!" he said in Pashto. "Peace be with you."

"And you, Mohammad Ali. But speak Russian, please, you need the practice anyway. This is Miss Elizabeth Sutcliffe. Elizabeth, Mohammad Ali Khalis."

"Most deeply honored." He bowed. "Toryalai Anwari, I hope you are well?"

Tor nodded curtly, hoping to forestall the traditional barrage of polite inquiries.

"And your honored father? He is well, may Allah protect him?"

"Everyone's well, Mohammad Ali. Everything's fine, so you can go on back to your dinner."

"But you must come and join our table! We cannot sit while you stand here in the cold."

Sighing, he turned to Elizabeth. "He'll keep at us till we do. Alright?"

She was smiling. "Of course. If they'll let us in."

As they picked their way to the corner table, she murmured, "He thinks you're wonderful."

Tor shook his head. "That's just our famous Afghan hospitality, Comrade."

But he couldn't conceal some awkwardness as the other two men scrambled to make room. "Ah, Toryalai Anwari!" Again there were introductions, and when they were finally settled, Mohammad Ali turned to Elizabeth with the one question Tor had been hoping to avoid. "Has Toryalai Anwari told you of his most illustrious family?"

"No," she said, "he hasn't."

Looking away, Tor signaled to the waiter. "At least let us order before you start gabbing." The Abdullahs would be shocked if he drank alcohol, but he decided they could go to hell since they insisted on speaking out of turn. He called, "Waiter! Vodka! And a bowl of lagman, and one of maniar." He told Elizabeth, "You should like this food after all those good Russian potatoes. The Soviet state has even embraced part of our Uzbek tribe, which is too bad for them but lucky for me. I couldn't live without this place."

She nodded, but turned back to Mohammad Ali. "What are you saying about Tor's family?"

"But surely..." He looked mystified. "Well, Toryalai Anwari is modest. His father is one of the greatest men in all Afghanistan! He was a cabinet minister under King Zahir, but he resigned over some point of honor, and our fathers agree he is the only man of that government whose hands are completely clean. Well, there were many honorable men. But when a person makes such a sacrifice, then you can be sure, and of Omar Anwari, Afghanistan is sure. Now his first son, Mangal, works for our first president, Mohammad Daoud Khan, and surely in time, if Allah wills it, Tor Anwari will also help lead our country. Tor Anwari may one day become as great a man as his father!"

Tor felt his cheeks burning as he furiously peeled the foil top off the vodka. Before he had always managed to keep the Abdullahs clear of his private life in Moscow, and now all his compartments were breaking down. He filled the two small glasses without looking at Elizabeth. "To Afghanistan, then. To the beautiful country we all miss so much." Glancing at each other, the Abdullahs raised their teacups. "To Afghanistan!"

Mohammad Ali said, "We will go now. It was a great honor to meet you, Miss Sutcliffe. Good evening, Toryalai Anwari, may Allah guard you both." Tor nodded as they trooped past him toward the door.

He was saved by steaming bowls of soup descending in front of them. "Ah, lagman, you have that. The maniar takes some getting used to, but we'll share. That's just meat and noodles with a little spice. This has egg and pastry in it too."

She said dryly, "So your father keeps bees."

"Now he does." Tor poured some more vodka and threw back the shot.

"And your brother ... Mangal? Does he keep bees too?"

He shrugged. "Do you want me to quiz you about your family?"

"If you like. You know about my father. My mother teaches music at a girls' school in London, and my brother David's an anthropologist working on a dig in Cornwall. Why did you lie to me?"

She sounded hurt as much as angry, and Tor cursed himself. A while ago she had come close to liking him, he knew that, and now her face was hard again.

He chased the vodka with a spoonful of maniar. "What difference does it make? We're here. We're not them. What difference do they make?" But the fragile thread had snapped, and he concentrated on his soup.

They finished the meal in silence, then left to take the metro back across the river. Their car was packed full and he braced his hand above Elizabeth's on the pole, trying to find words to bridge the distance between them. After all, he hadn't lied, really. There were twenty hives in the garden now. But accuracy wasn't the issue.

When they got to the dorm he dropped off his card at the desk and insisted on walking her upstairs. At the door to her room, he said, "Could I come in for just a minute so we can talk?"

She shook her head. "No, Tor, I don't think that's a good idea."

"But why?" He knew the answer. "Didn't you want to see me too? And it was good, until ... at least let me explain that."

"I can't. Don't you realize the position you're putting me in? I really do need to trade my camera and tape recorder, and if you come in, we'll fight, and then I'll be up a tree. I'm not feeling very well, and I'm afraid I might say things I'd regret tomorrow."

"Such as what? Go ahead, I know what you're thinking, so you may as well get it off your chest, Comrade. Do you think I'm such a skunk that I wouldn't help you because of that?"

"I don't know what you are, Tor." She shook her head again. "You really take the biscuit. You pretend to be totally shallow, but you're not. You're charming and clever, and apparently rich as well. And you've taken all that and turned it to muck. Why, Tor? I don't understand that. You can laugh at those three in the restaurant, but they certainly think more of you than you do of yourself."

Tor hit the wall with the flat of his hand. "I don't laugh at them, really. I just wanted to make you smile. You looked sad."

"Yes, but that's the point, isn't it. Nothing has any value except for amusement's sake."

He waited for two students to pass. "I gave you credit to see through that! It's all 'pokazukha,' Comrade—just for show. I've looked after those Abdullahs ever since they came to Moscow. Listen, there are people out here. Could I come in for one minute, please?"

She stepped back and he shut the door behind them.

Switching on the stereo, he retrieved the bottle of sherry and sat down in the brown leather armchair. "It's just that I can't describe my family in a five-minute walk past the Kremlin. I don't know if I can talk about them at all. I've never tried. Your father's a historian? Mine hardly speaks anymore, and my mother spends most of her time trying to make him eat. My brother rides around in a Mercedes with generals who wear sunglasses night and day. I haven't heard from my sister in five years. You compare me to the Abdullahs? Fine. For them, this is a big opportunity. They'll go back to their villages and be heroes. But for me to take all this seriously would mean being a good Soviet running dog, Comrade. And with all respect to the bugs in your room, I don't want to play."

She said, "You can take off your cape."

Opening the hook, he let it fall back across the chair. "As for my business—everyone in Moscow's out to beat the system. It's the only thing that makes them feel human. What's so terrible about that?"

"Ah..." She was pouring sherry. "So you just give people what they want. Which is the best alternative you could find to being a Soviet shill."

"I didn't say it was noble. I'm just being honest, and you're right, I'm out of practice. But I'd like to try, with you."

"Why? Have you run out of other girls?"

Her echo of his own thought was unnerving. "I like you," he said. "Is that a crime too? I want to help you, and maybe you could help me a little. I haven't had anyone here to talk to before. Yesterday I thought you were stuck-up and you thought I was a devil, so maybe we were both wrong. Can't we get to know each other and then make up our minds?"

"I'm afraid it's a bit late to start."

She swung her legs over the arm of her chair, reaching back for an ashtray on the desk, and lamplight curved around her breast so soft under the sweater. He felt a spasm of desire. "I'm a hopeless case, right? Then shoot me in the head." But the edge in his voice surprised him.

"No, Tor, I didn't mean that. I'll probably be leaving Moscow soon. Perhaps just for a while, but my father's ill and I think he's getting worse. I'm not sure I'll be coming back here."

"Oh, no." He put down his drink. "I'm such a stupid donkey. I've been sitting here yakking about my family, when Nadia said you were worried about him. I'm sorry. I just didn't know how sick I was of everything until tonight. And now I'm going to lose you." Why did that suddenly seem unbearable? he wondered. There were lots of pretty blondes around and some of them were even smart too. What was so special about this one, who wore jeans and an old sweater and no makeup? She pretended to be so tough, but you could see all the feelings she was trying to push down, and holding them so tight made her a little blind, he thought. That must be why he wanted to protect her.

She took a cigarette, and one corner of her mouth curled up. "Knowing me would hardly change your life."

"It might," he said. "I don't care about anything here, Comrade. I only drink because I'm bored, and at least I wouldn't be alone."

"And what would I be, your perpetual entertainment squad? You don't have to be alone, Tor. That's up to you. And if you're offering me your weakness, I don't want it."

Tor considered the wet leather of his new Swiss hiking boots. He had forgotten to oil them and snow was soaking through. There would be a line on their finish now, like wing tips, he thought. What a waste. It might take months to get another pair. Why had he been in such a rush to come over here at all? His first instincts were always right, and they'd told him Queen Victoria was trouble. Now he would think about her even more, if he let her send him away.

She was saying, "But I have no right to judge you. As you pointed out, I really don't understand your situation."

"I think you do." He smiled and lit a cigarette.

Some pieces were starting to come together in the back of his mind... that note, and the way her face looked when she opened the door. Elizabeth was in trouble too, so she couldn't send him away. She needed him, and maybe she had forgotten that herself.

Standing up, she wandered around the room, her right hand making little circles. "There are other things you could do here, you know," she said. "I mean, with your talents."

"Such as?"

He saw her lips move again, but then she shook her head. "Oh, never mind. I just wish I could see into your brain, Tor."

"With all respect, I don't think you'd like the view, Comrade. How soon will you be leaving Moscow? We still have some business to transact, and by the way, I've been thinking about that and it doesn't make any sense. You can't need money so badly that you'd have to sell your camera, so what do you want? Before, you said you needed to trade it. For what?"

Now he'd struck a nerve, he knew. Her face had that scared look for a second and then she turned away to peer out through the window. "We haven't time to get into all that tonight, Tor. Nadia should be back soon and I don't want to go on report."

The cool dismissal in her voice made him angry. Did she really think he couldn't find out what her problem was if he wanted to? Women always used that trick of acting superior when you got close to something they wanted to hide.

But then watching her, he felt sad again. She was leaving, and he'd be miserable even if he never understood why. He wanted to go to her and knead his fingers into her shoulders and back, pressing her thighs hard against his own until they both fell over, unbalanced, on the bright quilt on her bed. She ought to be laughing in his ear, though, wrestling only in play. These days he was so thin she could probably knock him out with one punch.

He got up and went to take her arms, to make her look at him. "Aren't you being slightly hypocritical, Comrade? You're telling me I should be honest. Doesn't that go for you too? Why can't we try to be friends for however long you're still in Moscow, and I'll do my best to help you. I know you're up to something, but I'm not sure you realize how risky fooling around here can be for noble, honest people like yourself."

Pulling free, she said, "Thank you. Tor, it's kind of you to warn me. I'm sure you know what you're talking about. But I think you'd better go now. This time you did leave your card at the desk, and in another ten minutes they'll come looking for you."

He could have told her no one had ever been hauled out of Nadia's room. But then she would remember why he knew that.

"So how about it, Comrade, can we try to be friends?" He held out a hand. "You might find out I'm a good one to have."

"That sounds like an obvious bribe." Smiling, she gave him a shake. "Alright. Since we're both supposed to be so interesting."

"Then will you see me tomorrow night? Can I come over again? Only because we may not have much time, Comrade."

"And because you know Nadia won't be in? You may if you promise to leave at a decent hour. I have to get up early on Saturday."

"I'm going right now, see?"

It would be a mistake to touch her again, he thought. She might already be wishing she'd said no. Picking up his cape, he said, "Let's just sit and talk. I'll bring you some nice French wine. White or red?"

"White, please. And thanks for the sherry, Tor. It was awfully good."

"Till tomorrow, then." Clicking his heels in a salute, he slipped out through the door before she could change her mind.

Downstairs at the desk he let his wallet fall open to empty itself on the floor, and while the attendant picked up rubles, his eyes scanned the register. Her other visitor had come at nine o'clock and he had been careful, so he probably wouldn't have given the right room number.

Five people had come in at nine. Two were women. Two others gave a room repeated several times on the column—someone was having a party. The fifth had written 223, the reverse of Elizabeth's number. Very nice. If necessary, that could be explained as a mistake.

The name was unfamiliar, but it wouldn't be for long. By noon tomorrow, Tor felt sure he'd know a lot about Kostia Ivanov.

Ten

CHAMPAGNE TONIGHT, Tor thought. Dom Pérignon, Vintage 1964, from the cellar at the French embassy. Now getting that had been fun. Three cases, in exchange for a very ugly Byzantine cross.

Parting the curtains he looked out into a new flurry of snow. The temperature had been dropping all day and the forecast said a blizzard was coming. Maybe he'd be trapped in Queen Victoria's room all weekend, just the two of them, alone together.

He had oiled his hiking boots, deciding to keep them as a souvenir in spite of the hair-line stains, and his gray Ecuadorean alpaca sweater was thick enough to keep six people warm. It was time to go, or he might meet roommate Petrov coming back from dinner, but there was still the question of how to confront Miss Elizabeth with her mess. He'd been pacing the room for half an hour, sipping vodka to calm his nerves, not wanting to leave before he knew the answer.

It had taken just one hour to find out about Kostia Ivanov—a third-year student whose scientist father had been sent to a labor camp. So sonny wants to join him, Tor almost said out loud. They were all so self-righteous, these martyrs, and for what? They'd never change anything. And limited freedom was still worth a hundred times more than politics.

Elizabeth would be leaving soon. Kostia's note must mean they wanted her to carry something. She couldn't be so stupid. But if he told her that, she'd say he was a coward, and it would be like last night all over again.

Maybe if they got along for a while, he could convince her gradually. Fighting now might only spoil whatever time they had.

But if he didn't stop her... Tor put down the bottle of vodka. He'd have to see her to know what to do.

Walking to the closet, he unzipped the cloth bag covering his white suede Afghan coat, embroidered in black and lined and bordered with long curly black sheepskin. He had worn it only once, to an embassy party at home, and the effect was, even for him, a little dramatic. Then why tonight, in snow? But the hides could take that, and he knew the choice would explain itself later on.

He was wrapping two bottles of champagne in a sweater when the door opened behind him, and his neighbor Magdi's caressing voice said, "Toryalai! When will you sell me that coat?"

Tor turned, conjuring up a smile. "Magdi, my friend! You've been gone so long I thought you'd decided to fight for Sadat after all."

The Egyptian came to run his fingers sensually through the black fleece. "No, Tor, I bleed too easily. My flesh is made for gentler things, like this. Why won't you sell it to me? Or trade it, perhaps? I've brought back fantastic things this time. Exquisite things, that only you could appreciate."

Magdi's lazy dark eyes flickered to his arm as he pushed up the loose sleeve of his galabia, showing a dozen wide golden bangles. "You see that work? A master craftsman, from Luxor. Yet, they could be easily recast. And look at this." He opened the row of tiny buttons at his chest. "It's so heavy I can hardly hold my head up." A thick gold link chain gleamed like fire against his smooth brown skin.

He stripped off a bracelet. "Look at it, Tor. That's twenty-four-karat international currency. If one had the nerve... but of course, I have not." His voice drooped, but his eyes were teasing. "I'm only a simple merchant, like my father and grandfather."

Tor's right hand closed around the bangle, warm from Magdi's body, and held it toward the light. The workmanship was Islamic, precise and intricate in pale gold with no orange tint. It would be a shame to melt this piece down, or any of the others.

"You see?" Magdi clasped his shoulder. "There are buyers in Moscow for that. For all of this."

"My dear Magdi! Of course there are buyers. You know who they are as well as I do—which is why you won't go near them." He slipped the bracelet onto his wrist, feeling its pleasant weight.

"But not you, Toryalai! You have a reputation. No one would touch the Black Wasp. The other things I've offered you... bah. Merely trinkets. You were right to refuse. But this? And I want only thirty thousand dollars for the lot. They could bring fifty, easily."

Yes, Tor thought, if you didn't mind dealing with devils like Gregori Kirov, who left a trail of dead bodies behind them. Last year another student, little

Jani Kuznetsov, had tried to sell gold to Gregori, and come away empty-handed and half blind. Now Jani had a glass eye and was afraid of everything.

Reluctantly, Tor pulled off the bracelet. "My friend Magdi, I can't do it because you are my friend and I might just lose this for you. Right now, I'm very tired. I'm sick of the whole thing. It's no good, working that way."

"Tired?" Magdi hooted. "Sick? Of making thirty thousand dollars in one day? If you're planning to go out of business, Tor, do it with a splash. You won't lose. You never have."

Yesterday that had seemed right, even selling Magdi's gold, but since last night he'd done some thinking. Elizabeth could call him a hypocrite too, if he took such a big risk, and then he would lose his bargaining power with her. Slowly he shook his head.

Magdi grinned. "Tired from too much lovemaking, eh? Well, that won't last. I saw you walking in Red Square with the little English girl. Hah! I was wondering when you'd get around to her. Tell me, was she good?"

Tor stepped back and Magdi's hand dropped. "She's a wonderful person, yes."

"Oh, she was *wonderful*!" Laughing, Magdi poked him. "Congratulations, my friend. You disappoint me though, Tor, I swear it. I didn't think any woman could make you tired. And I thought for an Afghan fear did not exist."

"I'm half American, too, Comrade. They like to save their skins." He turned away to put the wrapped bottles into his leather pack.

"You think about it," Magdi said. "When you're bored with her, we'll talk again." He went out chuckling. "So Toryalai's finally getting soft!"

After a moment, Tor slung the bag over his shoulder and switched off the lamp.

Outside, snow blew at him like a hundred tiny headlights and he pushed up the coat's broad fleece collar, already wet and giving off an oily smell of sheep that reminded him of hunting trips at home. The fur of his old posteen had been white, damp with sweat as he scrambled up rocky trails to look back at his father's tall figure climbing more deliberately, a rifle slung over his shoulder. What had he been thinking, Tor wondered. It was still impossible to tell. Last summer, Daddy-jan had worked for hours every day with those beehives, and when asked about them, or anything else for that matter, he just said, "You do what you have to do."

Elizabeth's father, what would he be like? A jolly, fat historian spilling ashes down his tie, or someone more like Daddy-jan?

At the desk in her dorm, he signed the register slowly and did not find Kostia's name. When he wrote Elizabeth's number, the old attendant gave him a knowing grin. "But Nadia's gone out!"

"Careful, Comrade." Tor winked. "It's dangerous to have a good memory in the Soviet Union. Stalin goes, Nadia goes, and both should be forgotten!"

Folding a ten-ruble note, he handed it in with his card. "I hope you'll forget me too, in case I'm late picking this up."

The money was pocketed, and he climbed the stairs to the third floor.

She answered the door on his second knock and for an instant it did seem like last night again. Her face was pale except for bright patches of color in her cheeks that contrasted with her white sweater and black jeans.

"Tor, come in. What a beautiful coat." She shivered. "It's so cold."

Setting down his bag, he went to put on a record. "I should have brought vodka. I think you need it."

"Maybe you're right. I've had some bad news."

Trumpet music filled the room and he turned to face her. "Don't tell me you've been getting more little notes."

She took a step forward. "No, Tor, it's my father. I got a cable from my mother just after dinner. It said, come as soon as you can. Not, 'if it's convenient' or when I finish my exams. So I have to go right away."

"Oh." He swallowed. "That's too bad. I'm sorry." He felt blank. She looked like a ghost already, with that short blond hair standing out around her face. In his mind all day she had belonged to him, Elizabeth, smiling, doing things with him, and now those pictures fluttered away and it made him so sad he didn't trust his voice. "I hope your father's better very soon," he said clumsily. "Would you like me to leave?"

"No, I want you to stay. Take off your coat. I'll be alright in a minute. I guess I wasn't really expecting this after all."

There were shirts and sweaters piled on the bed, a suitcase standing beside it, and in fact the whole room was a mess—the closet seemed to have been ransacked and big books were strewn all around as if she had started packing in a frenzy. So they wouldn't have even tonight to enjoy. But that was a very selfish way to think. She must be feeling terrible, and if he was her friend he ought to try to help and cheer her up.

He threw his wet coat over the desk chair. "How soon is right away? Do you have a reservation yet?"

"Maybe, but I have to get an exit visa first. I'm hoping Nadia can do that for me. She said she'd pick up my passport first thing in the morning."

"And when's this flight? Tomorrow?"

Elizabeth shook her head. "At noon on Sunday, but it may already be full. Tor, if you've brought some wine, let's open it. Do you think she can really get me a visa by then?"

"Little Nadia? Of course. Her father will sign it. And I've got a friend in Intourist who can get you on that plane. But Comrade, I don't think you'll like my choice of wine. It's for celebrating. It's champagne."

"What?" She smiled. "Well, I don't suppose Dad would mind. Especially if he saw the state I'm in."

"Calm down. We'll get you home alright." That was something he could do, at least, manage the practical side. Knowing what to say was harder, though. Saira was the only person he'd ever tried to comfort, and last time that hadn't worked out at all.

He turned away. "Let me get you another sweater. You're shaking like Stalin's mother-in-law."

"Oh, Tor, are you going to take care of me? The Black Wasp is full of surprises. Shall I open the champagne?"

"If you want to. But be careful, it's probably pretty shaken up—like you and me," he laughed. He was sorting through her sweaters, inhaling their faint scent of perfume. Maybe he could steal one to remember her by? The soft rose cashmere turtleneck, that was his favorite, but she needed a cardigan now.

Behind him, she chuckled. "Just a jar of plonk, eh? I've never had Dom Pérignon before. Would you get down those two glasses on the top shelf over there?"

He set them on the table, thinking he'd never seen anyone attack champagne so fearlessly. With one long even twist she brought the cork up and let it shoot into the air, but her hand shook, spilling a few drops as she filled the glasses. "These came all the way from Marks and Spencer. Now, there's a store you wouldn't like. They'd put you right out of business. And speaking of that, we still have some negotiating to do."

She wanted something. How had he let himself forget that? And it probably had to do with Kostia Ivanov, dammit. If she was leaving in such a hurry, she should have given up that idea.

Running a towel across the table, she handed him a glass. "So, what shall we drink to with this lovely stuff?"

"How about, to a very safe, uncomplicated trip home?"

He was looking for a reaction, and found it in her eyes.

"Alright, to a safe trip. I hope I have one." She sipped the champagne. "This is wonderful. Sit down while I put the other bottle in the refrigerator. Do you really have a friend at Intourist?"

"More like a business associate." He stretched out in the chair and lit a cigarette, watching her. Was she going to spend their precious time together pumping him for that idiot Kostia's sake?

She sat opposite him, smiling. "Yes, I rather assumed it was business, but what kind? Does this Intourist person import your *Guardian* weeklies?"

"No. We really haven't started working together yet." On impulse, he said, "Let me tell you about it, and we'll see if you think it's a good plan."

He outlined the details of the Intourist scheme, and when he finished she was frowning the way he'd hoped she would. "Just how illegal would that be?"

"Very," he grinned. "Intourist memos are confidential. They might be called secret government documents."

"Then of course you shouldn't do it. Are you mad?"

"Maybe." He gazed back evenly. "Are you?"

The color in her cheeks deepened. "What do you mean?"

"Only that it's dangerous to have the wrong papers here. As you've just agreed. I know all about your friend Kostia, and what those people are up to. Tell me one thing. Is he your lover?"

"Of course not!" She was indignant. "And what do you mean, you know all about him? Have you been spying on us?"

Pouring them both some more champagne, he swallowed half a glassful. "A little bit. If somebody checks up on me, the least I can do is return the favor. Listen, can we get this over with? I don't want to spend all night dancing around. Why don't you just say what you need, and I'll see what I can do about it."

Drawing up her knees, she curled back into the chair. "Damn you, Tor. I wish I could."

"You have to! Do you think I'd turn you in? And as you may have noticed, trying to weasel things out of me doesn't work at all. It just makes me mad, Comrade, and if you do want my help I'd advise you not to do that. Here—" He put the full glass in front of her. "Drink this and then get it off your chest."

"I don't have permission to tell you, though. Oh hell, everything's going too fast." She ran her hands through her hair. "If I do, Tor, will you promise not to repeat a word of this, ever?"

"Not even if they torture me with boiled sausages for five more years. Come on, Liz, I'm trying to be your friend."

"Alright. I suppose I can't afford to wait much longer anyway. You're right, I do need your help very badly, and tomorrow night might be too late."

But while she was talking, his smile of encouragement faded. They must all be crazy. He'd thought it would be a message, a handful of letters, maybe a couple of essays. This was a book—and it might as well be a bomb. If Elizabeth were caught, she wouldn't go to any prison where English diplomacy could reach her. In fact, she'd probably disappear in a blue puff of KGB smoke. He was furious. How could she be so naive?

He said, "Why don't you just blow up Moscow? It would save you a lot of trouble."

"What?" She studied his face. "Well, that's nice. Thanks, but I'm not trying to save trouble."

"You don't know what you're doing." The shock had made his voice cold, and now her eyes were narrowing, resentful. So what had she been expecting, applause? He stood up to walk around the room. "I see, that's what all this mess is about. You thought you could hide it in your typewriter case or something. What did you want to trade your tape recorder for, an invisible briefcase with wings? Or was that just a lie to get me over here."

"I didn't know you, Tor. I didn't know if I could trust you."

"And now you don't have much choice, right? You really think I'm stupid, don't you. Maybe you were hoping I'd tell you the name of my Intourist friend in my sleep. Oh no, forgive me, I forgot! Then you'd have to be in bed with me and that would probably kill you."

"It doesn't seem to have hurt anyone else." She folded her arms. "Look, this other thing had to come first. I'm sorry I couldn't tell you straight off, but I'm not the only person involved."

"Yes, except you're the one who has to get past customs, which is crawling with KGBs. You can't bribe them for something like this. Do you know what they'll do to you if you're caught, or haven't you thought about that?"

"Of course I have! And I won't be. If there isn't any good way..."

"Good way? How could there be a good way?" Cursing, he punched the back of his chair. "Do you have any idea what happens to girls in prison, if you should live that long? If your pals are so crazy to get this out, why don't they do it themselves?"

"Because they can't get exit visas, Tor, remember? If you don't want to help me, fine. I'll do it on my own."

"Help you what? Be killed? Playing their stupid games?" He saw her, suddenly, surrounded by men, their hands moving toward her.... "I just can't stand to see you used!" He added lamely, "You're so sweet."

"Sweet?" She jumped up, glaring at him. "Is that your opinion of me? And you of all people talk about stupid games? Let me tell you about Yelena's 'game.' She used to be an editor of *Novy Mir*—the most important literary journal in the country. She was published all the time then, and sat on the Board of the Writers Union—meaning she had real power. Did you ever hear of Sinyavsky and Daniel?"

Tor shook his head. Her eyes glittered and her folded hands were very white.

"In 1966, they were sentenced to long terms at hard labor for publishing work in Europe under pseudonyms. Obviously, since they used false names, they knew they were being bad boys, right? A clear admission of guilt. Some other writers, including Yelena, protested. And they were ruined. The only way to get published in this bloody country is by going through the Writers Union, the Department of Culture, etcetera, etcetera, with censorship supplied for free by your friendly KGB. For the past twelve years, she's been printing her work illegally. They call that samizdat—self-publishing. She jokes that it lets her be her own editor, publisher and censor, but it means she has no real audience, and most of her poetry isn't even political. On top of that, she's already had to sign three warnings. So now with this psychiatric rubbish, she'll probably be locked up for five or ten years. Do you call that a stupid game?"

"Alright," he said, "I apologize. This Yelena's a hero. I still don't see what you've got to do with it."

"Fine." Elizabeth collapsed in a chair. "It has nothing to do with me. Forget it."

"Not until you do." Crouching, he looked into her face. "Wouldn't your father rather have you than this book?"

"Oh, please," she said sarcastically, "I only asked what you'd do in my place, not for a lecture on sentiment. I'm doing this *for* my father, Tor, can't you understand that? I said, if you don't want to help me, that's fine."

"You mean he'd let you risk getting arrested? He wants you to? That's the craziest thing I've ever heard." Tor stood up to get the second bottle of champagne. He had almost said: What kind of father is that? Daddy-jan would never ask Saira to do such a thing, not in a million years. Didn't anyone else care for Elizabeth more than this stupid manuscript?

The cork's wire fastener broke off in his hand and he told himself to quiet down, but he couldn't see any way of reversing the stands they each had taken. How could he cooperate? His own success came from measuring risk, and this was one he would never buy. Once you got into customs there were no exits in case the air smelled wrong, and that was an instinct it took years to sharpen. He turned. "How big did you say the thing is?"

She glanced up, surprised. "About five hundred pages. Probably the size of that dictionary."

"Oh. Great." Neither was there any place to dump a package that size. So there could be no fall-back plan—also a chance he'd never take. But he should have pretended to go along, suggesting and eliminating one trick, then another, until she herself gave up. Getting mad had only made her more determined.

She was thinking. She'd dream up something. And he was sure it wouldn't be good enough.

For the moment, he'd have to go along.

The cork popped and a geyser of champagne bubbled over his fingers. Elizabeth gave a half smile. Go with that.

He grinned back, filling the glasses. "Partner, a toast! To our first collaboration. I hope it's not our last."

"Tor!" She sat up straight. "Do you mean it?"

"Well—" He shrugged. "*If* you can get your hands on the thing, I'll give it my best shot. The trouble is, you're not a professional. You don't have the right tools. I'll inventory my equipment and see what I can come up with, but I wouldn't set your hopes too high. If Kostia hasn't been able to get into this Yelena's apartment so far, what makes you think he will by tomorrow? Once he knows you're leaving he'll probably break his neck trying, though. You'd better think about that too, Comrade." Perching on the arm of her chair, he handed her a glass. "What time are you supposed to meet him?"

"Around noon. Right after my history class."

"Then I'll meet you back here at four o'clock and we'll have a little class of our own. Only if there's a good way, remember, but I think I'll find one."

And if I don't, he thought, you won't have time to find a bad one. Because you won't have been worrying about it meanwhile.

Elizabeth tipped her glass toward his. "To success, then! Oh, lord, Tor, you don't know what this means. I've been going around in circles for months."

"Then you have to relax. That's ninety percent of it. Let's both start, right now." He sipped the champagne, tasting it for the first time all evening. Sunlight in a meadow.

She was smiling at him mischievously. "What will you do for champagne in Afghanistan, poor thing?"

"Probably the same thing I do here. There's a very nice French embassy in Kabul." But his eyes were tracing the shape of her face, the fingers balancing an empty glass for him to fill again. She had been insulted when he called her sweet, as if that were the same as weakness. But she *was* sweet, and strong, she was the only girl in five years whom he liked as much as wanted. They could have so much fun together if she weren't leaving, here in this room on weekends and walking all over the city. Maybe she'd come back, if the Soviets never figured out who smuggled the manuscript, but even so, she probably wouldn't want him. She must have a boyfriend in England who was studying to be a lawyer, and it was only because she still needed him that she was looking at him like this.

Bending, he kissed her very gently, her cheek, then her soft mouth open with surprise. "I feel like we've just been through the last Anglo-Afghan war, Comrade. Don't you think it's time our two countries started sharing love with each other?"

"I'll have to ask my ambassador," she chuckled. "Someday when I'm sober."

Her eyes were more blue than gray tonight, he saw, and relief or the champagne had brought some color to her skin. Putting down his glass, he held her face in both hands and kissed her, willing her to want him even if it was just for two days, because she had nothing to lose and it would make him so happy to pretend it was real. Then he knew he loved her. That was it, the same feeling of being sick and scared that he thought he had got rid of, and she was kissing him too now, her breathing slowing down, and he let his hand brush the tips of her breasts as he slid down beside her in the chair. "I'm crazy about you, Comrade."

"Oh, come on." She was embarrassed. "You've known me for all of one day."

"I've been keeping an eye on you for five months. Don't tell me what I know. I'm going to make love to you and then you'll see."

"No, Tor"—but her arms were around him. "I can't. It's too soon for me. Tomorrow I'd wake up and think I'd done it as my half of the deal."

"I don't care," he said. "It's the only chance we've got."

Things were spinning around inside him and he kissed her again, harder this time, stretching to fit against her so he could feel the whole warm length of her body, so aroused suddenly that he cursed the tight layers of cloth that separated them. Pressing her breast, he heard her gasp and slid his hand quickly under her sweater, but she pulled away. "Tor, don't."

He left his fingers resting on the bare skin at the curve of her waist, "Why not? You want me too. Why shouldn't we?"

"Because I promised my father I wouldn't," she smiled. "Really, Tor, I have to go to bed soon or I won't be good for anything tomorrow."

"You promised your father? Is that supposed to be a joke?" He tipped her head back. "What are you talking about?"

"Nothing. I'm just saying I can't do this tonight. I'm too confused with everything else now. Please don't ask me."

She was beautiful, he thought, with her hair ruffled up and her lips so soft and red. It was easy to imagine how she'd look if she were really excited, flushed and quivering like Karima had been when he gave her pleasure. Since then he hadn't wanted to see anyone's face in bed, and again he felt a twinge of panic. Maybe it would be better not to make love to Elizabeth, if just watching her now made him ache; but it seemed impossible to let go of her so soon.

"Alright," he said. "Can I just stay here then? I'll sleep in this chair like a little dog."

"No, Tor, Nadia's coming at seven. If she found you here I don't think she'd be quite so glad to help me. Nadia's generous, but she's also very possessive about you."

"So it's better for me to suffer than her? I don't give a damn about Nadia."

"Yes, but I do. I have to. Besides, your card's at the desk and I can't risk getting in trouble tonight."

"But you wouldn't! I bribed the attendant."

"What? And they know you came up to my room?" She sat up. "Oh no, they could be just waiting to catch us."

She was really upset and he said, "Take it easy. I can still get my card before curfew. If you'll kiss me good night first, Comrade."

Drawing her down against him, he ran a hand along her back to rub some of the tension from her shoulders. "I ought to give you a massage. You can't be a good spy when you're like this."

"If only you could smuggle it for me," she laughed. "And I could stay here and take all your exams, right?"

He kissed her, holding her very close. "Elizabeth, why don't you change your mind?"

"No, please, Tor, you have to go. Let's not have a fight."

Her eyes were cool now, and he stood up abruptly. "Alright, fine, I'm leaving." What was he doing, anyway? He didn't need to be a beggar. She wanted him to take all kinds of chances for her without giving anything herself.

"Thanks. And thank you for jumping in this with me. It's the first time I haven't felt alone with it."

"Good. Go to bed now, and be careful tomorrow. I'll see you at four o'clock."

Closing the door behind him, he put on his coat and turned down the stairs.

She was all mixed up, he thought, that must be why she made such a big fuss about his card. But this manuscript... he was beginning to hate it. Was it so much more important to her than he was?

Yes, of course. That was why she had wanted to see him in the first place, it was the only reason, and if she liked him a little bit better now, that might just be from gratitude.

Or, he thought, it could even be a fake.

The snow was coming down in sheets, and when he stepped outside it lashed his face so hard he had to shut his eyes. He bent his head down, walking against the wind, stumbling in soggy drifts that were almost knee high already. At this rate it would take an hour to get back to the dorm.

Reaching inside his coat, he found the emergency flask of vodka he kept in a secret pocket. Champagne was no good against this cold. The vodka was old and tasted of metal, but he took a long swallow anyway. Elizabeth was probably cozy and half asleep by now, dreaming of Kostia and being a hero. How could anyone that smart be so gullible?

Five hundred pages. The size of a dictionary. He took another drink. What did she think, she could stuff that in her hat? But now she had him worrying about it for her, so she wasn't stupid after all. It was up to him to get her home safely.

Well, there was one way he could make sure of that.

If he informed on Kostia, though, she would really despise him. That would have to be a last-ditch tactic.

All that fuss about Nadia and his card, when he could feel how much she wanted him. It must have been years since she'd made love with anyone, the way she let go so fast in spite of herself. It would have been good for her, too. He could have made her more relaxed than if she'd slept for a week. Maybe tomorrow after he solved her problems, she'd like the idea better. She wasn't in love with him, naturally, but she might do it as a favor, a little reward for helping her with the manuscript.

The flask was cold against his lips, even the vodka was cold now, and he let it slide down his throat. Maybe she had figured all this out—to tease him just enough so he'd come back again. She was smart enough to play his games, make him fall in love with her and then say: If you love me you must never, never, never. What if her father wasn't even sick?

Yes, he thought, the whole thing could be a lie, just like one of his own tricks. After all, here he was out in the snow, as if touching her made him a criminal. She was probably toasting herself with champagne for having got him to jump through all her hoops. Then she could tell Kostia, "Yes, Tor's in love with me, he'll do anything for me now." And Sunday she could get on the plane with a little wave and thank him so much for being a good dog.

Only it wouldn't happen like that, not if he could help it. "No, Tor, if we made love I might think it was my part of the deal." Well, so what? Nothing was free. If she wouldn't love him one way, it would have to be another, but he'd keep his promise first. There must be some way to hide that manuscript.

And after that, they'd have a little party. But not an English tea party, he smiled. That was what they always tried, to make you "civilized" and make you forget about anything you might need yourself. Some vodka would keep him from doing that again.

He still had a key to Nadia's room. He could be waiting for her when she got back from holding hands with Kostia. Tomorrow night she wouldn't send him away, and if the manuscript was there she wouldn't dare make such a fuss when he came to take what he wanted in return.

Eleven

ELIZABETH STOOD looking up at Saint Basil's through snow so fine it was almost a mist, glittering when sunlight broke through the heavy gray blanket of clouds. She hadn't found a seat on the metro and the swaying of the car seemed to echo Professor Turchin's stream of questions after class. He'd met her father three or four times and had even returned some comments on a draft of the book Dad had started before he got ill. Was it finished yet, he wondered, or close to being done? Was there any way he could help with that? How long would she be gone?

She had thought he was really saying: Perhaps I can use your father's work. Is he dying? How soon will he die? And after twenty minutes his probing had made her frantic, as if by asking he could make it true.

Tomorrow I'll be on the plane, she thought, and Monday I'll be home again. Poor Mum, she's probably been living at that clinic. At least I can give her a rest.

Unless Dad was so critical that none of them would be able to sleep in any case. She could picture his face only as she had left it. How would he look now? It might be hard to keep her own eyes from showing the horror she was certain she would feel, though if she brought him Yelena's manuscript they would smile no matter what. Even if he had to pass it on to one of his colleagues, it would remain their most extraordinary contribution, and he and Yelena would both have the last laugh.

Except that the bloody manuscript was still in Yelena's kitchen, and Tor might not come up with a magic solution after all.

Shivering, she turned to start across the icy swath of Red Square, pulling her blue stocking-cap down over her ears. A queue had formed along the elaborate stonework facade of the GUM store, no doubt for the sale on nylon bags. Kostia had known it would be crowded since everyone in Moscow carried shopping bags to house the unexpected find, and nylon folded small, didn't rip and was always scarce. The bright clothes and appliances shown in the store windows were what Tor called pokazukha—only for display, which made this a safe meeting place. Desirable goods came through the black market or the Party's Bureau of Passes, so there was little chance of being seen by Nadia or her betters outside the GUM.

Glancing at her watch, she stamped her feet to keep them warm. Kostia always materialized like a genii, right behind her, and last week she was happy to be absorbed by this crush, to watch and eavesdrop inconspicuously. But today the mob seemed to push against her with small threatening gestures, ordinary chatter amplified to a roar. She had to force herself not to turn again looking for Kostia's scarecrow shadow, his frowning eyes and slightly crooked nose.

Slowly, the queue wound into a three-tiered arcade as long as a soccer field. In the center, fountains reflecting light from the glass roof were circled with people eating a second Saturday breakfast, filling the cavernous space with noisy talk. Stalls on either side were dimly lit by chandeliers suspended from mirrored ceilings, and she smiled remembering that Tor had called this "the five-year-plan bazaar, Comrade, where they unload all the junk made in three days to fill some factory's monthly quota. They keep it dark so no one can see what trash they're about to buy."

Behind her the queue was swelling with shoppers who joined first and then asked what was for sale. Now she heard a rumor being passed down from the front: There were no bags left! They had all been sold! Someone grabbed her elbow, saying harshly, "It's as usual! Come on, there's no point in waiting," and looking up she found Kostia's thin angry face nodding toward the door.

He kept hold of her arm. "Do what I say and don't ask any questions yet. See that green car? When we get in, lie on the backseat as if you're tired. Where we're going is secret, understand?"

The Zhiguli stood at the curb with its motor running, and the driver did not turn to greet her. Kostia climbed in beside him, and as they pulled away she stretched and slid down on the seat.

For the first fifteen minutes she tried to keep track—out of Red Square down Gorky Street, turning west, but then it seemed they had come back onto Gorky again. Kostia said pointedly, "Moscow is circles, so we go around and around," and after that she watched blue sky as they drove quickly through the city. "He takes the chaika lane." Kostia chuckled. "He thinks he's a nachelstvo now, one of the bosses." The other man said nothing.

She guessed they were heading toward the aeroportski region, where the

Writers Union had communal apartments, but then the car stopped suddenly beside an ancient wall. The old quarter, possibly quite near Red Square. Kostia said, "We're at the door. Please keep your eyes closed, Elizabeth. The less you see, the safer for you." She felt his hand shielding her head as she climbed out, then guiding her up three steps. A bell rang. They were in a hall. Then a second door opened.

The familiar ironic voice said, "Hello, little English. Are you having a nice thriller?"

She opened her eyes to see Yelena leaning against a mantel with a glass in her hand, grinning. "Yes, that's right, it's me." A new pallor emphasized her green eyes and generous red mouth, but her chestnut hair was glossy above a thick brown sweater and there were no visible signs of the torture Elizabeth had imagined in her worst nightmares.

"So, I'm still alive!" Yelena came to kiss her, spilling vodka on them both. "Come, have a drink to celebrate. I don't know if it's night or day anymore. Kostia, let me kiss you too!" They were embracing with Russian fervor, and Yelena said, "Let's be grateful for now!" with such emotion that Elizabeth's laughter trembled close to tears.

Yelena cupped her cheek, "It's good to see you again. I'm sorry about the KGB tactics, but I'd like at least one day of freedom. Come, we'll drink. You sit here. Kostia, get some food and I'll open the other bottle." While she rummaged in a satchel, Elizabeth looked around the room.

It was part of a pre-Revolution apartment, more intact than most, but as crowded. In one corner, a clothesline dangled laundry over a sink filled with dishes. The floors were stained to a greenish gray, the walls gouged beneath their covering of tattered opera posters. The couch no doubt became a bed at night, another cot stood along the wall, and every flat surface was stacked with books—Greek drama to astrophysics. The curtains were drawn. Two floor lamps cast an eerie yellow glow.

Kostia handed her a glass of vodka, smiling for the first time since she'd known him. His eyes were a lighter brown than Tor's, and clearer. "Fresh bread, cheese, and..." Reaching into his jacket pocket, he took out a small tin. "This!" He watched as Yelena opened it, uncovering small luminous black beads.

"Caviar? Kostia!" Yelena turned to her. "Do you like this?"

"Oh, yes," she smiled, though she had rarely invaded the huge tins Nadia kept in their refrigerator.

Yelena held up her glass. "A toast! To Dr. Valentin Panov, of the Serbsky Institute of Forensic Psychiatry, who's trying against all odds to be an honest man. I might say, against all reason, but at the Serbsky, lunacy reigns. You know about this place, Elizabeth?"

She nodded. "How on earth did you get out of there?"

"First, we drink. To the Doctor!" She tossed the shot back, chasing it with bread. "Poor Panov was encouraged to diagnose me insane. That way, no public trial, no embarrassment. But what am I, psychotic? Schizophrenic? Maybe a little neurotic, I won't deny that. Slightly paranoid, after so many searches. That's all he would say. And it's not enough to lock me up right now and forever. He must be crazy himself, that man."

"I'll send him a basket of fruit," Kostia smiled.

Yelena touched his hand. "Kostia, that only means I'm here with you right now. By tomorrow, my case will have been reviewed by a more ... cooperative doctor, and I'll be back there bribing orderlies to bring me vodka. In fact, they'll probably pick me up as soon as I go home, and maybe Dr. Panov will be committed as well. I can't think how he came to be working at that place."

"But what sort of trial could there be?" Elizabeth asked. "If they haven't found the manuscript, what else could they charge you with?"

"Impeding the development of some other case." Yelena shrugged. "But it won't come to that. Insanity is easier, you see? They might believe I'm insane too, I laughed so hard when they came to get me. Five little men in blue raincoats, tearing up my house! Then we visited Major Malov, Senior Investigator of Heretics like myself. Major Malov is very fat, and he has a big desk. He says sweetly, 'Yelena, this isn't your problem. Someone else gave you this problem. Now pass it to me, and we can reinstate you in the Writers Union. You'll be able to eat at the Writers Club again! And wouldn't your sick mother like to see you published once more before she dies? Yes, we know about your mother. We even know you ripped your dress and swore about it this morning.' And all the time he was yammering I could hardly keep from grinning, because the night before that, Kostia had come over the roof to visit me and we had a big fight about the manuscript right in front of their little bug." Laughing, she spilled caviar on the table. "Kostia wanted to take it away, and I wouldn't let him."

"But I was right," he smiled. "They did pick her up. I couldn't yell at her, of course, we were passing a pad back and forth. But I almost punched her in the nose, I was so angry."

"You were being unreasonable," Yelena said mildly. "Now, have some more caviar. See how nicely I've piled them this time? Only a madman would drop caviar, or refuse a chance to eat at the Writers Club with Yevtushenko."

The oranges Elizabeth had eaten for breakfast were no defense against vodka. Caviar was better, with moist black bread smelling of earth, and she ate hungrily to calm a sense of unreality. At two o'clock in the afternoon they were drinking vodka by lamplight, while Yelena laughed at the prospect of being committed to that place?

And now, Elizabeth thought, I have to tell them I'm leaving and spoil the party completely. But we'll have to move quickly if they still want to try to get the manuscript out.

She said, "I didn't know your mother was sick. That puts us in the same boat. My father's very ill now, and I have to go back to London. Probably late tomorrow morning."

"No! You've heard from home? Oh, Elizabeth, I am very sorry. Forgive me, I should have asked about him right away, but you see? These monsters make me a monster. Asher can't leave us yet. What does your mother say?"

"Only that I should come. The question is, what do you want to do about it? I'm willing to try to be courier if you can get the manuscript to me."

Yelena's face was slowly registering the news. "Tomorrow morning. But how could you carry it?"

"I'm not sure yet. Listen, I've done something you won't like, so I may as well just tell you. Kostia, do you know Tor Anwari?"

He looked perplexed. "Everyone at the university does. Why?"

"What do you think of him?"

"Well—" Kostia smiled. "If Tor were Russian and not a drunk, he'd probably be on the Central Committee by now."

She turned to Yelena. "Tor's a smuggler. A very clever one, and I'd been hoping I could ferret out some of his conduits on my own. Then I got my mother's cable. I thought there was still a chance Kostia could get into your kitchen, so I took Tor into my confidence last night and he said he'd find some way to help me. I believe him, but we can't be absolutely sure he'll come through, and he needs the manuscript first. He has to see how big it is."

"So." Yelena's brows knit. "Is he...sympathetic?"

"Politically?" She shook her head. "He's just perverse on principle. He'd try it for the challenge, not for love." Then she wondered if that were true.

Yelena fished a battered pack of cigarettes out of her pants pocket. "Perversity can be useful at times. But this Tor, can he be trusted? What do you say, Kostia?"

He was gazing down at his folded hands as if they contained an answer. "Not to talk? I guess so. He lies amazingly even when he's drunk. But Yelena, I've tried to break into your rooms, and those shutters are so strong your neighbors always stuck their heads out to see what the racket was. You'd have to give me your key."

"Wait, now. We need to think about this. People risked their lives stealing those records. I'm not sure I want to hand them over to some drunken smuggler I've never met." She got up to put a kettle on the hot plate. "First, we must balance one risk against the others. For me, the cards are dealt and maybe for Kostia too by now, but I owe Asher Sutcliffe too much to lose his daughter for him. On the other hand, with these damned Olympics coming, no place in Moscow will be safe soon, so the timing of this might almost be a blessing." Lighting a cigarette, she exhaled a gust of smoke. "Besides, I have no one else to leave it with."

"That's not true." Kostia sounded hurt. "I could hide it somewhere."

"But for how long? And if you were arrested, it might be as good as lost. Oh, Elizabeth, if only you could get the documents out! I don't care so much about the analytic section. I haven't finished editing the biographies anyway, and that part's harmless by itself—the ravings of a lunatic. But those records ...do you see how important they are? Most of the 'cases' they describe are people known to the world, and it's time the world found out what's happened to them. Not one little report here, another leak there, so people can fool themselves that these are isolated incidents. The Americans are pushing human rights now. This is just the moment for the West to hear our story. And if they're going to lock me up anyway, I'd like to be slightly guilty."

Yes, Elizabeth thought, so when they shoot you full of sulfazine it will at least be bearable. She said, "Please let me try, Yelena. Nobody suspects me yet, and I really want to do it. If my father could, he would. The KGB must know the manuscript exists, since they talked about your 'problem,' so if I can get it out perhaps they'll leave you alone. Why close the barn door after the horse has gone? Some publicity in London could protect you."

"Hah!" Yelena laughed. "I'm not Sakharov, you know! No, I thought I might stay here and have a holiday for a few days before they collected me again, but now I'm wondering if they didn't let me out on purpose. I can be very stupid sometimes. No one followed me here, I made sure of that, so you're still safe, Elizabeth. And if you want to be an idiot like the rest of us, alright. I've made up my mind. This is our only chance, so we have to take it."

Turning away, she poured boiling water into a teapot. "Listen to me, Kostia. I'm going home. And at the same time you'll come over my roof, and the minute I get inside I'll hand it out to you. Even if there is a little man in a blue raincoat waiting on my doorstep. Then you'll bring it to Elizabeth quickly as you can, and we'll see if her friend can find a way to hide it."

Kostia went to take the pot from her. "No. You'll give me your key. You can't go back there now. I won't let you!"

"Oh? And who are you to give me orders? Don't you be silly too. My building's being watched, and if they see you go in they'll come right after you. I'm too old to crawl across the roof myself, can you picture that? No, Kostia, you'll do as I tell you." Her face was grim, and then suddenly she threw her arms around him. "Don't you see I can't lose you either? You're my one link to the world. You're the only one here who will know what happened to *me*."

His shoulders sagged and Yelena pressed her cheek against his. "My friend, do you think I want you on my conscience? Why postpone the inevitable, when by giving up the battle we can win it. Do you really want to spend three days talking about what a pair of fools we were to let this opportunity go by?"

"But what if Tor doesn't find a way?" he said. "Couldn't we ask him first?"

"Elizabeth's said he needs to see it. That makes sense to me. And if they can't manage, we may as well toss it in the river."

Yelena stepped away from him. "Elizabeth, I want you to go now. From here, you must use your own judgment. It would be nice to bring your father this thing, but don't be an idiot. He needs you even more than we do. If you can't carry it, leave your curtains closed tomorrow morning and Kostia will come around to get it again. Put on your coat now," she said abruptly. "Let's not waste any more time."

When Elizabeth had slipped into her parka, Yelena came to zip it up. "If you do succeed, and they trace the manuscript to you, they won't let you back into the country. I'm going to give you just the documents, but if by some chance you can come back here, I'll try to leave the rest with Kostia or someone else and they'll contact you. I don't think you and I will meet again, little English. At least"—she smiled—"not this year. Maybe next year, in Jerusalem, eh? No, Elizabeth, don't say anything more. Just go. And tell your father I send him a Russian kiss."

Giving her a hard hug, Yelena pushed her toward the door. Kostia called to her, "I'll come late tonight. Don't go to sleep." But his voice broke, and she did not turn to look at him when she said good-bye.

Outside, snow was billowing in the gray air and she was startled by the Zhiguli pushing up in front of her. The driver said, "Get out of sight, please," and she slid down in a daze, thinking that now Yelena and Kostia would probably make love, which somehow didn't seem strange in spite of the twenty-year difference in their ages.

No, that was crazy, of course they wouldn't. Yelena must just want to calm him down. Or was that a comforting, puritanical British rationalization? Perhaps despair was erotic, because last night it had felt very good kissing Tor Anwari, and given one more glass of champagne she could quite easily have gone to bed with him. Two days ago that would have been unimaginable.

Now they were all three dependent on Tor, who didn't care a bean for the substance of what they were doing. His family must be pro-Soviet if they'd sent him to school in Moscow, but Tor clearly was not, so how could he be so indifferent? Still, if he were in her place he'd have come up with something by now, and maybe he cared more than he let on. Why else would he help her when she was leaving and could offer nothing in exchange?

He didn't love her. How could he, after so little time? But he had a streak of tenderness he took pains to hide even from himself, as if behaving well would represent some kind of capitulation to the Soviets—which might be true, for all she knew about Afghan politics. Maybe doing this would give him an alternative to drowning himself with drink. It would be interesting to ask at what point in his five years here the Black Wasp had been created.

Snow was streaking by the windows as the Zhiguli turned onto Gorky Street, wet heavy snow that would be hard to move. What if Kostia brought the manuscript and the airport had closed? Then she might have to hold it, hide it for a day or so, and Nadia would be back in the room tomorrow.

Moscow

Well, Tor could probably find an answer to that too. It was odd, since Thursday she had never once doubted his ability to do the job, given enough time and the inclination. Tor had his own sense of honor, though it was hard to decipher at first, and last night she had fallen asleep quickly for a change, feeling stronger for his company.

I must trust him as a person, she thought, not just as a smuggler, or else I wouldn't have kissed him, so why did I make him leave? Was I actually afraid of being distracted today, or did I want to prove I'm not easy?—as if anyone here would care. Because he was right when he said I wanted him too.

Rara avis. Skin the color of sun on the cliffs at Cornwall. Half the women in Moscow weren't blind. He was lovely to look at. But until last night he had held the same attraction as a Russian lacquerware box—something exquisite to examine, not desire. Then after a bottle of champagne some wall of resistance to him dropped away, and the real warmth in his brown eyes had let her enjoy their bit of cramped passion in Nadia's chair. Tor knew what to do with his slender body, and perhaps that's what had put her off—his list of conquests, which might have left her feeling like just another notch on his belt. But it wouldn't have been that way.

"I'll let you off at the next corner," the driver said. "Sit up now."

It was darker than she had realized looking up through the snow. Her watch read five o'clock. Tor would have gone to her room an hour ago and had probably been worried not to find her there. How soon would he come back?

Thanking the driver, she stepped out into a bank of freezing slush. It would be fascinating to see what Tor had found to disguise the manuscript. He was proud of his work—proud, period. Sending him off last night had made him angry, and she'd thought: Tough luck, you twit, I'm not a piece of merchandise to trade.

But that had been her own pride speaking and it was beginning to seem a luxury, belonging to a different world of fine distinctions where time could be spent carelessly. Seeing Yelena and Kostia today had been a lesson that had nothing to do with politics.

Twelve

TOR'S EYES SLID over to Elizabeth's clock. Dark, almost six, she was two hours late, the liar. It didn't matter now. Put down the bottle and get started.

Soft black and helpless under his hands, woman's hair, a female sheep. Metal shears rasping, one point, two, closing in a beautiful crunch...furrows of naked scalp surprised, embarrassed, screaming, "Toryalai!"

Too bad. You can't stick it back again. Never.

He smiled at the dark cloud. Now he would have it—cover his face with her hair. Elizabeth's bed came up to meet his shoulder, knocking him into the vodka. Black floated up all around.

His face was wet. The hair stuck. Smelled wrong. Last night it was like incense. Gray eyes. Mummy's eyes. Never, never, never.

"I promised my father I wouldn't do this."

Saira's fingers clasped the bottle. "It's cognac, Tor, not whiskey."

"Karima and Nadir have named their son Zia...."

Cool night air from the garden shining on soft hair, again.

Saira smiled. "A *great* love, Tor?"

"My dear sister, I beg you to forgive me...."

"Dear Saira, Five letters now and still you haven't answered."

Gray eyes, laughing at him. "I promised my father I wouldn't." But he wanted her too much to understand then. "I do need your help...please go. You have to leave." So cool. "Go away, Tor. Go."

She'd made a fool of him. He let her. Bigger fool. The scissors winking, hard and sharp. Good, he'd show her this time, the liar!

Scraping in the door lock. Six o'clock, exactly! Opening, gray eyes in a pale face, different, some kind of disguise? A blue cap to hide her hair, showing little bones, so sweet, how did she know? Like a towel...Saira's towel, all her feathers wet and laughing...that mole by her ear, she'd been hiding that too, but he saw it now.

Gray eyes, widening. "What's...wrong?" Her wrists felt thin enough to break like straw. Good, let her hurt this time. "What's that...on your shirt?" She pulled off the cap, hair falling on white skin, the door slammed—an explosion in his skull.

"Tor!" Her smile was coming apart. "Drunk?" She squinted—he'd seen that before too. "What have you done? Oh, Tor!"

Oh, Toryalai!

"...help with your coat..." His hands at her neck and ripping, spinning against the bed. Her face was even whiter. Good. "What's the matter, scared? Afraid your game didn't work?"

Backing away from him. Right. He was right. Her face twisting as he crept toward her, slowly. She knew what was going to happen.

"Tor! How could you?"

Oh, she was disgusted?

Smiling, "I haven't done anything, yet."

To distract him—"But your coat...all that..."

He grabbed her wrists, turning them hard. "We made a deal, right? But I'm expensive, whore. You didn't pay enough."

A wail. "You're hurting me, Tor! You're drunk! Are you mad as well?"

He let go a wrist to slap her face, the pink mark reddening. "Drunk? And who makes me? Your cognac, you liar!"

Bending to cover her head with a shriek. "What are you talking about?" Yes, she was getting it now.

The bed. He pushed her backward. "Liar! You love me, sure. Until a better plug comes along. Make love, why not, if it gets what you want. Then marry someone else, you liar!"

Catching her ankle with his foot, he knocked her onto the bed. Gray eyes, so close, white all around them, breasts heaving under his chest...she thought she could fool him. They all did, but he knew.

Her voice in little gasps, wheedling, "Tor! I don't understand! What are you saying? Oh, no, look!" Her eyes bulged toward the door.

His followed and her knee jackknifed, pain between his legs. Rolling, he grabbed her arms, her shoulders, but his jaw snapped back hard...her knee, then he was falling, something slamming his temple again and again.

She was sitting on him, pinning his arms with her knees and shaking his head by the ears. "You stupid little shit! What, were you trying to rape me? Who the hell do you think you are? Or I am?"

Two of her, slowly meeting now. He glared. "Get off me, cow."

"No, you tell me what the devil's going on! How did you get in here to begin with!"

Not frightened anymore. Self-righteous. Sitting on him like a whore.

"You planned it all, didn't you? Sweet Elizabeth! Who helped you? Your father, who's supposed to be so sick? Or your little boyfriend, Kostia?" But his voice was shaking. Fool.

Her mouth hung open, crookedly. "Planned what?"

"To use me! Don't lie anymore. You promised your father you wouldn't make love to me though, but you even lied to him. Are you so late because you were fooling around with Kostia too?"

She let go of his ears. "So that's it. You were jealous, so you got drunk? You really are predictable, aren't you. Just for the record, Tor, I never said anything about love last night, let alone marriage."

His head throbbed sickeningly. Now the words didn't seem to fit. "Not ...that. I didn't mean...you."

"Quite! And cognac? What was that all about?"

Spreading his fingers on the floor, he made his body rigid. "Why don't you just leave me alone."

She grabbed one ear again. "Don't worry, I will. But first, I want an explanation, damn you!"

Now he could see her clearly...pale hair, a hot red cheek. His throat closed and he tried to swallow. "You made a mistake, Comrade."

"Obviously. What did you do to your coat?"

The lump stayed, hopeless. "Just gave it a haircut." But it was Saira he had been remembering, the night of Mangal's wedding—knocking over the coffee table and seeing her face more shattered than the crystal globe by his feet. Yes, it was coming back now for the first time since...this was the only time he had been so drunk since then, and now Elizabeth's eyes, furious, not hurt, as if she saw what had happened too.

He raised a hand to touch her cheek, but dropped it in midair. Saira had never forgiven him. Never.

She was shaking her head. "Oh, what difference does it make. I must have been mad myself, to count on you at all." Climbing off him, she picked up his coat. "Why don't you just clear out now. I've got work to do."

Elizabeth...

He sat up in a panic. "Wait!" There was still one chance. "Let me show you...I figured out how you can carry that thing." He sounded weak, despicable. Too weak even to leave.

"After this? Thanks, Tor, but I'll manage on my own."

"No!" Grabbing the edge of the bed, he stood, pain stabbing where she had kicked him. "So, I disappointed you. Fine. That's what I do best. Next best I'm a smuggler." He held his head to stop it spinning. "Don't be stupid. I don't want anything back."

"I thought I didn't pay you enough. For a whore, that is."

"Elizabeth..." He stepped forward, but she moved away. "You don't have to be afraid now. Let's do what we planned, please, or else it's a total loss. Please, you need... what I'm making. Punch me again if you want."

She was twisting the coat in her hand and suddenly threw it onto the bed. "Damn you, Tor! I'm really in a fix, and now this! First you say you love me, then you attack me, and now you tell me I need you. Not that much!"

"No," he said, "I didn't mean to hurt you, honestly. It's just... I do love you, but it's all mixed up."

"To put it mildly!" She was shouting, then turned quickly to put a record on and trumpet music tore into his skull. "You tell me what's changed since last night to make you act this way! I believed you last night. And I'm *not* stupid."

"Please..." He reached for her hand. "Let me try to explain. It might not make any difference, but... it wasn't you. Honestly it wasn't."

"What do you mean, not me? I don't understand any of this. You frightened ... your craziness frightens me, Tor. You shouldn't drink at all."

"I haven't really been drunk in five years, Comrade. Will you listen to me for one minute? I just started to remember something, and I think I'll lose it again if I don't talk about it."

After a moment she shrugged. "Alright. Since I really want to know." Sitting down in one of the armchairs, she lit a cigarette. "Go ahead, I'm listening."

His cheeks burned as he paced the room. Never would she love him after this. Karima... all that seemed clear enough, but when he thought about Saira it was confusion. He barely recalled Mangal hitting him, then falling into the table, blood on his shirt, but what happened before that he could piece together only from things other people had told him. He had shown Ashraf Saira's letter from Jeffrey, so the next day Saira left Kabul and Ashraf's father died of a heart attack, so Ashraf married his cousin... but that wouldn't make sense to Elizabeth. If he started at the beginning, going through it bit by bit, maybe he would remember better.

"It doesn't matter," he said. "But I fell in love with you last night, Comrade. That's only happened once before, with the daughter of our servants at home, and everyone in my family treated it like a dirty joke."

An hour later, ten cigarettes had burned from red to ash in the darkening room. Elizabeth watched him, keeping back her questions, but toward the end she had to hold the arms of her chair to keep from going to him. All this time he'd been punishing himself for something he couldn't even remember doing when he was eighteen and drunk for the first time. It was terrible, what he'd done—no wonder his sister hated him for it—but it wouldn't have been fatal if his brother hadn't got involved in that coup and this Ashraf's father hadn't been so ill. Those parts weren't Tor's fault... unless the heart attack was brought on by the letter. And wouldn't the coup have been a bad shock too?

She said, "So Ashraf married his cousin because his father told him to? Maybe he didn't love your sister very much after all, then."

Tor shook his head. "Ashraf's the eldest and he has a lot of sisters. His father asked him to get married quickly for the sake of the family, and by that time Saira was gone."

"But his father couldn't have known that, if it all happened on the same day. So it must have been Saira he meant Ashraf to marry. Do you really think Ashraf would have told him about that letter while he was on his deathbed? You didn't kill him, Tor."

He was standing with his back to her and his whole body looked clenched. "I don't know. So what? I still ruined Saira's life. If it weren't for me, she wouldn't have left Kabul."

"Then why didn't Ashraf go after her? Is it such an unforgivable crime that she had a boyfriend in college?"

"But he did try to find her! He wrote to her at my grandparents' in Boston, but she didn't go there. No one heard from her for months. It turns out she was staying with some Indian friend of hers in Cambridge, and by the time she got his letters, he'd married his cousin. That's traditional at home, and I'm sure his uncle pushed him into it, since Ashraf's side of the family has more money. He probably told Ashraf it was his sacred duty to honor his father's dying wish."

"Oh, lord." Elizabeth switched on the lamp, wondering what Tor's sister must be like. He said she was living in New York and working at the United Nations now, so she couldn't have been completely destroyed. And if she was as pretty as he claimed, she must have found someone else to love. It was difficult to imagine wanting to marry the boy next door after four years of being away, but in England lots of people did that too.

She said, "Well, you haven't been home much either since then. Perhaps next summer you could meet there again and make all this up. It really is a shame, when you were so close."

"No. You don't understand." Turning, Tor gave her a pained little smile, "Saira won't go back to Afghanistan. Girls like her are supposed to get married, and then if they want to do some work, it might be alright. But not alone. Kabul isn't London, Comrade. She couldn't rent an apartment there and go out on dates, and she wouldn't want to live with my father. I don't blame her. I don't either, and I'll have to after next year. Anyway, Saira isn't my only problem. It's all of them. See this?"

He drew a gold chain from the neck of his sweater. A crescent of glass hung suspended from it, and she stood up to take a closer look. "So that's what was sticking into me last night." There was a white fragment of something that looked like carved ivory imbedded in the pendant. She made a guess. "Is this part of that globe you said you smashed?"

"Very good," he nodded. "My mother had one of these made for each of us. When she sent it, I didn't know that. I thought she was trying to make me feel guilty."

"You're doing a fine job of that by yourself. Look, everybody does things they regret. You can't let something that happened five years ago run the rest of your life. Get over it, by doing better things, and I don't mean just on your family's terms. You've managed to survive here all this time without swallowing the Party line."

"That's easy for you to say. You like being good. I don't see anything to like or want. But you." He dropped the necklace back into his sweater. "Besides, I wasn't sent here to learn the Party line. It's my punishment, and in 'all this time' none of them has cared about me."

"Well, I do. And I'm sure when you go home again you'll find a niche of your own. You've certainly done that here."

"Shhh..." He covered her mouth with his hand. "You don't know. Come visit me in Kabul someday, and we'll see if you can find a place for me."

Moving her head, she kissed him. "I might just do that."

But he stood with his arms stiff by his sides. "Stop it. I feel like a beggar."

"Why? Because of what you just told me? I like you better right now than I ever have, Tor." It was ironic, she thought, that Tor had always seemed so free, almost oblivious to the rules that worried everyone else in Moscow, when in fact he felt crushed by a set of expectations she would have imagined he'd cheerfully ignore.

He pulled her hair gently. "You British always sent your misfits to Asia, Comrade. At least, until the empire started disintegrating. Maybe I should be the first one to work that in reverse."

"Be my guest."

"I just might do that."

"Now will you tell me what you've done to your coat?"

"Ah..." He smiled. "It's my best invention, but it still might not be good enough. I don't think there's room to pad the sleeves. See, we cut the fur off, shave the hides, and then sew in your papers and glue the fur back on top of them."

"You mean, I should wear it home?" She looked from Tor to his coat, then back again. "You know, it just might work. The manuscript will only be half as long as I said. But Tor, your beautiful coat..."

"Bring it back to me, Comrade. As soon as you can. Why don't you try it on now and we'll see where there's room to spare." He held it for her. "I'm sure they won't body search *you* at the airport. I'll give you my lighter too, and while they're going through your bags, you drop the lighter and pretend not to know you've done it. They'll be so eager to get their hands on it, they'll run you through on wheels." He stepped back. "There. You look like a princess."

"Hardly." But she had to smile at her reflection in Nadia's mirror. "It's very long on me, and much too elegant."

"Mmm…" He was bending to measure the hem. "We'll put most of the ...insulation down here, and a little in the shoulders. We'd better wait till we've got the manuscript to shave this, though, or we'll have fur all over the room. Are they going to bring it here to you?"

She nodded. "Kostia said he'd come late tonight."

Tor glanced at the clock. "It's only eight. Are you hungry? Shall I get you some dinner?"

His voice was soft and polite and she realized he was trying to behave "properly," just as she had last night, and after seeing his pain that seemed even more ridiculous and sad, as if he thought she would remember him best for the state of his manners. That must be how she had made him feel.

Taking off the coat, she folded it across the back of the chair and slid her arms around his waist. "I don't want dinner. I want to fool around. But Tor, if you ever raise your hand to any woman again, I'll know it, and I will find you and kill you."

"I swear I won't. I'm sorry. I'll never forgive myself, Comrade."

"No, don't turn me into your sister. I think you were just waiting for a chance to let those demons out, whether you know it or not, and if they're gone once and for all now, I'm glad I could help you somehow too. In a funny way, I think you trusted me to slap them down, or else you wouldn't have done it. So, I'm going to trust you. You may be used to sleeping with people you've known for two days, but I'm not."

"It isn't the same," he said. "I've never been with anyone who knows me. I'm just as scared as you are." Lifting her chin, he studied her face and then his arching lips came down to meet hers and she closed her eyes.

At first, he barely touched her with his mouth, the tips of his fingers, but then he crushed her tight against him. "I love you, Liz. Please say you believe me."

"Alright. I do. Shall we get in bed? I'm freezing."

As she bent to fold back the quilt his hands moved under her sweater, and straightening up, she let him slip it over her head.

"Yours too."

He pulled his own off, and rather shyly opened the clasp of her bra. "I knew you'd look like that."

"Like what?"

"A mermaid on a rock."

"How do you know about mermaids, Tor? Besides, my hair's too short." Smiling, she reached down for the lamp, but he stopped her arm. "No, don't."

"Then let me close the curtain. But I have to open it again later, remind me."

When she turned back he had got in bed and was holding up the covers.
"That's cheating."
"I'm a cheater. Come here, I'll get you warm."

The dark planes of his body looked exotic against the sheets. Kicking off her shoes, she went to lie beside him and he covered her with the blankets. "May I steal your jeans, Comrade? I can get a fortune for them." She lifted her hips and he pushed them down. "So much for the class system."

The lamplight made Tor's skin golden. He ran a finger up her arm, then slowly across her shoulder. "Why couldn't we have met before this? I wanted to. Did you?"

"I think so. I'm not sure."

"You thought I was the devil. Do you still?"

"Not such a bad one, anyway. Sort of a good one."

He took her hands, pressing them down against the mattress. "I don't want to be good." His lips moved along her cheek, her neck, then lower and she closed her eyes again. He seemed to want her to be still, to give her pleasure, and that was hard at the beginning without alcohol to blur the edges of her mind, but Tor did that himself, as if he knew her reservations, breaking them with a counterpoint of sharp and soft sensations that erased thought, brought her down into her body.

"Now the Afghan is invading England! You're mine," he said. "Admit it, Liz. And I'll admit the same."

But he kissed her so she couldn't speak, had no desire to speak.

His eyes were golden, teasing her, as if he knew . . . and he was lighting out for the territory, coming back with news. A thousand stars and his hot breath, Tor calling to her as if he were lost.

She lay curled with her head on his shoulder. "Do you always make so much noise? I thought they'd come knocking the door down."

"There's a first time for everything, Comrade," he grinned. "But you're right. I'll put on another record and get us a cigarette."

He came back with the sherry too, drinking it straight from the bottle. "Now you'll see what a barbarian I am."

"I suppose we should really get dressed."

"Oh, no. Are you afraid I'll go crazy again? I told you, I don't get drunk, just a little fogged up, and I'm too happy even for that tonight. Kiss me, and see if I don't taste good." Putting down the cigarettes, he slid in beside her. "We aren't finished yet. By the time we are, neither of us will be able to walk across the room." His hand moved to her waist, "I can't resist you, Comrade. I've never made love with the lights on before, and I never will again so I can always pretend it's you. Relax now, we have enough time for this . . . and this . . ."

A while later, he said, "Does Nadia still have all that food?"

"Yes." She laughed. "But I don't think I can walk across the room."

"I'll fix it. What would you like?"

"Anything. Everything. But I'll get up too, it's almost eleven."

"Then wear this sweater." Tor reached down into the pile they had knocked on the floor. "This rose one. I love it. And please don't wear your bra, you don't need it anyway."

She smiled. "Do you have any other instructions?"

"Only that you stay with me forever." He stood to put on his trousers. "Maybe I'll talk you into that some day."

Dressing, she watched him fuss over the food—neat little chicken sandwiches, a plate of fruit and cheese—whistling to himself as he arranged it on the table, then pouring out the sherry like a housewife serving tea.

"So, the Black Wasp has a domestic side."

Giving her a hug, he pulled her down on his lap in one chair. "You'd better eat it all, too, because I'm going to have you for dessert."

"Actually, I think I will. I'm ravenous. Would you please stop feeling me up? It's very distracting."

She was halfway through a second sandwich when it struck her. "Tor, it's awfully quiet for eleven. I wonder if the clock's stopped."

Getting up, she went to check it. "No, I'm wrong."

"About the clock, maybe." He had risen behind her and was looking out through the window. "But it's quiet, alright. Come here, and you'll see why. It looks like the North Pole out there."

His mouth tightened and she had started toward him when a knock came on the door.

"Let me," he said. "I'm in this too now."

"You aren't really jealous of Kostia."

"No."

But it wasn't Kostia whom Tor pulled into the room. Another student, blond, with frightened eyes behind thick glasses, clutched a damp green sack bulging with books.

She moved to turn up the music. "What's happened? Where's Kostia!"

"He's been arrested. I saw them take him, right outside my dorm. He came running in and asked me to bring this to you, and then he went out and they grabbed him. I'm going too now. I don't know what this is and I don't want to know." Shoving the bag at her, he spun toward the door but Tor caught his arm. "Wait. Who grabbed him?"

"The police! I told you!"

"But which... what color was the trim on their uniforms? Could you see? Was it blue?"

"I'm not sure. I think there was red on the shoulders. Now let go of me!"

Tor held the door, closing it behind him. "He's French, did you hear the accent? I wonder what Kostia's got on him."

"What difference does it make? Oh no, if they've arrested Kostia, they must have Yelena too."

"Not necessarily. Red epaulettes mean they're MVD—from the Ministry of Internal Affairs. There's just a chance they were after him for something else completely, since it wasn't the KGB. But you still have the hot potato, Comrade. Let's have a squint at it."

While she emptied the bag, he went to look down the hall, then out through the window again. "It's quiet on the eastern front so far."

Three science textbooks had been gutted, and the manuscript pages taped loosely inside. When she broke one seal, documents spilled out on the floor.

"What a mess," Tor said. "What is all that? It looks like they're all different sizes."

"They are." She glanced up. "Admission slips, treatment records, file notes. ... That's the whole point, they're originals, and now I've got them scrambled up."

He sat cross-legged opposite her. "That's alright. We'll have to put ones the same size in piles anyway, and fit them together like a puzzle. You can straighten it out in London. If you get to London. What I'd recommend is that you give this to me and I'll go bury it somewhere. I'm willing to bet the airport's closed and you'll lose your reservation. And if the MVD *was* after Kostia for this, they'll be here before noon anyway."

"No. I've got to try, Tor. If Kostia went to so much trouble to get it to me, he won't tell them where it is."

"Not even if they torture him?" He took her wrist. "Don't kid yourself. I can hardly stand being in this room with it myself. Elizabeth, let me get rid of it, please. I want you to see your father again, and maybe even me."

"Don't you think I do too? But this is the only chance now. I can't just back out when it's my turn to take some risks."

"Are you listening to me, Liz? Go look at that snow, and then tell me you'll get out of here tomorrow!"

"I could take the train. The Red Arrow always runs, and it leaves early."

He shook his head with disgust. "They search everything on it. At the border they come in and pull everything apart. It's not like the airport. I won't let you take it!"

Remembering Kostia, she smiled. "Are you trying to give me orders? No, Tor, you listen now. I'm sure what you're saying is right. I believe you. But I also believe I'm going to bring this to England with me—that I'll make it. You've told me how I can do it, and I believe it will work. Furthermore, I can do all that cutting and pasting on my own, so there's no need for you to be involved any more. I don't want you to get in trouble on my account. I'm sure when I go through customs, wherever, I'll be a total wreck, but right now I think I'm emotionally saturated. I feel like a horse with blinders on. I just want to go ahead. Why don't you leave me to it, and wish me luck."

His lips twisted. "Oh, sure. Do you think I would? Alright, if you're going to be stubborn, let's at least get this stuff off the floor. It will take a lot of time to fix the coat, and then the glue has to dry. Sort out those slips and I'll finish my barbering job."

Flushing angrily, he spread his coat open on the rug and started cutting off hanks of black fleece, laying them out side by side. It was as long and wavy as his own hair, and she laughed. "If there isn't enough, I could always scalp you." He grunted, and she bent her head to the scattered papers.

Three hours later she apologized for having said that she could do it all herself. It was two o'clock before the razor finished stripping away what the scissors had missed, and when the hide lay bare they calculated its area and laboriously stitched in the documents, concealing the new thread in the black embroidery. Tor ripped apart a bed sheet and sewed that in on top like a lining, and for another hour they sat hunched over, gluing the fur back in straight rows, working up from the hem to hide the seams.

"That's amazing!" She smiled. "It really doesn't show."

"I've only seen three coats in my life with fleece as long as this. You should be grateful for my extravagance, Comrade. But you'll have to wear it carefully. I'm not sure about this cement. At home we use some American stuff called Elmer's Glue-All you can get in the bazaar."

"You mean you've done this before?"

"Only on my old vest. Just for repairs. May I ask how you were planning to get to the airport?" His voice was tired and he would not look at her.

"Nadia said she'd send a car. Tor, please don't be angry at me. I have to do this. It's what I came here for."

"Fine. Then you'd better call Nadia and ask her to send the driver at six, if you want to take the Helsinki train. You've got what you came for and you don't want my advice, so why cry about it? I'm going to make tea."

He stalked over to the hot plate and she followed him. "Look, if Kostia told, they'd be here by now, wouldn't they?"

"Maybe. If he talked right away. If they didn't leave him sitting in a hall somewhere by mistake. If he went through channels, just like that. But this is the Soviet Union, remember? Since they do everything the hard way here, they may be watching all these dorms right now. Tell Nadia to send you a Zil limousine, with a general at the wheel."

"Do you really want tea? Let's have a drink instead. If you're trying to get me rattled, you're succeeding, damn you. Are you happy?"

"Yes. Call Nadia."

When she came back from the hall phone, he was holding up the coat. "This ought to be dry now. Try it on. What did Nadia say?"

"That she'd send her father's driver. And that she'd been up all night so I wasn't *really* bothering her, nudge, nudge, wink, wink."

Tor smiled thinly. "I'm sure that's true."

"Oh, you mean you know it from personal experience. Shall we both get nasty, and spoil our last two hours?"

He pointed to a glass of sherry. "There was only one drink left, and I've had my share already. Come on, let's see how the coat looks."

In fact, since it was cut for a man, it fit her better than before with the shoulders padded. But it was heavy.

"Walk around," he said. "Does it rustle?"

She experimented. "Only when I sit."

"Then take it off before you sit." Circling her, he pulled at it here and there. "It's alright. It's good."

"Thank you, Tor. You know how much this means to me. Can we go back to bed now and be friends again?"

"We're friends. I just wish it could last a little longer." The coldness left his eyes and he came to hug her fiercely, "I hate this. I hate you for leaving me, that's all." Shrugging, he opened the coat to see if the wool was intact, then slipped it off her and draped it over the desk.

Watching him, she guessed he was shutting her out already, and perhaps that was best. But was it what Tor really wanted?

She went to put her arms around his neck and kissed him, softly, deliberately, and for a moment he stood still, withdrawn.

"Don't you have to pack your things?"

"I want to pack *you*. The hell with my clothes."

"Well..." The corners of his mouth turned up. "If that's how you feel, Comrade, we'd better get rid of them." His hand moved to cover her breast, "I have a confession to make. For the past three months I've dreamed about touching you through this sweater."

She grinned. "Yes, I had that idea."

"But now I only want to take it off."

"Come here." She led him over to the bed. "This time it's my turn. I'm going to give you a backrub."

They undressed quickly, and when he had stretched out on his stomach, she said, "Close your eyes and don't move a muscle unless I tell you to." Last term, Nadia had giggled, "Toryalai makes love like a tornado!" And even then, she'd thought: yes, without subtlety, without risking exposure. If he could work through that now it might heal him a little... if she could get down to where he'd been hiding all those things and leave something else in their place. Then nothing would be left unfinished, whatever happened. She started with the back of his neck, "I'm going to exorcise all your devils and pack them in my suitcase and take them back to England. But you have to let me do it. Will you, Tor?"

"I'm not in a very good position to argue with you, Comrade."

"Then keep your eyes closed and kiss them good-bye."

Kneading his shoulders, she talked to him silently, trying to send the sense down through her hands, telling him that he was stronger than he knew, and better, and very lovable, and that he could be and do anything if he'd only just let go and let himself like other people again, and after a while her fingers knew where to move and how deeply to touch him, and it did not seem silly at all to be making this a meditation. Even with her eyes closed she could tell he was opening to her. Each breath seemed to grow longer and there was no tension in him now, except that she knew he was very much aware of what she was doing, and turning him on his back, she saw he was smiling.

"You're a genius, Comrade."

"Shut up. I'm not through yet."

Now everywhere she had touched him she kissed him, breathing into his body, willing him to be free and happy, to find someone soon who would also love him without his magic show, and there was resistance only when she took him in her mouth, but even then she refused to let him hold back, thinking: come on, Tor, come out in the open for once, and he did, slowly, helplessly, curling around her until she felt his breath warm on her back.

"God save the Queen," he said. "I think I'm in heaven. But it must be hell, since that's against the law."

"A sin, you mean? Forgive me, I didn't know. Is it worse than drinking alcohol?"

"No, it's better. Much better. I think from now on it's my favorite sin, but only with you, Liz. You'll have to marry me now."

"Let's get untangled here. I want to see you."

Tor's face was bright, his eyes delighted. "If you'll give me five minutes to rest, I'll memorize *you*."

"No, you know what I'd really like? Just to go to sleep together till the sun comes up, as if I weren't leaving at all. I want to remember us being human for a while, along with everything else." She pulled the quilt up around them. "Alright?"

He nodded, curving to fit her. "I'll do anything you say, Comrade. I love you. Remember that too."

His head fell back on the pillow, and when she knew he was asleep, she sat up to look at him again. Making love might not work miracles, but it was powerful when it was real, and in trying to find Tor she had also given herself to him, opening a channel between them that ran both ways, that made her strong too. What else might they discover if they had all the time in the world?

Maybe I will come back here, strange person, she thought. Maybe I can somehow.

Pale blue light was sifting through the edges of the curtain, and slipping out of bed, she picked up her clothes. She hadn't brought much back to Moscow after Christmas, to leave room in her case for the manuscript, and it took less than an hour to shower and pack.

At quarter of six, she sat down beside Tor, brushing the hair back from his slanting cheekbones. He opened his eyes. "Oh, no. What time is it?"

She showed him her watch. "I didn't want to wake you at all."

"Wait, I'll walk out with you." He started up. "Let me get dressed."

"No, you can't come down, Tor, and it's too late anyway. But I'm going to miss you badly, my friend of three days."

He drew her down. "Not half as much as I'll miss you."

"I've left you my little tape recorder, so you can smuggle me messages."

"They'll all say the same thing. Come back soon." Holding her tight against him, he said, "Be very careful on that train. Not too friendly, or too cool. And take my lighter, it still might come in handy."

She smiled. "If only for your cigarettes, which I've already stolen. Tor, I have to go now...."

"I know." His mouth stopped hers with a long kiss. "Don't forget me, Comrade."

"No chance." She stood up to put on the coat. "Will you please take care of yourself?"

"I'll think about it. And I hope things are... better at home. Write to me as soon as you get there so I'll know you're safe."

"I will. Thanks for everything, Tor. Especially this."

"That's only a loan, remember. You have to return it in person. Goodbye, Comrade Elizabeth. Good luck."

"To you too, Mr. Anwari. Go back to sleep now."

She went out quickly so he wouldn't try to get up. Even the single case was awkward on the stairs because of the length of the coat. Tor wore it with so much more grace.

At the front door of the dorm, she smiled inwardly. Nadia *had* sent a Zil limousine—not black, but metallic gray, and its heavily swaddled driver got out to put her bag in the trunk. "The storm isn't so bad now, but it will get worse again soon. I'll take care of your ticket. Intourist has it at the station."

As he held the rear door for her, she remembered: the curtain. She was supposed to leave it open, and Yelena still might be waiting for that signal.

Scanning her floor to pick out the window, she saw Tor standing in it, shirtless, looking down at her. He lifted a hand, and climbing into the car, she turned to keep him in view, a small figure, fading, then disappearing in the powdery snow.

Resting her head on the back of the seat, she closed her eyes. Three days of Tor and no sleep. How was it possible to get so used to somebody in that time? Tor was closer to her now than anyone had been in years, except her own family. She fingered his lighter in her pocket. It was like him—hard, compact and beautifully made. Would they ever see each other again? No ...yes...when...

She woke to a strange voice saying, "Everything is arranged. Come, I'll show you to your compartment."

Still half asleep, she followed the driver through the crowded station, onto a platform and down the long steel train toward the front. He helped her into the carriage. "I'll have tea sent to you. It will be a long journey, but still shorter than waiting for Aeroflot to get straightened out again. Yours is the second compartment on the left."

"Thank you so much. And please thank Nadia and her family for me too."

When he saw her face at the window, he vanished into a crush of people, and she took off the coat, spreading it carefully on the berth above her head. It would take sixteen hours to reach the border once they got under way, and that wouldn't be for a while yet. Stretching out on the seat, she thought: move me if you have to, but I'm going to take a nap.

The sound of a whistle jolted her awake and she sat up in a panic. What was...the train, and the windows were dark already. In the dream she'd been riding in Wiltshire with Dad.

"You sleep as if you are dead! It is the wheels, I think. My name is Uta, from Helsinki. Do you like some herring, please?" The plump girl held out a reeking jar, "I think you brought no food."

"How did you guess I'm English?" She used Russian, assuming it would make conversation easier, but Uta shook her brown curls. "I don't speak that language. I thought you are American."

Elizabeth smiled. "But you understood what I just said."

"I don't speak it." She extracted another chunk of fish. "Ugh, there is too much fat on these. Everything in Moscow is too this or too that. Not like our herring at home. Are you going home now too?"

Reluctantly, Elizabeth half responded to a seemingly endless list of personal questions and offers of food and drink. No, she did not want any vodka, thank you. Yes, there was no night life in Moscow to speak of, but no, she was not a tourist, so not too disappointed, and no, she had never dated any Russian men. At that point, Uta described in detail every "Soviet" whom she had been involved with over the past three years, and Elizabeth gave up any hope of going back to sleep. If Uta had crossed the border by train as often as she claimed, she must have developed good instincts for the process by now. Still, so many questions...What had Yelena said? "There is always an informer near you, English."

And this Finnish girl was certainly an odd duck. Her cycles of chatter built to crescendos, and then, just when they became unbearable, she'd lapse into a morose silence and stare off into space.

Elizabeth studied the compartment, wondering if it was an advantage that there were two passengers rather than four. Uta had tossed her numerous bags and parcels on the upper berths instead of storing them under the seat with her own case. Perhaps it had been a mistake to bring so little herself. After all, smuggling *something* must be very common, so their attention would focus more sharply on what she had.

Maybe it had been another mistake not to drink any vodka. It was ten o'clock, they'd reach the border soon and her mouth was dry.

She accepted half an orange. Where had Uta found an orange in Moscow, in February? "What a storm!" she said. "With the airport closed, I'm surprised the train isn't more crowded. The station certainly was."

"Do you know"—Uta smiled—"only three times I am alone with one person like this. Because you are English, or if you are American. They put foreign women together, always alone. But you are not Jewish?"

"No. Why do you ask?"

"Well..." She shifted uncomfortably. "One time, it is bad. I am alone with a young Jewish girl, an...émigré—the last in her family to go. They do things to her which they have no right. They...touch her. But I know the lieutenant, and I tell him I will not like him anymore if they don't stop it."

"And did they stop?" She was wondering what Uta's "liking" included. Her flesh could warm any number of cold hands.

"Yes, they do!" The broad face smiled in self-congratulation. "I give them a big salami!"

Elizabeth laughed and Uta seemed vastly relieved. "I ask if you are Jewish because you look unhappy of this search. I think maybe you carry someone in your suitcase! Also, this is not the time for student holidays. If you carry something, tell me where it is so I can help you hide this."

Her blue eyes were sympathetic, and for a moment the offer was tempting. But Tor would never trust anyone. On the other hand, if Uta had been helpful to that Jewish girl, a confidence now might not be amiss.

"No," Elizabeth said, "I'm just upset because my father's ill. That's why I'm going home in the middle of term."

She watched Uta's forehead crease with concern. Everyone had a father. In any other circumstance, her own would be appalled at his condition's being used to spark maternal feelings.

"Oh, I am sorry, Elizabeth. But you will be home soon. I think we slow down already. Now you see. At the airport, it is nothing, yes? They open your suitcase, only take a peek. Not much trouble, because maybe someone too important is waiting behind you. But on this train? A real show. The poor boys here do nothing but freeze. And they like very much girls' things," she grinned. "I put my nightgowns and underclothes on top, and they always look at my panties, each."

Uta's monologue reverted to men, and Elizabeth looked out through darkness at the Leningrad forest. She could distinguish tree trunks separately now against their field of white. Yes, the train had slowed a good deal.

Two piercing beams of light shone through the woods, becoming brilliant as the train pulled to a stop by a low metal blockhouse.

Immediately, dark figures approached through the snow, cradling rifles and shouting to one another across the barbed-wire fence.

"They come two on each carriage," Uta said, "a lieutenant and a corporal, or a sergeant and a private—usually one speaks English and one not." But she also was straining to see out the window, and not smiling at all now.

The car trembled as it was boarded, and they heard footsteps in the corridor. There was no window in the compartment door and Elizabeth leaned against it. A faint knock up ahead, then muffled voices. Five minutes later, a repetition. But the searchers so far couldn't have been very thorough. She rubbed her palms across the brown fabric seatcover as Uta stood up to answer the door.

The two men wore KGB gray—the same color as every drop of paint inside the train.

"Lieutenant Ivanov..."

Elizabeth told herself: he might be Kostia's cousin. Yes, pretend he is, forget you know that Ivanov is the Russian equivalent of Smith.

It was the lieutenant who spoke bad English. "To see passports, please?" Dark hair, shrewd eyes, a big man, cold and impatient. A small scowl for Uta—of recognition? Taking her cue, Elizabeth decided to speak English, in case fluency in Russian might be cause for suspicion.

"Svenson, Finnish." His scowl deepened. "Soot-cleef, English. You will wait, please." The blond, bug-eyed private held the door, closing it quickly behind them. A moment later he opened it again to return their documents.

Elizabeth exhaled. "That wasn't much."

"No"—Uta shook her head—"they come back to search." She was chewing on her lower lip. Her high spirits had vanished.

They heard scuffling in the corridor, then a cry. Uta's mouth puckered nervously and she sat down, mumbling in Finnish. But when Lieutenant Ivanov reappeared, she went through a second transformation—swinging her bottom as she climbed up on the berth to hand her satchels down, pointing her breasts and giggling, to the private's obvious admiration.

It seemed she had a hundred bags filled with toys and food, and all were being carefully examined... a flat cake in the lieutenant's large hands. "Forgive it, please..." He broke the cake in half, and Elizabeth cursed herself for not having brought something they could easily destroy.

Uta's suitcases were thrown open on the seat and Elizabeth tried to get out of the way without leaving the compartment. A rifle butt jabbed her side, the private stepped on her foot twice, and since the train had stopped, the air had got progressively more stuffy. The searchlight gleamed on the coat's white suede. They would have to look at it soon. Was it wrong to hover, instead of pacing the corridor as some other passengers had? What would Tor do? Perhaps she should pretend she *was* Tor.

But in the close air, the smell of sweating bodies was maddening, setting her nerves on edge, and when the lieutenant glanced at her she was sure the look in her eyes gave her away.

"Is it all, Miss Svenson?"

Uta began to nod, then changed her mind and suddenly jumped up on Elizabeth's berth, scrambling over the coat. "I have a little bag up here."

The two men were working seriously now, pulling up the seats and looking under them, sliding out the writing table. But Elizabeth saw only the coat in Uta's hands, her arm drawing back to throw it, heavily, onto the luggage rack over the door. The private gave her sack a quick search and tossed it back to her.

Then it was Elizabeth's turn, and if she'd been carrying so much as a contraband nail file in her case they would have found it. Watching them, it was all she could do not to run away, out through the forest. If they found the papers, they'd drag her into the blockhouse, slap her, strip her... could she stand that with any dignity? And Tor would be caught too. Nadia would be questioned and she'd know the coat was his. Poor Tor, he must have thought of that. Perhaps it had figured in his argument about not taking the train.

No, it was no good trying to be Tor. He could be flip and make chummy jokes, but for her that would be acting "too friendly."

The private ran through each page of every book, then measured the depth of her suitcase against its interior, spilling sweaters on the floor. Yelena would say something wry now, and faintly contemptuous, but Yelena was a fatalist with years of practice at this.

I'm just scared, Elizabeth thought. I wouldn't be any good at getting tortured.

Lieutenant Ivanov was frowning his way through her notebooks. "I must take these, Miss Soot-cleef. Very sorry, but much is said of the Soviet Union and there is not time to be sure." His eyes were penetrating. Had he noticed how good her written Russian was?

She tried for mild indignation. "But those are only my class notes! I'm a student at Moscow University. Can't you see they're all on Russian history?"

He shrugged. "If you wish to get off and wait for the next train..."

"I can't do that! I have a connection to make." Sighing, she said grudgingly, "Oh, alright. Take them." Perhaps now they'd feel they had bothered her enough?

"Very sorry. What else do you bring, please?"

"Nothing. That's all I've got."

Uta was standing on the seat again, rearranging her belongings. "Why don't you officers take some of those cookies down there?" And then Elizabeth's stomach turned. Uta had reached to pull Tor's coat back on the berth and it caught on the side of the luggage rack. A handful of black fleece dropped onto the seat just by her foot. Looking down at it, she turned to meet Elizabeth's eyes, then tried to push the coat back, but now it was firmly stuck on the hook. Had the others noticed anything? If Uta let go, it would fall down like a curtain in front of the door.

Yes, dammit, the lining had ripped and a strip of paper was showing. Could she move to hide it somehow? Dad, she thought, I may not see you again, but you'd better send me some inspiration. I should have been thinking of you all along here. Well, what would you do now?

He might give Uta a small, apologetic smile, but his eyes would say very sternly, "Stay exactly where you are." He would will her to, because this was too important for anything to go wrong, and she would feel the strength of his insistence.

The lieutenant was latching the writing table and Elizabeth gazed steadily at Uta, looking away only when he turned toward them again. Uta made another stab at pushing back the coat, but her balance faltered and her foot slipped on the seat.

"One moment," the lieutenant said. "You will show that coat here, please."

Uta stared at the coat as if she'd just realized it wasn't hers.

"Hold it up, please, and shake!"

Elizabeth thought: she'll rip it even more, and that will be that. Or she'll tell them it's stuck and let them pull it down.

But then, with a faint quizzical expression, Uta managed to wrench it free, shook it, and without being asked, turned the pockets out. A few kopeks and Tor's red lighter... the lieutenant's hand was reaching out to touch the curling fleece, and he jostled the private. "Look, we should confiscate this ...your sister..."

They were joking in Russian as Uta folded the coat, smiling flirtatiously, and placed it back on the berth. "You can't have it anyway, because it is hers, and you'd get in trouble. Here's my coat. It's only wool." She thrust it in their faces. "Just like your sister's, yes? But you can have some of my cookies if you want."

The private took one and they were gone.

Uta collapsed ashen-faced on the seat and bent over, listening, but Elizabeth was choking back laughter. I've done it, she thought dizzily, we've done it, Tor, and Yelena, and Kostia, we did it, and Dad, you're going to have the surprise of your life. It's over now, I know it, and I'm free.

"Uta," she said, but the girl stood up to climb past her onto the berth. What now?

A second later, she peered down, smiling, with a rag doll clutched in one hand. "Not even touched!"

"You mean... you were hiding something too?" Elizabeth felt the laughter rising inside her and knew it would be uncontrollable. This was all so unreal....

"Yes," Uta chuckled, hanging over the berth upside down. "She's full of my grandmother's jewelry, and you almost got me hanged. You should have told me you had something, so I could help you. This is my tenth trip, my last trip, and it's foolish to take any chances at this crossing. It's one of the worst."

Where had her broken English gone? Uta wasn't what she pretended, either.

Elizabeth held her aching sides. "So we're a pair of crooks? Uta, where's your vodka!"

Thirteen

WHEN THE GRAY Zil limousine drove out of sight, Tor walked over to the bed and put on his shirt and sweater. It would take Elizabeth sixteen hours to reach the border. Anything could happen in that time. A phone call or a wire sent even late tonight could intercept her. That was what she hadn't considered.

A hundred times he'd started to say: If they catch you, if you're arrested ... But that might jinx her, and she was determined to go, and at least the papers were out of her room. If Nadia stayed away too, it might take the MVD all day to find out Liz had left the city.

Turning on the hot plate, he made a strong pot of tea and poured the last glass of sherry into it. She had looked so fragile climbing into that car in his white coat, so pale against the snow.

If no one went after her, she'd make it alright. She would know what to do when the time came. She might be scared, but she was more intelligent than the border guards, with their onion breath and big peasant hands....

They couldn't have Elizabeth, they must not touch her. And if no one called after her, she'd make it through. If Kostia kept his mouth shut.

Kostia Ivanov. Who was this idiot? A martyr, with a father in a labor camp. So they'd threaten to work his father to death in some frozen potato field and ruin the rest of his family, and if that had no effect they'd attach electrodes to his testicles, or torture Yelena in front of him while reading out a list of her foreign contacts over the past few years. And the name Sutcliffe would be on that list.

No, he thought, that would happen only if Kostia reached the KGB. It was the MVD who had him now, and they were a different story. It was possible to bribe the MVD.

At least, that was said to be true. It might be easier to try to get past them and just strangle Kostia Ivanov.

If they tortured Yelena, Kostia would talk eventually, thinking Elizabeth's plane had already left. So he must not get to the KGB today, if he wasn't there already. Maybe the Internal Police *could* be bribed. Who had good connections at the MVD?

Only Nadia. And going through her was out of the question.

Then it would take a lot of money. This had to happen fast, to beat Liz's train to the border. A dozen clerks and secretaries might have to be paid off just to find out where Kostia was being held. Then three or four junior officials and their boss and a couple of guards. And all of them would want hard currency—large denominations of dollars, pounds or yen, if they had to move quickly. Say, twelve hundred dollars for the clerks, the same again for the guards and little bureaucrats and twice that for the big shot.

Five thousand dollars. There was only one way to get that much cash on short notice—by selling Magdi's gold to Gregori Kirov.

Tor forced a stale sandwich down his throat and collected his things. Her things, really, since she had been smart enough to notice that he hadn't brought another coat to wear. Her parka looked silly on him, but it would get him back to his dorm, and she had left her rose cashmere sweater on the chair along with the tape recorder. Maybe she read his mind? But no, she'd left other things as well, which Nadia would inherit. It would be strange to see Nadia wearing Liz's clothes... unbearable, if Elizabeth were caught.

Walking back through the snow, he decided to send Gregori a message right away, and then worry about the mechanics of getting through the MVD. Even this early, Gregori ought to be lounging at Café National. And little Jani Kuznetsov knew Gregori by sight, though with his glass eye, Jani was hardly the ideal go-between. Gregori had already beaten him once.

Still, it would look worse to show up at the café himself, and this time Jani would be only a messenger boy, not the dealer.

Jani's room was on the ground floor, and standing on tiptoe, Tor could just see over the windowsill. There was Jani, working on a model plane on the floor. It would be better not to tell him what the message was about.

Rapping on the glass to get his attention, Tor waved and went in through the hall. Jani smiled, "Toryalai! Have some tea! And some of this sweet bread my mother sent me."

Tor put a record on Jani's miserable excuse for a stereo. "I've already had breakfast. Give me a piece of paper instead. And a pen. I want you to take a message to Gregori Kirov at the Café National, and bring his answer back as fast as you can, alright?" He made himself look straight at Jani's false eye. "You aren't afraid just to go down there, are you?"

"Gregori! No, Tor! Don't be stupid like me!" The crooked pink scar zigzagged out across his temple and the dead glass made Tor's skin crawl.

"Don't worry," he said, "you'll be doing me a favor. I owe Gregori a lot of money, and I want to pay him back now before he starts getting ugly about it. He'll be happy to hear that. He won't bother you."

"Well then, good." Jani smiled with relief. "It's bad business to owe money to Gregori. And you shouldn't go there yourself. He's jealous of you, Gregori, and his friends might jump you just to make him even happier. They only make fun of me now. I'm not scared to go. But Tor, you'd better hurry and write your note. My roommates will be coming back from breakfast any minute."

"I think I'd like some tea after all," Tor said to put some distance between them. Jani went to turn on his electric kettle, and quickly Tor scribbled a list of Magdi's pieces, figuring their prices by breaking down the total that Magdi had said he wanted for the bangles and chain. By cutting his own profit in half, he could offer Gregori a terrific bargain, but in nonnegotiable terms: Jani must not be harmed or bullied, and the deal would have to be settled by noon. That gave Gregori three hours to come up with the cash. They could meet at the Pushkin monument. That should be safe.

"Be sure to get a receipt for this. And bring it to me in Magdi's room. His roommates are always out on Sunday morning. Mine won't even be up yet." Swallowing the scalding tea, he smiled. "Thanks, Jani. I'll pay you for your trouble when you get back."

"You'll be glad to get this off your chest, won't you?" Jani smiled. "So, I'll hurry, Tor."

Climbing the stairs to the second floor, Tor thought: now to get Magdi up. And that might be the hardest part of all.

After five minutes of wearing out his knuckles on Magdi's door, he heard a muffled voice call, "Go away, you obscenity! It's Sunday!"

Tor kicked the door and kept kicking it until Magdi let him in. The Egyptian dove back into bed. "Leave me alone, Tor. Come back later. I'm too cozy to wake up now."

As usual, Magdi was covered with the three quilts that made him "just warm enough to dream of Cairo." Switching on loud music, Tor tried to pull them off, but Magdi held on tight. Tor ran a hand underneath them to give his balls a hard squeeze. "I'm telling you, sit up! Come on, I don't have time to sing you songs today. I'm going to do you the honor of selling your gold."

"You bastard!" Magdi fondled himself, laughing. "These are more precious. Don't you wish you could buy them?" His heavy eyelids drooped, but he propped himself on an elbow. "So, you've finally come around. I knew you would. What is that little jacket you're wearing? You look like a piece of candy."

"Shut up, or I'll give you another handshake. Now listen. Does this sound right?"

He repeated the estimates he had made, and Magdi nodded. "Close enough. I'll be glad to get it out of here, too."

Opening the tape recorder case, Tor said, "Do you have a belt that hooks instead of buckling?"

Muttering in Arabic, Magdi scrambled out of bed and across the room to pull on his galabia. "Somewhere here I do."

"And a sharp knife?" Tor took out the small machine. A Sony. Very nice. He'd have to remember to come back for it later or it would disappear. "Lock the door and bring your gold here."

Magdi forced a chair under the knob too. "I don't have a knife. Is a razor blade all right? What are you doing?" Dropping the razor by Tor's hand, he went to drag his bed away from the wall and reached up inside the springs. A metal box was chained to them with a padlock.

Tor cut two slashes in the tape recorder case and threaded it onto the belt. He would wear the case at his back under his cape. Hooking the belt, he practiced opening it in one smooth motion, sliding the case inconspicuously down into his hand. When it was weighted, that would be even easier.

Magdi had unlocked the metal box and took out a scale. "Now we do some business, my friend. Are you selling this to Gregori?"

Tor nodded.

"Does he want it all?"

"I hope so, Comrade. I need the money."

"Well, we'll do a little inventory, just in case. I'll give each piece a number and you can write down what it's worth. Or what we want, which won't be the same figure." Magdi smiled. "And tell me, how's the little English girl? Are you here because she threw you out after all?"

"Do you want a punch in the face? Get to work."

They had just finished packing the gold in the case when someone tapped on the door. Magdi jumped, but Tor grabbed his sleeve. "It's Jani Kuznetsov, and he doesn't know about this. Let me handle him."

Pulling back the chair, Tor opened the door a crack. "Jani, did he give you a receipt?"

"Yes, I've brought it." He looked proud of himself. "It's only ten o'clock and Gregori's drinking already."

"I think Magdi's got the Russian flu. He's sick. You better not come in." Tor took the envelope Jani offered and handed him fifty rubles. "Thanks, Jani. You have more guts than I do." Smiling, he closed the door.

Gregori's note said: "I'll meet you at eleven outside Sokolniki Park. The Pushkin monument's too dangerous for me. I'll have your price in dollars. Be sure you aren't followed."

Tor sat down on the bed. Sokolniki Park. Sure, that would be safe for Gregori, alright. In this weather, it would be deserted. Meeting him there alone would be suicide.

He glanced up at Magdi. "Comrade, you do look sick! I think you need some nice fresh air."

"What?" Magdi frowned. "That's from Gregori? What does it say?"

"He wants to meet at Sokolniki Park. Have you ever been there?"

"No. Where is it?"

"All the way on the other side of Moscow, and it's huge. I'm going to need your help."

"Oh, no, Tor..." Magdi held up his hands. "If I had the nerve for that, I wouldn't need you."

"But I'll take all the risks, Comrade. You don't have to go near Gregori. Just stand across the street, and if they try to rob me, point and scream like an outraged citizen. You'll only be protecting your investment. If I go alone, he'll kill me, and I don't have time to renegotiate. This offer is good only today, this morning, so if you don't come, the deal's off, permanently. Gregori doesn't know you and he'll get out of there too fast to see much of your ugly face."

"It's my father I'm scared of," Magdi said. "If I get arrested, *he* will kill *me*."

"Forget it then." Unsnapping the case, Tor started to take out the bangles.

Magdi's eyes followed his hand. "You mean... I could be a safe distance away? Just watching? Wait, Tor, stop that, I haven't said no."

"Then say yes now, or I'm leaving."

"Alright, you Afghan bastard, piece of excrement, son of a whore. I'll do it. The Black Wasp is still the best."

An hour later, Tor stood huddled against the wall of Sokolniki Park, trying to stay out of the wind that blew light snow into his face.

Across the street, Magdi was faking conversation in a telephone booth.

Tor clapped his cold hands together. Would Gregori come himself? Probably not, if he was drunk. And now the whole plan seemed shaky. There was too much money involved. It was Sunday, and snowing. Where could Gregori have got that much money so fast? And if he couldn't find it, he'd still come after the gold. It might be better just to leave right now.

Because if Gregori's goons tried to rob him, Magdi would be a failure in his role as "outraged citizen." They'd take one look at his tan face and know he was not.

What was Kostia Ivanov doing now? Skinny Kostia, he couldn't stand up to much. If he had to choose between protecting Yelena or those papers... and Elizabeth... Tor took out his flask of vodka and swallowed a mouthful. It was his own job to worry about Liz, and this was the only way to make sure Kostia wouldn't talk. Who would that idiot think had set him free?

Magdi was afraid of being arrested. Hah, that was a laugh. The street was empty in both directions, and there wouldn't be any police patrols in the park in all this snow. That was too bad, since going to jail would be nicer than being murdered. In fact, right now it might be a relief.

But then they'd send him home to Kabul, and if Elizabeth came back here ...he might never see her again.

No, if there was any chance to make her crossing safer, he'd stand here until he froze solid.

Suddenly, Magdi took off his hat. That was their signal. Someone was coming.

Stepping out from the wall, Tor stood in plain view. There were two of them, huge men, and Gregori was slight. Then behind them, he saw a snowplow turn onto the street four blocks down. If it worked its way up fast enough, Magdi wouldn't be the only witness.

The two men both wore thick wool coats and knit caps pulled low on their foreheads. "Tor Anwari? I'm Yuri and this is Stephan. I think you have a package for us?" Yuri was young, but his face was mapped with scars that made Jani's seem minor by comparison.

"Maybe, Comrades." Tor smiled. "Do you have one for me?"

"Oh, yes! Forty large green souvenirs of the United States of America, with Gregori's compliments. Let's walk into the park a little way."

"Forgive me, Comrades, I don't mean to offend you, but I happen to be allergic to parks. Especially in the winter." The small case strapped around his waist felt heavy against his spine.

"But your cape is so memorable," Stephan said. "We're afraid to be seen with you." He jerked his head toward the snowplow. "They're watching us. Come into the park."

Magdi had turned his back to them. What the hell was he doing?

The two men moved to flank him and Tor stepped out of reach. Yuri smiled. "Just a little walk, Comrade. No problem."

"If you touch me, no deal," Tor said. "Besides, I don't have the gold on me." The plow was three blocks away now.

As they grabbed his elbows, Tor spun away but Yuri hooked an arm around his neck. "Quick, the driver's not looking!"

Stephan nodded toward the phone booth. "There's someone..."

Tor started to scream and Yuri jammed three fingers down his throat. "Pick him up, come on!" Biting hard, Tor heard a groan of pain, but the big fingers stayed, making him gag, and he kicked wildly as they lifted him, dragging him into the park.

They threw him down in a stand of trees on the other side of the wall and Yuri punched him in the mouth. "Shut up or I'll kill you!"

Swallowing blood, Tor gave no more resistance to their search. If they thought Magdi was calling the police, they might not risk more than robbery.

Pulling off Tor's belt, Yuri opened the case. "Here it is! I've got it!"

"Hurry up!" Stephan was peering over the wall, "I don't like the look of this."

Straightening up, Yuri strapped on the belt and Tor scrambled away from him, but Stephan came around on his other side, and a knife had appeared in his hand.

"This is stupid," Tor said as they closed in on him. "You don't need to..." Wheeling suddenly, he raced past them, leaping for the wall. And at the instant that Stephan's blade entered his back, Tor saw Magdi's coat flapping as he ran.

MARCH 1978
New York

Fourteen

SAIRA CAUGHT A cab on First Avenue outside the U.N. Secretariat and gave her address on West 86th Street. It was the second time this week that she'd taken a taxi home—a ridiculous extravagance even with the new promotion.

But this was only the fourth time in the year she had been seeing Andrei that he would be able to visit her at night. Russians at the U.N. were forbidden to have a social life outside of their own coterie. Andrei had managed to steal several long lunch hours each month, but it was much harder for him to find excuses to evade the buses that came to collect the Soviet staff every evening. And tomorrow Mummy and Daddy-jan would be here, and then Devika.... No, this cab fare would be worth the hour or two of peace and quiet it would buy. Her six o'clock ritual with the birds had grown to be too important to miss even for Andrei's sake. It was an antidote to New York, the U.N., feeling bad, even to Andrei himself.

Though it was the birds in their tree-lined flight cage, the Oriental rugs and tapestries in her apartment that had captured Andrei's interest when he'd stopped by with his aide one night to drop off some late copy for her newsletter on the Year of the Child. Andrei's mother was a French Communist whose family had lived in colonial southern India for generations, and he'd grown up with stories of that lost, exotic past through the long Moscow winters that finally had destroyed his mother's lungs when he was thirteen. Andrei looked more French than Russian, with his high color, narrow body and shrewd, amused dark brown eyes. His mother had read him Rousseau as well as Chekhov, and he believed, as she had, that the greatest failure of the Soviet state lay in its suppression of literature and art.

What did Andrei's wife feel on that subject, Saira wondered. He had married the daughter of a diplomat, and though they were legally separated, the small black and white photograph of her that he'd produced at Saira's insistence seemed to have left a nagging shadow between them. Trying not to think about Andrei's wife took up a good deal of her time lately.

Saira rapped on the Plexiglas partition, pointing to the right, and the cab driver swerved across a moving lane of traffic to stop just short of the entrance to her building. In the lobby, the doorman handed her a yellow envelope, which she opened in the elevator—a cable from Mummy-jan, confirming their travel arrangements from Paris and saying they'd meet her at the U.N. at noon.

Please, Saira thought, let this visit go well. It's been so long since I've seen them I won't be able to stand it if we can't get along.

They ought to approve of her apartment, at least, since it was furnished with things sent from home—a white and gold Istalif carpet, the framed Chinese scroll that had been a diplomatic gift from Premier Chou En-lai, the row of Persian miniatures above the teak desk, and the sandalwood screen concealing the kitchen area. The rust velvet couch opened out to sleep two, but she had decided to give them her bedroom anyway. Otherwise, the birds might wake them up, in spite of the blinds she'd installed to regulate light inside the flight cage.

At the tenth floor, she turned the key in her lock, trying to see the living room through their eyes. The parquet floor and windows gleamed, and against beige walls the standing green plants seemed brighter from last night's careful washing. On either side of the low glass table, cushions covered in woven Kashmiri wool made a color bridge from the rug to the couch that faced the floor-to-ceiling aviary set in the bay window.

Unzipping her boots, she called, "Hello, birds! Hello, funny birds, I'm home."

She went to pull the blinds fully open to give them the last of the afternoon light. Calculating the changing arc of the sun had been a problem at first, but gradually she had figured out which slats to screw down tight, according to the weather and season, to provide shade in each section of the cage, as well as some natural light at dawn. Because really, there were five separate parts, divided by mesh screen to protect the territorial claims of each species: the red-factor canary Tor had given her and his mate and offspring; a pair of white mourning doves; two male gray-cheek parakeets that were completely tame now; a half-dozen zebra finches and a pair of miniature cockatiels, whose high spotted crests stood out against the foliage twined through the wire grating. Twenty birds, each with enough space to fly a healthy distance and appearing to share a single area, thanks to her painstaking design. At night, thick white draperies shielded them from lamplight in the living room, but when she felt lonely or wanted to show off, she could draw them back a precise length and listen to the canaries, whom she'd taught to sing with exposure as their cue. Tarana, the youngest virtuoso, could follow a side of Haydn string quartets almost faultlessly with the record now, and smiling at him, she went to put it on. "I'm getting sick of these, you hear? Soon you'll have to learn to like Louis Armstrong. That's your father's favorite."

Hanging her coat in the hall closet, she walked into the bedroom and stripped off her gray silk blouse, black pleated skirt, bra and nylon stockings, and took a yellow robe into the bathroom to turn on the shower. Clouds of steam fogged the mirror as she unpinned two combs from her hair and twisted it under a plastic cap. The spicy scent of Roget & Gallet carnation soap rose up—another luxury, but an indispensable one. It foamed beautifully even in this hard water, and the smell made her happy and then disappeared by the time she put on perfume.

Maybe I'm sick, she thought. Lady Macbeth, are you suffering from a compulsion? Or is New York really as filthy as it seems?

Out of the shower early tonight, so the ritual could be finished in step: crossing the living room to boil water for tea, then back to the bathroom when the mirror had cleared to clean her face with cream and a hot washcloth. Conservative dress and subtle makeup were camouflage at work, but this face was for private scrutiny.

Her olive skin could have gone with no foundation and very little blush. Would that still be true in five years? The sheer stroke of amethyst eye shadow, gray liner and mascara didn't make her feel more attractive, but rather protected somehow until she could get home to take it off and resume this silent dialogue with the mirror. There you are, Saira, not so rosy anymore, and with faint wrinkles starting, called crow's feet here. At home you'd be considered old at twenty-five, and no wonder, look at those bony cheeks and impertinent brown eyes. Even Ashraf would take one look at you now and know you were trouble. But isn't that why you like yourself better? You can't have it both ways. Remember that. You can't be a shrinking maiden when there's no man around to play hero, and if one offered, you wouldn't trust him anyway. Remember that, at least until tomorrow night, and then I'll tell you this all over again, so you won't begin to hope for some bright future with Andrei, or too much comfort from Daddy-jan.

It was safe to expect a wonderful time with Devika though, she thought, pouring water over the Darjeeling tea her friend had sent from Calcutta. This seemed to be the year for family reunions. Devika had been in India for six months now, and it was pure luck that she was flying in the day after tomorrow, so that, even if things went badly, they could lie around on the cushions and laugh about parents, men, and living in the States while putting forth solutions to all the problems at home. Devika's last letter had said: Don't worry, I'm coming back, Saira. Will it surprise you that I've discovered I still don't like being interfered with?

Five years ago, it was Devika who had taken her in when she'd arrived at Logan Airport, feeling suddenly unable to face the Lowes and their dark house on Beacon Street. Devika had met her at the kiosk in Harvard Square, brandishing a newspaper. "Do you know there's been a coup in Afghanistan? Read this. Tell me what it means." And later, "So, you have two Leftist parties, and it seems one's got in at the expense of the other. What's their platform? What kind of changes will they make?" Of course, that was before the Afghan ambassador had returned Saira's urgent phone call, telling her that her family was safe and her brother Mangal was the new president's press aide.

How had the coup changed people's lives? Outside of the family, the answer was very little. Negligibly. Daoud's chief campaign in office had been systematically to purge the Leftists who'd brought him to power, sending Babrak Karmal's Parchami followers out into the countryside to "supervise" provincial affairs in competition with the local khans. Instead of King Zahir and Omar Anwari, Afghanistan now had President Daoud and Mangal Anwari— the self-appointed natural heirs to the kingdom.

At least Daoud had some credentials to offer, even if they'd proved to be worthless. Mangal had only his name to contribute, and his willingness to sacrifice everyone else in the family, including Roshana, who had not led any more demonstrations. And how she must have wanted to by now. Because in five years Daoud's government had done exactly nothing. The coup had just put a fresh coat of paint on the old monarchy, and that was what he and Mangal had been stirring up at the wedding dinner.

Within the family, though, life had changed enormously overnight. For Ashraf too, since his father had died the morning after the coup. Did he think that she or Tor or Mangal or all of them had killed him?

If Tor hadn't shown him Jeffrey's letter, she might be living in Kabul now, surrounded by Ashraf's love and their children.

If Mangal hadn't sent her away, she would have gone to Ashraf's father's funeral, and surely they would have made things up between them. But Tor and Mangal had changed her life, carelessly, as if it didn't matter at all whom she loved or where she lived. For months after the coup, she wouldn't have been able to go home even if she'd wanted to. Unless Mangal arranged it, which he could have had no intention of doing since he'd sent her here in the first place. Maybe Ashraf was happier married to his pretty cousin, about whom no one would whisper at tea, "Disappeared. Ran off! She must have known what was coming. Her poor father."

And when finally she had gone to the Lowes', there was a letter from Mangal saying: We did this for your own good, Saira. And believe me, given

Daddy-jan's resignation, there would have been a different coup soon anyway, and the mullahs might be running the country now.

Why hadn't he added: Admit it. Be grateful.

That was the standard refrain.

Had Mangal needed to use his influence to get Tor out of Afghanistan? But he would have been happy to do that. And in the early years after the coup when Daoud was close to the Soviets, going to school in Moscow must have been like a pilgrimage. Only now Tor was lying in some Russian hospital bed, and Mangal still didn't want him to come home. According to Mummy's letter, he'd convinced them Tor was getting the best care available, and it would be better not to visit him, since it was high time he learned the consequences of his behavior.

That had produced one good effect, though. When she heard it, she'd finally been able to write to Tor herself. Until then, his letters had only brought back the whole wedding night so painfully that she felt nothing but rage. How could she say, "You almost killed me, Tor, but, oh sure, I forgive you." Now she had written, "I'm alright here. No one interferes with me, and I like that very much. I've asked a Russian friend of mine to see that they treat you well, so scream your head off if they don't. Your little bird seems to love New York. Here's a picture of his cage."

Tor's eyes must have popped when he saw that photograph.

Setting her teacup in the sink, she walked over to the aviary and lifted out one of the gray-cheek parakeets. From his perch on her finger, he climbed up her arm to give her chin a peck. He was a parrot, really, almost as large as a dove and bright green except for the gray fuzz by his beak. It was too bad Americans had no feeling for birds. She'd begun to dislike showing Western friends the aviary; their compliments were usually followed by some murmur that it was sad to see birds caged up, or a sidelong glance that told her they found it all terribly symbolic. She wanted to answer: I didn't trap them, I just rescued them from some filthy pet store, and they have more room for their size than you do, and they're probably happier too.

But they wouldn't have understood.

She set the parakeet back in the cage. Andrei had loved this, from the first minute. His eyes had shone with recognition.

Bending to adjust the blinds, she saw that the cats were out on the ledge again. The big gray Persian just lay watching, as if the birds were cat television, but the little black and white kitten still tried to claw its way through the glass. They didn't seem to upset the birds, so she had slowly grown to like them. Tapping the window, she smiled. "Go home. Your supper isn't here." Then she took the thin hose down from its hook, went back to the sink, turned on the water and began to wash the cage.

At the bottom, a slanting tub ran to a baseboard siphon that carried water over to the kitchen drain, and she was proudest of this part of the design because it solved the problem of cleaning the foliage. The hose was meant for watering house plants, and starting at the top she let its warm spray cascade down over the leaves and even a bird or two who chose to stay in its way. The canaries sang loudest while the water ran. Would Haydn like their tribute?

And what would Andrei bring for supper tonight? He said he loved her only because she lived so near Zabar's, even though at this point it would make their life much easier if she moved closer to the U.N. Lunchtime taxis were costing them both a fortune. But having the river two blocks away was another safety valve—walking under the arching trees along its bank, catching snowflakes on her tongue before fumes belched from trucks and gratings turned their white to dirty gray. This month it was so warm most of the snow had melted, so Devika would not have to curse about her sari getting stained.

Twisting the small nozzle, Saira hung up the hose and shut the water off. The birds hopped with excitement, reclaiming their branches.

Now, what to wear. Having time to change was a luxury in itself. Not slacks tonight. The long soft moss-green Kandahari dress, embroidered with black silk at the neck and hem. In the bathroom, she drew a thin line of black along her eyelids and smudged it, then touched her cheeks and lips with gloss. Ten years in this country, she thought, and the longer I'm here, the more I seem to need these things from home.

The buzzer rang. Andrei was early.

Crossing the hall, she pushed the intercom button. "Yes?"

"It's your delivery, miss. Enchiladas. Okay?"

"What? Come up here." Andrei loved saying okay. He did it often and with relish, even when he was speaking Russian.

He stepped off the elevator grinning, "*Hola, señorita. Yo tengo* . . . How do you say surprise? My Spanish hasn't got that far. At this rate I'll never be able to infiltrate the Panamanian High Command."

"That's just as well. The mosquitoes down there are as big as pigeons."

"Saira, what a beautiful dress! You look wonderful in it." Setting down the large brown bag, he put his arms around her. "But then, I've never seen you look anything else."

"Hmmm. That's the one advantage of this situation. You don't have to face me in the morning."

"But I'd like to." He kissed her, lifting her off the floor. "Look, you have no shoes on. No wonder you seem so little."

"I wasn't expecting you till eight."

"That's no reason to go barefoot. This is only a false thaw. You have to be careful."

"Thank you, my babushka." Taking off his steel-rimmed glasses, she rubbed the red indentation they left on the bridge of his nose. It was his eyes she had fallen in love with, once she'd seen them without the shield of glass that made him look forbiddingly serious. When he had first come to work in UNICEF's Asia Program section, people said he was unfriendly, an arrogant numbers-man who thought he was smarter than everybody else. After watching him for a month, she had decided he was shy and absolutely committed to his work. Then, when she was moved over to the Year of the Child Newsletter staff, he'd brought her some figures one afternoon along with a cup of tea, and while they were talking he had taken off his glasses and she found herself looking into tired sensitive brown eyes that crinkled warmly at the corners. He said, "They all hate me over there."

"That's because you don't gossip enough." She smiled. "Try standing by the water cooler."

"You never did that, and everyone likes you."

"Oh, come on, Andrei. You don't really care whether they like you or not."

He shrugged. "Maybe. So long as you do. Where did you learn to speak such good Russian?"

And then a week later he had found it necessary to drop by her apartment, and the next day asked her to lunch.

Then, she'd been close to despairing of her feeble day-to-day effort to find reasons for getting up in the morning: shopping with Emma, dinner with Lori or a movie with JoAnne, and the random dates with men that just made her feel rigid because all they wanted was sex, and it was impossible to be very intimate with someone who thought Afghanistan was in Africa. For the first three years in Manhattan only Devika's rare visits had eased her loneliness, Devika's laughter bubbling up through hours of serious talk about their semivoluntary exile. When she called Devika to tell her about Andrei there had been a long silence on the phone, and then, "Well, I don't suppose it will isolate you any more than you are already. Just don't expect him to divorce that wife of his. Not if he wants to rise in the Party. I said socialism had a marginal benefit, not a major one."

But Andrei was the first man who had helped her believe in herself. Ashraf had loved a girl, his childhood sweetheart, the daughter of her father's household, and once she stepped outside the safety of tradition, that context ceased to exist. Andrei saw her as an individual, apart from her family and social position, encouraging her to grow beyond self-pity and her role as crippled victim. He said she was strong, intelligent, precious, and now she drew his head down to kiss the sore red mark left by his glasses. "I love you very much, *petit* Andrei. No matter how bad your Spanish is."

"Tu es petite!" Lifting her higher, he spun her around. "And no matter how good your Spanish is, my French will always be better."

"You didn't really bring enchiladas?"

He nodded. "From that Mexican place in the Village you told me about.

If Mohammad can't go to the mountain...But I have to heat them up." Setting her down, he smiled apologetically, "I wish we could go there together, Saira. There are so many things I wish."

"It's not that bad here, is it? I'll light some candles. Don't give me your tortured Russian look. Do you want to risk getting sent back to Moscow because we had to go out for tacos?"

"No. But I know you mind this. Anyway, it would be fun." Raking back his fine brown hair, he put on the glasses and looked down at her feet. "Do you want to risk getting pneumonia because you're too stupid to wear slippers? Go put some on this minute."

She came back just in time to stop him from putting the guacamole into the oven. "I can tell you've had a bad day. You're supposed to eat that cold."

"It looks disgusting. What is it?"

"Avocado salad."

Andrei wrinkled his nose. "I only got it because I remembered you said you liked it. That's the first word of Spanish you taught me." He had taken off his jacket and was rolling up his sleeves. "Enchiladas verdes, coming up, señorita. Did you start learning Spanish at Radcliffe too?"

"Yes, but just in my last year." Opening the cupboard, she took down plates and got out some cloth napkins. "I think I only went into languages because my freshman adviser told me I had an aptitude for them, and that was the first time anyone said I was especially good at anything. Here," she scooped some guacamole onto a tortilla chip. "Try this."

He ate it, looking at her with suspicion. "Are you sure this isn't garbage? Well, I guess I'm not in a very receptive mood right now. If I'd had to get on that bus tonight, I would have blown a fuse. We were going over the budget, and no one could agree on which set of figures we were supposed to be using. You may have a gift for languages, Saira, but you're an absolute genius at program work. You should be running the whole office. Do you know, you're quite famous in the Asia Section? They all say: If only Saira Anwari were still here!"

"Flatterer! I don't believe that."

"Okay, you don't have to, but it's true." He ran the tip of one finger down across her cheek. "I don't think you know how good you are. With people, as well as on paper. I miss you very much. Professionally."

Turning, she put silverware on top of the napkins on the plates. "I'm not sure I could stand working with you now, Andrei. Personally, that is. Everyone would see it in a day."

"Some of them know already. My assistant does, at least. He's just being quiet about it because he's afraid I still have enough power to hurt him more than he could me."

"Because of your important father-in-law." Her hands closed around the yellow plates. That photograph again.

"Hmmm." Pulling down the oven door, he picked up a corner of the tinfoil

New York

covering the tray. "These must be done now. I'm going to have some Scotch, but I've brought you a bottle of Mexican beer. Dos Equis. And I bet you'll only drink half of it." He glanced up. "Haven't you ever been drunk? Not even once?"

"No. And I never want to be."

"You wouldn't last very long in Moscow."

"I don't want to live in Moscow, Andrei." She carried the dishes over to the glass table and lit three white candles. "Did your mother start drinking when she moved there?"

"I don't think so. She drank wine, when we could get it."

"You could get it there now, couldn't you? Because of your father-in-law?" What a child I am, she thought, I ask for it, over and over, and then tell him it doesn't matter, I don't care.

"Yes, because of him. Unless I got divorced, of course." Andrei had come up behind her and she felt his hands on her shoulders. "I'm sorry, Saira. I don't know what to say when you ask me those questions."

"No, forget it. Keep answering them. I need to be reminded you really belong somewhere else."

"I want to be with you all the time." He rested his chin on the top of her head. "Wouldn't you consider living in Moscow if I got divorced?"

He had never asked that before, and she turned slowly to find him nodding.

"I mean it. Would you marry me?" Smiling, he reached to take her hands, but she stepped back.

"That's not fair, Andrei. You know you can't. Don't tease me to feed your vanity."

She went to pull the blinds closed behind the flight cage. He followed her. "It isn't so impossible. I wouldn't ask if it were. Here I propose to the woman and she acts as if I've insulted her!"

"Oh, sure. When you've told me a hundred times your father-in-law would wreck your career. Your wife's still in love with you, isn't she? So what would we do after he got you fired? Live in a little room while we worked as file clerks in some Soviet bureaucracy? You're as tied to your family as I'd be to mine if I lived in Kabul. Why don't you get away from yours too? Why can't we both admit we're hopeless mongrels and stay here in the melting pot? I think you should defect."

"What?" He shook his head, laughing. "I'm only an administrator at UNICEF, Saira, not a nuclear physicist. They wouldn't want me here."

"I have dual citizenship. Now you're getting frightened, aren't you. I could change that to American and you could marry me here."

"And then do what? Lead tour groups around the U.N.?"

"No. We have eight languages between us. We could open a school."

"You're serious about this!" He caught her arm. "I mean, you've thought about it. I'm glad. It feeds my vanity."

"But?"

Pulling her close, he wrapped her in a bear hug. "But, my darling Saira, I don't think teaching languages would be much more fun than working as a file clerk, in the long run. We both love what we're doing now, and being at the U.N. Besides, you'd never give up your Afghan citizenship."

She pushed him away. "Then why ask me to marry you? Just to see if I'd say yes?"

"Well, that would be nice to know." He looked bewildered. "Why do you think I'm working so hard? If I can establish myself in my own right, as an Asia Specialist, which if I may say so, I'm well on the way to doing, I'll be too valuable to demote. Last year my father-in-law could have sabotaged me easily. This year, it would be more difficult. And if my evaluations keep improving, which they will, by next year or the year after he won't be able to touch me. And my wife will have found somebody else by then. To feed her vanity."

"I'm sorry, Andrei. I didn't think you were serious. Did you mean to ask me that tonight?"

He came to steer her toward the kitchen. "Let's get the food before it's cold. I'm starving. No, I hadn't planned to, but I've been thinking about it so much, I guess it escaped. Will you keep thinking too, Saira? My wife wouldn't want me in Moscow if we divorced, so I could stay here for a few years at least, but after that there are no guarantees. I could be posted abroad for the rest of my life, or we might end up in Moscow, which wouldn't be as bad as you think. Your brother seems to have enjoyed himself enough there."

"You asked about Tor!" She stopped. "What did they say? Is he really alright?"

"More or less. But we're going to start eating before I tell you the rest. You always get hopeless when you're hungry. Oh, it's good to be here! This is all I have to look forward to."

"Me too. But I'm not feeling hopeless, Andrei. I'm just nervous because my parents are coming."

He was wrapping the foil tray in a dish towel. "So you're being defensive in advance? Bring those chips, I'll carry this."

In the living room, he set one cushion up against the couch and sat down on another, taking off his glasses. "You've made this place so beautiful I think you could live anywhere, but you're getting me too used to eating well. I get cranky now when the food's bad, which it usually is at Riverdale."

She sat opposite him, cross-legged, watching his face in the candlelight. Andrei never let his guard down at work and their lunchtime meetings were brief and passionate, so it was still surprising to see him like this, relaxed and animated and tender. Had he ever shown anyone else but his mother his vulnerable side? He said that in the twenty-three years since her death, this was the first time he hadn't been lonely; that he'd realized soon after his marriage that his wife's affection depended on how well he met the ambitions she had for him, and he'd needed to leave her to rediscover his own motives and interests.

Well, New York seemed the right place for that, and he looked so happy now. *I love him,* Saira thought—*why can't we both just stay here and forget about everybody else?*

"Half of these are chicken and half cheese," Andrei pointed with the spatula. "Which would you like? They smell delicious."

"How about one of each." She offered a plate. "I'll bet your mother was a good cook, since her son likes his food so much."

Smiling, he spooned out rice and beans. "You're right. In fact, she said half the problems in the Soviet Union could be solved if all the members of the Politburo would stand up and admit they wouldn't eat what most of our citizens have to live on. She said in France there would have been a second revolution by now, since no one would put up with such a diet."

"Why did she put up with it? Was she madly in love with your father?"

Andrei served a second plate, then pushed the tray aside. "She loved him, yes, and they had many things provided to them. They met in Paris, after all. If you mean, how could she live in Moscow after France, I think the answer is, she wanted to be where important things were happening and try to influence those decisions. She succeeded too, in some things, according to my father. Not that she had any illusions. But she thought exporting socialism was more estimable than supporting fascist dictatorships."

"And her son feels the same."

His fork stopped in midair. "Don't you?"

"Theoretically, yes. But I'm not trying to 'influence' anything, Andrei. I help edit a newsletter and write charming reviews of books and films on kids. And speaking of children, what did you find out about Tor?"

"Oh, yes." He took a swallow of Scotch. "Well, as we suspected, the official story wasn't the whole story. He wasn't just mugged. Sokolniki Park is a favorite trading place of one of our more visible social parasites, who has a sideline selling his victims back to the KGB. In this case whatever he took from your brother was too much to risk getting caught with. Tor's been known to sell national art treasures, so it may have been that, or gold or jewelry. The point is, Tor's graduated. He's not just dealing in blue jeans anymore."

"Then why is Mangal leaving him there! Does he want him to be sent to prison? That's all my mother needs now." Spreading sour cream on the enchiladas, she plastered it down like mortar. National art treasures! Didn't Tor have any conscience, or respect for other people's values? If that was still true after all this time, he probably would never change, but then he ought to be in Kabul, where he could be watched. Andrei had told her long ago about the string of girls who had followed in Karima's footsteps. Tor wasn't dangerous only to himself.

"My father's home most of the time now," she said. "If he and Mangal can't supervise Tor, how do they expect the university to do it? Punishing doesn't work with him. You have to bribe him to be good, and my parents could do that if they'd take the trouble. Do they know what you've just told me?"

"Mangal does. He may not have wanted to upset them any more until Tor's better."

"Yes, or because they'd bring Tor home, which would be inconvenient for Mangal. Never mind who else suffers in the meanwhile. He didn't even want them to visit Tor, since they might have felt sorry for him. What right does Mangal think he has to run everyone else's life? He's been doing it for years, and they let him!"

"In this case, he may have a point."

"How can you say that!" She put down her fork. "You don't know them. You can't teach Tor 'lessons,' and if he gets in serious trouble, it's only going to make my mother more miserable than she is already. I'll talk to them about it tomorrow and see if I can't change their minds."

Andrei sat up straight, moving one of the candles so he could see her better. "Then I should tell you the rest. And don't get angry with me. You asked me to look into this, so I did. I had a long talk with our ambassador to Kabul last night, who happens to be in Washington this week, and there are a couple of other things your brother Mangal's keeping quiet about. First, I heard from another source that Tor's injury is worse than your parents know. Apart from the lung wound, his heart was nicked and there's extensive muscular damage, so he'll be in pain and in need of excellent care for several months. Moscow's better than Kabul for that. And if he isn't moved, he's expected to recover completely."

"Expected to? You mean, there's a chance he won't?"

"Just a small chance, Saira. If his heart got infected... But I tell you, he has one of the best cardiologists in Moscow. Mangal knows that too. *Petite* Saira, he'll be all right. I have ten people looking after him now."

"No, I'm just furious!" Pushing away the plate, she shook her head. "My parents should have been told he's so sick! Is Mangal trying to protect them?"

"Possibly, in a sense." Andrei ran a hand along his jaw. "If they knew, they'd insist on going to Moscow, wouldn't they? I think Mangal's afraid they might not be able to get an exit visa."

"But he could get one for them. This is crazy! He works for the president."

"I didn't mean from Kabul, Saira. I meant from the Soviet Union. We aren't on good terms with Daoud's government now—in fact, less so than ever. He spent his first three years in office taking every bit of development aid we offered, and these last two turning his back on us in favor of the Saudis and the Shah of Iran, whose policies are only going to bring that mullah Khomeini back from Paris. Your President Daoud betrayed the Afghan Left, and then the Soviet Union, and the irony is that by doing so he's united your Leftists for the first time in history. And the greater irony is, our ambassador thinks they're ready to stage a coup, and we don't want it. Not if there's any hope Daoud can be persuaded to give the Left a voice in his government. Your brother's one of a very few aides who still have influence with him, which puts Mangal in a delicate position. He may be afraid that pressure could be brought to bear, through your parents. I'm not sure, I'm just guessing, but it's possible. Frankly, I doubt that Daoud listens to anyone anymore, and since our people in Kabul would know that, Mangal's wrong to be afraid. Of us, at least, right now."

"We've been afraid of you for a thousand years, Andrei. That's why we've always tried to balance your help with someone else's—to keep you from taking over. Are you telling me a Leftist coup wouldn't be in your interest?" Saira realized she was twisting her hands underneath the table, and folded them together. This shouldn't be a personal argument.

"What I'm telling you is what our ambassador said in all sincerity. Which is that our aid to Afghanistan was designed to serve as a model for other countries: development without intervention. It still might work, and in any event, Daoud's a better bet than your Left, because if they got in they'd start fighting among themselves again, and we'd be faced with having to choose one limited faction over another. So, we don't want that to happen, but there's a good chance that it will. Do you know the saying: My enemy's enemy becomes my friend?"

She nodded. "But if the Left is so strong now, how can Daoud afford to ignore them?"

"You should ask your father that question." Andrei shrugged. "I'd like to know the answer. I'd like to know how Mangal rationalizes all that rhetoric about the 'republic's revolutionary program of social and political reform,' when what he's actually serving is an oppressive, right-wing administration. Next they'll put the women back in veils."

"You should join us for lunch tomorrow. I can't talk to my father."

"I wish I could." Getting up, he brought the bottle of Scotch back to the table and poured out a little. "What do you mean, you can't talk to him?"

"I just can't. I never could." She scraped a tortilla chip along the guacamole. Even thinking about Daddy-jan made her tense.

Andrei smiled. "But you're older now. Do you imagine that if you ask him questions, he won't answer you?"

"Only in monosyllables. I'll always be a child to him, Andrei."

"Then draw him out and show him you're not. I've seen you work on people in meetings. You're very diplomatic when you want to be. And I think your father is a very...forward-looking man. I'm not sure you saw what was happening under your nose five years ago."

She looked up. "What do you mean?"

"Nothing. Never mind. Eat your supper." He was frowning into his glass and she saw that his face was flushed. "We've got so little time together. Let's not talk politics."

"No, don't patronize me. I want to know what you meant."

He passed his finger through the candle flame, once, then again. "I'm not patronizing you, Saira. I just don't want us to fight. Well, I've been listening to you talk about all this for months now, so naturally I've put some things together in my mind. But I may be wrong, and I know you'll think I'm presumptuous."

"Like? For example?" She took a taste of his Scotch and shuddered.

"You're sure you want me to tell you?"

"Yes. I just said so."

"Okay. But you won't like it. What I think is that it takes great vision to resign just before a coup. To leave a government one minute before it falls. As your father did."

She sat back. "What are you suggesting? That he knew the coup was coming?" Mangal's wedding was still a blur, everything had happened so quickly. The Nikka, Daddy-jan's announcement, Tor... and the next day she was gone, because Mangal had planned it that way. She said, "Mangal wouldn't have told my father. They were on different sides. Anyway, he had a reason for resigning."

"And that was...?"

"I've told you, Andrei, I don't know, except that it had to do with his honor."

"Hmmm." Andrei smiled gently. "Is it considered honorable for a minister's son to overthrow his king? But for that matter, would it be honorable for such a son not to warn his father? Who could support a man who had caused his own respected father to be killed? Coups are violent. They can't be entirely controlled. If your father had been killed, would Mangal be where he is today?"

Saira felt sweat on the palms of her hands and picked up a napkin. "No, that's impossible. If my father had known about the coup, he would have tried to stop it. You don't know him. He doesn't make accommodations."

"Not even if he knew it couldn't be stopped? Your king was in Italy then, remember. Warning the army might only have ensured a month-long bloody battle, which otherwise could be avoided. There was remarkably little bloodshed, if you recall."

Looking down at the candles' reflection in the glass table, she tried to remember exactly what Daddy-jan had said after the Nikka. Could he really have made that sanctimonious speech about honor... but he had certainly made another to her that night.

"It may even be—" Andrei went on. "You understand, I say this only as an example of things that sometimes happen—but it may even be that your father and brother are better friends than they pretend. None of the old ministers would talk to Mangal now, but I'm sure they do talk to your father. I wonder what they say to him about Daoud's fine government."

"No." She stared at him, appalled. "My father would never inform on them. Is that what you're saying? No."

"Saira"—he pinched her arm—"I only meant that your father could act as a voice for their opinions, if Daoud had enough sense to listen, which apparently he doesn't. I myself would be curious to know what those people think, and if you care about the fate of your country, you should be interested too. What happens in the future will depend on what's happening now, in the minds of a few men."

"I *am* interested, Andrei. But I've told you, I can't talk to him." Her voice sounded tight and strange. "Why don't you come to lunch with us, and then we'll all learn something."

"He intimidates you? Still? Is he that frightening?"

"I don't know. He used to be. He makes me feel like everything I say is aggressively stupid."

Andrei laughed. "Then I don't want to meet him. But you've changed, Saira, just since I've known you. I don't think that will happen again. Try, and see."

"You mean, impress him with my political astuteness? I can't even do that with you."

"Yes, you can. You do it all the time. What are you talking about? Ask him whether the government's going to fall or not. That's simple enough. Ask him what the old cabinet thinks—who supports Daoud, and who wants the king back, and who might like a real republic. Where do the intellectuals stand, and how do they perceive the strengths and weaknesses of each side? Those are the questions you've been wondering aloud to me for over a year now. So, open your mouth and ask them of someone who can tell you the answers. I can't. I wish I could. As long as I've known you, you've been agonizing about conditions there, and whether you can ever go back and live as an independent woman. You say you wish you could go back to work for women's rights, but don't you have some responsibility even from here, as an educated woman? You're not helpless. I know you think you are, but you're not. Your friend Devika would agree with that, I'm sure. Now she's someone I'd really like to meet. When will she be here?"

"The day after tomorrow. Twenty-four hours after my parents leave for Boston. They're coming back again later, but my mother's afraid if my father stays in New York too long now he'll have a breakdown."

"Yes, I know that feeling." Andrei cocked his head, smiling. "Have you told Devika about me? I want the truth."

"I always tell you the truth, Andrei. Yes, I have. Her and no one else."

"And what did she say about it?"

"That I shouldn't expect you to divorce your wife if you wanted to rise in the Party."

"Then she doesn't know I'm brilliant."

Saira grinned. "Let's just say she wouldn't take it on faith."

"She'll eat those words one day. But I still want to meet her. I'm sick of us living like mice in a wall and never sharing our friends. How about if I take you two out to lunch on Friday?"

"I'm sure she'd love it."

"I love you."

He held out an arm, and she moved around to rest her head on his shoulder. Hugging her, he smoothed back her hair. "Now, would you like to hear another story of my misbegotten boyhood? Have I ever told you about the white nights in Saint Petersburg? My grandmother lived there and she refused to call it Leningrad, to my father's deep dismay, so when I was little I thought they were two different places. I'd always visit my babushka for the white nights. The sun never sets at all, but the light is eerie, a kind of misty glow, and she'd take me swimming in the river. Well, I'd swim. She'd sit on the bank, cackling and screaming at me."

Saira looked up at him. "Poor little Andrei. All by yourself? It must be lonesome to be an only child."

"That's why I'm so jealous of your family. I hope someday you can introduce them to me."

"In a year or two? Maybe. Or else tomorrow. Or in six months you'll open an envelope and find out you've been assigned to Helsinki."

He kissed her forehead. "Then I'd convince you to come with me."

"To Helsinki? As your concubine? What would I do there, open a language school? Didn't we just have this conversation?"

"No, we'd marry and have a child and transfer out again quickly. The first time I told you I loved you, you said: Don't, you can't marry me and I want to have children. That's haunted me ever since. It makes me sick, because every day you meet men who could marry you tomorrow, and one day you'll get sick of waiting. You might start thinking you'll always come second to my work, or that you really couldn't marry a non-Afghan, let alone a Russian bureaucrat. I feel you're more my wife than Galina ever was, so all these obstacles are just technical problems we have to negotiate, but that's self-serving, since all the obstacles are on my side. Every time I leave you, that fantasy gets punctured. I think: how must Saira be feeling now, all alone in her apartment. It doesn't have to be this way for her." Holding her head in his hands, he gave her a long kiss. "Maybe it's too unfair to you. I don't want to hurt you, Saira. You could find someone else. A thousand men. Do you think we should stop?"

"Stop what? One night together every three months? You've never even slept here." His face looked pinched and white, and she drew him down beside her. "No, Andrei, even if we tried, I know I'd last about a week before I called you again. I don't want anybody else. I love you too. But let's not talk about our families anymore. It scares me."

He stretched out next to her on the cushions, pulling her against him, and she thought that his long, sheltering body was the closest thing she had known to a home in years.

"Then we should just go on like this? Week to week, with no commitment, waiting for the envelope to come? Is this really enough for you, Saira?"

He kissed her deeply, and feeling his urgency she knew that tonight there would be no long caresses, or kisses where no other mouth had ever touched her, but only a hard, brief joining of their bodies that would leave her bruised and empty when he left, as all their meetings did, but yes, she told him, yes, it was enough for now.

Fifteen

IN THE SECRETARIAT lobby, Catherine stood looking up at the turbulent blue Chagall stained-glass window, contrasting its fractured waves of color and light with the ocean they had just crossed. Behind her, U.N. staff members were drifting out to lunch, nodding to each other, bright in saris and dashikis. Yet in spite of the noisy crowd and solid concrete walls, the Atlantic still seemed to yawn beneath her, choppy in the early morning mist.

As they flew out of France it rose up suddenly, vast, gray and desolate. Ever since they started planning this trip, she'd dreamt of high surf throwing rainbow spray against the rock coast at Bar Harbor, and long white combers rolling in to meet the sand dunes of Plum Island. In Afghanistan, she had strained to recall the smell of kelp and the taut feeling of salt on her younger, sea-washed skin. From the airplane, though, the ocean had appeared as no miracle of diamond water, only a dim outstretched surface measuring the distance they would have to return.

Now the Chagall window offered itself in brilliant consolation. A passing tour guide had said it was a memorial to Dag Hammarskjöld, "expressing his ideals of peace and brotherhood." But the artistry was less formal and ordered than any description could tell, tossing up figures of men, angels, animals, in a flickering vortex as if to defy the medium's usual iconography. Here, God and man were joined together: on the right, a crucifix descended or arose from a crowd of faces that had to represent the struggling masses of the world, yet they were smiling, clasping each other, certain of victory.

A scattering of women, or madonnas, rocked their infants while other children flew toward the sky, and even the serpent seemed benign. Catherine wondered whether Omar would find this highly Christian imagery offensive. But he only glanced at the window, saying, "Yes, it's blue, just like a church, so they can all feel sanctified. Blue's the U.N. color because it's supposed to symbolize freedom of the spirit. Do you feel that here? I don't." Then he went back to his impatient forays up and down the hall.

It was not quite noon. They had reached the U.N. earlier than expected and called Saira only to discover that UNICEF was quartered in an office building on the other side of the plaza. Never mind, she'd come across to meet them at the Secretariat. Hearing the low, nervous pitch of Saira's voice, Catherine wanted to warn her: your father—be gentle, be careful with him. But Omar had stopped close by to listen.

Pacing the corridor, hands thrust deep in his pockets, he had alternately studied the flow of international complexions, then hunched his shoulders as though to avoid recognition. She had suspected he was torn between the hope of meeting old associates and a dread of answering their inevitable questions. After ten minutes a voice had called, "Dr. Anwari! Is that Dr. Anwari?" And the slight figure of a Thai diplomat sprinted toward them, smiling over the enormous pile of papers he was carrying. His grin was infectious; Omar relaxed, and she urged him to accept Mr. Lin's invitation to tea in the Delegates' Lounge. She and Saira would follow very soon.

Turning her attention back to the Chagall, she let its wit restore her composure. The animals all had human heads or wry, ironic smiles, and in the center a tiny sun was balanced on a mass of flowers from which a face emerged to kiss a child. Maybe life wasn't this cheerful, but now she felt willing to trade all reality for a few minutes of peace. Organizing the trip had taxed her already strained emotions, and their cab ride through Manhattan had assaulted sense and memory until neither of them could speak. If she were alone, it would have been easy to surrender to those changing vistas—the rink at Rockefeller Center, where she had skated once with Dad; the Biltmore, where she and cousin Meg had drunk their first illegal daiquiris in the lounge below the clock. But with Omar pale and gaunt beside her, she could only compare this visit with the last time they were here as a family, when everything seemed possible and the children had run screaming with excitement, "Mummy-jan, Daddy, look at *this*!"

She was nearly desperate about Omar's state now. For two years after the coup he had kept up a convincing front—the elder statesman gentleman-farmer dispensing cryptic, sardonic commentaries on the new government. Then, shortly after Roshana became pregnant, he fell into a depression. He had always been fond of her and was delighted by the prospect of adding "grandfather" to his list of other titles, until he realized that would require him to alter his distant relations with Mangal. "I can only teach this child what I believe to be true," he said. "But if I do, his father won't like it. Or should I be a hypocrite, and congratulate Mangal for smashing several lifetimes of work?" Roshana, who had never stopped trying to reconcile them, teased, "In that case, I'll have a girl. Which wouldn't trouble you half so much, eh?"

Her baby was a boy, and within days Omar's reservations disappeared, so for several months the tensions of both households were supplanted by wonder and joy at little Yusef. The child, whom Omar had defined as an emblem of the country's future, presented himself as a squirming, happy creature with no interest in political lessons. Yusef weighed almost ten pounds at birth, had a full head of black hair and huge dark eyes so mournful that even Omar would make faces to coax a smile from him. By the time Yusef could crawl, he had become a real comedian, as though he understood their need for laughter; and then just when the future was beginning to look hopeful again, Uncle Yusef died, and Omar erupted with a rancor and bitterness that never had truly left him: the coup was responsible, Mangal was responsible, he had destroyed them all.

As if to fulfill Omar's prophecy, Mangal withdrew in a grief of his own that his father refused to honor. Roshana brought the baby to visit, but Omar would not say Yusef's name. The depression returned and grew deeper. For the last two years, there had been brief periods when he seemed better, when he would start new projects or go off hunting in the mountains. But gradually Catherine recognized a pattern, and knowing these good days would be followed by weeks of even darker despondency, she no longer welcomed the sight of his rifle leaning by the door. In fact, increasingly, that rifle frightened her. As a last resort, with Mangal's collusion, this trip had been arranged: they would stay with her parents, so Omar and her father could resume in person the political debate they'd carried on by mail all this time. She smiled now, remembering how much their arguments had upset her when she first brought Omar home for the family's scrutiny. Then it had seemed as if they were fighting for possession of her soul, but through the years even that conflict had evolved, like a mirror of her marriage, through stages of passion and reason to settle finally in an attachment that gave unique satisfaction to both men.

She had decided this initial visit with Saira should be brief, so that before Omar had time to dissect and pass judgment on his daughter's life, their stay in Boston could do its healing work. Though he loved the children dearly, too often his regret about missing so much of their growth emerged in tones of accusation. Mangal and Tor were easy marks for criticism, even rage. But oddly, she felt most worried about his effect on Saira now.

Omar blamed himself that Saira had left home again, to work, unprotected, in New York, and given his current pessimism, that regret might spew forth as invective against her world, injustice and failure in general. Mangal could shout back: You're talking about yourself now! But Saira had never seen that. And here Omar had a larger target as well, surrounding them, a glass and concrete monument to all the shattered hope of his life.

She could recall him as a graduate student, scowling across the seminar table at Professor Kern, who was expounding with postwar euphoria on the "vision of Dumbarton Oaks." Omar had pushed his chair back irritably. "Yes, it all sounds admirable, except that it's not going to work. The Soviets are the only major force to contend with now, and they won't conduct their business in an open forum. It's naive to think so, just in view of their war diplomacy." Dr. Kern's blue eyes had turned on him. "And what about Afghanistan's war diplomacy, Mr. Anwari? Your much vaunted neutrality, which in fact provided a base for Axis espionage? Of course, I forget that in return Hitler called you the original Aryan race." She had watched Omar's mouth tighten and been surprised by his silence, but later, walking back through Harvard Yard, he explained that Kern was a Polish Jew, "so he's entitled to all the hatred he wants. What makes me so angry is that this United Nations idea might actually have a chance if people would face the hard issues. Instead, they want to close their eyes and pretend we're all good fellows together. Which, at this point, everyone in the world should realize is a pathetic illusion."

For over three decades since that hot spring afternoon, his ambivalence had grown in step with the development of the U.N., through conflicts solved, resolutions disregarded, and the various effects of missions that he himself had frequently served. But his opinion of its essential value remained unchanged: the U.N. was a chimera, a dream panacea without power to realize its mandate. In thirty years, words on paper had become this sprawling complex, and today, gazing up at the Secretariat, she had thought Omar seemed bowed beneath its weight. Perhaps he too was remembering the time when its delegates and projects had formed a network summoning him from Kabul to Cambodia, Aden, Yugoslavia, and then north into western Europe. His talent for bringing compromise from deadlocked negotiations had become legend. And watching his lined and sleepless face in the morning light, she had felt a wave of anger that in Kabul now, Omar was seen by many as a ghost of the past who had no place in the new configuration, while here he was still Dr. Anwari, friend to Nasser and Sihanouk, Tito and King Faisal—a luminary of so-called third-world politics—even if that respect must be too gratefully received from men like Lin, who were junior officials during Omar's best years. No wonder he hunched his shoulders, feeling, in his very eagerness, demeaned.

Whom would he have found in the Delegates' Lounge? she wondered. With any luck, no one from the Afghan contingent.

A voice came from behind her, "Mummy-jan!" And she turned to see Saira leaning over the gate to the front lobby, waving with one hand and fumbling in her purse with the other. She took a card from her wallet and showed it to the guard, smiling over his shoulder, but Catherine did not move, could only stare at this daughter who had changed so much. On the phone her voice was girlish, and Catherine still had pictured her as that rather awkward late adolescent, trusting, anxious, trying on images, lovely and shy. Now, even in this swirl of foreign faces, Saira glowed with exceptional warmth, and the delicate beauty she had owned at twenty was in full exotic bloom. Quickly, she moved through the crowd, holding her head high, and Catherine put out her arms to her, feeling almost faint with relief; her daughter had grown into a stunning woman, she was alright, she was fine. But looking up into that beaming face—for Saira was the taller now—she thought, and I've missed that. My only daughter, and I've hardly known her since she was seventeen. Why?

Stepping back from their embrace, Saira brushed the side of her own cheek. "Mummy-jan, are you *crying*?"

Sixteen

"I CAN'T BELIEVE you're really here! Where's Daddy?" Saira hoped she sounded less anxious than she'd felt a moment ago when she caught sight of her mother standing alone against the concrete wall, seeming small and frail behind the high-school group just passing. Under the fluorescent light her skin looked colorless, and there were streaks of gray now in the ash blond hair rolled up into a chignon. But her eyes were clear as ever, and her arms were strong, Saira thought, hugging her again. Mummy would never be old. When she was ninety, the rest of the family would still be leaning on her.

"You must be tired! That flight's always awful. Daddy *is* here somewhere, isn't he?"

"Yes, dear. He's in the Delegates' Lounge with an old friend of ours. Saira, if you're half as well as you look, you should run for mayor of New York."

"*Je suis un bête.* How was Paris?"

"Seen through a fog. And I don't mean the weather."

"Oh, Mummy-jan, it's so good to see *you*. I know I shouldn't say this, but I almost wish we could go to lunch alone. There's so much I want to ask you. Have you been going crazy, living with those lunatics over there?"

"A little bit. Not so much as your father has. But what about you, jan? Will you hate me if I tell you how much you've grown?"

"I'd hate you if you didn't. I'm fine, Mummy, honestly. You can take me off the long list of people you have to worry about. How's Roshana doing these days? She writes about everyone except herself."

"I'm not surprised. That's like her. Roshana's not on my list either. She's caught between a rock and a hard place, but she's managing very well."

"With the baby, you mean."

"Yes, that, and not being able to do the kind of work she wants."

"Because of Mangal's job? Isn't that a family tradition?" Saira smiled. "No, I was only kidding."

"If it is, you've broken it. Congratulations on your promotion! I got that letter the day we left."

"Then it took a month to get there."

"I'll have to speak to Mangal about that."

They both laughed, and Saira picked up her suitcase. "I wanted to show you my new office. It actually has three walls that go all the way up to the ceiling."

"And I want to see it. We'll make a date for that on our way back." Taking Saira's arm, she began walking aimlessly down the hall as if trying to blend into the crowd. "Do you know how proud I am that you're working at the U.N. and living on your own in Manhattan? It sounds so exciting! I like to think that's something I might have done myself. But you belong here more than I do now," she added, "my sophisticated daughter!"

Saira wanted to ask, Why didn't you? You could have done anything you wanted. But then, she had fought with her own father to go to Afghanistan. To marry Daddy-jan.

Nodding at a secretary from her floor, she steered them closer to the wall. "You didn't miss much, believe me. Even this new job is only a job. New York's a pretty cold place, really."

"Then why don't you come back to Kabul! We could use your expertise. At least think about it, Saira? There's nothing I'd love more than to have you near me."

Saira looked past her through the window at a brown patch of grass. "Don't, Mummy-jan..." She shook her head unhappily. Every letter from home made this suggestion one way or another. "I have thought about it. I miss you too. But it's just... impossible. I couldn't get a decent job there unless it was through Mangal, and I still don't want to be anywhere near Ashraf and his little bride. Besides, I can't live at home again now."

"Because of your father? Give him a chance, Saira. He was very upset that night."

"I know. I'm not blaming him. It was my own decision to leave." She shrugged. "So here I am. How *is* Daddy, anyway? I think Roshana's been more honest than you have about him. Her last letter said he didn't want to come. That he wasn't going out at all, lately."

"Well, yes. But he'll be alright. It's more of the same story: when he's overtired, he says things he doesn't mean. That's why he needs this trip so badly. And Saira, darling, I want you to promise me that no matter what, you won't get into an argument with him. You might not think he minds when you fight, but he could spend the rest of the visit flagellating himself and go home even more exhausted. We can't afford that now. None of us can."

Saira opened the top buttons of her coat. Was Mummy suggesting that she'd go out of her way to cause trouble—Saira, the perpetual brat?

"I don't want to fight either. Is it required by law?"

"It's not you I'm worried about, dear." Her shoulders sagged, and Saira gave her a quick apologetic hug. Mummy always had to be the go-between.

"Alright. I solemnly swear that under no circumstances will I raise my voice one decibel above sweet. Is that what you want?"

"Something like that. For the duration, at least. Now I suppose we should find the Delegates' Lounge. He'll be wondering what's happened to us."

"Okay." Saira grinned; the word resurrected Andrei's face in her mind. Willing it away, she took her mother's arm. "We have to turn around, then. Back this way."

The left wall of the lounge was glass, looking out on a courtyard by the East River, and standing against the light, her father looked so thin and stooped that Saira walked more slowly toward him. Then his arms were around her and for an instant she felt like a child again, as if he had just come home from one of his endless missions with a trinket for her in one of his pockets.

Smiling up at him, she saw surprise, then, yes, admiration replace the guarded look his eyes had first held. He murmured, "My little Saira?"

"Hello, Daddy-jan. Just now, I almost felt little. I was thinking you must have a present hidden, remember?"

"Ah! And you are right! But let me introduce you to Mr. Lin. Forgive us, Mr. Lin, this is my daughter, Saira." His hand still rested on her shoulder, claiming her, it seemed, and she saw relief in her mother's face.

Mr. Lin took her hand, bowing over it slightly. "Delighted, Miss Anwari. I'll go now, and leave you to your reunion." He bent to pick up a stack of papers. "Dr. Anwari, to see you here has been splendid. And Mrs. Anwari, too, of course. Perhaps when you come back...?" Nodding and smiling, he moved away across the crowded room.

They sat down around the low table. Saira said teasingly, "Do you really have a present for me, Daddy-jan?" Her nervousness had dissolved in a wish to make him smile again, to soften the deep lines that had appeared at the sides of his mouth.

"Most certainly I do!" He also seemed eager to take up their old game, as if it could dispel more recent memories. Drawing a folded square of tissue from the pocket of his jacket, he handed it to her, and feeling its weight, she was sorry to have forced this now. It should have come later, in his own time, after they had talked. But the package lay on her knee and he was waiting for her to open it.

Unwrapping the tissue carefully, she found two identical bracelets—smooth dark bands of flawless lapis hinged with gold. "Oh, Daddy-jan, they're beautiful!" She leaned to give him a kiss. "Should I wear one on each wrist?"

"No, no." He patted her arm, and she remembered that he had never been easily affectionate in public. "The other's for your pal Devika. You said we might meet her this time. I thought such great friends should have handcuffs."

"Devika loves lapis too. She'll be overwhelmed. Thank you, from both of us! Now, tell me all the news. How's my fat little nephew, for instance? No, wait, first let me get you something to drink. What would you like? They make very good cappuccino here."

"Fine," he said. "Your mother's been wanting decent coffee all day."

Standing in line at the coffee bar, Saira watched them through the screen. Daddy-jan didn't seem depressed. He was sitting up, peering around as if all the other people were minor guests at one of his afternoon teas. Could he be physically sick? Was that the reason they had come here now? But Roshana would have written if that were true.

"Cappuccino, right?"

Startled, she looked up at the young black man behind the counter. "Yes, three, please."

"See? I never forget an order." He turned away and she heard a hiss of steam infusing the coffee with hot milk. There were no trays left, and paying him, she balanced the cups in a tier, but coming through the narrow partition door her grip tightened suddenly and the top cup and saucer fell, smashing on the floor.

Below the green tapestry of the Great Wall of China, Andrei was standing alone and still, with one hand raised in a gesture that just then had seemed like a warning. He glanced over to the table where her parents were sitting, and she realized he had been telling her not to speak to him, but now Mummy was coming to help and when she looked for Andrei again he was gone. He had been smiling, she recalled. Was this an intended coincidence?

"I'll take care of it, miss." A janitor started mopping the broken china into a dustpan.

"It's all right, Mummy-jan," she said. "Why don't you take these two and I'll get another."

"No, don't bother now. Let's just go to lunch." She nodded toward their table, and Saira saw that Daddy-jan had turned his chair away from them.

We all want to get out of here, she thought. "Alright. I've chosen a place, if you don't mind a little exercise."

U.N. Plaza opened onto First Avenue and the wind came in broad gusts, chasing papers at them as they walked toward 54th Street. Mummy wound her scarf a second time around her neck, but Daddy-jan strode along with his face turned up into the wind and the arrogance of his profile was maddening. Had spilling coffee been such a sin? Whenever the slightest thing

New York

went wrong, he disassociated himself. When as children one of them cried or fussed he would stalk away as if it were Mummy's problem to solve. Then everyone had to tiptoe around until he decided to forgive them. Saira felt like mimicking Tor: "A thousand pardons, Your Excellency!" But remembering her promise, she smiled instead, "I'm taking you to the India Pavilion. I eat there a lot, and I wanted to show you one of my real haunts. Anyway, I thought it might help your culture shock. Here, we turn left at this corner."

She led them downstairs to the basement restaurant, hoping it wouldn't be crowded—they were early for her reservation for one of the banquettes in the back. The room was long and comfortable, gleaming with white linen, and she had imagined sitting across from them while fragrant plates of food were served in several courses. It was quiet here, though not too expensive. ...But why am I making excuses? she wondered. Am I still so afraid of criticism?

The host said a booth was free, and when they were seated, handed each of them a menu. Daddy-jan stared down at his with a faint scowl, and she thought, oh fine, now he's in one of his moods, so we'll all have to be quiet. Never mind that he hasn't seen me in years.

Seeming to read her expression, Mummy-jan said, "Saira, why don't you choose for all of us. You must know what's good here."

"Is that alright with you, Daddy?" Her voice sounded colder than she meant it to be.

"What?" He looked up blankly. "Oh, yes, whatever you like. Go ahead."

Pretending to study the menu, she tried to collect herself. They had come over here because he wasn't well. It was important to keep that in mind. He shouldn't have to be on best behavior with the family, but why did he have to withdraw? He always did this, put up a wall to keep everyone away, and if only he wouldn't, he might not be so unhappy. If just once he let them climb over it, he might find out he had friends.

A waiter stood poised and Saira held up her menu. "First, the vegetable pakoras, please. Then chicken tikka, poori, and pickle. And then beef vindaloo and tandoori shrimp and dahl. Oh yes, and some yogurt."

When he had finished writing it down, she leaned across the table. "So, tell me all about home. How's the wonder child? Has Mangal got him studying economics yet?"

"I've brought you pictures of Yusef...somewhere in here." Opening her purse, Mummy took out a square blue envelope.

"Just a minute," said Daddy-jan. "Do you have your bracelets?"

The irritation in his voice was unmistakable. What was wrong? Hadn't she praised them enough? Before she could answer, her mother touched his arm. "Yes, Omar, she's got them, don't worry."

Saira bent to the pile of photographs. There were enough, she guessed, to provide at least an hour of harmless conversation.

A running commentary was served along with the lunch: Yusef without teeth, with one tooth, with four. Yusef wearing tribal clothes, on horseback, supported by Mangal. Roshana and Yusef in their garden, digging a hole and squinting in the sun. Then they were joined by Karima and her children, and Saira stared in amazement. Tor's little "beggarmaid" had become a handsome woman, and her older son, Zia, stood tall as her hip. Zia, her five-year-old premature baby... had it occurred to anyone else that Tor might have beaten cousin Nadir to fatherhood?

"Are they close friends now?" she asked. "Roshana and Karima, I mean."

Mummy-jan nodded. "When they have time to be. They're both busy, but they get along very well. I'm glad. Roshana's in a difficult situation socially right now."

"Because her husband's in a bad situation professionally." Exhaling, Daddy-jan threw down his napkin, pressing his lips together, but glancing at her mother, Saira knew she shouldn't question him. She raised her hand for the check.

On the street, she suggested taking a cab to her apartment, then ran ahead to the corner of First Avenue to find one. Her neck and shoulders were aching with tension, and she breathed the cold air gratefully. Three more hours, she thought. In three hours they'll get into another taxi and I'll get in bed and pull up my quilt and wonder what this was about.

But a familiar silence as they rode uptown made her rebellious again. How long had Mummy been on tiptoe, and for what? Daddy's cherished sense that he alone carried the fate and weight of the world on his back, which gave him the prerogative to bully everyone else. Mangal felt that way too, of course. So much preciousness! But if this taxi blew up, would anyone outside the family really care? If Kabul disappeared tomorrow, and Mangal and Daoud with it, would the rest of Afghanistan suffer much from the loss?

I've been gone five years, she thought, and nobody seems to have noticed, but then I'm just a lowly female. Daddy-jan, why don't you get down off your camel and rejoin the human race. We may not be perfect, but neither are you, and it's warmer on the ground.

In the lobby of her building, he said, "A *doorman*? Well, very good, Saira."

"Oh yes." She tried to match his sarcasm. "And an *elevator* too. But speaking of servants, how's Ghulam-Nabi? Did Raima get those etchings I sent?"

"She did, and she's making her own frames for them." Her mother looked pale. "But I've got news about them too, jan. Raima and Ghulam-Nabi have gone to live with Mangal and Roshana. With little Yusef, there's so much more work...."

"Ghulam-Nabi's devoted to Mangal," said Daddy-jan. "And you know how much Raima loves babies. We have Uncle Yusef's servants now."

Saira pushed the button for her floor and watched the lights flash as they rose. So Raima and Ghulam-Nabi had been sent off to Mangal, after thirty settled years with Mummy-jan, because they were disloyal in their affections? Who was really being punished there? And he made it sound like a reward.

She opened her door with a flourish. "My exciting New York apartment!" and went to pull the aviary blinds.

"Saira!" Her mother followed her. "Your photographs don't do it justice. I can't believe you built this cage yourself."

"That orange bird's the one Tor gave me," she grinned. "I smuggled him through customs, which was quite a project. I had to give him airings in the ladies' rooms, and he kept getting away. He sings the Pashtun version of 'I Left My Heart in San Francisco.'"

She took them on a tour of the tiny kitchen, bedroom and bath, and when Daddy-jan was out of earshot, whispered, "Have I done something? What's wrong with him?"

"No, it's just difficult for him, coming back here now. Please be cheerful. I know it's hard, but try."

"For you, I will." In louder tones, she began to joke about the characters who lived on her hall, while her mother looked for each treasure she had sent from home. Daddy-jan was watching them stonily from the couch, and Saira asked, "Do you want tea? Devika's sent me some wonderful Darjeeling."

He shook his head. "No, thank you."

"Then maybe you'd like to see the newsletter I'm helping to edit. It reports on I.Y.C. programs all over the world." Yes, she thought, that's a good idea, find some common ground. There were a few copies in her desk.

She brought them to him. "This first one was done before I came. We haven't changed the format, but I did most of the writing in these two, and it's better, if I may say so myself."

He held and opened them awkwardly, as if he'd never seen such things before. Saira watched him scan the pages, but for a while his face showed no reaction. Then softly, he started chuckling.

"What are you looking at?" Smiling, she peered over his shoulder. There was nothing funny on the page he was reading, and now his laughter rose to a giggle and the newsletter slipped out of his hands.

"Omar!" Saira turned to see his name repeated through her mother's whitening lips. "Omar! What is it?"

"Nothing! Everything! Catherine, isn't it wonderful?" He was almost choking. "Isn't it fantastic? Those enormous buildings, tens of thousands of people, all that money, and *this* is what it comes to. Christmas cards and stupidity. The International Year of the Child. What idiocy. What supreme and utter nonsense. But why should I complain? My Saira has a *doorman*. Shouldn't every father want that for his daughter?"

"Oh, for heaven's sake, Omar." Mummy-jan crossed the room to sit next to him. "Saira, he doesn't mean that the way it sounds."

"Then how does he mean it?" Bending, she picked up her newsletters. No, they weren't much, he was probably right. Just words on shiny paper. Her words, and she'd taken trouble with them, but so what? She felt her fingernails dig into her palms. "How did you mean it, Daddy?"

"I doubt you could appreciate the irony. All the hopes we had... some of us had, and what a symbol that... organization was to my generation. I'm glad if you like your job, Saira, but just don't confuse the good it does for you with any... greater value. Don't start thinking it's real, or important, or..."

"Serious? Oh, no, how could I ever be serious!" Her voice shook, and Mummy looked so—Damn, she had promised. Promised!

Leaning back, he covered his face with his hands. "My God, haven't I taught my children anything? I don't understand what any of you are doing, playing games, but that's alright, as long as you're enjoying yourselves. When I was your age I didn't know the meaning of the word. Mangal sits in the President's Office talking about 'the people,' Tor's majoring in theft and bribery, and you write book reviews and have a doorman. Fine. Afghanistan may be falling apart, but why should that concern the Anwaris? We've all skimmed cream off the top."

Saira said, "I'm going to make tea." Because unless I get away from you, she thought, I'm going to break my promise. I'm going to tell you that you're blind and selfish and wrong, and if you don't understand us you have only yourself to blame. I care, and I'm not *enjoying* myself, and I'm not a "child" either. If you weren't so busy being a martyr, you might look around and notice that.

Behind the sandalwood screen, she filled the kettle and then rested her head against the wall. How had she ever hoped this could turn out well? Andrei had drawn a picture and she had almost believed it—that after so long they could meet as equals and share their thoughts and feelings. But Daddy-jan would never take her seriously. The harder she tried, the louder he'd laugh.

Measuring out the tea, she remembered that Devika must have gone through something like this in Calcutta, though it was impossible to imagine her cringing and grinding her teeth. Then how would she have handled it? Calmly, first of all. By stepping back and taking a cool look. "Consider the source," she always said, and Saira peered around the screen. They were whispering, and Mummy's face was angry... poor Mummy. She was the one who needed a rest.

Think of Mummy and consider the source. Daddy-jan. Alright, he was like a stranger. No use crying about that. How could he know her, when they had hardly seen each other in ten years and not much before then. The last time she was home, they had spoken only about Ashraf, about marriage, since that was supposed to be her one significant decision. If she had married Ashraf, Daddy would respect her as an adult, as the wife of a man of affairs, and if he couldn't see her in any other light as yet, that might be a problem of geographical as much as emotional distance. Because behind his wall, he loved her, and she had always known that. He loved them all and he must be lonely.

Pouring water over the tea she thought: maybe I can do it. Maybe I can make the peace and then we'll all feel better. What have I shown him so far? Only objects—books and furniture, and that's not what I've become here. That isn't what I'm proudest of or like most about myself. Maybe just for once I can climb over the wall and talk to him, and then he won't scare me anymore and he'll have some faith in me too.

But her stomach churned with the beginnings of panic. Andrei made that sound so easy. "Draw him out and show him you're serious! I've seen you do that in meetings." In the past, he had answered her efforts with a verbal slap in the face and she had disintegrated, like the last time, when she ran crying out of the room instead of staying to defend herself. Now Andrei might smile. "If he barks at you, will you go hide under the bed? Coward. Silly coward."

She put the teapot on a tray with cups and saucers. And so what, baby Saira? Even if you succeed, do you think you'll get Daddy-jan's approval? Are you still holding out for that? Because you'll just be disappointed again. Haven't you learned anything?"

Well, it couldn't be left this way. Another fight that would take five more years to get over. When they walked out the door, she had to be feeling strong, with the satisfaction of having held her own ground. Daddy-jan always acted as if he owned the keys to the country and she had no rights in the matter. But Andrei said, "Don't agonize with me, when he can tell you what you need to know. Open your mouth and speak."

She carried the tray out to the living room and set it on the table. This time things would be different. Diplomatic. And she was the only one who had to know it was a contest. A private victory.

"I'm sorry, Saira." He helped her set out the saucers. "That...establishment simply infuriates me, but I didn't mean to make a scene about it."

"That's alright. I understand." Yes, she recalled, he had always been good at apologizing after the fact. "Daddy-jan, I don't think my work is so important, I'm just trying to learn some skills. Which I'll need if I'm ever going to do anything worthwhile. Right now this is a better place for that, for me, than Kabul, but don't think I'm not homesick. Can't you remember what it's like to be cut off from your family?"

"But you don't have to be! We want you to come home."

"It's not that easy. As a woman, I couldn't be independent there. I hope that's changing, but..."

"The burden of being a woman! That's all I hear from you and Roshana, who happen to be privileged beyond belief. Don't be naive, Saira. You can't separate out one problem and use that as an ultimate standard. If everybody's starving, are women the hungrier?"

She poured the tea, smiling at Mummy. Well, that had certainly been the wrong tack to take. Women's problems always came last with men, and putting him on the defensive would only make matters worse. It would be better to start with one of his old bêtes noires, let him rave for a while, and then he'd congratulate her on her intelligence.

"I was talking about myself, Daddy-jan. Not the female sex." She decided to use shock tactics. "So, how do you feel about our president these days? A Russian friend of mine at the U.N. says our government's about to collapse."

"And what would you expect! Even Mangal can see it now. He was always painting Daoud as the great liberal, which shows how little history he knows. If I'd come home a few years later than I did, when Daoud was prime minister in the fifties, I would have been thrown in jail by His Excellency. That's how he dealt with ambitious, potentially threatening young men. Mangal wanted a free press? There's more censorship now than ever. And no elections. The literate can't express themselves, and people in the countryside can't vote."

His face had colored and Saira put down her spoon. "Then what do you think will happen?"

"Wait and see." He gave a stiff shrug. "There have been three countercoup attempts already, from the Left and from the Right. Someday, one will succeed."

"What do you mean 'someday,' Daddy-jan? Do you mean soon? How soon?" She couldn't stop herself. "Is that why you've come here now?"

"Calm down, Saira!" Mummy had been watching them tensely. "Of course he doesn't mean that."

"I'm sorry." She sat back. "I must be tired too. Daddy-jan, did you anticipate the last coup?"

"Only in principle. I wish I had."

"Do you believe what Mangal says about his getting involved at the last minute?"

"If Mangal tells me so, I must believe it." Drawing up his legs, he folded his arms and made a show of looking at the birds.

"Daddy-jan," she said, "you have to talk to me."

"Am I not?"

"You have to tell me what's going on. I have a right to know."

"Why don't you come home and see for yourself?"

"Because I can't." She glanced at Mummy, who had folded her hands on the skirt of her gray dress and was wearing her resigned-to-the-battle expression. "And since I can't, you have to tell me. You're my father. Who else should I ask?"

He poured another cup of tea. "Exactly what do you want to know?"

"Just what you *think* about it all. You say Mangal doesn't know history, but did you ever tell him those things? Do you think he learned them at the Sorbonne, or me at Radcliffe? But you sent us there."

Apparently, she had tapped some vein. He sat up, crossing his legs. "You see, Saira, it's all connected. It's the patterns that count. I've watched those men for thirty years. I know what they really believe. Do you remember the trade unionist, Mir Akbar Khyber? Babrak Karmal's mentor in the Parcham faction? When I came back in the forties, he was a leader of the Youth for Reform movement. He's moved with the times, not changed his nature. It's the same with Daoud."

"And what about you, Daddy-jan?" His eyes were bright for the first time all day, and even Mummy seemed more relaxed.

"Me? I wish His Highness would come back from Rome. He'd be welcomed with open arms."

"By part of the family, at least." Mummy smiled, and looking at her, Saira knew she had been hoping this would happen. A reconciliation, of sorts.

It's working, she thought, I could ask him the combination to his safe and he'd tell me now. Andrei was right. Does that mean I've been wrong all these years?

"Do other people want the king back too? The Afridi family, and the Durranis? And what about the old cabinet? My Russian friend claims they'll be the decisive factor."

"I think your friend is wrong. They've all been pushed aside like me. It's the military that needs watching. Daoud trusts that they're still with him, but he's living in the past."

"Tell me," she said, and for the next two hours, he answered her questions in detail and at length. Mummy threw in wry comments, and when they had to leave, Saira thought of going with them up to Boston. But she hadn't been invited. This was their vacation. And it might be better not to tempt the gods.

After seeing them off in a taxi, she began her ritual with the birds, but it wasn't comforting, and she found herself pouring some of Andrei's Scotch. It tasted like mouthwash, but the apartment seemed too clean to fall asleep in, almost cold once she'd drawn the aviary curtains.

Daddy-jan. He had enjoyed it too. On their way back, she would persuade them to see Tor.

Seventeen

THE TELEPHONE WAS ringing again, and extending a bare arm, Saira lifted it up onto the bed. "Hello?"

"Saira?" Andrei was almost whispering. He must be in the office, of course. Yes, through the noise of her headache she could hear a typewriter in the background.

"Saira, why haven't you answered before? It's eleven o'clock. When I asked your secretary, she told me she wasn't sure when you'd be in. You shouldn't let her say that, you know."

Smiling thinly, Saira wrote with her finger on the quilt, "Eleven o'clock. Mustn't let her tell..."

"What happened? Are your parents still there?" He sounded exasperated.

"No, Andrei. I drank some of your Scotch and it made me sick, so for once I didn't call in. Report me, like a good Russian."

He cleared his throat. "I'll come to see you."

"Now?"

"Yes, I can do it now."

"Alright, but don't expect me to be very articulate. I'm still not feeling well."

"That's the point," he said. "Isn't it."

After she hung up the phone, she pulled the quilt around her again. It had been past dawn when she got to sleep, five hours or minutes ago. The bedroom windows faced north and the light they gave was always cold. It would have been impossible to guess the time if Andrei hadn't announced it. At 3:00 AM she had unplugged the clock to stop the clicking of its digit panels. Now she was lying on her back swaddled like a mummy, suspended in a pale cocoon that made the world outside seem pleasantly unreal.

If only I could stay this way forever, she thought... warm, and quiet, and peaceful. I should have disconnected the telephone too.

Last night she had wanted to hear Andrei's voice, though. Instead of deadening her nerves, the Scotch had brought up waves of frenzied energy, and the afternoon's events had played through her mind over and over like a loop of film, until she started scheming "official" excuses for calling him at the Soviets' walled apartment complex in Riverdale. But the phones there were tapped, and anyway it seemed wrong to ask him for comfort after a visit from her own parents. He would think it had gone well, as she had when they left, because of their long conversation.

"What happened?" he had asked. That was a very good question, with probably a dozen answers. Finally, though, one thing seemed painfully clear: whatever ground she had held or won was a desert, a demilitarized zone, safe but sterile and without value of its own. She had pleased everyone except herself with that debate, backing away from anything controversial, and what had her real motive been? To help Mummy? To prove to Andrei that she could stand up to Daddy-jan? Or simply to manipulate the situation, for revenge, because she was hurt and angry and wanted to get the better of him, but sneakily, a weak, dishonest, very little girl.

Well, that was hardly Andrei's fault. He wouldn't understand what she was upset about, either. If he came and found her lying here like a patient wrapped in gauze, he'd accuse her of feeling sorry for herself.

Pushing back the covers, she got up slowly and put on her robe. He had been worried about her. It still was strange to realize that someone else felt involved with her life on a daily basis.

By the time the buzzer rang she had dressed in black slacks and a mauve sweater, fed the birds and boiled water for tea, though the wedge of pain in her forehead was no better.

Andrei closed the door and stood against it, taking off his gloves. "Why on earth would you want to drink my Scotch?" He touched her cheek. "I'm sorry I made you drop that cup, Saira. I didn't know what to do."

"Andrei, I'm not mad at you. Is that what you thought?"

Reaching up, she kissed him and he held her tight. "It was a hard day, wasn't it. Your father struck me as a very unhappy man."

"He is. Now don't make me cry. I'm all polished so you'd think I was the Rock of Gibraltar."

"You can't expect too much from a five-hour visit."

"I know. But that's all I have with them." He smelled of the pipe tobacco his assistant smoked, and she ran a hand down his spine. "Thanks for coming."

"Are you still sick?"

"Just a little. In the head, as usual. Do you have time for tea?"

He nodded. "Cheer up, now. Devika's coming tonight, and I know she's good company for you."

"So are you, Andrei. I didn't mean to grouch at you on the phone."

Following her to the kitchen, he took the kettle out of her hand. "What did you fight about? Tor? Or the fact that you aren't married?"

"We didn't fight. We had a reasoned political discussion. You would have been proud of me. And that's probably just why I did it."

"I was proud of you yesterday morning when you spilled coffee on your foot. You looked as if it had happened to someone else."

She sat down. "Did you follow us into the lounge?"

"When I saw you in the lobby, I couldn't resist."

"I told you what time they were coming in."

"That's why I thought you'd be mad at me."

"But I'm not, remember? I'm glad you saw them. What did you think of my mother?"

"I liked her. Immediately. I'd like to talk with her someday."

"No, you'd like to talk to my father. He said some fascinating things."

"Then if you didn't fight, what are you so sad about? Come on, let's sit in the living room."

Setting down the tray, he tucked pillows around her. "The tea will help your head. Aren't you even a little bit glad you could have that kind of conversation with him? I thought that's what you wanted."

"So did I. But you know what I've decided? Being taken seriously in my family means that you can talk about politics. Not anything more important. That's what he and Mangal always do—use it as a substitute. I almost wish we *had* fought over Tor."

He was pouring the tea. "Maybe they don't agree with you that Tor is more important."

"To me he is."

"Yes, now that you've reconstructed him." Andrei smiled. "A year ago, you told me he was a monster."

"And one month before that, I felt the same about you."

"Touché. Drink this now."

"Do you want to hear what my father said or not?" She took the cup. "You'll be proud of yourself, Andrei. You were right. You knew more than I did. As usual."

"Only because you don't want to know."

"That isn't true!" She sat up. "I care. More than you ever could."

"Then what are you afraid of? As soon as you jump over one fence, you put up another. But if you got over this, what makes you think the next will be so bad?"

"The perpetual optimist." She smiled reluctantly. "You're very smart, aren't you, Andrei?"

"About you, I try to be. And yes, I do want to hear what your father said, and what you said. I think you might find it interesting too, from this distance. Do you want something to eat first? You've got some English muffins in there."

"Please, don't mention food."

"Okay." He stretched his long legs out parallel to hers and took off his glasses. "Did they like the India Pavilion?"

"I'm not sure. Lunch wasn't a wild success. Until we got back here things were tense, and then they almost blew up. My father thought my newsletters were the funniest comics on earth. I've never seen him laugh so hard."

"You mean, he didn't find them brilliant?" Andrei held up his hands in mock amazement. "Don't forget, Saira, the cost of those letters may be more than Afghanistan's education budget. It's one more thing to feel bitter about, if a man's looking for reasons. You know your work is excellent."

"Maybe for what it is. I guess that was his point."

"Did you punch him on the nose?"

"No. I made him talk to me. And I take it back, Andrei, you weren't right about everything. My father didn't know about the coup beforehand. I believe him. And he believes Mangal."

"And he's worried what will happen to Mangal."

"We didn't talk about that. I told you, no soft emotions were expressed. It was strictly a history lesson. But he does think another coup is on the horizon, from the Left. Your ambassador has good information. Taraki and Karmal have mended their fences."

"Karmal's the Parcham faction, right? And Parcham means Banner?"

"Yes. Babrak Karmal. Very urban. The son of an army officer. Taraki and Amin lead the Khalq faction—the Masses. They're more rural. You might call them professional Pashtuns."

"Do you have a piece of paper?"

She smiled. "Really?"

"Yes. I want to get this clear for once."

"Alright." She got up and went to the desk. "Just so long as you don't tell Uncle Leonid about it."

"If he doesn't know this much already, he's in serious trouble."

Andrei listened intently to her monologue, taking neat columns of notes, and it seemed all this did make more sense to him, from the expression on his face. At the end, he said, "Your brother should quit. Why doesn't he? It sounds as though he's been compromising his loyalties for a long time."

"Maybe he can't admit that to my father."

"Or to himself? That's possible. But if so, I've had the wrong impression of him. Well, so much for your great experiment with democracy. Even a bad socialist government ought to be an improvement."

"You believe that, don't you."

"I suppose so. When you consider, for example, that our Uzbeks are more literate, have longer lives and a lower infant mortality rate than their cousins across the river in Afghanistan."

"So do the Pashtuns in Pakistan, and they aren't Communists."

"Not by much."

"Maybe so. But at least no one else owns their souls."

"Our Uzbeks can still practice Islam, Saira, if that means so much to you. Don't believe everything you read in *Time* magazine. We both come from countries that restrict the individual in favor of a larger group: in your case, family and tribe, in mine, the state. The question is, if you were sick, would you rather have a mullah or a doctor?"

"If I were a village woman, I wouldn't be allowed to see a male doctor, Andrei. And that won't change for a hundred years, if ever, no matter who's making the laws."

"Then there should be a push to graduate woman doctors as quickly as possible. I'm just saying, there are obvious things that could be done, if Daoud cared to try. Since he hasn't, someone else will. Wouldn't you rather have a stab at a real republic than slide back to Islamic fundamentalism?"

"That was Mangal's excuse in '73. I told you, I have trouble sacrificing human beings to ideology. I'm an Afghan, alright?"

"So's your brother, and he had no such difficulty."

That was true enough, she thought. Dear old Mangal. He'd walked over all of them with no apologies. Was Daddy-jan glad or sorry to see him struggling now?

"Yes, Andrei, but I don't pretend to speak for 'the people.' I'm a Leftist by inclination because I'd like to be able to live there on my own terms. Which makes me just another selfish Anwari." She stood up. "I'm going to take some more aspirin. Would you like to see the decadent, expensive bracelets my father brought me?"

"Saira, forgive me." He caught her hand. "I forgot about your headache. We shouldn't argue. Not today, at least. Yes, of course I'd like to see them."

Ruffling his hair, she went to wash her face in cold water, pressing the folded cloth to her forehead and temples. Maybe it would be a relief to have a screaming fight for a change, with Andrei in place of Daddy and Mangal. She could see him now in the mirror, bent over his notes, frowning. What was he writing about so feverishly, making arrows from one column to the next?

Putting down the cloth, she turned to face him, but he was oblivious, drawing lines, linking names and allegiances....

A drop of water trickled down her neck and she raised a hand to brush it away. No. That couldn't be. But he looked so odd. And all those questions, in such detail... "Too blind," he had said. "You were too blind to see what was happening under your nose." If he agreed with Mangal that politics were all-important, then why shouldn't he use her? Daddy-jan wasn't his father. And she had run back with the answers like a puppy hoping for a pat on the head.... No, no, she thought, I'm mixing him up with Mangal now. I must really be sick.

But Andrei's posture seemed almost furtive. And he was Russian, after all. A Soviet true believer.

She walked over. "What are you doing?"

He glanced up as if she had interrupted a complicated train of thought. "Just fleshing this out. I'm so terrible with names. When I talked to our ambassador he mentioned people I knew I'd heard of from you, but I couldn't recall who they were."

"I haven't told you that much, Andrei."

He put down the pen. "Is something wrong?"

"No. I don't think so. I just want to get this straight. Would you tell your ambassador those things?" She pointed to the paper. "Yes, you would."

"Are they state secrets?" Taking her hand, he pulled her down beside him. "Saira, he knows all this and more already. That's what I've just said."

"He didn't ask you any questions? About me, for instance?"

Andrei's brown irises contracted, and he pushed the paper toward her. "Here, take this back. I won't remember a word of it by tomorrow."

"No, Andrei, talk to me! I just want to understand. Why are you so interested in specific names? My father says it's the military you should be watching, not these people."

"Yes, that *I* should be watching. Brezhnev doesn't need to. Your officers come to him. If you're asking why I care at all, it's partly because of you, and partly because I have program responsibilities in the Asia Section and a change in your government could flush several million dollars down the drain, and also because I felt like an idiot talking to that ambassador for the first and probably the last time in my life."

"Alright. Don't get angry. You're the one who's always telling me to ask questions, so answer one more: If there *were* a coup from the Left, couldn't that information also be used as an enemies list?"

He looked down at the paper, then met her eyes again with his mouth set in a line. "Do you imagine they'd call up UNICEF to solicit my opinions, given our network in Kabul? Is that why you think I'm here? Saira, when we met you hadn't see your father in years."

"I know that, Andrei. I'm not accusing you of anything. I just don't want to be careless anymore."

"Okay." His face was dark. "You want to hear what you've given me? You should know it yourself, but I'll tell you. The rock-bottom value of this conversation is as follows: It's interesting to know that in your father's view the military is tilting Left, even though our people could judge that better than anyone else. Because what he says is true: if another coup happens it will come from there, not from his friends. They've tried one and failed already, according to our ambassador. Still, it might be useful to know if they'd support Daoud over the Left, since we'd like him to stay in power, and you should be concerned too, if you don't want Mangal to get caught in the crossfire."

The words hit physically in her chest. "You mean, it's coming to a choice?"

He shrugged. "I'm just guessing, but that's possible."

"Well, what decision would you make, from that list?"

"None. I wouldn't be able to. It looks to me like a three-way split and I'd tell President Carter that. Now take this back and forget about it."

"I don't want it, Andrei."

"Then burn it. Grind it up in your garbage disposal. Do you know why you're doubting me all of a sudden? Because you feel guilty yourself. If you were at home, you'd know these things without asking, so you're blaming me for your own embarrassment yesterday."

"That's what my father said."

Andrei still looked hurt and she gave him an apologetic smile. "It's true. I have this idea that I should be driving around in a jeep in the countryside, organizing clinics or something. But I'm not like Roshana. I couldn't. I'm not brave enough."

"She isn't exactly running for office either, in case you hadn't noticed. Your brother married a symbol and co-opted her. No, Saira, I can't see you on muleback, but living here doesn't give you the right to cry your way out of any responsibility. Your father's colleagues are on the outside too, and what they think still counts. Who knows where you'll all be in five more years? Just because you feel powerless now doesn't mean you can cut yourself off."

"But I *am* cut off, Andrei. I can't do anything."

"What can your father do? Only watch and think. Before the coup, what could your brother do? Wait and plan for a time when he could act. But you feel paralyzed. Why? Because you're still more a daughter and a sister than a woman in your own right. You still think you need your father's permission to have ideas of your own. You're trying to live in America and call yourself Afghan, and talk about change without being willing to risk anything for it. Women's rights? The first one should be to have an independent mind. But you've come ten thousand miles to avoid the consequences of that, and it still isn't far enough, is it?"

Pain began jabbing in her temples again. "Are you saying I should go back?"

"Not unless you want to. I just think it's time you made a few commitments. You can't make any kind of progress without losing things along the way. Your brother knew that, and he made his stand."

"I'm not trying to compete with Mangal, Andrei. He doesn't care about anyone but himself and his damn politics."

"Whereas you're so terrified of conflict that you'd rather cut out your tongue than say something unpopular. But if you could once get over that, you'd feel much happier, more than you've ever been. I don't want us to live in a soap bubble. How can I hope you'll ever really be with me, if you can't turn around and look behind you?"

"I will. I'm trying to, in my own way." She smiled bitterly. "I just don't have your network in Kabul."

"And besides, you still expect me to hurt you the way your father and brothers did."

"No, Andrei. That isn't true. Here..." She folded the paper and put it in his pocket. "Please. You have to trust me too."

"Saira, if I take this and I talk to our ambassador again, I'm sure I'll try to impress him with my overview."

"Hmmm. Devika said you wanted to rise in the Party."

"Oh, no," he laughed. "I only want to be an Asia Specialist. Someone of value, but no visibility. Likely to be well placed geographically, and otherwise ignored."

"Except during coups? That's the point, Andrei. Since I don't want Mangal to get 'caught in the crossfire,' you have to return the favor. If you hear anything, any inkling, you have to tell me. Will you promise?"

"Of course! I'd like to be part of your family some day. If I could help your brother, nothing would make me happier. Now I think you ought to try to get some sleep. Without a nightcap this time. What time is Devika due in?"

"At six." Saira grinned. "You know, when my parents were here, I remembered about your Scotch. I was afraid my father would find it and we'd have Mangal's wedding night all over again."

"But you said that's what you wished had happened. A real fight?"

"So, you and I had one instead. I'm glad, too. I feel better. With all respect, even if it came out of your skin."

"That's what we superpowers are for." He scratched the bottom of her foot. "Just scapegoats for everyone else's problems."

"You poor things. Andrei, can you stay a little while longer? If you go now, I'll sit here worrying that this has spoiled things between us."

He glanced at his watch. "At least long enough to tuck you in bed. I have another budget meeting at three."

"Then you should have left half an hour ago."

"I can be late, Saira. They'll be delighted to start without me."

Standing up, he held out a hand, and after a moment she took it. Andrei was not Mangal, or Brezhnev, or Daddy-jan. He was every bit as alone here as she herself.

In the bedroom, he pulled the shades down tight. "I want you to be asleep when I go. You aren't meeting Devika at the airport, are you? I'll set your clock for six, and you'll have plenty of time to dress."

"You're so efficient, Andrei. You should be secretary-general."

"Send my name in." He twisted his fingers in her hair, clasped her shoulders, and she kissed him, desperate suddenly to know if they could find each other again. It was too dark to see his face, but his mouth was warm and questioning—Andrei, who also always expected to lose everything without warning.

Pulling her down on the bed, he covered them both with the quilt. "You should marry me, Saira. You love me, believe it or not."

"Shhh, don't talk anymore."

He curved around her and slowly the darkness came down, moving into her, the same and also different from before. Indefinably, their balance had shifted, as with Daddy-jan last night, and it was just as unnerving and exhilarating.

Whispering her name, Andrei moved a hand to her hip, and when she woke again he was touching her there and kissing her good-bye.

The alarm was still buzzing when the phone rang, and groping by the bed to shut it off, she picked up the receiver. "Hello?"

"Saira, it's Devika. Listen, you're going to be mad at me. I have to go straight to Cambridge. I got a letter from my thesis adviser two days ago, and if I want to see her before her vacation it has to be tomorrow."

"Oh, no. But *I* need to see you! Couldn't you fly up in the morning?"

"No. I have to go over my outline, which is a hideous mess. I'm sorry. What's the matter? You sound upset."

"I just woke up. But I think I am. I don't know, that's just the trouble. Couldn't you even take the last shuttle tonight?"

After a minute, Devika said, "Well, I wouldn't get to your place until eight, and I'd have to leave by nine. If an hour would help, I'll do it."

And then what would I say to make your cab fare worthwhile, Saira thought. That I'm confused? As usual.

"Never mind, Devi. I'll be all right."

"But you aren't now? Wait, I'm going to put in more money."

There was a cascade of beeps followed by a recorded message.

"Now tell me what's going on."

"Andrei asked me to marry him. That's the first part."

"Oh?" Devika gave a surprised laugh. "And what did you say?"

"I accused him of being a spy."

"For wanting to marry you? Wouldn't that be slightly above and beyond the call of duty?"

"Then he asked me for information, and I gave it to him. From my father. Nothing their real spies wouldn't know, but..."

"You're afraid you gave it to him because you're still so angry at your family."

Sitting up, Saira almost dropped the phone. "No! I don't think so. That's what we argued about. He claims I'm incapable of doing anything they wouldn't approve of."

"So you showed him he was wrong?"

"Oh, God, Devika, that's why I wanted to talk to you. I can't sort it out. Which, according to Andrei, is exactly my problem: that I can't separate abstract principles from my emotional attachments."

"Well, good for you. There's no such thing as an impersonal motive, in my opinion. But Saira, I wouldn't worry too much about it. You haven't committed an act of treason. And he'd be stupid if he weren't curious. I want to hear what your father said too."

"But you aren't a Soviet bureaucrat."

"If you don't trust him, how can you love him?"

"Trust him to do what? Change his stripes? The funny part is, it goes both ways. He might be able to warn us if something were about to happen at home."

"Or he might distinguish himself at his next high-level meeting, and they'd give him more ... freedom of movement?"

Saira lay back on the pillows, straining her eyes against the darkness. "Devi, how can you do this to me? You're making me feel awful."

There was silence, then a long exhalation. "I'm sorry, Saira. I just spent six months in Calcutta, and I'm not sure of anything anymore. I'm Bengali, I've never felt that more strongly, but I don't want to live there under a microscope. So maybe I've been fooling myself. We both feel like deserters, but it could be just as well if we work out our upper-class 'destiny' by staying here and doing the least harm."

"In spite of our expensive educations?"

"Our Western educations? That's the white man's burden. You come by it honestly, since your mother's American. What I want to know is, are you going to marry Andrei?"

"Not unless he defects. We'd need to have neutral ground."

Devika chuckled. "How long are you prepared to wait for that phenomenon to occur? He's happy right where he is, isn't he?"

"Yes. I'm not waiting. When you were gone, I put myself on a diet of not hoping anymore. Except to see you, dammit."

"I'll come next weekend, if that's all right. We've never been depressed at the same time before. Maybe telling stories will get us both laughing again."

"Oh, yes, please do! My father brought us presents. Handcuffs. He wants to meet you too. So does Andrei."

"Good. We can have our own U.N. And I bet we'll all vote the same way."

Saira laughed. "I wouldn't count on it, but I think you'll like them. Alright, my friend. I feel better now. I'm so glad you're back."

"Me too. Just don't tell anyone at Harvard that. I'm still trying to intimidate them. Lots of love, Saira. I'll call you later in the week."

"The same to you. Bye, Devika."

She had almost hung up the phone when she heard a sound from the receiver and held it to her ear again. "What?"

"I said, I meant to add, congratulations on your promotion."

APRIL 1978
Kabul

Eighteen

CARRYING HIS TEACUP out to the garden, Mangal breathed the warm spring air. Overnight, apricot and cherry trees had burst into early blossom, and now buds of almond and pear were coloring too. In the flower beds, fine grass had started that would have to be turned under, but for a few days this green looked more fresh than anything else in nature. Even in the years of drought, he recalled, there had been one week each April when it seemed the land would be forgiven.

The trees were young, just a tracery against their compound wall. In another month, vines would conceal the mud brick, but it would be twenty years before the garden looked alive in every season, as his parents' did. Still, he had planted this orchard himself, and today he felt like calling birds down to nest in its branches.

"Daddy-jan!" Yusef shrieked, indignant that his mother had stopped him to button his red sweater. "Wait! I have something to show you." He ran out, pushing back his tasseled hat, "Daddy-jan, the tulips are opening! You were waiting for them, weren't you?"

Roshana followed him, drawing her long hair from the folds of a white wool shawl, and smiling at her, Mangal swung Yusef's light body into the air. "Yes, Bechaim. But I trusted you to tell me when they were out."

They walked to the far wall, where three scarlet blooms were showing in the cluster of high shoots. "Yusef," Roshana said, "do you remember our surprise? Daddy's poem? How does it begin?"

The boy's smile shifted to a frown of concentration.

Roshana prompted, "'Where does...'"

"I know," Yusef cried. "'Where does the spring come from?'"

"'Anemone...'"

"'Anemone, basil, lily, thyme.' But why 'time,' Mummy?"

"No, silly." Mangal tickled him. "That's a plant. An herb to use in cooking. What's the next line?"

Yusef fingered the curved crystal pendant under Mangal's shirt. "I forget. Will you say it, Daddy?"

He put his lips to Yusef's ear. "'Where does the spring come from? Anemone, basil, lily, thyme. Jasmine, white rose, narcissus, pomegranate. But most beautiful everywhere is...'"

"'The dark red tulip!'" Yusef finished triumphantly.

"And who wrote that poem, Bechaim?"

"The famous Pashtun warrior poet..." he stammered, "Khushal Khan Khattak."

"Good. Next spring you'll know every word."

Yusef scrambled down to prowl the garden. "And here, tomato plants will grow, and here already is rhubarb, Mummy? And in the fall we'll cut them up and put them into jars, right? And eat all winter long?"

"Don't be in such a hurry," Roshana laughed. "Let's have the summer first." She stretched her arms up and back over her head, and the shawl fell open. Until this week, her pregnancy had not been noticeable, but now the front of her yellow dress swelled slightly below her breasts. Soon Yusef would have to be told that when the harvest came there would be another mouth to share it, and Mangal wondered how that news would be received.

He put an arm around her waist. "Do you have a boy or a girl there?"

"A girl this time, I think. I'd like to name her Rabia."

"So we'll have our own poet in the family?"

"Or a heroine, at least. I have a feeling she'll need to be."

Roshana's voice was brittle and he kissed her temple. "Yes, like her mother. One day I'll tell her how you got that scar."

"And scare her to death? Mangal, I want to bring the wicker table out."

"Now? But we can't sit here with Karima."

"Oh, heavens, no. Anyone might think we were equals." She reached to pull the tassel on Yusef's hat. "Jan, why don't you go into the kitchen and Raima will give you a cookie."

"Yes, I will!" He went to pry open the door, and Mangal looked at his watch.

"What time is she coming?"

"Soon. Around noon. And she can't stay long, of course. Now that she's supposed to hate us so much."

"But her parents live here too."

"You were the one who made such a point about her keeping away. Being careful."

"Only for her safety, not ours. Oh, Roshana, I've put your best friend out of reach, haven't I? But it was her idea and it's just for a few months."

"And then what? Karima's spying for us, Mangal, on Leftists who ought to be our friends. But they aren't our friends anymore, and I don't see how she can be either. If she turns around one hundred and eighty degrees, don't you think they'll know it was a false conversion? How safe will she be then?"

She was staring past him, and he dropped his hands from her shoulders. "When I came back from Paris, you didn't consider Babrak Karmal and Taraki our friends. You said they had one foot in Moscow. And as long as they're most interested in running cults of personality, they can call themselves nationalists all day and you'll still be right."

"I wasn't thinking only of them. Zalmai's with the underground now. And Professor Durrani would be too, if he didn't hate Babrak so much for what he did at the university."

"For exploiting his precious students? That gets easier by the year. You just have to tell them exactly what they want to hear, which is that they should get everything free. Babrak's their great hero because he's been in jail, and in Parliament, where he did nothing but cause trouble, and Taraki's a romantic who writes Marxist fiction. What other qualifications should anyone need to be president?" Shrugging, he kicked a pebble off the path. "I wish we could have a minor Western sexual revolution. Sap isn't the only thing that rises in the spring, and Babrak's well aware of that. He'll use it. He and Taraki haven't joined forces out of love for each other, I promise you."

"I know. But we were used too, Mangal. Daoud used your brains and name and he still is. We were students in '73. What better credentials did we have?"

She was right, of course, he thought. The parallels were so obvious it was laughable, except that five years ago neither he nor Roshana had wanted to take power, until there seemed no alternative, and now they were captives of that choice.

"Well"—he touched her scar—"you had this. I'd just learned about government at my father's knee. The difference is that Babrak's father's a general in the army. What do you suppose he learned at home? Roshana, if we make it to September I'll quit, but the way things are, I can't now. We have to know what's going on, for everyone's sake. And in the meantime, maybe I can pour a little ersatz oil on the waters."

She took his hand, walking into the orchard. "What would that consist of?"

"Putting out some official disinformation. The most important thing is to give an illusion of strength, so the Russians won't get nervous. When I tried to convince Daoud the army's crumbling, he had General Rasuli 'investigate,' and his report says just the opposite: no widespread defections. The Left may claim otherwise, but if Daoud can swallow that, maybe the Soviets will too, with my encouragement. The Khalqis exaggerate so much, they've lost credibility. If they're saying they own the military, they'll need corroboration."

"Hah!" Roshana shook her head. "They could get that from your father, any day of the week. He positively gloats about it."

Mangal picked a white petal from her hair. "That's why I was hoping he'd stay in the States another month. So he could talk it all out of his system with my hawk of a grandfather."

"Yes, you were very helpful planning that trip," she grinned. "And then they came back too soon to suit you. But Mangal, he'd hardly tell the Soviet ambassador the things he says to you in private. Don't worry. He doesn't want a coup either."

"Oh, good. That makes six of us! Isn't it hilarious, though? We went with Daoud because we thought he could handle the Russians, and since he's turned to the Islamic bloc, I'm the one who plans how to manage the Soviet ambassador. It's just another public relations job: not the truth, only what can be made to seem true. Maybe Karima will give us the reality. In fact, we'd better go in."

"No, wait." Roshana held his arm. "I want to ask you something. Out here, where Raima can't hear us."

"What?" Her skin was glowing in the sun, and he recalled that she had also been especially lovely while she was pregnant with Yusef. He folded the shawl across her chest. "What would you like to know, my beautiful wife?"

"It's whether... I'm afraid Karima's taking risks for us out of some sense of obligation. Do you think that could be the case? When she was carrying Tor's child, you found her a husband and gave her a dowry, and if Zia's starting to look like an Anwari, that's fine, since Nadir's your second cousin. You've given them a lot of help, and they're proud people. Do you see what I mean?"

"The way you say it, she ought to hate me! Roshana, I didn't bribe Nadir to marry her. Karima wouldn't let me. He was so blindly in love, she could have passed Zia off as his, and at the time I thought she was foolish not to. All we've done is keep their secret. I may have made her some promise on our wedding night, but it's only thanks to luck and chemistry that no one's been dishonored. Not even Tor, for once, though I hope to God he'll never guess it. He was always bad at arithmetic."

Roshana's crooked smile was skeptical. "You don't think he's ever wondered?"

"No. If he even suspected, he would have written me a screed. Come on, let's go in. And as for Karima, I think her involvement with the Left is as pragmatic as mine with Daoud at this point. If there's a coup, it will be a bloody mess and she might not come out of it either. She has three kids, I've got a baby, a pregnant wife, one sick brother and a crazy father. I can't picture us running very fast, can you?"

"If you resigned, we might not have to worry about that."

"Then I'd just be a coward." Opening the door, he thought, Roshana, don't you see it yet? There's no way out for us. It's too late to go back to graduate school and start all over again.

Down the hall, Raima was setting places in the small sitting room that Roshana had decorated with Shiraz carpets and blue and green cushions and bolsters. A white cloth covered the low table and beside it an antique samovar was already steaming. For the rest of the house she had chosen more modern furnishings, but this was the room where they always came to talk out of earshot of the household, and later they would speak in English for added privacy.

He said, "Raima, you genius, whatever you're cooking smells delicious. Will you forgive us for stealing your daughter away for lunch?"

"Only this time. And she will leave hungry. Karima can never eat if she's in a hurry. But it's very kind of you to help her with her term paper. She's been working too hard this semester."

When she left the room, Roshana closed the door. "Some term paper. Aren't we wonderful? Mangal, that reminds me, you'd better write to Saira. I had a letter from her yesterday, and she has some idea that your father made Raima and Ghulam-Nabi come here because he couldn't stand how fond they are of you."

Slipping off his shoes, he stretched out on the cushions. "Well, he wouldn't have told her he didn't trust the servants we had. I still don't know whom he saw Sayyed talking to in the bazaar, but it's just typical of him to look for that, and find it."

"He's been at this much longer than you have." Roshana sat down carefully. "I wish you two would make it up. He could advise us better than anyone now."

"In his own way, he *is* helping, though." The spigot on the samovar jammed, and Mangal cursed as the tea came in a rush. "Anyway, if we seemed much closer, he might not keep getting such good information. Most of his friends are scared to open their mouths, since Maiwandwal's coup failed."

"Can you blame them?" Twisting back her hair, she added sugar to the tea. "They don't want to get beaten to death in prison. So, neither do I."

"Ah, but that was a tragic mistake, remember? Which gave Daoud just the excuse he needed to get rid of 'unreliable' Leftists—meaning almost everyone but me. That's when I should have quit."

"Then why be a hypocrite? Your father resigned when the king wanted him to stay on."

He sat up. "For the tenth time, it's not a question of Daoud's wanting me. He doesn't anymore, I've fought with him so much, but I'm a token liberal with limited influence, so he'd lose more than he'd gain by firing me. I'm a thorn in his paw. Where else should I be? Right now his brother Naim and I are the only ones pushing him to make concessions. We can't let him burn all his bridges. That's why I have to see your Uncle Aziz this afternoon. He won't talk to anyone else in the government. And when one of the most powerful khans in Paktia feels he's been treated like a peon...doesn't that frighten you a little?"

"Yes, of course it does. And it upsets me more that for the best reasons in the world, we always seem to wind up on the wrong side. I agree the Left isn't ready to take over now. But what if we'd worked with them for the last three years instead of trying to prop up Daoud?"

"Do you think they would have welcomed us? Karmal and Taraki? We'll always be a threat to them, Roshana."

She closed her eyes. "Even if we moved to Paghman? Maybe I just want to build my nest, Mangal, but it seems to me you're gambling our future on your ability to control an incredibly volatile situation. What if you can't?"

Then we'll probably all die, he thought. No matter where we're living.

He took her hands. "Are you thinking you married into the wrong family?"

"Not yet." She gave a slow smile. "After all, there's my family too. If Uncle Aziz heard me say one good word about Taraki, he'd saw my tongue out with a rusty knife. Why does he want to meet you in Mirzaka, anyway? That's right in the middle of nowhere."

Outside, a car door banged. He said, "That must be Karima," and stood up. Roshana's question was not one he wanted to answer.

Karima's high, clear voice came from the kitchen and he stepped back as she walked down the hall. "Jan, what have you done!"

"Yes, my mother's crying into your soup," she smiled. "I've cut my hair and I like it. Don't you?"

"What?" Roshana leaned back to look out at her. "I don't believe it. Come in here."

Karima shook her head forward, laughing. "See? It dries in fifteen minutes. And I think it looks nice, though it does feel very peculiar to be bald."

"Please, sit down," Roshana said. "It takes me half an hour to get up these days." Hesitantly, she put a hand out to touch the short curls. "Oh, your beautiful hair! But this is pretty too, on you. It shows up your eyes more. Is it also supposed to advance the cause of socialism?"

"If you mean, did I do it as a statement, yes, but I think I was curious as well."

Mangal set a cup of tea in front of her. "What does Nadir think?"

"That it will grow back, and the sooner the better. Really, this sort of backfired. Taraki was shocked. Do you know why? He wants me to start spying on you, and he's afraid it might make you suspicious."

"Then at least they've accepted you." Mangal realized he was staring and lowered his eyes. Karima had always looked young for her age, but now with her long neck bare she seemed taller, her features stronger.... If he had met her in the bazaar, he thought, he wouldn't have recognized her.

She crossed her legs. "Well, why shouldn't they? I'm a Tajik. There's no room in the government for anyone but conservative Pashtuns. I was your servant. Why shouldn't I want to reverse our roles?"

"I've been wondering that myself," said Roshana dryly. "Maybe you will, before long. Taraki's an eloquent man."

Pulling her bright orange dress around her knees, Karima nodded. "In principle, I think he's right. But Daoud isn't a fascist and Afghanistan's not Cuba. We don't have a few rich families exploiting our nonexistent natural resources. They talk about revolution, but it's for themselves they want it most, and I won't help...." She struck the table, unintentionally, he thought, from the look on her face. "I won't help them start a war and kill people. ... That's what they want to do. I'm sorry. I think I know too much now, and I'm just as scared as you, Mangal."

He glanced up as the door opened and Raima came in with a tray, but she didn't seem to notice the angry color in Karima's cheeks. "I've made the squash you like, and there's lamb pilau and yogurt. Will that be enough?"

"More than." Roshana put up her hands to take it. "Thank you. We'll serve ourselves."

"I'll come have tea with you later, Mummy-jan." Smiling at her, Karima reached out to shut the door. "Do you think she heard me?"

"I'm sure not. What do you know, jan? Something more than last time?" A nervous throb started in his temple. Her eyes had already answered him.

"Just since yesterday, yes. You wanted me to find out if there was some kind of ... committee? That could make the decision to fight if an opportunity came up?" She was almost glaring at him. "Well, it's gone far beyond that, Mangal. Plans? Oh yes, they have them. Down to the last detail, on paper—maps, charts, chains-of-command of Khalq cells in the military—it's amazingly complete. I'll bet they could mount a coup in twelve hours. Maybe less."

"That's wonderful," he said. "So much for Rasuli's report. I knew it." When she looked quizzical, he explained, "One of Daoud's generals just gave the army a clean bill of health."

"Then he must be deaf and blind. I only had three minutes alone with this ... document, but the military section's the largest part. There are ten pages of names. How could the generals not know what's going on right under their noses?"

He shrugged. "Some of them must. They may just have mixed feelings about it. Daoud was brought to power by officers trained in the Soviet Union who expected him to be Moscow's best and most moderate friend. Well, it hasn't worked out that way. But the older men can't be too enthusiastic about a civilian like Taraki. They probably just want to be sure of coming out on the winning side."

Roshana asked, "Do you think the Soviets are behind this?"

"I doubt it." He shook his head. "If they were, they wouldn't be leaning on us so hard to put Leftists in the cabinet. They'd act as if everything were fine."

"It's such a good plan," said Karima sardonically, "they're very impatient to use it. All they need is the right excuse. Taraki's strongman Hafizullah Amin is the one who scares me most. He's in charge of this scheme and he seems absolutely ruthless."

"Yes, Amin's a real opportunist." Mangal felt a spreading cold sensation in his chest. "What about the Parchamis? Are they so eager too?"

"Babrak is, but he still listens to Mir Akbar Khyber, who's much more sensible. Khyber says that as a trade unionist, he's responsible to all his men. And Babrak treats him as if he were his father."

"Well, that's something, anyway." Roshana folded her arms across her belly. "I find this incredible. I never thought Karmal and Taraki could agree on what time of day it was."

"You can thank the Russians," he said. "I hope they're happy. They made a marriage of convenience to put pressure on us, and now it's out of hand. In '73, Babrak was on top, and now Taraki has the edge, and they're going to keep at it till one of them's dead, no matter what their instructions are." He gestured at the untouched tray of food. "What's wrong, ladies? Aren't you hungry?"

"Mangal"—Karima touched his sleeve—"do you think this will help you? To persuade Daoud it's not just talk anymore?"

"I don't know. I'm not sure what to tell him. He hasn't listened so far, and if he didn't believe me, he'd go around crabbing about it. Which might only put the Khalqis on warning and expose you into the bargain."

"Listen, Karima"—Roshana's voice was sharp—"if you feel anything odd ... strange looks from anyone, pretend you're sick and get right out of it, please. I worry about you all the time."

"Thanks." Karima patted her knee. "But I'll be alright. I'm just a peasant. It's you who should be taking care, Roshana. My children need another cousin to play with, not a houseful of guns. Can't you eat even a little? Come on."

"You sound just like your mother," she smiled. "To tell you the truth, I'm ravenous."

"Well, I'm not." Mangal stood up, "I don't want lunch. I have to get out to Mirzaka, which it may take me all afternoon to find. If we're going to keep a lid on this, Uncle Aziz may be the man of the day, since the Khalquis have been trying to start trouble in Paktia all month. Now I think I know why."

Roshana put up her cheek for a kiss. "Aren't you going to change your clothes?"

"No." He brushed off his khaki pants, "I'm taking the jeep. These match it." Resting a hand on Karima's head, he smiled. "I admire your haircut very much. And everything else you've done. Now that you're supposed to be spying on us, at least you two can have a good visit."

"I'll tell her all your secrets," Roshana chuckled. "Good-bye, Mangal. Give Uncle Aziz my love."

He closed the door and had started up the stairs when the telephone rang, but turning back, he heard Raima answer it in the kitchen. She came hurrying down the hall, "Mangal, it's Prince Naim!"

"Shame on you," he teased. "We don't have princes in a republic!" Yet of all the Royal Family, he thought, Naim had proved most truly noble—a wise patriot, without pretensions, who cared more for the country than any one man's right to run it.

In the study, he picked up the extension on his desk, and there was a click as Raima hung up her receiver.

"Mangal, I'm glad I found you!" Naim had grown so deaf he had taken to shouting lately. "Mark this date, Mangal: April 17, in the year of Hijra 1357—the day my brother Mohammad Daoud has been blessed to see one ray of light."

Laughing, Mangal tried to match his volume. "Really? Did it shine from paradise?"

"I'm not sure where it came from," Naim said. "After so many years of talking to him with no progress.... He visits Saudi Arabia, he wants to visit America, and all this time I've been telling him that it's here, his home, he should be worried about.... Ah, he's out of touch, that's all. I'd almost given up hope. And then one hour ago my brother brought the family together to say, at last, he's going to reform the government completely, and bring in sound administrators and technocrats even if they won't shine his shoes every morning. Mangal, can you believe this? A brand-new administration! I'm calling you because my nephews are in such an uproar they might let something slip, even to the press, and I don't want you to be embarrassed by ignorance."

No, Mangal thought, you called because you needed to crow yourself, and if you knew what I've just heard, you'd dance and sing as well. But still, this will have to happen very fast if it's going to save our necks. When was the last time Daoud moved quickly?

"Mangal?"

"I'm just breathing a long sigh of relief, sir. I'll explain why when I see you. And who knows, maybe the light your brother saw was shining from your eyes. He must have realized your advice has always been the best, and he may have begun to wonder why, if he could depose your cousin, you might not simply follow that example."

"Ah." He could sense Naim's gratification. "But I would never do that."

"I believe you, sir. But doesn't a poet think everyone is capable of writing verse?"

"Every Afghan can write poetry, Mangal." Naim was laughing now.

"As in a republic, everybody can hope to be president."

"Yes," Naim chortled. "I think it finally occurred to him that might present a small problem."

Nineteen

A HAIL OF PEBBLES rattled the windshield as Mangal turned the jeep off the tarmac onto an unpaved road leading southeast. On either side, where fields had caught the rain, brown furrows were already being plowed through the pale grass, and he found himself looking eagerly for a glint of sun on metal blades.

Ahead, the road churned downward, then up again to spare ridges climbing to mountains, and in places the shoulder had crumbled so precipitously that he had to stop to use the wooden wedge for traction. Still, if the drive were easier, Roshana would have insisted on riding along, and she read his face far too well. There was no point in alarming her further now, but if what Karima said was true, maybe plans for getting the family out should come before anything else. Nothing immediate. Not yet. Just some arrangements that would be in place if the time came.

He laughed out loud. Nothing was ever ready. Me least of all, he thought. Roshana and I weren't ready when we had our little newspaper and Daoud wasn't ready to be old. I always saw him the way he looked fifteen years ago in his uniform at the Great Assembly. Indestructible. Brilliant. And what is he now? A man so crazed with power that he has to make every decision himself, so nothing ever gets done, and who surrounds himself with toadies because he can't stand criticism. Macbeth, buried in obsessions. And what am I? His public apologist, getting squeakier by the day as I announce that elections really will be held in another eighteen months.

If the world were still the way it was in '64, Daoud-jan might have been great again. But the cities exploded with newly educated people from the countryside looking for work, and there were no jobs. For six years, crops had been good, yet there was nothing to export and, lately, not even enough food for the markets here. In rejecting his natural allies on every side, Daoud had eliminated competence from government, and by refusing to legitimize his opposition, he made them immune to any real test. Karmal and Taraki could claim or promise anything without having to produce, while urban legions of the disgruntled beat their breasts in agreement.

Naim was forecasting miraculous changes now, but Roshana's instincts might be better. Just one month ago, planning a speedy exit would not have been difficult. Immobilized, Tor was safer in Moscow than he would be in Kabul if a coup came. Saira was in the States, and sending Daddy-jan there had held the double value of isolating his "opinions" for a while and keeping him out of harm's way. He'd never go into exile voluntarily.

Then neither can I, Mangal realized. I can't just abandon them. Maybe Roshana's right that what I do won't make a difference, but I have to try. If things get worse, Uncle Aziz will give her and Yusef his protection while I stay around to pry our parents loose.

A small avalanche of rocks scattered down from a ledge, and swerving to avoid them, he heard the jeep's tires grind dangerously close to the edge. Now the sun was almost blinding, and he tightened his grip on the wheel. Mirzaka, of all places. Aziz lived closer to the Pakistan border, where the authority of tribal khans had always been higher than any dictate from Kabul, but today they would not meet at his home. Aziz's message said both their reputations might be safer if this visit were held secretly.

Mangal glanced down at the map he had sketched. The turn should come very soon now... a knife-backed ridge curving off to the left. Here the earth was the color of wheat set against a radiant blue sky and looked so dry as to be uninhabitable. Then just ahead he saw the mud-brick wall Aziz had described, fringed with crusts of dry grass starting with new green blades, enclosing the lower end of the tiny village. It was at this first house that he was to stop.

Pulling the jeep in close to the wall, he turned off the ignition and got out. On the doorstep, a weathered old man in a white turban and long vest sat napping by a clutter of tin milk pails, but before Mangal could speak to him, Aziz's imposing figure materialized on the threshold—tall and ruggedly built, with dark, penetrating eyes, and above the full black beard, cheeks that were scored like bark from exposure to wind. As Mangal climbed toward him, though, Aziz's laughter held the unrestrained pleasure of a boy's, and he stepped down, opening his arms with the quick grace peculiar to mountain tribesmen.

Even on the rare occasions when Aziz wore Western dress he could be intimidating, but today the man had put on half his arsenal. A bandolier of bullets was slung across his chest, a pistol and dagger stuck out of his belt, and no doubt a rifle or two were standing just inside the door. The display was effective, and Mangal surmised that this had been his uncle's intention.

Aziz crushed him in a ferocious bear hug. "Nephew, may you never be tired!"

"And may you live long, Uncle." The exchange made Mangal chuckle—another of Aziz's tests: his place, his terms, and usually also the conclusion that he sought. He understood the subtleties of power better than anyone in Kabul.

"Ah, but you're getting too thin." Aziz pinched his arm affectionately. "Isn't Roshana feeding you enough? Or are you spending too much time in your gray little office with all your little gray papers? I should set you out in the sun here, but no—we must have privacy inside. People might wonder what Mangal Anwari wants in their humble village... if anyone here knew who you were, which I fear in all honesty they do not. So, come in. We have only green tea, I'm sorry to say, not the black tea you like to drink, but you must be thirsty after your drive, so perhaps green tea will serve?"

Mangal followed him into the house and the old man limped behind them to fuss with an ancient dented samovar. The small front room was bare except for two worn cushions placed on either side of a brass tray table.

They sat cross-legged, facing each other, and while the old servant poured tea, Aziz inquired politely and thoroughly about each male member of the family—and then, in a departure from customary delicacy, about Roshana. He had no daughters of his own, and claimed to have passed on his temperament to her behind the back of her businessman father.

"So, a second child!" Aziz's eyes flashed. "That's wonderful news. I suppose this one will be named for your honored father, and the next for my brother. How long will I have to wait for another namesake? Aziz Anwari. It's a fine name, now that city people are taking two names."

"I agree, Uncle. But Roshana thinks we're going to have a daughter next, so you may have to wait quite a while."

"Well, I'm a patient man, Mangal. And I'm glad to hear of this child. All the years she was working, I told her: what is a woman without sons? You and I may be dead in ten years, but if she has sons growing up she'll soon have men to defend her. Of course, Roshana herself has proven that daughters can be just as strong. While they are young, at least."

Aziz folded his arms with self-satisfaction, and Mangal decided this was not the time to explain Roshana's motive for retreating into motherhood: Increasingly, at the university, she had become a target for animosity because of her connection with a government that she could neither defend nor publicly oppose. But it was typical of Aziz, he thought, to feel no conflict between his love for her and his hatred of the Leftist policies she espoused.

Remembering the night she had made that choice, Mangal said, "She wants to start a new dynasty, Uncle. With her own rules and laws. When I asked if she'd rather be queen or president of it, do you know what she answered? That she'd like to be khan, like Uncle Aziz—the one whom everyone comes to for help, so she could give people what they need to make them happy."

"Did she? Really?" Aziz's face warmed with emotion that he quickly hid in laughter. "What a rosy view of my function! But as always, I admire her aspirations. By any chance, are you hoping I'll prove her right about my powers?"

"With all respect, Uncle, it was you who asked for this meeting."

"And you agreed because you know we're both in trouble now."

A vertical line appeared in the center of Aziz's forehead, and motioning for his servant to leave, he drew himself up straight, signifying an end to cordial formalities. Then, in a transformation that Mangal had watched before, he seemed deliberately to relax. His face was smooth again, and he clasped his arms loosely around his legs as if centering his balance.

The length of his silence now would suggest how deeply he was disturbed, and the room was quiet for a full minute before he spoke again.

"Mangal, I'm very worried." He smiled genially. "Things are very bad. You must tell your president this deal he has made with Pakistan will be his downfall. For twenty-five years he has sworn he would never seal the border with Pakistan, and now our Pashtun people will be trapped on either side of a line he still admits should never have been drawn." The false smile vanished. "He has broken faith with us, this man whose own great-great-grandfather ruled in Peshawar. What kind of Pashtun is he? For twenty-five years, Mohammad Daoud Khan encouraged our fight for independence. But now those in Pakistan who have fought—Pashtun and Baluchi alike—will be jailed or executed because they can no longer flee to Afghanistan. Where is the honor in that? I'll grant you, he has enemies in Pakistan. Leaders of the Islamic Brotherhood whom he persecuted into exile. But is he so frightened of them that he'd betray the rest of us? Is he that weak?"

"More than you know, Uncle. But he's not afraid of Niazi's people in the Brotherhood. He's trying to break with the Soviet Union, and a trade route through Pakistan would be very helpful in that. Our Islamic allies are rich now, and they're pushing him to make peace with Pakistan. The Shah of Iran has been giving us twice as much aid as the Russians, and he wants these border wars to end."

"The Shah?" Aziz laughed. "I wouldn't call him a mullah. If he prays at all, I'd be very much surprised."

"As would I. His concerns aren't religious. If our monarchy could fall, then his might too, so it's in his great interest to keep the Baluchis quiet. And the Pashtuns, since their cause is the same."

"Not quite the same, Mangal. The land at stake is different. Theirs belongs to them, and ours to us." Aziz was scowling. "Does the Shah think he can command us? When I could call up a hundred thousand rifles in one week?" He made a gesture of disgust. "But that's not the worst of it, Mangal. If this deal were only on a paper in Kabul who would care? Who would even know of it yet? But now the little Communists come, creep, creep, with their nice haircuts, very clever little city boys who say they come to visit relatives and always speak from both sides of their mouth. They're raising very much hatred against this agreement with Pakistan, and we don't need a war now either. No one wants them here, the little barber boys, but in places they are taking hold, only because of this stupid deal with Islamabad. You must stop it! I know these troublemakers speak for the Russians, but all people don't understand that. They even pretend to take the side of the mullahs against your new civil laws, but if their time comes, the mullahs will be the first to suffer, am I not right? Did not one of these burn the Holy Koran in public, saying there is no God?"

"Yes, Uncle. That man's name is Babrak Karmal, and you're right to be worried about him. So am I. Even more, after what you've just told me. I'm glad you sent for me."

"So." Aziz was studying his face. "It's serious, then, in Kabul. What's happened to Daoud Khan that he can't control these children with shiny shoes?"

Stretching out his cramped legs, Mangal shrugged. "I don't know. The diplomatic colony's passing around a joke that it's his teeth. He's been having a lot of trouble with them for the past two years." Could that literally be true? he wondered. A constant toothache, combined with constant headaches? He smiled. "You tell me, get rid of the Communists. And they say, tear down the khans. The new constitution hurts the mullahs, so they scream, and when we try out land reform, the Left says it isn't enough."

Aziz nodded. "What an old story. Maybe that's why you can't understand it. Don't those boys who are bothering us follow Nur Mohammad Taraki? I know him. He grew up not far from here. A Ghilzai Pashtun. They've always had a feud with Daoud's Durrani kinsmen. Or have you forgot that such matters are still important?"

Of course this would be Aziz's interpretation, he thought. Ancient bad blood as Taraki's driving force. It made as much sense as government-by-toothache.

"I know tribal loyalty's important," he said. "Why do you think Taraki sent those people? Raising Pashtunistan as his banner gets him automatic support, here and even in Moscow. If we can't go through Pakistan, we're captives of the Russians, and they're so frightened of losing power they may help him into the palace just to keep their hold on us. It's Taraki you should be fighting, Uncle, not Bhutto or Daoud Khan."

Aziz slapped his palm hard against the dirt floor. "What are you asking me, Mangal? Three times, Pashtunistan has been sacrificed to Kabul's politics. What have you ever done for us? Do you imagine I could tell my families to forget their relatives over there, because you want to ship pistachio nuts to our enemies?"

Looking into Aziz's narrowed, angry eyes, Mangal thought: Roshana's right, everything's turned upside down. Sometimes when I hear myself lately it's like listening to Daddy-jan.

"Uncle, I share your feeings," he said. "I'm a Pashtun too. But can't you at least make your people wait until they're hurt before they start shooting? Just for a few months. We can work on this deal. When diplomatic channels are better..."

"Diplomacy!" Aziz kicked the table and teacups clattered against the tray. "Tell me this, Mangal. Where have the crazy Americans gone? The ones who send us all their old clothes for the Russians to fight over in the bazaar? Who expect..." He shook his head. "Who expected our kuchi nomads to become nice little farmers in the Helmand valley? But all they ever grew there was opium poppies! I thought these Americans were supposed to handle the Soviets."

"The U.S. abandoned us long ago, Uncle."

Standing up, he went to the door to gaze out at the jagged barren mountains. "Every time we've asked Washington for that kind of help, they've said no. First to a U.N. agreement that would have given us other trade routes, then to Afghanistan's joining the Western Alliance—because they don't need us enough to promise to defend borders as 'difficult' as these. And then six months ago..." He smiled down at his own polished shoes. "Six months ago, the American secretary of state, a man named Vance, invited Daoud Khan there for a visit. But when their ambassador started making arrangements, he was told by some junior official that President Carter didn't have time anymore for 'minor foreign dignitaries.' And every time the U.S. snubbed us, the Russians came with their arms full of gifts. Afghanistan has a hundred varieties of grapes, and the U.S. only sends us grape jelly."

Turning back to the room, he crouched in front of Aziz. "Listen to me. I swear on Roshana's head, what I'm telling you is true. If you value our freedom, you have to keep peace here now. Otherwise, we may all have to learn to speak Russian."

"Your freedom, you mean," said Aziz bitterly. "We have always been free, Mangal. Allah is our superpower, not your Americans and Russians. Kabul governments may come and go, but in Paktia things will never change."

"You could be wrong about that, if Taraki gets in. The Soviets are more efficient governors than we are. They won't let a border province like this be run by local men they can't trust. Uncle, you can't separate yourself from Kabul anymore."

"How would I ever do that, while my brother and niece are there!" Aziz drew a hand through his beard. "Alright. Since you swear, I'll risk my honor and talk to our people. Where I live, they're so angry at your government, I didn't want them to see you come. I didn't want them to think I could listen to any word of this deal. And yet, when a man like Mohammad Daoud calls for justice for twenty-five years, I knew there must be some reason for this treachery in the end. For now, I'll do what you ask, Mangal. But tell your President Daoud that when the first ten Pashtuns die in Pakistan, the fighting will begin and I'll join it. Tell him I have cousins there, and I intend to visit them every day for the rest of my life, if I choose."

"I understand that, Uncle." He got up and Aziz rose with him.

"Good. Come here. I want to show you something." He pointed through the side window. "Down there, at the end of the wall."

In a patch of shade thrown by the gnarled single tree, a tall boy in a blue turban stood cradling a Soviet-made automatic rifle.

"Do you recognize him?" Aziz smiled. "He is also a Ghilzai Pashtun, but from the other side of the country. From a farm near Herat? He dislikes you very much."

As if hearing himself described, the slender figure shifted the rifle and turned, looking up at the house. Not quite a boy anymore, Mangal could see now, though his thin face was still as tense as it had been that night in the back of Khalid's shop when he cranked out copies of *New Homeland* on the mimeo machine. Nur-Ali, the avenging angel, whose fits and rages had been so much like Tor's.

"I found him in a teahouse," Aziz went on. "His eyes were red from smoking hashish and he was shouting about the government. I considered him a vast annoyance. Then he mentioned you. He calls you the Voicebox. I thought I had better help him out of there before he got arrested or started in on Roshana. Well, I didn't need to worry. He loves Roshana, and he ought to love you, since you did him the excellent service of making him cynical about all politicians. He's not a bad boy, but he needs to grow up more and I've been thinking about what kind of responsibility to give him. Now I have an idea."

Below, Nur-Ali shouldered his rifle and walked out of sight. Mangal kept his eyes on the spot where he had been standing.

"With all respect," Aziz said, "you can't be in four places at once. If there's trouble in the city, you'll be involved at the palace, won't you? And there are three households to consider. Do you know the stall in the bazaar that sells only Istalif pottery? With your permission, I'll put Nur-Ali there, so if there's anything you want me to know on short notice he can carry your message. And if there's trouble in the city, get Roshana and Yusef out right away. Nur-Ali will bring them here, if you can't. My brother and your parents are welcome too, of course. I can't offer them the comforts of Kabul, though even my simple fort might seem appealing under the right circumstances."

"I wanted to ask if I could send them to you. Thank you, Uncle. I hope that day won't come, but I'm grateful to know I can trust them to your care."

"Always, Mangal." Aziz clasped him in another powerful embrace. "Goodbye. May Allah go with you."

"And with you, Uncle."

After he had started up the jeep, Aziz walked back into the house.

Releasing the clutch, Mangal coasted around the hairpin turn, then braked to a sudden stop. In the small backyard, Nur-Ali was unrolling a rug for evening prayers and he did not look up as Mangal got out and came toward him.

"What happened to you, Nur-Ali?" Mangal rested his elbows on the wall. "Roshana and I tried to find you. She even wrote to your parents asking why you'd left school, but we never heard anything."

"Because they can't read or write. I was there when your letter came, but then I left again. My father wouldn't forgive me for giving up the university." He bent to straighten the corners of the carpet. "They couldn't understand that all I learned there was deception."

"But we didn't lie to you. Till our wedding, we didn't know a coup was even a possibility."

"And when you found out, you had the rest of us thrown in jail."

"No. I just couldn't stop that. You may have an inflated notion of my influence with Daoud. It was never very much."

"You live in a beautiful house though, so what does that matter."

"And you live here now? How long have you been with my uncle?"

"For six months. I'm lucky he let me come. I was defiling my body with hashish and opium when I met him, and he taught me not to try to blame my sins on anyone else." Facing Mangal, he pointed to his blue turban. "Do you remember this? You gave it to me, the night we put out the paper. I wash it, wear it, wash it again.... I'll always wear it, to remind myself not to believe the promises of clever men who don't pray to Allah for guidance. What god do you worship, Mangal?"

"Then you'd like the mullahs to run things? Five years ago, you wanted to revenge your brother's death by shooting a few conservatives. Do you remember that?"

"Yes. You told me: 'Words are better than guns.' But they're just tricks politicians use to take away what we have. Now, your uncle is the only man I trust and he thinks guns are most important."

"Well, I see you've got a fancy one there. Maybe that's what you really wanted."

"And you have a million words, Mangal. I wonder which of us is happier with our choice." He knelt on the rug. "It's time to pray, if you have no objection. Do you think I'm facing the right way?"

"Toward Mecca? I don't know, Nur-Ali. Maybe we've both lost our sense of direction."

When Nur-Ali pressed his forehead to the ground, Mangal walked back to the jeep. The sun was setting, so the descent would be more dangerous than the drive up, and he was anxious to get home. Turning out, he caught a last glimpse of Nur-Ali prostrated on his rug, the Kalashnikov rifle leaning by his side.

In the gathering dusk, the jeep felt precariously balanced on the narrow road, and relaxing his hands, Mangal tried to sense the earth's surface through the motion of the steering column. Balance... how often had he cringed at that word spoken by his father when it had seemed to mean stagnation, old men's caution, the enemy of progress. Now the country had been carved up by the mullahs and the Leftists, and if Nur-Ali could find no middle ground, then what of all the other students who had sifted through the university? Which way would they jump if a decision had to be made?

Tor would choose these mountains and a horse and gun over any government-issue job. And with brown land opening behind the jeep it was easy to imagine Tor on Aspi riding up off a trail here. He wouldn't pray like Nur-Ali, but he might be a better shot and he certainly hated politics as much. And his brother also? Tor and Nur-Ali had that in common too.

What would be different now, Mangal wondered, if Tor had been the eldest son. Maybe nothing, since then Tor would have carried the burden of obligation, but the idea was interesting. Tor, on horseback instead of a jeep, but driven with the same compulsion, planning and scheming—his devious nature might well have made him the better strategist. It still could, if only Tor would use the talents he wasted so infuriatingly. He had nerve, brains, a warm heart.... Tor wouldn't want to trade places, though. Would he be astounded to learn that his elder brother the ogre envied his freedom and spontaneity?

Tor, Mangal thought, sometimes, like right now, I wish you were here and we could talk as brothers. You'd be very good at this kind of crisis.

Sending Tor to Moscow had at least protected the honor he would someday want to reclaim, just so he could marry. But in every other way, Moscow had been a mistake. New York could have absorbed Tor at his worst without anyone's blinking an eye, and he and Saira would probably have grown to be friends again, once they'd decided all their problems were really Mangal's doing.

It was hard to picture Tor married, though, because Karima came into it and that wasn't finished yet. When Tor returned to Kabul he would have to be around Karima and her children—her first son, his own child, Zia. After a while Tor might sense it, or Karima's attitude give her away. Saira refused to come home because she knew she couldn't avoid seeing Ashraf and his wife socially.

Or was that more her way of getting even with the family? "See? I'm still in pain and it's all your fault." But it was Tor who had done her the greatest harm... and he must have had some provocation. That night everyone was half crazy, and if Saira had been injured most, she had made up for it since with her chilly silences, with the letters she wrote exclusively to Roshana, who said, I've told her it was my idea to give her our plane tickets, and it's a bit insulting that she won't believe me.

Below, the lights of Kabul spread out like a star against black ground, and reaching the paved road, he pressed the accelerator closer to the floor. Tor and Saira... did either of them ever think well of him, when they were lonely or homesick or just remembering childhood days? Wasn't there anything he had done right in their eyes? If the answer was no, that would be punishment enough, whether they knew it or not, because he loved and missed them. And before long, they might have to change their minds. They were safe now. If worse trouble came, they would be clear of it. Whatever happened, they would live.

Wearily, he turned the jeep down the driveway and into the garage. Roshana would be glad to hear that Nur-Ali was well, though the rest of Aziz's news would not delight her.

Closing the garden gate, he squinted against an unexpected blast of light. The side door of the house was open and Roshana stood in silhouette, with her arms folded tight to stop the shivering he could see even at this distance.

He shielded his eyes. "Roshana?"

Something in her posture quickened his step and catching her shoulders, he turned her toward the light. "Roshana-jan, what is it?"

Her face looked carved and hard as a piece of sculpture. He thought of the old wooden statues Kafirs had buried with their dead. "Roshana, speak to me."

She raised her eyes. "It's here, Mangal. It's already begun." Her voice was deep and toneless.

"What has?" He lifted her chin. "What are you talking about?"

Taking his hands, she seemed to relax, but in resignation more than relief.

"What Karima said... the right excuse. The opening the Parchamis have been looking for. Mir Akbar Khyber was murdered today at the Microrayon apartments. Remember she told us Babrak Karmal treated him like a second father? Khyber's been popular longer than any of the others, so they won't have much trouble raising a riot over this. And according to your father, cars have been streaming out to Microrayon all evening."

Twenty

IT WAS, Mangal had decided, a sort of tribute to Khyber that every faction in Kabul blamed another for his assassination. The Leftists, not surprisingly, accused Daoud, who pointed to the Islamic Brotherhood. Some of Khyber's friends suspected his killer stood closer to home—a rival in his trade union or the underground itself. But the murder seemed too politically convenient to be the fruit of impulsive violence, especially when the next day Taraki applied for permission to hold a funeral procession.

Ever since then, the streets had been swelling with crowds made up chiefly of students, who looked, Mangal thought, even younger and more obdurate than he had been five years ago.

Permission was granted over his loud private opposition. Daoud, in his new conciliatory frame of mind, wanted to appear to sanction what he felt he could prevent only by force. And, he said, he could use the demonstration to identify hidden Leftists in the government. Photographs would be taken along the route: after studying them, he'd know whom else to fire.

For hours, Mangal had argued that pictures would just establish who was curious—a questionable benefit, compared to the advantage the Leftists would gain by taking over the city. If the "procession" were forbidden, only students and the Leftist leadership would dare risk arrest or an open fight. As it was, their sympathizers, the concerned and the merely inquisitive might fill Pashtunistan Square in what would seem a major show of strength. There had not been a demonstration of any scale in Kabul for years now, and the Leftists could be counted on to resurrect old grievances, the pent-up anger and energy that had been denied other means of expression.

Photographs. Mangal threw his comb at the bathroom mirror. Here was the chance for Daoud to prove to the Soviets that he was in control. Before, paranoia had made him too heavy-handed, but now in a burst of misplaced optimism he was dropping the reins completely.

The procession would start at Microrayon, the Soviet-built housing complex in eastern Kabul where Khyber had lived—and only political loyalty could have kept him there, Mangal thought. It had to be the ugliest development on earth. A grid of concrete boxes dropped on a dismal site... even the lure of plumbing and electric lights couldn't compensate for a shoddiness and sterility that seemed designed to be demoralizing.

There was no reason for him to drive out to Microrayon. He wouldn't be a convincing mourner. It made better sense to meet the procession near the palace and then go on to the cemetery.

Downstairs, he opened the garage door to find Ghulam-Nabi running a dustcloth over the spotless black Mercedes. Squaring his shoulders defiantly, the old servant reached for his keys. "I will drive you today."

Mangal shook his head. "I'm taking the jeep. It's less conspicuous. Or at any rate, it will keep people at a distance."

Ghulam-Nabi pushed the turban cap further back on his lined forehead. "Four eyes can see more than two, Mangal. It's good to know what's behind you."

"I need your eyes here. And your mouth. There's something I want you to do." He hesitated. It was an arrogant plan; he would be furious if it were done to him, and involving two servants was less than noble. But this was hardly the moment to start getting delicate about family protocol.

He said, "I want you to phone my father's driver and tell him to disable their car. Nothing serious... something he can fix again quickly if he has to. My father's known Khyber for thirty years, but there may be trouble at the funeral, and he'd get right in the middle trying to stop it. Do you see what I mean?"

"You're just as bad as he is." Ghulam-Nabi stamped his foot. "You're careful for everyone but yourself!"

"Will you please ask my father's driver to take his spark plugs out?" Mangal climbed into the jeep. "You don't have to, nor does he. Tell him that too."

"Alright." The old man stepped back with a scowl. "We all will do just as you say, as usual. Go ahead, if you're in such a rush."

"Thank you," he smiled. "Take care of them for me."

"You don't need to tell me that. Go."

Reversing the gear, he backed the jeep quickly down the driveway.

Long before he reached Pashtunistan Square, he had to get out and walk. The streets were impassable, choked with people, animals, cars and carts of all descriptions. The tall bright trucks he loved so much for their painted landscapes seemed to have been intentionally placed to obstruct the small side roads he had meant to use.

The crowd swirled and eddied in changing patterns around young men who were calling out praises of Khyber for his devotion to the country, his sense of justice... and Mangal walked on through a welter of papers trampled underfoot that he did not need to read. They were broadsides, hastily printed and no more legal than *New Homeland*, but these were scarcely more than lists of slogans, promptings for the herd.

Here, on the fringes, the mood was still more festive than funereal. The sun shone, the judas trees were in bloom, and if not for this excitement families might have taken the afternoon off anyway to picnic or just to wander through the public gardens. Instead, they bought kebab from stalls and speculated on the action, while children climbed up on their parents' shoulders for a better view.

But as he came into Pashtunistan Square by the corner of the barracks lining the front wall of the palace, tension boiled up around him. The children were replaced by students with hard angry faces, not praising any longer, but denouncing—Daoud, Naim, the United States, Pakistan, the economy and poverty—in a harsh rhythmic chant that was being taken up by the people looking on. The Palace Guard was out in force. He didn't sense immediate danger, but the sheer mass of bodies—straining, shoving—the low rumble of voices building to a crescendo of shouts and jeers, the renewed onslaught of slogans and raised fists... yes, the potential for violence was real, only the weapons were missing.

Suddenly, the crowd surged to the right and a hush spread from that direction. The funeral entourage must be passing. With effort, Mangal elbowed his way closer to the procession as it wound by the palace and the Ministry of Planning toward the cemetery behind the Shor Bazaar.

Circling around the Dutch embassy, he crossed the river ahead of the rest, walking quickly to keep a respectful distance.

He could never see this graveyard without thinking of the Montmartre cemetery in Paris, where worn ornate headstones fell together at angles suggesting a drunken party was continuing underground. Here, there were no markers at all, since in Islam men are equal in death, kings and Communists alike stripped of any ornament and wrapped in six lengths of unbleached muslin. Their burial ground had to be worthless too, and this was a brown, rocky, arid plot without trees or flowering plants. Mourners brought only sweets and small coins to distribute to the beggars who were men so handicapped they couldn't approach, beseeching, as their brothers in the bazaar did, but only sit and wait like crouching guardians of dust.

Climbing the aimless path, he looked for the hillock where he had stood while Grand-uncle Yusef was buried, his body in its winding sheet seeming small as a child's. In Paris there had been a casket that appeared to be made of gold, and the one American funeral he had attended was bewildering—so much painting and packaging; even the open earth had been masked with a grassy green cloth, to conceal or deny what, he wondered. Then he realized even he must have some need for a marker, because here were traces of the crumbling wall he had picked out so he could find Grand-uncle Yusef's grave again.

This was a good vantage point. The procession had come in to stop on a low rise a stone's throw away.

Taraki, Amin, Karmal. Now that his mentor Khyber was gone, Karmal would have lost power to the others. A gust of wind carried away the words the mullah was saying, but their faces were eloquent in the sun. Taraki, slim, erect, almost professorial with his aquiline profile and gray mustache. It was impossible to dislike the man. As much as they disagreed politically, Mangal could not question the integrity of his motives, and now he saw real grief in the curve of Taraki's back, the slow incline of his head as Khyber's body was lowered into the ground.

To his left, Babrak Karmal stood staring down at the grave, fists clenched in the pockets of his coat. He looked stunned and shaken, but he had most to mourn here. Khyber had been his worthy friend and ally, a steadying influence... without him, Babrak himself would be diminished.

Just behind them, Hafizullah Amin was shifting his weight from one foot to the other, as if impatient for the rites to be finished. His eyes searched the crowd—calculating their number, Mangal thought, remembering what Karima had said about his ruthlessness. At a guess, Amin was the most dangerous of the three, sleek but cunning and more hungry for prestige than socialist five-year plans.

Instinctively, Mangal had felt there would be a lesson to learn at this burial. Now he saw it—the odd thing: Taraki, Amin and Karmal held the place traditionally reserved for the mourning family—proclaiming it as more a political event than personal ceremony. If they also stood as hosts at the mosque for the customary three days of mourning, and used that time to whip up even greater hysteria, Khyber's death could be the first of many.

Mangal cursed. Daoud was not here, and he should have come to see these tight, determined faces. If he felt the seriousness of it, would he hurry to announce the reforms he had in mind? But even that might not be enough to defuse the threat of bloodshed, and any outbreak of fighting would bring troops to the streets, arrests, and then a government backlash more repressive than the last.

Unless the Left won, of course. The Soviet ambassador must be looking on too, wondering if Daoud had lost all support, and he might have to answer that question in a vacuum, since lately Daoud was refusing to meet with him. What would his assessment be? Like Daoud's own generals, the Soviets wanted to come out on the winning side, and his vacillation now might lead them to shift their backing, however reluctantly.

Maybe arrests ought to be made, and the sooner the better. But Daoud could not be convinced he had lost ground.

Now Taraki had turned and was speaking to the crowd, hands upraised and fingers spread out dark against the sky. He was shouting and Mangal caught random words and phrases... "Our comrade... as we are equal in death, so should we be in life... not die in vain... come follow us." Then his hands dropped and the crowd moved forward in a wave, surrounding him, bearing him off.

Buttoning his coat, Mangal walked down the way he had come. He would not follow them to the mosque. Today was less important than what would happen tomorrow and the day after that, but no time could be wasted. He decided to go back to the bazaar and see if Nur-Ali had arrived from Paktia yet, and then he would drive home and tell Roshana to get ready to leave the city.

Twenty-One

"No, Mangal, not without you." Roshana looked out to the garden where Yusef was playing, and pulled the window shut. "Do you think I could sit in Paktia, not knowing what's happening here? To you? And what about our parents?"

"Your father may see the wisdom in taking a short vacation. I'm going to tell mine it might be a good idea to start his planting at the Paghman house early this year. Which will just make him more determined to stay in Kabul. Roshana, this is only a precaution. I couldn't manage ten people on short notice."

Her back stiffened. "I'm not helpless. If it's bad, then we should all leave, including you, Mangal. You aren't responsible for Daoud's mistakes."

"Yes, but I've worked with him for five years. I've collected my salary. How honorable would it be to walk away now? It would look like a vote of no confidence. I'm supposed to be a public servant, which means staying at my job especially when it's difficult, but none of that's true for you. Why shouldn't you make a New Year's visit to your Uncle Aziz? He sent Nur-Ali here so he could drive you."

"And you think it's your sacred duty to go down with the ship?" Roshana's face colored. "When you said yourself Daoud hasn't taken any of your advice?"

"No! I've told you, I'll come later on. The rest of us could fit in one car if we have to. But I can't just give up without a fight. Besides, it will take time to persuade my father. Don't you see how much less worried I'd be if you and Yusef were safe?"

She leaned back against the green bolster. "I want you to worry about me.

Otherwise you might not leave at all. You have to come with us, Mangal, and if that's blackmail I don't care. It's up to you to say when, but if you have us on your conscience too, you'll make a better decision about that."

"I should divorce you." He shook his head. "Four days ago you accused me of gambling on my ability to control the situation. Now you expect me to be able to anticipate it day by day. Wives are supposed to obey their husbands, remember?"

"And husbands to respect the counsel of their wives. You used to value my judgment."

"I still do and you know it."

"Then don't try to send me away when you need me. I won't leave. In fact, I'm going with you to the mosque this afternoon. The last day of mourning should be the most telling, and I want to see what Taraki's up to. Maybe they've even got Karima passing out leaflets. We have to think about her as well."

"You're the most stubborn woman in this city, curse you. Alright. But we should go soon if you want to get close enough for a view. It was already crowded down there when I drove home."

Setting aside the lunch tray, she smiled. "Go ahead and say it."

"What?"

"I divorce thee, three times."

"Then I'd really be in trouble with your uncle. No, thank you. He's angry enough as it is."

"Poor Mangal." She stood up and stepped into her shoes. "My Uncle Aziz, then Nur-Ali... no wonder you want to get rid of me."

He kissed her forehead. "If that's true, why do I feel so relieved I won't be alone this week?"

Half an hour later they stood by the river embankment across from the pale green Mosque of Two Swords, while Hafizullah Amin cried out against Pakistan in the same terms Uncle Aziz had used. It seemed to Mangal, irrationally, that Amin's head had grown larger.

"... Two hundred thousand kuchis used to migrate back and forth to Pakistan every year! Did they need passports? No! I ask you in the name of Allah, if they didn't need passports, is that a national boundary?"

The crowd gave the inevitable answer.

From Pakistan it was an easy leap to the United States and the CIA, which Amin claimed controlled half of Afghanistan, since so many upper-class Afghans had been educated there. And Amin too, Mangal recalled, had gone to college in America, though few people listening to him now would know that.

"I don't like this 'in the name of Allah' business," Roshana said. "The little hypocrite! But it's working. What's your father's latest recommendation, by the way? Did you see him this morning?"

He nodded. "Briefly. And he doesn't agree with me about making arrests. He says Daoud should propose a coalition with Taraki first, which is fine, except that will never happen."

"But for him even to suggest that... Your father's frightened too then, Mangal, so maybe he won't be so hard to persuade. Let me work on him, will you?"

"With my blessings. I've got to go back to the palace. Have you seen enough?"

"Yes. If I stay here any longer I might start shouting myself. Well, things ought to quiet down a bit now. In a few days we should have a better idea of what to expect."

For once, she was only half right. The crowds dispersed slowly with the end of public mourning, but that just lowered tensions from a boil to a simmer. The army and security forces were kept on alert, and meetings went on so late he hardly saw Yusef for a week.

Among cabinet ministers, the debate went in a circle: the Left had won public sympathy, so moving against them now might only play into their hands. Yet not to act was weakness and perhaps folly, given the existence of the plan Mangal insisted Amin had drawn up. Daoud developed his photographs and fired a handful of officials. Naim tore his hair in frustration.

Every night, Mangal made the same speech until he felt like a tape recorder: We have to talk to the Soviets and find out where they stand on this. Each time, Daoud rejected his plea. He said it would be a display of fear, requiring subsequent concessions.

Then, inexplicably, the president made up his mind with no further consultation.

Mangal was sound asleep for the first time in days when the call came, and he sat up to hear Naim shouting that Taraki had been arrested and six other Leftists were being brought in or placed under house arrest. In the morning, a meeting would be held to decide what the next step should be.

Roshana followed him downstairs to make tea in the dark kitchen while he stood in the study dialing one number after another. His father refused to predict which way the wind would shift, but there was apprehension in his voice. Still, he saw no reason to leave Kabul immediately. The Left were so incompetent that if they started a fight, they'd probably shoot their own feet off.

Roshana's father's phone was out of order.

Naim had not known much about the arrests, and through a series of connections, Mangal finally got General Rasuli on the line. Yes, he said, all the leaders were in jail now. Amin? He'd been under house arrest for most of the afternoon. No, his papers hadn't been searched, but there was a guard at his house and that would be done. Had he been allowed to communicate? Not with anyone outside the family, and his phone was disconnected. Shouldn't that be sufficient?

After some prodding, Rasuli agreed to ask Amin's guard if any member of the household had gone out during that time.

Roshana had turned on lamps in the sitting room and sat wrapped in her white shawl. "Did you get them all?"

"Except for your father. Mine won't say whether he thinks I'm being an alarmist or not, and he won't leave either. Roshana, I want you to come with me tomorrow. And Yusef too, you can visit with Daoud's family. I'm sure his wife could use some level-headed company by now."

"Today, you mean." She held up her watch. "It's three o'clock already. No, Mangal, I'll stay here and pack. If this meeting doesn't go well, you have to resign and we can send Nur-Ali to kidnap your parents at gunpoint if necessary. I'll be the coordinator."

"No, you're coming with me, and this time you have to do what I say." He sat beside her, "I'm not so worried about my father anymore."

"Why?" She grinned. "Because he's such a mule?"

"That, and a precious national resource. Oh, why did I give up smoking. Do we have any cigarettes at all?"

"No. But Ghulam-Nabi must have some tobacco. Mangal, will you please tell me what you mean?"

He shrugged. "I've just decided that if anything happens, my father will be the safest man in Kabul. He's the only one left of any stature who turned against both Daoud and King Zahir, and Taraki needs all the names... all the legitimacy he can get."

"What?" Roshana squinted. "But he'd never speak for them."

"No, but I think they'd settle for his just keeping quiet. And he would, he hates them all equally. Besides, they'd have a hostage."

"Yes, your American mother! That's why we should get them out now, Mangal. Let me go down and talk to Nur-Ali."

He gave a sharp laugh. "I didn't mean my mother. I was referring to Tor, my sweet. And how would you propose to rescue him from Moscow? Don't you see? They're all each other's insurance policies."

Someone was moving in the hall, and he stood up to open the door. In the gray light, Ghulam-Nabi's face looked seamed and haggard, and wondering how much strength today would need, Mangal said gently, "I hope you and Raima slept well?"

Ghulam-Nabi looked startled. "Yes, well enough."

"Good." He smiled. "My friend, do you have any tobacco?"

"Ah, my *friend*, so that's how it is. I heard the phone ring before. It was bad news?"

"We don't know yet. It could be a good thing, or it might be very bad, yes." Remembering how Aziz had smiled while delivering a similar pronouncement, he thought, why does it make people so happy when their most awful prophecies come true?

"Here." Ghulam-Nabi pulled a small pouch from the pocket of his loose shirt. "If you've been up a long time, you must be hungry. I'll tell Raima—"

"No," he interrupted. "There's something I want you to do. Right now, before it gets light." He turned back. "Roshana, will your father go if we ask him to?"

She came to the door. "He might. It's worth a try. His phone's broken, Ghulam-Nabi, so could you give him a message? Tell him he should leave this morning and go to Aziz Khan in Paktia. Mangal thinks he may be in danger, so make him understand he must not wait."

"Yes," Mangal chuckled. "Tell him his Mercedes dealership is the biggest capitalist symbol in Kabul and the Commies don't like it. No, I was only joking." But Roshana had cringed and he took her hand. I can't start laughing now, he thought, if I do I'll never stop. "I'm sorry, jan. It's just my rotten nerves. Alright, Ghulam-Nabi, off with you, and don't spare the horses."

The old man scowled. "Will I drive you today?"

He nodded. "May Allah protect you, yes. You can take us to the palace as soon as you get back."

Turning, Ghulam-Nabi hurried away.

Roshana said, "I'll go see to Yusef."

"No, let me do that." Mangal put his arms around her. "If only one of us has breakfast, it had better be you. And Rabia, of course." He felt the warmth of her breast through her nightdress. "Roshana, what a mess I've got you into. Can you forgive me?"

"You? It's my fault too, Mangal. I was stupid to get pregnant. I just didn't see what was happening. We were both so . . . optimistic when I carried Yusef, I wanted us to be that way again. Now I feel useless, I'm so tired all the time and you're worried about me. But don't be. I'm fine, and I can still run if I have to. Or even shoot, for that matter."

"I know." He kissed her old scar. "You're ferocious. That's why I love you so much."

She was looking into his eyes. "You think there really will be a riot today, don't you. Why? Couldn't this also have the opposite effect?"

He shouldn't have tried to protect her, he knew. It was unworthy of her and impossible now in any case. "Maybe," he said. "But I failed to mention one thing. With his usual genius, Rasuli left Amin under house arrest for hours before they brought him in, and Amin's the one who's got the plan. There's a chance he could have sent instructions to the others. I just didn't want to talk about that until we had a plan of our own."

"I see." She stepped away from him. "So we're supposed to hide behind the Palace Guard and let everyone else take their chances?"

"No, listen to me. I told you, I'm not so worried about my parents as I am about you and Yusef. If there's a... demonstration today, they won't go to my father's house, but they might very well come here. And I don't want you to be home. Alright?"

He started up the stairs. "Have some breakfast now, and I'll get Yusef dressed. I'd like to take a quick drive around the city before we go to the palace."

When she had gone down the hall, he climbed to Yusef's bedroom.

"Daddy-jan!" The boy was standing up in his crib, screaming with delight ...or with some of the tension that filled the house like smoke.

"Good morning, Yusef-jan, did you have nice dreams?" Impulsively, he picked the boy up and swung him high over his head, the way he had when Yusef was younger.

"Daddy-jan!" Yusef squealed. "Are we going out? I heard you tell Mummy..."

"Yes," Mangal smiled, feeling crazy laughter in his chest again. "We're going to the palace to see the president." He recalled an old nursery rhyme his mother had recited: "I've been to the palace to look at the Queen...." And, "a cat may look at a king." The king, Zahir Shah, what must he be doing now? What time would it be in Rome? But Yusef was staring. "Alright, Bechaim, let's find you some clean clothes."

Pushing down the side of the crib, he watched Yusef scamper unsteadily around the room. Karima... would she be dressing her children now? Or was she in a meeting of her own, hoping for a break when she could slip away to call him?

There was a third possibility, of course. She might have tried that already and been discovered. Then what good would her haircut be?

Laughter crept up, escaping through his lips, and Yusef looked up. "What, Daddy?"

He crouched to button Yusef's shirt, forcing his fingers to make small careful movements. "I was just thinking, Yusef-jan. Someday your Auntie Karima might be president!" His tone was wrong, though. The boy's smile vanished.

"Alright." He lifted Yusef to his hip. "Let's go down and see Mummy."

They left when Ghulam-Nabi returned from what he claimed was a successful mission. He said he had left Roshana's father praying while his servants packed a case.

"Good," Mangal said. "And after you drop us off, I want you to go to my father. I'll call and tell him you're coming. If there's trouble later, I may ask you to put a gun to his head and take him to Paktia too."

"Guns," Roshana said quietly. "That's what it comes to, isn't it? All our ideas, and all their ideas, and all that matters is who has more guns."

"That, and deciding whom to shoot," he grinned. "Here, Ghulam-Nabi, go east now. I want to check the traffic. If people are massing anywhere, it's probably at Microrayon."

Five minutes later, he was relieved to find little activity on that road. In fact, there seemed many fewer cars than usual coming into the city's center, as though the heat of the demonstrations had spent itself. "Okay, fine," he said. "Let's go on to the palace."

"Mangal..." Roshana turned, pointing through the rear window. "In that blue car we just passed... isn't that Jonathan Straight? The American with the limp whom Tor called Mr. CIA?"

Ghulam-Nabi slowed to let the small Ford overtake them, and Mangal recognized the bony profile, and the shock of red hair blown back from his face. Straight had left Kabul shortly after Daoud's coup and hadn't been seen since. Glancing over at them, he looked startled and then shouted out his open window, "What the hell's going on, Mangal?"

"Nothing, for a change, as far as I can see."

"Then why's the road to Pakistan blocked? There are tanks from the Pul-i-Charki cantonment, just past our embassy."

Mangal shrugged. "As a precaution? I don't know."

"Then find out, will you? We should have been informed!"

The blue Ford sped off going north, and Ghulam-Nabi turned left toward Pashtunistan Square.

The palace stood backdropped by a snow-streaked mountain ridge, but the sun was warm, and around the pool at the entrance pots of red tulips had been set out—by order of the president, no doubt. The inelegance of the angular stonework compound was a standing joke in the family, but this morning its thick walls looked as welcome as the flurry of soldiers at the gate.

Raising one hand in vague salute, the familiar guard waved them through and Ghulam-Nabi drove past a row of barracks to stop by the presidential offices. Roshana was gazing back across the courtyard at the family quarters, as if measuring the distance that would stand between them.

"Yusef-jan." Mangal shook him gently. "Yusef, you go with Mummy now while I do some work. After that I'll come find you, but till then I want you to be very good. Will you promise me?"

Roshana squeezed his hand. "You be good, Mangal. Be brilliant, and don't worry about us. Tell Daoud if he won't listen, you're leaving today, and then do it. We'll be right there waiting for you."

Why didn't I kiss her before, he thought. A real kiss. I can't do that with ten soldiers staring at us.

Reaching under his collar, he untied the silk cord holding his crystal pendant, then knotted it around Roshana's neck. "I want you to wear this now."

She smiled. "Like a kuchi woman, keeping the family jewels?"

"No. Just to remind you that I love you."

He got out and watched the car pull away, Roshana holding Yusef, who knelt up on the seat to wave.

In the large office on the second floor, Naim was sitting alone at a long polished mahogany table. His hands were folded and there were no papers in front of him.

Mangal sat down opposite him. "Where's everyone else? Or is it only you and I?"

"No, they're wandering around somewhere. Waiting for *him* to come out." Naim stabbed his thumb toward the connecting door to the president's private office. "It would be better if it were only you and I."

As if in response, the door opened and Daoud's stocky figure filled its frame. He waved away Mangal's greeting. "How did things look driving in?"

Mangal met his gaze. "It seemed quiet enough at Microrayon. We ran into Jonathan Straight out there. He says tanks are blocking the Pakistan road. Have you heard something I don't know?"

"Only that we've brought in Hafizullah Amin. Wasn't he worrying you? The Americans must have been nervous too, and misinterpreted what they saw. I didn't order any roadblock. I simply directed the army to celebrate these arrests."

"You mean, you've taken them off alert? When there were twelve thousand screaming people in the Square last week?"

"Oh, so you fancy yourself a military adviser now! We've got two thousand soldiers in the Palace Guard, Mangal. Don't you think that should be sufficient for today?"

Seeing the president's fatigue, he swallowed an indignant answer. Daoud's massive bald head seemed too heavy for his body, and his face was deeply creased. Offending him now would only make him more intransigent. Honey might work better.

"With all respect," Mangal said, "the best advisers in the world can be wrong. For instance, General Rasuli's report on military infiltration..."

"And what do you have to refute it? Another report, written by Taraki? Naturally he'll say they can do anything. Colonel Qadir agrees with Rasuli, Mangal—the Air Force chief of staff agrees with him. And Qadir was with me in '73 too, out in front, not back in that office with you. Are you saying I shouldn't trust him? Naim, why isn't Qadir here? I told him what time we'd start."

Pushing a chair back from the table, he sat down. "Well, I won't be kept waiting by anyone. Call in the others, please, Naim."

Only three ministers had assembled. Kayoum, Abdulillah and Nuristani filed in, followed by Naim and General Rasuli, who said Colonel Qadir must have gone out to "examine the situation." Mangal watched the five men with a curious sense of detachment. It was plain from their strained faces they had reached no private consensus in the hall.

The discussion proceeded to take up the fate of Karmal and Taraki; what charges could be brought against them, with what penalties. But as Mangal came to understand the logic that had led Daoud to order the arrests, he felt chilled. Obviously, the president viewed this as an end rather than a beginning: the Left was scheming against him, so he'd take their leaders and they would stop. He had written a script that said so. If Taraki had a different agenda, he would will it out of existence.

"Mr. President"—Daoud's secretary had come to the door—"the Soviet ambassador's on the line."

"Really," said Naim, catching Mangal's eye. "This might be the right time to talk to him... better than having to call him later."

Glaring at his brother, Daoud repeated, "Tell him I'm in conference. Now, can we continue?"

Mangal guessed Daoud was applying that same rule to the Soviets: if he didn't talk to them, they could not act. And the president was in no mood for debate. Again and again, Mangal tried to turn their focus from legal questions to the immediate problem: these arrests would bring a reaction. What might that be? What should be done now to anticipate the worst?

Half an hour later, he was ready to give up. But resigning now would leave Naim without any real support. Probably Roshana was just sitting down to lunch with the family. Why not wait till two then, and let her finish.

Daoud's secretary stood in the doorway. "Mr. President, the Soviet ambassador is calling again."

"Please," Mangal asked, "may I talk to him? At least let's find out what he wants."

Daoud ignored the offer. "I'm in conference. Would you make that clear? And Rasuli, find out where Qadir is. Tell him I want him here right now."

"I'll go," Mangal said, and stood up gratefully.

In the hall, the secretary stopped him. "Mangal, is the president expecting Colonel Qadir? Then there's something I don't understand. The colonel had me put through a call to the Begram Air Force Base, and I heard him say he was on his way. By helicopter. He left some time ago."

Wonderful, Mangal thought, another crossed signal just when we don't need it. "In that case, you'd better call Begram again. Get me the commander's office."

The secretary went to the switchboard and started dialing. "There's no answer in the C.O.'s office."

"Then try a different line. And keep at it till you get someone who knows what's going on. I'll be just down the hall, getting some air."

He walked to an open window overlooking the Square. No gathering crowd. It was even strangely quiet for the middle of the day. The Khyber restaurant seemed to be deserted.

Word of the arrests must have circulated by now, and he'd expected an outraged mob to form, at least the hard-core faithful calling for the release of the three leaders. Instead there was this eerie nothing.

And Qadir had taken off for the Begram air base, without orders and by helicopter? That didn't make sense either.

Neither did Jonathan Straight's mistaking a "celebration" for a roadblock. He'd been furious, and he wasn't prone to nervous exaggeration.

Mangal turned as General Rasuli came up, frowning. "The secretary said to tell you no one answers at Begram. The phone lines must be down."

"They were working a few hours ago when Qadir called there."

"What are you afraid of, Mangal? We've cut off the head of the serpent."

"So the body will die? I don't agree."

"You're the one who wanted them arrested in the first place."

"Yes, *before* there was trouble. Now we need a remedy. Fairly minor charges could be brought, with a promise of negotiations. They've made themselves heroes, thanks to you. We can't just lock them up now and pretend that never happened."

Rasuli's face darkened. "Just a slap on the wrist? So they can go on to more dangerous conspiracies in the future? What kind of example would that set?"

"General, I don't give a damn about teaching anyone lessons when the city's ready to blow up."

"Look outside, Mangal. It's a peaceful, sunny April day." Smiling, he pointed through the window, then suddenly bent in a crouch. "What in God's name is that?"

Down the Bibi Mahro road, a cloud of dust showed in the distance. Mangal could just make out the shape of a tank—the first in what seemed a long column.

Peaceful? Sure, it had been too damn quiet, starting with Microrayon.

He grabbed Rasuli's lapels. "Did you ever ask Amin's guard? If they let anybody leave his house yesterday?"

"Yes, but..." Rasuli looked confused and scared. "Only his young sons ...went out to play."

"To *what? Why didn't you tell us that before?*"

Cursing, Mangal ran down the hall into the conference room. "Mr. President, did you order tanks from the Pul-i-Charki cantonment?"

Daoud glanced up. "No. Why?"

"Because we have visitors coming. You'd better have a look at this. All of you, hurry!"

Quickly, Daoud followed him out to the hall window and stood still as if in disbelief. His dry lips parted, and Mangal noticed a stain on his usually immaculate necktie. Daoud was old now, falling apart; it was all too much for him.

Then Mangal clenched his fists with anger. The man had no right to be surprised. Only the fondest, most wishful thinking could have blinded him to the likelihood of this.

"Rasuli," Daoud said, "get down to the barracks and call out the Palace Guard."

Saluting, Rasuli turned and left.

Daoud ran a hand along his jaw. "Let's not panic. There may have been trouble elsewhere, and one of my generals is second-guessing me, providing extra security."

"Or some of them could be Khalqis, in spite of Rasuli's little report. Amin's guard let his sons out last night, and he's the one who kept the plan, remember?"

As the sound of the tanks grew louder, Mangal moved to block Daoud from exposure. The president seemed to read the gesture and refuse it. He stepped away. "I'm going to call Pul-i-Charki myself. The rest of you wait in the conference room. I'll be there in a minute."

The others did as requested, but Mangal stayed behind, transfixed as the brown tanks' outline sharpened—Soviet-built T-62s plowing into the Square, while beyond them, incongruously, a yellow taxi stopped to let someone out. Absurd, the whole thing, from start to finish. Soviet money, advisers, munitions, and the man charged with protecting that enormous investment couldn't get a phone call through to the president.

Below, the Palace Guard came out at a run, fixed bayonets flashing like toys in the sunlight. From this height, their phalanx seemed to protect only the small pool with its border of red tulips.

The mud-colored tanks rattled closer, like hideous insects, he thought. And there was Lieutenant Watanjar, another veteran of the '73 coup, waving for them to settle in a line. Daoud had been right; their steel snouts were pointing away from the palace walls. Watanjar must have shared his own doubts about the President's complacency today.

Leaning out, Mangal peered down, bewildered by what was happening. Watanjar had circled in front of the line and was moving from one tank to the next, speaking to each crew. When he reached the last, he drew his pistol, aiming it across the Square at the Ministry of Defense.

One sharp crack, then an ear-splitting volley as the tanks fired in unison, and Mangal stared incredulous at the wreckage of the ministry. Watanjar must be mad.

He raised his pistol skyward. Now engines were revving and the tanks moved forward, curving in an arc until their guns had turned fully back to face the palace.

Watanjar fired again, and instantly the report was answered by an explosive blast of noise, a jackhammer impact of shell against stone that threw Mangal into an acrid cloud of choking gray-white smoke.

He didn't remember hitting the wall, felt pain first, something wet on his cheek, and then the building shook with another series of explosions that plunged him into darkness. He started crawling with his head down and eyes closed against the hot air until he reached the hall doorway where he lay flat, fighting for consciousness, dizzy, stunned and bleeding.

Cries were coming from all sides, a fresh blast from the Square.... Not mad, he thought, no, highly organized, as Karima warned us... We who are about to kill salute you. And Amin had used his own children as couriers to set this in motion.

"If he won't take your advice, then leave." Roshana had been saying that for months, but he "knew better," he had "responsibilities" that made the risk worthwhile, and now there could be no escape from this insanity, for her or any of them.

A wave of pain made him gasp. He struggled to see down the corridor. Several pairs of legs were moving out of the conference room, climbing away into smoke. Suddenly, the floor erupted under him and he felt himself slide hard into an open crevice.

He lay rolled into a ball, trying to clear his head and get oriented. The others must have gone to take shelter downstairs. They hadn't abandoned him—they hadn't realized he was there; but he wouldn't have followed anyway, to be crushed by a mountain of stone. The tanks seemed to be leveling the palace block by block, he felt every shock in his body. Why would they go to be buried? And then he knew why, heard a different sound... not tanks this time, but MIG jets.

From Begram! So Qadir was part of it too. He must have taken over the air base... Qadir, whom Daoud had trusted above all.

The jets were swooping down, diving, strafing, and he pressed himself against the wall. Still, he would lie very still until he figured out the quickest way to get across the compound. Listening, he smiled after a moment, because the planes weren't hitting at all, and he remembered Sukarno's visit, the planned air force display.... They'd missed every target then too, shamefully, until Soviet pilots were sent in to bail out their Afghan trainees. The Soviets hit those targets every time.

He began edging forward painfully on his elbows. So many phone calls from the Soviet embassy... They would hit this target too, since Daoud had given them no other choice. If only... but it was too late to think about anything but Roshana and Yusef, whom he had brought here for *safety*. Ahead, he could barely see the stairs, had to turn and crawl down backward through dense white smoke, fine particles flying into his face as if the stonework itself were disintegrating.

Yes, now the planes were coming closer. They sounded right overhead. He collapsed at the door to the courtyard and watched bullets drive into stone, rows of crackling hail throwing up bright fragments at eye level. Somehow, he had to get across. What would Roshana have done... followed the family to some inner room? Would it be possible to find her in all that rubble?

The planes were turning again. He would time this circuit, starting across the yard the second it ended.

Covering his face with his forearms, he saw his sleeves soaked with blood and to his left three bodies lying at angles to each other, soldiers who must have been standing at the gate. He closed his ears with wet hands against the clatter and whine of bullets, then crouching in a stoop, ran out blindly. Halfway, he thought, I can make it that far before the next strike hits.

It caught him in an open space and he rolled for cover with as much strength as he had, but looking up at Daoud's residence he felt a hot blow on his hip, then searing pain, and heard himself scream at the sight of Roshana standing by the window, Yusef in her arms smeared with blood and limp. The planes were looping back and he waved her away, but Roshana's hand was stretching toward him, her face speaking horror, lips calling soundlessly, and just before the round of bullets tore into his body, he saw one, two, three scarlet blossoms burst across her chest.

Part Three

Enter ye in the company of
The Peoples who passed away
Before you—men and jinns—
Into the fire. Every time
A new People enters
It curses the People who went before
Until they follow each other, all
Into the fire.
      —Holy Koran, Sura VII, v.38

APRIL 1979

Twenty-Two

"DEAD, TOR. All three of them were killed in the coup. I'm sorry. Your brother and his wife and child. I hate to have to bring you this news." The Afghan ambassador leaned over his hospital bed. "Do you understand what I'm saying, Tor?"

Mangal? No, it must be a trick. The coup happened years ago, before Yusef was born.

He shook his head. Of course, he had been very drunk that day. It felt like Stephan's knife was still stuck in his back, the pain was so bad and nobody cared except Magdi with his vodka.

"Your parents are alright, but they're under house arrest. Listen to me, Tor. You have to behave yourself now, for their sake. No more of this, do you hear me?"

Oh, did it look like he was going somewhere, when he couldn't even sit up? Mangal. What was that about Mangal?

When he tried to sit up, the pain had made him scream.

Now, after a year, it hurt only when he moved his right arm or shoulder— a dull, hot stab that took about a minute to subside. Reaching the library door, he clenched his teeth and raised his hand to the knob. As the weather grew warmer, this was getting easier...one twist, then a quick pull against the pain. He would make it go until it was gone.

That hospital. Mangal. And since then every letter from home had been cut to gibberish by the censors. Just to remind him who was in control of all their lives.

It worked, too. He was still afraid some old sin of his might come to light and cause trouble for his parents. The ambassador said their friends had either been executed or were in jail or also under house arrest, but having Tor in Moscow gave a guarantee his father wouldn't support the growing rebellion in Afghanistan. On the other hand, the Russians didn't need Tor now. If he became a problem again, they'd ship him back to Kabul, and that might make President Taraki nervous on two counts.

So the Black Wasp retired in the hospital and when he was discharged back to the dorm—to a new room with only one Komsomol spy—he began studying for a change. It wasn't so hard. Sending good marks home would be better than making promises, and anyway, what else was there to do but get upset and drink himself to sleep? One by one, he waved away the nosy faces who came to his door, except for Magdi, who brought tubs of hot food from the Uzbekistan Restaurant so he could hear Tor say again: It's alright. I probably would have run away myself. I told you I'd lost my nerve.

Magdi had convinced his father that having gold "stolen" was a misfortune that might happen to anyone. But he did not think his cowardice could be forgiven.

Magdi kept bringing bottles of vodka that Tor touched only on weekends, and in spite of three months in the hospital he had finished the spring term's work by the end of summer. By then, three little notes from Elizabeth had come, all sliced up like her first, even though she'd written knowing the authorities would read them:

> Dear Tor,
> I was so sorry to hear XXXXXXXXXXXXXXXXXXXXXXXXXXXX XXXXXXXXXXXXXXXXXXXXXXXXXXXXXXXXXXXXXXXXXXXXXX XXXXXXXXXXXXXXXXXXXXXXXXXXXXXXXXX. My father died last week and I can't write much more than this now. XXXXXXXXX XXXXXXXXXXXXXXXXXXXX. Please take care of yourself.
>
> All good wishes,
> C. Liz

Only Saira's letters were pretty much uncut—long ravings about how they had been too young to appreciate Mangal and the difficult choices he had made, and now there was no chance to tell him she finally understood that, and she and Tor must never be so stubborn again, or let anything come between them, and poor Roshana, and little Yusef whom she hadn't seen once, and did he think that Daddy-jan XXXXXXXXXXXXXXXXXXXXXXXXXX XXXXXXXXXXXXXXXXXXXXXXXXXXXXX.

His own handwriting was so crooked he guessed even the censors couldn't read it. He didn't tell Elizabeth why. She wouldn't be coming so what was the point? She was probably engaged to someone else by now. Ashraf got married when he lost his father.

Answering Saira took weeks because he didn't know what to say. Thinking about Mangal just made him drink too much, and then he'd lie there, unable to study, wondering how long it had taken them to die.

No one knew how Mangal died. Well, maybe one person did. According to the ambassador, the bodies in the palace compound had been hacked to bits and buried in a common grave, except for Roshana and Yusef and some members of the Royal Family, who were found dead indoors after the assault. Even tough old Ghulam-Nabi had been killed trying to get through, and his body wasn't returned for a funeral either. Later, the ambassador said that a week after the coup, a stranger told Daddy-jan he had buried Mangal's corpse himself, secretly and with great respect, to keep it from being "defiled."

Mangal's corpse. His open eyes seeing nothing. And before that? A bayonet in his stomach or a bullet in his head, or maybe he'd been crushed to death in his three-piece suit. Roshana had been shot in the chest, which must feel something like being stabbed—that dizzy sensation of blood rushing out, taking everything with it, terrifying because no one could stop your shrinking into darkness and you knew it was all finished, too late to change your mind. Did Mangal have time to wish he hadn't been so smart after all?

It was better to study than to think about Mangal or Elizabeth, or plaster on a smile for the Abdullahs and Jani Kuznetsov. No matter how nice they meant to be, he still didn't want to see them, and most of all he couldn't stand anyone touching him. He had to step back, pointing to his sling for an excuse, but he knew it was more than that. Being alone and numb and dry was the only way to keep the inside things from getting out, or the other way around. He could never read *Pravda* when he had been drinking, because it was full of stories about the "glorious April revolution in Afghanistan" and pictures of the broken palace walls, the new flag that was solid red, as if the old Islamic green stripe had been murdered too.

Until last fall, when he threw away the sling, his roommate Nikolai had helped him to dress and that was torture. He couldn't bear even to have people very close to him. Maybe they thought it was Black Wasp pride, but the arm would heal only as he used it, and since he couldn't lift it too high he broke bottles, cut himself shaving and knocked over lunch trays in the cafeteria. If he hadn't been so clumsy, though, it would have taken Elizabeth longer to find him, and he smiled now as he walked down the path to the Administration Building, seeing the bench, the exact spot where she had rescued his notes, and him. Since then, they always met here after class.

It was by this tree that his registration folder had blown open last September and he ran stooping to collect a trail of cards scattered on the sidewalk, glancing up to see a hand cuffed with white suede and curly black fleece. "Toryalai Anwari, Physics II. There must be some mistake." He sprang up to face her. But for a minute he could only stare, shaking like a fool. Elizabeth, the one person who could touch him, devastate him.

He wasn't the only one staring at her, either. She was more beautiful than his best memory of her in that coat. Her skin was golden tan after the summer and her short blond hair streaked pale by the sun. Then, looking more closely, he saw a new tightness around her eyes and mouth, which he recognized from his own mirror. At least they had one thing in common now.

His fists clenched, crumpling paper. "Why didn't you tell me you were coming?"

"But I did, Tor. I wrote to you last month. Didn't you get my letter?"

He shook his head.

"You don't look glad to see me."

"I am. I'm just... surprised." Already, he was lecturing himself: hope for nothing but her friendship, even that will be a miracle, just to have someone to talk to. But then another thought came. Maybe she was going to leave as soon as she got the rest of the manuscript?

"How long have you been here? Is it just for a visit?"

She smiled as though his questions were transparent. "I got in yesterday morning and I'll be here all year, I think. Yelena and Kostia have been in prison since last March, so there's not much chance of having to rip up your beautiful coat again. See? I took it to a Bond Street tailor to have the fur sewn back in. He thought I was stark, staring mad. Tor, you're looking as if you hate me."

"No. I'm just in shock, Comrade. That's too bad about your friends."

When she moved to hug him, he flinched instinctively to protect his sore arm, but then they were holding each other in the middle of the path, Elizabeth chuckling against his shoulder and Tor stiff as wood. It didn't mean anything that she was here. She must be glad to find an old friend, that was all. Elizabeth always acted cheerful, so it could happen just like before. But now he wouldn't be able to be casual, to pretend he didn't need her, and he couldn't risk falling apart again even for her.

She said, "Are you really taking physics? Oh, no, what an ass I am, Tor, I haven't even told you how sorry I am about your brother and his family. I didn't know they'd been killed till Nadia told me yesterday. Of course you're in shock. So am I."

Tor began feeling almost ill. Here was Elizabeth, who would understand most of what he'd been through, looking at him as if they could start right here to know and care for each other again. He wanted so much to believe it that he couldn't help drawing back.

He saw himself put out a hand, formally, heard his voice say, "It's very nice to see you again. I hope we can get together soon."

Her gray eyes got darker but she took his hand. "Yes, I think that can be arranged. How about right now? I'm rooming with Nadia again, and I'm almost sure that at this very minute she's entertaining your roommate Nikolai."

Moscow

"What?" He smiled. "So that's where he's been hiding, the little rat."

Elizabeth grinned. "Clever old Nadia. She kept telling people I was coming back so they wouldn't put anyone else in her room. Nadia's a girl that likes her privacy... but of course, you know that."

"Comrade Sutcliffe"—he pretended embarrassment—"which one of us has not sinned?" His kinks of worry and fear were dissolving in a memory of the last time they'd joked together. If nothing else, Elizabeth could make him laugh, and maybe that was what he needed more than anything.

He rocked back on his heels. "Well, Liz, as the Party dictates: To each according to her need. If your room is taken, I humbly offer my own. I even have a bottle of sherry I saved to remember you by."

"Then on behalf of the struggling masses, I accept." She took his arm. "And I could use a drink now, so let's go."

In his room, he turned on a Rolling Stones record while she took off the coat and held it up. "Almost good as new. Tor, how are you, really? When I didn't hear from you for so long, I thought I'd caused trouble for you."

"No. I did that all by myself. I couldn't write because I was sick for a few months. You might say I got stabbed in the back."

Elizabeth sat down on Nikolai's bed. "Nadia told me about that last night too. Was it censored out of your letters? I didn't know you were hurt. I thought you must have written to me only while you were drunk."

She was thinner now, he saw, and more nervous than she had seemed outside, rubbing her hands together and then folding her arms as if she didn't know where to put them.

Giving her a glass of sherry, he sat next to her. "I couldn't send you the real story, Liz. And I didn't want you to think I was up to my old tricks the day after I promised you to be quiet for a while."

"Did you promise me that?" She smiled. "What a victory. Even if it didn't stick. Cheers, Tor. So, what is the real story?"

He told her his idea for bribing Kostia free and the attack at Sokolniki Park, trying to make it funny so she wouldn't feel responsible. "It's a good thing I was hooked up to that EKG machine when I finally got your note, Comrade. Otherwise, I might have had a heart attack. I thought you'd forgotten all about me and it came right on top of the coup."

"But I wrote to you my first day in London! What a bloody mess. They must not have passed on that letter. All yours were so cut up I knew they were harassing you, trying to isolate you. It made me furious. You couldn't have said so many sensitive things. After the coup, I was afraid you'd just given up and gone to hell again."

"And I thought you were mailing me lace doilies. Tell me, did your father get to read the manuscript?"

The sherry stopped halfway to her lips. Nodding, she tipped the glass toward him. "That was the only good thing. Oxford University Press is bringing it out with great guns next fall. The first documented exposé, etc.

Dad chose the editor. We couldn't have done that without you. Thank you, Tor."

She put down her drink and turned it slowly on the table. "I wonder which is worse. Watching someone you love disintegrate right in front of your eyes, or hearing about it all of a sudden when you're this far away from anyone who cares."

"I don't know. Whichever one you get, Comrade. To me, it's totally unreal. I have to keep saying it and I still don't believe it. Also, I ought to warn you, I'm a wreck now. I'm scared of the dark, just like Jani Kuznetsov, and I don't even have a glass eye."

"So am I, Tor. What a horrible year. My father's gone, Yelena and Kostia are in prison, and almost all your family's dead or under house arrest."

"This room is my jail. Do you like it? I hope you'll come visit me once in a while."

She was holding her head differently, he noticed, hunched down and forward a little. He touched her shoulder. "Your back's hard as a rock. Turn around and let me give it a rub."

"Right now?" Her eyes flickered self-consciously. "It's true, though. I feel like Quasimodo. Perhaps I came all the way to Moscow so you could give me a massage." She swung her legs over the foot of the bed.

Her muscles were in knots under the soft wool of her sweater and the fine hair at the nape of her neck tickled his fingers as he kneaded the tight tendons along her spine. Last time, it was Elizabeth who knelt over him, telling him to close his eyes. Was she thinking of that too?

Not yet. He would know when it happened and that shouldn't be too soon, or it might scare her. Maybe if he was careful, he could make her trust him again and then remember.

What a joke, he thought. It's me who's scared.

She let her head drop forward. "That's heavenly, Tor. But you have to do the talking. How much have you heard about what's going on in Kabul?"

"More than I wish I had, from the Abdullahs. You met them." Pressing his thumbs between her shoulderblades, he worked down slowly. "First there was a nice honeymoon when Taraki went to mosques on Friday and said Allah every five minutes. That didn't last too long. Then he executed two or three thousand people and put ten times as many in prison. He's trying to make it the sixteenth Soviet Socialist Republic. Kids have to learn Russian. He's taken away all my family's land except the Kabul house."

"How very Marxist of him. That must be awful for your parents."

"It's the least of their worries, Comrade."

Holding the top of her arms, he shook them. Now she was loosening up. He could smell her perfume, that same kind, like incense.

"What does it mean that your father's under house arrest? Are they locked in with guards at the door?"

"I'm not sure. They can't tell me the truth. Probably their new servants are all spies, sneaking around and eavesdropping, and he has a 'driver' who takes him out once a week to prove he's still alive. That's what's making me crazy. I don't know." His hands rested on her shoulders.

"So you're taking physics to show your parents you're alright?"

"It's a good anesthetic, Comrade. Vodka doesn't work anymore."

"The poor Black Wasp. Reduced to studying." She brushed her cheek against his wrist. "Once you asked me what value there was in being sober when it just made you more conscious of how trapped you were. And I gave you a sermon, remember? Well, I went through a version of that with my father. How much to kill the pain if it also killed awareness, and then after a point his only reality was pain. Tor, was I horribly nasty to you?"

"Just nasty enough, Liz. You made me think I could pass physics."

Her shoulders began to shake and he cursed himself. But they'd have to talk about their families sometime, so why not now? Get it over with.

Bending to kiss the back of her neck, he slid his arms around her waist. "Let's sit here and cry for a week."

Then she leaned back against him and he realized she was laughing. "Tor, you should have seen what happened to your face when you saw me with your physics card! It's not fair, because I was trying to find you and I watched you walk down that path, but you looked as if I'd caught you out at something. Very guilty. That must be an historic first."

"Yes, I looked scared because I still love you. And if you want me to stop I wish you'd tell me now." Might as well get that over with too.

Her face was expressionless except for the dark gray eyes that held light the way lapis did. In Kabul, Elizabeth could walk around naked as long as she wore sunglasses.

One side of her mouth turned down and she put a hand on his knee. "As you once said to me, Tor, am I God? I don't know what should happen."

"Why did you come back here?"

"Because of you and Yelena. It wasn't finished."

"It is with her."

"For the time being."

"Would you have come if you were sure it was over with her?"

Elizabeth shrugged. "Where else should I go? My mother's in France with her sister. She doesn't need me. I still feel like I'm more here than there. It makes some kind of sense to me to be in exile in Russia with you now, as Yelena might put it. Not that I think we have much future after this."

"There's no such thing as the future, Comrade. Now is all I want."

Her hair was electric under his hand and he kissed her mouth. A taste of salt and sherry, the tip of her tongue, it was easy, very simple, he remembered all of it, and she remembered too, with the same jolt he had felt before.

She shivered, "Tor, it's so soon."

"No. It's so late. There's no time, remember? That's what you always said." Her ear was perfumed and the feel of her breast through the thin sweater made him giddy. Then he was touching bare skin, cool at her waist, and their clothes were thrown in a pile on the floor.

A minute of shyness, but both their eyes were hungry, hands wanting what they saw, a curve of muscle, cheekbone, hip, legs in a hurry, grazing each other, and the tightness in her softening with every breath. Trying to hold back was hopeless, stupid, too late, didn't matter. Live bodies, he thought. I must still be alive after all.

"This isn't even my bed," he laughed. "Do I look glad to see you now?"

She was tracing his scar. "So you got this on my account. It doesn't feel half healed yet. Oh, Tor, if you only knew how much I've missed you. How did we get so close in three days? Every night when I came home from that clinic I wanted to talk to you. And your letters worried me so much."

"Let's hope the censors agreed with you that I still seem like a drunk. Our ambassador says my bad reputation may have saved my life."

"Good." Smiling, she kissed him. "I have a confession to make. What really happened when I saw you outside was, I thought: He must have someone else by now, and I've been an idiot to come back."

"See? You do love me a little bit. Admit it!"

Her skin was browner than his own now, and warmer too, and she fit against him perfectly. Maybe this was a dream? How could it be true that all the time he was sure it must be over, finished, she'd been wanting to start again.

"Of course I do, you booby! I'm so glad they gave me a visa. I can't see you living in London, or myself in Kabul, but at least we've got this year, Tor. That's worth something, isn't it?"

"If it's long enough to convince you to marry me. I know, there I go again, but so what? You're too practical. You're always so busy planning ahead, you don't see what's right here."

Pressing her hands down against the pillow, he came into her again and neither of them closed their eyes. This time they hardly moved while waves of pleasure sparked and swelled on their own, as though their bodies knew each other well and had only been waiting to pick up an old conversation.

Afterward, Liz got up wrapped in a blanket to put on "Back in the U.S.S.R.," then brought the sherry bottle over, dancing.

Roommate Nikolai had not come back that night. Nadia's planning worked out well for all of them. She and Nikolai were Komsomol-spies-in-love, so a bargain was easily reached: Once a week they had dinner together and Tor and Elizabeth let themselves be inspected. Nadia smiled with moist quivering lips—if she was their warden, she saw herself as mother of their love, and Tor had to pinch himself to keep from laughing when she asked for the tenth time, "Didn't I make a good deal, Tor? Just like the Black Wasp?" It would have been a mistake to answer, yes, you got Elizabeth out of your room. Nadia was Russian, a romantic, and also an egomaniac, he thought. She wanted to be told over and over that if not for her, they never would have found each other again.

Now, Tor joked, they really were like an old married couple, meeting after class to shop and do the laundry, but lately his old nightmares had come back because things were getting shaky. Nine months of their year had gone by. They had each applied for another term, but the forms he filled out seemed like the prayer ribbons people left on shrines at home to be blown away by the wind. The decision would be made for him, and if it was that he should go home, that could mean much more than just losing Elizabeth forever. He dreamt of huge tanks and firing squads, and some other thing she called his bloody apparition—a shapeless, horrifying monster that woke him up in a sweat, that sometimes now he thought he saw from the corner of his eye in daylight too. No one was ever safe, anywhere, and if Elizabeth was one minute late meeting him, she found him twitching, angry, almost panicked. The solution he found was to come early and sit on this slatted bench, not glaring at the clock but peacefully watching the stream of passing students and looking for new green grass in the thawing, muddy quadrangle. Seeing Tor there so often, Magdi nicknamed him the Dean.

At four o'clock the sun was low and the tower of the Administration Building cast a long cold shadow on Tor's bench. Shivering, he felt a twinge of impatience. Today, she was very late. He scanned the path, but then quickly bent his head as if he were reading from his notebook. The disadvantage of this meeting place was that it had no privacy, and now he could see skinny Abdullah One hurrying toward him with his shoulders hunched and that determined look on his face. For days, this Abdullah had been trying to catch him alone, no doubt for some "serious" conversation, since he hadn't just come to the dorm room for a visit.

It was ungrateful to avoid him, since all three Abdullahs had fussed over him after Mangal's death, but that was exactly the trouble. If it was hard to believe Mangal was dead, how could he even pretend to agree his brother was in "the vision of Allah." So he refused to pray with them and curtly answered their polite questions, but these Abdullahs couldn't take the hint. Now, as Tor raised his head at the last possible moment to greet him, his eyes moved down the path for any sign that Elizabeth might be coming to his rescue.

"Peace be with you, Toryalai Anwari."

Yes, Tor thought, this Abdullah was feeling serious, alright. His bushy black eyebrows met in a thick line across his forehead.

"And with you...Mohammad Ali Khalis." Damn, if he didn't stop calling them Abdullah he would forget all their real names.

"I hope you are well, Toryalai-jan?"

"Yes, I'm fine. But I'll ask you again, please just call me Tor."

Abdullah One gestured as if the wooden bench were the doorway to Tor's home. "May I please sit down? No... it's better if we walk. Would you walk a little way with me?"

Tor smiled, relieved, "I can't right now. I'm waiting for someone here."

The Abdullah bit his lip. "But... just here we can walk. Forgive me, but you sit here very often...."

"And you're afraid by now my bench understands Pashto?"

So this Abdullah also worried about bugs. Moscow must finally be getting to him. Tor stood up. "Alright, Mohammad Ali, I'm freezing anyway. Let's walk."

The Abdullah clasped Tor's elbow as though to keep him from escaping. "Toryalai, do you remember when I spoke to you of Sher?"

They were going along the edge of the path and for a minute Tor silently watched his boots sinking into mud. Sher: Lion. The very name was odd. Usually, it was coupled with some religious name: Sher Ali, or Sher Mohammad. But no, this man, whoever he was, who had risen so quickly as a leader of the rebellion growing at home, called himself just Lion, without any other name even to indicate his tribe. And that, as the Abdullahs had laboriously explained, was half of this Sher's value. Many men had come together in groups to oppose Taraki's "reforms," but most were after some personal gain, so of course their interests conflicted.

The old Royalists—Tor could almost count those who hadn't been jailed or executed—must hope Taraki and Amin's brutality would make them seem truly noble by contrast, though what they really wanted was their lost land, money, power. Same with the mullahs, in spite of all their holy Allah-wailing. Islamic Brotherhood, he thought, equals religious blackmail. And as for the tribal khans—no one could be stupid enough to believe they'd join together in any fight bigger than sniping at traders in the Khyber Pass. It was all pathetic and predictable.

Then this anonymous Sher had appeared, and according to the Abdullahs he was having uncanny success—recruiting men across all tribal and regional divisions. He claimed to be only a nationalist, though they said he was a brilliant tactician—not like other tribal leaders running local wars.

The Abdullahs' reverence for this Lion had made Tor laugh, until they told him stories of the man's wild tricks and schemes, the lightning raids that had won him growing numbers of men and weapons. But they probably fought because they enjoyed it. All they needed was an excuse. They could never stop shooting each other long enough to kill many of Taraki's little red soldiers.

"Yes," Tor said. "I remember Sher. He's your favorite hero, right?"

Abdullah One seemed not to catch his sarcasm. "Ah, you speak the truth.

This Sher is heroic indeed. I believe he is the only man who can save us."

His solemnity made Tor want to laugh. These Abdullahs were driving him crazy with their holy versions of reality, and he was tired of humoring them with pious answers.

"Save you from what, Mohammad Ali? The godless Soviet machine? Where do you think you are, anyway?"

The Abdullah spat with sudden viciousness. "They can't touch my soul. I take their learning and give them nothing."

"Oh, sure." Tor felt his stomach tighten. "That's what Mangal used to say. 'You can take from them, it's perfectly safe, as long as you know when to stop.' But I guess they didn't agree with him, did they?"

"No." The Abdullah shook his head. "With all respect, your brother did not know when to stop. Daoud didn't know. So it's up to us to do it. There are five thousand Soviet 'advisers' in our country now, with their MIG jets and helicopter gunships. We have a twenty-year Treaty of Friendship with the Soviet Union. And do you know what these good friends are helping Taraki to do? Cut up the land and give it to people who have no means to farm it, and who think taking it would be a great sin of theft. Telling us whom we may marry, and when. Forcing children, girls even from the smallest villages, to go to schools that teach there is no God but communism. They turn our mosques into offices and spit on all our ways."

"So?" Tor shrugged with irritation. "What are you going to do about it, Mohammad Ali? Fight tanks with rifles and knives? Maybe it won't be so bad. They took away all our land too, but I think we can get along without it. And at least girls are learning to read for a change. My father worked for that, and you honor him."

"But by force and as an insult... it is unbearable!" The Abdullah's hand trembled on Tor's arm. "Even the Americans had enough sense to make their medicine seem like magic to people who believed in magic first. I don't think you understand the countryside, Tor-jan. Things fit together... so." He laced his fingers into a steeple. "And if you pull apart those pieces, there is only mass confusion. That's what Taraki's people want—to break our spirit, to turn children against their parents and to destroy all the old systems that have worked well for so long. Then we will be completely at their mercy. They go into villages and arrest the local leaders, who are never seen again, and in their place come new high-school graduates, hardly more than children themselves, who say: All these changes must be made right away. Of course, the people resist being told how to run their farms and families, and when they do they are crushed."

"That's my point," Tor said. "What can you do about it?" He stopped walking so the Abdullah would look at him. "With all respect to you, Mohammad Ali, asking villagers to fight with soldiers is like telling them to commit suicide. And what I do know about the 'countryside' is that all the tribes out there have never been able to agree on anything. Do you think they're just going to stop and shake hands because your Sher asks them to? Even if he's a genius the khans won't accept his authority, any more than they do Taraki's."

"I tell you, it's different now! If Taraki had set out to unite the country in hatred for him, he could not have done a better job. Now the people see what he's trying to do. We know our way of life cannot survive if he remains in power. In twenty-five of our twenty-eight provinces, the rebellion has grown from village to village. Is it 'suicide' to go to paradise protecting the honor of your family? Would you not die for your own mother and sister?"

"I hope I would, Mohammad Ali. If I were there."

"If you were there, you would see the truth of what I'm saying. And you would have courage. Why is it so hard for you to believe that your cousins in Paktia hate the Russians as much as you do?"

"Oh, you noticed that."

Tor was looking down at his boots again, trying not to smile, but the Abdullah said angrily, "Is this funny to you?"

"Only in a sense. My father always said education would unify the country, but not because people would rather die than send their kids to school. You've been in Moscow for three years and you aren't a Communist. Forgive me if I seem disrespectful, but I don't know why you're telling me all this. If you want me to feel rotten, I do already."

"Yes, because Taraki killed your brother, and your parents are in danger and you feel dishonored here. But what if I were to say you could do something very important? That your help is needed very much, right now?"

"What?" Tor stepped back, staring at him. "*My* help? Don't be stupid! I can't help anything except by doing nothing, or my parents will be in even more trouble. If you're starting some little college underground here, I don't want to know about it. I don't even want to be seen with you."

"Please," the Abdullah grabbed his arm again. "Listen just for one minute, Mr. Anwari. It's Sher himself who asks your help, with something only you can do...."

Tor pulled away, furious. "You listen, Mohammad Ali. As you just pointed out, my parents are under house arrest because of politics, and that's what killed Mangal and Roshana and my nephew. As far as I'm concerned you can take yours and..." He made an obscene gesture. "If you want to play stupid games with the Russians, fine, but leave me out of it!"

Elizabeth's breathless voice came from behind him. "Wait, Tor, are you leaving? Sorry I'm late. I got stuck at the GUM."

Turning, he saw her smile fade and she glanced at the Abdullah. "I've interrupted something."

"No," Tor said, "we're finished. Let's go."

"Toryalai-jan..." He was speaking Russian now. "Please, allow me to say just one more thing."

Tor scowled at him. If Elizabeth didn't like these Abdullahs so much...
"Alright, but hurry up."

"There is a legend you may have heard, that might have meaning for you. It is about some men who fell asleep in order to learn the truth. When the truth came, they awoke and saw it and knew the purpose of their lives. But this still happens, even today, because men are still asleep, and only Allah knows where they are and when they may awake. Remember... only Allah knows when one will awake." With a last sharp glance at Tor, he hurried off down the path.

Elizabeth's eyes followed him. "What on earth was that all about?"

Tor shook his head, not wanting to answer. "Nothing. It's insane." But walking across the campus, he found he couldn't push away the face those words had called to mind—memories were returning in a flood. It must be pure coincidence: Ghulam-Nabi had told him the story was an old one. Still, he was back in his room at home sick from throwing up, curled on his bed and miserable until the old man's gentle presence loomed above him, felt more than seen, then the touch of his hand. "Do you know what you did tonight?" He had brought a cup of tea and whispered the story, sending Tor off to sleep. "In the dark days before the Prophet, blessed be his name..." Tor shook his head again, violently, but the words kept echoing.

"Tor..." Elizabeth squeezed his arm. "What's wrong? You look ill."

He saw his reflection in her eyes distorted as in a toy mirror, grotesquely wide lips opening, spreading. He said, "It's only... a story."

"Come on." Her face was anxious now. "If it's that bad, wait till we're back in the room."

She kept her arm tight around his waist until they got inside, then taking his coat, pointed toward the couch they'd made of Nikolai's bed. "You sit. I'll put on water for tea."

"No, I'd rather have a drink. Magdi brought some vodka yesterday. It's on the windowsill."

"So long as you don't get too drunk to tell me what's going on."

"Never." He gave her a hard hug. "I can always talk to you. If I couldn't, I'd be finished."

"Good. I'm glad to hear it." Kissing him, she walked to the window and Tor watched her pull back the yellow curtain, then bend to raise the sash. He was here, in Moscow, with Elizabeth, and Ghulam-Nabi was dead. But when she handed him the shot glass he saw his fingers were shaking and quickly swallowed the drink.

She poured him a second. "Better now?"

"Much better, Comrade Doctor."

"So, talk."

"Alright. But it won't make any sense." He settled back against a worn brown cushion. "The night of Mangal's wedding, when I made my little scene, our servant Ghulam-Nabi told me that story. He didn't make it up himself, but I've never heard it before or since, and anyway, no one else knows he told it to me."

Elizabeth pursed her lips. "I guess I don't understand."

"I don't either," Tor smiled weakly, "but Abdullah One claims that Afghan Che Guevara I mentioned wants me to help him somehow. I'm just wondering why he said that story would have meaning for me."

"But the story itself has meaning? Like a parable?"

"Sure. Everybody has trouble waking me up, right?"

He didn't sound convincing even to himself, though.

"Wait, we need some background noise." She went to put on one of the records she had brought from England, the Doobie Brothers' "Minute by Minute."

Tor leaned forward. "Play the second track. It's about stupidity."

Moving the needle, she smiled. "Not appropriate in this case."

But as high, plaintive lyrics rose from the large speakers, Tor felt his head spin sickeningly. There were so many things he couldn't get clear, couldn't know, because no one could tell him. For instance, about Ghulam-Nabi's death. The old man had been killed trying to get through to Mangal, but nobody knew where or when. Did he reach the palace, to be cut up and thrown in a common grave with the others? Or had that strange man... what was his name?... the one who said he had buried Mangal... could he have found Ghulam-Nabi too? Was there a chance...?

The singers seemed to mock him, claiming not even a wise man could let go of his illusions if that left him with nothing at all. Which makes him a fool like me, Tor thought. That must be what I'm doing, trying to see what I'd like to believe. If there were any real doubt about Ghulam-Nabi's death, somebody would have told me. The Abdullah's story must be a coincidence. Why not just leave it at that.

He poured another drink. The bloody apparition was not invited to supper tonight. Skinny Abdullah One, Tor cursed, throwing down the shot, I should have run away the minute I saw that serious, holy face. Why can't they all leave me alone?

Elizabeth sat at the foot of the bed. "What else did he say, before he told you the story? About that Che Guevara?"

"I don't know. Not much. You came before he finished talking."

Someone knocked twice on the door and they both swiveled toward it. Elizabeth motioned for him to wait and went to answer it, but when he saw who their visitor was he jumped up, snarling, "What do you want now?"

Abdullah One stepped into the room, closed the door and stood against it. He said in Pashto, "I must speak with you."

"Get out." Tor used Russian. "Go away and don't come back."

Elizabeth held up a hand. "Just a minute, Tor. Let's solve this right here. I know you won't be able to forget about it, so ask him."

"Please," the Abdullah said, "Tor-jan, I must speak to you alone."

"Why worry, Comrade?" Tor laughed. "After all, women are only pieces of furniture—and only Russian furniture has ears. Anyway, she's the only one here who wants to talk to you, so if you have something to say, tell her." Walking to the window, he looked out at the hazy dusk, the cat dragging a bone down in the alley. Elizabeth was right. He needed to know the answer now. But he didn't want the Abdullah to see that.

He heard her say, "Mohammad Ali, who told you that story about the sleepers?"

Silence. Then, "The story is unimportant." The Abdullah's voice was a terse staccato.

"If you're afraid of bugs," Elizabeth said, "we've found ours and put the stereo on it, so no one can hear you. If you made such a point about that story, it can't be unimportant. Please tell us why. You may not have another chance with Tor."

The Abdullah made an exasperated sound. "Alright. I must trust you. Perhaps you can persuade him. Toryalai Anwari believes our rebellion is hopeless because he does not know the truth. And like him, miss, you may not understand why Taraki's programs are hated so much by our people, since you are also from a large city. So if I tell you, for instance, that our bride price has been lowered from, say, the equivalent of five hundred English pounds to only three, you might think it is a good thing, not realizing that by custom, the bride's family must supply many clothes and household things they could otherwise not afford. Toryalai Anwari's family can get along without their land because they have other means to make a living, but in the countryside there is only one way to survive—through the relationships we have always honored. Once Taraki has destroyed those, we will not be able to resist him, so we are doing it now, and with success."

"Alright," she said quietly. "I'm not challenging you. But I asked about the story you mentioned to Tor. What was the meaning of that?"

The Abdullah exhaled. "Yes, of course. The story. Shall I tell you one that will have meaning for anyone who is not a devil? Since we have done so well, Taraki is now only trying to survive himself, by 'pacifying' the countryside with his new 'Government of National Deliverance.' Does that sound like just more words to you, miss? Have you ever seen a Soviet commando squad at work?"

"No, Mohammad Ali, I haven't. Don't you want to sit down?"

He seemed to ignore her. "Let me tell you this story, then, that you will never read in *Pravda* or *Izvestia*, even though it is being duplicated all over our country as retaliation for our resistance. In the Kunar region of Afghanistan there is a village called Kerala, of perhaps five thousand people. Toryalai Anwari may have heard of this place, it's about fifty kilometers northeast of Kabul. When I tell you what was done to the families in this village you will understand why our mujahedin can fight and win against all odds."

His voice was choked and Tor turned to listen respectfully. He could not help Sher, but Afghanistan was still his country.

Elizabeth sat down on the desk chair, fixing grave eyes on Tor's face, and he nodded to say he was alright. "Go on, Mohammad Ali."

The Abdullah shook his head with disgust. "In this village, Kerala... on the Sabbath day last week, thirty Soviet tanks came and circled the houses. With them came one hundred Afghan soldiers, a hundred policemen and twenty Soviet advisers. They asked all the men of the village to join them in a *jirga*, a meeting, miss, in a plowed field. Toryalai knows what this means."

He stood waiting, and Tor said slowly, "I guess the point is, the villagers brought no weapons, right?"

"Yes. You see, miss, it would be a great insult to bring guns to a *jirga*. And those Soviets knew that. So one thousand men and boys came into this field, and the soldiers ordered them to shout 'hurrah' for this Taraki government. But instead of that, the men of the village cried, 'Allahu Akbar!' God is great! There was a Soviet helicopter flying overhead, and a Soviet adviser spoke to it by radio. Then he called out, 'Open fire!' The soldiers shot point-blank with automatic rifles. In three minutes, one thousand men lay dead. And as their women and children looked on, weeping, a bulldozer dug the bodies into the ground. The Soviet adviser shouted that next year's potato crop would be good."

Tor bowed his head in disbelief. It was impossible. He had never heard of Kerala. There was no such place as Kerala, and no massacre that could be spoken of in Moscow through a wall of rock music blaring on the stereo. A village in Kunar province... they all looked more or less the same, mud-brick houses with a few loose goats and chickens running around. How could those men have been stupid enough to walk out without their weapons? But the Abdullah said their leaders had been arrested, so they had only their code of honor to go by in that field, and even when they must have known what would happen... with their women watching. Women who might never have seen tanks or a bulldozer before.

He heard Elizabeth saying words he couldn't understand and looked up to find Mohammad Ali gazing at him with pity. The Abdullahs... For months now he'd been sending them away with their stories because his own problems had seemed so much worse, so much more delicate and interesting. And all the time he was mocking them, they had probably been despising him underneath their courtesy, the rich boy from Kabul who did not pray, but who might be of some use anyway later on.

Elizabeth was staring down at her hands.

"Forgive me, Mohammad Ali," Tor said. "I'm... grateful you've told me this. I had no idea...."

"The world has no idea, and wouldn't care if it did. That's why it's up to each of us to do whatever we can. But no Afghan has ever run from a fight, is that not so, Toryalai-jan?" He glanced at Elizabeth. "Even the British could not colonize us, though they tried for a hundred years."

Tor thought he saw a gleam of amusement in Mohammad Ali's dark eyes now. Could Abdullah One have a sense of humor after all?

"True, but they didn't have helicopters then. Or tanks, or submachine guns, and our people are still fighting with the same weapons they used a hundred years ago. I honor their courage, Mohammad Ali, but if this rebellion's growing from village to village, the Russians will kill it the same way. You can't stop them. Not the whole army."

"Ah, but they don't have the whole army. Not now. And it isn't just a countryside war anymore." His eyes shone with excitement. "In this last month, it has spread to the cities also and there have been many defections. Recently, our mujahedin took the city of Herat—the third largest city in Afghanistan, miss. Two thousand Afghan soldiers have joined in the fighting with us, and even Soviet bombers have been unable to crush the rebellion. In Jalalabad, too, our troops mutinied when they were ordered to fire on the mujahedin, and killed instead their Soviet advisers. Now in Kabul we are planning... but I must not speak of that yet. Aren't you surprised, though, Mr. Anwari? Of course the Soviets would not publish these facts in *Pravda* or let them be told in letters. So, how could you know?"

Herat, the city of nine hundred poets... Leaning back against the window ledge, Tor tried to picture the streets he had walked along on family visits now filled with farmers and shopkeepers shooting up at Russian planes... and in Jalalabad the same? So he had been all wrong, because he was a coward who couldn't imagine that a few hundred fools together could add up to a counterrevolution, and since they were too stupid to know it was hopeless, they would keep on and become thousands of fools who might be very hard to get rid of.

Kerala, he thought, I'll bet that's what they say now. Remember Kerala, and go to God.

"Yes, I am surprised," he said. "I'm proud of them and ashamed of myself, but how could I help you, Mohammad Ali? You know my situation. Even if I could move freely, what could I do from Moscow?"

"Not from Moscow. From Kabul."

Tor stared, "I can't go home."

"An exit visa might be arranged. Even a ten-day leave. Especially since your mother has been ill. Wouldn't you like to see her?"

"What?" Tor stood up straight. "Why didn't you tell me that before?"

"No, no, it is nothing," the Abdullah smiled faintly. "Only it is a matter of... interpretation. A bad cold. But we have one person in the government who will say that she may be dying of pneumonia."

"But why bring Tor back?" Elizabeth asked. "There must be people there who could help you more easily."

"No, my dear Liz"—Tor mimicked Abdullah One's voice—"this is something only *I* can do. Sher himself has said so." He poured the largest drink he had allowed himself in months and swallowed half of it. Vodka didn't even taste good anymore. "Alright, tell me what you want. But I'm not making any promises."

"I'm afraid that's what you must do, Toryalai." The Abdullah stepped closer and there was new authority in his voice. "You must promise at least to try to help before I can tell you our plan. Otherwise, if you refused, you would have knowledge dangerous to everyone and there would be no gain to us from that risk."

Tor looked up at his jutting chin, the dark eyes that were narrowed and unreadable.... The Abdullah's face had changed again, from simpleton to holyman to someone else now, strangely threatening. He felt his cheeks warming from the vodka. "You're crazy, Mohammad Ali. Yes, I want to see my parents, but I don't know how things are with them. I won't do anything that could put them in more danger. So forget about it, alright?"

"But there will be no risk to them, if you follow Sher's instructions. That is sworn. We have a man working as your father's driver who is willing to take any blame that might fall on your house. Does that surprise you too? He would even die in your father's place. Sher is not our only hero. If, when you get home, you find you cannot do this thing, at least you will give comfort to your parents. But you must promise to try, with all sincerity. This is a most important mission. Our future depends upon it."

"And my parents' safety depends on me! How do you think I got stabbed, Mohammad Ali? My plan wasn't as good as I thought. I counted on someone else and he wasn't there when I needed him." Tor willed his anger to grow to cover his confusion. "Now you're telling me I should trust some martyr who's fighting a holy war? He'll think we should all go to paradise tomorrow, as long as he gets what he wants. How can I trust even you, if you have so little regard for my family?"

"Little regard?" The Abdullah said softly. "No, the opposite is true. Do you know why I always call you Toryalai Anwari? Always that, instead of Tor? As a sign of respect, to remind you of the honor of your family. You ... you have taken all the privileges of power, but so far not one of its burdens. Do you think your father and brother have paid your debt? They understood their power was a gift from the people and they used it well. While you..."

"Just a minute," Elizabeth said. "Tor doesn't owe you his life. I think he's right to be worried about his parents."

"Not as an excuse for doing nothing, miss. Not when I have guaranteed their safety. Again, this is something you may not understand—another reason why Taraki will fail. He expects the poor to hate the rich and turn against them, but he of all people should know that in Afghanistan, strong and wealthy families lead and protect their weaker cousins. The poor accept this order and benefit from it more than from all your English socialism. In our country, ambition is tied to obligations, so Toryalai does owe us whatever he can contribute."

"I'm not ambitious, Mohammad Ali. I didn't choose what house I was born in." Tor found himself instinctively reaching for the bottle of vodka.

The Abdullah stopped his hand. "So you refuse?"

"Yes. I refuse." Deliberately, he poured more vodka than he wanted. "You can tell Sher I'm not on this earth to live up to his expectations."

"Ah, he expected you to refuse, Toryalai-jan. But he said that even if you care nothing for your debt to your country, there might still be one other debt you would wish to repay. And so he sent you something to remind you of that one."

Tor had turned to see Elizabeth's reaction, but she looked past him, raising a hand to her cheek. "Tor," she said, "isn't that yours?"

The Abdullah was holding up a thin black silk thong with a curved crystal pendant. Then it seemed to divide until there were two, three, half a dozen of them, glittering like the Abdullah's black eyes in the airless room. Tor was afraid to touch it; there was something wrong about it, a trick, he was sure, but he took two short steps to look more closely.

No, not his, but like his. How many had there been? The globe held five shards and his own was ivory. This one was red, maybe the lacquerware piece. He couldn't remember very well.

But anyone could have copied that or stolen it from home.

Yes, he thought, that must be it. Old stories and new lies ... They knew how to get to anyone. They'd only been waiting for the right chance to catch him, to trap him....

Elizabeth reached out for the pendant. "No, this one's different. But you said there were others."

"That was taken from Roshana Anwari's body, miss. We have cherished it as highly as her name."

"Liar! You liar!" Wheeling, Tor grabbed it from Elizabeth's hand. "Don't you see what he's trying to do? Lure me back to Kabul. Sure. Then they'll have all of us. He's probably got six bugs on him for proof I conspired to overthrow the government. They'd need a good excuse to execute such an 'honorable' family, right? That's why I have to agree in advance, isn't it, Mohammad Ali?" But glaring into the Abdullah's eyes, Tor saw genuine amazement.

"No, in the name of the Prophet, I swear..." His face had lost its color. "By everything holy, I have spoken only the truth. That is given to you in Roshana Anwari's memory, to remind you that murders must be avenged according to our law and honor."

"Then how did you get this, Mohammad Ali? If everyone in the palace was killed, whoever took this from Roshana must have been on the other side. I think you're one of Taraki's friends and you've been spying on me all this time." But before he had finished the speech, he knew he only half believed it. None of the Abdullahs would take a sacred oath in vain.

"Tor..." Elizabeth said, "there's an awful lot of coincidence here. Remember Ghulam-Nabi's story? Who told you that story, Mohammad Ali, and who gave you this necklace? Was it Sher himself? Have you met him? Could he possibly be an old man?"

The Abdullah's eyes jumped between them. "Old? I don't know. And yet ...it may be so, because I've heard he never goes out with the men. I have never met Sher, miss. That necklace was passed to me by someone whose name would have no meaning for you. How he got it I cannot say, but not all the Palace Guards were killed. Many of them have come to join our cause. And you may search me to see that I have no 'bugs.' I have spoken only the truth, I swear it. There are good reasons why Toryalai must agree to help us before I can tell him more, and I think he would understand why if he were not afraid."

He turned to Tor, "I will leave you now, so you can think about this. In one hour I'll come back and you can give me your decision. But consider well, Toryalai-jan. Remember the people of Kerala. Remember whom you have lost."

Opening the door, he was gone.

"Now I want a drink," Elizabeth said. "Tor, are you alright?"

"If I hear this record once more, I'll smash it." He went to the stereo and made up a new stack, beginning with Jimmy Cliff. If he turned the volume high enough maybe it could drown out all the Abdullah's words, and even the Abdullah himself, so he could never come back and it would be four in the afternoon again, time for tea and cake.

Behind him, Elizabeth muttered, "Damn, the vodka's warm. I should have put..." Suddenly, Tor felt himself turning to grab the bottle from her, and opening the window, he threw it hard to shatter against the building across the alley. He collapsed on the couch running his fingers through his hair. "I'm sorry," he said. "There's sherry.... Oh, why did this happen now? I don't want it."

She came to crouch in front of him, covering his hands with her own. "We'll sort it out, Tor. It just needs talking. First, you'd better tell me about Ghulam-Nabi. Is there any chance he isn't really dead?"

Tor shook his head. "My parents think he is. They never found his body, but they heard he was killed in the fighting in Pashtunistan Square."

She nodded. "But what if he wasn't? Would he have any reason just to disappear?" Getting up, she brought over the sherry and some bread and cheese. "Come on now, you have to eat something, or you'll have Black Wasp belly again."

He broke the round loaf of black bread in half and sat staring down at its twin crescent shapes, smooth on the outside, but underneath, a honeycomb of dark twisting tunnels....

"Well," he said, "with Ghulam-Nabi gone, his wife, Raima, and my father might be safer. His loyalty to my father wouldn't rate him high on Taraki's popularity list. Raima's living with my parents again, and if Ghulam-Nabi were there too, the Khalqis wouldn't trust any of them. They'd have to watch him all the time to be sure he wasn't carrying messages. And their daughter Karima... let's not forget the beautiful Karima... she's working right in Taraki's office, the little traitor, but I don't think even her connections would be good enough to give them much protection. Anyway, she's a real Comrade now. What's a father, more or less, when politics are involved."

"Alright, let's say he isn't dead and that explains the story. If he left Kabul, he might have gone to Sher. Now the necklace. Do you know if it was Roshana's?"

Tor drew his knife across the waxy surface of the cheese. "No. I've never seen the others. All I know is, my mother made five of them. She could even have given one to Ghulam-Nabi—he's almost a member of the family. He saved my father's life twice when he was in the cabinet."

"Listen..." Elizabeth put down her glass. "Maybe this is daft, but while we're speculating about Ghulam-Nabi... is there any chance at all that your brother might still be alive? He would certainly have had one of these."

Mangal. Tor jammed the knife into the cheese and left it there. "No, not even a slight chance, Comrade. It doesn't work that way. Taraki would have had to see his body to be sure. He probably stuck his fingers into the bullet holes. If they thought for a minute he might be alive, my parents would have been thrown in jail as bait to smoke him out."

"Alright, sorry. I didn't mean to upset you. Then we have three possibilities. Mohammad Ali could be lying. Or, he could have been lied *to*, if Ghulam-Nabi got captured and Taraki took his necklace to trap you. Or, it might really have come from Sher, by way of Ghulam-Nabi or someone in the Palace Guard, in which case this whole thing is legitimate. And I can't believe Mohammad Ali is your enemy. I think he really loves you."

"Not as much as Ghulam-Nabi does. If they tortured that stubborn donkey for months he'd just decide to die before he'd betray my family."

"So? And if that's true...?"

"I don't care! Even if it isn't a trap, I'm not going. My parents need me to be a little sheep, and I need you." Then glancing down at the necklace lying on the table he had to force away the thought of it on Roshana's body, a soldier bending with his hand at her throat....

"What your parents might really need right about now is to see you."

He looked up. "You mean you want me to go?"

"Hardly. It scares me to death. But I know how worried you are about them, and if Mohammad Ali's plan is safe... He said you only had to try. If you don't go, you may regret it."

"And if I do, I could get us all killed, or make some mess that would keep me from coming back here. I'm afraid to leave you, Liz. I don't trust it. Something would happen."

She closed her eyes. "Alright. That's a possibility too. But tell me this: would you go if I weren't here?"

Tor pushed his drink away. How could he answer that question? If the Abdullah had brought that story, the necklace... but he'd still be his parents' safeguard. What else would he be now if Elizabeth had never come back to Moscow? Still numb and self-controlled? Or would his old despair have gotten worse, until he had to do something, anything, out of sheer frustration?

He said, "I'd stay right here, Comrade."

"I don't believe that, Tor. I think you would go, just to prove you weren't afraid. Or because for all you know, something else could happen to your parents and this may be your only chance to see them again. For other reasons, too... that atrocity in Kerala? I'd like to do something about that myself."

"I can't believe you're saying this. Are you trying to get rid of me?"

"Only for ten days."

"But what if I can't come back!"

"I know. But I have faith in you. And Tor, in two months we may have to leave Moscow anyway—out of our little hothouse. Perhaps we could both go and live under house arrest, though somehow I can't see that. Or you could come to England if you want to. If they'll let you. But first you have to figure out where you want to be, and that might be a good argument for going home all by itself. Besides, you don't have to sign a contract. If you get there and your job seems too dangerous, you can simply say: no deal."

He stood up to walk around the room, trying to imagine what it would feel like to be in Kabul again... their compound with the Paghman mountains rising up in back, the spring garden, Mummy-jan's face, Aspi. He hadn't let himself think about home for almost a year, and now he could almost smell the house—Raima's pilau, the wood basket under the stairwell and the sandalwood screen—but even those things might have changed. This wouldn't be like coming home from Lawrence College. They were under house arrest.

And he could never replace Mangal in their eyes.

"I wonder what Sher wants," Elizabeth said. "What is it only you can do?"

He shrugged. "I don't know. Lie in four languages at the same time? Maybe he wants me to kill Karima. I might even enjoy that."

"Or maybe he wants you to translate secret Russian codes. Tor, you could see what's really happening there. Aren't you excited at all?"

Smiling, he turned to look at her. She always knew. His scalp had started tingling while the Abdullah was talking about Jalalabad and Herat. And something in Kabul next? Being there would feel like a slap of cold water, waking up all his senses.

But what good would they be without Comrade Liz?

She was sitting on the carpet, bracing her back against his bed and her hair looked pale as cornsilk in the lamplight. How could she want this? If there was even a chance that it might mean the end of everything... But fourteen months ago they had sat together planning a job she had to do, and he'd let her go then.

She cocked her head, "I still have a few diplomatic connections myself, you know. If you get stuck there, I'll come after you if I have to bring in the queen on horseback."

"Better give her a helicopter," he smiled. "Demazang prison has high walls."

"Tor, you're going? You've made up your mind?"

"I guess so. If Che Guevara wants to give me a ten-day leave, I can take it and consider anything else I do a favor."

"That's right. Only I'm sure you'll find the challenge irresistible, so be very careful, will you please?" She was starting toward him when a knock came on the door. Making a face, he went to open it.

The Abdullah had changed into a heavy coat and sweater and thick leather boots. Tor smiled. "Are you planning to march to Kabul tonight, Comrade?"

He shut the door. "What I'll do now depends on you. What is your decision?"

"Sit down, Mohammad Ali." Tor pointed to the desk chair. "I'll go. But I'm promising only to try. If my parents are in danger I might not touch your job. So, you can take it or leave it."

"That is only what I asked. But you must swear to try in all sincerity, Toryalai-jan."

"Didn't I just say I would?" This Abdullah was getting impossible, he thought. "What's my sacred assignment?"

"You have sworn? Praise be to Allah! And this should not be too difficult for you. Here is what you must do. In your father's files are the plans... blueprints for the Pul-i-Charki cantonment. The arsenal there could supply a thousand men for months, so Sher is going to raid it. Your task is to find these plans and pass them to our man."

Tor sat down abruptly on the couch. So this was what only he could do ...but they must be crazy. Pul-i-Charki was crawling with soldiers twenty-four hours a day. Then he had a second thought. "You mean you want me to steal from my own father? Plans only he could have?"

"Unfortunately, yes. That is why his driver's sacrifice is so necessary. If the plans are somehow captured before the raid, our man will say he stole them. In fact, he has tried to many times and failed. They are not filed where they should be. But it is essential that your father know nothing of this, since he would try to stop you. We have approached him already and he refuses to help us because he is a man of peace and wants no involvement in our struggle. I honor him, Mr. Anwari, but our future success depends on those plans. The man whom you will pass them to is one of our best. You need have no fear of him."

Tor wondered if he looked nervous. His palms were sweating, but he felt a cold clarity returning to his mind. His part seemed easy enough. If the rest of them wanted to go to paradise, that was their own business. For ten days he would be home. Anyway, why shouldn't this Sher have the plans? Taraki ought to be sent to paradise as soon as possible too.

"Is it settled?" The Abdullah held out his arm and Tor clasped it.

"Yes. I'll do my best. Will you explain all this to my father if he kills me?"

"He would do it, if he were younger. And you are his son, Toryalai-jan. In two days the embassy will call you. The ambassador should have your exit visa and a flight will be arranged. I must go now, to fix these things."

"You're sure my father has these plans?"

The Abdullah dropped his arm. "Yes. And one final thing. You will give them to our man at sunset, in the bazaar stall that sells only Istalif pottery. He will wait there every night for a week. If you don't come, we will contact you, but I know you will not fail us. Your father's driver, Rashid, will take you to this man, since otherwise your movements will be closely watched. He is young and always wears a blue turban. His name is Nur-Ali. Good evening. Thank you very much, miss."

He turned in the doorway. "May Allah protect you both."

"And you, Mohammad Ali Khalis." Tor closed the door behind him. The Abdullah, who was not what he seemed.

Nur-Ali. Collapsing in the armchair, Tor put his feet up on the table. Wasn't that name familiar? So many memories, pieces, fragments, it was hard now to separate one from another, and yet... he was sure he had heard the name before—not recently, but not very long ago—sometime in the hospital? And then he knew when it was.

"Elizabeth," he said. "I just remembered something. I think Nur-Ali was the name of the man who told my father he buried Mangal."

Twenty-Three

As the plane descended to Kabul a glimpse of familiar mountains drove Tor to his feet, and bending he peered through one tiny window at the city's sharpening outline. First the skyscrapers at Pashtunistan Square, then the ancient fort, Bala Hissar, the blue wisp of the river and, beyond the Shor Bazaar, the old quarter of haphazard mud-brick houses climbing up the rock face. There was the long clean slice of the Jada-i-Maiwand, and now he could just make out the maze of smaller streets where he had lost most schoolday afternoons in games and exploration, in spite of the scolding he always got for coming home so late.

Surprisingly, not much seemed different. A few ugly Soviet boxes sprouted here and there, but after the awful sameness of Moscow, Kabul looked almost wild, and unpredictable.

"If I were Russian, I'd cry now." With a shock he realized he had spoken out loud and sat back down in his seat. The "rodina"—the motherland—even sophisticated Russian students used that term with awe, so when he scraped mud off his boots he'd joke, "Don't sweep that away, Comrade, it's part of the rodina!" But now, looking down at the valley as the plane banked in a curve, he guessed their pride must be like his own hunger for this place, for its spice and music, and for people who weren't crushed by monotony but moved quickly through the narrow crowded streets, calling greetings or naming goods for sale, their eyes and hair dark as his own.

Now the plane was circling over Carte Char and Seh, and he could almost see into the high-walled family compounds. Such parties, so much mischief ...did that still go on? he wondered. Further east, the houses thinned out and just as the airport came into view a roar rose from the ground and the plane shuddered. Grasping his seat, he stared at the gray streak that had taken off from the runway—a Soviet MIG jet, trailing smoke across the clear blue sky.

When they landed and taxied to a stop, the door opened onto an April sun so brilliant his eyes couldn't adjust for a minute. Then he saw five soldiers armed with submachine guns standing at the entrance of the low concrete building.

Picking up his bag, he felt a bulge where the two liters of vodka were packed. With luck, they'd confiscate the vodka and laugh at him: See what happens to these rich boys? But after that, they should worry about him less—just a drunken baby without his bottle.

Inside, the passport control desk had been replaced by a barrier stretching the width of the room. Six more soldiers stood in a line behind a senior officer who sat at a long table. He stuck out a hand without looking up. "Passport?"

Uneasily, Tor put his small black folder on the open palm. If they kept it he'd be completely in their power.

"Why, it's Toryalai Anwari!"

The officer raised his head and Tor stepped backward. The man had spoken Russian and his eyes were blue. Turning toward the soldiers, he said in Pashto, "This is the *Soviet* Anwari. It's been a long time since he's been home. Which means he has a lot to learn, but we'll be glad to teach him, won't we. I'm Lieutenant Brokhin, Special Adviser for Internal Affairs. Put your bag up here, please."

Setting the vodka out on the table, the lieutenant smiled. "I'm happy to see you appreciate our national drink so much. Too much, perhaps, for such a short visit, but that's not my affair." He spent twenty minutes going through every pocket and page of the few things Tor had brought, holding up a cashmere sweater for the soldiers to touch. "We don't sell these in Moscow! He must go to the U.S. to do his shopping. Alright, Mr. Anwari, you can pack this up again. And don't forget the vodka. I hope your father will like it too. Sergeant, bring his driver in here."

If you want to humiliate me, Tor thought, you'll have to try harder, Comrade.

But he picked up his passport quickly.

A plump young private came to take his case.

"Here's your package, Rashid," the lieutenant said. "Be sure you don't lose him. And Mr. Anwari, I'm to inform you that *if* you're allowed to move about, which unfortunately isn't my decision, a curfew is in effect from eleven PM to four AM. If you're found outside during curfew you'll be shot with no questions asked, so *if* you're wise, you will stay indoors from sunset to sunrise, understand?"

"Yes." Tor shoved his fists in his pockets. "I'm sure that's good advice." He followed Rashid out to the parking lot.

The Mercedes was barely recognizable, grimy and dented—Ghulam-Nabi must really be dead if the car could look like that. When Rashid held the door for him, Tor avoided his gaze. This was supposed to be the person who would die for them, but he was awkward, almost beardless, probably more unreliable than Magdi in a tight situation. No wonder the Abdullah had made him swear an oath to try "in all sincerity."

Rashid also seemed to be taking his measure through the rearview mirror, but it wasn't until they turned onto the Bibi Mahro road that his round face opened in a smile. "Welcome to the first anniversary of our glorious revolution! To celebrate, they're painting all the public buildings red, just like our new flag. Do you like the color red, Toryalai?"

"On some people." He returned the smile warily.

Rashid nodded. "But not on me, and I think not on you either. Green would suit us better, don't you agree?"

The color of the Islamic flag. Tor leaned back in the seat. "Is there much green yet this spring?"

"In Kabul, no. It's too early. But the provinces are full of new grass."

"I'm glad to hear that."

They were driving past the U.S. embassy and Tor saw the shutters were closed. Then he remembered. "Is it empty now? Did the Americans all leave when their ambassador was killed?"

"Ah, poor Mr. Dubs! He was here such a short time, and I believe he loved this country. But he was either very brave or very stupid, since he would have no bodyguard. They grabbed him on his way to work one morning and held him at the Kabul Hotel. It's too bad the soldiers rushed that room so quickly, trying to rescue him. Our Soviet adviser must have miscalculated. An unfortunate accident."

"I seem to recall *Pravda* said his kidnapping was 'a spontaneous act of hatred for American imperialism,' or something."

"Spontaneous? No, merely stupid," Rashid chuckled. "The kidnappers were Shi'ite extremists who wanted to trade Mr. Dubs for friends of theirs in prison. But no one in this government would give five afghanis for the life of any American, and poor Mr. Dubs presented them with a great temptation. If he hadn't died, you would never have read that story in *Pravda*, and the U.S. might still be giving us aid. Which would be unwelcome competition now."

Tor was looking straight down the road to where Pashtunistan Square opened in the distance. The palace... they would go right past it, and it was too soon for that. Seeing Mangal's old room would be hard enough.

"Can you go around the Square," he said. "If we met President Taraki, I might faint with joy."

Rashid turned right at the Ariana Hotel and skirted the downtown area. Here many buildings had been gutted by fire. Armored vehicles were stationed at each intersection and every blank wall had been covered with revolutionary slogans. Their detour brought him past the Ministry of Health, which had not yet been painted red, but a handful of soldiers with fixed bayonets stood along the sidewalk.

"There are machine guns set up right inside that door," Rashid said. "Which is healthy only for some people." He started down the Sher Shah Mina road leading into Carte Seh.

In a few minutes now they would reach the house.

Tor asked hesitantly, "Rashid, how are my parents?"

"They're alright." Rashid met his eyes in the mirror. "I think they are... unbreakable. But courage goes only so far these days. I must tell you something now that you won't want to hear. For the last month, there have been midnight raids—mass arrests, mostly of Royalists like your father. And I can't think of one single person who has been released afterwards."

A small black car was parked outside the gate to their compound and Tor could see two heads behind the windshield. As they turned past it into the drive, Rashid smiled and waved. "That's the guard. At least they're not inside anymore. But if you try to leave, except with me, they'll make you wish you hadn't. I mean it." He stopped the Mercedes in front of the garage. "Your parents want you to meet them on the second floor. They even take their meals up there now."

The house looked shut in on itself, Tor thought, abandoned and desolate. All the curtains on the ground floor were drawn and vines fell in a ragged mass over the garden wall. The kitchen door needed painting. At Mangal's wedding three hundred guests had come to eat and dance while a band played in the reception hall. Where were those people now?

As Rashid handed him his case Tor felt warm fingers press his own. "Good luck. I'll be out here when you need me. But we'd better not go on any tours until our work is done. It's not good weather for sightseeing these days."

"Alright. Thank you, Rashid." Walking up the path, he opened the kitchen door.

It was orderly, spotless, exactly as he remembered it, even to the row of bright enamel pots hanging from a wooden dowel over the work counter. He'd expected the air to be stale, but the garden windows were open and looking out, he dropped his suitcase. If the outside of the house had been neglected, the garden was more beautiful than ever. In the orchard, all the fruit trees had grown and their white petals shivered like handfuls of snow thrown into wind. The flower and vegetable beds were already crowded with young green plants that must have been started indoors during the winter, and shiny garden tools stood in a row against the shed by the grape trellis. At the center of the rose garden, the fountain installed for Mangal's wedding shot an arc of spray that rained down to a copper basin, and two wicker chairs, set side by side, seemed to admire the effect.

This was Daddy-jan's work—he'd never let the servants do much in the garden—so he must really be alright. Tor draped the heavy coat he was carrying over the back of a chair and started down the hallway, calling, "Hello up there! Mummy-jan, it's me, I'm home!"

She was leaning over the bannister and he ran up to wrap her in a bear hug.

"Tor. You've grown a foot! Oh, listen to me ... as if you were a baby! Jan, what a wonderful surprise. We couldn't believe it when we heard you were coming. Omar, he's here!"

The door across the landing opened and his father came out wearing baggy pants and an old black sweater. He looked almost shy and Tor went to give him a hard hug too. "I saw the garden, Daddy-jan. Now I'll never want to leave."

"Bechaim." His father held him tight, and Tor swallowed back a sudden aching lump in his throat. "My son. Welcome home, such as it is."

Mummy-jan clapped her hands. "Thank goodness you got through. They told us you'd be here at noon and it's almost four o'clock. We've sent all the servants away, Tor. For this afternoon, just the three of us." Her voice was hoarse, and Daddy-jan said, "Catherine, don't try to tell him everything at once, or you'll be back in bed for another month."

She'd been sick, Tor remembered, and turned to look at her again. Her gray eyes were shining. "Nonsense, Omar, I'm much better, really, Tor." But bending over, she coughed sharply. "This thing just seems to hang on. Come in and have some tea now, while I heat up the pilau. We've turned the room next to ours into a study so your father can work in peace up here."

The study where the blueprints were supposed to be? Oh no, he thought, those file drawers screech. This is too close to their bedroom. Then he hated himself. It wasn't the time to worry about that yet. When she opened the door, though, he saw just armchairs set around the fireplace, a few bookcases and a desk. So the file cabinets hadn't been moved upstairs, and if this was the only living room they used now it would make his task even easier.

"Catherine, you sit with Tor. I'll bring up the food. But keep an eye on her, Tor. Don't let her get too excited."

She waved him away, "I'm fine, Omar. Alright, I'll let you wait on us for once. Raima made Tor's favorite yogurt drink and it might need to be stirred." When he'd left, she grinned. "Your father's the one who's excited. He spent all morning fussing in your room, putting out books you might like."

Yes, Tor thought, I can just imagine what kind they are too—Rules of Good Behavior. He said, "Mummy-jan, being sick must agree with you. Right now you look very pretty."

It must be those clothes that made her seem more relaxed—a pale blue skirt with a darker blue silk pullover. Her hair was pinned up in a casual coil and he could never remember her wearing sandals at home before. She rested her elbows on the arms of her chair and a gold bangle slid down one thin wrist. He saw that she wore her wedding ring loosely too.

Usually, she had dressed formally in stockings and a dress. This was like seeing a blurred picture of her when she first came to this house, young, not always having to attend to Daddy-jan's work or their screaming children. Her blond hair was still glossy, but it was shot through with gray and her skin looked very white. Maybe not relaxed, he thought, just tired, beaten up, not caring about formalities anymore.

She pointed to the fireplace, where a lattice of kindling was set. "We thought you might like a fire. It's been cool this year, and it can get chilly very quickly late in the day."

When he crouched beside her to light it, she said quietly, "Listen, Tor, if you don't mind, let's not talk about Mangal and Roshana tonight. This is a celebration. But I have to tell you about Aspi, before you go running down to look for him. After the coup, we had to send him to the Paghman house. He was just too much to handle without Ghulam-Nabi. When the Paghman farm was confiscated, Aspi went with it. I don't know who has him now. I'm very sorry."

"You'd better hope I don't see anyone riding him." He squeezed her foot. "That's okay. I had a feeling he was gone. Now I can tell Taraki I've already made my contribution to the revolution. Heil Hitler."

There was a crash in the hall, and he jumped up to collect the silverware that had fallen off Daddy-jan's tray.

For the next few hours, while they ate and drank pots of tea, he also fed the fire as the sunlight faded. Even up here the shades were partly drawn, so it was darker than it had to be and the shadowed furniture looked heavier. Probably they spent most of their time right here and he could almost see paths worn in the carpet from the few trips their feet could take now, like the caged pheasants in the garden who paced up and down along the wire mesh all day, every day, hoping for the gate to be opened.

At least he could try to make them laugh.

"Have some more tea, Daddy-jan. Are you still keeping bees? Or did Taraki have them executed for holding secret meetings?"

"Still?" Mummy-jan smiled. "He has four new hives!"

"What do you do with all the honey?"

His father shrugged. "We haven't had any honey yet this year, Tor."

"Well, what did you do with it last summer?"

He touched his chin. "Nothing. Last year we did nothing. And this year the same."

"Omar! That isn't quite true. We've done an awful lot of reading. Guess what your father's devouring now. English fiction. A Jane Austen novel I love called *Mansfield Park*."

"A friend of mine in Moscow has some books by Jane Austen. I don't know her work at all."

"Maybe some day you will. But tell us about the university, Tor. Or living in Moscow. What do they have on TV?"

"Brezhnev!" Tor held his palms up flat. "'My comrades, let us all remember our glorious mission, and fill our monthly factory quotas for the greater good of the oppressed peoples of the world!'"

"Does he amuse you, Bechaim?"

"No, Daddy-jan." Tor dropped his hands. "Well, sometimes he does. They roll him up there like a statue. I think he wears makeup, too."

"Yes. They're all old. Soon they'll be dead, whether they like it or not. We've been very pleased by your grades, Tor. Congratulations."

"Thanks. But I have to report that Moscow University isn't really so hard, except for science majors."

"If you had discovered that four years ago, you'd be graduating with honors. You simply never tried before."

"No, not at schoolwork, I didn't."

He doesn't mean to sound that way, Tor thought. He just can't help it. That's how he feels. He's glad to see me with my A in physics. Hoping for a miracle. But he'll never trust me. He can probably smell the vodka in my case. And now I have to steal his files, just to prove him right. Damn the Abdullah and his holy vows. The sooner I get that over with, the better.

"More Moscow stories!" Mummy-jan was trying to patch things up. "Have you met any dissidents?"

"Wait a minute, Catherine. I want to finish. I'm proud of what you're doing, Tor. You and Saira are both working seriously and that makes us very happy. Especially when I know Ashraf spent last winter skiing in Gstaad with some friends. His family's living in Kashmir now, with relatives. I'm not saying he doesn't care. But when I think of Mangal's wedding... it's like a merry-go-round. Mangal's dead and Ashraf's skiing in Switzerland. Babrak Karmal made that coup with Daoud and now he's living in Prague, branded a traitor. He'll be executed if he ever comes back. Well, there's nothing Ashraf could do here. In the countryside, people are fighting. But in Kabul, in the cities, you can't walk down the street. We all sit around and watch the plaster crumble." He stood up. "I must go to bed now, Bechaim. I think I'm catching your mother's cold. I just wanted you to know how I felt."

Tor got up too. "Thank you, Daddy-jan. It's so good to be home."

"I'll see you both in the morning. Don't keep your mother up too late."

When he'd left the room, Tor tiptoed with mock defiance to the fireplace and threw on another log. "Is he okay? He seems sad. Is he always like that?"

She shook her head. "Believe it or not, he's been in good spirits lately. He's just embarrassed for you to see him this way. Idle, helpless, without much to do. It's frustrating, when he's been so busy all his life. But he is enjoying reading and working in the garden. He's earned a rest. And he was thrilled about your visit, Tor, believe me. But I think it's made him realize the hopes we've had for our children have gone up in smoke." Stretching back in the chair, she yawned. "And speaking of smoke, don't put on too much wood. I'll have to turn in soon myself."

"Not yet! What about our celebration?"

He thought, I've got to do this thing tonight. They're both tired, so they'll sleep soundly. By tomorrow, Daddy-jan will look at me with his X-ray eyes and know I have a guilty conscience. Tonight if they hear me making noise downstairs, they'll think I'm just looking around. But first I have to know some things, before I have to start worrying about the servants' spying on us.

Sitting in the opposite armchair, he unbuttoned the top of his shirt, exposing the crystal and ivory pendant.

"Do you really wear that?" She smiled, "I wasn't sure you would."

He nodded. "Ever since you sent it. I never take it off. At first it made me feel awful, though."

"That wasn't my intention, Tor. Maybe it's just as well you broke the globe, since now you each have something to remind you of Uncle Yusef. It's funny. He used to give me lectures till I wanted to strangle him, and now I miss him terribly."

"I miss him too," Tor said gently. "But I'm sort of glad he didn't live to see Kabul painted red." He leaned forward. "How did you decide which piece of that globe to give to whom? I'm sure you didn't send me white because I'm the most holy."

"Maybe not at that time, but since then... as your father said, we're very proud of you, Tor."

"Thank you, but it's not exactly heroic to be good when you don't have any choice."

"No, but you could have just gotten by. You've done much more than that."

Her praise was making him feel worse, like an impostor. Finish it, he thought, get it over with.

"I'll bet you gave the Phoenician glass bit to Saira," he said. "That was the prettiest piece."

"Mmmm. And I kept the bronze and gave your father the Roman stone. Then Mangal had..." Her voice broke suddenly and she bent her head as if listening to something far off. It was the closest he'd ever seen her come to tears.

"Mummy-jan..." He moved to sit on the edge of her chair. "Forgive me. I'm so stupid. You've been trying to make me feel good, when it must have been ten times worse for you."

"No." She was coughing again. "I'm fine. Don't worry about me, Tor. Sometimes things... catch up with me, that's all. It doesn't last. But I wish you could have seen little Yusef. He was such a dear. You and Saira will have to give us grandchildren someday. They're much more fun than you think."

"I'm working on it," he smiled. "Remember my friend who likes Jane Austen? I'm trying to convince her to marry me."

"No! She's not a Russian, I hope."

He shook his head. "English. And you asked about dissidents? She got me involved with a whole nest of them. Well, only two, really, but it seemed like there were twenty. I helped her smuggle out some of their work." Now why had he said that? To make her think he was Mangal? "I mean, before the coup, of course. I haven't taken any chances since then."

But her interest was so obvious he began to tell her about Elizabeth, and when he finished she was beaming.

"That's wonderful, Tor. She sounds like a fine person, and I've hated to think of you there all by yourself. How odd! Here I thought my past was gone, and now Saira lives in New York and you go to Moscow and fall in love with a girl you wouldn't be able to talk to if you hadn't had a Western mother."

"She speaks Russian too," he grinned. "But now I know why you're so pleased. Your Pashto was never very good."

"That's true. But there are so many ironies. Like that crystal globe. Do you remember all those shards came from an archaeological excavation at Begram? Well, the Begram base was where the planes came from—the planes that strafed the palace during the coup. Colonel Qadir sent them, do you remember him? Taraki made him Minister of Defense afterwards, and then had him arrested. Along with many others—from the Left and the Right. It's like Alice-through-the-looking-glass around here lately. 'Off with their heads,' for no discernible reason. They're afraid of the rebels on the one hand and their own people on the other. Taraki sent all the top Parchamis away as 'ambassadors' before he declared them traitors, and they were his allies during the coup."

"Too bad he can't send the rebels away. Especially this guy Sher?" Tor found himself waiting anxiously for her reaction.

After a minute, she said, "I'm surprised you've heard of Sher. It's very strange.... Raima just told us a rumor about him she picked up in the bazaar. I probably shouldn't repeat it...."

"Please tell me." He forced a smile to cover up his curiosity. "I miss hearing all those stories from the bazaar."

"Well"—she wagged a finger at him—"don't *you* repeat it, but apparently, some people think Sher is Roshana's Uncle Aziz, and he's using that name to neutralize old enmities. Whoever Sher is, he's definitely working out of Paktia province, and it seems that some of his lieutenants have been recognized as friends of Aziz Khan."

Looking into the fire, he tried to recall Aziz at Mangal's wedding... tall and muscular, with an energy that filled whatever room he was in. He had made Tor feel scrawny and insignificant.

"I mean it, Tor. Don't you repeat that. I can't believe it, but if it's true... the walls have ears these days."

These days. That's what Rashid had said. He wondered if she knew about Rashid, but there was no safe way to ask.

He said, "I won't even think it. But it doesn't seem so incredible." Then he was afraid she might wonder why he thought that.

Instead, she stood up. "I ought to go to bed now, or I won't be any good tomorrow. Your room's just the same, Tor. Do you want me to help you unpack? Or would you rather stay by the fire a while longer?"

He got up to kiss her. "I'll watch it till it's out. I may go down and get some more of that pilau, too, so don't worry if you hear me banging around."

"I'll get some for you now, if you like." She smiled. "My always hungry son."

"No. You go to bed. I want to get used to the house again."

"Alright. Good night, Toryalai. I know you're excited, but don't stay up too late. You must be tired too."

"I won't. Good night, Mummy-jan."

He watched her walk across the landing to the bedroom.

Closing the door only part way so it wouldn't creak later on, he went back to kneel in front of the fireplace, banking the ashes in a mound. His head was pounding and his mind felt crowded with questions, but it seemed he would have to pose them one by one. She might too easily follow the thread of his interest to what was already dangerous ground.

Maybe tonight was too soon to look for the blueprints after all. His shoulder hurt from stoking the fire, and the layout of the study could have been changed while he was away. Fumbling in the dark might even alert the guard outside.

Nerves. Scared baby, he told himself, it's Daddy-jan you're afraid of. Home less than a day and already in disgrace. Good old dependable Tor.

No. It had to be now. This would only get harder as the days passed. Besides, he might not have to ask them questions that this Nur-Ali could answer. That's right, Nur-Ali should be able to tell him many things.

Maybe a little vodka would help. One quick drink, in the kitchen?

But if Daddy-jan caught him at that, it would be unforgivable. Mangal's wedding all over again. At least stealing the plans had some kind of honorable explanation. And vodka still turned his eyes red.

Flexing the bad arm, he pulled off his boots and walked over to the door. No light came from the room across the landing. He turned out the lamp and went quietly down the stairs.

There was no sign of life in the kitchen either, or the servants' quarters beyond. So there was only the guard to worry about. The study opened off the front hall, and if they were parked right outside the gate, they might be able to see the lights go on. A candle would be softer, but could also look more suspicious. Was Daddy-jan not supposed to use the study? There were curtains in there, though. Yes, candlelight would be best. The bottom pantry drawer had always held a box of tapers.

He smiled at his silence opening the kitchen door, remembering every creak that had betrayed him sneaking in late years ago. But when he carried one lit candle back to the entryway, his amusement evaporated. The study door wore a shiny metal padlock he hadn't noticed earlier.

Instinctively he blew out the candle and stood for a moment in darkness. The key—where would Daddy-jan keep it? Probably on the bureau with his other keys at night, in his pocket during the day. So there would be no better chance than now to get it. This was nothing the Black Wasp hadn't done before. Don't think, just move quickly.

The stairs were quiet, but he rubbed sweat off his hands before opening their door. A thin shaft of moonlight fell across the bed and he waited for any sign of movement from the two huddled figures. Then cautiously, he moved around the bed to the bureau on the opposite wall, and though he could see no glint of metal, the first pass of his fingers settled on the coiled end of a chain. He felt along it, closed his fist around the mass of keys, and taking a step backward struck the bedpost hard with his foot.

His mother's sleepy voice said, "Omar?"

"No," he whispered leaning over her. "I just came in to kiss you good night."

"Good night, dear. Go to bed now."

He pulled the door almost shut.

Downstairs, he sorted through the keys by candlelight. Only one was small enough to fit. Turning it, he cupped the padlock to keep it from rattling, then slipped it into his pocket and opened the door.

Here, the air really was stale. His small flame shrank against it. Setting the candle on the edge of the desk, he looked around the room.

Nothing had changed. The rifles hung in their old order in the gun case, and across from that six steel file cabinets stood in a row. The first three were labeled MINISTRY FILES, the next two SPECIAL PROJECTS, and the last PERSONNEL.

This, he thought, is my punishment for not being interested in politics. Come out, wherever you are.

The Pul-i-Charki plans could fall in either of the first two categories. The Defense Ministry—he pulled that drawer and discovered it was locked. Of course, they were all kept locked, and those keys... no, not on this chain... there had been another ring in the desk. Holding the tangled chain close to the candle, he found the desk key and bent to unlock the top drawer, pulling it out gently. There was the ring. As he reached for it, the study door swung open and his father stepped into the room.

"Have they sent you back here to steal from us, Tor?" He sounded incredulous, but also teasing. "If it's money you're looking for, I'm afraid you won't find any."

Their eyes met above the candle and Tor's hands closed around the drawer. Already a few lies had come to mind. The Black Wasp was getting stronger. But none of them were good enough, not now. His father's haggard face and hesitant smile seemed not to want to believe what he was seeing... though no lie could pass for truth to those eyes anymore, Tor realized. And Daddy-jan's trust was a price he couldn't pay again for any reason.

"If you mean, did the Russians send me to steal, the answer to that is no." He had meant to return a joke and was startled to see his father's face relax in genuine relief. "Daddy-jan, you can't think I'd do that?"

"I think anyone might do anything. My assessment of human nature has been revised sharply downward since the last time I saw you, Tor." He walked over to switch on the desk lamp, turning its shade low to dim the light. "If I include myself in that, why not you? Suddenly, your grades are good and you're allowed to come home. I can interpret that in one of three ways. First, that you've matured and had a stroke of good luck. Second, that you've defected, for some inconceivable reason. And third, that they have a hold on you, as they've held you against me. Any combination of these might be true. I prefer to choose the first explanation, without discounting the third."

"No, I'm not spying on you! I know, it seems funny...."

"Then what are you looking for?"

Tor slid the drawer shut. "I can't tell you."

"Why is this?"

"I can't tell you that either. Really, I'm sorry, but I can't."

He raised an eyebrow. "So many secrets, Tor!"

"I wish you could trust me, just for once."

"I'd like to, Bechaim. But you've made that difficult."

"I know. It's not your fault. But I'm getting good marks now. Doesn't that prove anything to you?"

"I've never doubted your intelligence."

"Just everything else."

"Chiefly, your judgment." His eyes had that look that said: You are a disappointment, but I try to love you because you are my son.

Tor put his hands in his pockets. "It hasn't always been so bad. Daddy-jan, I know I'm not Mangal. I can't help that. If I could be dead instead of him I'd do it, to make everyone happy."

"Don't be melodramatic, Tor. No one wants you to be Mangal."

"Yes, you do! Or else, that I should disappear. When you talked about my marks before, it was the first time you've ever praised me—for something Mangal's good at. That isn't all that counts. There are things I do well, too."

"You can't spend the rest of your life riding horses, Tor. Good marks aren't an abstraction. What you'll be able to do in the future depends on what you're doing now. We care about you, so naturally we've been concerned to see you wasting your talents."

"That's what I'm saying! I have other talents."

"And I'm saying, I know that, but what are you going to do with them in five years, or ten?" Tipping his head back, he smiled bitterly at the ceiling. "Not that I'm sure any of us will be around that long. But if we are, you may have two aged parents to support. No, I'm joking, I hope it won't come to that. But you will have to work, Tor. I'm afraid I don't have a Swiss bank account for all of us to fall back on."

"I know that, Daddy-jan. I'll run your honey business. Anwari Apiaries."

"Oh? Then what would I do?"

"Watch me constantly. Pick out all my mistakes."

"Don't feel too sorry for yourself, Tor. You've had a thousand chances. Maybe two thousand. And now I wish you'd tell me what you're doing in my study."

"I can't. Honestly, Daddy-jan. But do you think we could just talk for a while, without getting each other mad?"

"We could try, Bechaim. It would be a new experience for us both." He took a cigarette from the box on the desk and offered one. "They're very stale."

"No, thanks. I don't smoke anymore. Is it safe for us to stay in here?"

"I think so. Shall we sit down? If we have a midnight visitor, it won't matter which room we're in." Taking the ashtray to his reading chair, he pushed over the ottoman and Tor sat on it cross-legged.

"Are you expecting that?"

He shrugged. "So far, we've been lucky. If Taraki can be believed, we'll be alright, given certain limitations. But ever since the Shah fell, there's more pressure on him. Not to mention the trouble here. He's not handling it well. And if Amin takes over, as he'd very much like to, God have mercy on us all. Amin's been behind the worst of what's happened. But you don't know about all this."

"I've heard some things. What's the Shah got to do with it? Brezhnev can't be scared of Khomeini."

"Of losing all that oil to Shi'ite fanatics when it's already scarce in Russia? Soon two-fifths of the Soviet population will be Islamic, and they've always had unrest in their southern Muslim republics. They need us to keep this border secure. And as a doorway to Pakistan. They've always wanted a warm-water port. Sometimes I wish Taraki all success, because I'm so apprehensive about what the alternative might cause."

"How could it be worse than this? Kabul looks occupied right now."

"Yes, that must have come as quite a shock to you." He tapped his cigarette on the ashtray. "Never mind, Bechaim. If you want to see something truly impressive, you should read Taraki's official biography—a wonderful piece of fiction! After all, he was a novelist once. Now he's just a man of the people with his very own Politburo and enough Marxist rhetoric to make even Lenin sick. Meanwhile, the country's going up in flames, and the Russians won't let that happen. They won't lose what they've gained, of that you can be sure."

"But isn't the rebellion getting stronger? At least, that's what I've been told."

He was lighting another cigarette and blew out the match with disgust. "Strong? It's idiotic. You can't hope to fight Soviet hardware with nineteenth-century rifles."

Tor thought, that's what I said too, but it's better than doing nothing if they're going to kill us anyway.

"Do you know how much matériel they've brought in, Tor? You saw those armored vehicles downtown? There are almost a thousand of those, along with eight hundred tanks that cost a million dollars apiece. But worst are these helicopter gunships—they're trying them out here for the first time, aren't we very lucky? Inventions of the devil! They shoot six thousand rounds a minute, not to mention bombs and rockets, and they can cross the country without stopping to refuel. In an uprising in Herat last month, they killed more than twenty thousand people."

Tor sat up. "You mean, that's over?"

"Of course it's over. *Barre duroz Shah*. Do you remember what that means?"

"King for two days, isn't it?"

"In this case, for five days," he nodded. "They did well to last that long. But now the punishment will come, you see? Indiscriminate bombing of villages. Wholesale slaughter of peasants who had no part in the rebellion."

"Like at Kerala," Tor said softly.

"Of course as at Kerala, Bechaim. The Soviets aren't playing games here. They've sent us Alexei Yepishev, chief political commissar for their armed forces. Last month, the rebels took the upper Kunar valley and declared it Free Nuristan. Kerala was in payment for that. And so now in Herat province, and anywhere else a stand is made. And even where no stand is made, as with so many of our old friends, whose only sin was working for His Majesty or going to college in the West."

"Both of which you did." Tor stood up to walk around the room. "I don't understand this. You hate the Russians, but you won't support the rebels either. Maybe this rebellion could mean something if all of us..." He stopped in mid-sentence. For the second time he was echoing the Abdullah.

"So, are you a nationalist now, Tor? Is that your new adventure? What excitement have you found here in my study?"

Tor turned to see his father leaning toward him through the yellow light.

"It was the mujahedin who sent you here to steal, correct? What do they want of mine?" He glanced around the study as if appraising its contents. "My rifles? Why bother, for so few. Money? I no longer have any. Records of an obsolete government, then. Why would they want them?" His eyes returned to rest on Tor's face. "You can't tell me. But maybe I can guess. Could it be the Pul-i-Charki plans? Yes, I can see I'm right. They aren't here, so you may as well admit it."

"Daddy-jan, I've taken a sacred oath. I can't say anything."

"And I have sworn to Taraki that I will do nothing against him. That's why we're all still alive."

"But you can't trust him! He killed Mangal!"

"Not out of spite, Bechaim. Mangal lived by the sword himself. He wasn't a private citizen."

"Neither are you, Daddy-jan."

"Your mother is. And so are you. Let's keep it that way, shall we? Your friends approached me for those plans and I refused. I still refuse. And you are still my son."

"Your eldest son now, remember? And I've sworn an oath too. There's no risk involved, except to me. If I can help kill a few Russians, just for Mangal's sake I want to."

"You never had great affection for Mangal, Tor."

"Maybe, but if he were here right now, I'd kiss his foot."

"I see." He smiled grudgingly. "Death is a wonderful teacher, isn't it."

"So are you, Daddy-jan. I've just been very slow."

"If you think the rebels can win, you still are."

Tor shook his head. "But if they keep doing well, other countries might help. The Chinese, or the Americans..."

"Unfortunately, you don't know your history, Bechaim. With you, everything is romance. In the fifties, we asked the U.S. for military aid, and turned to the Soviets only when they flatly refused."

"Aren't things different now, though? Like what you said about the Shah? They might support us just to keep the Russians away from that oil."

"And King Zahir might return from Rome, and Taraki might fly up to heaven."

Tor smiled. "I'd like to arrange that trip for Taraki myself. Then maybe you really could bring the king back. If you tried, and the Durrani family and the Mujadidis and... are they all still alive?"

"In Peshawar. They've all escaped to Pakistan. Perhaps they'll form a government-in-exile. I wouldn't be surprised. I'm just as glad to be here, though. In Kabul, where I can assess the situation. The groups in Peshawar are fighting among themselves already. I don't want any part of that. And I'm not sure they'd choose King Zahir to lead them now."

"But you would."

"I think he's the best hope we have. In fact, on the day I decide and truly believe all is lost... on that day, I will leave here no matter who's standing at the door."

He was smiling almost secretively, Tor thought, and then he remembered the garden—all that careful work. Maybe Daddy-jan also had a dream and a scheme to go with it. He'd always been mysterious about his dealings.

Tor sat down on the footstool. "Daddy-jan, when I agreed to come back, I didn't want to help the rebels. I promised just so I could get home. Now I don't think I'll be able to stand living in Moscow again—being a little sheep—if I haven't tried. How can I grow up if you won't let me? You've always accused me of being irresponsible. For the first time in my life, I don't feel that way. And I swear, there's no risk to either of you. I'm twenty-four years old. I have to make my own decisions too."

"We've already lost one child, Tor. Do you think we could stand to lose another?"

"You won't! This is what I'm good at. You can't protect me anymore. Tell me one thing. Honestly. If I were Mangal and I wanted to do this—something on my own..."

"I'd give the same answer."

"Even now? If he were standing here, would you say no to him, Daddy-jan?"

Leaning back in the chair, he closed his eyes and said nothing for a few minutes. Then, "Uncle Yusef didn't want me to marry your mother. I'm sure we've told you that. He said no. He had good reasons. And I was like his only child. His eldest son. But of course, he had taken no vow. So even though these plans are where a thousand eyes can see them, I must forbid you, Tor. And you must honor my reasons in the same way that I still honor his." He got up. "Bechaim, it's almost five o'clock. I have to go to sleep now, and I think you should too. I've never liked your ugly face in early morning light. But first perhaps, after all this bad air, you'd like to step out into the garden. For the sake of your health. I know you think I'm hard with you, but it's only because I love you. Good night, now. Pleasant dreams." He picked his keys up off the desk and went out toward the stairs.

Listening for the upstairs door to be closed, Tor took a cigarette from the box and touched one end to his tongue. What was all that about Uncle Yusef? Daddy-jan had certainly not obeyed him.

The tobacco was dry and crumbling. Daddy-jan had sworn...it was a blessing! A secret message that didn't break his vow: honor me as I did Uncle Yusef.

Striking a match, he lit the cigarette. A message. Then what about the plans? They weren't here. He had moved them, maybe after Rashid tried to steal them. Away from the house? No, he was watched too closely for that. Besides, where else would he be able to guard them?

Not "here." Not in this room. The smoke tasted like dark gray dust. "Where a thousand eyes can see them."

Plastered into the compound wall? On the roof? But who could see them there? Maybe they were glued onto the bumper of the car, and Rashid could have taken them all along.

Only outdoors could there be a thousand eyes of any kind.

So they must be in the garden. "For the sake of your health..."

Crushing out the cigarette, he went down the hall and through the kitchen door. The sky was just in danger of getting light and the plants were straightening up. He stood while his eyes adjusted to the dark, breathing in the sweet smell of the orchard. A hundred million blossoms, not a thousand.

He sat down in one of the wicker chairs. A thousand eyes of what? There weren't any potatoes, and no daisies yet. The most birds they'd ever had was twenty.

Which left only the bees, whose white wooden hives were showing along the wall now. How many bees were there in a swarm? More than five hundred, but so far, that idea came closest.

Going over to the tiers of rectangular boxes, he felt along the wood. How could you hide anything in a beehive? Already they were waking up, buzzing in alarm. The front openings were biggest, but only just wide as a hand. If the blueprint was really inside a hive, it would have to be dismantled first, at night, and that would make a lot of noise.

Stuck between them, maybe? There were three hives in each stack. Gently, he lifted one uppermost box and jumped as a dozen bees gusted out angrily. Somewhere, Daddy-jan kept a hat and veil, but the sky was streaked with pink now. No time to go hunting around. Even a smoking cigarette would help, if he'd thought to bring one out.

Working down the row, he twitched and dodged as more bees tumbled out. Nothing in the first two sets of tiers. He pulled the sweater up over his head so only his eyes were showing and kept lifting and probing with his fingertips, cursing as one, then a second bee stung him, but there was something here, an edge of oilskin, deep under this hive.

Wiggling it out, he watched a third bee settle on his wrist. His hand was free now and he shook it hard, before the barb sunk in. Oilskin, and inside that blue paper. Was Rashid watching through the gate?

Tor stuck the package inside his shirt. His hand was hot and swelling fast, hurting more by the minute.

Cradling it against his chest, he walked back to the house.

Twenty-Four

THERE WAS LAUGHTER coming from the garden, but Tor didn't want to wake up until he remembered the question again, buzzing around in his brain like one of the bees that had stung him last night. When he turned his face toward the window it flitted farther out of reach, and it was important not to let it get away.

Not about Elizabeth. She'd just been in his dream. This was something ... He opened his eyes a crack to see his right hand, red and swollen. It didn't hurt so much now, but something was making him mad and he pulled the quilt up over his head. A woman's laugh ... why was that so irritating?

When he woke again it was quiet and bright sun glinted on the studs of Aspi's bridle hanging by the door.

Sitting up, Tor ran his fingers underneath the mattress. The oilskin folder was still there and now he knew the question too: If Rashid was willing to say he'd stolen these plans himself, why couldn't he take them alone to the bazaar?

Why do I have to go with him? Tor thought. It doesn't make sense.

He slid out of the blankets and got dressed. It was three o'clock already—how had they let him sleep so late? Hunger mixed with the annoyance settling in his stomach. Maybe Rashid could not be trusted completely? But if that was true, the risk to all of them could be greater than the Abdullah had admitted.

Pushing the plans deeper under the mattress, he hurried down the stairs and stopped abruptly in the hall. A small boy was sitting on the kitchen floor trying to string a kite, and for a second Tor imagined it must be Yusef. But no, this child was older, he could see that now, and as he came closer the boy looked up, frowning over his mass of string.

"Can I help you with that?" He crouched next to the sturdy brown legs stretched out on the floor. "I used to be pretty good at making kites."

Behind him, a side door opened and the boy grinned in recognition, but before Tor could turn he heard a familiar voice. "Hello, Toryalai."

That laugh, no wonder it had bothered him. His hands froze on the kite and he stood up holding it in front of him as if the plans were sticking out of his belt.

"Karima, hello." He smiled. "What a nice surprise to find you here." Good, that had just the right tone. But watching her, he felt the thin wood bend between his fingers. Taraki's little assistant! How dare she come, how could she be so beautiful? Soft brown eyes to spy with, the mouth he used to kiss now full of lies.... Already he wanted to touch her, feel her warm throat under his hands and then squeeze harder, choking that fake smile off her face.

She said, "Zia-jan, I want you to meet another Anwari uncle. Tor, this is my eldest son, Zia. His grandmother just gave him that kite."

"How nice!" Tor kept the light tone in his voice. "So that's why you're here. I was sure there must be a reason." He kissed the boy's cheek awkwardly. "I'm your Uncle Tor, jan. Has your mother told you about me? Well, Karima, three children in five years! My cousin Nadir's a lucky man. But then, you're a very... talented woman."

Her eyes narrowed. "Zia, why don't you take your kite out to the garden and see if Bibi Anwari can help you with it."

Squinting up at them, Zia shrugged as if he were used to being sent away, took the kite and ran outside.

"Are my cousin's other children here too?" Tor asked. "And Nadir? I should congratulate him. Especially since his dear wife was kind enough to visit me on my first day home." He was wondering why she had really come—to write a report on him? Or could some hint of Sher's scheme have leaked out?

"I wanted to see you, Tor. Is that a crime?"

She was pretending to be friendly. Did she think they were all stupid? "My dear Karima, I'm not Taraki, and who else can judge crimes? Anyway, I couldn't keep you out. You tell us what to do now, right?" But he had to cool down. This was no time for a fight.

"Nadir's in Pakistan, if you're really interested. Working at the port of Karachi. His sister Salima and our two younger children are living with him there. They aren't in school yet, so it's—"

"Healthier," Tor interrupted. "All that sea air must be very healthy for anyone named Anwari. But I'm glad to see you've stayed behind to keep the country on track. It would make Roshana so happy to know that women can get such good jobs here." He smiled sweetly. "By any chance, are you working right now?"

The color in her cheeks darkened. "Life isn't always as simple as you'd like to make it, Tor. People do things for all sorts of reasons. I was hoping we could have a conversation. It's long overdue."

She stood facing him, hands clenched by her sides, and just then he also wished they could talk. Not about her marriage—he had explained that to himself a thousand times. Unwillingly, he'd left her and she had turned to someone else. Now he also had someone else, and no right to be bitter about Nadir. But about other things, yes. He wanted very much to know how she could have lived in this house for so long, claiming to love them and finally even marrying their cousin, and then turn against them in favor of Taraki and his bunch of murderers. Maybe she had been taken in by Communists at the university, but to join them so wholeheartedly, spying on the family ... No, that couldn't be excused or forgiven, and now everything in him wanted to drive her away. Talking could be dangerous for many reasons, and the blueprints had to be passed on by sunset.

"Ask me whatever you want," he said. "I await your orders."

She shook her head. "You really hate me."

"How could I? You're a total stranger. But tell me one thing. Why did you come here today? To remind me of what?"

Karima winced, but then her face hardened. "Never mind, Tor. Just forget it. You think you know so much, but you don't understand anything. It's your loss, not mine." She brushed past him toward the garden door.

Looking through the kitchen window, he saw her bend to speak to Raima, who was playing with Zia. Then his own mother came up to them, seeming to ask a question, and when Karima shook her head Mummy-jan glanced sharply toward the house. He stepped back from the window and stood waiting until the sound of Karima's car had faded down the street. Then slipping through the side door, he walked up the driveway into the garage.

Rashid was sitting on a low stool beside the Mercedes, his head hidden by the newspaper he was reading. Peering over the top of it, he grinned. "You were up late last night, yes? I heard the back door open."

Inexplicably, Tor felt like sinking a fist in the soldier's wide belly. "Tell me something, Rashid. Why do I need to go with you? Wouldn't it be safer for you to make this delivery on your own?"

"Ah, then you had success?"

Tor said nothing, staring at him. Rashid's smile quivered. "Toryalai, I have only my instructions. And no authority to change them. I was told to bring you, that's all."

"Then they don't trust you to do this alone."

A line of concentration appeared in the middle of the man's forehead. "No, I don't think that's the reason. For the guard to see me leave without a passenger would not be good. And a new message may have come down for you that I couldn't carry. The less each person knows at every stage, the better."

They all act as if ignorance were a badge of honor, Tor thought. Or am I just too used to being in charge?

"I have to be back here in time for supper. How soon can we leave?"

Rashid checked his watch. "Now, if you like. It's a little early still, but better soon than late with this curfew."

"Alright. I'll be back in a minute."

Upstairs, he put the plans in a cloth market bag that he could flatten under his shirt and discard inconspicuously. Then he went down to the garden. His mother was sitting in one of the wicker chairs, gazing up at the fountain, and when he touched her arm, she jumped. "Oh, Tor, good. I have to talk to you."

"Can it wait an hour?" He smiled. "Your driver says I'm allowed one tour of the city and I've asked him to take me now. I need to see it."

"Oh, no. Can't that wait till tomorrow? There's something I've got to tell you—"

He stopped her with a guilty kiss. "Mummy-jan, he might change his mind by then. I'll be home soon, honestly. We'll have lots of time to talk later."

And, he thought, I'll be able to think about something besides these blasted plans.

In the drive Tor found Rashid sitting behind the wheel, and as they backed out he repeated his jolly waving act with the guard. "They think I'm a fool," Rashid chuckled. "But you see? It's better to be thought a fool than a clever man these days."

As they drove down the Sher Shah Mina road, though, Tor saw in the rearview mirror that Rashid's face had grown tense and he was licking his lips nervously. Had it been a mistake to trust him, just on the strength of what the Abdullah said? If the Abdullah was not what he'd seemed, Rashid might have surprises for them both.

But if this was a trap, why should Rashid be afraid? Maybe it was a good sign after all.

Once Rashid had parked the car and they were walking through the bazaar, Tor felt his anxiety ease a little. There were only a few soldiers here, none of yesterday's scars of battle, and he let his senses open to the smell of roasting lamb, charcoal and dung, tanned leather and tobacco, while the high ring of the tinsmith's hammer beat a counterpoint to voices bargaining urgently or with indifference, dark eyes set in weathered skin following him as he passed stalls offering nuts, spare car parts, silver jewelry, bags, rugs and a hundred other wares displayed according to the merchant's own sense of design and color.

Every kind of thing, Tor thought, what a wonderful mess. I could spend the rest of my life here and be happy.

"It's just here," Rashid smiled.

Tor felt the cloth bag snug against his chest.

The Istalif stall seemed to explode with pottery of bright blue and green, and he touched one large azure bowl fondly. Their glazes were brilliant, but too fragile to travel well, and he'd missed this color in Moscow. Maybe on the way out he could find something for Comrade Liz.

Rashid said, "Go straight through to the back."

Turning from the bright path to the darkened stall, Tor almost collided with the owner, who stepped forward out of shadow.

"I'm looking for someone called Nur-Ali." Tor swallowed. His throat was scratchy.

Wordlessly, the man lifted a heavy curtain in the rear, and Rashid followed Tor into a small cluttered storage space. The curtain dropped behind them.

A turbaned wiry young man whom Tor judged to be near his own age was sitting cross-legged on an old footlocker, rolling a cigarette. He looked Tor up and down. "Good. You found the plans." Then coolly, "Can I have them, please?"

Tor took out the bag and watched him as he flipped slowly through the blueprints. So this was Nur-Ali. He looked fairly intelligent, cunning, physically tough, and something else... maybe not quite so confident as he acted? Yes, Tor thought, I could teach him a few things. For instance, that a little charm works better than a trunkful of arrogance.

"They seem to be complete," Nur-Ali looked up. "And you haven't tampered with them."

"Of course not. What would be the point of that?"

"You've been in Moscow a long time."

"Not by choice," Tor said tightly. "But I learned more there than you'll ever know about recruiting people."

"Oh yes." Nur-Ali smiled sardonically. "We've heard all about your famous exploits. Did you carry a gun there?"

"I didn't need to."

"Well, I do." His hand moved and then the snout of a small Mauser was pointing at Tor's chest. "Please don't make us knock you out. Rashid hates hurting anyone. Zafar..." he called. "It's time for Tammim, please."

Tor glanced at Rashid, who shrugged apologetically. "I'm sorry, Toryalai, but we can't let you go yet. Not until these plans are safely in Sher's hands."

"You mean, you're going to hold me here?" But then another man slipped through the curtain and Tor could only stare. This new person looked so much like himself that from a distance they might have been mistaken for each other.

Rashid said, "This is Tammim. He's my little cousin, thin like you, and we have made his hair like yours also. Now you can see why I wave like a fool at the guards each time we pass? They look at me and make fun of me, maybe, but they don't look so closely at you. So tonight they will see Tammim come home and think his name is Tor."

"My mother won't!" Reluctantly, though, Tor felt admiration softening his anger. They had done a very good job with this boy.

Tammim grinned, "I wouldn't try to fool your honored mother. But I will try my best to assure her that you'll be returned unharmed tomorrow night. Please understand, you're the only one who knows we have these plans, and every care must be taken."

"No, he doesn't need to understand." Nur-Ali motioned with the gun. "Take off your shirt, pants, sweater and shoes. You can keep the rest. Tammim, give him your clothes."

Quickly, Tammim stripped off his baggy tribal pants and shirt, and after a moment Tor did the same. He didn't want to give them any excuse to touch him. Nur-Ali's eyes surveyed his bare body as if matching Tor's strength against his own.

Fumbling with the loose trousers, Tor realized he hadn't worn such clothing since he was a child, and even after he fastened the last button he felt undressed and clumsy.

Nur-Ali lifted the curtain flap, then turned to Rashid. "It's not dusk yet, but I don't want to wait. Take Tammim now, and tell Zafar to bring the truck around to the back." Again, he aimed the gun at the center of Tor's chest. "We're going for a ride in the countryside. I won't tie you, because if we're stopped that would be awkward to explain. Your name is Siddique, and..." Grabbing Tor's hand, he studied it. "Pah, you've never done any work, have you. But we can't say you're a schoolteacher, not the way you look. So, we'll call you a schoolboy," he smiled thinly. "You could pass for a backward boy, so soft and pretty you are. But that means if you have to speak you must use simple language. Leave the talking to me as much as possible."

Tor had been watching him in silence, considering the gun. It would be tricky to disarm Nur-Ali, but not, he thought, impossible, so long as he could keep these insults from affecting his judgment. If Nur-Ali was going to drive in the country, he'd need both hands for the wheel.

Zafar's voice came from the other side of the curtain. "The truck's outside now."

"You go first," said Nur-Ali. "And remember, if I shoot you in those clothes, no one will know who you are. Or care. You'll drive east down the Jalalabad road... Why are you smiling?"

"Because I don't know how to drive. We've always had a driver." Stealing the Mercedes had been his biggest sin in high school, but Nur-Ali wouldn't know that.

"Pah!" Nur-Ali spat on the ground. "The elite are good for nothing! Alright, I'll drive, but I can shoot with either hand and I'd really enjoy killing you if you give trouble. We have the plans so we don't need you now, and you're no good to anyone else. And if I can't shoot you I'll stick this in your throat"—he touched the dagger at his belt—"or strangle you with my peasant fingers. Afghanistan wouldn't be in this fix if it weren't for you aristocrats. Now move."

Tor walked lightly around to the back of the stall. In spite of Nur-Ali's threats it should be simple enough to jump out at some intersection. Nur-Ali wouldn't want to risk losing the plans by attacking him in public.

A high square truck painted with bright scenes of animals stood with its motor running, the cab doors open. Climbing into the passenger seat, he watched Nur-Ali position the gun carefully in his left pants pocket. Then he shoved his face close to Tor's. "Remember this too. If you escape, these plans will be no good to us. We couldn't trust you not to talk. So if you get away from me, Rashid will take them to your parents' guard and say he saw your father give them to you. For his sake, don't be foolish."

"With all respect, I think you're lying, Comrade. Sher wouldn't let you do it." But looking into that lean face with its beaked nose and thin hard mouth, he thought Nur-Ali might enjoy making other people suffer no matter what his orders were.

Throwing the shift forward, Nur-Ali joined the stream of traffic hurrying to leave Kabul before sunset. Tor relaxed in the seat. He wouldn't try to escape yet. Apart from the threat to his parents, he was beginning to think a visit to Sher's camp might be interesting. In the meantime, maybe he could learn some things from his bad-tempered escort.

He asked, "How long have you been with Sher? When did this rebellion start?"

Nur-Ali glanced at him sideways. "You know nothing, do you. I've been with Sher a long time, for years. And the rebellion—that depends on what you mean. I worked against the king too. We've had enough of tyrants of any name."

Looking over his shoulder, he turned the truck off the road and pulled up behind a stand of poplar trees. "We'll wait until it's dark to go farther. Get out, and sit down over there."

Tor walked to the small rise and after he had reached it, Nur-Ali climbed out carrying a leather sack. He sat on the opposite side of the path, unpacked three containers of food and began to eat noisily with the gun close by his side.

Tor said, "Could you share a little of that? I haven't eaten all day."

Breaking off a piece of flat bread, Nur-Ali aimed it to fall on the ground beside Tor's feet.

If they had to go a long way, he couldn't afford the luxury of going hungry, and he brushed off the dust with seeming unconcern. In fact, the bread was delicious—the first nan he'd tasted in years, and for a second, glancing up, he thought Nur-Ali had smiled at his obvious relish. He used that opening to say, "What have you got against me, anyway? I'm doing your Sher a favor. And aren't you the man who buried my brother out of 'great respect'?"

Nur-Ali stopped licking his fingers. "You aren't your brother. You're no better than most of the Mohammadzai princes who should have been shot years ago. That's why I'd like to kill you. And as for doing favors—if you worked for us for ten years you still wouldn't have paid one-tenth of your debt to our country. What I have against you is that you're a parasite, and before this night is over I'll have the pleasure of hearing you scream."

"Shooting people and calling me a parasite—you sound like quite a Communist! Maybe you ought to work for Taraki." But the man's hatred was unnerving. How much authority could he have? In the dim light his eyes shone crazily and for the first time Tor wondered if he was supposed to reach Sher's camp alive.

"It's time to start now. Get in the truck." Nur-Ali made a wide circle around him and a few minutes later they were heading up into mountains. The truck seemed much too heavy for the narrow unpaved road, and Tor was glad Nur-Ali's large hands were maneuvering the gearshift and wheel. However many times he had stolen the Mercedes, he'd have trouble making this climb, and watching Nur-Ali from the corner of his eye he also began to doubt he could beat him in a fight. Under the brown skin of Nur-Ali's forearms, taut muscles moved like rope.

A three-quarter moon had come up and the landscape was eerie now—on one side gleaming ridges stood against a background of thorny scrub, while to the right the edge of the road plummeted into darkness. There were no villages, no sign of life beyond an occasional sparse row of trees marking the path of a stream.

How could people manage to live up here—and most of Paktia was like this or worse. A whole day could be spent just carrying water up a hillside for cooking, plants or livestock—Daddy-jan had told him that. When they were young he often used to take them to the country to teach them how karez wells brought water to irrigation ditches, and how land was plowed and seed cast down in an even line. It had been fun watching the peasants work—his peasants, he had liked to think, imagining that if he rode up on his horse they'd all bow down before him. But glancing over at Nur-Ali, he guessed that given the right chance they might cheerfully have pulled him off into the dust instead. Or maybe not so cheerfully—why else would Nur-Ali want to hear him scream?

Now Nur-Ali had the tail of his blue turban clenched between his teeth, and he was cursing softly as the road grew rougher. They were very high and the rocky earth falling away behind them seemed more hostile even than Nur-Ali. Feeling cold sweat under his arms, Tor realized he was frightened, though not of violence. It was simply that he didn't know how to operate here. Given one ruble in Moscow, he could make a fortune in a week, and in the Kabul bazaar he might do even better. But his best asset was his tongue, and charm had no value in these mountains. His family name might be more a liability than any guarantee of help.

Grudgingly, he had to admit that given a ruble in Moscow, Nur-Ali might do almost as well, and in this terrain he'd have the upper hand.

They had slowed down and Nur-Ali was peering out the side window. Then suddenly he gave a small grunt and swerved the wheel to the left. A mass of branches rose up to crash against the windshield and sing along the paint. When Tor lowered the arm he'd raised to his face, they were in total darkness.

"Get out," Nur-Ali said. "Back on the path, where I can see you."

Opening the door, Tor swung his feet to invisible ground and walked toward the moonlight shining through a battered lattice of branches masking the entrance to the cave. Nur-Ali followed him at a safe distance, the gun glinting in his hand. "Now," he said, "cover up that hole the way it was before."

There couldn't be many good shelters in such barren country, so they had to be near the camp. And if Nur-Ali had brought him this far in safety, his tough talk must be just that. All those insults! Tor said, "Do it yourself."

Nur-Ali transferred the gun to his left hand and drew the dagger from his belt. "Give me one good reason to use this. Just one."

Tor couldn't see his face. "If you had permission to kill me, you would have done it by now."

"I need only one good reason." He stepped closer in a slight crouch. "Give it to me, please." Quickly, he strapped the Mauser into a holster under his vest. "I won't shoot you unless you run. I prefer my knife anyway. Or my hands."

Seeing a flash of teeth in the shadowed face, Tor knew they were going to fight and that he had wanted this. Even if he lost, it would be better than marching up that hill like a little sheep, and he could keep some honor if they both arrived bloody at the camp.

In the moonlight, Nur-Ali was silhouetted by a pale cascade of rock, and watching for his first movement Tor felt the cool night air bristling his scalp. If he died here no one would find him in the dark cave at his back, and Nur-Ali was armed and stronger. But, Tor thought, a year's frustration ought to count for something now. I wouldn't have run from Stephan if he'd been alone.

The blade moved and in that instant he lunged, swinging his right leg up in an arc to hit Nur-Ali's knife arm, and as they fell he felt a hard blow numb the left side of his head. He came out on top, but Nur-Ali still clutched the knife and used his knee like a lever, throwing Tor off to scramble to his feet.

Again they faced each other on the path, but this time Tor had the advantage of light. Nur-Ali came toward him slowly, making playful strokes with the knife. "Why don't you just put the branches back. I don't want to carry your corpse uphill." As the blade passed his left shoulder Tor caught the arm, throwing all his weight against Nur-Ali's chest to knock him to the ground, but Nur-Ali hooked his ankle, flipping him backward. Tor kept the hold, twisting Nur-Ali's arm back, and then they were rolling over each other down the dusty slope, the sound of their panting harsh in Tor's ears as he punched the hard body again and again while answering blows rang on his own head with a force that was almost blinding. Then Nur-Ali was straddling him, pinning both his arms and grinding his knees into Tor's shoulders, and his body arched away from a searing pain in his old wound.

Freezing every muscle, he willed it to subside, but something had torn in his shoulder and the hot stabbing got even worse until only the pain was important—that, and concealing its power from Nur-Ali. Tor lay still, trying not to breathe, concentrating on a sharp edge of rock pressing through his shirt.

Nur-Ali was holding the tip of the dagger next to Tor's left eye. "Have you had enough, or shall I blind you too? My sister made this shirt for me and I don't want to spoil it." Blood trickled from the corners of Nur-Ali's mouth, his gasping made the knife blade tremble closer, and Tor felt a rush of panic stronger than pain as the bright point seemed to dissolve, filling his vision. Even by mistake, Tor thought, he could do it and then laugh about it, and he'd still be a sadist and I'd be half blind.

"You win," he said. "Get off me. You're bleeding on your friend Tammim's clothes."

Slowly, the blurred point of light sharpened to metal again. Nur-Ali climbed off his chest. "Now put those branches back like a good boy."

As Tor sat up, new currents of pain shot down his right arm. "You'll have to wait awhile," he said thickly. "Since I can only use one hand, it might take all night." Hunching over, he pulled himself to his feet, covering his grimace with a smile. "Would you like them to go up and down or sideways?"

Watching him intently, Nur-Ali took out the gun and stuck the dagger in his belt. "Just do it, will you?" But his tone was softer and he followed Tor to the cave, using his free hand to screen one side while Tor worked on the other. "Two arms," he said when they finished, "so it only took ten minutes. Now climb straight up there on the right until I tell you to stop."

Grasping the low shrubs with his left hand, Tor pulled and scrambled his way up the slope, his teeth clenched against the raw ache that ran from his neck down to his hip. As they reached a clump of trees, Nur-Ali said from behind, "Stop right there. And kneel down."

He was gasping and Tor guessed his own punches had taken effect in the climb. But then the implication of the order hit like a cold fist in his stomach: Nur-Ali didn't want to carry him uphill, so obligingly Tor had walked up to be shot. He would fake it, he thought, pretend to bend and then roll away with all the strength he had left. In the dark, he might have a chance.

"On your knees, I said!"

Squatting, Tor lifted his arms as if to cover his head, then tightening into a ball he sprang sideways and tumbled down the slope.

As he came to rest against the base of a tree, he heard a rifle bolt snap behind his head.

"Stop!" another voice barked, and looking up he saw a man standing poised above him ready to fire.

"I've stopped," Tor said. "Go ahead and shoot me. I deserve it, for helping you filthy dogs." His shoulder was hurting too badly now to care about anything else.

"It's Tor Anwari," Nur-Ali called. "But watch out, he moves fast."

Lowering his rifle, the man peered at Tor, then extended a hand to pull him up. "Welcome. You've had a hard journey?" Then, "The camp is just up there. Can you walk without help?"

"I think so." He started climbing again, even faster, to put as much space as possible between himself and Nur-Ali.

Over the stony ridge he saw the glow of a small wood fire, and then dozens of men grouped around it. They were facing a tall man who had his back to Tor, with one hand raised as if he were speaking, and it was then Tor knew how tired he must be, because as he slid down the slope he felt no curiosity, or interest even, about this strange tableau, but only a bottomless need for food and sleep.

The tall figure turned, and Tor found himself crouching at his feet.

Twenty-Five

"TORYALAI-JAN!"

Tor staggered up, staring through the flickering light at Ghulam-Nabi's smiling face.

"So it is you! I said...it couldn't be." Then sparks seemed to fly through the black night and Ghulam-Nabi was embracing him.

"You're shivering. Nur-Ali, bring those blankets from over there. So, Tor, you thought I was dead and all of a sudden my old story found you. As you can see, my sins aren't over yet."

Nur-Ali returned draped in gray blankets and offered one to Tor. "I think I hurt him," he said to Ghulam-Nabi. "I didn't mean to, but..."

"Get away from me, you dog!" Tor raised his right arm, then held it still against a fresh wave of pain.

Ghulam-Nabi's hand moved to Tor's shoulder and he opened the row of buttons, pulling the shirt down away from his wound. "Yes, I see, you've torn the scar. I didn't know it was so wide. Those Russian doctors stitched you badly. That must be very painful and it's my fault, I should have warned him. Nur-Ali, get my kit please."

Tor glared at Nur-Ali's retreating figure. "Warn him? You should lock him up. Don't you have any control over your men?" He saw blood glistening on Ghulam-Nabi's fingers, while beyond them a circle of shadowed faces watched impassively.

"He isn't really a savage, Tor. He was told to be hard on you to test your nerve. And now..." he asked as Nur-Ali handed him a box, "how did Tor like your bad manners, my friend?"

Nur-Ali's sour face twisted in a grin that was almost sheepish. "I'm sorry about your shoulder, Tor. If it weren't for that you might have beaten me." He turned to Ghulam-Nabi. "He has courage, this one, and he kicks like a camel. I think I like this Anwari very much."

Tor saw a look pass between them, some understanding that excluded him. "I don't get it," he said angrily. "Why should you need to test me?"

"Wait," Ghulam-Nabi said. "This will sting."

As the alcohol swab burned into his flesh, Tor ground his teeth in frustration. He had hardly let himself hope that he'd find Ghulam-Nabi—or should he call him Sher—at the end of this stinking road, but now instead of joy there was only more distrust and even humiliation. It was Nur-Ali they valued, whom the men reached out to touch.... Tor felt the bandage tug as Ghulam-Nabi tied it, then fastened the buttons.

"You'll have to wear a sling," he said gravely. "Yes, I should think for several days or that wound will open again. But it's not as bad as it might be. Now, I have to take these papers in, but first, Tor, tell me, how is Raima? And how are your parents?"

Tor looked more closely into Ghulam-Nabi's face. He had never seen the old man in better health. And Raima too, he recalled now, seemed much happier than he'd expected. "Raima's fine," he said slowly. "She knows you're alive, doesn't she."

Ghulam-Nabi nodded. "But your parents, no. To them I'm still dead. Karima has told them so."

"You were lucky to fool her. She inspected me with a microscope today."

"Ah, then you saw her!" Ghulam-Nabi chuckled. "What a daughter! To think I used to wish she were a boy."

"I don't know how you can say that. Isn't she working for Taraki?"

Laughing, Ghulam-Nabi clasped Tor's good arm. "I guess it's you who were fooled, Tor. But I thought she meant to tell you...." The broad smile faded. "Didn't you speak to her?"

Again, Tor was standing in the hallway. "I wanted to see you, is that a crime?" She had stood with her fists clenched, leaning toward him.

"Not really," he said weakly. "There wasn't much time. What was she going to tell me?"

"No." Ghulam-Nabi shook his head. "That must come from her. But who do you suppose approved your exit visa? Now, forgive me, I must take these papers. You eat, and then go to sleep. We have hard work to do tomorrow." After another quick embrace he turned and walked beyond the circle of light.

Now Tor could see there were several low houses on the other side of the fire, the furthest dimly lit by a candle or lamp.

"Tor-jan," Nur-Ali said, "don't blame Ghulam-Nabi for my treatment of you. Those orders came from Sher, not the old man."

"What?" Tor spun around to face him. "But... he is Sher, isn't he?"

Nur-Ali's eyes widened with surprise. "He...? No, Tor-jan, he's not Sher."

"Then I'm going to find out who is!"

As Tor started forward, Nur-Ali grabbed him. "I don't want to stop you, Tor-jan, but if you try that, I'll have to. Sher won't see you tonight. And here you follow his orders like the rest of us."

Tor pulled away. "I don't believe this! You bring me here from Moscow, risk my life for a couple of blueprints, and now he's too tired to see me? That's a lot of thanks. You can all go to hell."

"I thank you, Tor." Nur-Ali bowed. "I thank you very humbly. Look, you're practically falling down. Come and eat and don't be so impatient. We have to act on those blueprints tomorrow, so tonight's for planning. But the hospitality of our camp is yours." He spoke warmly, but his body still was tensed, ready to spring.

Tor felt a nervous tic starting in his left eye. He might lose control now, he thought, he was tired enough, hungry and confused. Ghulam-Nabi was alive but he wasn't Sher, Karima had furnished his exit visa and even Mummy-jan wanted to whisper something.... It was like the matryoshka peasant dolls in Moscow that were really shells, you pulled open one to find another, and inside that, another.... Across the fire, the ring of faces seemed to blur together. Maybe food was more important now, so that later he could think. Nodding shortly at Nur-Ali, Tor followed him toward the others.

Ghulam-Nabi closed the wooden door behind him. "Tor and Nur-Ali are here."

"I don't like that fire. Put it out."

"Of course, Your Excellency." Ghulam-Nabi placed the small cloth bag on the foot of the cot. "Here are the plans you wanted so much."

"Thank you. Is Tor alright?"

"He's suffering from injury in more ways than one. If you look out now you can see him by the fire, I think."

"I want that fire out! I know they were waiting for Nur-Ali, but we're too close to the Gardez garrison here to go in for midnight picnics."

"Yes, I know, it's very upsetting," Ghulam-Nabi said as if to a child.

"Don't presume too much, Ghulam-Nabi. Is Tor really hurt? Or just his pride?"

"Nur-Ali was a little too enthusiastic," Ghulam-Nabi answered dryly. "He opened that scar on Tor's shoulder. But a sling might be a useful place to carry a pistol. Apart from that, Tor feels he's been abused, and I think I agree."

"You think I'm too hard."

Swinging his numb left leg off the cot, Mangal glanced toward the window apprehensively. If he saw Tor he might go out to him and that would be a mistake. Once the family was safely out of the country he could write to them, but if they learned he was alive now they might refuse to leave and Karima had sent a message that his father would be arrested in a matter of days. Tor was good at keeping secrets, but this one could be distracting when he would need all his wits for the desert.

Still... how long had it been? And since he'd let Tor suffer in ignorance, how could he justify sparing himself the opposite pain?

Pulling himself up, he dragged his braced leg over to the window. Tor was sitting apart from the others, balancing a chunk of bread on his knee and staring into the fire. His face was thinner than Mangal remembered, and as he watched, Tor drew a blanket up around his neck as if for protection. His seeming fragility and isolation made Mangal ache to embrace him, to drive away the loneliness they had both known for too long. Strange, he thought, if one year ago he had imagined this scene, he would have placed Tor as the leader and himself sitting on the ground in a business suit, waiting for what, a bullet?

Turning away, Mangal said harshly, "He looks wretched. You'll have to cheer him up."

"Oh, certainly. I'll tell him more stories."

"Stop that!" He brought his fist down on the table, "I had to find out if he could do this. Fine. Now we know he can function. He ought to be able to get my parents out. After that, he'll stay in the States or come back to us, and I don't want to influence that decision. I want him to be with me, but for his own reasons, and the only place he'll find them is out there."

"You're shouting," Ghulam-Nabi said. "I understand. You want me to believe what you think instead of what you feel. Or is it yourself you're trying to convince?"

"In the old days they used to shoot men like you from the cannon on Sher Dawaza."

"That was before the great days of the republic, I suppose." Ghulam-Nabi waved his hand in mock disgust. "Reasons of his own! It took Aziz Khan three months to convince you to get up off your bed after that coup."

"Since I couldn't walk yet then..." But Mangal had to smile.

"No, you couldn't face Aziz. As if he blamed you for Roshana! I think you were afraid of failing at this, in case his men ran out of mutton and decided to eat you instead. Sher Dawaza, Sher Anwari—lions all around! Don't forget whom you're talking to, Mangal."

"I know. You used to bounce me on your knee. Now tell them to put out that fire and go. When they get to the river I want those trucks completely plastered with mud. Right now, they're perfect targets. And if there's any trouble with the other groups, I need to know right away. Timing's everything in this operation. The diversionary charges have to go off at exactly ten PM so we and Tor can move on schedule."

"You don't want to go through it with the couriers again?"

"No. That would just give them another chance to argue and I'm sick to death of listening. But make Tor welcome, will you?"

"Certainly. I'll bounce him on my knee."

Ghulam-Nabi took his leave and was gone.

Mangal stood by the window till the fire was smothered and Tor became a dark shape indistinguishable from the others. Then he turned back to the room.

It was bare except for one old armchair, the cot and a small table. Lowering himself onto the bed, he turned up the oil lamp and watched its shadow pulse on the wall. The cot was uncomfortable, but he found it hard to rise from a lower bed or sit in straight chairs for more than a few minutes. Two bullets had been removed from his thigh but a third remained in his hip, and he joked with Ghulam-Nabi that his leadership was de facto: he had to stand fast since he couldn't run.

But it was Aziz who had helped him stand at all, after Ghulam-Nabi and Nur-Ali bribed their way into the palace to find him lying unconscious in the courtyard. They had curled him into the trunk of the Mercedes, and when he opened his eyes in that darkness he felt as if he were hurtling through space. The loss of blood sent him into shock and then he was sick for weeks with an infection spiking to his brain. Aziz told him later that in his ravings he'd tried to make a deal, exchanging his own life for his wife and son's. Instead, Aziz had offered a different bargain.

Whether Watanjar's tanks or Qadir's planes were responsible he had never learned, but Daoud and Naim had also been killed and with them the last hope for a free government. Taraki had been Daoud's prisoner, and the Khalqis claimed to have hit the palace so hard to prevent his murder. Now Taraki sat in the palace taking prisoners by the thousands, and Watanjar was the minister responsible for AGSA—the secret police who dealt in midnight raids and electric torture, who fed twenty men each evening to the firing squads outside the Pul-i-Charki prison.

Even Professor Durrani had been taken to Pul-i-Charki, and the prison was tomorrow's secondary target. They should be able to blow up part of its wall. If Durrani still lived... and how many others, Mangal wondered. Some of his colleagues had already been executed.

Opening the blueprints on the blanket, he drew the oil lamp closer. Aziz had said: "You plan strategy, and I'll raise us an army. A lion needs four legs to move well."

Now Mangal knew he was good at this work; Aziz hadn't misplaced his faith. Their men were young and disciplined, with little of the fighting and looting that plagued the groups headquartered in Peshawar. Mangal smiled.

He wouldn't go to Peshawar even if an alliance could be forged. The Islamic fundamentalists there—the Jamiyat and Hezbi-i-Islami—seemed to want only to duplicate Khomeini's medieval horrors. They might be as quick as Taraki to call him Western, elitist, a CIA puppet.

Why, he wondered, couldn't they see that Khomeini's success had no parallel here. The U.S. was thousands of miles away, not sitting on Iran's border. It was easy to call names from such a distance. But Russia had more than money invested in Afghanistan, and the Brezhnev Doctrine promised that once a country fell into Soviet hands it would be held at all costs—as Czechoslovakia had discovered to its pain.

No, Mangal thought, there was no Afghan Khomeini and there never would be. He wouldn't accept one if there were—any more than he shared the Royalists' aim of returning King Zahir to the throne. Rather he hoped, increasingly with each new success, that a strong persistent rebellion would force Moscow to seek a compromise: a man with clean hands who understood that five-year-plans meant little in a country like this. A man—Mangal smiled—not unlike his own father.

But the time for that hadn't come yet, and his father wouldn't live to see it if he stayed in Kabul.

With silent apologies to Prince Naim, who had called Jonathan Straight a CIA spy to his face, Mangal had contacted Straight in Pakistan. If the CIA had used Afghanistan, why shouldn't they return a favor? Nadir had carried the message and Karima delivered Straight's answer: Yes, he saw little problem in getting visas for the States since Mrs. Anwari had never renounced her American citizenship, and yes, he'd be happy to help if Mangal could get the family to Quetta.

That meant three days in the desert—which still seemed safer than taking the Khyber Pass route to Peshawar. There was less chance of arrest or ambush in the south. Anyway, if Daddy-jan surfaced in Peshawar the rebel leaders would fight for his allegiance like so many dogs with a bone—and the time for him to lend support or make enemies had also not come. Whether it ever would now depended on Tor.

Mangal glanced up as the door creaked and Nur-Ali came through it. "Are you ready for me yet?"

"Yes, sit down. How's my brother doing?"

"Sleeping like a stone," Nur-Ali grinned. "Do you know he wanted to beat me up, even though I was armed and he was not?"

"I'm not surprised. I often want to beat you up myself. But you may be the only armed man in this camp if we don't do well tomorrow."

Perching cross-legged on the end of the cot, Nur-Ali took out his tobacco and began rolling thin cigarettes, scattering brown shreds on the blue paper. "So these plans tell us everything but where the mines are laid, and where the guards are posted, and the other things we really need to know. You could have just drawn me a picture, right? If you hadn't wanted to torture your poor little brother."

"If you laugh at Tor anymore, I'll certainly have to beat you up."

"I laugh at all of us, Mangal. I laugh at the memory of you lecturing me about words being better than guns, and now guns are all you want. I bet you'd trade every word you know for a truckload of Kalashnikov automatics."

"Not when I have you to get them for me." He took the cigarette Nur-Ali was offering and returned his smile. It was only during their late-night talks that he was able to unwind. Nur-Ali could tease him, he'd saved his life—then offered himself as a substitute for the family Mangal had lost, as if blood had evened the old score between them. Nur-Ali had lost his closest brother to a government bullet too. His rage at that, chilled to ice and well preserved, made him the best fighter of the lot. But the need and grief that death caused had also remained intact, submerged, until Nur-Ali had given it and himself to fill Mangal's empty hands.

In these mountains, in the company of men who mistrusted every value of his former life, Nur-Ali had been his best companion. Through the long winter nights, as they huddled under blankets, Nur-Ali had made him outline all his courses at the Sorbonne, quizzing and cross-examining with a keen intelligence he'd never trusted in himself before. Teaching Nur-Ali was a pleasure, and he repaid Mangal with a new understanding of the country's western provinces and peoples, with a fierce, possessive loyalty and love. And if jealousy had let Nur-Ali be hard on Tor for a few hours on the road, Mangal knew he would also probably die for Tor in battle, just because Tor was weaker and Mangal's younger brother.

But Nur-Ali is my brother too now, he thought, looking at the thin face bent so seriously over the Pul-i-Charki plans.

As if feeling his intensity, Nur-Ali glanced up. "I apologize, I was wrong. These will be very useful. Look, see how this foundation's laid? I think that's just loose rock underneath. If I set my charges here, here, and here, the whole building ought to roll right down the hill."

"Good," Mangal nodded. "But time your fuses well. That's got to be the last thing to blow. I only wish we didn't have to rely on Zafar's men to start it. The first rule is always to use local people, but I don't know them well enough to trust."

"I do." Nur-Ali touched Mangal's arm. "I've been sitting in that stall till I can't stand up anymore. And because they're Kabul people, if they're caught out near curfew time they'll have some chance of talking their way out of it. I know you're worried about your family, but Zafar will come through, I promise. I'll check with him again on my way out."

Mangal felt exhaustion weighing on his shoulders like a yoke. They'd covered every detail of this a hundred times already. There was nothing to do now but let it go.

"Alright," he said. "So the plan is this: Zafar's people set the charges in the city—at Demazang Circle, the airport, the ministries, and so on. They blow at ten. With any luck, half the troops at Pul-i-Charki will take off to investigate. We'll give them fifteen minutes to leave, and then Suleiman's people take the barracks under fire. We'll finish the grenades for that tomorrow. As soon as his barrage starts, you blow the arsenal—which ought to make enough noise to draw the guard away from my parents' house. Then Tor moves them out."

"Yes, it should work," Nur-Ali nodded. "Rashid will tell the guards it's their patriotic duty to go with him to the fighting. That way he'll be away from the house when your parents leave, so maybe we can keep him working for us in the army. But Mangal... if the guards don't leave, Tor and your father will have to kill them. Can they do that, do you think?"

Meeting Nur-Ali's troubled eyes, Mangal had a sudden image of his father crouched and firing out the study window, and involuntarily he laughed. Daddy-jan and his precious dignity—he'd consider it beneath him to shoot any soldier under the rank of colonel. No, if killing couldn't be avoided that would probably also be up to Tor, who had no experience of it and a wounded arm.

"I think for my mother's life, Tor could do anything. But there's no way to be sure before it happens."

"I'll work on him tomorrow." Nur-Ali grinned. "You told me he used to be a good shot? I'll let him play with my guns. Before you know it he'll be dying to kill somebody. But now we both should sleep, because you're right— we have to do well tomorrow. I'm tired of chopping down beautiful trees to trap convoys on the road."

Folding the plans, he stood up. "Can I get you anything?"

Mangal shook his head. "Good night, my friend. I'll see you in the morning." He watched Nur-Ali's hard narrow back cross the room and leave it.

Yes, he thought, gritting his teeth as he straightened out his left leg, they'd need to do very well tomorrow. Nur-Ali's joke about the trees was an old one and no longer funny. How could they plan actions without a reliable source of arms? So far, most of their supply had come from deserting soldiers, and that should increase since the army was now filled with unwilling draftees.

Infiltrating the military, winning defectors... it had worked for Taraki.

His own plan was to aim for generals in the provinces, who could turn over all the men and weapons at their command. Already, Tor's old friend Farouk was using his ancient radio transmitter for hit-and-run broadcasts telling the troops Allah would not forgive them for killing their own people. But that would take time, and this was the moment when they had to move. Everything grew more quickly in the spring.

Snuffing out the lamp, Mangal tried to relax under his thin covering of blankets. If the rebellion kept growing, the Saudis ought to send money to support it, and the gunshops in Pakistan could duplicate even Soviet antitank guns. But how, he thought, cursing in the dark, how without weapons can we prove ourselves at all?

He had to sleep. Worrying kept him from it much too often lately, broke his dreams and woke him in the middle of the night to lie alone waiting for another dawn he didn't want to see, raw with the endless pain that was named Roshana.

Twenty-Six

Tor woke up shivering in the early sun and lay watching from under his blanket as the rest of the camp rose one by one, then kneeling, bent to pray. There seemed to be only twenty men left of the sixty he'd counted last night, and in the gray morning light they looked less formidable—even, he thought, pathetic. So these were Sher's brave warriors, wearing tennis shoes or sandals made from strips of rubber tire. One man threw down his coat as a rug—an olive green jacket stenciled in white: U.S. PARKS AND RECREATION. When he finished praying, he dusted it off as if it were his dearest possession.

The village was smaller than it had seemed too, just five mud-brick houses set at the end of a narrow box canyon. Now Ghulam-Nabi crossed in front of the fire, bringing tea to the last house on the right—probably to Sher, thought Tor—Ghulam-Nabi, still the servant.

Propping himself on an elbow, he cursed and rolled over on his back again. During the night his arm had stiffened so much it felt almost useless—except as an exploitable source of pain. And there was Nur-Ali, grinning at him as he fed twigs to the meager blaze. He must be very proud of himself.

The door of the far house opened and Ghulam-Nabi went back to the fire, stooping to pour another mug of tea. Then he came to squat in a crouch, masking Tor from the others, and holding his arm, Tor sat up awkwardly.

"Your morning tea, Toryalai, as in the old days. It's wonderful to see you here. I've brought some bread and cheese too, though the bread isn't fresh, I'm afraid." Breaking the nan across his knee with a crack, he offered one dry wedge.

The cheese tasted sour, but the tea was delicious—dark, strong and heavily sweetened. As he ate with his left hand, the old man examined the bandage on his shoulder.

"Good, this hasn't bled any more. I'm glad to see that. How are you today? You're not used to sleeping on the ground, and with that arm..."

"It's alright. If it gets any worse Rashid can take me to a doctor and say I fell downstairs. Is my face bruised?"

"Just along here." Ghulam-Nabi touched his cheekbone. "And so is Nur-Ali's. What did you fight about?"

"His manners. He had a knife, remember?"

"He wouldn't have used it."

"That's what you think. Just tell me how I'm supposed to explain all this to my parents. They must be scared to death by now."

"It may be well if they are, Tor." Crossing his legs, Ghulam-Nabi took a cigarette out of his turban. "I have something of great seriousness to discuss with you. Last night you asked why we needed to test you? I can tell you now. Karima's working for us. She was working for Mangal. And she says your father will be arrested within the week."

Tea splashed on the blanket as Tor set down his mug. "I should have guessed. She couldn't have turned against all of us. But Daddy-jan's sitting there waiting for it. Why?"

"He feels he has a special destiny," Ghulam-Nabi smiled faintly. "And so he does, and so do all of us, but it may come from a gun just as easily as from a king. At first the Khalqis thought they could use him, since he'd broken with both His Majesty and Daoud Khan, but I suspect now they've discovered what we already knew—that your father's the most stubborn honest man who ever lived. So, the time has come for you to take your parents out of the country."

"Me? You mean...now? Take them where? To Peshawar?"

"No, through the southern desert, across the border to Quetta. And from there to the United States. You'll leave tonight. I wish your arm hadn't been injured, but you've been covered with scrapes all your life. I know you'll succeed, Tor. Do you understand? This is the real reason you were brought here from Moscow."

Moscow. The Abdullah's face. "Something only you can do..." Stealing those plans had been too simple. Then he was seeing Liz's impish grin. "If you get there and it's too dangerous, you can always say: no deal."

But not to this. The house was like a tomb already. And outside, tanks and armored cars, two guards just waiting for the order to come through. ...I sensed it last night, he thought, I almost knew in Moscow, and the

Abdullah must have known from the beginning.

He said, "Why couldn't you have told me the truth? Do you think I'm a child?"

The old man looked incredulous. "Are you unwilling to do it?"

"I don't like being manipulated."

"Tor, many things were uncertain...."

"Such as whether I'm still crazy? Alright, I guess I deserve that. But since you have your answer, give me mine. You sent me that story like bait for a stupid fish. What about the necklace? It was taken from Roshana's body?"

Ghulam-Nabi bent his head. "By my own hand."

"She was shot? And Mangal too?"

"Yes, and little Yusef, may his murderer be crushed by Allah, the all-powerful."

"So then you came to Paktia, which just happens to be the territory of Roshana's uncle, Aziz Khan."

He groaned. "Tor, you guess well, you guess rightly, but I can't answer these questions. I've sworn."

"Then at least tell me where we are. This isn't Aziz's village."

"No." Fingers stained with nicotine combed his ragged beard. "Have you ever heard of a place called Mirzaka?"

Tor nodded. "I didn't know it was so small."

"Mirzaka is the next village down the mountain. So, I've trusted you that much, Tor. Now will you do this thing?"

"Of course. I'm not scared, if that's what you think. But I had a life. You took me out of it without a word of warning. Do you expect me to be happy?"

Ghulam-Nabi rocked forward. "Yes, I know. It's a horrible thing to have to leave your home. There can be nothing worse in this world."

"I meant Moscow," he said hopelessly. "I meant Elizabeth." The broken earth seemed to be stretching, splitting, pulling her away. Liz, who wasn't as tough as she thought, who'd come to Moscow needing him almost as much as he did her.

"You mean, you want to go back to Russia?" The old man scowled in disbelief.

"Not there. To someone there. A friend I love very much." He drew a line in the dirt with his finger, then wiped it away. This was pointless. She had predicted it too: "In a few months, we'll have to leave anyway. Out of our hothouse. And then...?"

Ghulam-Nabi touched his arm, and Tor looked up to find him smiling. "A woman, you mean? Of course, a woman! We can send her a message in the same way we contacted you."

"Sure. A very short one. Good-bye forever." The Abdullah would knock on her door. "Toryalai Anwari is sorry to say..."

"If she's the English girl we've heard about, she won't always be in Moscow.

We'll tell her where you are. You might be able to meet again."

But a move to the States seemed so far, so irrevocable. He said, "Why can't my parents stay in Pakistan? They have friends there now."

"So you could return to Moscow? The Russians won't have you back again. Be realistic, Tor."

"I am! And this will get her—my friend Elizabeth—in a lot of trouble. They'll think she knew what my plans were, and they're already suspicious of her. You should have told me about it in the first place."

Ghulam-Nabi sighed. "I didn't know it was so serious between you. But what difference could that have made? If we'd told you, would you not have come? Don't you understand how important this is? Your mother's been ill all winter. Can you see her living in two rooms at Peshawar, or in a refugee camp? Because they won't be able to take anything out, except a few pieces of jewelry. In the States they will have help, and I believe your mother has a dowry in some bank there?"

Tor smiled. "It's called a trust fund, and it's pretty small, I think."

"And Saira's in New York. Just imagine, being all together again."

He tried to picture Saira and failed. It had been so long he wasn't sure what he felt about her anymore. Closing his fingers around a handful of pebbles, he sat looking down at them as if he'd never seen gray stones before.

Ghulam-Nabi cleared his throat. "Toryalai, I'm sorry about your friend. We'll do everything we can to let her know you've left here before the Russians hear it, so she can make up an excuse for herself. But you can't go back, Tor. You have to go forward, along a dangerous path. And that means putting this woman out of your mind completely, until you're all safe again. Worrying won't help her. And if your thoughts are divided, it will only put you at greater risk. Can you hear the truth of what I'm saying?"

Slowly, he nodded. The old man was right. It was too late to argue now. And Elizabeth was smart, she'd come up with some story if they reached her in time. If not, at least her denials would be genuine. She could curse him and mean every word of it. But they'd probably make her pay for it anyhow, one way or another.

"Are you listening to me, Tor?"

He glanced up. "Yes. My parents have to get out of there, and I want to be the one to take them. I just hope they'll go. My father doesn't trust me any more than you did."

"After this, he will."

"Tell me what your plan is."

Ghulam-Nabi smiled with relief, "Tonight, you'll drive to Kandahar. There you will meet a kuchi caravan that will take you most of the way through the desert. Rashid will give you the details. You'll leave when we hit Pul-i-Charki, which should get rid of those guards. And if your father objects, then tie him up and put him in the trunk of the car. Your mother would help you do it, I'm sure. Now, if you want, to keep from being bored today, you can help us put together some grenades. We won't be going to Kabul for several hours."

Tor had to laugh then. This must be a joke. Here was Ghulam-Nabi politely asking him if he'd like to make some grenades? It was ridiculous.

"If you can use just my left hand, I'll be glad to help."

"Good. Finish your breakfast, and then go to Nur-Ali. He'll show you how." Ghulam-Nabi got to his feet. "I'll see you later, Toryalai."

Past the old man, he saw Nur-Ali dragging boxes out of one of the houses.

Tor swallowed the rest of his tea. In a few minutes, he would join them. But first he had to say good-bye to Liz, get her out of his system cell by cell . . . their room in Moscow, her warm gray eyes . . . good-bye, I can't take you with me. Instead there will be Daddy-jan's eyes, that pained look, needing convincing. And selling him on a camel caravan through the desert was going to take genius.

He could show no doubts. Not a blink of hesitation. Starting now, pretend to be sure, and by tonight it will be true.

He closed his eyes to feel the sun on his face. There was nothing but today, the smooth stones in his hand, being ready to move. Even meeting Sher seemed unimportant.

When his mind was clear, he stood up and went over to Nur-Ali.

Through the afternoon, he sat on a shelf of rock with Nur-Ali and two other men introduced as Bashir and Wahab, turning a pile of metal pipes into what he began to think of as Afghan Molotov cocktails. His job was to steady each pipe with his knee while Bashir cut it in sections, then pass the pieces to Nur-Ali, who capped one opening and drilled a small hole to fit the fuse. After tamping in explosive powder, Wahab closed the other end and carefully packed the devices in a crate.

For a while they worked in silence, but then Bashir—an older man whose face was as scarred as the rock cliff around them—turned to Nur-Ali and started making statements that Tor understood were really questions aimed at himself. It could be an art, this manner of speaking, and he knew they wanted agreement less than a reasoned discussion proving the superiority of their views. He was Omar Anwari's son, but educated in Moscow. What then would he have to say?

"Ah, how I pity the Russian people!" Bashir rolled his eyes at Nur-Ali. "For were they not once People of the Book, who worshiped as devoutly as ourselves? And now see how their women are degraded, as they would like our women to be. For if a man receives no dowry with his bride he can divorce her far too easily, without having to pay back a single afghani to her father."

"Yes," Nur-Ali answered. "Unhappily, that is true."

Passing him a length of pipe, Tor said, "If I may make an observation from my time in the Soviet Union, Russian women are not so dependent on fathers and husbands for support. They're educated and hold jobs, so if they lose both father and husband they can still survive and raise their children."

"Ah, but here our respect for women assures that they will always be cared for. So education is unnecessary."

Bashir was still addressing his remarks to Nur-Ali, and feeling mischievous, Tor decided to join him. "Do you agree with that, Nur-Ali? How about the sister who made your shirt? Wouldn't you want her ever to learn to read?"

"Why? So she'd be good enough for you to marry?" Pushing a cap onto the pipe, he glared around the circle defiantly. "Alright, yes, I do want her to learn. But from other women, or our chosen teachers, not from young men wearing red armbands."

For the first time, Bashir turned to Tor. "Have you heard about these men? No, they are boys, some not as old as you, and they know nothing, yet they pretend to teach us. Through many generations, my family worked a farm that the Khalqis have chopped up in pieces. Now they come to tell us how to use this land, though they've never farmed themselves. They're even ignorant of our tradition of sharing water from the karez wells. Imagine, making such a change without understanding irrigation!" He laughed derisively. "Are people like that also running the Soviet Union? If so, we will surely win."

"Maybe Tor's a Communist who'd like a share of our land too," Wahab chuckled. "Or maybe he's still wealthy enough to buy it instead. Would you like my land, Tor Anwari? Because I have to sell it. Taraki has done away with moneylenders, which is very wonderful. Now I don't have to pay my debts! Only, there is one small problem." He wagged his black beard mournfully. "I can no longer borrow money to buy seed. And without seed, what good is land? I have to sell half of it to farm the rest. But it must be hard for you to understand this from so far away as Moscow."

"From as far away as Kabul," Nur-Ali spat against the rock. "It's because Tor's from Kabul that he knows nothing. To him this land is poor, since he's used to having richer farms and houses. But if we lose one dry field, we can always find another. What will Tor Anwari do when he loses even his Kabul house?"

"Maybe he'll take my pigeon coop," Wahab laughed, slapping Nur-Ali's thigh. Then his hand froze in midair. "Listen!"

In an instant, Nur-Ali was on his feet, pulling Tor down under the ledge.

As he watched, the other men ran to collect their guns and boxes while the droning coming from the west grew louder. Three planes showed on the horizon, but when they passed overhead a moment later, the hamlet looked deserted.

Nur-Ali's arm was tight around his chest. "Those are Russian planes, not Afghan. Can you understand the difference?"

Slipping free, Tor scrambled to his feet. "I'm getting sick of this. You're trying to make yourself look good by making fun of me. Only, it won't work,

Comrade. The others might think you're a hero, but I don't. These grenades won't touch the rocket and machine-gun fire you'll be getting back. And even if you're fast enough to survive, what about the rest of them? At least I'd never lead good men on a suicide mission."

"Lead them?" The brown eyes creased with amusement. He pushed back his turban. "No, Tor, I follow them. What men have earned they'll gladly fight to keep, though I can't expect you to know that. And when a man has lost his land and family to Russian guns—this you should understand—honor demands they be avenged. Taraki's grown as ignorant as you from living too long in Kabul. He forgets that violence always brings more violence. And you forget that a machine gun works the same in any hand. Come, I'll show you. I have one—perhaps the very gun that killed your nephew, since I picked it up at the palace."

He started toward the middle house and reluctantly Tor followed.

"This is a Kalashnikov AK-47 assault rifle," Nur-Ali said, "And that's a Soviet grenade launcher. No, don't bother with it now. It's shoulder-fired. You couldn't handle it yet. But try this pretty gun." He stroked the rifle's dull barrel. "See the curved clip? It fires a thirty-shot round. After tonight I'll have a hundred of these. What will you have, Tor?" He held the rifle up in both his hands. "Come on, take it from me."

When he reached for it, Nur-Ali shoved the gun hard against his chest, knocking him backward, one step, then another. "Can't you take it? Try again."

"I've only got one arm, you dog. You made sure of that last night."

Nur-Ali had him up against the wall now, and Tor saw a gleam of sweat under his short black beard.

"Tor-jan, that was a mistake. But if I wanted to kill you, wouldn't you fight back even if it hurt, or are you really a coward?" He bared his teeth in a smile. "So, you think we're teasing you? Making fun of this poor little boy? Being unfair? Why don't you cry then. Everyone will feel sorry for you. I'm not picking on you, Tor-jan, I'm trying to make you angry. I want you to hate the way we do, as you should, enough to kill with only one arm. Because tonight I think you'll have to do that, so your body and mind must both be ready."

"I'm not going to Pul-i-Charki. You're the one who likes killing people."

"I'm talking about your parents' guard. Didn't the old man tell you? If they don't leave, you'll have to kill them, or your father will never leave the country alive." Nur-Ali stepped back. "It's going to take you two days to reach the border. Every hour they know you're gone weakens your chances. So you can't just knock these soldiers out or lock them up in a closet, even if you could get their guns away from them—and with one arm that would be impossible. You must shoot them, before they sense any risk from you. Can you do it, Tor-jan?"

Tor's face was hot and his arm sore where the rifle had pressed against it.

He walked around Nur-Ali to the center of the room. "Is that another order from Sher?"

"If you need it to be, yes. If you don't like orders, no. It's what you must do, whether the idea pleases you or not. Unless you want to see your mother in chains and your father killed before your eyes. Unless you want to die yourself. You'll need a pistol and I'm going to give you mine."

Reaching under his shirt, he unstrapped the small Mauser and held it out, flat and silvery. "You can carry it in your sling. Go on, see how well it fits."

The gun was warm from Nur-Ali's body. Tor curled a finger around the trigger. "Maybe I'll start with you."

"I thought you might feel that way," Nur-Ali laughed. "It's such a friendly gun. A copy, made in one of the shops at Darra, but the workmanship is flawless. Now see if you can slip it down your arm under the sling."

After a few clumsy attempts Tor found that if he hunched over a little, the sling loosened enough for him to slide the gun into his hand with a single motion. The steel grip fit his palm snugly.

"That's good. But practice when you get home. You have to take them by surprise. Now give it back to me and turn around."

He heard Nur-Ali step away behind him. "Now Tor-jan, let's say you're one of the soldiers and I'm you. Either you'll be facing him, so you can use your sling trick, or you'll come up on him suddenly like this."

Tor stumbled back as Nur-Ali grabbed him and pushed the gun into his chest. "Get the soft spot right under the ribs and shoot up into the heart. Take your shoes off first, if you try it like this. And don't look at his face, Tor. That's the most important thing. Especially, don't look in his eyes." Lowering the gun, Nur-Ali embraced him. "We both have so much courage because we're crazy. But at least we have it. When the time comes, yours will serve you."

His arms dropped. "Now I've taught you all I know."

Embarrassed, Tor straightened his shirt and sling. "Thank you. I appreciate it. Could we work on that some more?"

"You mean, can you stick it into me? No, it isn't a pleasant sensation. You might not want to repeat it. Anyway, we must leave now. It's almost dusk. But I wish you well, good luck, and the blessings of Allah for tonight. May he protect you and your parents on this journey."

Handing him the Mauser, Nur-Ali turned and walked outside.

Tor fit the gun near his elbow under the sling and went after him.

As if by some silent signal, the rest of the men had already gathered around the dead brush fire.

"We'll pray now and then go," Nur-Ali said. "May the Prophet, blessed be his name, be with us."

Tor stepped back, confused. It would offend them if he didn't pray too, before such a dangerous mission, but he refused to be a hypocrite in front of Nur-Ali.

"So, you have no religion, either," Nur-Ali crowed, kneeling in the dust. "No land, no houses and no religion. If we die tonight, we'll be martyrs, highly honored in Paradise. But if you die, Tor...?"

Walking down to the truck, Tor thought smiling: this subtle person is trying to tell me something.

Twenty-Seven

"GHULAM-NABI SAID so himself," Tor shrugged. "We have to go. But they've planned it well. Once we're away from the house there's not much danger."

His mother took a step forward. "Tonight? And we can't bring anything with us?"

She had been twisting the wedding band around her finger since he began to talk, and now he reached to stop her hand before its nervous motion wore through his own thin shell of composure. "Just some jewelry, if we can hide it. I'm sorry, Mummy-jan."

They were in the second-floor study, lit only by two candles that cast moving shadows on the ceiling. His father stood by the window with his back to them, looking down at the garden.

Tor watched her glance move from that still figure around the room to rest on the row of family photographs lining one bookcase. "I could hide those too, if I took them out of their frames."

He shook his head. "If they were found, nobody would believe we were kuchis. Saira must have pictures in New York."

"Not this of Uncle Yusef, or your grandfather..."

"Catherine, what difference does it make?" His father pulled the window shut. "If what Tor says is true, all that's finished. We may as well forget about it." He started toward the door, "I'm going to call Karima myself. I don't understand why this should happen now."

"You can't ask that on the phone, Omar." She turned to Tor. "It's been tapped for months."

"Daddy-jan..." Tor stepped into his path. "Would Ghulam-Nabi lie to you? Please, I don't like this either, but we have to do what they say. We're not the only people involved."

"That's what *you* say, Bechaim." He hurried past them, out of the room and down the stairs.

"No, don't go after him, Tor. I think he just needs a few minutes to get used to this. How soon do we have to leave?"

"In about an hour. What if he won't come?"

"He will. Don't worry, I'll talk to him."

"I have to see Rashid now. Are you alright?"

She kissed his cheek. "Yes, dear. Once I've digested it, I'll be fine."

But looking into her tired eyes, he wondered whether any of them would be fine again.

Halfway across the landing he remembered there was one more thing to do.

Instead of going downstairs he went through the hall and opened the door to Mangal's old room. Drawing the window curtain shut, he groped for the desk lamp and turned it on.

The room looked like a shrine. All the clutter was gone, and then he recalled it had been cleaned up the week before Mangal's wedding. He and Roshana had spent their wedding night here and Mummy-jan had brought in special things—the Tibetan mandala painting, a round silver tray that held a candlestick with a stump of wax, and over the desk, a modern picture of colored spots and squiggles that she called her Miró. An embroidered satin quilt was folded across the foot of the bed. Maybe Mangal and Roshana had made love here.

But there was nothing else of Mangal in the room. He must have taken all his books and photographs to their new house, which had already been confiscated by the government. In a way, it was comforting to find this room so bare. Leaving the last bits of Mangal here would be like losing him a second time.

Saira's room might be harder to face.

Outside her door, he stopped. This could be baggage of the worst kind ... a cognac stain on the closet floor, a torn piece of silk, her scattered shoes.

Turning the knob, he went in. There might not be another chance.

Light was coming from the garden so he didn't turn on her bedside lamp. He could see well enough to know that this room had also been tidied. Everything in the closet was stored in clothing bags and a single perfume bottle stood on the dresser. Saira had spent only three days in this room after her last two years in the States... thanks to me, he thought. Thanks to Mangal. None of us has lived here since that night.

Then on the windowsill he spotted the little bamboo cage that had held the orange canary Saira had smuggled into the States. Crossing the room, he picked it up—and bent to look out the window. In the garden below, his father was crouching by a patch of light from the kitchen, doing something peculiar with his hands. They were moving steadily, separately, flashes of white against the dark ground.

He ran out and down to the kitchen. Had Daddy-jan gone crazy? He couldn't be praying. He shouldn't be out there at all now.

Quietly, Tor pulled open the door. His father had gone farther into the shadows, but on the path where he had been a heap of green plants lay uprooted and wilting. By the fountain, the rose bushes were thrown in a pile.

"Daddy-jan? What are you doing? We have to go soon."

He glanced up, "I know that, Bechaim. I'm almost finished here."

"But the guards might hear you!"

"I'm not making a sound, Tor. You can help me, if you're in such a rush. Since Taraki will hardly keep this house as a memorial to us, I have no intention of leaving him my vegetables to eat. I only regret I can't cut down every tree in the orchard as well." His voice was even but he kept on working, ripping up plants and tossing them aside.

Looking down at the stripped beds, Tor rubbed a hand across his chest. It felt so tight it was almost hard to breathe. He had not considered what would happen after they left, but of course the Khalqis would take over the house, ridicule and destroy whatever they couldn't use or sell... and there were many things of value Daddy-jan could smash to pieces if he cared about the money. Destroying the garden was a gesture of defiance.

Tor touched his shoulder. "Please, let me finish here. It's twenty of eleven and you haven't changed your clothes yet. Please, Daddy-jan, I want to do it."

"Alright, Bechaim." With a sigh, he stood up. "I just have to take the nozzle off the fountain." Putting it in his pocket, he walked back to the house. "Be sure to get all the tulips, will you, Tor?"

There were rows of them in bloom by the garden shed, and going over Tor wrapped his fingers around two stalks. It seemed unfair to kill the plants. This wasn't their fault. But he pulled them up, bulbs and all. These were Mummy-jan's favorites, so why should Taraki's wife have them on her breakfast table?

Then he found himself tearing at the flowers in a frenzy, throwing them against the garden wall. We'll come back to Kabul someday, he thought, we have to, but not to this house. Not after they've been here. If I could burn it to the ground right now I would.

He jumped as a thud came from indoors. Could Daddy-jan have had the same idea? But they must call no attention to the house tonight. Their headstart would be small enough as it was. He'd started toward the kitchen when the garage door creaked and Rashid's voice said, "It's almost time. Are you ready to go?"

"I guess so. I just hope I'll remember all the names you gave me."

Rashid stepped into the square of light and Tor saw he was licking his lips again, the way he had when they'd driven into Nur-Ali's trap in the bazaar.

"Comrade! This isn't another trick?" But the edge in his tone made the joke an accusation.

Just then the first explosion came—a dull blast and a tremor rising through the earth that shook his bones and made Rashid appear to dance before him, wide lips drawing back from his white teeth.

"No trick, Tor. That was the Demazang charge." Patting down his clothes, Rashid smiled nervously. "Four more should come pretty quickly now. Get up there and watch so you can see if the guards go with me. I'll run out after the next one. Good luck, Tor."

"And to you." Tor clasped his hand, "I won't forget what we owe you, Rashid."

He went in and up the stairs.

His mother was waiting on the landing and pulled him into their bedroom, where his father stood looking out the front window. The top of the guard's car was visible over the compound wall and as another explosion sounded in the distance, Rashid hurtled down the driveway pulling at his collar as if he were terrified. They heard a babble of voices—Tor couldn't catch the words—followed by a third muffled explosion to the north. Then to his relief the car started, pulling out and down the street. But just as he was turning from the window, the front gate opened and a soldier came through it with a hand on the clip of his automatic rifle.

The back of Tor's neck prickled—in anticipation more than fear. He would have to act quickly now. There could be no challenge from his parents. Purposely, he'd been vague about the specifics of the plan so anything might seem a part of it. Even this.

"That's fine," he said. "Let's go downstairs and get you out to the garage. I'll be there in a minute. I want to see where our friend is first, but we'll leave so fast he'll have to curse our dust."

Shepherding them out through the kitchen, he waited until the garage door had closed with a faint rasp. Then mimicking Rashid, he mussed his hair and clothes, slipped the pistol into his sling and ran to the front of the house breathing in gasps. The guard was standing just outside the door and he swung around as Tor threw it open.

"Please, Officer, it's my mother! I think she's had a heart attack. She fell down when the blasting started and we can't wake her up!"

The young soldier stepped away uncertainly and Tor lowered his eyes.

"Please!" He faked a sob. "Will you come help my father? I sprained my arm so I can't lift her and she's very ill!"

The guard pushed the door back, still undecided. The gun wavered in his hands. He held it up. "Alright. You go first. Where is she?"

"Upstairs," Tor pointed. "Thank you very much! Daddy-jan," he called, "we're coming!"

He scrambled up the stairs and when he was sure the guard was following, pretended to fall against the bannister and slid back, colliding with him. Groaning as if he had hurt his arm, he doubled over and slid the Mauser into his hand. When the guard reached down to help, Tor pressed the gun into his chest and fired a muffled shot.

The soldier fell on top of him, crushing him into the woodwork, hot and suffocatingly heavy. His face was buried in Tor's neck, but there was no sensation of breathing. Sweating in a panic, Tor struggled to move the flaccid body—the pain in his arm was sickening, but he had to get free before someone came to see what the delay was about. Finally, grasping the bannister and kicking his feet for traction, he managed to pull himself up and out. As he got to his feet, the guard slid down the stairs, his loose jaw snapping hard against each step.

Climbing past him, Tor stumbled into the kitchen and bent retching over the sink. He'd been too nervous to eat any dinner and his stomach shuddered with dry convulsions. Turning on the faucet, he let cold water wash over his face until the heaving in his belly stopped. It was only then that he saw he was covered with blood.

He had put on Western clothing for the drive to Kandahar, but getting a clean shirt would mean crawling over the body again. Tammim's pants and shirt were in a sack on the table—his dress for the desert leg of the trip. Why not wear them now instead, and act as his parents' driver?

Stripping, he sponged off his chest and arms, then pulled on Tammim's clothes and retied the sling. The only thing left was to close the front door, and going down the hall he swung it shut. But turning, he stopped at the sight of the guard splayed across the stairs. There was a mole on his cheek the size of a coin. A black mole he had seen some time before.

That face. A little older now, but it was the boy who had grabbed Aspi's reins at Dar-al-Aman the day before Mangal's wedding. The soldier in the greasy uniform who had glared at him with so much hatred.

I shot him without looking at him, Tor thought, just like Nur-Ali told me. Sher's plan. What a good comrade I am.

It was stupid to have regrets. The plan had worked and he was grateful for it. Now, though, it seemed hideous to leave the guard like that. He was Afghan, not Russian, and he was following orders too.

But there was nothing else to be done.

Turning off the hall light he went back out through the kitchen.

His father was sitting behind the wheel and Tor forced a smile. "Since when do you drive yourself?" He gestured at Tammim's clothes, "I thought it would look better if you had a servant."

"What happened in there, Tor? We heard some noise."

"I invited your guard in for tea." He opened the rear door. "And then since I'm a bad host, I locked him in the study."

Climbing out, his father glanced up, startled. There was only one key to the study and he kept it in his pocket, as they both had reason to know.

Tor let the Mercedes coast down the drive and only turned on the headlights when they were out of Carte Seh. A barrage of artillery fire had started from the direction of Pul-i-Charki, and as they drove west its reports carried more clearly—a relentless tattoo of machine-gun fire broken by salvos of grenades and an occasional rumbling thunderclap of mortar. On a rise at the edge of the city, he stopped the car to look back.

The night sky had an eerie beauty—red tracer bullets arcing within the broad white circling beam of the five-kilometer searchlight. His parents watched in silence through the rear window, and he wondered if it also reminded them of fireworks on festival days.

Nur-Ali wouldn't be thinking of that or maybe anything else as he tossed his powder-filled pipes into the arsenal. He'd light a fuse, throw one and then run for cover, trusting his instincts to save him. In the backseat Daddy-jan muttered, "Murder and suicide!" and Tor recalled making the same accusation. But he no longer felt detached from what the rebels were doing. In spite of himself he had listened, knelt to steady those pipes, and when the hour came he'd killed a man. Without Sher's help they might all be facing a firing squad tonight, but if Daddy-jan deserved the safety of this car, what right had he himself to its protection? Nur-Ali had scorned his soft hands, calling him useless, a pretty boy better sent out of harm's way. But we aren't really so different and he admitted that, Tor thought—just a pair of crazy fools. So good luck, my grouchy friend. Aim well and win. I almost envy you.

Starting the engine, he turned back to the road.

The eight-hour drive to Kandahar seemed twice that long, and to distract them, he told stories of the rebel camp and his meeting with Ghulam-Nabi. Yes, he told his mother, it did seem possible Sher was Roshana's Uncle Aziz after all, and that he'd stayed inside the house so he couldn't be identified later on if something went wrong. And wouldn't it be interesting to travel with the kuchis? They had such a sense of freedom. Their women wore such wonderful clothes. While he was talking he scanned the highway with an intensity that made his head ache and his father kept a similar watch out the back. But the patrols they strained their eyes to see never materialized.

Near the outskirts of Kandahar, he slowed the car and began looking for his contact—the high truck with jet planes painted on its sides that Rashid had described. It couldn't park and wait without inviting investigation, so it was supposed to drive back and forth along this stretch of road like a tradesman's van endlessly starting out, then returning for something forgotten.

For twenty minutes they drove at a crawl, but the van failed to appear. It would be dawn soon and not safe for them in Kandahar—better to find a hiding place than go into the city. Then, just as he was about to give up, a horn sounded behind them and through the rearview mirror he saw headlights flash as the truck swerved to come abreast of the Mercedes.

A turbaned boy leaned out the passenger window. "Can you tell me where the turn is to Mizani?"

Tor supplied his half of the password. "You've come four kilometers too far."

Grinning, the boy nodded to the man who was driving and the truck passed the Mercedes, pulling up on the shoulder. Tor stopped the car close behind it.

Now, he thought, I can only pray you won't say the wrong thing to my father—or he'll turn around and walk straight back to Kabul.

"We'll go with the truck," he said. "They'll take our car and leave it on the Jalalabad road to give us a false trail." In fact, the Mercedes would be kept as payment for services rendered, but they might lose confidence if they saw this chiefly as a business deal.

As they got out, the trader came to meet them. Stopping an arm's length away, he examined them with interest. "It is our great honor to serve you, Omar Anwari. I'm Akbar, and this is my son Nangyalai."

"Peace be with you both. My wife and I are most grateful for your help."

Tor picked up their cloth bags. "We'd better hurry. It's getting light and I know you want to hide the car."

Reading his glance, Akbar nodded. "Yes. You see, we must preserve the secret of your path so others can use it when necessary. Now I offer you a seat in the back of my truck, with apologies for its discomfort."

While Akbar was settling them on a pile of rags, Nangyalai went back to walk in a circle around the Mercedes, reaching out to caress its curved fenders and grinning as if in disbelief at his sudden good luck.

The truck door slammed shut and for half an hour they rode in darkness. When Akbar opened the door again the sky had a red glow. They had stopped by a stream near the crumbling walls of an old caravanserai, where twenty or more camels were hobbled with a few donkeys and horses beside a ring of six black goat-hair tents. As Akbar led them toward the sleeping camp, four mastiffs with clipped ears and tails ran out snarling to hold them at bay until an old man stepped out of one tent and the dogs turned in answer to his call.

"Mehdi," Akbar said, "may you not be tired. Here is your new family."

"Peace. Live long." Mehdi's white beard and turban, his slight dignified bow marked him as the patriarch here. Tor watched with amusement as the chief and his father exchanged respectful greetings while their eyes held a more direct conversation, and almost at once they both relaxed. It must have been hard for Daddy-jan to follow the lead of Rashid, Akbar, even his own son. But this man Mehdi's authority he could honor.

After Akbar had been sent off with a string of thanks and good wishes,

Mehdi called, "Aliya!" and a tall young woman slipped out of the next tent as though she had been waiting for her name. Tor looked away, trying not to stare, but she made a strong impression—silver jewelry, curly jet black hair framing a face more handsome than beautiful, a print dress concealing all but the gathered tips of her red pantaloons. Feet brown and bare.

"Catherine Anwari, this is my second granddaughter, Aliya. She will do everything for you now. Remember," he told the girl, "you must show her how to cover her face in exactly the right manner, in case we meet any sons of Russian devils."

Even the kuchis know who's calling the shots now, Tor thought. Taraki hasn't fooled them either.

Mehdi smiled. "Don't worry, Bibi Catherine. I'm more afraid for your skin in the desert than I am of soldiers. Go with Aliya now, she'll dress you. And Omar Anwari, please rest in my tent for what little time we have. I'll bring other clothes to you."

"That's very kind," he said. "Thank you, but I have what I need right here." Bending, he disappeared with his small bag under the tent's goatskin flap.

"And you, Toryalai Anwari..." Tor thought he saw a twinkle in the old man's eye. "You can help us with the camels."

The rest of the camp was waking up, women with black head scarves over long bright dresses coming out of their tents to start fires for bread and tea. The coins sewn into their clothing tinkled as they moved, and when they passed Tor they smiled or nodded with none of the shrinking timidity village girls would have shown. But kuchi women had never been veiled. Their wide scarves protected them from sand and wind as much as unwanted attention, and their grace of movement and easy laughter fascinated him now as they set up their tripods and curved plates to cook dough over the fire.

There were sheep and goats too, beyond the circle of tents, and as the men rose more slowly to untie the hobbled herd, Mehdi introduced Tor and offered his help to Ghafar, his eldest son, a giant in a black turban who wore an enormous black mustache. As at the rebel camp, it seemed taken for granted that Tor's sling was a small handicap, even that he would feel insulted to be excused from work. Though he was glad of it, he hoped they didn't really want him to handle the camels, who were snorting bad-temperedly and straining at their leads. The closer he got, the bigger they looked.

Ghafar was grinning down at him. "Do you know these animals?"

"Not very well. I've never...led one, if that's what you mean." He had almost said "ridden," but only old kuchis or babies actually rode the camels. And he also remembered hearing how dangerous the beasts could be.

"I will tell you"—Ghafar bent to untether one—"the camel is the stupidest and most stubborn creature Allah in his wisdom ever made. But I'm going to show you how to lead this one because you must look like the rest of us, and also a camel can be excellent protection from many things in the desert." He looked sideways at Tor. "From bullets, even." Speaking softly, he placed Tor's left hand on one quivering flank. "This camel, now, is a magnificent animal, and I think she'll be your friend. Her name is Zora, she's my sister's camel, and Zora is also my sister's name." Ghafar laughed loudly at his joke. "My sister never gave her a name and it made this camel angry, so one day I started calling her Zora too, and from that day she has loved me. Now, take her lead and say her name and see if it doesn't make her smile."

Gingerly, Tor took the reins and looking up at one brown rolling eye, said, "Hello, Zora. My name's Tor." He felt like an idiot.

Wagging her loose jowls, Zora curled back her neck and spat neatly between his feet. Beside him, Ghafar exploded with laughter. "Good, now walk a little way with her."

Tor pulled on the lead and to his surprise the camel followed him—then jerked the tether out of his hand and galloped away toward the stream. "Get her," Ghafar called. "She's going for water, but she can't have it till you let her!"

Cursing, Tor ran after her, conscious of the women watching and smiling at his initiation. He caught the lead again and with the strength of anger, led her back to Ghafar, who was applauding now. "Fine, Zora is yours. Give her some water and then have breakfast yourself. My daughter Aliya will serve you." He pointed toward the fire and Tor turned to see her standing beside an older woman, whom he recognized with amazement as his mother.

She was wearing a flowing black head scarf edged with coins, and her forehead was hidden by a silver band crusted with tiny colored glass beads. A long black dress fell almost to her ankles, exposing the ends of the blue pantaloons that married women wore. As Tor watched, she began to smile, then with a quick modest gesture drew the scarf across her face. Aliya grinned triumphantly at her father.

Ghafar nodded. "Yes, that's very good. Now let's hurry. Eat something, both of you."

By the time Tor finished his bread and goat's milk yogurt, the tents had been struck and kneeling camels were being loaded with a mountain of cooking pots, trivets, lamps, poles, rugs, and finally puppies, lambs and infants, who were lashed on top like any other goods. He looked around to see his father in loose traditional clothes herding sheep with an impatience that said he could have done this every morning of his life. Managing livestock was a skill Tor had refused to learn, to his father's great disgust, and now it was embarrassing to be sitting by the fire while Mehdi's old eyes followed Daddy-jan, approving what he saw.

I've shamed him again, Tor thought. I always will.

The camp was dismantled in less than an hour. They started out before the sky was fully light. He counted ten men and twelve women but lost track of the children, who ran up to peer into his face before darting off again. Mehdi had said today they would push hard to cover forty kilometers, and Tor wondered if Mummy-jan's strength would hold up after her sleepless night. Turning, he saw her laughing and talking with Aliya at the rear of the group. He went up to walk behind his father and Mehdi.

"I don't like stopping near Kandahar," Mehdi was saying. "But the younger ones insist upon it. They always want a bit of silver filigree or something else from the shops. And yet, since we have little to trade now, the townspeople like us even less than they did in the old days."

"Ah..." Daddy-jan nodded gravely. "But they must recognize how much they still need the dung of your camels for fertilizer. In the Soviet Union, when they drove away their kuchis to make 'virgin lands,' the earth died and nothing has grown there since."

Mehdi smiled in satisfaction. "Anyway, the open air is the place for us, not the smoke of towns or those pathetic little farms in the Helmand valley. As if we would ever be farmers! And as if the government owed us nothing..."

For the next three hours, the old man entertained them with stories of kuchi valor, while the sprawl of Kandahar grew smaller and faded to the north. They were in true desert now, parched rocky ground stretching out of sight with only tufts of withered grass cropping up here and there. As the sun climbed, the day grew hotter than Kabul ever was in April, and Tor put on the black turban Ghafar had given him. No wonder the kuchis could go so long without bathing or changing clothes. It was too dry to sweat at all. Heat rose in waves that made the sand shimmer; at times even the brown hills seemed to be floating in midair.

The sun on his skin felt wonderful after a winter in Moscow's close rooms. His legs found a rhythmic stride. He smiled at the children picking up camel dung and fighting over who had collected more of the precious fuel. If only Elizabeth could see this! It was easy to imagine her walking beside him, also exhilarated by their escape from the prison of Kabul. They'd all been captives, and if leaving meant losing everything, as Nur-Ali predicted, freedom was still worth more than what they had given up. Then he realized Nur-Ali would heartily agree, could almost hear that sharp voice saying, "So, Tor, you have finally discovered what we're fighting for?" He was sending back a mental salute when the hot thin air was broken by a distant metallic grind of heavy engines.

Squinting, Tor could just make them out in the east—a line of tanks looking like mechanical toys that an invisible hand was rolling through the dust.

Ghafar came up behind him, leading the largest camel and offering a pair of shiny binoculars. "Don't worry yet. They're a long way off. If they were looking for you, they'd be here by now."

Tor peered through the fine lenses and the tanks sprang into focus. He could even read the numerals painted on their sides. Cursing, he handed the glasses back to Ghafar, who grinned. "You thought you were through with them, eh?"

"I don't understand what they're doing out here."

"Test maneuvers." Ghafar shrugged. "Is it true you speak Russian?"

Tor nodded, hoping he didn't look shaken. He had thought they were through with that, yes, and now he felt his lack of sleep in every muscle.

"I'm glad," Ghafar said. "We've been stopped by soldiers before and the officers always speak Russian. I never know what they're saying. Toryalai, do you have a gun?"

"Just a pistol. Yes."

"It's difficult to hide out here, and sound travels far. Don't use it unless you have to." Jerking on the camel's lead, Ghafar went up to speak to Mehdi. Tor checked the Mauser in his sling and waited for his mother, who was talking less gaily with Aliya now. He heard the girl say, "Yes, we've seen them other times, though never, never so many. But don't worry, my father is much cleverer than the Russians."

Maybe, Tor thought, but Ghafar can't understand them, so that's going to be up to me, and I don't want to make his decisions.

"Tor dear, walk along with us." His mother put a hand out to him and her gold ring glinted in the sun. Suddenly he was furious. If they'd overlooked something that basic, they must have made worse mistakes too. He said, "Kuchis don't wear wedding bands, do they?"

Aliya looked startled and followed his gaze. "No, not like that, no."

"Can you get it off, Mummy-jan?"

She was already pulling at the ring, but though her fingers were thinner the knuckles had swollen and it wouldn't come. Aliya ran ahead to get a spoonful of oil, and with effort they forced the ring up off her finger.

"Forgive me, Mummy-jan. I'm sorry if I hurt you." He couldn't meet her eyes.

Aliya started chattering nervously about kuchi weddings, and he pretended to listen, but all his attention was fixed on the long brown line crawling in the east. Then, as if his fear had called it, one dark shape broke away from the rest to move toward them at high speed.

Ghafar raised his glasses. "It's a jeep! Two men with machine guns."

Tor ran up to him. "Listen, Ghafar. If they speak Russian and I think it looks bad for us, I'll say something. I'll say..." He remembered Kerala, "I'll shout: Hurrah for the Taraki government! And the second I do, you shoot the soldier on the left. I'll get the other one."

Ghafar frowned. "Only if it's unavoidable."

Tor felt like screaming: Of course, you idiot! Instead, to calm them both down, he smiled up at the huge man with the Black Wasp's oily sweetness. "Why worry, Ghafar? Allah knows where we are."

Smiling, the man turned both palms up as if to ask a blessing. "Allah!"

When the jeep had almost reached them, Mehdi raised his hand for the caravan to stop.

Two officers got out of the jeep, cradling Kalashnikov rifles. They both wore Afghan army uniforms, but the colonel's eyes were blue. The lieutenant looked about twenty-five and his smile showed crooked teeth. "What are you doing so far east? Not going to Pakistan, I hope." His Pashto was bad and heavily accented.

"Pah!" Mehdi said. "We no longer travel to Pakistan, not for many years. We're going to my grandson's wedding in Spin Baldak."

The lieutenant translated for the colonel, who answered in Russian, "I doubt it. Tell him he's lying."

"He says he doesn't believe you."

Mehdi glowered at the insult. "Just look at the gifts we're bringing! These lambs, and silver jewelry for the bride..."

"Be quiet, old man." The lieutenant was watching his commander, who had come closer to look into each face. "There's something wrong here," the colonel said in Russian. "I can smell its stink."

He stepped in front of Tor. "What's this one's name?"

Tor made his face a blank till the translation came, then bobbed his head. "Siddique, Your Excellency."

Siddique, the idiot child.

"You see?" The colonel moved down the line. "Some of these people are too white. The older man at the front, for instance." He gave Aliya a broad, misleading smile.

Tor thought, he means Daddy-jan, but he isn't looking at him. He just doesn't want to put us on guard, and Ghafar won't understand that.

Aliya was supporting Mummy-jan with one arm as though she were very old. They both had drawn their scarves across their faces.

"And this woman," the colonel said in the same pleasant tone, "look at that pale hand. If she's a kuchi, I'm Leonid Brezhnev."

The lieutenant struck himself on the forehead. "The attack on Pul-i-Charki last night! When I talked to Kabul this morning they said an important prisoner had escaped. Not from the prison. A man under house arrest... a former minister and his family. They killed their guard."

"Did they? How interesting."

"Yes, but the police are searching for them on the highway to Peshawar."

Tor kept smiling serenely.

"Perhaps they're looking in the wrong place then," the colonel said. "I'm certain these people are running to Pakistan."

"Shall we take them back to Kandahar?"

"What, the whole stinking bunch?" He shook his head. "No. Since these kuchis are helping them, they're also guilty—of treason. I think we can dispose of them right here. I can't spare the men it would take to escort so many back. They want to leave the country? Good. We'll help them to do so, permanently."

For a split second Tor caught Ghafar's eye and was chilled by the man's expression. He looked puzzled, even frightened, but his body held no hint of tension.

"Of course"—the colonel grinned—"since there *are* so many, we must do this with care. Hit the men first. Start in the middle, work out to your left and then go back to finish the women. Begin when I count three."

Tor cleared his throat loudly. "Your Excellency," he called in his idiot voice, "all of us here say, Hurrah for the Taraki government!"

Waving his sling for emphasis, he fired at the colonel's face.

Where a nose had been a moment before, a black hole spurted blood even though the colonel's mouth continued to open as he fell to his knees, teetering, and Tor raised the gun again. But there was no need. With a choked wheeze, the thick body folded sideways and lay sprawled and limp under the rifle his hands still clutched.

If I'm alive, Tor thought, Ghafar must have killed the other one. But I didn't hear his shot.

He turned to see Ghafar straddling the young lieutenant, whose brown eyes looked up sightless at the sun. A stream of blood beside his head was soaking into the earth. Somehow, in spite of the machine gun, Ghafar had cut his throat with the dagger that lay next to him now, red along its blade.

Standing up, Ghafar muttered unhappily, "I told you, sound carries in the desert. And men in tanks also own binoculars."

"Yes..." Mehdi nodded. "So quickly, quickly, put them back in the jeep." He motioned to his men. "Come on now, hurry!"

"They were going to shoot all of us," Tor said. "I had to do it. I'm sorry."

He watched as Mehdi supervised the positioning of the bodies. A length of rope was passed across their chests and lashed to the doors to hold them upright. Then the lieutenant's hands were bound to the steering wheel and his right foot to the accelerator. Aliya had led a camel behind the jeep to screen it from the tanks. Maybe at that distance it would look as though the soldiers were bargaining with the kuchis for something.

Mehdi beckoned to him. "Come here, Toryalai. I don't know how to start this thing. I want you to aim it, fix it to go that way." He pointed across the desert. "And if those sons of devils haven't seen what we did, they won't know why their friends are leaving them."

The steering column had been tied too, so the jeep wouldn't swing on its path. And this old man didn't know how to start it? Swallowing his queasiness, Tor leaned over the lieutenant's body and used his rifle to depress the clutch. When the ignition fired, he threw the shift into gear and gave the jeep a push. Slowly, it moved away from them in a straight line.

He smiled at Mehdi. "You should join the army."

The old man shook his head. "They may follow us. We may die soon. Let's go quickly now."

They started walking again, and after long suspense Ghafar reported that the tanks were nowhere in sight. He felt sure there wouldn't be others this far out, but the caravan kept up a brisk pace through the afternoon and there was little talk until they stopped to make camp.

At night, the desert air was freezing. Tor shivered as he helped Ghafar hobble the camels and donkeys while the women raised the tents in a ring. Then he went to warm himself by the dung fire where his mother was already seated. They had walked together, holding hands, for the past few hours and he'd felt her tension, but she had said nothing about the shooting and now he needed a sign that she could accept what he had done.

For a while they sat looking into the fire, sharing its heat in silence as they found each other's presence again. It was something they had always been able to do, even after serious fights, but tonight he sensed a calm in her that he hadn't expected. It must have been the threat of more danger that had troubled her earlier, and his doubts dissolved. He gave her a hug. "I hope you live forever. I don't think I could stand this life without you."

"When I die, my spirit will stay with you and it will never leave you."

He was stunned by her answer. Hesitantly, he teased, "Only me? What about Saira?"

"Both of you." She was looking down at her hands. "I'm sorry you had to do that today. I didn't raise my children to kill people. But I'm not sorry you did it, understand that too. I didn't bring you into this world to be murdered, either. I'll even admit, after you shot that man I felt some anger go out of me, and I've had so much for so long that if you lined ten Russians up against a wall I could probably kill them all and then sit down to supper. Yes, this is your mother speaking. But there's only so much one can take."

"I know," he said. "I've been thinking I ought to feel worse about it. At least, that it had to happen, but I don't."

"You and Ghafar saved our lives, Tor. Quite bravely, I might add. You should have seen your father's face. He was very proud of you."

"Or of himself, for making me learn Russian. Look, I think Aliya's bringing us dinner."

The kuchi woman was balancing cups of tea with a dish of bread and dried mutton. "We'll have a better meal tomorrow night, Bibi Anwari. There wasn't time to cook today."

"Since we almost didn't live to eat this one, nothing will ever taste more delicious. Thank you, Aliya."

Tor chewed a piece of tough meat mechanically. He couldn't agree with her there.

When they had finished, he dozed off in front of the fire until Ghafar prodded him up to lie on a pile of rugs in his tent. Tor turned them so he could see outside. The moon was almost full and the sky was alive with milky, swirling constellations. The desert floor spread out flat and pale, then blurred into the darkness.

After a second day's walk on sore feet they made another camp, within sight of the Khojak Pass to Pakistan. Mehdi had driven them even harder, as if anxious to be rid of so great a liability, but it meant tomorrow's hike would be less grueling. Aliya had insisted her new friend Bibi Catherine ride on horseback, and in spite of Mummy-jan's protestations, Tor thought she looked better for it. There was no more risk now, so dinner became a feast lasting many hours. Aliya danced with a tambourine and tried to coax the others to join her while Tor lay back laughing, loving the color and music, even the camel, Zora, and printing new sights and sounds over those he didn't want to remember.

In the morning it was hard to leave the caravan. Ghafar would be their only guide through the pass. Tor saw his mother press a gold necklace into Aliya's hand, and smiling with frank pleasure, the kuchi woman stripped off her widest bangle in return.

When farewells had been exchanged with each member of the band, Ghafar led them away.

Looking back, Tor saw Aliya standing apart from the rest, a bright figure growing dimmer against the sweep of earth and sky. She stayed like that, facing their trail and waving, until he lost her on the horizon.

At the border, they left Ghafar with many thanks and crossed without incident to Pakistan and the railway station at Chaman.

When the crowded train lurched into Quetta four hours later, a throng of waiting passengers surged forward to find seats. Tor linked arms with his parents, and struggling out into sunlight, they walked two blocks east to the Jinnah road—a tree-lined avenue of low pastel-colored shops, hotels and office buildings, where vehicles of every kind competed with each other, tooting horns and clanging bells.

He had been told that Jonathan Straight would be staying at the Farah Hotel, and as they passed through the Suraj Ganj bazaar it was obvious how subdued the Kabul bazaar had been by contrast. Here, there were no soldiers and the merchants didn't watch every passerby suspiciously, but rather called out the excellence of their goods or the superiority of their kebab.

The smell of roasting lamb made Tor's stomach growl. He hurried his parents toward the pale green hotel and the orange sign over its awning that read: RESTAURANT.

Settling them at a table, he went out to the reception desk and asked for Mr. Straight. A boy directed him to the front room on the second floor. He had half expected the man would be out in the middle of the day, but as he reached the landing the door across the hall opened and a familiar, listing profile was silhouetted by light. Straight waved him in with one hand, grasping the doorknob with the other, and Tor guessed his limp must have grown even worse. Lame Mr. Jonathan CIA—or was his handicap as phony as his cover?

"Hello, Toryalai. I saw you from the window. I'm very glad you all arrived safely." His face was bonier than ever and his hair an almost purple red.

Tor stepped into the seedy room and shook the hand offered to him. He said with a warmth he didn't feel, "It's kind of you to help us."

"But?" Straight smiled. "I think I hear a 'but' in your voice." He pulled the door shut.

There were no chairs in the room. Tor sat down on the narrow bed. This might be his only chance to talk privately with the man, and his questions would sound ungrateful. Still, they were safe now and this American couldn't send them back to Kabul, so why bother being polite? The CIA wasn't doing this out of love. He said, "But why are you letting them take over!"

Straight was watching him shrewdly. "You mean, why is the United States allowing Afghanistan to handle its own affairs?"

"The Soviets run the country now. You know that as well as I do."

"Every Soviet adviser there was invited in by the Afghan president. Are you suggesting we overthrow Taraki?"

"Oh, heavens no! You'd never try such a thing. Not in Viet Nam, or Chile..."

"Listen to me, Tor. There's no chance in the world that my government will get involved in a civil war on the Soviet border. Don't you understand what that would mean?"

"Yes! I'm not saying you should send in troops. We can fight our own battles, but not with sticks and stones. You could find a way to ship guns to the rebels."

Straight was toying with his cane. "If there were a Communist uprising in Mexico, and Moscow supplied it with arms, don't you think we'd consider that an extremely hostile act?"

"If they did it out in the open. Come on! It happens all the time."

"Look, let me show you something." Opening his wallet, he took out a scrap of newspaper. "It's from last Sunday's *Washington Post*."

Tor read the few lines with disbelief. The article said, without comment, that a Soviet battalion was massing by the Afghan border.

He looked up. "Does this mean they're going to invade us?"

"I imagine they'd love a reason to do just that, given Taraki's ineptness. And what better excuse could they have than American intervention? I'm afraid your guerrillas may have done too well. They'll probably be slaughtered for their pains."

Tor put down the article. His fingers were shaking. "So the U.S. is just watching and not saying a word, is that right? You might as well send an engraved invitation to the Soviets."

Straight turned away. Tor couldn't see his face. "I only heard about this a few days ago myself. I can't speak for President Carter. All I can do, all we can do here, is help men like your father get out and hope that with the next turn of the wheel they can get back in again. It isn't over yet, Tor."

But his tone said their conversation was finished.

"Fine." Tor stood up. "I guess we're lucky we still might be useful to you. I have to go downstairs now. My parents are waiting for me."

"Your tickets and State Department visas are in this envelope. I don't think you should have any problem."

Straight fumbled in his wallet again, then pushed some money into Tor's hand. "Don't tell your father. This is just in case you have trouble on the other end. New York's an expensive place."

Tor was confused by the gesture. Perhaps he shouldn't accept it? He counted four five-hundred-dollar bills.

"That's not a bribe, Tor. If you don't spend it, you can give it back to me one day."

His eyes looked dull and Tor wondered if he might care more than he let on. After all, Straight had lived in Afghanistan. It might hurt him to see it disintegrate too. And he was helping them, whatever his reasons.

"Thank you." Tor shook his hand firmly this time. "You're very generous. I'm sure we'll need some extra money at first." And if we don't, he thought, I'll send it to Raima for Sher, so you'll buy him guns in spite of yourself.

Straight held the door and Tor went out, slipping the green bills into his pocket. They were so new their surface felt like silk.

Twenty-Eight

SAIRA HUNG UP the telephone and after a moment was conscious of her secretary, Johnetta, watching through the glass partition. The State Department had never called before. Johnnie turned away discreetly, but Saira pressed the intercom button and their eyes met through the pane of glass.

"You'll have to cancel everything I've got for today and tomorrow, Johnnie. Maybe longer than that. I'm not sure yet."

"Alright. Is there anything else I can do?" She said softly, "You don't look well."

"I guess I'm in shock. That phone call said my family's flying into New York tonight. It's the first I've heard about it."

Johnnie cocked her head. "But isn't that good news? I know how worried you've been."

"Yes. It's just so sudden. Listen, I'd rather no one else here knew about this for a while. Will you cover for me?"

"Sure. I'll hold the fort. I'll tell Personnel you've gone home sick. You're supposed to see Mr. Sahni at one. Let me try to head him off." Her brown hand moved toward the Rolodex and she switched to an outside line.

Saira looked down at the notes she had made. Could this possibly be a mistake? Mr. Robert Graeber, at the State Department. She hadn't thought to ask for his extension. The five-thirty flight from Karachi. Air India. Daddyjan, Mummy and Tor. Better for her not to meet them, Mr. Graeber said, since clearing them might take an hour or so. But someone would escort them to her home, and was this the correct address? She hadn't asked how he knew that, either.

Andrei had contacts in Washington. He might be able to check out Robert Graeber. Or was that just an excuse to call him up? It was her fault things had gone sour between them after Mangal died. Andrei said she blamed him for Mangal, and maybe he was right. Still, he cared about her and he might understand what this meant. There was no reason not to tell him.

She dialed his number. Yes, the male secretary said, he was in, and who was calling, please? Of course, Miss Anwari, just a minute, please.

How many people here know about us, she wondered. Everyone at the U.N. thinks their love affairs are secret, but the secretaries always guess. They laugh about it at lunch.

"Saira?"

"Hello, Andrei. Can you talk?"

"For the moment, yes. Is something wrong?"

"I'm not sure. Someone just called and said my parents have left Kabul and they'll be in New York tonight. Including Tor, who I thought was still in Moscow."

"Really? Well, that's a surprise." He sounded as uncertain as she felt. "Who was it that called? Someone from the Afghan Mission?"

"No. A Mr. Robert Graeber. He said he was at State."

"Hmmmm." She could almost see Andrei writing down the name. He would think she was stupid not to have got a telephone number.

"Saira, shall I call our embassy and try to verify this?"

No, she decided, she'd ask for nothing. "You don't have to do that, Andrei. I just wanted to let you know. We were supposed to have lunch this week, remember?"

"And they'll be staying with you... indefinitely?"

"I don't know how long. It's going to be quite a trick to fit four people in my apartment. They'll probably go up to Boston after a while. Meantime I have to clean house and buy some food. I left things in a mess."

"I don't have anything urgent on this afternoon. Could you use some help with that? You know I'd love to see you."

She hesitated. Since their last meeting she had been wanting to see him again too, and this might be their last chance for a long time. The family wouldn't get uptown before seven. Six hours. She was already nervous.

"If you can really spare the time, I'd love it, Andrei."

"In forty-five minutes then. Okay?"

He hung up without waiting for an answer.

Johnnie had moved away from the glass. Quickly, Saira took her purse from the drawer and stood up, smoothing her gray wool suit. With one more promotion she might get a separate office with plaster walls. It was odd, when she first came to UNICEF the vast open floor had seemed friendly, with all those desks set head-to-head and gossip at the Xerox machine. Having a partitioned side office with a window had seemed the height of status then.

Knotting a blue scarf around her neck, she slipped into her trenchcoat. Sunglasses, where were they? She always wore them now. Johnnie had begun to tease her about it. But they'd get her down the endless aisle of cubicles and desks, high metal cabinets and typing stands whose sharp hidden corners seemed designed to injure. The glass partitions were meant to bring a glimpse of sunlight to the clerical pool, but instead they worked as mirrors, bouncing cold fluorescence from one hard surface to another. There was no privacy or color, except in the clothing of the staff, and for months all the noise had been grating on her nerves until she wanted to scream at each slammed file drawer, the constant racket of typing. Andrei thought her annoyance was temporary, part of her personal troubles. Instead, it was getting worse. If it became impossible to stay here, waiting for a closed office that might never turn up, what would she do then?

Johnnie was nowhere in sight. Scribbling a note that she'd call her in the morning, Saira walked out to the elevator bank. Outside, the sun was brilliant, the plaza flocked with tourists. A Checker taxi stopped as soon as she put out her hand.

Carrots, raisins, rice. She would make a pilau. Eggplant, onions, yogurt, butter. Had Taraki just let Daddy go? Then why would the State Department be involved?

Tor must have gone back to Kabul first. Maybe he was sick again. Or maybe he had never got very much better. He was supposed to have become a model student, and that didn't sound like him at all. It was hard to believe that even Mangal's dying could have changed him so completely. Knowing Tor, it would just have made him wilder—made everything worse, the way it had with her.

But Tor always went from one extreme to another.

A whole year had gone by since the coup, and if it had affected her so much, living here, how could she claim to know any of them now? None of their letters said anything revealing for the censor to read. They were all like shadow people on the other side of a curtain, and that was how she had felt too.

I've put myself under house arrest in sympathy, she thought. Under soul arrest. If I let Andrei think I blame him, he can call me irrational, but I don't have to treat him fairly. I don't have to worry about how he feels. Except that the minute I'm in trouble I go running to him and expect him to comfort me.

No. The last time he came over, there was a spark of something real again, honest and worth exploring. And last time Daddy-jan was here, we at least talked like human beings. Things can change, I ought to know that by now. Five years of hating Mangal and Tor. Then Mangal died, and Roshana and Yusef, and Tor got hurt, and everything looked different overnight. It's as if I got them back, the way we were as kids, only too late and from too far away to do any good. Maybe I've just been waiting since then to start being a person again. Maybe that's why I called Andrei. A good thing, not a bad one. Practice for Daddy-jan and Tor.

How would they be feeling? Exhausted and probably grouchy. Hungry. A little in shock too, since they must have left home quite suddenly. When Tor was upset he needed careful handling, and that would not have changed.

Saira looked down at her hands, surprised. Her fingernails had cut red crescents into the flesh of her palms. If thinking of Tor was still so painful, what would seeing him be like?

She knocked on the taxi's plastic divider. "Let me out at the next corner, please."

The cab swerved and stopped with a jolt. Climbing out, she passed ten dollars through the window. The market was six blocks away, but a walk would help calm her down. And if it didn't, she told herself, choosing the vegetables would.

Ten minutes later she stood in front of a pyramid of eggplant, trying to pick out the best ones by eye before testing the choice with her hands. She could stand, hypnotized, at the produce counter for half an hour sometimes, judging the ripeness of avocados, melons and tomatoes. Andrei said it was proof of peasant blood. The eggplants were always too big here, and the melons tasteless compared to the lush fruit in the Kabul bazaar, but their color and soft weight in her hand never failed to soothe her. For someone who had grown up in a house with a cook, she wasn't a bad one herself, she thought, and tonight would be a celebration feast. Everything had to be perfect.

She put the vegetables in plastic bags and carried them to the checkout counter, collecting lamb and yogurt on the way. It was funny how things worked out. Six years ago, when Kabul seemed the safest place on earth, she had been forced to leave, thanks to Tor. But if that hadn't happened she wouldn't be here to help the family when they needed her most, to start over in a country that might seem strange even to Mummy-jan. They had been forced to leave too, and now she was the eldest and able to give them safety. In the long run, it could all make sense.

She walked home smiling. Their plane must be in Europe now, maybe just taking off across the ocean from Paris or Rome. No more guards or sleepless nights or having to ask permission.

But would Daddy-jan be happy living here?

Inside, she set the brown bag on the kitchen table and took a close look at the aviary. The cage had just been cleaned, thank heaven. Tor would love it. Had he ever tasted avocados? she wondered. They looked peculiar on the blue Istalif plate, like huge lizard eggs.

It was a shame to cut up the eggplant so soon. Usually it was hard to find them this tiny, their purple skins without a single vein. But a few minutes later they were draining in a sieve while she melted butter and started slicing carrots into matchsticks. The last time she had cooked a real Afghan meal was months ago, for Devika. Andrei liked to buy steak.

Damn, now this carrot was cut crooked! Had calling Andrei been a bad idea? Seeing him last time was almost like the old days, lots of joking, and it was even alright when he kissed her good-bye. Poor Andrei with a crazy woman on his hands, wanting him there all the time after Mangal died, and then beginning to push him away when the first letters came from home, because, so he said, she blamed him for being Russian.

But he was French too, and he also liked Mexican food, and he'd never stopped loving her. Poor Andrei, just a human, looking as miserable at the office as she must have, until she had to admit it was silly not to see him, at least to talk, since the crazy woman couldn't handle more than that, not trusting either of them anymore.

Maybe now that the family's safe I could love him again, she thought. If they weren't coming here.

She was starting on the biggest carrot when the doorbell rang. Putting down the knife, she went to buzz him in.

He stepped off the elevator holding an enormous sheaf of florist's paper up in front of his face, and didn't lower it until she closed the door behind them. "Now no one can tell your father you've been entertaining the enemy."

"You mean none of my friendly neighbors whom I never see?"

"That's right. But maybe the birds will tell him. I meant to bring you flowers for your New Year, but I haven't seen you since then. You call it New Day, isn't that what you said?"

"Yes. *Now Roz*. You're only two weeks late, and today might be more appropriate anyhow."

He nodded. "There is a Robert Graeber on the Afghanistan Desk at State. Furthermore, your parents escaped from Kabul four days ago, while your brother was home on leave. So we can assume the rest is also true."

"Oh, Andrei. I just can't believe it." Suddenly, she didn't trust her voice to say more.

"You may not believe this, either, Saira, but I'm almost as relieved as you are. It was only a matter of time before your father would have been arrested." He hugged her awkwardly. "I thought you said you left things in a mess here."

Remembering her unmade bed, she took the flowers and went over to the counter to unwrap them—a mixed bouquet of blue irises, daffodils and pale yellow tulips.

"Some competition for the birds," he said. "Happy New Day, Saira. I hope this year is very good to you."

"And to you too, Andrei. Thank you. May you never be tired."

He smiled. "What?"

"Now you're supposed to say: May you live long."

"Oh, are you rehearsing? Do you really speak that way with them?"

She shook her head. "The flowers are lovely. I'll bet you picked each one yourself."

"Of course. I drove the shopkeeper crazy. It was fun." He took off his tweed jacket. "Now tell me what to do. Aren't you going to change your clothes?"

"Yes, I forgot. You hate this suit."

"Only because it's gray. You never wear colors anymore. Is that to punish me too?"

"I'm not a glorified secretary anymore, Andrei. I have to look professional, even if I don't feel it."

"That's ridiculous and you know it. You've been 'professional' for three years. Maybe once your family's here, you'll relax and I'll see you in the halls looking radiant and ignoring me."

His brown hair was too long now, she thought, at least for Andrei, curling around his ears. He had new tortoiseshell glasses that showed his eyes better, dark and tired today, unhappy. Andrei had no vanity about his looks, so it was easy to read his mood. Either that, or he was smart enough to know she'd take pity on a slightly neglected schoolboy.

"Please—" She touched his hand. "Let's not argue. I've been wanting to see you all week."

"And I've been wanting to see you for months. Why did you have to wait till now?" He kissed her forehead. "Never mind. You weren't expecting them to come, and we're both glad they're out, so why fuss about it? You know it's true though, don't you."

"Right now I don't know anything, Andrei. I'm just the cook."

"Then I'll be your scullery maid. I hope I don't get fired."

She walked around the counter into the kitchen. "I'm going to put these in a vase. They'll look beautiful on the glass table. If you really want to help, take that knife and start chopping. The rest of those carrots, or the onions if you'd like to be a hero."

"How many would I have to cut for that?"

"About six."

"Okay." He shrugged. "It's cheap at that price."

Taking down a vase, she filled it with water and found her sharpest knife. First the blue sprays of iris, each stem cut at a slant and to a different height. Then the daffodils, and last the tulips, their soft heads nodding around the edge of the arrangement. "Look. They're gorgeous. Now can I pour you some of your Scotch? I'll have to throw the bottle away if you can't take it with you."

"Okay. Maybe a short one then. Am I doing this right?"

"You're hired." She set the flowers on the coffee table and came back to make his drink. How many other things were here that ought to be hidden, she wondered. Andrei's old shaving kit, still in the medicine cabinet. A few books and letters. There must be nothing for Daddy-jan to use against her. Or for Tor to find.

"It's going to be strange, seeing Tor again," she said. "I haven't, since our fight."

Andrei looked up, his eyes teary from the onions. "Well, before you canonize him, there's something I should tell you. The guard at your parents' house was killed—shot in the chest. That sounds more like Tor's work than your father's, don't you think?"

The ice cube tray was burning her hand and she put it down. "I don't know. I guess so. If he had to do it..."

"I'm sure he did. I'm only saying, don't expect to meet the same Tor you left six years ago."

She handed him his glass. "Didn't you also say, that doesn't sound completely out of character for Tor? But I don't suppose he enjoyed it."

He might have though, she thought, if he was angry enough. Under those circumstances, I could have done it myself if I had Tor's nerve.

Andrei scraped the onions into a bowl. "It's a mystery how your family got out. The CIA, maybe. That's not impossible. Another of your father's last-minute leaps."

"Let's not get into that again. If he'd known about Taraki's coup, they wouldn't have gone back to Kabul last March. Do you think he'll be able to get a job here?"

"I'd say that depends on how friendly he's been to officials of this government. Or the U.N. might hire him. Then you'd all be here together and I'd never see you at all. Isn't that true?"

"I don't know, Andrei. Maybe. I'm sure we won't all live together, but it wouldn't be easy." Just now he looked very lovable sitting on that stool with a towel on his lap and a huge carrot in his left hand. She brushed a wisp of hair back off his glasses. "It might just mean I'd have to sneak around and keep you a secret the same way you've been doing with me for two years. I need to change my clothes before I start frying things. I'll be back in a minute."

In the bedroom, she took the mauve sweater he loved out of a bureau drawer, and a pair of gray slacks. A little let's-pretend, Saira, now that it's safe and you know you can keep him at a distance? Is that why you feel so warm to him today? Last time it had not been safe, and she'd wanted to kiss him, but there were other things to think about this afternoon.

She and Mummy would sleep in here. Daddy-jan would insist on that, and he and Tor would take the couch. She could make it up after Andrei left and then close it again till they came. Two sets of clean sheets. There was no time to do laundry. But they'd be too tired to notice if the pillowcases didn't match.

Pulling the sweater over her head, she hung up her suit and began to strip the bed. Pink sheets for in here, something cheerful for Mummy-jan. And the new white summer blanket. She was folding the quilt over a chair when she heard Andrei behind her, and quickly turned around.

"Why do you always do that?" he said irritably. "You act as if I were a burglar. I just wanted to ask you what else to cut up. Do you think if I come in here I'll attack you? Look, you're blushing."

He was still holding the wet knife and she pointed to it. "You don't look exactly harmless at the moment."

"No, I'm serious, Saira. We've been being so polite to each other, but if this is my last chance to see you in God knows how long, I want to get some things said. You're the one who's been keeping the secrets. You won't tell me what you're feeling, you just let me read it between the lines. You want me to see you're suffering and respond to that, but not in any intelligent way because then you might have to give it up. You blame me and yourself for things we had nothing to do with. Nothing! Now your family's coming, so you'll lock me up in a closet like your private skeleton. Okay. It probably would have happened anyway before long." His head was tilted back angrily.

"I'm sorry if I've been such a burden to you, Andrei. You offered to come here today. What am I supposed to do, send my family back to Kabul?"

"Will you listen to me? Did I say either of those things? The only way you've been a burden to me is that you won't let me help you. I love you. I hate to see you suffer for no reason. When you were little, did you play a game that if you stepped on a spot on the sidewalk you could break somebody's neck? You think because you told me a few names last year, it's our fault what happened to those people. And Mangal. That's just a superstition, can't you see it?"

"Will you please put down that knife, Andrei? You look like you're about to kill me."

"I'm sorry." He set it on the bureau. "Now will you please give me an answer?"

She pushed the quilt down into the chair. "Alright, I can't. Maybe I overreacted, but I couldn't help it. When I gave you that information it all seemed so... theoretical. Then one month later there's a coup and everyone on that list is arrested. To you they're just a bunch of faceless casualties. But I used to know them very well and now most of them are dead."

"So? I'm sorry, but there's no connection. Taraki and Amin killed their natural enemies. They didn't have your list. They didn't need it. Why don't you blame those two, or even your brother, for that matter?"

"I do." She took a step toward him, "I know I haven't been fair to you. I've just been too confused. I don't blame you if you hate me. You ought to."

He shook his head. "You do that much too well yourself. That's what I wish I could change. Maybe your family will succeed where I've failed. Are you going to tell them about me? Of course not."

"Why do you sound so bitter about them? I'm not, about your wife."

"Not anymore, you mean. Because now you know I care for you. I can't compete with your whole family, Saira, but if I won't be seeing you again, I'd like to leave things clear between us." He was pressing the tips of his fingers together the way he used to in meetings at work, when he was on the verge of losing an argument.

"I'm not sure I can't see you, Andrei. Except for a little while. It sounds as if you want to stop seeing me."

"I only said, I want to leave here with things clear between us."

"And what would I have to say to make that true?"

He rolled down his shirt sleeves, avoiding her eyes. "Well, maybe that we've loved each other. That it probably won't work out because I'm not acceptable to your parents and I won't defect to please you. That's okay if it can't be helped. But I don't want to be a bogeyman. I don't want you to rewrite history and pretend you never loved me and I haven't been a good friend to you. I want you to stop feeling guilty that when your brother died, you weren't very fond of him. Who knows, maybe in time you'll reconstruct me, the way you have Tor and Mangal."

She sat down on the bed. It was just too much. One phone call from the State Department, and a year's unfinished business had to be settled. And he made it sound so final.

"Come here, Andrei. Will you sit down for a minute?" She put a hand out to him. He took it and sat next to her. "So now it's your turn to beat me a little?"

"I should have done this months ago, Saira. I wanted it out in the open. I just didn't think you were ready before, and now my option's been called."

"That's what you say. It's scaring me. I wasn't ready for this. I know you've been a good friend to me—the only one I've had except Devika. I've been awful to you. I admit it. But lately things have been better, haven't they? Look at me. Why do we have to stop trying?"

He gave her a dry smile. "Because the world's on a different schedule than we are, and it's not going to let us catch up."

Taking her face in both his hands, he kissed her, almost coolly at first, deliberately, but then his arms were around her, lifting her onto his lap, and his warm breath against her cheek made her shiver.

He pressed his lips there. "You smell like jasmine. Saira, I've missed you so much."

"Me too, Andrei. I think about you all the time."

The hard circle of his body rocked back so they were lying on the tangled sheets. "What a waste. You silly girl."

She smiled and he kissed her again, long and deeply, until his probing mouth and the pressure of his body made her tingle. When his hand moved down the front of her sweater she arched her back, dizzy with the sudden feel of him.

"Come on, let's mess the bed up some more." His fingers were at the belt of her slacks and her legs stiffened.

"No. I can't."

"Why?" He pulled back to look at her. "It isn't even three yet. You've got lots of time."

"I know. But I'd feel like they were all standing over there watching."

"Forget them for an hour. Be here with me." His thumbs coaxed the tips of her breasts. "I've waited ten months, and I need you too."

She took his hand away and kissed it. "That's why I didn't want you to come in here. I'm sorry. I just wouldn't be comfortable."

"You were a minute ago." He traced her lips with his finger. "What if you knew we might not have another chance?"

"Because my family's coming? Or because you're sick of waiting?"

"Neither." Groping for his glasses, he put them on. "It's what I said before. I think the world has other plans, and there's nothing I can do about it."

She propped herself on an elbow. "What's that supposed to mean?"

"Just this." He stood up and went to the window. "I'm ninety percent sure that, before long, my country's going to invade yours. If you've been blaming me about Mangal, how will you feel about me then? Not too friendly, I'd guess."

"Andrei, are you serious?" Pulling her sweater straight, she moved to the edge of the bed. "What have you heard? You told me sending that battalion to the border was just saber rattling, nothing to worry about. Just to put some pressure on Taraki."

"Maybe it was then." He shrugged. "But Taraki's useless now, and we can't control Amin. They've got an ideal program and they're ramming it down people's throats as if it were deadly poison. In one year, they've managed to turn literacy and land reform into dirty words. Now this rebellion has got to the point that if we don't move in, we may lose twenty years' investment, and according to my father-in-law, the Kremlin's not about to let that happen."

"Well, your father-in-law ought to know." She found her shoe under the blanket and put it on. "Wouldn't that be a fairly absurd case of overkill? Bringing in a whole battalion to shoot a few villagers?"

"Yes, if it were a few. Apparently, it's not anymore."

"Come on, let's go in the other room. I don't want to fight in here."

"Look, it isn't my fault. I told you, we didn't want that coup just because it might have this kind of result." He followed her back toward the kitchen. "Brezhnev doesn't like to go around invading little countries. It gets him bad press. This won't help us in Africa or South America. But he'd get in worse trouble at home if he lost a border state to a bunch of Islamic fundamentalists. Those holy gentlemen who squirted acid in your sister-in-law's face. I hope you saved your chadris, Saira."

"I've never owned a veil, Andrei. Lucky me." Turning away from him, she took down a pot and filled it with cold water. "Aren't you exaggerating a bit? Maybe your 'twenty-year investment' has all been leading up to this."

"I'm only telling you what I was told. Because I thought you might be interested. The opposition's serious and it's growing."

"Well, at least it's not coming from my parents' 'elite' friends. But then they're all dead now. I forgot."

He picked up the glass of whiskey and took a swallow of it. "They're mostly alive and living in Peshawar, Saira, planning a government-in-exile, no doubt. It's the fanatics inside the country who are causing trouble. Them and their holy war. Inciting the peasants. Allah, Allah, kill a Russian and go to heaven."

"Those mullahs *are* the peasants, though. That's what you don't understand. They're our rural aristocracy. They aren't like priests. They have real power."

"And they're using it. What's the word in Pashto for lion?"

She smiled. "I think it's *sher*. Why do you want to know?"

"That's what their leader calls himself." Bending back, Andrei stretched his arms. "Sher. The Lion. And his band of sheep. But you can't make me the scapegoat this time. If Afghanistan's invaded, it will be on that man's head. Your very own Khomeini, shrouded in mystery, issuing edicts from on high. I wish you could tell me why the rest of your people should be willing to die for him. The worst is over. Soon they'll start to profit from Taraki's reforms."

"You mean, if there are any people left by then."

He slapped his hand on the counter. "If we could only get rid of Amin! He's the worst problem, and he's trying to take over now. If we could get rid of Amin and this Sher, Taraki would still have a chance."

"Then why don't you put your assassins on the job?"

"They probably are. Wouldn't that be better than sending in a battalion?"

"If it worked, it would be, yes. Kill a mullah for Brezhnev and go to Moscow. What could be more heavenly than that?"

He reached across the counter and pulled her sleeve to make her look at him. "You liked Roshana very much, didn't you."

His face was angry and she nodded, "I didn't know her very well, but when I was at Radcliffe she was like a heroine to me."

"So they burned her face with acid. Remember that, Saira. If our troops go into Kabul, consider that the alternative is a government of mullahs condemning anyone who has more than three independent ideas."

"You mean, not like in Mother Russia, where people can do whatever they want."

"That's right, or here, where everyone is free. I thought you passionately wanted women there to learn to read, and the marriage laws to be changed."

"I do. Are you saying to get that we have to let you pull the strings? That can't be right."

"If not us, who? This Khomeini-Sher, who'll wipe out all your family's achievements?"

She ran her hands through her hair in exasperation. "No. I don't know.

You're asking me to choose between a mullah and your army. There must be some other side to be on."

"Maybe, but if Taraki can't put down those rebels, Commissar Yepishev will be glad to do it. Him, not me. Just remember, I'm not the government."

"Your father-in-law's government? I bet he's in favor of it."

"Yes. They're all too old. They want to own the world before they die."

"I thought they didn't believe in private property." She wiped her hands on the kitchen towel. "Andrei, I think you should go now. This is really upsetting me, and I've got work to do."

"And as usual, you'd like to get rid of a problem by moving it somewhere else. Especially in my case."

"What else is there to say? You want me to forgive you in advance, is that it? Absolve you of responsibility? Fine. If there's an invasion, I'll read all about it in the *New York Times* and look at the pictures and tell myself: It isn't Andrei's fault, and since my family's out of there, why should I worry about it? Let socialism march over the mullahs, and good riddance. Is that how I should feel?"

He put on his jacket. "This is hopeless. I'm not telling you how to feel."

"Yes, I know. I'm totally unreasonable."

"And I love you anyway. And I wish I felt you could care for me despite events I can't control. That's what I meant when I said I wanted to leave with things clear between us."

"Alright, Andrei. I care for you. I also think it's easier to be you than me when things like this are going on. That's about as clear as I can see right now."

He held up his hands. "Okay. I hope your family arrives safely. If there's anything you need, call me at Riverdale and I'll get back to you on an outside line."

"Thanks. And I'm sorry not to be more grateful for your news report. Maybe I resent the fact that I hear what's going on at home only from you."

"Well, that won't be true after today." He kissed her cheek and she went to open the door.

"Good-bye, Andrei. Thanks for offering to help me, anyway."

"Then we're right back where we started?"

"I don't know."

"Then we'll have to wait and see. Good-bye, *petite* Saira. I hope this isn't our last good-bye."

He passed her quickly and she closed the door behind him without waiting for the elevator to come.

So it had happened again after all. Lead in the pit of her stomach. Politics, fighting, no love-making, because she was too "immature" to separate one thing from another. Even if he was right about that, it left no direction to go in. Maybe it was just as well the family was coming now, before she fell in love with him all over again.

Andrei's shaving kit, in the medicine chest—maybe she was sacrificing him to the family, but if so, she couldn't do it any other way.

She took a piece of newspaper into the bathroom, wrapped up Andrei's kit and threw it down the incinerator next to the elevator. Then she went back to turn on the shower. Pulling off her clothes, she stepped under the spray, made it hotter, and scrubbed herself with the loofah. She thought of Tor after Mangal's wedding, waving Jeffrey's letter around, falling down on the rug, and all because she wouldn't tell him how wonderful he was for taking Karima to bed. And Andrei acting superior because she wouldn't make love to him. Women were supposed to just roll over and say yes, yes, yes.

One of Mummy's letters had said Karima was working for Taraki, and maybe Tor was the reason why. To give other women some rights and protection. Even if Taraki had killed Mangal.

What would Roshana make of all this?

She remembered coming home from Radcliffe that sophomore summer and seeing Roshana's burned face, purple scars running down her cheek like trickles of blood. Roshana comforting *her*: "Ho Chi Minh says nothing is more important than freedom and independence. I think that goes for women too, Saira."

And Royila, that same summer, announcing that her parents refused to let her go on with her studies. Was that when she first had the idea of killing herself?

The next summer, when she did, I was swimming at Plum Island, getting ready to fall in love with Jeffrey, Saira thought. If it weren't for what happened to Royila, I wouldn't have slept with Jeffrey and Tor would never have found his letter. Then I'd be living in Kashmir with Ashraf now. If I hadn't laughed at Tor, he might have gone to Columbia and he'd be here making dinner instead of me.

Dressing in a different sweater and slacks, she made up the beds and started frying onions. Tor had been in Moscow for more than five years now. How would that have changed him? If he had to choose between a mullah and the Red Army, which one would he pick?

To calm down, she put on Chopin's Nocturnes. The birds started singing wildly, in perfect pitch with the record, and she found herself smiling again. Tonight would be a new beginning for them, here, together, and Andrei had even cut the onions for her.

Six steps to Raima's recipe, one after the other. It took a long time to make this pilau. You had to be careful.

She was just mounding the rice on a platter when the doorbell rang.

Twenty-Nine

"Won't you have a little more rice, Daddy-jan?" Saira touched his shoulder gently, offering the platter. It was painful to see the effort it had cost him to finish one small portion.

"Tomorrow, jan. I'm very tired, forgive me."

"Your bed's all made up. I hope it's comfortable. Mummy? Would you like more?"

"No, dear, thank you. What I really need now is a bath." She touched her hair, then dropped the hand back to her lap.

"Of course!" Saira put down the dish. "Let me run one for you. Tor? I've never known you to refuse a second helping of anything."

He looked up from under swollen eyelids. "It's very good, Saira, honestly." But he didn't even glance at the pilau.

In the bathroom, Saira turned the taps on full and sat on the edge of the tub twisting a washcloth in her hands. They're like robots, she thought, they must be in shock. Maybe I can get a doctor in to see them tomorrow.

A personal escort from the State Department! Somehow she had imagined them arriving well dressed and with large suitcases. But they had nothing at all. Daddy-jan was wearing a crumpled brown suit that smelled faintly of dung, Mummy had on her old blue dress, and Tor... Tor looked like a village boy in his black turban and baggy clothes.

They had come through the desert with a kuchi caravan and met Jonathan

Straight at Quetta. That was all they had told her. They could hardly speak.

She poured oil into the bath and set out a bottle of shampoo. Daddy-jan and Tor would need her razor. What else? A clean nightgown for Mummy. Tomorrow they could make up a shopping list. Tor would probably want some jeans.

She looked up as her mother came to the door. "Your bath's ready. I'll get you a nightgown."

"Thank you, dear. Be quiet on your way. Your father's gone to bed." She was leaning heavily against the wall. "If I don't come out in ten minutes you can assume I've fallen asleep."

"I won't let you drown." Saira hugged her. "Your suntan's very becoming." She touched the kuchi bangle on her mother's thin wrist. "Was it really awful, Mummy?"

"Coming out? Yes and no. In one sense, it was a vindication. But leaving home, leaving everything... even my pictures," her voice broke. "We may not ever be able to go back."

Over her mother's shoulder, Saira caught her own reflection in the mirror. Never to go back. Having lived with that might be the best help she could offer.

"I know, Mummy. But at least we'll all be together and you won't have to worry about Daddy-jan anymore. I want to look after you for a change while you figure out what your plans are. Besides, *you* left Boston for Kabul, remember? It's meant a lot for me to know that since I've been here. And you had to leave everything then too."

"Yes." She smiled. "When I was young, and adaptable, and enthusiastic."

"Come on! You have more energy than the rest of us put together."

"Once upon a time, maybe. At the moment, I feel ancient and not very wise. I don't know how those kuchis manage in that sun day after day, but I'll tell you all about them in the morning. Right now I'm going to have a soak and get into bed. The thought of a bed was the only thing that kept me alive today."

"Good." Saira kissed her. "I'll toss you in a nightgown. I want to talk to Tor for a while, so just go to sleep. I'm so happy you're here, Mummy-jan." She went out, closing the door softly.

Across the hall, Tor was prowling in the kitchen restlessly, and she moved the sandalwood screen to shield her father from the light. Thank heaven she had remembered to throw out Andrei's bottle of Scotch.

"Can I get you anything more, Tor?" she whispered. "Another pot of tea? I don't have any men's pajamas, I'm afraid," she stopped, embarrassed, but he didn't seem to notice. He was looking straight through her as if thinking of something else.

"Could we go out for a walk?" he said suddenly. "I feel like I've been in one box after another for the past two days."

She smiled. "You want to go out in those clothes?"

"What's wrong with them?" His tone made her wince. "They're Afghan clothes. So what? I thought everyone was supposed to be welcome in New York."

"Shhh. They are. But they might get stared at." She tried another tack. "You look really good, Tor. I mean, I can see how tired you are, but you're also very handsome, little brother."

"Handsome?" He gave a short laugh. "Well, let me return the compliment, Saira-jan. You look like a movie star. And this is quite a palace. You should have seen my room in Moscow."

"Oh, now don't you start," she forced a smile. "When Daddy was here last spring he made me feel guilty for having a doorman."

"Daddy's had a doorman in Kabul lately. But I had to fire him. Come on, Saira, let's go out."

"Alright." She hesitated. "Tor, I'm really sorry you had to go to Moscow. It would have been fun to be here together."

He was staring at her oddly again. "Or there, or in Kabul. But we weren't. Look, if you don't want to come, give me your key and I'll go alone."

"No, just let me get Mummy a nightgown." She took one from her bedroom closet and passed it into the bathroom, trying not to show her irritation. Tor's eyes were always easy to read. She was too fancy, the apartment too grand, and he was a noble savage. So that was his new passion, after three days with the kuchis.

Outside, a cool breeze blew down the length of 86th Street and she inhaled it gratefully, turning toward the river. Try, try again, she thought. Mangal put up with more than that from me.

"I just want to show you this place for a minute, Tor. It's sort of dangerous at night, but it's my favorite spot and tomorrow we can bring a picnic here. I love the way those trees look against the sky."

"Sky? Is that the sky? Thank you for telling me. All the way here in the taxi I was wondering where it was."

He stood gazing out across the river with his long shirt flapping, and she reminded herself how exhausted he must be. Of course he was tense and grumpy. She'd just ignore his sarcasm. Just ignore it.

"Come on." She took his elbow—then stepped back startled as he wheeled, snarling.

"My arm!" He looked like a stranger. "Sorry"—he cradled it—"but that hurt. And I guess I'm still pretty edgy."

"Just a bit." She smiled with relief as the wildness left his eyes. "We ought to go, though. It really isn't safe here now."

"Or anywhere else. Haven't you figured that out yet?" He followed her to the crosswalk. "Is there some place we can get a drink?"

"You mean, as in alcohol?"

"Yes. Don't worry, I won't get drunk and ruin your reputation."

"No, I'm just thinking. There's a restaurant called The Library over on Broadway."

"My, no wonder the Americans are losing the arms race. They drink in the library!" He was smiling at her sideways, apologetically. "No, I'm kidding. That sounds good, I've always wanted to see Broadway."

"This is the wrong end though, Tor. Don't expect much glitter." She buttoned her jacket. There was nothing wrong with Tor's wanting a drink. Anyway, it might help calm him down.

The Library was crowded for a Tuesday night, but twenty minutes later they were seated at a round oak table that gave views of both the street and the bar. Tor studied the list of cocktails on the back of the menu. "My God, what are all these things? You'd better order, Saira-gak. What's a Tequila Sunrise?"

"Oh, that might be a good idea. I don't know what most of them are myself, but my friend Devika always gets a tequila drink when we come here. It's called a margarita, and it's very good."

"I'll try anything once." Tor waved at the waiter. "Now doesn't he look cute."

Taking in Tor's costume, the waiter pointed to his name tag as if they wouldn't understand him. "Hi, my name's Todd. I'll be your server tonight."

"It's alright, comrade, we aren't deaf. Two margaritas, please."

"Straight up, or on the rocks?"

"On the rocks," Saira smiled.

When he left, Tor said innocently, "Is it alright if I fish the rocks out of mine? I'm afraid I'll break my teeth."

Now he was turning on the charm, to make up for his rudeness before, and she grinned. "Rocks are ice, silly. That's your first lesson in American English. By the way, don't look now, but that blonde over there wants to eat you up."

Tor's eyes swiveled. "My second lesson! Americans are cannibals. Do you know, in Moscow you'd wait six hours to get into a place like this? Except it wouldn't be like this and all they'd have is vodka."

"Ugh. You must have hated it there."

"Till last year," he shrugged. "I've got a girl there now. A friend."

She teased, "From Mummy's letters, it sounds like you've had several. Tor, th3 e scourge of Moscow University."

"Yes, I've been a great sinner. How about you? Have you committed any new sins here?"

"Oh, a few thousand. Just not the same kind as yours. I only did one of those, but it was a big one."

"You'd better watch out, Saira-jan! The last time we had this conversation it didn't turn out too well. My," he said as the drinks were delivered, "these look interesting. Do they all come covered with sugar in the States?"

"That's salt, Tor. It's a Mexican drink." She lifted her glass. "Well, here's to your escape. Thank goodness you all made it."

He was licking some grains of salt off his hand. "And to the revolution. May it never be tired."

She took a careful sip to cover her confusion. The revolution? Which one was he talking about?

"Whew! That's salt alright, but it's good. I feel halfway to Mexico already."

Something in his voice just then reminded her of the other time she had seen him drink... holding out the cognac bottle. "Oooh, Saira, it burns!" Maybe it had been a mistake to bring him here after all. Daddy-jan would blame her if anything happened. Again.

She put down her glass. "So, tell me about your adventures. Mr. CIA came through in the pinch?"

"In the last pinch, anyway," he nodded. "You probably won't believe this, but I wound up almost liking him. He's really upset about what's going on at home. In fact, I wouldn't be surprised if he knows the countryside better than we do. I thought I'd been all over Paktia, but... have you heard of a place called Mirzaka?"

She shook her head. "I thought you went through Kandahar."

Tor drained his glass. "That's right, we did. But first I got kidnapped to Mirzaka, or a little village right on top of it. To the camp of this maniac, Sher. You probably haven't heard of him yet, but believe me, you will. I think I'd like another of these drinks, if I can catch our toy waiter. How about you?"

"You'd better take it easy, Tor. They're stronger than they taste."

She didn't know what else to answer. If she admitted having heard of Sher, Tor would keep digging at her until he found out who had told her.

"Saira, are you there?"

"Yes. I'm just trying to decide..."

"Bring two more," he told the waiter. "Women can never make up their minds. And how about some of those crackers all the other tables have?"

When he turned back to her she tried to smile. "I didn't know you were kidnapped!"

He nodded, "I got tricked at my own game again, but this time it was alright. I spent a night on the moon with some rebels and learned how to make grenades. God, they have guts. I felt like a sissy."

Saira frowned. "They may be brave, but they're pretty shortsighted. All that fighting will just bring in the Red Army."

"My dear Saira, the Red Army's there! In Kabul there are tanks on every street corner."

"But not troops! And even the tanks will probably leave when things quiet down a bit."

Tor shook his head. "With all respect, I don't think you know what you're talking about. You haven't been home in years."

Yes, she thought, and whose fault is that? Don't tell me what I know. "So you were home for a week, which makes you an expert, right?"

She was joking, but Tor nodded seriously. "You can learn a lot in a week, if it's from the right people. I've wanted to murder Taraki ever since he killed Mangal, and now I have other reasons too." He hunched forward in his chair, "Have you ever heard of a village named Kerala?"

As he moved, his crystal pendant slid through the opening of his shirt and Saira closed her eyes for a minute. "What is this, a geography lesson? Tor, the 'people' you've just discovered are going to get themselves killed. I hate Taraki's tactics too, but you have to separate that from the real progress he's trying to make."

Tor stiffened. "Easy for you to say. The people just want to live the way they always have. What's so bad about that?"

"Even if they have no jobs or doctors and girls don't go to school?"

"It's better than what's happening now. Everyone's going nuts."

"At first, maybe. But when things settle down, it should be better than before. Afghanistan has to join the twentieth century, Tor. Not just us. People like my friend Royila—and Bibi Nawabi, remember her? Having a nineteen-year-old girl brought in as her husband's second wife? And that's in Kabul. In the countryside, it's about a hundred times worse. Those are problems that don't affect you, so you never think about them. You've always had more freedom than anyone else I know. But it isn't like that for most people. Just look at the difference between you and me. In Kabul I'd be considered unmarriageable, but you wouldn't."

A tray descended between them and they watched each other in silence while the waiter set two more salt-rimmed glasses and a basket of fish-shaped crackers on the table.

Tor took a long swallow of his drink. "It's really funny that you say I've had freedom, considering where I've been at school. If you think that kind of government's so wonderful, you should try living in Moscow for a while."

"I'd do better there than I would in most of Afghanistan."

"So, good for you. Go live in Moscow."

"I don't want to, Tor. That's exactly what I don't want. But let's not go backward, either. Besides, if Taraki's overthrown, the Russians will take right over."

"See," Tor smiled thinly. "That's what I meant about your not having been there. My dear Saira, Afghanistan's as good as a Soviet state already. They're painting Kabul red right now. And I don't know what 'progress' you're talking about. Every change they've made so far is a joke. Why don't you root for Taraki, and I'll take the rebels, and we'll see who wins in the end."

She hid behind her glass. Another drink she didn't want. But of course Tor would think those reforms were a joke, having never wanted for anything.

Naturally he'd romanticize the rebels—that was what he loved—camping out and shooting guns, making grenades with the boys. What fun.

"Tell me," he said, "what makes you think those tanks will leave? You sound so definite. I don't believe it. Who told you that, somebody at the U.N.?"

Involuntarily, she drew back as if Andrei had materialized behind him. But that was just more stupid guilt and it opened into anger. The truth was, Tor wouldn't believe she could reach any conclusions on her own.

She said coolly, "It stands to reason, Tor. They don't want to be there."

He was eyeing her untouched second drink. "I thought maybe the Afghan Mission was pushing propaganda at you. Look, I couldn't tell what was going on from Moscow either, but Saira, it's not a few tanks. It's MIG jets, helicopter gunships, Soviet 'advisers' wearing Afghan army uniforms. You know how the villagers feel about people from Kabul, let alone the Russians. What right does any outsider have to tell us how to live?"

"Us? You're including yourself in this?"

Tor glared. "Yes, of course I am. I still consider myself Afghan, even if you don't."

"As it happens, I do. But we aren't the point of this. Would you live in one of those villages? Never. We're able to live very well no matter what anyone tells us, but most of those people are trapped. A lot of them don't like it anymore. If you want to blame someone for Taraki, why not try your holy men? It's the mullahs who are telling the people: don't learn, don't read, Allah is the answer. They've held back the countryside just to maintain their own power. Mangal knew that, and he tried—"

"And Taraki killed him for it! Are you saying those tanks have a right to be in Kabul? You don't know what you're talking about, Saira. It's not your fault. I have to believe that. The alternative is—"

"What?"

He shook his head. "I don't like to say it."

"Go on!"

"No." His eyes challenged her. "I might regret it later."

The blonde at the next table was watching them with open interest now. Saira lowered her voice. "This is so typical of you, Tor! You spend two days in a village, hear one point of view from some wildmen who love fighting more than anything else, and since that appeals to you too, right away you're ready to start a war. If a thousand innocent peasants happen to get caught in the crossfire—well, that's tribal honor for you."

"Yes," he said softly. "At Kerala, it was a thousand." He was staring at her, shaking his head. "Forget it, Saira. You don't know. If Sher's a wildman, I'll take him any day over a third-rate ass like Taraki. But I guess since he's killed off all the real brains in the country you think he's some kind of genius. It must take brilliance to murder little babies like Yusef and girls like Roshana."

"Roshana was hardly a girl, Tor."

"Oh, well, that's alright then. Was it okay for him to kill Mangal too?"

"Take my drink if you want it. I don't. Has it ever occurred to you that Mangal helped start all this back in '73?"

"That's a year I try hard to forget," he smiled tightly.

"Good luck. I wish I could. My life broke in two pieces that night, and so did yours."

"You were here before then. For four years."

"And you've been in Moscow for almost six. Does that mean you want to live there forever? It's different from being a foreign student. Knowing I couldn't go back home happened for me after Mangal's wedding. For you, it's been less than a week." The tension in her chest was easing. Tor had just come out of the desert. It was wrong to expect him to see more than that now. How could she say, "But my ex-lover's father-in-law spends every other weekend at Brezhnev's dacha, and he tells me if Taraki goes, we'll be invaded." That would just make Tor madder and he'd never believe she was even more furious about it.

She took a deep breath. "We've been together three hours and we're already fighting."

Across the room, someone laughed loudly and beer mugs rang together in a toast. Tor's fingers closed around the crystal pendant. "So what am I going to do here? I was thinking about it last night, and I'm sure the Soviets won't release my transcript now. In three more months I would at least have had a diploma to prove I was there."

He looked dejected suddenly and she touched his hand. "This is supposed to be the land of opportunity, remember? With your talents, you'll find something interesting." And I'll bet Andrei can arrange to get your records sent out, she thought. "What have you been majoring in?"

"Oh, lots of things! Journalism, physics, history. I switched to history last year so I could go to class with my friend Liz."

Saira couldn't help smiling. But Tor had never got by on his grades. "And they let you? Then you don't have a major."

His eyes flickered. "Go ahead and laugh. I'm not like you and Mangal, but that doesn't mean I'm useless."

"That's just what I've been saying."

He settled back a little, sipping from her drink. "Alright. Then give me some ideas."

"Well, you could apply at the U.N. . . ." To do what, she wondered. Translators had to be trained at the Geneva school. No, he wouldn't qualify for anything there without a degree. "Tor, New York's full of exciting things. Film studios, newspapers, even a few stables, if you're still so crazy about horses. I'm not saying it's going to be easy. You'll have to work hard. No one cares who we are here."

"You mean, you don't think I can." He flushed. "Maybe you're right too, Saira. I'm not sure I even want to try." He was sticking his chin out stubbornly. Tor, who'd never done any work in his life except when forced.

She folded her hands. "Since we aren't rich anymore, you won't have a choice for once."

"No, that's how *you* think!" His nostrils flared. "You haven't changed, Saira. You're always such a good little girl, but you aren't any better than I am. I remember Mangal's wedding too—Saira with her French perfume and Commie newspapers. Now here you are, all dressed up, with your New York apartment, telling me I have to be like you. But you don't *do* anything, you just yak about it from a nice safe distance. Compared to my friend Elizabeth, you're just a baby, crying about things that should be forgotten! Go ahead, rub it in some more. If I'm bad, that makes you good, right? Responsible, and—"

"Oh, stop it, Tor! I knew this would happen! You're so holy now? You always find some romantic excuse for acting like a child. I think you're just jealous. You were jealous of Ashraf and me, so you wrecked things for us then, and you're jealous that I came to the States and you had to go to Moscow. You're the one who always loved expensive things, being lazy and having the best clothes and horses. You must hope if you side with the mullahs they'll get it all back for you so you can be a little playboy again. But they won't. We're out of it, whether you like it or not. You'll just have to work for a living like the rest of us peasants, and you'll find out how 'easy' it is to make it in New York...."

"Good-bye, I'm leaving." He stood up and drained his glass. "I'll get your doorman to let me in later."

"No," she grabbed his wrist. "Sit down, Tor. Let's get the check and go. You can't just walk around here at night. Come on, we're both upset. Please."

"Let go of me." He wrenched his hand away, "I want to be by myself now. But Saira, I think you're the one who's jealous. You've been 'out of it' for years, so you want the rest of us to join you. So what if the Russians take over? Just turn your back and walk away. Well, if you can do that, so can I to you." He put his face close to hers. "And as for it's not being safe here... I've already killed two men this week. That takes care of Mangal and Roshana. But I need one more to make up for Yusef, so I hope somebody jumps me tonight. Good-bye, dear sister."

He pushed his way out through the bar and the swinging door closed behind him.

She had half risen, but sat down shaking. Following him would mean a worse fight in the street. Tor was ready to blow now, better left alone.

And me too, she thought. Oh God, where did all that come from? Am I still so angry at him?

He wouldn't get lost. He was too smart for that. Tor was the only one who thought he was stupid.

But he could be so cruel, as if he had the right and everyone else was supposed to smile at his tantrums no matter how much they hurt.

Not me though, Tor. Not anymore. I don't care how tired you are. I haven't been feeling so wonderful myself.

Why did it always turn out like this? The only way to get along with Tor or Daddy or Mangal was to agree with everything they said. That was the same as admitting they were right and you were wrong, making yourself a liar. But the alternative was arguing, and they'd use any insult to shut you off, to keep from losing, and it worked every time.

Tor was so afraid of having to work and not being special anymore. He shouldn't worry. One of Daddy-jan's old friends would probably hand him a job out of sympathy, and then Tor could run around charming everyone and never lift a finger.

He'd do just fine in New York. In those clothes, telling stories that made him the hero of their escape. The blonde girl at the next table was still staring after him—Tor, so attractive with his pretty brown eyes and his dangerous smile. If he'd snapped his fingers and said, "Come with me," that blonde would have followed him into the street.

Killed two men this week, he said. The guard at the house and who else? He seemed to have enjoyed it after all. Tor had always loved shooting rabbits and bringing home their bodies to wave under her nose so he could hear her squeal. Now he must picture himself as Genghis Khan, or Tamerlane, or Abdur Rahman.

Saira laughed out loud. Tor as Tamerlane? He was much too skinny. Sher, this Mr. Lion, what would he look like? A mullah with a long gray beard and turban, taking Tor on his knee. "My son, we want our land back. Here is a grenade. Join our Holy War and whatever loot you get, we'll split it fifty-fifty." Where did Tor say his camp was? Someplace called Kerala? No, before that. In Paktia...Mirzaka, that was it. How funny. All those soldiers looking for Sher, and she knew where he was. At home they didn't have any idea, but here the location of Sher's camp was talked about in public bars. It was true, you could find anything in New York.

"...chair?" a voice said. "Do you mind?"

She looked up at a blue and gold Yale sweatshirt, a blond head, light blue eyes. He said, "If your friend isn't coming back, we'd like to borrow this chair." He was grinning, great big perfect teeth. She said, "He is coming back." The boy stepped away, raising one hand. "Okay, sorry to bother you." He turned to the blonde girl. "If you aren't waiting for someone..." A matched set, Saira thought. I must seem crazy, or else why did he look at me so strangely?

Maybe Tor really would come back. He might even apologize. He was good at that, and being cruel. Turn her back and walk away! It was his fault she had left home in the first place.

But staying here was my idea, she admitted. And not only because of losing Ashraf. I didn't go back, because for me there was no alternative to getting married or living at home. That doesn't mean I don't care. It doesn't mean I have no rights now, does it?

Devika says living here causes the least harm. But you can't even be sure of that. I did give those names to Andrei, and there's always the chance they made a shade of difference at some point. I'll never know.

Still, I do know something Tor doesn't seem to understand. The alternative to Taraki is a mullah or an invasion. Khomeini's been in Tehran one month and they're back in the Middle Ages already. But an invasion would be even worse, so we're stuck with Taraki. Maybe some Russian assassins will get rid of Amin soon. And Sher. Then the government could be saved. All they'd have to do was come to a bar called The Library on the Upper West Side of Manhattan island and several people could tell them where Sher's camp was. That blonde girl, for one.

Saira picked up her drink and put it down again.

And me for another, she thought. I could tell them too.

The palms of her hands went cold, then burned, and she flattened them against the sides of the glass. This wasn't good or funny at all.

Tor must not realize the difference between a few tanks and a battalion if he thought things were bad at home now. And he accused her of being out of touch. "My dear Saira, I have to believe you don't know what you're talking about. The alternative is..." What? That she did know.

Sher, whom Andrei said could bring the invasion. Sher and Amin.

Saira turned toward the window and looked out at the street. There were knots of students wearing T-shirts on the corner, and older people walking by. Everyone looked happy it was finally spring.

In Kabul, it would be warmer now. Petals all over the ground and fruit starting to set. This year there were also brown Soviet tanks. Tor had seen them and they scared him.

I don't want to do this, she thought. I can't. Everybody says I never stick my neck out and they're right, I don't.

Except that last time. The list of names. But I didn't know what I was doing then. This time, I would. If I tell Andrei where Sher's camp is, I'll be responsible for people getting killed. The peasants I've been telling Tor he ought to care about.

Andrei said, "If Afghanistan's invaded, it will be on that man's head." Then thousands more would die.

And on my head too, if I could have stopped it?

But why should I do anything to help Taraki keep on making mincemeat out of everything? He killed Mangal and Roshana. And Yusef. Besides, Sher probably wasn't at Mirzaka anymore. Didn't guerrilla fighters move around all the time?

Better not to know and to do nothing.

So many alternatives. If I tell Andrei, I'll be a murderer too. If I don't, and the country's invaded, I'll think maybe I could have prevented it.

This had to be decided.

Telling Andrei would mean never seeing him again, because this time she would know what she was doing. Giving secrets to the enemy. Betrayal. Right here in this bar, since she couldn't call him from home.

There was a phone booth by the ladies' room at the head of the stairs. If she turned to look back, she could see it.

"Miss?" the waiter set another drink in front of her. "This is from that fellow over there, to apologize for bothering you before."

Saira followed his glance. The Yale sweatshirt was grinning at her. She said, "Take it away, please. I don't want it."

"But it's paid for."

"I told you, I don't want it!"

Shrugging, the waiter cleared the table and walked away.

Her cheeks were hot. What did that sweatshirt expect? That having one full drink, she'd take another and then let him sit down? Did she have a mark on her forehead saying: Woman of no virtue? Why hadn't he tried the blonde girl?

Roshana was a woman of no virtue. And Royila and Devika. There must be thousands then, getting out or killing themselves, and a few million more who couldn't do either. At least Taraki was trying to change that. He might not be a great administrator, but he was a patriotic Afghan and not a mullah, grabbing land and burning women's faces. Tor *would* find a self-righteous bandit to worship.

Roshana and Mangal had stuck their necks out. The '73 coup wasn't very violent, but it easily could have been. They took that chance into account. The few, risked for the many.

I can walk out of here and go home, or I can call Andrei, she thought. Maybe it's time I stuck my neck out too. Given what Taraki's done to our family, no one could accuse me of acting in our interests.

Tor had probably gone home to bed. She would creep in and hear them all breathing.

This would mean standing alone, though, out in the cold. Not so simple as throwing grenades. That's what Tor couldn't see. The hard part was figuring things out the way they really were, and then deciding what to do about it. Not having fun, but making these decisions.

Tor had killed two men to revenge Mangal and Roshana.

Why not for Royila?

No, the killing wouldn't be for Royila. Only the hope afterwards. She had a younger sister living in Kabul.

New York

It would take a lot of change to call the Soviet complex in Riverdale. Saira looked in her coin purse. Two dollars or more in change.

First she would ask him again: This Sher is really the worst threat? He had been very convincing this afternoon. So she'd tell him Mirzaka, and I can't see you again. No games this time. No offer of a choice between herself and a piece of information. No ambiguity. Just her own decision, and then walk out to the street and step in front of a fast car.

If Mummy-jan wasn't here now, that would be tempting.

Picking up her purse, Saira walked quickly toward the phone booth.

By the time Tor reached the river, he knew he had to go back. Not to The Library or Saira's apartment, but back home and soon, before he lost his taste for dusty blankets and sour cheese.

Coming out of the bar, he had run against the light across the avenue, waving his arms at a red Mercedes that screeched to a stop, honking angrily. Behind its windshield, two women looked startled at the sight of him caught by their headlamps, and grinning, he called, "Forgive me, friends, my camel got away!"

After the stuffy air in the bar, he felt as if he could fly. The river, that was where he wanted to be, and he even remembered the turns they had made. New York, after the desert.

Maybe it wasn't nice to leave Saira back there alone, but there were taxis in the street that she could take, and if he'd stayed one more minute he would have started shouting at her. What would be the point of that? It wasn't her fault she didn't know what was going on. She was here because he had wrecked her life and she'd never forget that.

None of them ever let him forget anything.

As soon as they got to Pakistan, Daddy-jan had taken over. For two days in three different airports he'd made it clear that he was in charge again. So now they were here, and that was good for them, but it already felt like living in the Kabul house—Saira telling him what to wear and lecturing him: "You have to work hard, Tor!"

As if the desert could be forgotten and Moscow had never existed.

Let Saira talk. She hadn't seen anything. She wouldn't have heard what happened at Kerala. He should have told her about that.

But it had taken the Abdullahs one whole year to get him to listen to their stories. Maybe she didn't want to know any more than he had.

Turning onto 86th Street, he saw the expanse of the riverbank up ahead and walked more quickly. What would Comrade Liz be doing now? Eating lunch while Nadia watched, asking for the tenth time: "Are you sure Tor didn't say he might not come back?"

Since he hadn't, Liz would really be surprised. Nadia ought to be able to tell that. And they couldn't do more than question her, could they? She was sponsored by the British ambassador.

Every time he thought about her, he felt worse. He'd been risking her too, without seeing it. No use curling up in a ball and pretending they were still in their room. That was over, and it could be finished this time. Remembering just made him ache for her warmth, her low voice: "Tor, we can sort it out." He might never hear those words or feel her arms again.

Unless somehow she could come here or he could go to England, months or years from now. Till then he'd go crazy missing her, taking orders from Saira and Daddy-jan, who liked putting him in his place.... Be responsible, get a job, Tor. It doesn't matter what.

Be a camel. Carry boxes.

Maybe he could be a toy waiter. You didn't need a diploma for that. If the whole family stayed in Saira's little apartment, working at The Library would be more fun than going home at night. He could wear a name tag and waltz around the tables, smiling at that blonde girl who made cute faces whenever Saira turned away, her shiny lipstick and gold neck chains winking at him in the dark. Someday he'd be too lonesome to keep walking past her. Those sweet drinks—sneak a few of those on the side and then Daddy-jan would start smelling his breath when he came in. "Oh, Tor!"

Oh, Toryalai, you could get in a lot of trouble here. After what's happened, it's too soon to try to be a nice little boy. You'll start drinking again, and by the time Liz comes, it will be too late.

Because I am going to see her again, he decided, even if it takes five years. So if I'm going to make trouble in the meanwhile, I might as well be where it can do some good.

Crossing to the riverbank, he slid partway down the grassy slope and sat by a clump of bushes that hid him but gave a broad view of the path. There was no sign of anyone else around.

Why not go back? Liz would understand that. She'd respect it, if nobody else did. Even if he only helped Nur-Ali make grenades for three months, till Liz got back to England. And he could write to her. That would be better than saying, "Yes, I'm a toy waiter now. Don't you want to come and live with me?" It was people like Yelena she admired, and Kostia Ivanov. She'd probably like Nur-Ali too.

Kostia and Nur-Ali. They even looked alike. And he'd said the same about both of them: idiots. Kostia was a martyr alright. He'd been rotting in Lefortovo prison for over a year. But a few fools could do something even in Moscow. Liz had brought their manuscript out, with a little help from the Black Wasp.

Liz was smart in Saira's way, and she thought he had talent. No one in the family would admit that. "Get serious, Tor. You can't ride horses all your life."

But for a few months, why not?

Nur-Ali was doing something at home. And the Abdullahs and Karima. Even Daddy-jan had wanted to stay in Kabul instead of running to Peshawar.

He was no coward, either. He knew it was better to stay on the inside where you could see what was happening than to believe how things looked from a distance.

Tor rubbed his cold hands together. In Moscow he had known that, before the coup. Before Elizabeth.

Too used to being in charge? So what? If you were good at it.

Even with his bad arm, Ghulam-Nabi should welcome him, after he fussed about it, and Nur-Ali would give him a thin smile. "Did you take good care of my nice pistol?"

Yes, until I used it, Tor thought. You were right, I didn't like shooting the guard. And that Russian wasn't happy to lose his nose. Let me sit around and make grenades now.

Going, without having been here. Pulling him, sucking him back. Because it was closer to Liz, who might already have left Moscow?

He slipped his hand into his pocket—he even had enough money. Then, under Straight's folded bills, his fingers touched a sharp edge and he drew out the few gray pebbles he had picked up at Sher's camp. For a minute, looking down at them, he tried to recall what automatic gesture had saved them.

Standing up, he tossed the stones one by one into the river.

He climbed the bank, starting to picture the scene his decision would cause. By the time he reached the crosswalk it seemed it would be best to leave tonight. If he told them, they'd try to stop him. Mummy-jan might cry, and then he could wind up being a waiter and slowly going nuts. Talking about it would only end up in an argument. They'd had enough of that already.

He touched the money again. There wasn't any reason to go back to Saira's apartment. On Broadway, lots of shops were still open. He could buy some paper, write them a note, and break one five-hundred-dollar bill.

Three stores said they couldn't give him change. At the fourth, a small market, he offered a deal: He'd pay twenty dollars for the service.

The manager's hair was gray but he looked ready for a fight. "You printed this up yourself, kid?"

"It's real." Tor smiled sweetly. "I've just had an emergency."

The bill was being held up under a brilliant purple light. "Yeah, this looks okay, I guess. What are you, Indian?"

"I'm half American and half Afghan, and I'm offering you free money."

"Hey, my sister makes Afghans!" He grinned. "George, did you hear that? This guy's an Afghan." The pale lips twisted, "You got some I.D.?"

Tor's hand moved toward the pouch at his belt, but then he changed his mind. Never again would he put his passport into a strange hand. He said, "Nothing in New York, if that's what you mean."

"Then I'm afraid I'll need a little more profit, kid. To cover the risk I'm taking. Give me fifty, take it or leave it."

You bastard, Tor thought, you better pray I don't come back here. But it was late and there might be no other choice. He said, "I'll take it and some paper, if I can write a letter here."

"Sure. You can write all you want."

Standing at the counter, he scribbled,

Dear Daddy-jan, Mummy and Saira,

No, I didn't rob anyone. This money came from Jonathan Straight to help the U.S. economy, so I hope you'll use it.

You won't like this, but I've decided to go back. You'll be better off without me for a while and I need to be outdoors. I'm going to where Ghulam-Nabi is. He'll keep an eye on me. Don't worry, I'll be careful, and I'll see you in a few months.

Love,
Toryalai

Turning his back on the counter, he slipped two of the three bills left into the envelope.

Five minutes later, he climbed the front steps of Saira's apartment building. The doorman pocketed ten dollars and promised that in exactly an hour he'd slip the note under her door.

Tor walked back to Broadway and caught a cab. In Moscow he would have bargained for the fare. Asking for Kennedy airport, he settled back on the seat, telling his sore muscles to relax. In two days or less he'd be home again, which right now meant Sher's camp.

Thirty

THE TRIP TO London took six hours and then there was a wait of three more while British Airways #174 became flight 147 to Karachi—a switch from a Boeing 707 to a Lockheed Tri-Star that Tor watched half asleep through the plate glass wall fronting Terminal 3. England, Elizabeth, but he couldn't think of her now. It took all his energy just to change a few dollars and fill his pockets with candy from the vending machine outside the gate.

At Dubai and Kuwait his streaked window framed nondescript views of night sky and tarmac, and pulling a thin blanket up against the artificial light, he made himself deaf and blind. He had never been so tired, as if the close bad air were drugged, and he wondered if he'd ever wake up and what day it was. He wore no watch and, after London, had lost track of the time.

A voice announcing their descent to Karachi said it was 1:30 AM, and half an hour later, standing in the passport line at the sprawling, seedy airport, Tor realized that Wednesday had been lost in travel and he had just a hundred and fifty dollars left. Nervously he began to figure how much he'd need to reach the northwest frontier. The train trip to Peshawar was more than a thousand kilometers, and first he had to get to Karachi station.

Examining his passport, the young control guard mumbled something in Urdu to his colleague and Tor interrupted, "It's alright, I speak English. I'll just be in Pakistan for two days, taking the Khyber Mail on my way back to Kabul."

"Hmmm." The guard stabbed a finger at the small black folder. "Would you explain how you have a Pakistani exit visa dated two days ago, but no previous entry visa?"

His face hardened and a spasm of fear brought Tor fully awake. No, he thought, this can't happen now, I don't have any money to spend on bribes. The guard was wearing an Islamic symbol on a gold chain around his neck. Maybe the truth would work better than a lie.

"I had to leave Afghanistan informally," he said. "My government didn't want to lose someone of my...sympathies."

"Ah." The dark eyes flickered. "Will they be willing to have you back?"

Tor smiled. "Much too willing."

"You were in the U.S. for only twelve hours. Was that a business trip?"

Now he thinks I'm a smuggler, Tor cursed silently. "No, I was escorting my parents to New York. My mother's an American citizen. I haven't brought anything back, no luggage at all."

"That's for customs to see. My concern, Mr. Anwari, is that we have many Afghan nationals coming into Pakistan who are engaged in subversive activities against their government. Of course we cannot officially support this."

Had there been a slight emphasis on the word "officially"? Tor looked down at the black passport held firmly by that small brown hand. "By the Prophet, blessed be his name, I swear I have no intention of staying in Pakistan or abusing the hospitality of your country. I only want to go back to my home."

He had imitated Nur-Ali's tone, but the tremor in his own voice was authentic if not pious, and it had the right effect. The guard's mouth hinted at a smile. "I really should detain you, but the line's very long today. So I'll give you a fifteen-day transit visa with requirements for police registration and hope that you'll remember this oath, Mr. Anwari. Unless you want to go through the city, there's a juncture for the Peshawar train across the road."

Thanking him, Tor made his way out through the crowded lobby where whole families leaned together sleeping. It was a relief not to have to go into Karachi. The only pleasant memory of his stolen visit there seven years ago with Satpal, his Lawrence classmate, was the night they had lain on a spit of sand curving out from the harbor and watched huge turtles creep out of the sea to lay their eggs by moonlight. The only interest the city held for him now was the fact of cousin Nadir's presence—that skinny, serious boy he'd seen half a dozen times and not for years, who was now a man and Karima's husband.

On the plane, he'd toyed with the idea of finding Nadir and asking his help to get across the border. If Karima was working with the rebels, Nadir must be too—but then why was he living in Karachi with their other two children? To funnel contraband coming through the port? At least he ought to know the local black market in forged documents, and a second passport would be good insurance. But it could take days to find Nadir, and then he might not be a welcome guest—if Nadir knew all Karima's old secrets. Cousin Tor, his wife's first lover, showing up to beg a favor.

When he'd changed his money, a thick roll of rupees and some coin paisas filled the pouch at his waist. It would be enough to pay for the cheapest seat—a wooden board in a reeking car that would make sleep impossible—and still leave him with a few extra rupees. Crossing the street, he dozed for a while on the dark platform until a vendor jostled him on his way to service the train.

Then it was there, the Khyber Mail, and most of the cars looked as if they dated back to the British Raj. On this leg of the trip the train was still fairly empty, so after buying a ticket to Peshawar, he stretched out on a bench in the ancient rear car. It would take a full day to reach Lahore and the plains could be blisteringly hot. His candy bars would melt, he'd have to buy food and it would probably make him sick, since he was used to living with different germs in Moscow.

The passengers from Karachi were speaking Sindhi and Urdu and some of the women wore saris without the covering of a burqa, but as they went north out of Sind province across bleached earth colored here and there by early sunflower crops, farmers in tightly rolled turbans added Punjabi to the babble and women were fewer and more often veiled. All the carriage windows stood open against the heat, so now black soot streamed in to mingle with fumes of tobacco smoke and sweat, and yet Tor found himself smiling in spite of his hollow stomach and the grit stinging his eyes. I'm like a bee myself this week, he thought. Coming from Moscow to Kabul wearing a Scottish cashmere sweater, then leaving desert sand all over Saira's rug in New York, and now back here with English chocolate getting stickier by the minute. He traded one for a cup of curry from a boy sitting on the floor and stopped worrying about germs.

Daddy-jan said the Russians wanted Karachi? A Soviet system wouldn't last for more than a week here. There were too many kinds of people and it was hard to picture many of them running grim little committees. Brezhnev would have to build the biggest steamroller on earth, flatten the whole region and then colonize it. Even if he did, after a while the sand would start drifting, and vines would grow to cover a lot of rusty machinery no one had learned to use right, and people would go back to their old habits.

King for two days, Daddy-jan said. *Barre duroz Shah*. That's what Taraki would be. Saira was wrong to think he could change things. Cities like Kabul could be held by force, but not all this crazy landscape.

Then what about Kerala? he thought. Will there be a thousand Keralas?

Looking out at the green Punjab he wondered uncomfortably how much damage those troops at the border could do—supported by tanks, rockets, MIG jets and the helicopter gunships that his father had called inventions of the devil. He could still hear the hysteria in Saira's voice: "People, Tor, thousands of peasants, and dying for *what*?"

The train slowed coming into Lahore and passengers scrambled past him to get out and say prayers before the sun had fully set. Lahore, the city Granduncle Yusef called "extremely wicked" before India was partitioned and Hindus and Muslims started murdering each other. Then, now and later what mattered most here was religion, not politics.

A vendor came to the window and Tor exchanged twenty paisas for a glass of yogurt and a few pakoras, which he devoured watching the porters in red turbans move luggage through the crowd. The British had built this and a hundred more brick railway stations and then Gandhi came to lie down on the tracks. But that would never work in Kabul. Afghans weren't passive, and after Kerala no Pashtun would listen to Saira's excuses. They'd want to follow the peasants who'd died there, and go to paradise.

Tor's stomach turned. Maybe I'll join them, he thought, whether I want to or not. Maybe I'll be shot and chopped up by a bulldozer, and I don't believe in Nur-Ali's martyr-heaven.

Closing his eyes, he turned the idea over in his mind: I might die here, I might die soon, do I want to die for this?

The answer was no. Just one sore arm had turned him into a coward and in the mountains there wouldn't be drugs to kill the pain. From here on, the most important thing was to stay alive and in one piece.

Now the train was going forward, its slow wheels grinding in an even rhythm. He rested his head on the window and when he opened his eyes again it was six in the morning and they were coming into Peshawar.

He had planned only this far. Taking the railway road over the bridge, he wandered through the Khyber and then the Qissa Khawani bazaars in the old quarter of the city, looking up at the tall narrow houses and overhanging balconies as if some familiar face might appear to tell him how to cross the border. Then with a shock he realized that could actually happen. Darting into a tea shop, he sat concealed behind a large brass samovar. Lots of Daddyjan's friends were in Peshawar now, and he wasn't his father's agent here, though he wouldn't be able to convince them of that. They might help him, but they'd also be very curious about where he was going and why. There was a chance he would be followed.

If they were all fighting in the same cause, why should that seem threatening? It was just an instinct. Sher was inside the country and these men were not, so they must be playing by different rules. And there were sure to be informers in the Peshawar groups by now. It wasn't safe to stay here one more minute.

So, the only choice was to take the bus through the Khyber Pass and hope they didn't haul everyone off for separate inspections this time. Half the money he had left should be enough of a bribe to help the driver lose count of the passports he collected.

Touching his cheek, Tor felt a film of soot. Good, his clothes were dirty too. He needed to buy sandals—these would never stand another climb in the mountains. And some food to keep him going through Paktia.

He reached under his shirt and pulled out the British Airways blanket folded over his belt, then knotted its corners to make a small pack that fit his shoulders snugly.

Walking through the bazaar he filled it with dried meat, fruit, a plastic jug of water and a pair of the thick leather sandals—chappals—he always wore in the summers before Moscow.

The bus left at eight o'clock. On his way to the station, he rehearsed his pitch to the driver—a flash of folded rupees with the largest bill facing out, a claim of great fatigue, a sigh, a smile—but no transfer of money till he was safely across the border.

There was the white bus with its blue stripe, almost full already. As he joined the crowd still waiting to board, he caught sight of the driver—and spun around to hide his face. That same stupid donkey had pestered him with talk on every trip home from Lawrence.

Tor stood aside until the last man climbed on, then touched the driver's sleeve and made a quick gesture to stop his greeting. "If you speak, it could mean my life." He smiled warmly. "I hardly dared to hope I'd find you here, my friend. But knowing how you esteem my father, I thought I'd take the chance. You used to tell me for hours on end I'd never be his equal, remember?"

"But what rags you're wearing! Your father... is he well? We've all heard—"

"Yes," Tor hissed. "And he asks a favor of you. That you forget I'm on your bus today."

"At the pass? But it's become much stricter there."

"I have to take that chance, if you will. If they catch me, I'll say I snuck past you."

"And they'll have my job anyway." He shook his head. "For your sake alone, I shouldn't let you try it. But since you've asked in the name of your father, how can I refuse? That excellent man..."

Tor brought a finger to his lips. "Thank you. I'll tell him what you've done." Smiling again, he scrambled up to find a seat at the rear of the bus. It was sickening to use Daddy-jan's name, but the driver would have recognized him sooner or later—which meant by tomorrow everyone in Peshawar and Kabul would know that Tor Anwari had come back. He couldn't explain enough to win a promise of silence.

Settling the pack on his lap, he told himself this might be a piece of luck. If there was new pressure on these drivers, they might even be rewarded for betraying anyone who tried to bribe them. After the crime was committed, of course. After he'd been delivered to the Afghan side of the border.

Uneasily, he glanced up at the back of the driver's turban. Had it been a little bit too simple? People always praised Daddy-jan to him, but how much did that really mean? Especially from men like this, who probably agreed with Saira that her little brother was a spoiled brat. Tor smiled. Across the border he could be worth the price of a camel now. He'd have to watch carefully at the checkpoint.

They were going west out of the city toward the Suleiman hills and the old fort at Jamrud that marked the start of the Khyber Pass. Farm lands had faded in the distance and the so-called tribal areas began, the "disputed" areas that had always been beyond the reach of any civil law, as travelers carrying luggage still discovered if they tried to take this road alone at night. The terraced rocky slopes climbing into mountains were not so abandoned and lifeless as they seemed.

From Landi Kotal it was about three kilometers to Tor Kham at the Afghan border, and adrenaline or the altitude was turning his blood into soda water. He sat up straight as the pass opened out in a sweep of blue sky and chiseled mountains, glinting rough edges of stone plummeting down into chasms. This was his rodina—the heart of the unofficial state of Pashtunistan. Maybe the Kremlin was enough to overawe the people of Moscow, but here that force came from the land itself. And as Ghulam-Nabi had often said, pointing out some dramatic view, "Who is the architect of this? Allah."

For the first time Tor could understand the upturned, shaking hands. Wouldn't Nur-Ali be happy to think he'd made a conversion. But religions cut the world up as hatefully as governments, as ruthlessly as the tribes. The only thing that made Islam any better than the rest was that the Prophet, blessed be his name, hadn't declared all other faiths invalid, since People of the Book had wisdom that was "merely incomplete."

The bus swerved around a hairpin curve and he caught sight of the square two-story customs building. Now my wisdom's incomplete, he thought, what's going to happen here? The driver had turned half around in his seat and was grinning like a jackass. Tor tried to look commanding.

Two soldiers armed with Kalashnikovs walked toward the bus as it pulled off the road. The driver climbed out and spoke to them, waving his hands and shrugging. Then he gave a high laugh, got back on and started collecting passports.

I don't have to worry yet, Tor thought, we're still in Pakistan. But he couldn't catch the driver's eye as he brushed past.

While their papers were being examined, he stared out at the visitor's lodge with its fake white crenellations, trying not to think about the other checkpoint, which he could see by turning his head toward the windshield. But as the bus began moving across the strip of neutral ground he felt sweat running under his turban and fumbled in his pouch for his remaining rupees. When the bus stopped, he held them ready to offer his self-appointed friend.

Again, two soldiers came forward wearing Afghan uniforms while behind them an officer waited at the door, his impatient gray eyes scanning faces through the windows. Tor shifted in his seat to talk to the man behind him so he'd seem to be relaxed, just another trader going home—and found himself confronting a giant Baluchi, who was raising a hand in greeting to one of the soldiers. This man could be a good person to be seen with. Clearing his throat, he smiled, "I wonder if you know my cousin? I have four cousins in Baluchistan and crossing the border at Chaman is easy," he jabbered. "None of this waiting while they eat their lunch."

The Baluchi's smile widened with incredulity. "A Pashtun, with so many cousins in Baluchistan?" His grin exposed three gold teeth. "You must come from an interesting family."

Now the Russian officer was walking around to the other side of the bus. Then the driver climbed back on, calling, "Everyone must get off! They say you all must get out here!" Again, he didn't meet Tor's glance.

Letting his pack fall to the floor, Tor bent down as if he'd spilled it. If he went out, it was finished. They'd take him to Kabul, charge him with murder and execute him. But if they found him hiding here they might shoot him on the spot as an example. Wouldn't that be a little better than being tortured in prison? He waited, fiddling with his pack until the others had filed past, then slid down and stretched out under the seats, wedging himself hard against the wall. Being skinny had some advantages. Now if only that Baluchi didn't tell them he was missing. Maybe it would be smart to get rid of his passport? No, they wouldn't shoot an Anwari, and on the way to Kabul he might be able to escape. Why hadn't he promised that driver money to begin with so he'd have a stake in what happened now?

Loud voices were arguing in Pashto. Going through the baggage, they'd found someone carrying opium wrapped in a paper from Landi Kotal. "If he had this, there may be more. Search the bus, look carefully. These Westerners think they can do anything!" With surprise, Tor heard American English: "No, somebody put that in my bag! It isn't mine, I swear!"

Even if those soldiers understood him, they probably wouldn't let on. And the American must be wearing tribal clothes, or Tor felt sure he would have noticed him. They wouldn't like that either. Now someone was coming up the steps... big dusty boots standing at the head of the aisle, then moving toward him slowly... one bent knee, the sound of fingers prying between the seats. In another minute he'll find me, Tor thought. Do I want to die now or later?

The soldier called out the window, "Where was he sitting? I don't know where to look."

There was muttering and someone answered, "Beside me, about halfway down on this side."

The boots came closer. He could touch them. The soldier was kneeling an arm's length away. Then with an exasperated groan, he called again, "Where? I don't see anything."

"Never mind. This is enough right here. Come down and take him inside."

The boots retreated and a parade of sandals shuffled down the aisle. Then the Baluchi was looking down at him, grinning. "You were very lucky, eh, my little 'cousin'? It's a good thing you spoke, or I might have thought you were with him." Holding out a hand, he pulled Tor up. The bus was moving. They had crossed to Afghanistan.

From the Khyber Pass a ribbon of highway wound through the desert to Jalalabad and green, irrigated fields. When they reached the turning for Paktia, he went up to the front and the driver scowled at him. "I thought we both were dead. My heart was jumping out of my mouth."

"I'm sorry." He offered him the rupees, smiling. "I'm very grateful to you. Especially if you can forget I got off here."

"What? Put that away. You shame me."

Tor dropped his hand. "I meant no offense. I only wanted..."

"In the name of your father! Did he teach you bribery? I don't think so." The bus screeched to a stop. "Whatever you're doing, I wish you well. May peace be with you always." He pulled a lever and the door opened.

"And with you too. Live long." Climbing out, Tor adjusted his pack and started walking down the dusty unpaved road. The sunlight showed up a ribbing of armored vehicle tracks.

Two hours later, he saw the stand of poplars where Nur-Ali had stopped his truck to eat and wait for sunset. Remembering that unshared meal, Tor thought of the fruit in his pack. There was a ditch of water by those trees too, so he could fill his canteen and soak the new sandals before putting them on his blistered feet.

Coming into the glade, he stopped short. It looked like a truck was parked there now, though no bright painting or movement was visible yet. Cautiously, he moved closer. If it was from Sher's camp this might save hours of walking.

Still there was no sign of activity—and then he saw why. The charred skeleton of an army supply truck rested at a slant where it had crashed into a tree. A blackened arm and leg dangled from the open passenger door.

A grenade or fire bomb thrown in the front while men hauled cargo out the back before the gas tank blew—but how had they lured it in here? He decided he didn't want to know whether the soldiers were Afghan or Russian. He was on the main road again, walking quickly and not hungry at all.

The land here was still flat enough to give a good view in both directions, so when a car or jeep came along he had time to run for cover. That wouldn't be true much longer. He tried flagging trucks to hitch a ride into the mountains but three went past ignoring his outstretched hand. Finally an old Volkswagen van painted with women's faces stopped and a man near his own age leaned out the window. "Peace. Is there trouble?"

Pointing to his ripped sandals, Tor smiled. "I can't go much farther in these. I only have a few rupees, but I'd pay them gladly for a ride out of this sun."

"I'm going on about ten kilometers more. If that's any use, I'll take you just for the company. Get in."

Tor introduced himself as Siddique and hoped this trader wasn't feeling too nosy. Nur-Mohammad didn't, he felt talkative, and for the next hour he went on about the beauty of the girl he wanted to marry whose father didn't think him rich enough, and then complained that he'd probably be drafted into the army instead, since he always had bad luck. As they drove higher in the hills, his chatter was broken by a roar of low-flying planes—not jets this time, but old air force crates—and watching them Tor realized there were only two, the same two, making long turns in the sky.

"What a racket!" he interrupted. "Is it some kind of exercise? Do they buzz around like that a lot?"

Pushing back an immaculate turban, Nur-Mohammad peered up through the windshield. "No, I've never seen such a thing and I take this road every day. Perhaps they're teaching pilots, or searching for something."

Tor rubbed his hands along his thighs. Of course they were looking for something, for someone. If the Pul-i-Charki raid had gone off well, they must be combing the countryside for Sher. Before, when even jets flew over the camp it was made to seem deserted—maybe by now it really was. He hadn't thought of that. But these planes were circling again and again in the area of Mirzaka, their turns growing shorter with each pass. Yes, there was the tall dead tree he remembered marking the trail.

"Let me out, please. By that path on the right." The planes had banked off to the west and he wanted to be out of sight when they came back.

Jumping down, he ran up the shoulder and crouched in the bushes until they flew over; then pulling on his pack, he started climbing toward some trees that paralleled the road on a higher ridge. If he was right, these trees followed the stream to Mirzaka. From there it would be a straight climb to the camp. What had those pilots seen up there? An empty hamlet—it must be, or wouldn't they have bombed it?

Ahead, a small ledge lined with shrubbery overlooked the road. Squatting there, he opened his pack, chewed on some dates and watched the planes. They seemed to be losing interest finally, moving in wider arcs... but now the sound of another engine came up from below, a car, he guessed, from the trouble it was having with the gravel. Here the road was so steep each turn would be a fight.

A small red car. A Fiat, maybe. Without a traction wedge it wouldn't get much farther. There was something bright orange inside, a dress? That woman must be crazy.

As it came broadside the wheels caught stone, propelling the car forward and for an instant he had a good view of its interior. That was *Karima* driving, and beside her two short brown legs stuck out on the seat, and the tail end of a kite. Standing up, he shouted, "Stop! No!" But they had already made the curve. He grabbed a rock and chased the flash of red as far as the narrow ledge would allow, then shot the stone hard and fast. It landed in the dust thrown up by her tires as she drove out of sight.

Looking down, Tor saw he was standing just above the village of Mirzaka.

Behind him, the rock face was almost sheer, with only scrub and cracks for leverage. Unless Karima got stuck further on he wouldn't be able to catch up to her, but there might be another juncture with the road where he could stop her from leading the planes right to the camp. How could she not have seen them? Or was it possible... no, her own father was there. But a red car against this pale ground? Why hadn't she just flown an Islamic flag from her antenna?

Discarding the pack, he began to climb, hugging rock with his knees and clawing at crevices, then scrabbling against some loose shale as he lost his foothold and slid down to start again. Twenty minutes later his fingers were raw and his legs bruised, but the hardest part was over. Somewhere close by must be the cave where Nur-Ali hid his truck—would Karima know about that? Maybe, if she'd been up here before.

Since she had come now, the camp must still be in use, and climbing again he remembered her face bent over the steering wheel, tight and determined, as though she could move the car by strength of will alone. What a donkey she must have thought him that morning in the kitchen, clenching her fists. "You think you know so much, Tor!" Well, he understood a little more now. At least he had come back.

Here was the grove of trees where he'd rolled away from Nur-Ali into the muzzle of a gun—a sentry point, and given the planes, this time they might really shoot him. Standing out in the clearing, he called, "It's a friend! Tor Anwari!" He waited, feeling the short hairs prickle at the back of his neck. Someone was moving through the underbrush, but except for the random snap of a twig, everything was silent. The planes had not returned.

"Stand where you are!" Bashir stepped out. "Hold your hands where I can see them."

"Bashir!" Tor laughed. "It's me, Tor, don't you remember?"

"Turn and walk." Circling behind him, Bashir prodded him with the rifle. "Walk, I said."

Sher's great soldier, thought Tor, smiling as he climbed up over the rise. Sentries must not be able to take chances.

Reaching the top, he was stopped by the sight of the empty camp springing to life. It was like changing scenery in a play—men were coming from every direction carrying machine guns, rocket launchers, baskets of grenades. The Pul-i-Charki raid must have gone off very well. Then at the door to the far house Nur-Ali appeared clutching a handful of papers and shouting for Wahab, and sliding down the slope Tor called to him, waved and called again.

Nur-Ali froze, then slowly turned, and shoving the papers at Wahab, ran forward screaming obscenities with his arms bent and raised like two clubs.

Before Tor could move he was on him, battering him crazily and Tor was too startled to do anything but try to fend off the blows. The next moment he was on the ground, and Nur-Ali had pinned him. "Swine! Defiled one! Illegitimate child of your father! Son of a Russian whore..."

"No!" Wahab grabbed Nur-Ali's arm. "That's not for us to judge. We must bring him to Sher."

"I'll kill him!" But another man joined Wahab and between them they held Nur-Ali back as Tor sat up painfully. There was a ringing in his head, and shaking it, he found himself looking along the barrel of Bashir's rifle again while a circle of men glared down at him with contempt.

"We may all die today," Nur-Ali spat. "But you go first, by my hand...." He was fighting the men who held him and Bashir said, "Move quickly or I'll let him have you."

Tor found his voice. "What is this? I don't know what you're talking about!"

"You betrayed us! Do you think we're fools?" Nur-Ali jerked his head back at the sky. "You and no one else, and you'll die for that, you pig."

"Betrayed you? I came back to fight with you! I saw those planes on the road...."

"Tell Sher your story," Bashir jabbed him with the rifle. "We have work to do."

"Gladly! Over there?" Tor marched ahead of him trembling with anger. He hadn't even been in the country. How could they blame him for those planes? He'd done everything they asked, and now... Yes, he'd tell Sher his "story" alright, he would tell him many things.

Bashir knocked on the cracked wooden door. It opened slightly and he said, "Tor Anwari's here."

Karima's voice said, "Tor? No..." She threw the door open. "Tor!"

Her face was white and disbelieving eyes stared at him in horror. "But *why*, Tor, why did you do it?"

He reached for her. "No, jan, it's a mistake...." But she drew back toward another man who was turning from the window. So this was Sher, the biggest moron of all time.

Tor took a step backward and slammed into Bashir, who caught him by the arms.

"Mangal?"

The room shrank, looked as flat as paint, but it was Mangal behind that thick beard and turban, his dark eyes round and startled. "Hello, Tor. We weren't expecting you."

He was sweating. Tor could see beads of it running down his cheek.

"You..." His throat closed. The word was a croak.

Bracing his hands on the table, Mangal leaned over them smiling like Mangal, amused, sardonic. "You'll never know how glad I am to see you right now, Tor. Are you alright? Ghulam-Nabi, give him a chair, please."

The old man was standing just inside the door, holding Zia on his hip. He set the boy down gently. "I told you Tor had nothing to do with this. Will you never listen to me?" But the statue of Mangal didn't move, said nothing until Nur-Ali screamed a curse through the window. "You!" Mangal pointed toward the sound. "Calm down or have your fit somewhere else. Can't you see? If Tor had done it, would he be here? We were wrong."

Tor sat down breathless. "*You're* Sher? You mean, all this year...?"

"I wanted to tell you, Tor. I couldn't. Not unless you came back. I hoped you would, and now I wish you hadn't. Someone's given us away. There's going to be trouble here very soon."

"The planes...Mangal, I didn't!"

Ghulam-Nabi brought another chair and Mangal sat down heavily. "As I said, you wouldn't be here if you had. But Tor, you must have told someone where we are. Taraki got a cable from the Afghan Mission in New York, and you're the only candidate. Karima works in Taraki's office. She's sure of the source."

"No...Mangal, I was there only three hours! I didn't even tell Straight, I wouldn't have."

"Think. You told someone. Who? Daddy-jan? One of the kuchis? Did you call your girl friend? Karima, what did the telex say?"

She looked from him to Mangal. "It went from New York to Moscow and then back to New York again. At least it was cleared through Moscow. I can tell by the codes. It said that as of a week ago you were camped in a little village north of Mirzaka."

Mirzaka...that name...he'd said it after all. In the dim bar. "I thought you went through Kandahar...."

He said, "Saira. I told Saira."

Mangal rocked back in his chair. "Saira. Yes. Who works at the U.N. Why didn't I think of that? I wonder who she told, and why."

The scene in the bar seemed unreal now. "She was talking about Taraki. How great he is."

"And what else?"

"The mullahs. Her friend Royila. She must be a Communist."

"Saira?" Mangal smiled, "I doubt it. She must have told your story to some friend of hers, not realizing it could be used." He began to laugh. "How did Daddy-jan ever get away with it? He was out of the country seventeen years, and he's never made any big mistakes. Look at his children. What a bunch."

"Mangal," Karima said, "you and Tor can talk later. We have to hurry now!"

"Later? This is later! Do you know what I'm saying, Tor? Saira wanted to come home and we sent her right back there. You, me and Daddy-jan. Never mind, we're paying for it now."

"So you're saying that makes it okay for her to sell you to Taraki?"

"I'm sure she didn't sell me, Tor. Saira's not a traitor any more than you were. Any more than I was when I came back from Paris and fell in love with Daoud Khan. Political science at the Sorbonne! What did that have to do with this?" He opened his hand to the small room and the brown square outside. "The funny part is, we want the same things. If Daddy-jan hadn't been in the cabinet then, I might have joined the Khalqis myself. Karima and I could be sharing an office now, hmmm?" He smiled dryly at her.

"Mangal—" She stamped her foot. "Please!"

"Alright." He nodded. "Let's get moving. Tor, take Zia out for a minute. I'll talk to you after I see Nur-Ali. Would you ask him to come in please?"

Tor stood up, confused. He wanted to clasp Mangal's arm, or at least to touch him, something more than watching him from just out of reach, but that order and the tension growing around them made it seem impossible. He held out a hand to Zia, who took it grudgingly, looking back over his shoulder as they went out.

The square was empty but there was noise from beyond the trees: clipped voices, a clang of metal, the sound of shovels driving into the ground. Nur-Ali was waiting just outside by the window and gave him an embarrassed smile. "If I've wronged you, I apologize. Forgive me."

Tor caught his arm. "But it is my fault, isn't it. What do you think they'll do? Why did those planes leave?"

"To send troops from the Gardez garrison. A few bombs would only scatter us. Troops down there"—he pointed—"and more planes, maybe even a gunship if we're unlucky. Their reconnaissance was clumsy. I don't think they believed your sister. Why should they? This might have been a trick to distract them from some other target. It doesn't matter. They know we can't get down quickly enough. Not all of us, anyway. I must go in, excuse me."

Zia had wandered off to the other end of the house and Tor followed him numbly. How could they even hope to fight an army? Why weren't they trying to escape? Gardez was quite a distance away—it would be an hour before the troops could get here. In that time... but no, Nur-Ali was right. It took half that long just to climb to Mirzaka, and further down there were few concealing trees.

His chest tightened with the start of panic. Were they just going to sit here and let themselves be slaughtered? Them, he thought, and what about me? I'm a coward. I'm scared already. But it's my fault this is happening. I can't cry about it. Besides, Mangal is Sher, who's supposed to be a magician. He'll know what to do. Maybe only a few troops will come, and there are plenty of guns this time. Karima got here just before I did, so he didn't hear about it till then. They must be planning our way out right now.

Looking down at the quiet valley, he thought, this is ridiculous. Nothing's going to happen. Not on this bald ugly mountain with that little kid pulling up grass.

He crouched by Zia. "What are you doing, jan?"

As the boy looked up frowning, Mangal called, "Tor! Zia! Come here quickly."

He was standing at the door of the house. Next to him, Karima was flushed and crying. Tor got up and Zia ran ahead of him.

"Tor, you have to do what I say now." He smiled faintly, but his voice was hard. "I'm in charge here, remember. I want you to get in Karima's car and take her and Zia down right now. Just get in and drive. You'll make it."

"No, Mangal," she was sobbing. "You have to come with us! I won't go without you."

"Jan, I can't leave the others. In your position, you're worth any ten of us. I can't risk you, or Zia either." Taking her shoulders, he made her look at him. "We lost Yusef. We can't lose Zia too."

Mangal's face held a softness Tor had never seen there.

She shook her head, "I had to use Zia as an excuse to get away."

"Then you have to save him now."

They're close, Tor thought, they're really comrades.

He heard himself say, "I won't leave, Mangal," and realized he wasn't frightened. "I just got here. Don't ask me to go. I saw Karima drive up. She doesn't need my help."

"I'm not asking you, Tor, I'm telling you! With that arm you can't fight. I'd just be worried about you. Where I'm going to be there isn't room for you. I want you out of this, understand?"

"Mangal!" Nur-Ali shouted. "Look there!"

His finger aimed at a cleft between the mountains where three specks glittered like black stars against the cloudless sky.

"Gunships!" Mangal cursed. "I didn't think there were three in Paktia yet. Forget the car. They'd pick it off like a berry. Tor, you know that cave down below? Take Karima and Zia to it. You'll have to carry him on your back, but it's a natural shelter, you should be alright there. Take a gun and move now, those are closer than they look."

Tor's vision blurred to a white field of sunlight. Mangal was ordering him again, sending him away—sorry, Tor, I don't want you.... Suddenly Mangal grabbed the front of his shirt. "Damn you, Tor, I'm telling you, defend them! I left my son to be murdered! Save your own! Yes, your son! Just look at him. Can't your see it yet?"

Karima had clapped her hands to Zia's ears and he peered up at her anxiously—a little boy with straight black hair—what was Mangal saying?

"Didn't the Russians teach you to count? For years I've been expecting you to ask. Karima, tell him!"

Slowly, she raised her head and the look in her eyes brought it all together—Mangal's terse letter to Moscow, Mummy-jan's face in the garden, Karima leaning forward in the hall. "You don't know, Tor." Or had he refused to understand?

"Happy birthday," Mangal said. "Now move, or I'll shoot you myself."

A high metallic whine was growing in the west. The specks turned into three dark shivering blotches. Squatting by Zia, Tor lifted him awkwardly. "Climb on, wrap your legs around me, that's good. Hold on tight." A voice in the back of his head still said none of this was true, but Zia's red sneakers looked real and his small arms were hot.

Passing Karima a rifle, Nur-Ali said, "Allah be with you!"

Mangal put out his arms. "Go carefully, little brother." His beard scratched Tor's cheek and the power of his embrace was dizzying for a minute. Mangal's smell, but different now, stronger and somehow cleaner.

"You take care, Mangal. Don't make us lose you twice."

"Not even once, Tor, or you wouldn't be here. Good luck. I'll see you later."

Hitching Zia up on his hips, he started after Karima down the rocky slope. When he looked back, Mangal was gone.

"Keep down!" Karima pulled him into a clump of bushes. "Through here we should be covered most of the way. Zia-jan, I want you to shut your eyes tight and don't open them till I say so. Promise?" She touched Tor's arm, "I tried to tell you about Zia. So did your mother. The way things are, Nadir wants you to know."

"Nadir's a man. I'm just a donkey. Karima, I'm sorry."

"Don't be, Tor. Our life is good. Look, we have to scramble here. I'll go first so I can catch Zia if he slips off."

The expanse of bare ground straight below them ended in a sparse row of poplars. Overhead, the rotors were pulsing like a swarm of bees. Shouldering the rifle, Karima braced her feet sideways and slid down in a crouch, then turned and waved for him to follow. He reached her on his knees, choking from the pressure of Zia's arms around his throat.

Tears were streaking through the dust on her cheeks. "Mangal!"

The wail sent a thrill of fear through him. "He's not alone, Karima!"

"But with that leg, what chance does he have? Oh no, Tor, the *car*!" She pointed down to where the camp trail met the road, and a small red roof gleamed in the sun.

"I forgot about that! There wasn't time to climb up from the cave. I have to move it, Tor. If they don't have the right bearings they might hit Mirzaka. But not with that sitting there."

"I'll do it. Here, take Zia."

"No!" She pushed him back violently. "There's a trick to the clutch, I couldn't tell you fast enough...." Throwing off the rifle, she skidded beyond his reach. "Stay with Zia! I know where to hide." Before he could stop her, she was out of the trees and half staggering down to a ledge that had only a narrow shadow for cover. Her sandals cut long grooves in the dry earth.

Tor cursed. With Zia and the rifle he could only move clumsily, draw more attention, but everything told him to go after her. She had reached the ledge now, and below it there was the jutting lip of another. For an instant she turned, thrusting out a hand to say he shouldn't follow, then jumped down out of sight. The whining in the sky became a roar and looking up he had a clear view of the gunships.

They were coming very fast—not blotches anymore, but bulbous monsters with long rotor blades flashing light. Then two ships fell away from the third to swoop down at different angles with a throbbing electric buzz that vibrated inside his skull. They didn't move like any helicopters he had seen before.

So there might not be troops from Gardez. If Daddy-jan was right, these should be more than enough with their bombs and rockets, machine guns firing six thousand rounds a minute. "Defend them," Mangal had said. "Where I'm going to be there's no room for you." Where was that? A bunker he had already carved in the mountainside?

If the best defense was cover, their only hope now was the cave. Better to leave Nur-Ali's rifle here than Karima.

He pulled Zia around to face his chest and pressed the boy's head into his shoulder. "You promised to keep your eyes shut, remember? Hold on tight even if I fall, alright?" Stooping, he ran in a zigzag down to the ledge.

The red car hadn't moved, but just below them he saw a flash of orange—Karima crouching by some rocks, probably trying to guess what track the gunships would take. That was hopeless, though, they were dropping straight down like spiders from a web or hideous dragonflies, and now one came whining and angry, its plastic bubbles the swollen head and chest of a huge insect, dipping so low he could make out the missiles clustered like eggs on its belly.

Above, the mountain rocked with an explosion raining gravel hard on his back. Curving around Zia, he saw Karima run out across the road.

"No, it's too late!" He held Zia tight. Even if they hadn't seen the car yet, she'd never get to the cave. Now she was inside, the engine turned and then that sound was drowned by a shriek of rotors as the gunship dropped, reversing its course to come back at her with a burst of gunfire that turned the car into a spinning ball of blood and flames.

He was shaking, tasting vomit in his mouth, crouched with Zia between his legs, the small face hidden in his shoulder. There was nothing left of the car now but fire and blackened metal. They had to get down from here and find the cave, but horror would not let him move. The burning car looked like it was hanging by one tire, the earth under it blasted to a crater.

The mountain was coming to pieces, falling around them in an avalanche—boulders, hail stones, a cloud of smoke and dust, but no shouting, just one explosion after another and machine-gun fire screaming down in an endless blast. No shouting because three hundred bullets a second had made them human mincemeat?

The rubble of the car lost its grip and fell, bouncing out of sight. He felt like waving to it.

Was Mangal dead now too? Were all of them?

I have to find the cave while there's still smoke for cover, he thought. I can't think about what's going on up there, if anything is left. A bunker in the mountain—they'd take the roof right off that too.

Zia's fingernails were clawing at his ribs. My son, thought Tor. I don't believe that. Mangal just said it to make me bring him down.

"We're going to run now, Zia. Hold on like a monkey." He held the boy's legs around his waist again. "There's a hiding place down there, but it's hard to get to. Ready?"

Turning around, he dropped to the next ledge. From here to the mouth of the cave the climb would be easier but uncovered, and looking back for the gunships, he stopped in amazement. One of them had been hit. It was incredible—Nur-Ali must have caught the top rotor with his clumsy shoulder-launcher, and the ship was plunging in a dive. For a second it leveled off, buzzing like a hornet, but then its shuddering fall continued and it vanished.

When the explosion came, he smiled. Only Nur-Ali could have done that. Nur-Ali was alive.

Reaching the cave, he pushed through the branches and had a second surprise. Nur-Ali's truck was parked inside. That didn't make sense. Why hadn't Mangal taken it down with the best of his men? He wouldn't have had to leave them all behind. Maybe it was a hard climb, but they must be used to that.... No, wait, there was something about his leg.

Karima crying, "But with that leg, what chance does he have?" Then seeing the car had taken their attention.

Tor opened the passenger door and set Zia on the seat. Mangal standing at a table, sitting in a chair, leaning against the doorframe—never walking any distance. Ghulam-Nabi said he'd been shot. He must have been wounded badly and didn't want to show it.

The bombing sounded indiscriminate now. Shaking earth rattled the truck on its springs and dust was sifting down in bucketfuls. No more target practice after losing a third of their number—they were blowing the mountain to bits. And Mangal was up there, unable to move. I have to go back, Tor thought, I have to find him.

And leave Zia here to be buried alive if something happens to me? Mangal ordered me to defend him. My son. Was it only Zia he was protecting, or me as well?

If Karima had climbed down alone with Zia, she might still have tried to move her car and Zia would be dead now too. He'll be safe here, and lots of people heard Mangal send us to this cave. If I get killed, someone will come and get him out. Unless the cave collapses and he suffocates first. Unless no one survives.

Tor beat his fists on the truck in frustration. Mangal on the mountain, maybe alone, a target. Zia here alone except for him. He said hopelessly, "Zia-jan, do you know how to dig, like this, with your hands? If some dirt fell down in front of the cave, do you think you could dig through it?"

The boy was staring at him owl-eyed and so pale his face gleamed in the dim light. The words seemed not to register at all. Then his mouth opened and he turned to look back at the road. Tor followed his glance. There was nothing there. And no sound but a whining in the distance.

He ran out and saw the two gunships shrinking against the clear blue sky. Blobs, then specks again. They wouldn't be back, not for a while.

"They're gone, Zia!" He found the boy sitting still, without expression. "I want you to stay right here until I come to get you. I have to find your uncle Mangal now."

Zia looked through him and Tor pulled the doorlock. "I'm sorry, jan, I have to leave you alone, but don't be scared, I'll come back soon."

He'd be safe in the truck. His body at least, Tor thought, sprinting to the ledge. But he must know what had happened to that car, and his mother. I didn't even try to save her.

He climbed the rock face like a madman, barely aware of the shredding flesh on his arms and legs. From the next ledge he caught a glimpse of the twisted wreckage that had been the gunship, sent it an obscene salute and then, grasping the precipice, levered himself over it to fall gasping next to the shattered corpse of Bashir.

Only his clothes and gray beard were recognizable. His head was red jelly blanketed with flies. Two other bodies lay by the splintered grove of poplars, and Tor stood up and went to them, choking back the bile rising in his throat. These men he had not seen earlier.

Everywhere around him flies were buzzing as though they had been waiting for this. Moving through the broken shrubbery, he bent to many bodies, each time afraid he would know the face. Relief turned to disgust that it should matter. They were dead, and he had been protected.

The village was gone. There was hardly a sign it had stood there an hour ago. The ground was so blasted and littered with cartridge shells and branches it looked like a munitions dump. Scraps of wood, maybe a door or table, were burning among the mud bricks that had been the last house on the right.

He waded toward it through the rubble, calling. "Can anyone hear me? It's Tor! Try to make a sound so I can find you!"

Stopping to listen, he looked down into the blind face of Nur-Ali.

The thin lips were still curved in a smile and a rocket launcher lay by one outstretched arm. The rest of his body was covered by a fallen tree. Lifting it, Tor found Wahab curled behind Nur-Ali, and a scattered basket of grenades. Both bodies were almost severed at the waist.

Crouching beside them, he chased away the flies and straightened Nur-Ali's blue turban.

"You saw the hit, didn't you." His voice sounded as if he were crying.

"You know you got that ship, don't you." It wasn't his imagination. Nur-Ali was smiling, as if dying were just another and not the last of his jokes.

"Tor Anwari, come here!"

A man in a bloodstained shirt called from the ledge behind the house. "Come! Hurry up!"

He waved frantically, and scrambling to his feet Tor ran to him and swung over the edge.

Below, on a shelf of rock, Ghulam-Nabi was bending to wipe Mangal's face.

Tor slid down, sinking to his knees. Mangal was alive.

"Toryalai." His breathing was ragged. "What a blessing! Are they alright too?"

"Zia is. He's fine."

Ghulam-Nabi pressed his turban cloth hard against Mangal's side, but the circle of blood kept growing steadily.

"Karima?"

"She tried to move the car, Mangal." Tor slipped an arm under his head. "Forgive me, Ghulam-Nabi, I couldn't stop her."

Mangal's dry lips moved again. "Stubborn. Never listens." A trickle of blood started at the corner of his mouth and with effort he moved his tongue to touch it, then closed his eyes. "So, so."

Ghulam-Nabi bowed his head, weeping.

"Tor..." Mangal whispered, "take care of them now. All of them... Saira ... this worthless old man... Swear it."

"In paradise you couldn't lose me," Ghulam-Nabi said. "In hell you'll never be rid of me, Mangal Anwari."

"Promise, Tor..." The dull eyes flickered open. "Take Zia out, to Mummy-jan, take him... all we have now. Swear."

"I will, I promise. I love you, Mangal...." Tor bent to kiss his forehead and a shaking hand touched his throat.

"Have another child, Tor... many. Teach them well."

The hand fell back across his broken chest.

After a minute, Ghulam-Nabi stood up and stripped off his shirt. "Put him down, Tor. He's with Allah the all-merciful now. And my daughter. Where is she?"

Tor brushed some dirt off Mangal's cheek. Mangal and his three-piece suits. Why hadn't he ever worn these clothes before?

"Toryalai?"

He looked up. Gray hair on the old man's chest. "With Allah, Ghulam-Nabi. The car fell straight down, burning. Don't look for her here."

"But she must be buried." His face was like rock now. "And your brother too."

"Honor me. Let me do it." The man who had waved him over knelt and took Mangal's body onto his lap. "You all must get away quickly. A truck will come from Gardez soon, to see what they've done. I know every way off this mountain, Tor, but with a child and his grandfather...."

Folding his arms, Tor glanced at him. A face that looked like his own.

"Don't you know me, Tor? You're sitting in my clothes."

"Yes. You're...Tammim?"

He gave a strange smile. "No. I'm Sher. Or someone else will be for as long as we can fool them. Forgive us. Soon your brother will be honored as a martyr. But right now, he'd rather we let Taraki and his generals think they've failed."

"He's right, Tor." Ghulam-Nabi wrapped his shirt carefully around Mangal's head. "We must go now. Take Zia out. Do what Mangal said. Everything we promised, we must do."

"Do you mean, to New York? What about his...Nadir? And Raima and you?"

"I have promises to keep here. We can't go to America. Nadir's two children are living with his sister. He's coming back to fight. I want my grandchild with his father and grandparents, not in someone else's household. You swore to take him there and you must do it."

Tor looked at Mangal, remembering the strength of their one embrace. He lay limp on the ground now and his shirt was soaked with blood.

"Farewell, my brave daughter," Ghulam-Nabi said. "Make a place for me beside you."

Climbing the ledge, he put out a hand and Tor reached up to grab it, his sense of failure already turning to rage.

I couldn't have defended them anyhow, he thought. Not against those gunships.

At the edge of the clearing, he leaned down to take the pistol out of Bashir's belt. It wasn't as well made as Nur-Ali's, but the shot would be at close range.

Saira.

She had sent the planes.

Saira.

Thirty-One

"Saira, please, try to drink this at least." Catherine set the teacup in front of her on the glass coffee table. "You haven't eaten anything in days."

In a week, really, Catherine thought. Ever since Tor had gone. The next morning she had found Saira sitting in the kitchen, wearing the same clothes she'd had on the night before and staring down at a piece of paper. "What does he mean, Mummy-jan? How can he go where Ghulam-Nabi is, when Ghulam-Nabi's dead?"

After the explanation, such as it was—"No, Tor says he's alive, jan. At the camp of this Sher who helped us"—Saira had sat for several more hours, mute and hollow-eyed, then walked out to the living room. "You have to call someone. We have to stop him! Tor's going to be killed and it's all my fault!"

When she told them why, in three sentences, Omar screamed, "A *Soviet*? You have a Russian *friend*?"

As he went on about it, Saira shrank further back against the wall, getting thinner and more sallow by the hour, it seemed. Since yesterday there was more concern than anger even in Omar's eyes when he looked at her. Whatever had broken inside her had shattered a long time ago—thin cracks showing deeper fissures that she had covered up too brightly on their last visit, Catherine saw now.

At first Catherine was nothing but furious at Tor for running off half-cocked as usual, but then the fear had set in. The stillness. Saira left the blinds in the aviary drawn to keep the birds from singing, and they sat like little statues too, glancing out at the artificial twilight. "There isn't anybody we can call," Omar said. "We might do him more harm than good."

But now he was dialing the telephone in the kitchen.

"Yes, I'd like to know about flights to Pakistan, please. To Karachi. As soon as possible."

Pushing aside the hassock, Catherine ran to take the phone from him. "No, Omar! You can't! Not yet." She hung it up. "What could you possibly do there?"

"More than from here, anyway. We can't wait forever." He shook his head. "Alright. Why don't we ask Saira's Russian? Maybe he knows what's happening. Or Taraki. I could call him."

"Stop it," Catherine whispered. "Can't you see how bad she is?" She was looking at Saira's face when the downstairs buzzer sounded.

"Maybe that's her friend," Omar said. "Shall I ask him to come up?" His body was slack again, indifferent. The desert had aged him, or made more apparent the strain of the past year. Saira had not moved from her armchair.

"I'll get it, jan. I think we'd better answer it." Catherine crossed to press the intercom button. "Who is it, please?"

"Toryalai, Mummy-jan."

Her thumb was on the buzzer, stayed there, and she called, "Did you hear that? It's Tor! He's here!"

They stood by the elevators, Saira wrapped in the blue shawl that she'd been hiding under for days. Her mouth was pale as marble and her eyes only somewhat interested, as if the voice they had heard belonged to a stranger.

The door opened and he was standing there, dirty, with Zia asleep across his chest. If Catherine hadn't put out her hand the door would have closed again, taking him away. He made no attempt to stop it.

"Tor! My God, Tor!" She put out her arms for the boy. "And Zia? We've been frantic!"

Omar shepherded them into the apartment. "Saira, if you have any alcohol, I think your brother could do with..."

"Yes, Saira-jan," Tor mimicked him. "Don't you have any cognac? Or margaritas?" He lunged for her. "You traitor! I'll kill you! Murderer!" His hands were at her throat....

Stunned, Catherine shifted Zia's weight but Omar moved more quickly. Saira stumbled back into the couch, barely catching herself, and Omar was holding Tor by the shoulders. "Stop, Tor! You're alright now!"

"Yes. I am." Tor's sunburned face strained toward his sister, bloodshot white showing all around the dark irises of his eyes. "And Saira's fine, and you might be, but a lot of other people aren't. That's why I have Zia. Karima's dead. Is he really my son or was that just a trick?"

Catherine bent an arm around Zia's head. "Karima? Killed? By the military?"

Tor was still glaring at Saira.

"Toryalai, answer me!"

"Yes." He lifted his head to her. "In Paktia. At Sher's camp. You were wrong about him, Mummy-jan. Sher wasn't Aziz Khan. He was Mangal." Tor stabbed a finger at Saira. "She killed him. She sent helicopter gunships that blew him and Karima to bits. Mangal couldn't even walk, but I didn't know that. I let him be killed. I brought out a gun to shoot her too, but Mr. CIA took it away from me."

Omar let go of him and Tor rocked back and forth unsteadily on the balls of his feet.

"Mangal? How could it...did you see him?" Omar spun Tor around to face him. "What are you saying, Tor?"

"Yes, I saw him. I talked to him. I watched him die. And Karima. She killed them. Mangal is Sher, Daddy-jan. He was. He got shot in the chest."

Catherine breathed into Zia's shoulder. He didn't wake up. He felt stiff. Tor was saying more things.... "All last year...after Roshana...Aziz Khan ...I heard in Moscow..." In a cold voice, he kept building his story of Mangal.

Holding Zia, watching Tor, she began to believe him. Mangal and Aziz Khan. Mangal had been alive all this time. Tor had shot a Russian's face off in the desert and Karima was burned up in a car. Little Yusef and Roshana killed, now Mangal *again*, and Uncle Yusef, and the boy who said he buried Mangal.... Why shouldn't it just keep going on? How could it stop? Eating up everyone.

"Mummy-jan, is he my son or was that a trick?"

She looked up and saw only the horror in Saira's face. "Yes, Tor. He's yours. Saira, we didn't know Sher was Mangal."

"Yes, Saira-jan," Tor mocked her, "you killed him, but that's alright. Even Mangal said you aren't a worse traitor than I was for trusting you at all. It was me you wanted to get rid of, wasn't it? Not the rebels. Tell the truth."

Saira's back sagged. Catherine thought she might be fainting and reached out for her.

"Mummy-jan!" She pulled at her hair, "Mangal! And Karima! I didn't mean to! I didn't!"

"Wait, I have to put Zia down, jan. Wait, I'll just be a minute."

"Don't bother," Tor said. "Zia can't hear you. He can't speak. He's almost dead too."

"Saira, come with me, please." She tugged Saira's sleeve. "Please, jan. Come in here."

Omar said, "I don't believe this. Why wouldn't Mangal have told us?"

Because he couldn't trust us either, Catherine thought, drawing Saira into the bedroom. Mangal always played his own hand. Like his father. Like his mother. He just made up his mind and disappeared.

She put Zia down on the bed. He curled an arm over his face, but didn't stretch out. Saira said, "He's really Tor and Karima's? Oh, Mummy-jan, I murdered her!"

"No, no, jan. You didn't." Catherine held her brittle body gently. "It's war now, Saira. They've been after Sher for a long time. If he was Mangal... I believe Tor. He saw him. It must have been Mangal. But we didn't know he was alive. He didn't tell us." Suddenly, she remembered how Mangal had looked on his wedding night—open, radiant, even playful—and the next day they'd listened to him reading President Daoud's notices on the radio. A brilliance that in the next moment seemed blindness, and each unaware of the other.

On my wedding trip too, she thought. I said I could accept everything then. But not the loss of it. Not again. How can you mourn a person twice?

"I killed him though, Mummy-jan. And Karima. I told Andrei." Saira shuddered and Catherine hugged her tighter.

"And Tor shot two men face-to-face. All my children. It's insanity. I don't know why."

In the next room, Tor's voice was rising again. She clasped Saira's forearms. "Listen to me. You've never purposely done a malicious thing in your life, Saira. Why did you tell your friend about Sher? Did he ask you?"

"About Mangal, you mean? No, I did it all by myself. On purpose. I knew what I was doing."

Through the open door, Catherine saw Tor jump up from the sofa.

"Daddy-jan, please, just give me the money! I have to get out of here! Do you want me to kill her? I have to go back."

"Because this Tammim's saying that he's Sher, and you feel he's stolen your prerogative?"

"No! I want to fight! I didn't do anything when I was there. I hid in the cave with the baby. I was a coward."

"So now you want to prove you're not? With only one arm? Walk into a bullet? No, Tor, if anyone goes back it will be me."

"Why? You wouldn't help Sher when he asked. You're not any stronger than I am. With all respect..."

"Tor, do you have a son?"

Catherine couldn't see his face.

"Yes, Daddy-jan. It looks that way."

"And does your son have a mother?"

Tor didn't answer.

"Did Ghulam-Nabi give Zia to you so you could make him an orphan? Really, Tor, what could you offer over there? You'd just be one small piece of ammunition." He shook his head. "You have responsibilities now. You're not going anywhere."

"I don't believe it," Saira said. "They want to go back? Already? Why don't they just shoot each other instead. It would be a lot easier."

She stalked out to the living room. "Do you want to hear my side, Tor?" Her spine straightened, "I thought Sher was a mullah. That's what I'd heard. And even if that was wrong, I wanted to stop the fighting, not make it worse. All right, now I'm a murderess. Don't worry, I'll probably kill myself too. I wanted to, after you left. Why don't you do it for me? Go ahead."

"Stop it, both of you!" Catherine shouted. "Don't you even talk that way, Saira. Tor, sit down. I said, sit down, Tor!"

Saira was crying. "No, I haven't finished. I'm telling my side, remember? You'll never need to have a baby hanging over a hole in the ground, or jump into the river like Royila. If I won't live that way, how can I pretend anyone else should? At least the Khalqis stand for something. Not like the king and Daoud-jan, making promises and breaking them the next day. So I betrayed Mangal. That was my mistake. And I'm very sorry...." Grabbing her purse from the kitchen counter, she was out the door before they could stop her.

The hall was empty, but there was the sound of footsteps running down the stairs. Catherine went out into the stairwell and saw her hand on the bannister three flights below. "Saira! Come back!"

"No, Mummy-jan! I'll be okay. Leave me alone now, *please!*"

Tor was standing in the doorway, glassy-eyed. "Do you want me to go after her? I'll bring her back." In this light he looked even worse. In shock. We all must be, she thought.

"No, Tor. But you have to forgive her. She had reasons. She was wrong. But that guard you shot might have a sister who's hating you right now. Saira will blame herself more than you ever could. Don't you know that?"

She went back in to check on Zia. He was still sleeping, rigid, arms folded across his chest. Karima's mouth and straight hair. Not much of Tor in his face yet.

The debate in the living room started again.

"Please, Daddy-jan?"

"No, Toryalai!"

"Omar," she called. "Will you come here for a minute?"

She pushed the door shut behind him. "What are you telling him? You can't go back there!"

"Not even if I could salvage something from this? Catherine, Tor says they know about Mangal in Peshawar now. I might be able to help pull them together, while he's still a symbol. It's high time someone did."

"Omar, do you have a son?"

"Yes. I used to have two. Do you want to see all Mangal's work wasted? Or Tor get used for cannon fodder? Don't you see? It's the only way I can keep Tor from going himself. If I stay here, he'll leave again. He isn't ready yet."

"And what about Saira and me? What if we need you? What if I'm not ready to start all over here with three kids who are half crazy? Isn't it also high time you gave them some thought?"

He was looking down at Zia. "Past time, Catherine. It's too late. It's you they need, not me."

"That's a convenient way to think, so you can decide to leave again."

"My dear." He took her hand. "Don't you know you're the only one who wants me here? *If* I go, it will only be to Peshawar and for a little while. Tor and Saira will do better without me breathing down their necks. And you won't have to play three-way referee. You can go up to Boston and tell your father all his predictions came true."

Omar smiled apologetically. That awful dinner. Their "engagement party," as he liked to call it, when Dad had shown the most violent emotion she'd ever seen in him.

"Yes, but you didn't take four wives after all. And I'm not a 'naive girl' anymore, with an 'exclusively romantic' view of life."

Yet, in spite of everything, she would have wanted no other. Not a lawyer for a husband and three children whose greatest problem was choosing which country club to join. Even if Omar had been at home more, would Mangal have done one thing differently? The house he was born in and his grandfather's wedding shirt carried as much weight—the same onus Omar had borne for fifty years.

In time, little Zia would want to know how his mother had died, and then it would begin for him too.

"Poor Catherine." He took her face in both his hands. "Are you cursing the day you met me?"

"No, Omar. I'm just amazed at how well I kid myself. That when this thing or that gets settled we'll be able to live in peace. I thought coming back here would mean starting over. We should be that lucky. It's a good thing I love you all so much."

"When I was stuck in the house last year, you were dying to get rid of me."

"We didn't have children there."

"We don't now. They're grown, Catherine." He squeezed her shoulder, nodding at Zia. "Except this one. I have a grandson again. That's why I won't stay away long."

"I don't believe you, Omar. It will be the same. A little better or worse, maybe, but not much. Will you at least wait till we're sure Tor and Saira aren't going to come to blows?"

"Yes."

His voice was gravelly and she looked up, surprised, then put her arms around his neck. "It isn't so bad. If we've done it before we can do it again."

There was no point in wishing anything had been different. Only that these present wounds would heal. Even that was asking a miracle, but they could try.

Her gift. Not a small one. To love the people she loved most in the world. And let them go. And welcome them back, so they could go again, because that was their gift or curse. A hundred departures. A thousand. Circles of life. Even she had come back to her beginnings, and would leave again when the day came.

If it came.

Was that to be feared or hoped for, she wondered.

Tor could hear their voices through the bedroom door, but not what they were saying. He stood up and pulled the blinds on the aviary. The canaries started singing, jumping up and down. Too noisy. Time to get out of here.

Saira would be at the river. He'd strangle her. But he couldn't. Mangal had made him swear. Even dead, Mangal was running things.

Spreading blood on Mangal's shirt. "Your son, Tor. Can't you see it?"

No.

But before Liz, every time he'd touched a woman he thought of Karima, the summer nights when she came to his room. Now he could recall that sharply again. Zia. Karima on fire. The car falling. All mixed up.

Walking around the couch, he looked down through the open window. Across the street, a solid wall of buildings mirrored Saira's block—no mountains and no garden, but no microphone under the stereo either. Just slightly better than a dorm in Moscow.

He counted up a row of windows. Twenty floors. Maybe there was a door out to the roof.

They were still talking in the bedroom. He went out quietly. The roof door was locked with a metal bolt that didn't want to give. He kicked the door, then tried again. Kicked and pulled. It was coming now.

Sunlight poured down on the tar. He squinted. Let his eyes unfocus. Brown stone, pale as the mountains, with a chasm like the one where the gunship crashed.

Liz said I'd find my niche at home, he thought. She was right. And I guess I'm a father. She'll love hearing that. If Mangal spent a year figuring out how to trap me, he couldn't have come up with a better way.

"Promise, Tor. Swear it."

Get a job.

Be a father?

If they wouldn't let him go, he'd have to leave without permission. There was just the problem of money.

"Everything we've promised, we must do."

Well, hadn't he brought Zia out? They were all safe now. But not killing Saira would be harder. Mangal should be alive....

It was my fault too, he thought. If I hadn't gone back, Mangal would have died blaming me. "Take care of her," he said.

That was a laugh.

Daddy-jan might win at first. They couldn't both take off. How many months would it take to save a thousand dollars? Liz would be back in England by then.

He went to the edge of the roof and looked down. On the sidewalk, tiny people were walking dogs on leashes. Not kuchi dogs. Little toys.

So many things to be decided. If he made the family miserable enough, they might be glad to send him back.

Leaning out, he felt dizzy, almost drunk. So many serious decisions to be made! Sweep floors or wash dishes, save a thousand dollars, take a stopover in London and maybe stay there.

A low wall ran along the front of the building, pointing toward the river. In places it was crumbling, like the rocks. A tightrope, if he let his eyes swim. Why not walk it to the end and back?

He smiled. His spine was tingling. Yes, so many decisions to be made about life. But there was no harm in putting them off for a while.

Once he had walked out and back, then he would choose.

Saira fished in her purse for a tissue. People were noticing her, but she couldn't go back to the apartment. The river looked very brown today. Spring mud seeping in. If only she had the courage to jump.

Crying for Mangal again. And Karima instead of Roshana. No, I haven't felt this scared since Jeffrey, she thought. Like I'm losing my mind. But I wasn't just an idiot this time. I killed them. I told my lover how to murder my brother. What does that make me? Fratricide. There was a name for it.

Mangal.

Sher-the-mullah, so Andrei had said. Had he been lying, or just wrong, too far away? Even if she asked him she wouldn't believe his answer.

He would say: If Sher hadn't been someone you knew, would you think your reasoning was bad?

A nice hypothetical question.

She folded her arms tighter. Stop it.

Mangal wouldn't like being mistaken for a mullah.

Then who was he? When he went to Paris, she'd been twelve, and the next and last time she saw him was six years ago, at his wedding. Tor got drunk. Ashraf went away. But Mangal was more like an idea of a person. A miniature Daddy-jan. It was only since the coup that he'd seemed real again.

Now that would get worse. Keep seeping in. He'd known it was her fault too. Had Karima?

Saira shivered. Jump in the river or start walking. She got up from the bench. Tor would make sure to tell her every detail so her nightmares would be right.

I'm going to explode, she thought. Spontaneous combustion. It's not funny. What can I do?

Not back to the apartment. A long fast walk. A stiff drink? That would be Andrei's solution, and Tor's, and probably Jeffrey's by now.

I called them arrogant, she smiled. Me. I was just as proud. I thought I knew best. Roshana and Karima are dead, and I'm making phone calls to Riverdale. At least Devika's honest enough not to do that.

I can never go back to Afghanistan, though. The one time I stopped running away, I turned around and killed my brother.

She stopped and looked down at the muddy river.

No. Try a stiff drink.

Crossing the street, she started toward Broadway.

The Library was almost empty and the hostess said she could have the table where she and Tor had sat last week. When the waiter came, she ordered a Rémy Martin.

Even if the water in the river were clean, she wouldn't jump in. Couldn't picture it. Royila had worn a velvet dress to pull her down. But she didn't need to buy groceries.

Working at the U.N. would be for money now, and seeing Andrei there would be a penance.

The cognac came in a medium-sized snifter glass. Holding it near her nose, she felt the fumes. Take a drink, not a sip. Try to get drunk.

She swallowed and waited for it to hit her stomach. Hot, then radiating out. So this was Tor's great thrill. Living with him would be hell on earth.

Being with Mummy-jan could be good, though. And Zia.

Saira choked. Except that I killed his mother, she thought, and sooner or later he'll find that out.

She ordered another cognac. How had Mangal stood it? He'd taken Roshana and Yusef to the palace to be shot.

Maybe I did him a favor.

She turned her chair to face the window. Mangal stood it by being Sher. To revenge him, she'd have to kill Andrei and herself. Running away wouldn't work.

The second drink was just as rough, snapping her awake. In a while it might be possible to go back to the apartment. Zia was almost the same age as Yusef, whom she'd never seen. Tor's son, if he wanted him. Karima's oldest child. Tomorrow he would wake up in New York.

Daddy-jan and Tor.

Mummy and Devika and Zia.

Saira took out her wallet. Let the men go off and fight. They loved it so much. They could have it. All their politics. All their schemes.

For her, it was too dangerous to pretend to know anything.

The small plane had sat for almost an hour on an outlying runway and was now coasting slowly along as if on a sightseeing tour. Yes, this is Pakistan,

Omar thought. Isn't it wonderful to be back where nothing works.

He'd better get used to it. This was just the beginning. Patience was a necessary virtue here, one he had never mastered, and if he was going to achieve much at Peshawar it would be good exercise to practice detachment now—ignore the asinine bickering of the Saudi boys behind him and look benignly on the steward who so far had made half a dozen conflicting announcements.

After all, he was no longer a minister, measuring performance. In Peshawar, the strength of his authority would depend on how well he could translate the interests of each group into a common language, and how long he could stand to wait, watching for the moment when concessions might be made in desperation.

The Gailani family over here, the Mujadidis there, a handful of mullahs representing different degrees of orthodoxy. I suppose we'll have to spend a week arguing about the shape of the table, he thought. As if we were superpowers at a summit. Too many chieftains, literally, and no king and no cabinet. If a government-in-exile could be formed, might Zahir Shah be their chosen leader?

Mangal wouldn't have worked with these people. In a young man though, moderation was not such a good thing. When he himself came back from the States in 1946 he had been obstinate about his work, and that was the making of his career. Youth must reach beyond age, sons supersede their fathers. But why couldn't Mangal have let him know he was the Sher who had asked for help? Just before the coup, hadn't they found the friendship time should bring to fathers and sons?

Too little and too late, he thought. We teach what we know, and in my case that was only principle. By refusing to join the struggle, I hoped I could keep it from happening, and instead my children went on and respectfully left me out.

As I had left them, over and over, just announcing I was going away for a while. They weren't supposed to mind. That was what served me. If they did mind, they were not allowed to show it.

After a time, they were happier without me, and that will be true now. They'll sit up late talking, Tor might drink alcohol—only Catherine will really miss me. At least this past year gave us that.

He looked down at the canvas bag at his feet, filled with books he had borrowed from Saira's shelves. The volume of Montaigne on top would be saved for a dark night when he couldn't bear to hear one more word about Islamic law or the relative value of this or that coalition.

All winter, he and Catherine had shared books. Until then, their reading had been separate—her fiction, his utilitarian history and political science. But cut off from other sources, they turned to each other's libraries and he found Jane Austen and Henry James describing the families whose heirs he had known at school in England. Catherine had started Marx and Hegel, so

New York

their talks over dinner became hilariously incongruous with their situation, and he rediscovered the wise, complicated woman whom he'd had just enough sense to marry. Now, leaving again, he already missed her and all of them more than he ever had. Which, he thought, serves me right.

It had been easy, even pleasant, to sit in Kabul judging the power struggles going on at Peshawar. But there was no guard in front of Saira's building. No excuse for doing nothing in New York. Mangal hadn't left him a moral leg to stand on. It was as if he'd planned it all this way.

Catherine had said, "I don't want to lose you. I want us to get old together, will you remember that?"

"My love"—he lifted her chin—"I'm already old."

"No." She dismissed his humility as false. "You're rusty, that's all. If anyone can pull them together, it's you. But be careful, Omar, please, for all our sakes."

Making people be quiet, he thought. That's all I'm good for. I'm more limited than Tor with his horseback riding, and at least he has some fun.

But if things went well, there might be work for Tor soon, using his brains as well as his nerve. The first high mark he'd earned in Moscow was for journalism. He could get inside the country and tell the stories no one else seemed to care to report.

Beyond a column-inch about troops at the border. Who had even read that? Freedom of the press was a safe practice in the States. Americans get all the information. They just never think about it.

Kerala. That should be worth some attention. Afterward, the women and children had walked for days to get to Pakistan.

Pashtunistan. Omar smiled. Thirty-three years ago he'd taken an even shakier plane to Islamabad to pick up that fight, and if he had succeeded then, he might be cursing himself now. Pashtunistan was real to the people, so the border with Pakistan could never truly be sealed. A semipermeable membrane for arms and refugees. But the Soviets would have to respect it as an international boundary.

Uncle Yusef, he thought, pray for me. We'll need better luck this time.

The microphone squawked and a steward announced in Sindhi, Urdu and bad English that their small problem had been solved and a gangway was being attached now, no worry, please. The plane dipped to one side, then righted itself, turning toward the hangar. A tall figure stood on the tarmac ... Ghulam-Nabi?

Now Omar could see him clearly. So there was one person here he loved. Catherine must have reached him through Nadir.

Picking up his canvas bag, Omar started down the aisle, looking out through the cabin windows. There were two more men behind Ghulam-Nabi, waving their hands at each other. One was a mullah from a fundamentalist sect, the other ... yes, an old colleague from the cabinet. What do you know, a welcoming party!

Naturally, neither of them could have an ulterior motive. They wouldn't be hoping to win his support before he made other commitments. No, it was just the famous Afghan hospitality that had brought them all this distance.

Omar stepped out into white sunlight. Hot wind lashed his face with dust. The three men smiled, then hurried forward.

He braced himself to meet them.

Afterword

*A man took revenge after one hundred years,
And all the Afghans said he was impatient.*
—Ancient Proverb

THROUGH THE summer of 1979, resistance to the Taraki government spread in Afghanistan. The Soviet Mission in Kabul gave repeated warnings of the dangers involved in forcing sudden, drastic reforms, but all pleas for moderation were ignored.

On the way home from a conference of nonaligned nations in Havana in September 1979, President Taraki visited Moscow, where he was enthusiastically received. Leonid Brezhnev urged him to broaden the political base of his party, to appoint non-Marxists to the cabinet, and perhaps even to reunite with the Parchamis. (Babrak Karmal and other exiles may have been present at this meeting.) Taraki was also told to get rid of his strongman prime minister, Hafizullah Amin.

Unfortunately for Taraki, his bodyguard Taroun was in the service of Amin and warned the prime minister of a possible threat to his life. Amin then agreed to see Taraki only after the Soviet ambassador vouched for his safety.

Their subsequent meeting indeed proved an ambush, but it backfired—Amin was prepared. To the dismay of the Soviets, Amin rallied the Palace Guard and seized control. A few days later his new government announced that Taraki had died of an "undisclosed illness."

(An Associated Press dispatch from Kabul later cited Afghan radio broadcasts of "confessions" by members of the Palace Guard responsible for Taraki's death: Captain Abdul Wodood said Taraki had asked that his party card be delivered to Amin, and some money and jewelry to his wife. Taraki was then held down, strangled and smothered with a pillow and "martyred after ten or fifteen minutes.")

Through the fall, Amin and the Soviets worked to suppress the resistance while wrestling with each other for control of the army and administration. General Viktor Paputin, a senior KGB officer, tried to form a joint strategy with Amin, arguing that only a large infusion of troops could save his government. Amin refused, perhaps suspecting that such a force would be turned against him. This defiance may have been pivotal in the Soviets' decision to move into the country.

(In the London *Sunday Times* of December 28, 1980, Anthony Mascarenhas wrote that according to a source close to Amin, the Russians in fact had asked him for complete control of the Shindand air base near the Iranian border, believing the Carter administration would launch a military response to the Iranian hostage crisis. Soviet interest in Shindand, rather than the extensive army and air force base at Begram, suggested their concern was more with events in Iran than Afghanistan. And, to quote Mascarenhas, "The Indian Foreign Minister, Narasimha Rao, and his delegation during a visit to Moscow last April [1980] ... heard the Russian Foreign Minister, Andrei Gromyko, admit that the Soviet troops had gone into Afghanistan in a bid to pre-empt the Americans.")

By December of 1979, Amin was filling high government posts with close personal relatives. (His nephew, Zalmai, reportedly told the *Sunday Times* that after the demand for Shindand, Amin "secretly began to plot to throw out the Russians as President Sadat had done in Egypt," and approached, among others, the embassies of West Germany, Japan and Pakistan.) After another nephew, Asadullah, chief of the secret police, was assassinated in December, General Paputin convinced Amin to move his headquarters to the Dar-al-Aman palace outside Kabul, where he met his death in disputed circumstances just before the invasion.

The Soviet leadership has said that in accordance with their 1978 Treaty of Friendship, Cooperation and Good Neighborliness with Afghanistan, they rushed in troops in response to a call for help from the Afghan Revolutionary Central Committee, who had arrested and executed Amin and elected his old rival, Babrak Karmal, to succeed him. However, a Soviet parachute unit took the precaution of ensuring that Amin was dead before the "call" for troops was made, and Karmal's first announcements were broadcast by Soviet radio from Tashkent. He was then flown to Kabul in a Soviet transport plane.

That all this was handled so clumsily suggests a felt need for control at any cost. Facing a petroleum crisis at home, Moscow may have decided that if a show of strength could win leverage in the region—particularly in Iran and the Persian Gulf states—as well as Afghanistan's supply of cheap natural gas, it would be worth a loss of favor in world opinion. But as with the American experience in Viet Nam, the forcible installation of a puppet government proved inexpedient after all. The manner of Karmal's accession to power made him an object of scorn from the first, and served to galvanize the insurgency.

As of this writing, the war is going into its seventh year.

The Russians have kept a rotation of approximately 115,000 troops in Afghanistan and used it as a proving ground for new generations of specialized weapons. The mujahedin are armed with whatever guns they can capture and through covert aid from the U.S., China and sympathetic Islamic countries. Principal Afghan cities and highways are under Soviet control. Over 75 percent of the countryside remains in rebel hands.

Still, it is a war of scorched earth, attrition and perhaps gradual "sovietization." The government has been entirely restocked, tens of thousands of Afghan children are being educated in the U.S.S.R. and famine is making the countryside uninhabitable. Thirty thousand Soviet soldiers may have been killed, by contrast with as many as one million Afghans; exact figures are unavailable.

But Afghanistan has never been successfully colonized.

There are now about four million refugees from Afghanistan—more than from any other country in the world. Most live in makeshift camps along Pakistan's northwest frontier.

One such camp is named for the village Kerala.

November, 1985

M. E. Hirsh has written for the *Boston Globe,* the *Washington Post,* and the *Los Angeles Times* on subjects ranging from Afghanistan to Native American affairs. She is the author of *Dreaming Back,* a novel, and is currently at work on two others.